MW00333896

Hilarious, exuberant, subtle, tender, brutal, spectacular, and above all unexpected: these two extraordinary volumes contain the limitless possibilities of the British short story.

This is the first anthology capacious enough to celebrate the full diversity and energy of its writers, subjects and tones. The most famous authors are here, and many others, including some magnificent stories never republished since their first appearance in magazines and periodicals. *The Penguin Book of the British Short Story* has a permanent authority, and will be reached for year in and year out.

This volume takes the story from the 1920s to the present day.

———

Philip Hensher is a novelist, critic, librettist and short story writer. *The Northern Clemency* was shortlisted for the Booker Prize. His most recent novel is *The Emperor Waltz*.

THE
PENGUIN BOOK
of the

BRITISH
SHORT
STORY

VOLUME 2

From P. G. WODEHOUSE
to ZADIE SMITH

———

Selected with a General Introduction by
PHILIP HENSHER

PENGUIN BOOKS

PENGUIN CLASSICS

UK | USA | Canada | Ireland | Australia
India | New Zealand | South Africa

Penguin Books is part of the Penguin Random House group of companies
whose addresses can be found at global.penguinrandomhouse.com.

This collection first published in Penguin Classics 2015
003

Introduction and editorial matter copyright © Philip Hensher, 2015
The acknowledgements on pp. 729–735 constitute an extension of this copyright page
All rights reserved

The moral rights of the editor and authors of the stories have been asserted

Set in 11.25/14.75 pt Adobe Caslon Pro
Typeset by Jouve (UK), Milton Keynes
Printed in Great Britain by Clays Ltd, St Ives plc

ISBN: 978-0-141-39601-9

www.greenpenguin.co.uk

MIX
Paper from
responsible sources
FSC® C018179

Penguin Random House is committed to a
sustainable future for our business, our readers
and our planet. This book is made from Forest
Stewardship Council® certified paper.

To A. S. Byatt

Contents

Contents

Contents

Contents

Contents

General Introduction

I

The British short story is probably the richest, most varied and most historically extensive national tradition anywhere in the world. But before introducing a *Penguin Book of the British Short Story*, it's as well to admit that every single substantive word in the title, apart from 'Penguin', is under fierce debate. Certainly I felt unclear about what 'British' might mean, and was completely unable to lay down rules for who might qualify as British. It might make sense to include everyone who wrote as an inhabitant of the British Isles and as a subject of the government in London. That would include all Irish writers until 1922, but it is most unlikely that anyone would expect to find a story from James Joyce's *Dubliners* in this anthology. Foreign-born writers resident in the UK I ruled out where there was a strong movement to regard them, as in the case of Katherine Mansfield, as conferring merit on their place of birth rather than their residence. On the other hand, I have chosen to include Elizabeth Bowen, whose subject seems indubitably British. There are undoubtedly writers here who, to some readers, will seem to contribute to the British short story, rather than belong to it; there might, indeed, be a strong argument for including Henry James in an anthology of this sort. But Britishness is slippery and debatable, as indeed the British short story often is.

'Short story' is still more problematic. What is a short story? Eager pundits queue up to explain that a short story must consist of a single situation, a short space of time, a small number of characters, be less than a certain number of words, and so on. These restrictive demands have been around for a long time, often ultimately deriving from Poe's grandiose suggestion, applying Aristotle to a new literary form, that 'unity of effect or impression is a point of the greatest importance'.[1] Although this

xiii

insistence comes from the same writer, who insists that 'the death then of a beautiful woman is unquestionably the most poetical topic in the world'[2], the point about unity has been taken very seriously ever since. Certainly, in this country, reviewers for an 1880s London journal, *The Athenaeum*, which took an interest in the American short story, were already regularly insisting on 'economy and unity of effect'.

The market for such restrictive explanations seems to have expanded with the rise of creative writing as an academic discipline, but they remain uncertain and unconvincing. All of these pundits would quickly find themselves having to explain away the existence of great short stories that seem hardly to have the slightest notion of any of the single situation, a limitation of time, a consistent tone, or anything else. D. H. Lawrence's 'Daughters of the Vicar' covers thirty years in its marriage of the sublime and the minute, and takes a detailed comparison of four marriages as its grand subject. Restrictions of length, too, seem unsustainable, and there are short stories by Conrad that press on to 30,000 words and beyond. Why 'Typhoon', at 30,000 words, is universally regarded as a short story and *Nightmare Abbey*, at 26,000 words and possessing a more uniform setting, is described as a novel is a question only answerable by the accidents of publication history. Practical concerns prevented this anthology from acknowledging the occasional expansion of the short story, which in general flourishes at between 4,000 and 15,000 words, into much longer forms.

If it is difficult to reach a conclusion about what the formal literary limits of the short story are, the debate about the historical phenomenon of the short story also shows no sign of resolution. There are two general views about the short story, one inclusive in tendency, the other more rigid. In the inclusive account, a story told in brief is as old as mankind, and there are short stories to be found in ancient Greek literature, and in the Bible, before turning up in the English language (one friend firmly told me) in a short story in the *Anglo-Saxon Chronicle*. A generous and open account might include a Canterbury Tale before moving on to Mandeville's fantasy travel writing, and starting in earnest with Elizabethan prose romances.

On the other hand, the exclusive and rigid account of the short story sees it as a very particular historical phenomenon. The term 'short story' only occurs towards the end of the nineteenth century, although it is difficult to be quite sure when: the *OED*'s first citations, which are from 1877 and (Trollope's autobiography) 1882, seem to use the phrase as an established usage. To a surprising degree, authors of the time do seem to regard it as a much newer form than the novel. In 1894, the short-story writer Lanoe Falconer talked about 'the literary capabilities of the short story, still in its infancy'. [2] In Britain, writers were relatively slow to perceive the possibilities of short fiction, both artistically and commercially. American writers were obliged to develop a practice in short fiction as early as the 1790s, and certainly by the 1820s, because the American public generally preferred cheap, copyright-evading editions of English novels. One authority explains: 'The American short story . . . emerged in the 1830s when the flood of British imports drowned the American novel and left magazines and gift-books as the only paying outlets for native fiction.'[3] Those English novelists, by contrast, found their principal markets in the long form. The restrictive history of the short story maintains that, despite foreign practitioners such as Pushkin, Kleist and Washington Irving, the British short story only seriously begins with the establishment of major, well-paying short-story magazines such as *The Strand* in 1891.

Both historical accounts have something to be said for them, and both are, in the end, wrong. There doesn't seem to be anything to be gained from regarding any piece of made-up narrative as a short story, even if it is in verse. Even such pieces of imaginative prose as the Elizabethan prose romances seem to me so different from the short story when it emerged under that name, and to contribute so little to its development, that nothing was to be gained by starting so very early. (I admit, too, to finding almost all of them agonizingly dull.) On the other hand, indisputable short stories were being written and published in Britain long before *The Strand* and even the mid-Victorian journals such as *All the Year Round* started taking an interest in short fiction. In this anthology, the Scottish writers Hogg and Galt will be seen to be writing perfectly shaped and conceived short stories by the 1820s.

It made sense, however, not to start at that point, but to go back somewhat, and examine the different and often intriguing ways in which prose pieces of short imaginative fiction were trying to make sense of themselves in relation to the novel. The first pieces in this anthology are not, in the modern sense, short stories. But they bear in a vital, animating way on the short story's historical development. They are trying to distinguish themselves from the long form, and are drawing on a number of literary counter-examples. The Fielding is a compacted, sequential romance; the Defoe a mock-documentary account of confected reality; a morality tale starts to get out of hand in Hannah More. In other stories, possibilities are set out which will bear fruit long afterwards in the history of the form: Mary Lamb's entrancingly static idyll is a story about a life with no story. I include Swift's extraordinary 'Directions to the Footman' in part because it shows how narrative was always lurking, ready to rip up the most morally directive of stories, and partly because it foreshadows in an unmistakable way a tendency of recent years, to cast short stories in the form of non-fictional lists, instruction booklets and other secretly story-telling sequences of prose (Lorrie Moore's 'How to Talk to Your Mother (Notes)' from *Self-Help* is a good recent example). All these are working towards a definition of the short story in distinction to the emerging form of the novel. By the time Galt (and Scott) start to publish their short stories, the definition is clear, and confident; and it did not emerge from nothing.

2

Nowadays, when we read short stories, we read them in an unusual way, and one that may not resemble the way they were originally intended to be read. We read short stories in anthologies like this one, but mostly in substantial collected or selected editions, intermediate or summary accounts of a short-story writer's career. We are used to reading the short fiction of a single author one piece after another. Of course, the single-author collection can be a marvellous thing, introducing the reader to an author's world with intensity and power. Some of the most powerful encounters I had in the course of compiling this book, indeed, were with beautifully conceived and executed collections from which it was hard to choose a single example, such as Douglas Dunn's superb *Secret Villages* or E. M. Delafield's *The Entertainment*. But it's important to recognize that short stories were not first written to be read in this way, for the most part, but to be read singly and in very varied company. Short-story collections, and especially volumes entitled *Collected Stories*, I found, may be misleading, heavily revising short stories written much earlier, organizing an author's short stories in ways designed to obscure their publishing history, or even omitting most of an author's work under a title implying completeness. Some of the worst offenders in this regard are 'collected' editions compiled by the authors themselves. Sometimes, collected editions are calculated to make a particular effect by including works never regarded as within the author's body of short fiction. Readers were very surprised to see the huge bulk of Alasdair Gray's collected short fiction, *Every Short Story*, when it was published by Canongate. On investigation, Mr Gray had chosen to include an entire novel, previously published as *Something Leather*, under a new title. To gain an accurate sense of a writer's short fiction, it is often necessary to return to their first publication – usually in journals.

For the greater part of the short story's history in Britain, the main publishers of short fiction were the editors of magazines and journals. Even very distinguished and famous writers did not write their short stories to be first read in a collection between hard covers; their stories were submitted to the editors of magazines like – in roughly chronological order - *Blackwood's*, *Chambers's Edinburgh Journal*, *Household Words*, *All the Year Round*, *Cassell's*, *The Fortnightly Review*, *The Strand*, *Black and White*, *The Yellow Book*, *Adelphi*, *Life and Letters*, *Lilliput*, *Encounter*, *Horizon*, the *London Magazine*, *Granta* and very many others. There were journals to publish stories in very many different genres and styles, and each had its particular flavour. Some journals dabbled in short fiction and serial novels – *Country Life* published a short story from time to time, occasionally hitting gold or digging deep into its coffers to bring out something by a star author (it published John Masefield's 'Davy Jones's Gift', for example). Others were overtaken by fashion and broadened their scope to include fiction: *The Gentleman's Magazine*, published from 1731, gave in and brought out fiction between 1868 and 1890 before withdrawing from the fiction market in its remaining seventeen years. Fiction was a core part of the endeavour of many popular journals, even of daily newspapers – at first, usually novels or serial works, but as time went on, increasingly relying on the short story. The quantity of short fiction published by the *Daily Mail* in its early history beggars belief, none of it collected, all of it now effectively lost. Much of it must have given a lot of pleasure in its day.

The breadth of publications taking and paying for short fiction in this country, and the equally wide spread of possibilities in America and elsewhere, made it perfectly possible for a successful writer of short fiction to earn a good living, and even (like Conan Doyle) to become rich. In the 1890s, after the appearance of *The Strand* and *Black and White* as magazines that would publish only short fiction rather than serialized novels, at least twenty-three magazines were founded that published short fiction significantly or exclusively. In the decade and a half before the First World War, there were 'at least thirty-four high circulation magazines publishing substantial quantities of short stories'.[4] The primary market, and the primary source of income for these writers, was publication in the journals.

Some instances might reveal how, even without the consistently higher payments available from American magazines, British authors could attain real professional competence through selling short stories to magazines, and it was clearly worth investing a good deal in time, money and skilful craft. Some payments: Hardy's payments for a single short story went from £20 in 1878 to £100 in 1894. Twenty pounds was a fairly standard payment for decades. It is what Stevenson was paid for *Dr Jekyll and Mr Hyde* in 1886, and by the 1930s E. M. Delafield's customary price for a story had only risen to £30. There were still less well-paying journals – the *Yellow Book* paid Arnold Bennett £3 for a short story – but often hard-nosed and flush journals took a view about what an author could do for them, and paid accordingly. An interesting study by Reginald Pound has revealed the range of payments made by *The Strand* to authors in 1914 for single short stories, and it shows what they thought they could gain by star names. Britten Austin was paid £31/10s, P. G. Wodehouse £40, A. E. W. Mason £166/13/4, rising to £350 for W. W. Jacobs. It is complicated to translate these sums into modern-day equivalents, but it is worth noting that studies of the middle classes at the time cite a family doctor's average annual salary before the First World War as around £400. These, of course, are just the payments for first serial rights in Britain. Many, perhaps most, authors of short stories could also sell the story in the United States, and subsequently second serial rights in both Britain and the US, so that a story for which a British magazine paid £50 could easily end up earning three times as much merely from serial publication. These individual magazine payments, impressive as they are, fall short of Conan Doyle's extraordinary income. He was paid £50 each by *The Strand* for the four first four Sherlock Holmes stories, and then engineered a colossal increase. After 1895, the magazine never paid less than £100 per thousand words for anything he wrote. After Sherlock Holmes had been killed off and – through public demand – resurrected, Doyle was offered £3,000 for twelve stories by an English publisher and £6,000 by an American. Later still, Doyle received an offer of 75,000 dollars, or approximately £12,500 at the conversion rate of the time, for twelve short stories.[5] There was no question that magazine publishing of short stories could be among the most financially lucrative form of writing long into the twentieth century. This investment encouraged the most able and ingenious writers of the day to place it at the centre of their practice.

After the turn of the twentieth century, many and perhaps most of the best authors who published in journals found it possible to put together a volume for sale by a publisher. It is, inevitably, largely from these authors that the compiler of an anthology of this sort will find himself drawing. These collections would carry on supplying some kind of income to the author, and no doubt satisfy some authors in their sense of preserving their short fiction, as well as their novels, for the benefit of posterity. This was a possibility available to a good number of authors; according to the lists compiled at the time by Edward J. O'Brien, the editor of an annual 'Best Short Stories' volume between the wars, over a hundred collections by UK authors were published in the UK almost every year between 1925 and 1936. Publishers, however, were much more cautious than magazine editors, and often offered very small advances and limited royalty terms. H. E. Bates received £20 for a 1931 collection, and even a very successful writer like E. M. Delafield or Walter de la Mare might only receive £150 or £200 – about the same that could be raised by a single well-syndicated short story in the magazines. There was a strong belief among publishers that 'we reckon', as Victor Gollancz put it, 'that short stories [in collections] sell between a quarter and a sixth of an established author's novels – but with a very rigid maximum of about 4,000'.[6] The collection of stories, which is the way in which we read an author's work, was for most authors for most of this period a useful and prestigious, but not very profitable, addition to initial publication. The primary income, and the most exciting appearance of each work, came with the first publication, in magazines and journals.

Posterity has on the whole acted as it was supposed to, and kept an interest only in the short-story writers who stretched to published collections. Although only quite rare and aesthetically minded authors published their short fiction primarily in volume form in preference to journal publication of individual stories – George Egerton in the 1890s, Dorothy Edwards in the 1920s – this is the form in which the short story is invariably considered, and the way in which its history has come down to us. But to read the short story not in much later collections but as it first appeared is to gain a much more detailed sense of how it developed, and what it actually meant. Of course, it is beyond human capacity to read more than a few of the principal journals that published short fiction in the last quarter-millennium – *Chambers's Edinburgh Journal* was brought out between 1832 and 1956, and to read all the fiction it published is a major undertaking with doubtful reward. Moreover, the publisher taking a punt on an author who has made a splash in periodical form turns out to be quite an efficient filter of talent. In putting together this anthology, I have nevertheless tried to go beyond the *oeuvres* of celebrated and once-celebrated authors brought out in collected and selected form by mainstream publishers. In reading through a dozen or so journals, I have tried to gain a sense of how short stories initially appeared to the people they were written for, as well as looking for the occasional excellent story by an author who never quite attained the body of work or the popularity a publisher would need in order to bring out a *Collected Stories*. In this anthology, examples of fine stories that had, as far as I can tell, no life beyond first publication are those by T. Baron Russell and Jack Common – it may not be a coincidence that many such stories I read were by working-class writers. Occasionally, a story might be taken up by a well-meaning anthologist, such as Edward J. O'Brien's excellent *Best Short Stories* annual volumes during the 1920s and 1930s, giving a second wind, for instance, to the terrifying and heartrending short story by Leslie Halward I include here – Halward, in fact, did not include, or did not have an opportunity to include, this masterly vignette in his one excellent collection of stories, *To Tea on Sunday* (1936).

A key further point, certainly neglected by literary historians, is that single stories in journals by unestablished writers could be very much stranger and more experimental than stories in a collection for a mainstream publisher. This might seem to go against conventional wisdom, which suggests that a story written for a commercial magazine could only be conventional in type and execution. Certainly that could be true for many authors, and I grew to dread, in the 1930s and 1940s, the appearance of an H. E. Bates short story with its regular Stanley Baldwinesque allusions to a nightingale singing in the orchards. But the spread of financial and aesthetic risk could also encourage innovation and even wild eccentricity. A journal could find space for a single story about an underground kingdom peopled by unattached body parts and organs (1850s), or a talking dachshund (1930s), an unexplained dream sequence of locked rooms and female virginity (1870s), or a truly startling Calvino anticipation by Walter Besant in the 1890s. A distinguished author dabbling in fantasy could set off any number of bizarre imitations in journals – E. M. Forster's 'The Celestial Omnibus' (1911) inspired a good number of collisions between public transport and supernatural powers, such as Evelyne Buxton's 'You Change at Clapham Junction', published in *Blackwood's* in 1920. A journal would hardly lose anything if it didn't work, as most didn't; a publisher of a similarly *outré* collection might lose a good deal of money.

Short stories were not, mostly, read in the dignity of established authorship, but alongside some often sensational or comically inept illustrations. Successful authors found themselves being published, like Conan Doyle's later Sherlock Holmes stories, immediately adjacent to slavish imitations, of which (in the case of Conan Doyle in *The Strand*) the best are some ingenious but not very original detective stories by Grant Allen. Few journals were entirely devoted to literature, and the reader of what now seems a great late Victorian classic may turn the page to find a startlingly detailed and thoroughly researched article entitled 'Muzzles for Women'. The intricate level of interest in the facts of the world that many great short-story writers possess appeals, it becomes evident, to the same sort of reader that wants to find out curious and grotesque facts about the world's cultures, animal kingdoms and oddities of individual and mass behaviour, a reader whom the editors of many journals were happy to satisfy.

Even in the more aesthetically high-minded and literary journals, such as the *Yellow Book* (1894–7) or *The Adelphi* (1922–55), which supply two of the high points of the form, an immediate and vivid ebb and flow is apparent. You can see the writers of short fiction responding to each other, teasing, developing in response, and writers emerging in fits and spurts – the moment when the 'Eric Arthur Blair' who has been publishing fairly weak poetry in the pages of *Adelphi* suddenly emerges as 'George Orwell' is a thrilling one to experience in the reading rooms of the London Library. John Buchan and an 'Enoch Arnold Bennett' appear in the very unexpected aesthetic pages of the *Yellow Book* for the first time, and we feel the shock of interest as a reader must have, discovering a major talent. Most strikingly, reading the British short story in the pages of the journals that first published them makes one appreciate the most powerful feature of the short story as a form: its capacity for topicality.

3

While I was in the latter stages of preparing this anthology, the novelist Hilary Mantel published a short story in the *Guardian*, and immediately afterwards a volume, entitled *The Assassination of Margaret Thatcher*. In it, a middle-class housewife gives sanctuary to a working-class sniper in 1984, who after a long conversation shoots and kills the then prime minister from a window. It was not a very accomplished piece of work, and would probably have been passed over were it not for the substantial following Mantel's historical novels had acquired. It caused a definite stir of protest and disgust, some of which focused on the undeniable fact that its subject had indeed been the target of an assassination attempt around the time of Mantel's story, and had behaved with notable bravery. A number of friends and colleagues, including spouses blameless for government policy, had been killed in the (real-life) assassination attempt or had been crippled for life. Others defended Mantel and amusingly described her as 'brave' for taking on such a subject.

What unified detractors and supporters of Mantel in this sorry episode was a sense that a writer of fiction, and perhaps especially a writer of short stories, would not normally be expected to address a subject as controversial and lively as Mrs Thatcher's reputation, even thirty years on. Even though the story and its author had carefully waited until Thatcher had died before engaging with the reading public, it still seemed brave, shocking and above all, surprising to see a short story about (more or less) contemporary politics.

It is fair to say that this attitude would have greatly surprised previous generations. One of the very striking aspects of the British short story, as revealed by the experience of reading through weekly news-oriented journals, was its capacity to react immediately to the news of the most public order. Novels seem to take a few years to ruminate over events, to develop the impact of social changes or dramatic public events on lives – the great novels of Napoleonic upheaval are written between thirty and fifty years after his defeat at Waterloo. Short stories, on the other hand, may in some circumstances be written quickly, in the heat of the moment, responding with utter immediacy to a mere facet of a huge situation as it unfolds.

A large number of the best short stories are written as a sort of commentary on a changing social situation, as a writer thinks him- or herself into a new situation. Many of the stories in the *Yellow Book*, for instance, explore the new situation of women as independent-minded and perhaps even gainfully employed. From very early on, short-story writers saw the possibility for writers of fiction of the railway, and by the middle of the nineteenth century, railways are being exploited for all sorts of non-modern reasons, such as a hallucinatory ghost story – there is a good, standard example, 'Going Through the Tunnel' in *Chambers's Journal*.[7] Many of William Trevor's most interesting stories from the 1960s and 1970s are specifically about the human impact of social changes – wife-swapping parties in 'Angels at the Ritz' – just as Elizabeth Taylor and Samuel Selvon found the short story the best and swiftest medium to write about the impact of immigration in Britain in 'Tall Boy' and 'Knock on Wood'. In this anthology, one fine example of immediate response to events is a story by Adam Mars-Jones on an aspect of the AIDS crisis, written less than half a decade after the diagnosis of the first patient. To show how very swift this response could be, it's necessary to look at the impact of a huge public event on the pages of a fiction journal.

The Second World War quickly inspired a large body of first-rate short fiction, including Alun Lewis's marvellous accounts of the lives of ordinary soldiers, and there was no hesitation or delay between event and fictional rendering. In the first instance, full-scale novels of the conflict were either prophetic, written before anything had taken place, like Nevil Shute's *What Happened to the Corbetts*, written in the 1930s about a speculative air raid on Southampton, or out of date before they were published, like Evelyn Waugh's *Put Out More Flags*, whose subject was the phoney war but which had to be published as thousands were being killed in the London Blitz. The short story was much quicker and could more reliably speak to participants in a current situation. Mollie Panter-Downes, one of a number of British women writers whom the *New Yorker* has always supported, published the first of many short stories on wartime themes a mere fortnight after the outbreak of war in 1939 – its subject the outbreak of war itself.

This swiftness of response in the form of fiction now strikes us as surprising, and perhaps even indecorous. In a recent biography, the writer Adam Begley expressed some surprise that the American short-story writer John Updike regularly took real-life events from the very recent past and transformed them, as if transcribing, into saleable short fiction. There is no way of knowing how swiftly other short-story writers translated private, real-life experiences into imaginary prose, but we can see that when a public event occurred, its fictional representations in short fiction were never far behind. The First World War broke out in August 1914. At the earliest possible opportunity, in its September 1914 issue, *Blackwood's Magazine* published a story about a battle in the Great War, realistically written and edited almost before anyone had experienced one ('Five-Four-Eight', by Jeffery E. Jeffery). These responses to events were not automatically populist: another very early response in *Blackwood's* to the war, 'The Old Junker' by Charles Oliver, published in February 1915, goes to some length to expound the figure of the idealistic, kindly German, before 'he had taken the Moloch form that he wears today'. Such immediate responses have not gone away entirely. One of Graham Greene's last stories was a horrified warning against the imminent opening of a Channel Tunnel, first published in the *Independent* newspaper. But the effective separation of paying journal and practising short-story writer in recent years has diminished this important aspect of the British short story, and when it turns up, we are often rather shocked.

4

The possibilities for the writer of short stories have narrowed significantly in recent years. Where once there was any number of paying journals and magazines offering handsome sums for first serial rights, now the principal outlet for many writers of short stories is not publication but competitions. With no intention of mockery, I quote the acknowledgements page of a recent collection of short stories, published by a small press, the work of a writer who says she has been publishing short stories for twenty years.

> Placed 2nd in round 6 of The Whitaker Prize 2012; placed 1st in the live Write-Invite Competition 28th January 2012; placed 3rd in The Meridian Summer Competition 2012; 4th place in A Very Short Story Competition September 2011; shortlisted in Five Stop Story Competition 2012; one of twelve shortlisted in The Knock On Effect Competition 2012; shortlisted in the Erewash Writers' Short Story Competition; shortlisted in the Writers' Forum Competition July 2012; won second prize in the Greenacre Writers' Short Story Competition; placed 1st in the Word Hut Number 3 Short Story Competition; shortlisted in the Wells Short Story Competition 2000; longlisted in The Fish Short Story Prize 2011; specially commended in the Infanca Helene James Short Story Competition 2012 . . .

And so on. These competitions sometimes offer reasonable prizes – the Fish short story competition, for instance, offers a first prize of 2,000 Euros plus 1,000 Euros travelling expenses. Sometimes there are rather thinner rewards on offer. The Word Hut Prize offers only £70 for first prize. These prizes are funded by the eager contestants paying to enter – the Fish competition demands 22 Euros from entrants, and the Word Hut only £4. The possibility that anyone might pay in order to read these short stories seems hardly to be envisaged. But what alternative is there?

One Sunday newspaper offers an annual lavishly funded prize for the short story, culminating in a dinner for 150 or so and a first prize of £30,000. The winner is subsequently printed in the newspaper. The year that I went, the chair of the judges, a retired don, congratulated himself and his fellow judges for having produced a shortlist which contained no short story set in Britain, before handing over the cheque to an utterly routine piece of work by an American author about a tragically dead rock star and a terminal illness. It was, of course, in the approved present tense. There seemed no point in suggesting that with the same money, the newspaper could develop any number of short-story talents by, for instance, commissioning and running a short story every week for £1,000. Similarly, the BBC's annual short-story competition much prefers handing over £20,000 in prize money to paying writers properly to write stories for broadcast. I inquired about the fees payable by BBC Radio 4's short-story slot, *Afternoon Reading*. Enough to say that it would not pay for my weekly laundry bill. The sort of relationship, too, between magazine and author that existed in the past, permitting *Adelphi* to help to contribute towards the development of Jack Common as a writer and editor, or *Horizon* towards that wayward, fascinating experimentalist Anna Kavan, has completely disappeared.

There are very few outlets still able to pay a writer for a short story in a way that could encourage a writer to persist, and with the sort of editorial investment that will enable a writer to develop. Most of them are in the United States. The *New Yorker* has, happily, been able to develop the short-story writing careers of two of the best short-story writers now at work, Tessa Hadley and Zadie Smith. There is no British journal that would have published Hadley's stories, as the *New Yorker* has, twenty-one times, and paid properly for them. *Granta* very occasionally publishes a British short story; some newspapers, notably the *Guardian*, sometimes publish a short story by a very firmly established and celebrated 'name'; some popular magazines, such as *Good Housekeeping*, do still take short stories; others develop short, fervent periods of enthusiasm for short fiction before abandoning it again. The *New Statesman* is currently in such a fit of enthusiasm, publishing a short story every two months by, admittedly, very well-established authors. The stories now published by British outlets are, it must be pointed out, very rarely more than 2,000 words, which is at the very lower limit of the form's usual scale. If there is a paying British outlet for the classical short story of 7,000 words or so, I have not been able to discover it. The writer of short stories is largely reduced to persuading publishers to publish whole volumes in exchange for minuscule advances, making stories available for nothing or very little in niche journals whose editorial expertise may be uncertain and whose circulation is certainly tiny, or entering competitions. The result is a definite shift in the quality of short stories over the last fifteen years or so.

The problem with relying on competitions as a means of developing talent, rather than the response of a paying public, is that they reward what they think ought to be good, and not what contains any real energy. Repeatedly, reading short stories rewarded by competitions, I was struck by present-tense solitary reflections, often with characters lying on their beds affectlessly pondering; major historical events were considered gravely; social media were dutifully brought in to indicate an eye on the contemporary without disturbing the safely solitary nature of the character. Pondering preceded, by a very long way, the social interaction which is the proper subject of fiction. There was nothing there at all, apart from a fervent desire to win £30,000.

The insistence that short stories should be serious in theme, with an underlying contempt for anything not about major issues of public policy, and yet not permitting the short story of contemporary public events either, is nothing new. Lena Milman in the 1890s wrote that 'The contempt for the short story prevalent in England, but unknown elsewhere, is surely as traceable to Puritan influence as the destruction of the Mary Altar at Ely, and the shrine of St Thomas; for, insisting, as it has become our English bent to do, upon some serious side-purpose in art, we are not content with a beautiful suggestion, with a sketch be it never so masterly; the narrative must illustrate a principle, the picture, a fact.'[8] Not until the rise of literary competitions in the second half of the twentieth century, however, did the British hit upon a method ingeniously devised to suppress everything that had previously been good about a literary form.

The system of competitions replacing a system of commissions, payments, circulation and readers looks tempting as a guarantee of literary quality; no one, however, ever invited, or required Conan Doyle or V. S. Pritchett or Kipling or P. G. Wodehouse to put on a dinner jacket and shake the hand of a retired academic before they could receive a cheque for a short story. They might even have considered the idea somewhat humiliating. Moreover, no competition will ever produce or reward a 'Silver Blaze', a 'When My Girl Comes Home', a 'Wireless', or a 'Fiery Wooing of Mordred'. It is perhaps no accident that the dullest short stories I read from the last fifteen years were winners of competitions: a lot of the most exciting and interesting short stories, on the other hand, were science fiction, fantasy and horror. Clive Barker's *Books of Blood*, from the early 1980s, spawned a very engaged and argumentative readership which in turn created some brilliantly inventive writers – China Miéville, Neil Gaiman and Adam Marek are possible through a readership, a system of circulation, and not through the rewards offered by the conventional tastes of prize committees. If an ordinary newspaper took to publishing, once a week, a short story and paying the same that it currently pays for the celebrity interview that fills the same space, then the short story in all its forms would soon return to the energy and inventiveness that it possessed until recently. In the meantime, we can only be grateful for the British writers who are still nurtured by generous American magazines, the ones who can persist in writing collections of short stories for publishers for the same small advances that publishers always offered for collections, and the ones who are lucky enough to work in a field with an engaged and passionate readership.

5

With some embarrassment and some self-consciousness, I set out to suggest some of the qualities that distinguish the British short story in the last three hundred years, and make it worth reading.

In the 1990s, A. S. Byatt edited a groundbreaking and inspiring *Oxford Book of the English Short Story*. It was based on a principle which, curiously, had never been put into practice before: limiting its grounds to authors of English nationality. Byatt confessed to some doubt about setting out on such an endeavour, on the grounds that 'I feared that the great short-story writers were indeed from elsewhere ... I feared being marooned amongst buffers and buffoons, bucolics, butties and Blimps.' In the event, her anthology was a revelation of quality and a particular range of expertise. It came as such a revelation because the English, and perhaps the British too, *qua* British, are not accustomed to think of their own literary qualities. There is always a risk, in case some claim of supremacy starts rearing its head from the dark ages. It is as if the particular quality of writing from these islands cannot be considered because, inevitably, it will lead to distasteful claims of superiority that we signed away in 1947 with the end of Empire. Anthologies of English short stories, apart from Byatt's, tend to conflate 'writing in the English language' with 'writing by the English', as Byatt herself pointed out. Even Malcolm Bradbury's interesting *Penguin Book of the Modern British Short Story* mysteriously included a story by Samuel Beckett.

Not everyone shrinks away from national pride in this area, I wincingly discover. In fact, the practice of the short story appears to be, for much of the world, an opportunity for such jingoistic sentiments that one wonders that it hasn't been declared an Olympic sport. While I was preparing this book, the American short-story writer Lorrie Moore was reported as telling a presumably not incredulous Brooklyn audience that 'American short story writing is the best in the world really . . . partly because it has been nourished by universities.'[9] I was interested to read the unqualified opinion of the veteran Indian writer Khushwant Singh in an anthology of Indian short stories that 'Western short stories tend to be prolix, leaving the reader to guess what they are all about. That is why many critics believe that the West has lost the art of writing short stories. In India, on the other hand, the short story is as vibrant as ever.'[10]

No doubt very similar statements of national pride could be gathered from many nations, but it is simply impossible to imagine any British writer now asserting anything of the kind. That is not because of any serious doubt about the quality and the energy of the tradition, but because we just don't say that sort of thing. I don't want to enter into nationalist competitions: there is no point in trying to elevate one nation's writers in the form over another. Chekhov, Alice Munro, Kleist, John Cheever and Kipling are, in the best sense, freaks, and their genius is at once local and irrelevant to a local tradition. The consequences of this national modesty, or at any rate the refusal to bang the national drum, are that the British short story has been consistently underestimated and even dismissed. It is much easier, for instance, to find reviews of American collections in British newspapers than British collections. Reading some ill-informed accounts of British short fiction, I was reminded of the foreword to the first edition of the *London Magazine* in 1954, where the editor expressed a recurrent attitude through allegory.

> Two small boys came across a walnut tree one day at the bottom of a large, neglected garden. One of them said 'I can't see any walnuts on that tree.' The other replied: 'I bet you there are some, all the same.' And he swung up into the tree with his stick. The first boy was staring into the leaves where his companion had disappeared, when suddenly a walnut hit him on the nose and then a shower of them crashed into the grass all round him. A voice from the top of the tree shouted out in triumph: 'Who said there weren't any walnuts?' To which a voice from the ground replied: 'How do you know they aren't rotten? Rotten ones don't count.' But when the boy who had climbed the tree slithered down, he found that the other boy had walked away without bothering to look.

I found, preparing this book, that there were people who, like that boy, were prepared to dismiss the local tradition immediately; on investigation, sometimes this attitude came shortly before the revelation that they had never read, and sometimes never heard of, V. S. Pritchett, A. E. Coppard or Kipling's short stories.

But what is that local tradition? What do Britain's short-story writers do most characteristically? In some ways, I came to think of Arthur Conan Doyle's masterpiece, 'Silver Blaze' as the exemplary British short story. It is extraordinarily playful with the conventions of its own genre, beginning with an indication of the murderer that could hardly be more explicit or blatant. It is concerned with a huge range of significant and interesting physical objects, including the elaborate dress that is never seen and its owner never identified. It is about the actions of the overlooked and misunderstood. It is about social class, of course. Like many great short stories from Britain, it revolves around a general social gathering with its own rituals – William Sansom's wonderful 'A Contest of Ladies' is a good comparison. It appears to be telling a thrilling story while in fact being entirely contemplative and thoughtful about events in the past – the action of the story is mostly confined to two train journeys and a long walk. It is macabre, and draws some ingenious amusement from its grotesque elements – the cleverest and most enchanting surely the detail of the lame sheep that Sherlock so brilliantly intuits. (He tells us how brilliant he is, too.) It gives the appearance of being richly exact, while in fact being an utter fantastic fabrication – as Doyle himself noted, if the events had happened in real life, half the characters would have been in jail and the others banned from racing for life. And it shows no terror of literary genre, while doing with the conventions of that genre whatever it feels like.

Playfulness is never far from the British short story. This playfulness encourages the form in unexpected directions at different times; the brilliant outbreak of experimental short fiction in the 1960s, including Christine Brooke-Rose and J. G. Ballard – I should also like to have included Anna Kavan – started to influence quite unexpected people including Kingsley Amis. But long before that, the quality of playfulness never prevents the British short story from attaining real seriousness and emotional depth. Arnold Bennett's simply magnificent 'The Matador of the Five Towns' finds space for engaged amusement in its fabulous social panorama, closing down on meanness and tragedy in a little room. Kipling's 'The Village that Voted the Earth was Flat', surely the howling artificial pinnacle of Kipling's genius, was written and published a couple of months before the outbreak of the Great War; as a consideration of hysteria and wildness in the public mind, it has never been matched. Unexpectedly, it is both painfully cruel and fascinated by comedy in the most detailed way. More recently, the brilliant flippancy of tone of Georgina Hammick's masterly 'Grist' shading by degrees into real, wailing grief sustains a long-established tone in British writing. That interest in the overlooked, the apparently insignificant, finds a parallel not just in Dickens's great 'Mrs Lirriper's Lodgings' but in a flurry of superb and often richly orchestrated writing on proletarian subjects from the 1890s onwards – the *Yellow Book* stories and, here, Jack Common's beautiful story, are followed by the magical G. F. Green and Alan Sillitoe, one of the greatest of the writers here. In recent years, I very much admired David Rose, and would have liked to include a story by him about road-menders. Above all, the great British short story is outward-facing, analysing the world. *Chambers's Journal* promised, on its foundation in 1832, 'lots of nice little stories about travellers in Asia and Africa'.[11] As it moved into its heyday, the fascination with the outwardly exotic was supplemented by a much richer vein, finding considerable exotic interest in territories closer to hand.

There are sumptuous riches in the British short story, and the raucously exuberant piece of playfulness is only part of it. There is, too, an exquisitely withdrawn and precise vein, often claimed by women writers: these were among my most precious discoveries while reading, and I came to see the tradition that runs through Malachi Whitaker, Dorothy Edwards, Viola Meynell and Elizabeth Taylor to Shena Mackay – Jackie Kay and Jane Gardam should also be mentioned here – as a sublime, vulnerable one. Withdrawn exactitudes are an important part of the tradition, but only part. It often needs to be stressed that the British short story can be most itself when rumbustious, violent, extravagant, fantastical; above all, when it yields to a national taste for the theatrical.

So often, the great British short story seems to be fascinated by performance. A recurrent form is the narrator after dinner, who shares the best story he ever heard: as time goes on, and leisurely dinners become less universal in the real world, the story starts to turn towards the tale told in a railway carriage, like Graham Greene's thrillingly preposterous 'The Hint of an Explanation', or – surprisingly common – the tale told by a barber to his client, of which the greatest must surely be V. S. Pritchett's 'You Make Your Own Life' with its final brutal slash of the razorblade. Pritchett was the greatest of British short-story writers, and embedded in the art of performance, whether in the sardonic explanation of a stage trick in 'The Fall' that opens up a man's relationship with his absent brother, or the performance that has no idea that it's going on until its last line, as in 'When My Girl Comes Home', or the stage monologue which 'The Camberwell Beauty' initially seems to be. The monologue, as of a stage character, is a very common form in the British short story; I regretted not being able to include more after Dickens's 'Mrs Lirriper' set an unmatchable standard that only Pritchett began to reach. Too many others were ultimately rather limp interwar matinée offerings, but the indirect relationship with the stage, and with performance generally, animated many of the best short stories here.

The quality of performance drives two recurrent qualities of the British short story: its dependence on comedy in any and all circumstances, and its love of Grand Guignol. Wild and impossible violence often emerges from physical specificity, as in the Aickman or the great T. H. White story. The physically specific can be the source of comedy, too, and often these two very British modes combine. Adam Marek's eye-popping story 'The 40-Litre Monkey' has plenty of precedents. Even a writer as unfailingly sympathetic as Tessa Hadley can give a story of considerable suffering the detached and borderline flippant title 'Buckets of Blood'. Readers may be surprised at the things they are asked to laugh at by Somerset Maugham, Wilkie Collins or Max Beerbohm. The violence in the splendid Wodehouse story is always, it seems, waiting to break out. Sometimes the territory that seems to interest the writer is the exact moment when the laughter freezes on the lips, not just in the sublime and terrifying Kipling story but, in a minor key, in the A. E. Coppard and Rhys Davies. Both Coppard and Davies were masters of what A. S. Byatt very accurately calls 'mixed tones', and in their very best stories, as represented here, the reader is often moved to laughter before wondering whether laughter is quite the thing. The uncertainty, exactly pinpointed, is at the heart of their achievement.

It's common, in compilations of this sort, for the anthologizer to make a case for his general subject by playing down the comic element. Comedy is so much at the centre of the British short story that, by contrast, I've sometimes included a short story by a writer not primarily known for his or her humour. Elizabeth Taylor's virtuoso late 'In and Out the Houses' has all her social precision of detail (the ravioli!) but is cast as a broad farce where only one character ever goes anywhere – the technical command is stunning, like a Mozart rondo. I wanted, too, to highlight Elizabeth Bowen's gift for comedy with a savage edge with a relatively unfamiliar early piece rather than the acknowledged greatness of 'Mysterious Kôr'. That gift for comedy in surprising places continues: it beautifully lightens Zadie Smith's wonderful 'The Embassy of Cambodia' with some unexpectedly broad, Dickensian characters. I don't think it will ever go away, however superficially serious the subject of the short story.

From that valuing of comedy comes, I think, a characteristic of the British short story to entwine, reverse, overturn itself and take directions that nobody could foresee; this emerges most consistently in tone and flavour. The great British short story is often a ferocious ride with hidden traps and unpredictable bogs, explosions and patches of tranquillity or exhaustion. Surprise is a quality often prized; even the surprise offered by a story that never changes its tone, like Dorothy Edwards's or Mary Lamb's stories. In an extraordinary story by Penelope Gilliatt I came close to including, a well-planted fictional robot called FRANK does exactly nothing, but deserves the story's title. The surprise may be in the point of view, as in the wild shifts of direction in the Jean Rhys short story, or realizing that the person who places himself at the centre of the story has no significance whatsoever, as in Pritchett's 'The Camberwell Beauty'. Comedy, the tripping up of expectations, the overturning of an established world: these things have a tendency to shape the form even when laughter is not contemplated.

Some of these distinctive qualities are more or less permanently present in the British short story. Some, however, ebb and flow with fashion, and I have tried to suggest in my selection how the short story has a predominant flavour and urgent themes at different moments in its history. The feeling of growing hysteria with a diabolic edge before the Great War is striking – the feeling, perhaps, as Richard Strauss's Salomé puts it, that '*es sind noch nicht genug Tote*', there aren't enough dead yet. There is speculation about what women are to do with their lives in the 1920s that emerges in a spate of brilliant feminine two-handers. New subjects emerge; new themes interest the best talent at work.

A confident relationship with genre has never limited the British short story, though some genres have proved more fruitful to the form than others. The love story and the detective story were evidently very popular forms in magazine fiction: they did not seem to me to be natural candidates for short fiction, often requiring as they do a slow expansion on the significance of details and a warm growth of feeling over time. Perhaps for the same reason, there was no shortage of historical short stories, but, apart from Jean Rhys and the unique genius of Penelope Fitzgerald, very few I could much admire. Other forms, however, that could rest on suggestion and airy implication were natural. I sometimes felt, reading through the collected stories of classic authors, that an anthology of this sort could be made up of nothing other than the occasional ghost story that almost every British writer produced; there is at least one first-rate example from the works of many writers, including Saki, Elizabeth Bowen and Penelope Fitzgerald, as well as specialists like E. F. Benson and M. R. James. Ghost stories are British in the most conventional way; the great practitioners, like M. R. James and Robert Aickman, rely on a background of propriety and high respectability. When those moments of propriety are broken, sometimes with screaming terror, sometimes merely with the narrator being physically touched for the first time in the story, or by gatecrashing a party, a different, less orderly side of the British is revealed. Science fiction, too, which can rest on the suggestion of vast unknowable changes, was as natural to short fiction from the start as horror. Fine as G. K. Chesterton's 'The Honour of Israel Gow' is, it would be perfect if it ended before the solution started being put together, at the point of maximum bafflement, with all the horror and grotesquery in full untethered flight. Another point of genre possibility comes with the curious, dreamlike fantasy that sometimes overtakes the short story: the burst of allegorical mysticism in late-1940s short stories, including T. F. Powys and Sylvia Townsend Warner, is a very striking one – one should perhaps add Tolkien's long and beautiful 'Leaf by Niggle', a story it proved impractical to include.

Was there a regional aspect? Perhaps. The Scottish short story has aspects of folklore and a consistent interest in experiments with voice that is their own – I was sorry not to find space for Eric Linklater, and to have included some more early compilers of folklore would have taken the anthology in a direction too rich to be merely sampled. The Welsh short story produces profound mastery, and its fascination with the unexpected direction and the superficially relaxed, conversational purpose emerges in Rhys Davies and the breathtaking Alun Lewis story – a hearty, skirling, raucous quality, too.

It may be that the British short story offers the longest and richest national tradition in the world, and with its own particular qualities of genre, extroversion, confidence and improvisation escapes any kind of predictability. This anthology could very easily have been twice as long as it is. I was determined that I would not include famous writers on the basis of achievement that, in reality, lay elsewhere – neither Firbank nor

Virginia Woolf would command our interest on the basis of their stories if they had never written novels. E. M. Forster was a difficult case. The stories I most admired were published posthumously, ruling them out of consideration, and the ones he published in his lifetime suffered from the whimsy that his novels, at greater length, command and subdue. Nor was it right to include stories that were merely historically interesting; Scott's short stories are important, but I couldn't admire any of them as much as the best of Galt. I also thought that Walter de la Mare was in the unusual position of requiring lengthy submersion in his peculiar tone. It was impossible to imagine any of his stories making sense in an anthology of this sort, and I could not make up my mind whether he was a writer of genius or a writer of essentially entranced badness.

I thought it was my duty to shut my ears against the noise of fashionable approbation. Particularly in the case of contemporary writers, it would have been easy to have gone along with some lazily acclaimed writers. Of course, there are some writers at work now whom I omitted at the last with immense regret, such as Jane Gardam, David Rose, Gerard Woodward or Helen Dunmore. There were other highly acclaimed practitioners, however, who never came near a final selection. Reading through an author's successive collections of stories was a salutary lesson in discovering that a large reputation really had no idea how to put a story together, or had only one idea, much repeated over the course of decades. Other restrictions made themselves felt. It was agony to confine myself to a single story by a very varied and fecund writer. Worst of all, it sometimes had to be accepted that an author who had done something rather brilliant with a short story couldn't quite justify his or her space at the expense of a greater master. While not feeling much guilt about the omission of a fashionable name or a Woolf – they will survive my neglect – I do feel guilty about these unfamiliar names who had made something strong and beautiful and striking, and yet, at the last, I found that a J. E. Buckrose, a Margery Sharp, an Elizabeth Goudge, an H. A. Manhood or an R. Murray Gilchrist (much admired by Arnold Bennett) had to drop back into oblivion. With all that, the task of systematically reading thousands of short stories by hundreds of writers in journals, collections and magazines must count as the most rewarding and surprising of my professional life.

6

Many conversations, much correspondence and casual discussion over the years contributed to this anthology. I would like to thank John Mullan, John Sutherland, Tessa Hadley, Alan Hollinghurst, Nicola Barr, Harriet Harvie-Wood, Georgia Garrett, Georgie Hammick, Peter Parker, D. J. Taylor, Jane Feaver, Ginny Baily, Maggie Fergusson and Candia McWilliam for very helpful suggestions. The idea of the anthology was Simon Winder's at Penguin. Simon both confidently went along with the notion of an anthology on a very generous scale, and, just as importantly, kept the project within bounds. I should also say that he coped manfully with the loss of a splendid Ian Fleming story at the very last stage. The detailed investigation of both journals and collections of stories was only possible thanks to the London Library and the British Library. I would also like to thank Bath Spa University, which gave me time off from teaching at a crucial stage to allow me to get through a very large quantity of reading. Above all, the work of selection owes most to A. S. Byatt, who carved a pioneering path with her 1997 *Oxford Book of the English Short Story* and whose selfless interest and engagement in conversation and correspondence gave me a lot to think about. I am very happy to dedicate this anthology to Antonia, and to correct at least one glaring omission from her anthology; she modestly left herself out, and it is a pleasure to be able to include a superb story by my predecessor.

Notes

1. Review of N. Hawthorne, 'Twice-Told Tales', in Poe, Edgar Allen, *Essays and Reviews*, ed. G. R. Thompson (New York, 1989), p. 571 .
2. 'The Philosophy of Composition', *ibid*, p. 19.
3. *The Collected Stories of Lanoe Falconer* (Palo Alto, 2010), p. 13.

4. Baldwin, Dean, *Art and Commerce in the British Short Story, 1880–1950* (London, 2013), p. 8.
5. Baldwin, p. 43.
6. Lycett, Andrew, *Conan Doyle: The Man Who Created Sherlock Holmes* (London, 2007), pp. 298, 299.
7. Baldwin, p. 101.
8. *Chambers's Journal*, 3 June 1871.
9. 'A Few Notes upon Mr James', *Yellow Book*, vol. 7, p. 71.
10. Reported on Twitter by an audience member called Koa Beck, 1 February 2014, after a talk at Beth Elohim, Park Slope, Brooklyn.
11. *Khushwant Singh Selects: Best Indian Short Stories*, vol. 2 (Harper Collins, India), p. 9.
12. Quoted by W. Forbes Gray, 'A Hundred Years Old: *Chambers's Journal*, 1832–1932', *Chambers's Journal* (1932), p. 83.

THE
PENGUIN BOOK
of the

BRITISH
SHORT
STORY

VOLUME 2

P. G. WODEHOUSE

Unpleasantness at Bludleigh Court

The poet who was spending the summer at the Anglers' Rest had just begun to read us his new sonnet-sequence when the door of the bar-parlour opened and there entered a young man in gaiters. He came quickly in and ordered beer. In one hand he was carrying a double-barrelled gun, in the other a posy of dead rabbits. These he dropped squashily to the floor: and the poet, stopping in mid-sentence, took one long, earnest look at the remains. Then, wincing painfully, he turned a light green and closed his eyes. It was not until the banging of the door announced the visitor's departure that he came to life again.

Mr Mulliner regarded him sympathetically over his hot Scotch and lemon.

'You appear upset,' he said.

'A little,' admitted the poet. 'A momentary malaise. It may be a purely personal prejudice, but I confess to preferring rabbits with rather more of their contents inside them.'

'Many sensitive souls in your line of business hold similar views,' Mr Mulliner assured him. 'My niece Charlotte did.'

'It is my temperament,' said the poet. 'I dislike all dead things – particularly when, as in the case of the above rabbits, they have so obviously, so – shall I say? – blatantly made the Great Change. Give me,' he went on, the greenish tinge fading from his face, 'life and joy and beauty.'

'Just what my niece Charlotte used to say.'

'Oddly enough, that thought forms the theme of the second sonnet in my sequence – which, now that the young gentleman with the portable morgue has left us, I will . . .'

'My niece Charlotte,' said Mr Mulliner, with quiet firmness, 'was one of those gentle, dreamy, wistful girls who take what I have sometimes felt to be a mean advantage of having an ample private income to write Vignettes in Verse for the artistic weeklies. Charlotte's Vignettes in Verse had a wide vogue among the editors of London's higher-browed but less prosperous periodicals. Directly these frugal men realized that she was willing to supply unstinted Vignettes gratis, for the mere pleasure of seeing herself in print, they were all over her. The consequence was that before long she had begun to move freely in the most refined literary circles: and one day, at a little luncheon at the Crushed Pansy (The Restaurant With A Soul), she found herself seated next to a godlike young man at the sight of whom something seemed to go off inside her like a spring.'

'Talking of Spring . . .' said the poet.

'Cupid,' proceeded Mr Mulliner, 'has always found the family to which I belong a ready mark for his bow. Our hearts are warm, our passions quick. It is not too much to say that my niece Charlotte was in love with this young man before she had finished spearing the first anchovy out of the hors-d'œuvres dish. He was intensely spiritual-looking, with a broad, white forehead and eyes that seemed to Charlotte not so much eyes as a couple of holes punched in the surface of a beautiful soul. He wrote, she learned, Pastels in Prose: and his name, if she had caught it correctly at the moment of their introduction, was Aubrey Trefusis.

Friendship ripens quickly at the Crushed Pansy. The *poulet rôti au cresson* had scarcely been distributed before the young man was telling Charlotte his hopes, his fears, and the story of his boyhood. And she was amazed to find that he sprang – not from a long line of artists but from an ordinary, conventional county family of the type that cares for nothing except hunting and shooting.

'You can readily imagine,' he said, helping her to Brussels sprouts, 'how intensely such an environment jarred upon my unfolding spirit. My family are greatly respected in the neighbourhood, but I personally have always looked upon them as a gang of blood-imbrued plug-uglies. My views on kindness to animals are rigid. My impulse, on encountering a rabbit, is to offer it lettuce. To my family, on the other hand, a rabbit seems incomplete without a deposit of small shot in it. My father, I believe, has cut off more assorted birds in their prime than any other man in the Midlands. A whole morning was spoiled for me last week by the sight of a photograph of him in the *Tatler*, looking rather severely at a dying duck. My elder brother Reginald spreads destruction in every branch of the animal kingdom. And my younger brother Wilfred is, I understand, working his way up to the larger fauna by killing sparrows with an air-gun. Spiritually, one might just as well live in Chicago as at Bludleigh Court.'

'Bludleigh Court?' cried Charlotte.

'The moment I was twenty-one and came into a modest but sufficient inheritance, I left the place and went to London to lead the life literary. The family, of course, were appalled. My Uncle Francis, I remember, tried to reason with me for hours. Uncle Francis, you see, used to be a famous big-game hunter. They tell me he has shot more gnus than any other man who ever went to Africa. In fact, until recently he virtually never stopped shooting gnus. Now, I hear, he has developed lumbago and is down at Bludleigh treating it with Riggs's Superfine Emulsion and sun-baths.'

'But is Bludleigh Court your home?'

'That's right. Bludleigh Court, Lesser Bludleigh, near Goresby-on-the-Ouse, Bedfordshire.'

'But Bludleigh Court belongs to Sir Alexander Bassinger.'

'My name is really Bassinger. I adopted the pen-name of Trefusis to spare the family's feelings. But how do you come to know of the place?'

'I'm going down there next week for a visit. My mother was an old friend of Lady Bassinger.'

Aubrey was astonished. And, being, like all writers of Pastels in Prose, a neat phrase-maker, he said what a small world it was, after all.

'Well, well, well!' he said.

'From what you tell me,' said Charlotte, 'I'm afraid I shall not enjoy my visit. If there's one thing I loathe, it's anything connected with sport.'

'Two minds with but a single thought,' said Aubrey. 'Look here, I'll tell you what. I haven't been near Bludleigh for years, but if you're going there, why, dash it, I'll come too – aye, even though it means meeting my Uncle Francis.'

'You will?'

'I certainly will. I don't consider it safe that a girl of your exquisite refinement and sensibility should be dumped down at an abattoir like Bludleigh Court without a kindred spirit to lend her moral stability.'

'What do you mean?'

'I'll tell you.' His voice was grave. 'That house exercises a spell.'

'A what?'

'A spell. A ghastly spell that saps the strongest humanitarian principles. Who knows what effect it might have upon you, should you go there without someone like me to stand by you and guide you in your hour of need?'

'What nonsense!'

'Well, all I can tell you is that once, when I was a boy, a high official of Our Dumb Brothers' League of Mercy arrived there latish on a Friday night, and at two-fifteen on the Saturday afternoon he was the life and soul of an informal party got up for the purpose of drawing one of the local badgers out of an upturned barrel.'

Charlotte laughed merrily.

'The spell will not affect me,' she said.

'Nor me, of course,' said Aubrey. 'But all the same, I would prefer to be by your side, if you don't mind.'

'Mind, Mr Bassinger!' breathed Charlotte softly, and was thrilled to note that at the words and the look with which she accompanied them this man to whom – for, as I say, we Mulliners are quick workers – she had already given her heart, quivered violently. It seemed to her that in those soulful eyes of his she had seen the love-light.

Bludleigh Court, when Charlotte reached it some days later, proved to be a noble old pile of Tudor architecture, situated in rolling parkland and flanked by pleasant gardens leading to a lake with a tree-fringed boat-house. Inside, it was comfortably furnished and decorated throughout with groves of glass cases containing the goggle-eyed remnants of birds and beasts assassinated at one time or another by Sir Alexander Bassinger and his son, Reginald. From every wall there peered down with an air of mild reproach selected portions of the gnus, moose, elks, zebus, antelopes, giraffes, mountain goats and wapiti which had had the misfortune to meet Colonel Sir Francis Pashley-Drake before lumbago spoiled him for the chase. The cemetery also included a few stuffed sparrows, which showed that little Wilfred was doing his bit.

The first two days of her visit Charlotte passed mostly in the society of Colonel Pashley-Drake, the Uncle Francis to whom Aubrey had alluded. He seemed to have taken a paternal fancy to her: and, lithely though she dodged down back-stairs and passages, she generally found him breathing heavily at her side. He was a red-faced, almost circular man, with eyes like a prawn's, and he spoke to her freely of lumbago, gnus and Aubrey.

'So you're a friend of my young nephew?' he said, snorting twice in a rather unpleasant manner. It was plain that he disapproved of the pastel-artist. 'Shouldn't see too much of him, if I were you. Not the sort of fellow I'd like any daughter of mine to get friendly with.'

'You are quite wrong,' said Charlotte warmly. 'You have only to gaze into Mr Bassinger's eyes to see that his morals are above reproach.'

'I never gaze into his eyes,' replied Colonel Pashley-Drake. 'Don't like his eyes. Wouldn't gaze into them if you paid me. I maintain his whole outlook on life is morbid and unwholesome. I like a man to be a clean, strong, upstanding Englishman who can look his gnu in the face and put an ounce of lead in it.'

'Life,' said Charlotte coldly, 'is not all gnus.'

'You imply that there are also wapiti, moose, zebus and mountain-goats?' said Sir Francis. 'Well, maybe you're right. All the same, I'd give the fellow a wide berth, if I were you.'

'So far from doing so,' replied Charlotte proudly, 'I am about to go for a stroll with him by the lake at this very moment.'

And, turning away with a petulant toss of her head, she moved off to meet Aubrey, who was hurrying towards her across the terrace.

'I am so glad you came, Mr Bassinger,' she said to him as they walked together in the direction of the lake. 'I was beginning to find your uncle Francis a little excessive.'

Aubrey nodded sympathetically. He had observed her in conversation with his relative and his heart had gone out to her.

'Two minutes of my uncle Francis,' he said, 'is considered by the best judges a good medium dose for an adult. So you find him trying, eh? I was wondering what impression my family had made on you.'

Charlotte was silent for a moment.

'How relative everything is in this world,' she said pensively. 'When I first met your father, I thought I had never seen anybody more completely loathsome. Then I was introduced to your brother Reginald, and I realized that, after all, your father might have been considerably worse. And, just as I was thinking that Reginald was the furthest point possible, along came your Uncle Francis, and Reginald's quiet charm seemed to leap out at me like a beacon on a dark night. Tell me,' she said, 'has no one ever thought of doing anything about your Uncle Francis?'

Aubrey shook his head gently.

'It is pretty generally recognised now that he is beyond the reach of human science. The only thing to do seems to be to let him go on till he eventually runs down.'

They sat together on a rustic bench overlooking the water. It was a lovely morning. The sun shone on the little wavelets which the sighing breeze drove gently to the shore. A dreamy stillness had fallen on the world, broken only by the distant sound of Sir Alexander Bassinger murdering magpies, of Reginald Bassinger encouraging dogs to eviscerate a rabbit, of Wilfred busy among the sparrows, and a monotonous droning noise from the upper terrace, which was Colonel Sir Francis Pashley-Drake telling Lady Bassinger what to do with the dead gnu.

Aubrey was the first to break the silence.

'How lovely the world is, Miss Mulliner.'

'Yes, isn't it!'

'How softly the breeze caresses yonder water.'

'Yes, doesn't it!'

'How fragrant a scent of wild flowers it has.'

'Yes, hasn't it!'

They were silent again.

'On such a day,' said Aubrey, 'the mind seems to turn irresistibly to Love.'

'Love?' said Charlotte, her heart beginning to flutter.

'Love,' said Aubrey. 'Tell me, Miss Mulliner, have you ever thought of Love?'

He took her hand. Her head was bent, and with the toe of her dainty shoe she toyed with a passing snail.

'Life, Miss Mulliner,' said Aubrey, 'is a Sahara through which we all must pass. We start at the Cairo of the cradle and we travel on to the – er – well, we go travelling on.'

'Yes, don't we!' said Charlotte.

'After we can see the distant goal . . .'

'Yes, can't we!'

'. . . and would fain reach it.'

'Yes, wouldn't we!'

'But the way is rough and weary. We have to battle through the sand-storms of Destiny, face with what courage we may the howling simoons of Fate. And very unpleasant it all is. But sometimes in the Sahara of Life, if we are fortunate, we come upon the Oasis of Love. That oasis, when I had all but lost hope, I reached at one-fifteen on the afternoon of Tuesday, the twenty-second of last month. There comes a time in the life of every man when he sees Happiness beckoning to him and must grasp it. Miss Mulliner, I have something to ask you which I have been trying to ask ever since the day when we two first met. Miss Mulliner . . . Charlotte . . . Will you be my . . . Gosh! Look at that whacking great rat! Loo-loo-loo-loo-loo-loo-loo-loo!' said Aubrey, changing the subject.

Once, in her childhood, a sportive playmate had secretly withdrawn the chair on which Charlotte Mulliner was preparing to seat herself. Years had passed, but the recollection of the incident remained green in her memory. In frosty weather she could still feel the old wound. And now, as Aubrey Bassinger suddenly behaved in this remarkable manner, she experienced the same sensation again. It was as though something blunt and heavy had hit her on the head at the exact moment when she was slipping on a banana-skin.

She stared round-eyed at Aubrey. He had released her hand, sprung to his feet, and now, armed with her parasol, was beating furiously in the lush grass at the waterside. And every little while his mouth would open, his head would go back, and uncouth sounds would proceed from his slavering jaws.

'Yoicks! Yoicks! Yoicks!' cried Aubrey.

And again,

'Tally-ho! Hard For'ard! Tally-ho!'

Presently the fever seemed to pass. He straightened himself and came back to where she stood.

'It must have got away into a hole or something,' he said, removing a bead of perspiration from his forehead with the ferrule of the parasol. 'The fact of the matter is, it's silly ever to go out in the country without a good dog. If only I'd had a nice, nippy terrier with me, I might have obtained some solid results. As it is, a fine rat – gone – just like that! Oh, well, that's Life, I suppose.' He paused. 'Let me see,' he said. 'Where was I?'

And then it was as though he waked from a trance. His flushed face paled.

'I say,' he stammered, 'I'm afraid you must think me most awfully rude.'

'Pray do not mention it,' said Charlotte coldly.

'Oh, but you must. Dashing off like that.'

'Not at all.'

'What I was going to say, when I was interrupted, was, will you be my wife?'

'Oh?'

'Yes.'

'Well, I won't.'

'You won't?'

'No. Never.' Charlotte's voice was tense with a scorn which she did not attempt to conceal. 'So this is what you were all the time, Mr Bassinger – a secret sportsman!'

Aubrey quivered from head to foot.

'I'm not! I'm not! It was the hideous spell of this ghastly house that overcame me.'

'Pah!'

'What did you say?'

'I said "Pah"!'

'Why did you say "Pah"?'

'Because,' said Charlotte, with flashing eyes, 'I do not believe you. Your story is thin and fishy.'

'But it's the truth. It was as if some hypnotic influence had gripped me, forcing me to act against all my higher inclinations. Can't you understand? Would you condemn me for a moment's passing weakness? Do you think,' he cried passionately, 'that the real Aubrey Bassinger would raise a hand to touch a rat, save in the way of kindness? I love rats, I tell you – love them. I used to keep them as a boy. White ones with pink eyes.'

Charlotte shook her head. Her face was cold and hard.

'Good-bye, Mr Bassinger,' she said. 'From this instant we meet as strangers.'

She turned and was gone. And Aubrey Bassinger, covering his face with his hands, sank on the bench, feeling like a sand-bagged leper.

The mind of Charlotte Mulliner, in the days which followed the painful scene which I have just described, was torn, as you may well imagine, with conflicting emotions. For a time, as was natural, anger predominated. But after a while sadness overcame indignation. She mourned for her lost happiness.

And yet, she asked herself, how else could she have acted? She had worshipped Aubrey Bassinger. She had set him upon a pedestal, looked up to him as a great white soul. She had supposed him one who lived, far above this world's coarseness and grime, on a rarefied plane of his own, thinking beautiful thoughts. Instead of which, it now appeared, he went about the place chasing rats with parasols. What could she have done but spurn him?

That there lurked in the atmosphere of Bludleigh Court a sinister influence that sapped the principles of the most humanitarian and sent them ravening to and fro, seeking for prey, she declined to believe. The theory was pure banana-oil. If such an influence was in operation at Bludleigh, why had it not affected her?

No, if Aubrey Bassinger chased rats with parasols, it could only mean that he was one of Nature's rat-chasers. And to such a one, cost what it might to refuse, she could never confide her heart.

Few things are more embarrassing to a highly-strung girl than to be for any length of time in the same house with a man whose love she has been compelled to decline, and Charlotte would have given much to be able to leave Bludleigh Court. But there was, it seemed, to be a garden-party on the following Tuesday, and Lady Bassinger had urged her so strongly to stay on for it that departure was out of the question.

To fill the leaden moments, she immersed herself in her work. She had a long-standing commission to supply the *Animal-Lovers Gazette* with a poem for its Christmas number, and to the task of writing this she proceeded to devote herself. And gradually the ecstasy of literary composition eased her pain.

The days crept by. Old Sir Alexander continued to maltreat magpies. Reginald and the local rabbits fought a never-ceasing battle, they striving to keep up the birth-rate, he to reduce it. Colonel Pashley-Drake maundered on about gnus he had met. And Aubrey dragged himself about the house, looking licked to a splinter. Eventually Tuesday came, and with it the garden-party.

Lady Bassinger's annual garden party was one of the big events of the countryside. By four o'clock all that was bravest and fairest for miles around had assembled on the big lawn. But Charlotte, though she had stayed on specially to be present, was not one of the gay throng. At about the time when the first strawberry was being dipped in its cream, she was up in her room, staring with bewildered eyes at a letter which had arrived by the second post.

The *Animal-Lovers Gazette* had turned her poem down!

Yes, turned it down flat, in spite of the fact that it had been commissioned and that she was not asking a penny for it. Accompanying the rejected manuscript was a curt note from the editor, in which he said that he feared its tone might offend his readers.

Charlotte was stunned. She was not accustomed to having her efforts rejected. This one, moreover, had seemed to her so particularly good. A hard judge of her own work, she had said to herself, as she licked the envelope, that this time, if never before, she had delivered the goods.

She unfolded the manuscript and re-read it.

It ran as follows:

GOOD GNUS

(*A Vignette in Verse*)

BY

CHARLOTTE MULLINER

When cares attack and life seems black,
How sweet it is to pot a yak,
   Or puncture hares and grizzly bears,
    And others I could mention:
But in my Animals 'Who's Who'
No name stands higher than the Gnu:
   And each new gnu that comes in view
    Receives my prompt attention.

When Afric's sun is sinking low,
And shadows wander to and fro,
   And everywhere there's in the air
     A hush that's deep and solemn;
Then is the time good men and true
With View Halloo pursue the gnu:
   (The safest spot to put your shot
     Is through the spinal column).

To take the creature by surprise
We must adopt some rude disguise,
   Although deceit is never sweet,
     And falsehoods don't attract us:
So, as with gun in hand you wait,
Remember to impersonate
   A tuft of grass, a mountain-pass,
     A kopje or a cactus.

A brief suspense, and then at last
The waiting's o'er, the vigil past:
   A careful aim. A spurt of flame.
     It's done. You've pulled the trigger,
And one more gnu, so fair and frail,
Has handed in its dinner-pail:
   (The females all are rather small,
     The males are somewhat bigger).

Charlotte laid the manuscript down, frowning. She chafed at the imbecility of editors. Less than ever was she able to understand what anyone could find in it to cavil at. Tone likely to offend? What did the man mean about the tone being likely to offend? She had never heard such nonsense in her life. How could the tone possibly offend? It was unexceptionable. The whole poem breathed that clean, wholesome, healthy spirit of Sport which has made England what it is. And the thing was not only lyrically perfect, but educational as well. It told the young reader, anxious to shoot gnus but uncertain of the correct procedure, exactly what he wanted to know.

She bit her lip. Well, if this Animal-Lovers bird didn't know a red-hot contribution when he saw one, she would jolly well find somebody else who did – and quick, too. She . . .

At this moment, something occurred to distract her thoughts. Down on the terrace below, little Wilfred, complete with airgun, had come into her line of vision. The boy was creeping along in a quiet, purposeful manner, obviously intent on the chase: and it suddenly came over Charlotte Mulliner in a wave that here she had been in this house all this time and never once had thought of borrowing the child's weapon and having a plug at something with it.

The sky was blue. The sun was shining. All Nature seemed to call to her to come out and kill things.

She left the room and ran quickly down the stairs.

And what of Aubrey, meanwhile? Grief having slowed him up on his feet, he had been cornered by his mother and marched off to hand cucumber sandwiches at the garden-party. After a brief spell of servitude, however, he had contrived to escape and was wandering on the terrace, musing mournfully, when he observed his brother Wilfred approaching. And at the same moment Charlotte Mulliner emerged from the house and came hurrying in their direction. In a flash, Aubrey perceived that here was a situation which, shrewdly handled, could be turned greatly to his advantage. Affecting to be unaware of Charlotte's approach, he stopped his brother and eyed the young thug sternly.

'Wilfred,' he said, 'where are you going with that gun?'

The boy appeared embarrassed.

'Just shooting.'

Aubrey took the weapon from him and raised his voice slightly. Out of the corner of his eye he had seen that Charlotte was now well within hearing.

'Shooting, eh?' he said. 'Shooting? I see. And have you never been taught, wretched child, that you should be kind to the animals that crave your compassion? Has no one ever told you that he prayeth best who loveth best all things both great and small? For shame, Wilfred, for shame!'

Charlotte had come up, and was standing there, looking at them inquiringly.

'What's all this about?' she asked.

Aubrey started dramatically.

'Miss Mulliner! I was not aware that you were there. All this? Oh, nothing. I found this lad here on his way to shoot sparrows with his air-gun, and I am taking the thing from him. It may seem to you a high-handed action on my part. You may consider me hyper-sensitive. You may ask, Why all this fuss about a few birds? But that is Aubrey Bassinger. Aubrey Bassinger will not lightly allow even the merest sparrow to be placed in jeopardy. Tut, Wilfred,' he said. 'Tut! Cannot you see now how wrong it is to shoot the poor sparrows?'

'But I wasn't going to shoot sparrows,' said the boy. 'I was going to shoot Uncle Francis while he is having his sun-bath.'

'It is also wrong,' said Aubrey, after a slight hesitation, 'to shoot Uncle Francis while he is having his sun-bath.'

Charlotte Mulliner uttered an impatient exclamation. And Aubrey, looking at her, saw that her eyes were glittering with a strange light. She breathed quickly through her delicately-chiselled nose. She seemed feverish, and a medical man would have been concerned about her blood-pressure.

'Why?' she demanded vehemently. 'Why is it wrong? Why shouldn't he shoot his Uncle Francis while he is having his sun-bath?'

Aubrey stood for a moment, pondering. Her razor-like feminine intelligence had cut cleanly to the core of the matter. After all, now that she put it like that, why not?

'Think how it would tickle him up.'

'True,' said Aubrey, nodding. 'True.'

'And his Uncle Francis is precisely the sort of man who ought to have been shot at with air-guns incessantly for the last thirty years. The moment I met him, I said to myself, "That man ought to be shot at with air-guns."'

Aubrey nodded again. Her girlish enthusiasm had begun to infect him.

'There is much in what you say,' he admitted.

'Where is he?' asked Charlotte, turning to the boy.

'On the roof of the boathouse.'

Charlotte's face clouded.

'H'm!' she said. 'That's awkward. How is one to get at him?'

'I remember Uncle Francis telling me once,' said Aubrey, 'that, when you went shooting tigers, you climbed a tree. There are plenty of trees by the boathouse.'

'Admirable!'

For an instant there came to disturb Aubrey's hearty joy in the chase a brief, faint flicker of prudence.

'But . . . I say . . . Do you really think . . . Ought we . . . ?'

Charlotte's eyes flashed scornfully.

'Infirm of purpose,' she said. 'Give me the air-gun!'

'I was only thinking . . .'

'Well?'

'I suppose you know he'll have practically nothing on?'

Charlotte Mulliner laughed lightly.

'He can't intimidate *me*,' she said. 'Come! Let us be going.'

Up on the roof of the boathouse, the beneficent ultra-violet rays of the afternoon sun pouring down on his globular surface, Colonel Sir Francis Pashley-Drake lay in that pleasant half-waking, half-dreaming state that accompanies this particular form of lumbago-treatment. His mind flitted lightly from one soothing subject to another. He thought of elks he had shot in Canada, of moufflon he had shot in the Grecian Archipelago, of giraffes he had shot in Nigeria. He was just on the point of thinking of a hippopotamus which he had shot in Egypt, when the train of his meditations was interrupted by a soft popping sound not far away. He smiled affectionately. So little Wilfred was out with his air-gun, eh?

A thrill of quiet pride passed through Colonel Pashley-Drake. He had trained the lad well, he felt. With a garden-party in progress, with all the opportunities it offered for quiet gorging, how many boys of Wilfred's age would have neglected their shooting to hang round the tea-table and stuff themselves with cakes. But this fine lad . . .

Ping! There it was again. The boy must be somewhere quite close at hand. He wished he could be at his side, giving him kindly advice. Wilfred, he felt, was a young fellow after his own heart. What destruction he would spread among the really worthwhile animals when he grew up and put aside childish things and exchanged his air-gun for a Winchester repeater.

Sir Francis Pashley-Drake started. Two inches from where he lay a splinter of wood had sprung from the boathouse roof. He sat up, feeling a little less affectionate.

'Wilfred!'

There was no reply.

'Be careful, Wilfred, my boy. You nearly . . .'

A sharp, agonizing twinge caused him to break off abruptly. He sprang to his feet and began to address the surrounding landscape passionately in one of the lesser-known dialects of the Congo basin. He no longer thought of Wilfred with quiet pride. Few things so speedily modify an uncle's love as a nephew's air-gun bullet in the fleshy part of the leg. Sir Francis Pashley-Drake's plans for this boy's future had undergone in one brief instant a complete change. He no longer desired to stand beside him through his formative years, teaching him the secrets of shikarri. All he wanted to do was to get close enough to him to teach him with the flat of his right hand to be a bit more careful where he pointed his gun.

He was expressing a synopsis of these views in a mixture of Urdu and Cape Dutch, when the words were swept from his lips by the sight of a woman's face, peering from the branches of a near-by tree.

Colonel Pashley-Drake reeled where he stood. Like so many out-door men, he was the soul of modesty. Once, in Bechuanaland, he had left a native witch-dance in a marked manner because he considered the chief's third supplementary wife insufficiently clad. An acute consciousness of the sketchiness of his costume overcame him. He blushed brightly.

'My dear young lady . . .' he stammered.

He had got thus far when he perceived that the young woman was aiming at him something that looked remarkably like an air-gun. Her tongue protruded thoughtfully from the corner of her mouth, she had closed one eye and with the other was squinting tensely along the barrel.

Colonel Sir Francis Pashley-Drake did not linger. In all England there was probably no man more enthusiastic about shooting: but the fascination of shooting as a sport depends almost wholly on whether you are at the right or wrong end of the gun. With an agility which no gnu, unless in the very pink of condition, could have surpassed, he sprang to the side of the roof and leaped off. There was a clump of reeds not far from the boat-house. He galloped across the turf and dived into them.

Charlotte descended from her tree. Her expression was petulant. Girls nowadays are spoiled, and only too readily become peevish when baulked of their pleasures.

'I had no idea he was so nippy,' she said.

'A quick mover,' agreed Aubrey. 'I imagine he got that way from dodging rhinoceroses.'

'Why can't they make these silly guns with two barrels? A single barrel doesn't give a girl a chance.'

Nestling among the reeds, Colonel Sir Francis Pashley-Drake, in spite of the indignation natural to a man in his position, could not help feeling a certain complacency. The old woodcraft of the hunter had stood him, he felt, in good stead. Not many men, he told himself, would have had the initiative and swift intelligence to act so promptly in the face of peril.

He was aware of voices close by.

'What do we do now?' he heard Charlotte Mulliner say.

'We must think,' said the voice of his nephew Aubrey.

'He's in there somewhere.'

'Yes.'

'I hate to see a fine head like that get away,' said Charlotte, and her voice was still querulous. 'Especially after I winged him. The very next poem I write is going to be an appeal to air-gun manufacturers to use their intelligence, if they have any, and turn out a line with two barrels.'

'I shall write a Pastel in Prose on the same subject,' agreed Aubrey.

'Well, what shall we do?'

There was a short silence. An insect of unknown species crept up Colonel Pashley-Drake and bit him in the small of the back.

'I'll tell you what,' said Aubrey. 'I remember Uncle Francis mentioning to me once that when wounded zebus take cover by the reaches of the Lower Zambesi, the sportsman despatches a native assistant to set fire to . . .'

Sir Francis Pashley-Drake emitted a hollow groan. It was drowned by Charlotte's cry of delight.

'Why, of course! How clever you are, Mr Bassinger.'

'Oh no,' said Aubrey modestly.

'Have you matches?'

'I have a cigarette-lighter.'

'Then would it be bothering you too much to go and set light to those reeds – about there would be a good place – and I'll wait here with the gun.'

'I should be charmed.'

'I hate to trouble you.'

'No trouble, I assure you,' said Aubrey. 'A pleasure.'

Three minutes later the revellers on the lawn were interested to observe a sight rare at the better class of English garden-party. Out of a clump of laurel-bushes that bordered the smoothly mown turf there came charging a stout, pink gentleman of middle age who hopped from side to side as he ran. He was wearing a loin-cloth, and seemed in a hurry. They had just time to recognize in this newcomer their hostess's brother, Colonel Sir Francis Pashley-Drake, when he snatched a cloth from the nearest table, draped it round him, and with a quick leap took refuge behind the portly form of the Bishop of Stortford, who was talking to the local Master of Hounds about the difficulty he had in keeping his vicars off the incense.

Charlotte and Aubrey had paused in the shelter of the laurels. Aubrey, peering through this zareba, clicked his tongue regretfully.

'He's taken cover again,' he said. 'I'm afraid we shall find it difficult to dig him out of there. He's gone to earth behind a bishop.'

Receiving no reply, he turned.

'Miss Mulliner!' he exclaimed. 'Charlotte! What is the matter?'

A strange change had come over the girl's beautiful face since he had last gazed at it. The fire had died out of those lovely eyes, leaving them looking like those of a newly awakened somnambulist. She was pale, and the tip of her nose quivered.

'Where am I?' she murmured.

'Bludleigh Manor, Lesser Bludleigh, Goresby-on-the-Ouse, Bedfordshire. Telephone 28 Goresby,' said Aubrey quickly.

'Have I been dreaming? Or did I really . . . Ah, yes, yes!' she moaned, shuddering violently. 'It all comes back to me. I shot Sir Francis with the air-gun!'

'You certainly did,' said Aubrey, and would have gone on to comment with warm approbation on the skill she had shown, a skill which – in an untrained novice – had struck him as really remarkable. But he checked himself. 'Surely,' he said, 'you are not letting the fact disturb you? It's the sort of thing that might have happened to anyone.'

She interrupted him.

'How right you were, Mr Bassinger, to warn me against the spell of Bludleigh. And how wrong I was to blame you for borrowing my parasol to chase a rat. Can you ever forgive me?'

'Charlotte!'

'Aubrey!'

'Charlotte!'

'Hush!' she said. 'Listen.'

On the lawn, Sir Francis Pashley-Drake was telling his story to an enthralled audience. The sympathy of the meeting, it was only too plain, was entirely with him. This shooting of a sitting sun-bather had stirred the feelings of his hearers deeply. Indignant exclamations came faintly to the ears of the young couple in the laurels.

'Most irregular!'

'Not done!'

'Scarcely cricket!'

And then, from Sir Alexander Bassinger, a stern 'I shall require a full explanation.'

Charlotte turned to Aubrey.

'What shall we do?'

'Well,' said Aubrey, reflecting, 'I don't think we had better just go and join the party and behave as if nothing had happened. The atmosphere doesn't seem right. What I would propose is that we take a short cut through the fields to the station, hook up with the five-fifty express at Goresby, go to London, have a bit of dinner, get married and . . .'

'Yes, yes,' cried Charlotte. 'Take me away from this awful house.'

'To the ends of the world,' said Aubrey fervently. He paused. 'Look here,' he said suddenly, 'if you move over to where I'm standing, you get the old boy plumb spang against the sky-line. You wouldn't care for just one last . . .'

'No, no!'

'Merely a suggestion,' said Aubrey. 'Ah well, perhaps you're right. Then let's be shifting.'

'MALACHI' WHITAKER

Courage

Isabel Allat was twenty, plump, pleasant, and usually smiling. She had bright, very blue eyes, and small hands with soft palms. There were many things she did not understand, such as people biting their nails, or really liking beer or black coffee, or spitting in the streets; even though she pondered over these things for a long time, she got no nearer to understanding.

The day was a January one, light-skied but piercingly cold, yet she wore a thin navy coat and skirt and a small purple silk hat. Her underclothes were thick and cheap, without abiding warmth, but she had on a good pair of dark wool stockings. She had had to put on these new spring things because she had got a job at last, and the old – the very old thick coat which had been good enough for the eight o'clock job was certainly not good enough for the nine o'clock one.

She walked along, through Forster Square, looking about her, taking everything in. Because it was the first morning, she was a quarter of an hour early. Her stomach felt unquiet, she had had too little breakfast, had walked too soon, had slept too spasmodically. It had been alright to say jokingly the night before, 'if you're waking, call me early, call me early, mother dear', but that made for thoughts like chasms. Supposing mother should be late? Why mother should be late, with the two other girls still setting off at twenty to eight, she did not know. No, she was just terrified. Why had she left her old job for this new one full of perils?

She kept on walking dreamily along, glad that she was no longer to use her hands for making senseless paper ornaments.

'Who's going to buy these awful things?' she used to cry to Jem the foreman. 'I wouldn't.'

Yet for some reason, she made the things better and more quickly than anyone else.

There had been something fascinating in the long, close room, in the bent heads of the other girls and women, in the ceaseless chatter that went on in undertones. Now and then, everybody would sing, not very tunefully, but good-naturedly and happily. It depended on Jem's mood as to how long this went on. Sometimes he would scowl and grimace, and the song would drop dead. Other times, he would join in with apparent indifference.

'Oh, Jem,' thought Isabel, 'I shall miss you terribly.'

How could the world go on without Jem, without Mrs Holroyd, without Minnie Parkinson, and Beryl? (They all called Beryl Barrel, because she was so fat, yet Beryl was a lovely name.) The sun went behind an early morning cloud, and the keen wind struck through the thin costume and made gooselumps rise on the girl's skin. Her steps had slowed, she was afraid to go any further. Abruptly, she turned and walked back into the square again.

Surely if she walked along Swaine Street and down Leeds Road, she could go into the old door, up the old steps and slip into her old chair, gather up her old stock of paper and scent and gum, and just go on with her work where she had left off? But it was twelve minutes to nine. The girls would have been there over three quarters of an hour. They were always early because Jem's train got down early, and anybody arriving at five minutes to eight had a chance of talking to Jem for a little while.

Jem was married, and had two little boys, yet none of the girls except Mrs Holroyd has ever seen his family. The others just didn't believe in it. Jem was Jem, and he existed in this dreamy, scent-laden atmosphere. He was dark, and thick, and short – almost Italian-looking, with bluish teeth and a strong, nicotine-full breath. The thought of the roomful of girls hovered about him. Even the little fifteen-year-olds would seize any excuse to go up to him.

'Help me, Jem. I don't know how to finish this.'

'Get Mrs Holroyd to help you. Am I a wet-nurse? You young tarts give me a pain in the neck.'

'Young tarts!' The fifteen-year-old would sidle back, blushing. Didn't 'tart' mean 'sweetheart'? But Jem had spoken.

Isabel crossed over the station and looked at the bookstall. People were buying morning papers so quickly that the two men could scarcely cope with them. She could not understand why they should buy or want these papers. And yet, suddenly she took twopence out of her bag and bought *The Times*.

As soon as she had done it, the thrill that had entered left her. Why had she spent her only twopence? She had no more, not a cent. Each morning her mother gave her her expenses for the day. From Saturday's spending money (she had had to buy gloves and a scarf) there had been nothing left but this twopence. Why, then, have bought a *Times*? And the station clock said six minutes to nine. Folding the paper under her arm, she ran through Forster Square again and up the hill.

This, then, was the street? This was the office in which she had had her interview, in which she had said she could type (having practised on a friend's typewriter but five times), in which she had said, no, she could not do any shorthand, but she would learn; the office in which she had been praised for her clear writing (but I don't always write as nicely as this, she had said in a burst of frankness, I took a lot of trouble with that letter), the office in which she had grinned, and felt pleased, and sure at the moment that she could do anything that was asked of her.

There was a wide red door at the bottom of the steps. Isabel went through the doorway and upstairs, passing a woman who was kneeling on a rubber mat and wiping up water with a black cloth.

'Good morning,' she said politely, remembering that in the old fairy tales one had to be polite to everybody. But she did not like the look of the woman, who was young and fair and strong, and had an angry glare in her eye.

'Good morning,' said the woman abruptly.

Then something very strange happened. There were two entrances to the building. She had taken the nearer one, and had to walk along corridors. At the far end of the last corridor everything was in confusion. The girl kept skipping over streams of water which gushed along the linoleumed corridor. Men and boys were walking about with wet red ledgers in their arms. She simply stared at the things around her and then went and knocked at the glassed door of the suite of offices in which she was to be employed. It was certainly quieter here.

Nobody answered, so she opened the door and went inside. There should have been an office-boy ('the office-boy comes at half-past eight, Miss Allat'). The floor was not only wet and sodden, but the brown linoleum was ridged. Water was even in standing on the level backs of the sloping desks.

'I must be dreaming,' she thought. 'Or perhaps the angry charwoman does this every Monday morning.'

There was a small desk in the middle of the room, holding a typewriter with a tin cover on it. That was wet, too. There were six windows. One was broken. Also, water was trickling down the green-washed walls.

Isabel put down her *Times* and her black bag on the desk and took off her small blue coat and purple silk hat and the white, thin scarf she had bought on Saturday, and hung them up. Underneath, she was wearing a cotton blouse with dark blue spots on it. She looked with some dismay at the very shiny, round wooden stool she was to sit on, and wondered how soon her skirt would match its brightness. Then she looked slowly round the room again.

'It *is* a wet place,' she thought, 'but I suppose I shall get used to it.'

All at once the door opened and a very little, old, bald man came in. He was breathing quickly, fluffing up the ends of a huge moustache. He said 'Good morning,' and came running forward to shake hands. 'Miss Allat? I'm Mr Palfreyman, the head clerk, and the cashier too. Oh dear, oh dear, whatever's happened?'

'I don't know. Isn't it *wet?*' asked Isabel solemnly.

The little man ran here and there in creaking boots, while Isabel looked at him gravely. Every fresh wet thing he saw made him groan. 'How lucky, how lucky that we put everything in the safe at night. All but the big guard books and the letter books. They're sodden. Oh dear, oh!'

'There's been a fire, you know,' said Mr Palfreyman, looking at the young girl sharply. 'Now, why wasn't I informed? There'll be young Mr Julian worrying his head off, and nothing being done about it. I could have been down at five o'clock if necessary, you know. I've been with the firm for forty years. But Mr Julian will have the police call him if anything happens, and they always used to call me. He's been a different man since his father died last year. You must obey young Mr Julian,' said the old man, wagging his fingers and blowing out his large moustache with three sharp breaths.

'But where's that young boy, that Reggie?' he continued testily. Then he stopped to say approvingly, 'I see you hung your things on the proper peg. That's right, Miss Allat, that's right. Begin as you mean to go on. Now *I'm* privileged. I hang mine in the private office,' he said with gratification in his voice. Then the thoughts of fire and of the boy Reggie, who was still missing, overcame him, and he went into the private office groaning, 'Whatever will Mr Julian say?'

Isabel went to the door and looked hopefully for Reggie, but he was not to be seen. It seemed very damp and chilly in the office, in spite of the coal fire, which had been lighted for some time and was now black and rather caked. She wanted to poke it, but did not dare, so she went back and stood looking at it. Very soon another man came in. He wore glasses, and was so thin that his clothes hung upon him as if he were a coat-hanger.

'Hullo,' he said, 'I'm Bentley.' He glanced towards the private office where Mr Palfreyman, who had hung up his things, was now opening the mail with ostentatious cracklings. 'I've only been here fourteen years, so I hang my things beside yours.' He slid round the barrier, which stood like a mahogany counter a couple of yards from the door, hung up his things, coughed loudly and said, 'Anything for me this morning, Mr Palfreyman?'

'We shall see. We shall see,' returned the other, distantly. 'You realize there has been *another* fire, Mr Bentley?'

'No, I hadn't noticed it,' said Bentley, winking at the girl and rubbing his thin grey hair with a handkerchief. In spite of the cold, he was sweating. He went over and poked the fire. 'You're the first girl that's ever been in this place. Did you know?' he whispered. 'The old man wouldn't have 'em at any price. We've always had lads before, but they get sick of old Pompey Snuffbox in there and sneak off to better jobs with a list of our customers' names in their pockets. But young Mr Julian's got the business now.' He spun round on his heel, with the poker still in his hand, winked, and went on poking the dark coals.

'What do you mean "*young* Mr Julian"?' asked Isabel, speaking in a whisper. 'I saw a Mr Julian, but he was old and quite bald on the top.'

'That's young Mr Julian,' said Bentley. 'Give us a chance. He's not fifty yet. I'm sixty-two, Palfreyman's seventy-three, but you'd think he was ninety, wouldn't you?'

Isabel moved away from Mr Bentley, who smelt of old clothes, old fish, and cough medicine inextricably blended. Reggie came quietly in. Mr Bentley took off his outdoor glasses and put on another pair, which had a long black ribbon tied at the side of them, stared at him fixedly and said, 'Where have *you* been? I bet you left the office door open, and that means sudden death, you know.'

Isabel noticed that the boy was very small for his fifteen years. But he had upstanding fair hair, a stiff Eton collar on, very short trousers and very dirty knees.

'I've been helping with the fire,' he said in a rapt voice. 'You ought to see Peckett's place. It's soaking, and every window's broken. I've been on the roof.'

Mr Bentley leaned over towards Isabel and said in a croaking whisper, 'This boy doesn't exist yet. He's only been here a couple of weeks. But the last one was a corker. He was sliding down the banisters and fell between 'em, three flights on to a stone floor. His father was just coming in the door – a real coincidence this is, his father's an insurance man – and he says, 'Lay there, sonny, come back and lay down,' for this lad was bolting upstairs again, frightened to death of getting the sack at one end and a belting from his father at the other. He wasn't hurt a mite. He went back and groaned no end. But unfortunately somebody had seen him – seen what he was doing. And the case came to nothing. We don't employ boys who slide down banisters, you know.'

Isabel didn't know whether Mr Bentley was speaking the truth or not. She just looked at him with large eyes. Mr Palfreyman called from the other office, 'Less noise, less noise, please,' then 'come here, Reggie, take these envelopes out and cut them. And give these letters to Mr Bentley.'

Bentley went on talking to the girl in his croaking voice: 'Using up the insides of used envelopes as scrap paper. Dirty, messy old thing. You don't know where they've been, do you? Things like that want destroying, I say. And there'll be a hell of a mess over this fire. Excuse me, miss, I can't help swearing in a small way – my old girl at home, she swears like a trooper – but it's the second fire in three months, not that it's our fault; it wasn't started here; but any insurance company'd cut up rusty, what do you think?'

Isabel was warming her hands at the fire and looking round helplessly. 'Who tells me what to do?' she asked.

'Well, I don't, thank God,' said Bentley piously. 'But I can tell you one thing: dodge old Palfreyman like the devil. Stick to *young* Mr Julian, don't get across with the office-boy, keep on looking as pretty as you do now, and you'll get on all right.'

'Do you have any dusters?' asked Isabel, suddenly resolute. In spite of his friendliness, she did not much care for Mr Bentley. The older man was peculiar, but she liked his loyalty. She would do something to get on the right side of him, help him, be as nice as she knew how.

'You'll find any amount in the pattern room.'

'And where's that?'

'Through that door.'

She came back with an armful of dusters, soaked one in water, and began wiping the wet desks. She did not feel like the irresolute girl who had walked up to that bookstall. In a few minutes she was warm all over, her face flushed with the good work of clearing away an unwanted mess of water.

'I'm doing something without Jem or anyone having to tell me,' she thought happily. She had found a pail in the lavatory, and was busy wringing in her dusterful of water, when Mr Palfreyman called her.

She dried her hands on a handkerchief, and went into the private office. The old man was standing with his back to a very cheerful fire. There were two chairs, two desks, and an ornamental brass coal-box. Over the mantel was a curled map.

'Miss Allat, I'm going to let you do something. You shall look after Mr Julian's desk; see that the inkwells are always filled, blue-black, red, and copying. And that the nibs are in order. And fresh blotting-paper, plenty of it, always on hand. It is a great privilege; I have attended to this, and to Mr Julian's father's desk, for many years. Oh, and Miss Allat' – he lowered his voice – 'I should not talk to Mr Bentley a great deal. It is true he has been here for some years, but he has always acted as a stranger. He is not – Miss Allat, I grieve to tell you this – but he is *not* a gentleman. Miss Allat, he goes to funerals in a bowler hat. Now you may go back.'

'Thank you very much, Mr Palfreyman. I shall be very pleased indeed to look after the desk. I will begin in the morning.' She went out, wishing that the private office had been a sumptuous place and that Mr Julian would have flowers and a large picture of a very beautiful wife in a silver frame. But perhaps his wife was ugly. So many are, she thought wistfully.

She went back to her manual work, wiping up the water, wringing her dusters, looking brightly round for more wet places.

'Good morning!'

Suddenly, the whole place was alive. Mr Palfreyman was a devoted old slave, with his 'Good morning, Mr Julian.' The office boy was a kind of tolerated worm. Mr Bentley was simply Mr Bentley, the stranger who had been with the firm for fourteen years, and no more.

'Why, Miss Allat, whatever are you doing?'

Mr Julian had taken off his hat with a sweeping bow. 'What a long bald head. But what a nice bald head,' she thought. 'I'm clearing up after the fire,' she said in a clear voice.

'Don't trouble, please. Mrs Withy will do that.'

He looked in a very pleasant way at her young, fresh face, at her thin coat hanging on the peg, at her small hands competently wringing out the duster, and smiled. She smiled back widely, delightedly.

Yet she kept on wiping up the pools of water and hearing the droning voice of Mr Palfreyman, the hard, harsh cough of the friendly Bentley. Behind her, the boy Reggie sat at a dried desk cutting open the old envelopes, saving the smooth sides for the old man to make notes on. She felt little gusts of wind coming from the broken window, and every moment a little more of Jem and the girls and the scent and the coloured paper fell away from her memories.

'They'll be going on, close all together, feeling well, or ill, or hungry, or good-tempered or bad, and Jem'll be at the big machine waiting for them all to come up and flatter him and praise him.' She felt alone and exhilarated. 'But I've got away. I'm going to be my own self. There's no Jem here to take all the responsibility. I'm going to work well, and do exactly what they tell me. I'd love, yes, I'd simply love to be dignified. But nice, too. So many people are like marshes, slopping sluggishly about.' She laughed, and tried to whisper 'slopping sluggishly' to herself. 'But I'd rather be a lake,' she went on thinking, 'a lake with good, straight edges. A lake mightn't do much, really, but it is nice to look at, and marshes are such treacherous things. They run into one another, and rot everything that gets in the way.'

She went on thinking as she worked, about the dusters, about Mr Julian, about the copy of *The Times* on her desk, about her home and her family.

'I'm going to learn something here. Not business, not good arithmetic, not even shorthand. But some day, I'll – what will I do some day?'

She had not the remotest idea what she would do some day, but when she had washed down her wet desk and put away the dusters and the bucket, she opened her typewriter, got some paper from the top drawer and began typing figures, long columns of figures that she could add up. She did not add so very well. She began tapping, at first slowly, then with more and more confidence; and soon she was pulling out the filled paper, bending her head to it, frowning, looking the very picture of somebody who had plenty of fine work to do in the world and who knew exactly what she was doing.

JACK COMMON

Nineteen

When the curtain went down on the last act of *La Bohème* they stood up immediately, glad to escape the discomfort of a gallery seat and eager, too, to take a last look down at the little glimmering stage below where the performers now assembled to take their applause. That last glance was a sort of seal upon the night's entertainment, fixing it in the memory. There stood Mimi arisen from her deathbed but with the romance of her pathetic end still about her; and Rodolphe whom one does not love so well but who gains our sympathies at the last; and Colline the friend we all wish for. Romantic trinity, bowing themselves out of their parts before the dim-lit house and the rolling plaudits.

He stood straight, gazing at the stage but dissociating himself from the applause which, being too voluminous, affected him with a sort of shyness for the actors. She leaned forward and rested an arm on him to balance. He was proud to be her support. This was his first love, and he was nineteen.

Then, hurrying so as not to be caught by the national anthem, she gathered her things and they began moving along the aisle picking a way among people's knees and orange peel. Just as they reached the gangway the lights flashed on; the strange multitude of applauding shapes and white faces became an ordinary crowd of clothes, and spectacles, and limbs; and the introductory rumble of the anthem began. But Ella and he were safe through the doorway and among the advance contingent tripping down the stairs for the exit.

The theatre opened on a windy, silent side-street in which was a row of taxis, and a white globe of electric light with 'Gentlemen' printed on it over an underground lavatory. Beside the taxis stood three heavily-clothed men like Cossacks waiting for fares.

Ella shivered and fastened her little fox about her neck. He was lighting a cigarette against the wind and when he had finished she tucked her arm in his and they hurried off to the tram-stop.

'O-oh, it's cold,' she shivered, as they awaited the dilatory tram, which was just turning the bend in the road, losing its lights, while the trolley shot blue sparks, then steadying like a ship and blazing forth again. 'But wasn't it good?'

'Fine. Miles better than *Butterfly*. Better story.'

'Yes, isn't it? I love that last scene. She's a splendid Mimi. I'm so glad we went.'

'Here we are,' said he, as the tram ground its brakes and the line of windows with the dummy faces came to rest.

They pushed among the group of passengers, mounted the steps, and shoved along the gangway. There was only one seat which she took, while he grabbed a strap and swayed to the jolt of starting.

They did not talk on the journey, partly because of the difficulty of bending down, but mainly because he was a little shy of talking to her before strangers. He was immensely proud to be seen with her, to have a sweetheart and travel delightfully paired, but he was so new to it all that he was not sure he knew how to behave, and to talk would subject him to the criticism of these distantly malevolent passengers. This young man next to him, for instance, had a contemptuous glance and obviously thought *himself* much more capable of entertaining a pretty girl.

She *was* pretty; a dark fluff of hair curled on her cheek and through it one could just see the delicate shell of her ear. Oh, to be witty and keep her always laughing, or to be masterful, or admirable, so that one did not feel so uncertain about her affection! How is it that people in books find it so easy to make love, and one's acquaintances never confess any difficulty, yet oneself is such an awful fool that any conversation comes easier than the language of the heart. But then to Ella you couldn't say made-up things, and however much your heart ached no words came but stupid ones.

The tram-wheels ground on a steep bank and set up a long moan. Six great windows of a draper strolled blankly by. Ella looked up and smiled. It was time to get off.

The tram-lines shone in the light of a great moon which lit the roofs so plainly you could count the tiles and watch the shadows of thinning smoke from the chimney-pots waver there. But the other side of the road was a black wedge of shadow and in it a policeman was standing. Past him they hurried, not meeting his eye, the eye of the law. Ella stooped to avoid the wind.

'Oh, dear, dear! Aren't you cold? Come, let's hurry.'

'It's healthy weather, Ella. A splendid night, I think. Look at that moon. Isn't it marvellously bright?'

'It is a beauty; you can see the mountains on it. Wouldn't like to live there, though.'

'Wouldn't you? Why not? Just you and I, Ella. With a moon to ourselves. I think it would be wonderful.'

'Silly, you're making me shiver. It would be so cold up there.'

'I'd keep you warm.'

'Would you? I wish you would come along to our shop then. It's been freezing in there to-day. And Miss Hales would have the window dressed as usual. How would you like to stand by a cold shop-window with the draught from the door cutting through you? Miss Hales never notices the cold. She's so cold-hearted herself it doesn't make any impression on her. You know, Miss Carter's hands are in a terrible state with chilblains and Old Hard-as-nails, that's what Belle calls her, caught sight of them to-day, she says, "Look at your hands, Miss Carter, can't you do something about them?" Belle says, "Well, Miss Hales, it's the constant hot water, they never get a chance to heal." Halesie wasn't taking the hint. She says, "I've cleaned plenty of windows in my time and I never had hands like those. You must see about them. The sight of them is enough to drive customers out of the shop." Belle came across to me and whispered, "No, and I never had a face like hers. Something's got to suffer; I'm glad it's only my hands." Belle's a scream; if she wasn't there, I don't think I could stick it. And she'll be leaving in a few months' time.'

'Will she?' said he, thinking of other matters.

'Yes, her boy has got a good job now and they will be getting married soon as he has saved enough.'

He was thinking as he watched her bright face how curious it was that she took so much delight in relating the trivialities of the day, wasting the time precious to them which might be given to more significant conversation. Perhaps it was because he did not take the lead forcibly enough. Or was *her* love of a lighter, less-absorbing sort?

They turned the corner of her street and the usual little panic assailed him. The distance was so short to her door and sometimes she disappeared behind it after a brief goodnight. That left his evening pitiably truncated. What he wanted was a long pause in the shop doorway nearby, where he might hold her close to him, inhaling her fragrance, and taste the desirable no-taste-at-all of her lips. He walked in silence until they came to the doorway. Then he put his arm round her waist and said, 'Let us stay in here to say goodnight.'

'No,' she whispered, resisting, 'It's late and I'm so cold.'

'But I'll keep you warm. Just for a minute or two, Ella.'

'No longer, mind,' she whispered.

He caught his heel against the door and the noise startled him, it was so loud. Then he wedged an elbow into the corner and brought her close to him. He kissed her and felt full of pity because her lips were so cold.

'Poor little thing. Poor little Ella.'

But she pushed him off to arrange a strand of her hair which had escaped and was blowing about her cheek.

'Are you warmer now,' he whispered.

'Not very.'

'It is sheltered in here. Keep close and you will soon be warm.'

'But you are shivering.'

'It is because I love you, Ella,' he said, confused, and trying to stop it.

'Silly,' she said.

He kissed her again.

Then she drew her head away and looked over the silent roadway. He didn't know what to say next, he was so glad to have her close like that, and so aware that something should be said and that he should kiss her again and again many times, and that kissing was no use either. The moonlight lay on the pavement and on the cobbles beyond the pavement, a strange silent light. In the quiet, little things stood out like gems and were distinct. There were black streaks of frozen water in the gutters, and between the cobbles tiny wedges of shadow; a piece of paper fluttered but could not get away from the middle of the road, or would it not have sailed upward to the moon like a great white moth?

His back was turned to the street and all he could see was the angle of the shop window, an oval flaw in the glass sparkling, and a dusty pyramid of cigarette packets with a dead spider on one of the ledges. It was better to look at her; to watch the white curve of her cheek against the fur and her eyelids fluttering when she had stared too long.

'Wouldn't it be splendid, Ella, if we could go away to-night, and wake up to-morrow in a village miles away. Or, outside a village, a little cottage of our own. A little cottage on a slope with trees and fields all in front of it, and a river below where we could go for walks. And hurry back at night, run up the hill and have a big fire burning. You would look so pretty in the firelight.'

She looked up at him curiously, and he kissed her.

'Do you love me, Ella?'

'Yes.'

'Wouldn't that be better than working in a shop?'

'Rather. I'd miss Belle though. I'll miss her when she gets married. Do you think she's in too much of a hurry?'

'Eh? I don't know,' said he, taken aback.

'I don't believe in long engagements though. Do you?'

'Oh, no,' he said, pursuing his own thought and impatient of the interruption. 'There are so many marvellous places to live in. I'd love to take you round the world. If we could set off tomorrow—'

Just then a church-clock struck; its distant boom rippled over all the moonlit roofs. He held her closer.

'No, I must go. Half-past eleven.'

'One more kiss.'

She held up her face. Her lips were warm.

'There! Let me go now.'

He released her. They left the shop doorway, and a few paces further on she gave him her hand and said 'Good-bye.'

He said, 'Good-bye, Ella. See you to-morrow night.'

While he strode awkwardly over the cobbles, self-conscious lest she were looking after him, her door banged and simultaneously a cat nearby set up a long wail. In the following quiet he could hear the ring of his footsteps echoing up the sleep-bound houses and the gas-lamp on the corner singing to itself through a defective mantle.

He was very much in love; so much that he was unaware what it was that had come to him, for this emotion caught him up beyond analysis, and he did not in the odd ecstasy remember the creature he had been. The strains of *La Bohème*, which echoed in his ears once more now that he was alone, reminded him how sad a thing love is, and the memory of Ella's bright little face looking out on to the cold street seemed to confirm it. Why was the pleasure he got from her company such an unhappy one? The tenderness he felt hurt him, and seemed unreasonable. Perhaps it was because he was a poor creature tragically incomplete.

For instance, every fellow he met told tales of his conquests. 'Out with a wench last night,' they said. 'Had a good time. She was a hot piece of goods.' And he never spoke of Ella to anyone. Did girls talk like that among themselves? Well, she didn't. No.

He reached the hill leading down to his own suburb, and from the trees of the park on the other side of the road a trail of smoke came. Winter leaves burning. The pleasant smell of wood-smoke scattered his thoughts as he looked through the trees to a wide field of frosted grass. Above it the air was crystalline and one could feel the silent penetration of the moon's rays. One could imagine them raining down, a silent fall of electric radiance throughout the night, falling on roof-tiles and sheltered sleepers for the most part, but here and there on unprotected lovers making a miserable retreat from romance and beauty.

It was absurd that Ella and he should part and go the ways of office and shop. Suppose they had caught a train to London now, or – well, why not London? – and were even now sitting together by a train-window watching the silvered leagues slip away. And if they had a little house to live in – no hotels – what an adventure sitting by the fire would be! Then when they drew the curtains and looked out at the frost-rimed roofs, for once it would not be on distance that separated them but on a world easily shut out.

Easily shut out, he repeated mentally as he felt for his latchkey.

His bedroom was chilly and the tick of the clock reminded him of the oncoming morrow. Fortunately he was always quick at undressing and in a moment or two his trousers were folded over the bedrail, a chair pulled silently close to the bed, his cigarettes, matches and the clock placed on the chair, and he jumped into bed.

Slowly his body warmed; presently it was sufficiently warm for him to forget about it. He closed his eyes and soon the pale roses of the wallpaper which the moon had robbed of colour faded from his mind, and the endless problem of Ella came to occupy him again. And again. His thoughts ran in a sort of rhythm: first a dream of what they might do together, and he do for her; then a memory of what she had said or how she had looked; then a feeling of shame at his omission to be alert and witty or entertaining, and of reproach for being a fool and an incompetent; then again the happy dream.

When this had gone on as long as he could stand it, he got up and lit a cigarette. The room was brilliant with moonlight; it ran in a rippling line along the folds of the curtains, and plunged silver in the mirror of the dressing-table; but the moon itself was now out of view. He stepped over to the window and stood in his shirt looking out.

Was Ella sleeping or did she too think of her love? As he stared out at the chimney-pots and the bright shield above them, he remembered her standing in the doorway. She said, 'Do you believe in long engagements?' Odd things she asked. He nipped the end of his cigarette and sprang back into bed.

Half-a-mile away in a smaller, cosier room the creamy bars of light which broke through a latticed blind lay on a coverlet and on the face of Ella. She was sleeping. She had been asleep for an hour.

ELIZABETH BOWEN

The Dancing-Mistress

About half-past three at the end of November a sea-fog came up over the edge of the cliff and, mounting the plate-glass windows, filled the Metropole ballroom with premature twilight. The fantastic trees in the garden sank in like a painting on blotting-paper; the red roofs of surrounding houses persisted an hour in ever-ghostlier violet and faded at last. Below the gold ceiling the three chandeliers draped in crystal flowered reluctantly into a thin batch of lights: the empty floor of the ballroom was pointed with yellow reflections.

The door of the ladies' cloak-room kept creaking and swinging, gusts of chatter came out from the little girls being unpeeled from their wraps. Inside was a shuffle of feet on the muffling carpet, water gushing in basins, a clatter of ivory brush-backs on marble slabs. The mothers and governesses wanted elbow-room for their business with combs, for the re-tying of sashes and tugging of woolly gaiters from silk-clad legs. With their charges, they overflowed into the corridor. Here, all along, it was chilly and rustling with muslins; Shetlands and cardigans were flung over the radiators; little girls sat in rows on the floor to put on their dancing-sandals. Miss James, the dancing-mistress, hurrying past in her fur coat with her dispatch-case, with her frail forward slant like a reed in the current, was obliged to pick her way over their legs. This she did with stereotyped little weary amused exclamations: her pianist followed in silence, a sharper, more saturnine profile against the brocaded wallpaper.

Miss James and the pianist went into the ballroom, where they opened their dispatch-cases behind the piano and, holding the mirror for one another, dusted over their faces with large soft puffs. The pianist moistened the tips of her fingers to flatten her hair back; it was polished against her skull like a man's. Miss James took the mirror and, biting her lip, glanced once more at herself in the oval with a slanting, fleeting, troubled kind of reproach.

The pianist looked up at the chandeliers, then scornfully out at the mist. 'I'm so glad we've got back to artificial – it seems much more natural, I think. – I say *sure* you don't feel too rotten?'

'Not as rotten as all that, I suppose,' said Miss James, indifferent. She had taken two classes already today; before the second she had declared a headache.

Miss Joyce James had begun as a pupil of Madame Majowski's; she worked for her now. Six days a week she went all over the country giving lessons; in the mornings she got up early to perfect her dancing at Mme Majowski's studio. She had eight dancing dresses like clouds, in gradations of beauty, a black satin tunic for studio practice, and besides these and the fur coat to cover them nothing at all but a cloth coat-and-skirt that looked wrong in the country and shabby in town. She was twenty-one, pretty but brittle and wax-like from steam-heated air. All day long she was just an appearance, a rhythm; in studio or ballroom she expanded into delicate shapes like a Japanese 'mystery' flower dropped into water. Late at night, she stopped *'seeming'* too tired to 'be'; too tired to eat or to speak; she would finish long journeys asleep with her head on the pianist's shoulder: her sister received her with Bovril and put her to bed. Her eyebrows tilted outwards like wings; over her delicate cheekbones looked out, slightly tilted, her dreamy and cold eyes in which personality never awakened.

Miss James and Miss Peel the pianist sat for some minutes more in the window-embrasure behind the piano, side to side in jaded intimacy like a couple of monkeys. There was a radiator beside them. Miss Peel, having shivered out of her coat, kept spreading out her hands to the radiator, chafing them gently together, then spreading them out again, drawing in a reserve of warmth through the hands for her whole body. Her thin shoulder-blades rippled the silk of her dress as she bent forward. Miss James kept her eyes on the door, watching the children in, vacantly counting. As each came in its name jumped back to her memory as though a ticket had clicked up over its head. Though her mind was blank of this party of children from Wednesday to Wednesday, she never hesitated or was confused between the Joans and Jeans, the Margerys or the Mollies.

The little girls swung themselves in through the glass doors in twos and threes and skidded over the floor. The mothers and governesses sat down in groups round the walls with a resigned look of un-expectation. Their murmuring made a fringe round the silence, they nodded across at each other. The ballroom was gaunt in the vague smoky daylight, like a large church.

Three minutes before the class was due to begin, the hotel secretary appeared in the doorway, looking towards the piano. Miss Peel was sorting her music; she paused for a moment. 'There's Lulu,' she murmured.

'I know,' said Miss James.

Lulu, Romano-Swiss, fervent and graceful, looked away from them guiltily, looked round the room officially, switched on a dozen more lights. Miss James picked up a valse and frowned at it. She sighed, she was so tired. Two more little girls squeezed in past the secretary's elbow. The door swung to with a sigh.

'He's gone,' said Miss Peel and went back to her music.

'I know,' said Miss James.

A quarter to four. They both glanced at their wristwatches, sighed and admitted the hour. The dancing-mistress came round the piano, the pianist sat down in front of 'Marche Militaire', shook back a slave-bangle up either arm, and waited, her eyes on Miss James who stood at the top of the room and looked down steadily into a looking-glass at the bottom.

'Good afternoon!' she said, silvery. The little girls ran forward, shaking out their dresses. 'Fall in for the March! Grizelda leading . . . Skirts out, right foot pointed . . . GO! . . . *Right*, left – right – right – right – Heads *well* up – *that's* right! . . . Skirt, Phyllis . . . Toes, Jean! . . . Oh, *toes*, Margery – Margery, what *are* you doing . . . *to-o-o-es!*'

Miss Peel spanked out the 'Marche Militaire'. Grizelda, impeccable, head erect, face blank, toes pointed quiveringly, led the twenty-five twice round the room and up the centre. Then they divided, ones right, twos left, met again, came up in twos, in fours, and then spaced out for the exercises. That was that.

The five positions: they performed like compasses. First . . . second . . . third . . . fourth . . . fifth! For each a chord, a shock of sound tingling out into silence. The dancing-mistress kept them in the fifth position and melted down between the lines to look.

Margery Mannering never did anything right. Her week was darkened by these Wednesdays. She was perfectly certain Miss James hated her – Miss James did. She was an overdressed little girl who belonged to a grandmother. She had red sausage-curls tied up with lop-eared white bows and spectacles that misted over, blinding her, when she got hot. She stood crooked forward anxiously. A coldness fingered its way down her spine as Miss James came softly to her down the room in her blue dress that fell into points like a hyacinth-bell and fluted out.

'Now, Margery . . . Margery Mannering. What are you doing *now*?'

They looked hard at each other; all the rest waited. Margery thought, 'She'd like to kill me.' Miss James thought, 'I would like to kill her – just once.' Her face had a hard wistfulness. 'Just *think*,' she gently invited. The girls in front turned round. Margery looked at her feet. Just feet, they were, like other people's; boat-like in dancing-sandals. Oh, she had taken the *third* position!

'Yes,' said Miss James and nodded. 'Now do you see? . . . Now you can take those positions again by yourself. – Music, please – Go!' The chords clanged vindictively, like choppers falling. '*Now* do you see?'

Margery had pretty-child affectations that sat forlornly upon her. Now she flung back her hard curls; they bounced on her back. She peered up through misted spectacles like a plump small animal in the bite of a trap – like a rat, perhaps, that no one decently pities.

'Yes, Miss James.'

'Then please remember,' said Miss James, and walked away. The unrealized self in her made itself felt, disturbing her calm with a little shudder of pleasure. A delicate pink touched her cheekbones, she thought of Lulu, she was almost a woman.

Next the springing exercises, so graceful, from which the few little boys were excluded. Rows and rows of little girls kicking the air pointedly, showing the frills on their underclothes, waving their bent arms and fluttering fingers apart and together, tossing their heads. There were gleaning movements, throwing and catching movements, movements that should have scattered roses about the room. Miss Peel played 'Oh where, and oh where, has my little dog gone!' with a kind of saturnine prance.

Grizelda and Lois and Cynthia, Jean Jones and Doris excelled at varying movements; they were set to dance by themselves, to show the others. When someone was dancing alone as a glory the music was different, Margery Mannering thought; the choppers became curling feathers, fluttering in towards one and waving out.

The skipping began and finished; they passed the exercises with ribbons and Indian clubs. The fancy dances began. Little Cynthia was Spain itself in the Spanish dance; the grown-ups sighed at her, she was so sweet. Miss James told her that *next* Wednesday she could come, if she liked, with some castanets. Grizelda and Doris were best in the Irish Jig; so saucy, quite Irishly saucy. The Gavotte made two more couples illustrious; they were given the floor to themselves. 'If one could only teach you to curtsey,' Miss James sighed. If she could only, only teach them to curtsey. They went down on themselves all skewered; feet got lost behind them; knees stuck out in front.

'Just *look*, children: watch me' . . . But they all stood round sceptical; they knew they would never be able to curtsey like that. She sank with bowed head; with arms curved before her she melted into the floor. She flowed down into it and; flowing up again, stood. 'If I had a dress like that . . .' Doris thought. 'She's not like a person at all,' thought Jean Jones.

The hotel secretary stood looking in through the glass door. His eyes came a little nearer together, his face was intent. Miss Peel played a slow ripple; in her mind Miss James was curtseying.

After the fancy dancing there was an interval. The little girls flocked and slid to the chairs round the wall. Margery Mannering went back and sat by her grandmother's maid, who was knitting a bedsock. 'Got into trouble again, I see,' said the grandmother's maid and wetted her thin lips. 'You did ought to have practised that Spanish dance.' 'You mind your own business,' said Margery, who was rude to servants. She slid along three empty chairs and sat by herself. She watched Miss James go round the room, congratulating the mothers of little girls who had been dancing nicely. Governesses she did not congratulate; she was too tired.

Cynthia sat with her mother just beyond Margery Mannering; they were holding each other's hands excitedly and talking about castanets. Cynthia never seemed bare of being loved, it was round her at school, everywhere, like a sheath. Miss James came round to them, smiling.

Margery watched, her head well back on her thick neck, playing with one of her ringlets, and Miss James felt something catch at her, going by. She had again that shudder of life in her; a quick light came into her eyes. 'Don't kick that chair,' she said, put on her smile again and went on.

Miss Peel was back at the radiator. 'How d'you feel?' she said. 'Must you go round all those hags? Are you bad?'

'I suppose I'll get through . . . Did you hear me killing that Mannering child?'

'Which one?'

'Oh, you *know*. The red one.' She laughed a little and sat stroking one of her arms. 'She makes me feel awful . . . I – I don't know how it is.'

'Has she got anyone with her?'

'Only a maid.'

'Perhaps she'll die,' said Miss Peel brightly, and ran her eye over a fox-trot.

'Oh, she couldn't,' said Miss James, startled. She couldn't do without Margery Mannering; she wanted to kill her. She got up and said: 'Now all take your partners for the waltz.'

'Lulu's been back,' said Miss Peel hurriedly. 'When are you going to see him?' Miss James shrugged her shoulders and walked off. The music began.

By this time the fog had been stained to solid darkness; the windows were slabs of night. The chandeliers were in full flower. Children went round and round, smoothly spinning; the tall looking-glass at the end of the room doubled them into a crowd; they were doubled again on the outside darkness. She could not think why nobody came to draw the curtains. When she felt him again at the door, looking in at her with that straight level look of desire, she went towards him, pulled open the door, and said, 'Do please draw the curtains. The room looks so ugly; the mothers don't like it. People can see in.'

'You will give up your train, just once, just tonight?' he said. 'Yes?'

'No, I can't, I'm tired; I've got a headache. Besides, you know Peelie's here; she wouldn't go home alone.'

He skirted the floor and went round to the three windows, touching a cord somewhere so that the curtains trembling with movement slid over them noiselessly. Returning, he brushed Miss Peel's back as she played.

'I want her tonight,' he said over her shoulder. 'We all three have supper together – Yes? I put you both into the 8.40. Yes? Dear Peelie, yes?'

She nodded, in time with the music.

'Dear Peelie – *good!*'

She wriggled her shoulders, he hurried away.

'All arranged,' he said joyously. 'I get a taxi immediately. We all three had supper together down by the Pier.'

'Go away,' Joyce James whispered. 'You're dreadful; you'll ruin me – *One* two three, *one* two three. *Time*, Jean and Betty, time, time! What are you doing! – Mollie, don't talk while you're dancing! Margery Bates, remember you're a gentleman; what does a gentleman do with his hands? . . . *Toes*, Margery Mannering: *why* don't you *dance* on your *toes?*'

Lulu saw something wrong at the end of the room; the chairs were pushed crooked; he went to arrange them. Again he brushed past her. 'Till then, I keep watching. You are so beautiful. I would give my soul, my body, all that I have . . .'

She walked away, clapping her hands together – '*One* two three, *one* two three,' watching the couples go round. Then she suddenly cried to the music, to all the children: 'STOP!'

Of course it was Margery Mannering. She did not know how to waltz; she went bumping and hopping round on the flat of her feet, with her partner all limp. Miss James went over in silence and took her partner away.

'I shall have to take you myself. – All you others sit down for a moment. – We shall go on till I've taught you. And will you please *try*, Margery. You see you are wasting everyone else's time – Music, please!'

All alone on the empty floor, Miss James waltzed with Margery Mannering. They did not speak; they heard one another's breathing; the girl's light, the child's loud and painful. The thump of Margery's heart was like the swelling and bursting of great black bubbles inside her: now the bubbles were in her throat. Her hot body sagged on Miss James's cold bare arm. Her eyes, stretched with physical fear like a rabbit's, stared through the clouding spectacles at the mild white hollow of Miss James's throat. From her spectacles, light flashed up sharply into her partner's face as they circled under the chandeliers. Miss James's hand like a cold shell gripped the hot hand tighter.

'She really is patient and good,' said the mothers, nodding. 'She's so thorough.' They congratulated themselves. 'Look at the pains she takes with that poor little stupid. Wonderful; she keeps smiling.'

And indeed, she was smiling. Lulu watched through the door; his eyes got larger and darker and closer together, his face came closer up to the glass. Miss Peel played on mechanically; she watched him watching.

'I'm giddy,' said Margery suddenly.

'It's no good. I shall keep you on till you've learnt.'

In the taxi, the girls leant back silently. Lulu, his back to the driver, sat watching the town lights flash over their faces. The fog was lifting, but the taxi went slowly through spectral streets like a blind snorting animal. Sometimes the driver pulled up with a jar; the girls nodded forward, the window-frames rattled. Joyce's close-fitting hat was pulled over her eyebrows; her half-hidden face was impassive. Peelie sat with her hat on her knees, she looked over Lulu's head, sombrely humming. Joyce rolled her head with a sigh and an impatient movement; Peelie and Lulu both reached for the window-strap; Lulu was first there and let down the window. Mist came curling in, the air freshened; the taxi had turned down through the old town and the lonely crying of sirens came from the harbour. 'They're awful,' Joyce shuddered.

'She *is* tired,' said Peelie to Lulu across her.

'She will be better after supper.'

'She won't eat,' said Peelie, discouraging.

'Won't you eat dinner?' said Lulu, imploring. He touched Joyce's knee, left a hand there. Peelie eyed the hand sharply. Joyce took no notice. Peelie's foot felt a gentle pressure. 'That's *my* foot.' 'Oh, so sorry, Peelie.' The taxi crawled past a terrace of balconied houses and sharply drew up.

The 'Star' Private Hotel was modest and friendly. It was six o'clock; they went in and sat in the lounge. Peelie was pleased at Lulu's discretion; *here* they would meet no one who'd recognize Lulu and Joyce and go away talking to make scandal about the Metropole dancing class. It did not do for Lulu, who showed ladies into their bedrooms, or Joyce who spent hours in clumsy men's arms, to be patently man and woman; their public must deprecate any attraction. Poor Lulu was also distressingly beautiful; the shabby other visitors kept turning round to look – at the grace of his height, his dark-ivory forehead (foreign men do so much more with a forehead), the ripple-back of his hair, his gaze of shy ardency Joyceward, narrowed by low straight lids. He went off to order the supper – just supper, they said, fish or something, with coffee to follow. Peelie shook Joyce's arm suddenly.

'Do wake up,' she said. 'Can't you really love anyone?'

'I didn't want to – you brought me ... Well then, give me my powder-puff.'

'You've got heaps on – it's colour you want. Haven't you got—'

'No, you know I don't have any; Majowski hates it.'

'You may be thankful Lulu's Swiss. He wouldn't let you just sit there yawning if he were an Italian.'

'No. He's going to keep an hotel – isn't it awful. With two private funiculars. On the top of a glacier or something. Oh well, *he* won't melt any glaciers!' Joyce changed a yawn to a laugh; she laughed weakly, ruefully, almost in spite of herself, biting in her mouth at one corner and shrugging her slight shoulders.

'What are you laughing for?' said Lulu, coming back. They did not answer; he showed them into the dining-room. The room was empty, not a waitress there. He guided them to their table with an arm lightly round Joyce's waist; as he pulled her chair out she had to step back closer against him. Peelie's hard unabashed eyes contemplated them curiously. Each conscious of the two others they waited, then something in Peelie's eyes made it impossible, shameful for him not to press Joyce closer and kiss her twice on the cheek, high up, where the patch of colour sometimes appeared. Peelie laughed, Joyce laughed uncertainly, Lulu uneasily smiled: they sat down. Joyce unfastened her coat and let it slide down her shoulders, showing her neck and the soft rucked top of the hyacinth dress. Her eyes glittered under the hanging lights with their cold white shades.

'Did you see me killing that child?' she asked Lulu, eagerly turning. 'You were there at the door, you must have seen. Wasn't I dreadful – Peelie thinks I was dreadful.'

'Which child?' he said, while his eyes asked doubtfully, 'Who's there? What's there? *Are* you, at all? I want you.'

'Tell him, Peelie.'

'That fat Mannering child with red hair, she means. I only said: "Don't hate her so's the others can notice."'

'But I do hate her, don't I? Isn't it awful of me. I made her waltz till she cried. But I did teach her.'

Peelie eyed her exaltedness. 'She's quite awake now,' she said, congratulatory, to Lulu. 'I daresay she's quite hungry.' But soon the film crept back, Joyce faded like the roofs into this afternoon's mist; she let her hand lie coldly in Lulu's under the table. As Jean Jones had thought, she was not like a person at all.

When supper was finished they strolled back towards the harbour to look for a taxi. The salt air was milder, lamps made pale stains on the mist. It was high tide; under the mist, to their left, the dark, polished water sucked hard-lipped at the embankment. The edge of the road was protected by chains slung from posts; Peelie went to look over, stood idly clanking and swinging the chain with her knee.

'I wonder what you two would do next if I fell in and never bobbed up again.'

'Oh, *Peelie!*'

'Well, I won't – not *this* woman. All the same, I do wonder . . .'

Her meditation, tinged with contempt for them, broke up sharply when, hearing no more behind her, she turned to see where they were. Lulu had caught Joyce out of the lamplight . . . He was not so unlike an Italian. They stood as one figure till, with a gasp, he stepped back from her. Joyce stood vaguely, huddling up her coat-collar and looking round for Peelie. They started towards each other under the lamp. Peelie thought: 'Now what's coming?' but all Joyce said was: 'We must get that taxi. I can't go any further. Oh, Peelie, I'm *dead!*'

It was a long drive from the harbour up to the Central Station. No one spoke. Lulu's hands hung between his parted knees; he kept wringing and chafing his hands together. Joyce slipped deeper, deeper into her great fur collar, a swerve of the taxi flung her on Peelie's shoulder; she did not stir, she leaned there inert, asleep. Peelie slipped an arm along the back of the seat; supporting her; this was how they were going to travel home. Light from a picture-palace blared in, disturbing them like a trumpet-blast, on to the small set face of the sleeper, her hat pushed down unevenly over one eye. Lulu, startled, cried out: 'It's not fair!'

'Hush! . . . Nothing's fair.'

'In six weeks I go back to Switzerland. What does she care? – Nothing. And still you are having her day after day.'

'You and I, you and she, she and I, we'll forget each other anyhow – that's nature.'

'Don't you care?'

'Not so much.'

'Peelie . . .'

'Um?'

'*Peelie* . . . I . . . let me just . . .'

She beckoned. Two or three minutes were taken up by a cautious shuffling, balancing, edging; they rose and changed places like people passing each other in a boat. She sustained Joyce's weight till his arm touched her own, supplanting it, under Joyce's shoulders. Joyce never stirred, never woke; she lay quiet under their movements, their whispers and anxious breathing.

'Don't touch her head, you'll wake her – *don't*, Lulu; just let it roll – I do – it finds its own place. Just keep your arm – so – loosely; keep your hand on her other side so's she won't flop back . . . You'll be as stiff as hell in a few minutes – I am, always. Don't try moving, that's worse; just relax . . .'

Joyce sighed; her sleeping body crept closer against him, her head rolled into the hollow of his shoulder – 'found its own place'. She sighed again with her cheek on his breast; she was comfortable here. Lulu's face came down, scarcely breathing; his chin was just over her little black hat.

Joyce smiled. A new life, the self's, moulded her lips in a soft line. Her face was all broken up, vivid in sleep . . . She was dancing with Margery Mannering. 'I'll kill you, I'll kill you,' she said like a knife. Something burst behind Margery's stretched eyes; she fainted . . . Joyce smiled in her sleep.

EVELYN WAUGH

Cruise
Letters from a Young Lady of Leisure

S.S. *Glory of Greece*

Darling,

Well I said I would write and so I would have only goodness it was rough so didnt. Now everything is a bit more alright so I will tell you. Well as you know the cruise started at Monte Carlo and when papa and all of us went to Victoria we found that the tickets didnt include the journey there so Goodness how furious he was and said he wouldnt go but Mum said of course we must go and we said that too only papa had changed all his money into Liri or Franks on account of foreigners being so dishonest but he kept a shilling for the porter at Dover being methodical so then he had to change it back again and that set him wrong all the way to Monte Carlo and he wouldnt get me and Bertie a sleeper and wouldnt sleep himself in his through being so angry Goodness how Sad.

Then everything was much more alright the purser called him Colonel and he likes his cabin so he took Bertie to the casino and he lost and Bertie won and I think Bertie got a bit plastered at least he made a noise going to bed he's in the next cabin as if he were being sick and that was before we sailed. Bertie has got some books on Baroque art on account of his being at Oxford.

Well the first day it was rough and I got up and felt odd in the bath and the soap wouldnt work on account of salt water you see and came into breakfast and there was a list of so many things including steak and onions and there was a corking young man who said we are the only ones down may I sit here and it was going beautifully and he had steak and onions but it was no good I had to go back to bed just when he was saying there was nothing he admired so much about a girl as her being a good sailor goodness how sad.

The thing is not to have a bath and to be very slow in all movements. So next day it was Naples and we saw some Bertie churches and then that bit that got blown up in an earthquake and a poor dog killed they have a plaster cast of him goodness how sad. Papa and Bertie saw some pictures we weren't allowed to see and Bill drew them for me afterwards and Miss P. tried to look too. I havent told you about Bill and Miss P. have I? Well Bill is rather old but clean looking and I dont suppose hes very old not really I mean and he's had a very disillusionary life on account of his wife who he says I wont say a word against but she gave him the raspberry with a foreigner and that makes him hate foreigners. Miss P. is called Miss Phillips and is lousy she wears a yachting cap and is a bitch. And the way she makes up to the second officer is no ones business and its clear to the meanest intelligence he hates her but its part of the rules that all the sailors have to pretend to fancy the passengers. Who else is there? Well a lot of old ones. Papa is having a walk out with one called Lady Muriel something or other who knew uncle Ned. And there is a honeymoon couple very embarrassing. And a clergyman and a lovely pansy with a camera and white suit and lots of families from the industrial north.

So Bertie sends his love too. XXXXXX etc.

Mum bought a shawl and an animal made of lava.

Post-card

This is a picture of Taormina. Mum bought a shawl here. V. funny because Miss P. got left as shed made chums only with second officer and he wasnt allowed ashore so when it came to getting into cars Miss P. had to pack in with a family from the industrial north.

S.S. *Glory of Greece*

Darling,

Hope you got P.C. from Sicily. The moral of that was not to make chums with sailors though who I've made a chum of is the purser who's different on account he leads a very cynical life with a gramophone in his cabin and as many cocktails as he likes and welsh rabbits sometimes and I said but do you pay for all these drinks but he said no so that's all right.

So we have three days at sea which the clergyman said is a good thing as it makes us all friendly but it hasn't made me friendly with Miss P. who won't leave poor Bill alone not taking any more chances of being left alone when she goes ashore. The purser says theres always someone like her on board in fact he says that about everyone except me who he says quite rightly is different goodness how decent.

So there are deck games they are hell. And the day before we reach Haifa there is to be a fancy dress dance. Papa is very good at the deck games expecially one called shuffle board and eats more than he does in London but I daresay its alright. You have to hire dresses for the ball from the barber I mean we do not you. Miss P. has brought her own. So I've thought of a v. clever thing at least the purser suggested it and that is to wear the clothes of one of the sailors I tried his on and looked a treat. Poor Miss P.

Bertie is madly unpop, he wont play any of the games and being plastered the other night too and tried to climb down a ventilator and the second officer pulled him out and the old ones at the captains table look *askance* at him. New word that. Literary yes? No?

So I think the pansy is writing a book he has a green fountain pen and green ink but I couldnt see what it was. XXXX Pretty good about writing you will say and so I am.

Post-card

This is a photograph of the Holyland and the famous sea of Gallillee. It is all v. Eastern with camels. I have a lot to tell you about the ball. *Such* goings on and will write very soon. Papa went off for the day with Lady M. and came back saying enchanting woman Knows the world.

S.S. *Glory of Greece*

Darling,

Well the Ball we had to come in to dinner in our clothes and everyone clapped as we came downstairs. So I was pretty late on account of not being able to make up my mind whether to wear the hat and in the end did and looked a corker. Well it was rather a faint clap for me considering so when I looked about there were about twenty girls and some women all dressed like me so how cynical the purser turns out to be. Bertie looked horribly dull as an apache. Mum and Papa were sweet. Miss P. had a ballet dress from the Russian ballet which couldnt have been more unsuitable so we had champagne for dinner and were jolly and they threw paper streamers and I threw mine before it was unrolled and hit Miss P. on the nose. Ha ha. So feeling matey I said to the steward isnt this fun and he said yes for them who hasnt got to clear it up goodness how Sad.

Well of course Bertie was plastered and went a bit far particularly in what he said to Lady M. then he sat in the cynical pursers cabin in the dark and cried so Bill and I found him and Bill gave him some drinks and what do you think he went off with Miss P. and we didnt see either of them again it only shows into what degradation the Demon Drink can drag you him I mean.

Then who should I meet but the young man who had steak and onions on the first morning and is called Robert and said I have been trying to meet you again all the voyage. Then I bitched him a bit goodness how Decent.

Poor Mum got taken up by Bill and he told her all about his wife and how she had disillusioned him with the foreigner so tomorrow we reach Port Said d.v. which is latin in case you didn't know meaning God Willing and all go up the nile and to Cairo for a week.

Will send P.C. of Sphinx.

XXXXXX

Post-card

This is the Sphinx. Goodness how Sad.

Post-card

This is temple of someone. Darling I cant wait to tell you I'm engaged to Arthur. Arthur is the one I thought was a pansy. Bertie thinks egyptian art is v. inartistic.

Post-card

This is Tutankhamens v. famous Tomb. Bertie says it is vulgar and is engaged to Miss P. so hes not one to speak and I call her Mabel now. G how S. Bill wont speak to Bertie Robert wont speak to me Papa and Lady M. seem to have had a row there was a man with a snake in a bag also a little boy who told my fortune which was v. prosperous Mum bought a shawl.

Post-card

Saw this Mosque today. Robert is engaged to a new girl called something or other who is lousy.

S.S. *Glory of Greece*

Darling,

Well so we all came back from Egypt pretty excited and the cynical purser said what news and I said *news* well Im engaged to Arthur and Bertie is engaged to Miss P. and she is called Mabel now which is hardest of all to bear I said and Robert to a lousy girl and Papa has had a row with Lady M. and Bill has had a row with Bertie and Roberts lousy girl was awful to me and Arthur was sweet but the cynical purser wasnt a bit surprised on account he said people always get engaged and have quarrels on the Egyptian trip every cruise so I said I wasnt in the habit of getting engaged lightly thank you and he said I wasnt apparently in the habit of going to Egypt so I wont speak to him again nor will Arthur.

All love.

Cruise

S.S. *Glory of Greece*

Sweet,

This is Algiers *not* very eastern in fact full of frogs. So it is all off with Arthur I was right about him at the first but who I am engaged to is Robert which is *much* better for all concerned really particularly Arthur on account of what I said originally first impressions always right. Yes? No? Robert and I drove about all day in the Botanic gardens and Goodness he was Decent. Bertie got plastered and had a row with Mabel – Miss P. again – so thats all right too and Robert's lousy girl spent all day on board with second officer. Mum bought shawl. Bill told Lady M. about his disillusionment and she told Robert who said yes we all know so Lady M. said it was very unreticent of Bill and she had very little respect for him and didnt blame his wife or the foreigner.

Love.

Post-card

I forget what I said in my last letter but if I mentioned a lousy man called Robert you can take it as unsaid. This is still Algiers and Papa ate *dubious oysters* but is all right. Bertie went to a house full of tarts when he was plastered and is pretty unreticent about it as Lady M. would say.

Post-card

So now we are back and sang old lang syne is that how you spell it and I kissed Arthur but wont speak to Robert and he cried not Robert I mean Arthur so then Bertie apologized to most of the people hed insulted but Miss P. walked away pretending not to hear. Goodness what a bitch.

JAMES HANLEY

The German Prisoner

Just as dusk was drawing in, the battalion pulled into Boves. It had marched thirty kilometres that day. The men were tired, black with sweat, and ravenous with hunger. They were shepherded into one of those huge French houses, which now seemed more stable than house, alas. After some confusion and delay they were served out with hot tea, stew of a kind, and bread. The food was attacked with a savagery almost unbelievable. The heavier parts of kit had been thrown off, men sprawled everywhere. They filled the rooms with their sweat; their almost pesty breath.

'The Battalion will move off in three hours time,' announced a sergeant, the volcanic tones of whose voice seemed to shake the house itself. He also made the following announcement.

'Those who have not yet made out wills, had better see the orderly sergeant at once.'

Then all became silent as before. In the darkest corner of one of the rooms on the ground floor, lay two men. They were facing each other, and even in this recumbent position their physical contrasts were striking. The taller and more hefty of the two, one Peter O'Garra, said:

'I hope this "do" won't be as big a balls-up as the last lot.'

He spat upon the floor, following up the action by drawing the flat of his hand across his mouth.

'I don't think so,' said his companion, a man from Manchester, named Elston.

'You never know,' said O'Garra; 'these funkin' bastards at the back; you never know what game they're up to.'

'We'll see,' replied the Manchester man.

54

Peter O'Garra was forty-four years of age. He came from Tara Street, known as the filthiest street in all Dublin. He had lodged there with a Mrs Doolan, an old hag who looked more like a monstrous spider than a woman. O'Garra was very well known in Tara Street. In those fifteen years he had been known as, 'a strange man – a misanthrope – a Belfast Bastard (his birth-place) – a lousy bugger – a rake – a closet – a quiet fellow – a tub of guts – a pimp – a shit-house – a toad – a sucker – a blasted sod – a Holy Roller – a Tara lemon – a Judas – a jumped up liar – a book-worm – a traitor to Ireland – a pervert – an Irish jew – an Irish Christ – a clod.'

It was rumoured that he had never worked, and had at one time been crossed in love. It was known that he used to stand beneath the clock in Middle Abbey Street, stalking the women, all of whom are supposed to have fled in terror. O'Garra could never understand this, until he discovered it was his ugly mouth that used to frighten the women. It was his most outstanding characteristic. It made him something more than a man. A threat. The children in Tara Street used to run after him, calling him, 'Owld click', because he made a peculiar clicking sound with his false teeth. But all Tara Street was surprised when he went for a soldier. Not only the men, women, and children, but even the houses and roofs and chimney pots, the very paving stones, joined in song. They became humanized. And the song they sang was that Peter O'Garra's blood was heavy with surrender.

'His blood is heavy with surrender,' they sang.

As soon as the blood is heavy with surrender *Act*. O'Garra had acted. And Tara Street saw him no more. Perhaps what it had already seen of him was enough. Already there were a number of lines upon his forehead; the years had traced their journey-work through his hair; his eyes resembled the dried up beds of African lakes. But it was his mouth above all that one noticed. If one wished to know O'Garra, one looked at his mouth. Once Elston had asked him what he thought of the war. He had said:

'Well it's just a degree of blood bitterness, and bitter blood is good blood. Personally, it is a change for me from the rather drab life of Tara Street, with its lousiness, its smells, its human animals herded together, its stinkin' mattresses.'

Elston had yawned and remarked:

'My views are different. There is nothing I long for so much as to get back to the smoke and fog and grease of Manchester. I like the filth and rotteness because it is warm. Yes, I long to get back to my little corner, my little world.'

In Dublin, a fellow like Elston, a kind of human rat, would get short shrift. To O'Garra he was 'the Hungry Englishman' par excellence. And he had little time for Englishmen, especially the suck-holing type. Still he remembered that he was his bed-mate, his one companion in this huge mass of desperate life. When first he had set eyes on Elston, he had despised him, there was something in this man entirely repugnant to him. He had once written on a piece of paper, the following lines:

> There's an Englishman named Elston
> By the living Christ I swear
> Necessity has never hewn
> One like him anywhere.

'Have you any idea at all?' asked O'Garra – 'as to where we're goin'?'

The Manchester man smiled. His small ferrity eyes seemed to blink.

'Gorman thinks we're marchin' up to the jumpin'-off point, to-night. I suppose they'll want us to take back all the bloody ground the fifth lost, last year. God blast them.'

'Division you mean?' queried O'Garra.

'Yes,' replied Elston.

'I suppose we'll be met by a guide. Time they were movin' anyhow. See the time,' and he showed Elston his watch. 'Remember the last time, don't you? Confusion, delay, roads blocked up. Guide drunk and lost himself. Result. Caught in single file at daylight. One of his uckin' observation balloons at work. Next thing a salvo of five-nines and seven men lost.'

'Hope it won't be like that this time,' said Elston in a quiet voice.

A voice bawled out – FALL IN. And the men filed down the stairs and into the yard. O'Garra and Elston filed out too, and took their places in line with the others. Darkness, gloom, and silence. This darkness was so intense that one could almost feel it. It is just that kind of darkness which falls with the most dramatic suddenness. The men could barely see one another. By feeling with their hands they became aware that they were in line. All was in order. Gorman came out, though he was not discernible. But one recognised the voice. Names were called and answered LEFT TURN. QUICK MARCH.

The files moved. In that blackness they resembled the rather dim outlines of huge snakes, as they turned out of the yard and on to the white road. In the road they halted once more. Nobody spoke. The officers came up. Another order, and the men began to nose their way towards the line. One could not say they walked erect, but just that they nosed their way forward. In five minutes order had given way to confusion. This was inevitable. Roads were blocked. All space around seemed to be festered, suffocated by this physical material; by guns, limbers, ambulances, mules, horses, more guns, more wagons and limbers. And men. Suddenly O'Garra slipped into a hole.

'Jesus Christ! Already,' growled Elston.

He dragged O'Garra out, following up the action by falling in himself. One saw nothing. Nothing. There was something infinite about the action of feeling. One was just conscious that the night was deluged by phantom-like movements. That was all. Far ahead the sky was lighted up by a series of periodic flashes. Then a vast concourse of sound, then silence. The roads were impassable. The men were separated, relying on an occasional whisper, an occasional feel of a hand or bayonet, to establish contact with one another. Crawling beneath wagons and guns, now held up by mud. A traffic block.

'Elston man,' said O'Garra; 'how in hell are they goin' to get all this lot up before day-light. Its impossible. They'll never clear the road.'

'Think of yourself,' replied Elston. 'We have to go a mile and a half yet. And let's hope the guide is there. You know its not the trenches I hate. No. Its this damned business of getting into them, and out of them again too. Every time I think of those sons of bitches at the base, I get mad.'

There was no reply to this remark. The men wormed their way ahead. In that terrible moment when all reason seemed to have surrendered to chaos, men became as it were, welded together. Occasionally one saw a humped back, the outline of a profile, the shadow of legs. A huge eyeless monster that forged its way ahead towards some inevitable destiny. Nothing more. At last the road seemed a little easier. Elston spoke.

'I was over this same ground, last July. I believe we turn here. The trench-system proper commences somewhere about here. To the right I think. Funny though. I once saw an aerial photograph of these same trenches. Took it off a Jerry who crashed. Looked like a huge crucifix in shape.'

'You mean a cross,' said O'Garra.

'Yes.'

'H'm'. Cross. The bloody country is littered with them. I once saw one of those crosses, with the figure of Jesus plastered in shite. Down on the Montauban road.'

'Had somebody deliberately plastered it?' asked Elston.

'No. A five-nine landed behind it, and the figure pitched into one of those latrines,' replied O'Garra.

'Did you ever make a point of studying the different features of these figures?' asked Elston.

'Saw half-a-dozen. Didn't bother after that. Reminded me of the Irish Christ. All blood and tears.'

Again silence. Suddenly a voice whispered – PULL UP.

The order was passed down the line. PULL UP.

More confusion, babble of voices, whisperings, curses, threats.

'What's the matter?'

'Lost the way.'

O'Garra shivered. Pulled out his watch and noted the time. He said to the man from Manchester:

'Won't be long before its light. Must have been over four hours pawing about these blasted roads.'

Elston gave a kind of growl. O'Garra growled too. One had to do something. After all it was better than standing still, helpless. He, O'Garra, once said that the war had quickened his critical spirit:

'After all, the end of man is rather ignominious. No. I don't blame even the simplest of men for endeavouring to go down to the grave in a blaze of glory.'

Again an order. In almost a whisper.

'Get contact and move on.'

Once more the men moved along in single file. The road seemed clearer here, and the officer knew that but a thousand yards ahead a guide would be waiting to take them up to the old trenches of '16'.

That officer, whose name was 'Snow-Ball', was at present worrying over his men. He must certainly get them under cover before it got light. It might be too late in half-an-hour or so, and then progress was so slow. There were, of course, two reasons for this state of mind. Firstly, he might lose a few men; secondly, it might disclose (more important still), the movements of troops, going up for what, to the Germans, would be an attack on the grand scale. Far back, at the very tail end of this file of men, the Irishman was explaining to his English friend that:

'It looked as though the guide had failed to turn up, after all. I had a curious feeling something would happen,' he muttered.

'Cheer up,' said Elston.

'Its turned half-past-six, you fool. Cheer up. That bugger in front wants to cheer up. Doesn't know what to do, I'll bet. Same old thing every time. Flummuxed. I think they get a bug on the brain sometimes.'

'Yes. It's getting light now alright,' remarked Elston, and there was a frightfulness about the tone in which he uttered these words.

'We can't arse about here much longer. Wonder those fellows up in front don't have something to say to him.'

Down the line came an order. FILE MOVE ON.

The men moved on. And now, what had merely been a germ, became a disease, an epidemic. The torment was no longer private, but general. To all these men it became apparent that something had happened. When something went wrong the more sensitive spirits became agitated. One saw it in their eyes. Like a man conscious of Death, who begins to sense the earthiness of the grave about him. Elston remarked that it was about time they reached the trench.

'I know the ground well, at least I should think I ought to. To the direct North of this trench-network, you'll find a trench once begun but left unfinished. We used it for shelter on one occasion during heavy shelling. We were changing positions one night. It's not much in an emergency, but better than nothing. Only about three foot deep. No covey holes either. Jerry has it spotted too.'

Suddenly there was a low whine. Someone ahead shouted

LOOK-OUT, and the line was thrown into confusion once more. The shell exploded about twenty yards ahead of Elston and O'Garra. There was a scream.

'Christ!' exclaimed Elston. 'He's feelin'. Now we're for it.'

'I should think so,' growled O'Garra. 'Its gettin' light already. When is that bastard in front goin' to do something?'

'He can't do anything if the guide is lost, or failed to turn up.'

Already it was light. The men now began to murmur threats against the officer in front. Far ahead somebody had espied a balloon. Somebody shouted from the middle of the file:

'Has that soft runt gone mad? He'll get one bloody quick himself. I suppose he'll ask us to form fours and march in ceremonial style.'

It was quite light now. One could see the wilderness all around. Here and there a gnarled tree-stump. Far back one visioned the packed roads and became fearful of consequences. O'Garra thumped Elston.

'Let's go to him. The fool's crazy. Stark staring mad.'

'LOOK-OUT.'

There came another shell, exploding right in their midst so it seemed. Out of the smoke and stench there came sounds of moaning.

'That's only the beginning,' said Elston. 'Someone caught it alright.'

It got seven men. An order was passed down from one to the other. RUN FOR IT.

Both Elston and O'Garra made for a rise in the ground. Elston said: 'In here. Quick.'

Both men sprawled into this unfinished trench.

'This way, fellows,' shouted Elston.

Soon the remaining men had skeltered across the broken ground, and had jumped into the trench.

'We're here for the bloody day,' remarked a lance-corporal.

Elston and O'Garra agreed.

The Irishman still saw in his mind's eye, the mangled body of Gorman. Elston had helped him get the papers from his pocket. He had vomited too, for Gorman's brains were splattered on his forehead.

'Think I'll go to kip for a while,' said O'Garra. Elston agreed too. The other men were endeavouring to make themselves comfortable, when the sergeant, named Grundy, said he was going to post certain men. On hearing this, all and sundry broke into loud cursings and obscene oaths.

'If that son of a bitch – well by Christ – I – I—'

'I feel rotten tired,' sighed Elston.

As soon as darkness set in they were going to move out again, and continue their march until they reached the jumping-off point. An officer was expected up before they moved out. But Grundy knew that no officer would arrive. He was quite prepared to take the responsibility of getting the men up to the jumping-off point mapped out for them.

Finally Grundy had men posted every four hours until night-fall. He knew how lucky they had been to escape so lightly. And what a blasted rotten trench they were in. No protection from flying craft. Exposed to everything.

'If that officer gets here safely,' thought the Sergeant, 'it'll be a miracle.'

At ten fifteen the men broke cover, and continued on in single file across the broken ground, pitted here and there by yawning shell-holes filled with stagnant and stinking water. A voice was heard then.

'TAPE LINE HERE.'

And each man felt that at last he was near his final destination. O'Garra himself had espied this tape-line, well concealed in the grass. Only the bundles of twigs indicated to the men that that long line of white tape was their infallible guide.

'We follow this I suppose until told to pull up.'

'Correct,' said the Manchester man. 'It won't be long now.'

They gripped each other's hand and continued in this fashion until they heard the order to halt. No. They wouldn't be long now.

At two o'clock rations came along. These were handed down the trench from man to man. Bread, jam, tea. For three hours the men had been standing up to their thighs in water. O'Garra had loosed from his angry and tormented being a series of curses. Likewise Elston. All the men murmured. The orders were now known. Objective five thousand yards. On the right, the Aussies, on the left, the French. Centre body would make for the Albert-Roye road. The barrage would open up shortly after five. Something approaching awe seemed to hang over the trenches. All was silent.

But soon the secret rage lurking in the ground beneath their feet would burst forth. The attack opened up on the very stroke of five. O'Garra was half drunk. He had very rarely taken his ration of rum, but Elston had used persuasion to such effect that O'Garra had drunk another soldier's ration as well as his own. A whistle blew. The earth seemed to shake. They were over the top.

And now every sound and every movement seemed to strike some responsive chord in the Irishman's nature. He hung on desperately to the Manchester man. For some reason or other he dreaded losing contact with him. He could not understand this sudden desire for Elston's company. But the desire overwhelmed him.

It was not the sound, the huge concourse of sound that worried O'Garra. For somehow the earth in convulsion seemed a kind of yawning mouth, swallowing noise. No. It was the gun flashes ahead. They seemed to rip the very sky asunder. Great pendulums of flame swinging across the sky. In that moment they appeared to him like the pendulums of his own life. Swinging from splendour to power, from terror to pity, from Life to Death. More than that. There was a continuous flash away on his right. It was more than a flash. It was an eye that ransacked his very soul.

'Jesus! Jesus!'

The earth was alive – afire. The earth was a mouth, it was a sea, a yawning gulf, a huge maw. Suddenly Elston was drenched in blood. Like a stuck pig he screamed out:

'Oh funkin' hell. I'm killed. I'm dead. O'Garra. O'Garra. O'Garra.'

'Shut up,' growled the Irishman. 'Can't you see that bugger behind you. You got a belt in the back with his head. See. He hasn't any now. That whizz-bang took head and arse off him at the same time . . Phew! Everybody's mad.'

'If ever I get out of this,' screamed Elston, 'I'll – I'll—'

Grundy came up.

'Shit on you. Get forward. What the hell are you fellows standing here for? You bloody cowards,' he roared into their ears.

'What the bloody hell's wrong with you,' growled the Irishman. 'This fellow here thought his head was off. Everything alright, isn't it? We're going forward. Are you? You lump of shite. How long have you been in the line anyhow? When you've learned to piss in your cap, you sucker, you'll have room to talk.'

And Sergeant Grundy thought to himself.

'I suppose he thinks he was the only one in the first gas-attack. H'm.'

'I'll put a bullet in the first man who wavers,' he roared out.

The men struggled forward. It was impossible to see, to hear, to feel. All the senses were numbed. O'Garra's face was almost yeasty with sweat. He spat continually, at the same time cursing Grundy, and endeavouring to keep this man from Manchester upon his feet.

'Oh hell!' he yelled. 'Are you utterly helpless? Stand up.'

With the speed of terror Elston screamed out.

'Yes. Yes. I'm frightened. Oh, mother! Mother! Mother!'

'Shut it, you bloody worm,' growled O'Garra, and continued on his way, dragging the Englishman after him.

'Where are they drivin' us to, anyhow?' asked a man from Cork.

'Towards the bloody objective of course. Where in hell d'you think.'

'We fairly fanned his backside,' yelled another man from Donegal.

The screams of the shells, the plop-plop of the gas-shells, the staccatto drumming of the machine-guns, the shouts and squeals and blubberings, almost upset even a man like O'Garra.

'This is not so bad,' he murmured. 'The thing is – will these blasted sods come back? That's what we have to look out for.'

'Come back,' yelled a voice. 'Christ, you'll want running pumps to catch the swine.'

Then suddenly O'Garra stopped. He no longer heard the sounds of voices. True, the man from Manchester was at his side. But where were the others? And a thick fog was descending. For a moment he seemed to lose contact with the whimperer at his side. And O'Garra shouted:

'Elston. Elston. Hey Elston! Where are you. Something's happened. Can you see? Hey! Hey! Can you see? This bloody fog's thickening.'

Elston blinked and stood erect. Then his face paled. He said slowly:

'We must have gone too far. Lost contact somehow. We must search about quickly.'

'Too far. Too far,' shouted O'Garra, and he burst out laughing.

Yes. There was the possibility of that. He had seemed to eat up distance after that scrap with the sergeant. And then he must have dragged this

English coward some distance too. Before they were aware of it, the fog had blotted everything out. They were now conscious only of each other's presence. This fog had separated them from all that madness, that surging desperate mass of matter; that eyeless monster; that screaming phalanx. The fog became so thick it was almost impossible for them to see each other.

'We must do something,' said Elston. 'God knows where we landed.'

'Maybe into his bloody line,' growled O'Garra.

They both sat down on the edge of the shell-hole to consider their position.

They seemed oblivious of the fact that the attack had not abated. That to the right a team of tanks was shooting forward on to the machine-gun positions; that a thousand yards to the rear a mopping-up party was at work. Oblivious of war and life itself. A strange silence seemed to overwhelm them. O'Garra rested his head in his hands. Suddenly he sat up, gripped Elston by the throat, and said:

'I've a mind to choke you. To put you out of your misery. How funny that in the moment I first realized your cowardice, I became unconscious of my own strength. I must have pulled you a mile, you swine.'

The blood came and went across Elston's face in a sudden gust of fear and passion.

'What good would that do you. Especially at this moment?'

O'Garra once more buried his face in his hands, and remained silent. Elston was thinking. What was wrong? And had O'Garra really dragged him a mile? And had they really lost contact? Where in Christ's name had they landed? And did this man really mean to murder him? By God, then the sooner they found the others, the better. Perhaps he had suddenly gone mad? By God. That was it. He had gone mad. Mad.

'O'Garra,' called Elston to the man now seated on the edge of the hole. 'O'Garra! O'Garra!'

There was no reply, for the Irishman had fallen asleep. This discovery petrified Elston. The consciousness that he was absolutely alone; alone, save for this sleeping figure, caused a kind of icy mist to descend upon his heart, almost suffocating him. He too, sunk his head between his hands. The action was profound, for it seemed to the man to shut out thought, action, all external contacts with the world. But O'Garra was not asleep for long. He opened his eyes, looked across at the huddled form of the Manchester man, heaved a sigh, then fell back again into a kind of torpor. O'Garra suddenly began to think, and to think deeply. This process he found painful, as it always is for those who have ceased to think over a period of years. His was an atrophied mind. But now the whole of his past shot across the surface of that mind. He asked himself, if he would not have been better off in Tara Street after all. Even those lonely nights, those fruitless endeavours beneath the clock in Middle Abbey Street, surely they took on a richer texture now. Surely all those common-place things achieved a certain significance. Those times when his mind had remained simple; when he had been wont to enjoy those sweet charities of life itself. After all there was something in it. Why had he come into all this muck and mud and madness. He could not find any answer to the question. Then again, there was that after the war question. Would the men be compensated for all the inconveniences. *All* the inconveniences. All the men. Would they? He had a grudge. Only this morning he had had one against a foolish officer, and yet the sight of that officer's headless body had stirred something deep down in the bosom of his soul. He had borne a grudge. But that was forgiven. There were so many. Did not this state of affairs warrant some kind of vengeance? Perhaps it did. But how would a man get it? Everyone in the war must bear a grudge. But would they all demand retribution? Would they all wreak a terrible vengeance. Ah!—.

'Elston!'

'Yes.'

'Oh! you're awake. I say, we must have slept a hell of a time. My watch has stopped too. This blasted fog hasn't risen yet, either. We'd better move.'

'What's that you say?'

'What's up now. Got the bloody shakes again,' asked O'Garra.

'Listen,' said Elston.

Somewhere ahead they could hear the movement of some form or other.

'Let's find out,' said O'Garra, and jumped to his feet.

'No need now,' said Elston. 'Here it comes. Look!'

They both looked up at once. Right on top of them stood a young German soldier. His hands were stuck high in the air. He was weaponless. His clothes hung in shreds and his face was covered with mud. He looked tired and utterly weary. He said in a plaintive kind of voice.

'Camerade. Camerade.'

'Camerade, you bastard,' said Elston, 'keep your hands up there.'

And O'Garra asked: 'Who are you? Where do you come from? Can you speak English? Open your soddin' mouth.'

'Camerade. Camerade.'

'You speak English, Camerade?'

'Yes – a little.'

'Your name,' demanded Elston. 'What regiment are you? Where are we now. No tricks. If you do anything, you'll get your bottom kicked. Now then – where have you come from, and what the hell do you want?'

'My name it is Otto Reiburg. My home it is Muenchen. I am Bavarian. I surrender, Camerade.'

'That's all,' growled Elston.

'I am lost, is it,' replied the German.

He was a youth, about eighteen years of age, tall, with a form as graceful as a young sapling, in spite of the ill-fitting uniform and unkempt appearance. His hair, which stuck out in great tufts from beneath his forage cap, was as fair as ripe corn. He had blue eyes, and finely moulded features.

'So are we,' said Elston. 'We are lost too. Is it foggy where you came from? It looks to me as if we'll never get out of this hole, only by stirring ourselves together and making a bolt for it.'

'That's impossible,' said O'Garra. 'True, we can move. But what use is that? And perhaps this sod is leading us into a trap. Why not finish the bugger off, anyhow?'

The two men looked at the young German, and smiled. But the youth seemed to have sensed the something sinister in that smile. He began to move off. Elston immediately jumped up. Catching the young German by the shoulder he flung him to the bottom of the hole, saying:

'If you try that on again I'll cut the rollocks out of you. Why should you not suffer as well as us? Do you understand what I am saying? Shit on you,' and he spat savagely into the German's face. From the position the youth was lying in, it was impossible for either of the men to see that he was weeping. Indeed, had Elston seen it, he would undoubtedly have killed him. There was something terrible stirring in this weasel's blood. He knew not what it was. But there was a strange and powerful force possessing him, and it was going to use him as its instrument. He felt a power growing on him. There was something repugnant, something revolting in those eyes, in their leer, and in the curled lips. Was it that in that moment itself, all the rottenness that was his life had suddenly shot up as filth from a sewer, leaving him helpless in everything but the act he was going to commit? O'Garra was watching Elston. He too, seemed to have sensed this something terrible.

His gaze wandered from Elston to the young German. No word was spoken. The silence was intense. Horrible. These three men, who but an hour ago, seemed to be charged for action, eager and vital, looked as helpless as children now. Was it that this fog surrounding them had pierced its way into their hearts and souls? Or was it that something in their very nature had suffered collapse?

One could not say that they sat, or merely lay; they just sprawled; each terribly conscious of the other's presence, and in that presence detecting something sinister; something that leered; that goaded and pricked. Each seemed to have lost his faculty of speech. The fog had hemmed them in. Nor could any of them realize their position, where they were, the possibility of establishing contact with other human beings. What was this something that had so hurled them together?

O'Garra looked across to Elston.

'Elston! Elston! What are we going to do? We must get out of this. Besides the place stinks. Perhaps we are on very old ground. Rotten ground; mashy muddy ground. Christ the place must be full of these mangy dead.'

Elston did not answer. And suddenly O'Garra fell upon him, beating him in the face, and screaming out at the top of his voice:

'Hey. Hey. You lousy son of a bitch. What's your game? Are you trying to make me as rotten as yourself, as cowardly, as lousy. Its you and not this bloody Jerry who is responsible for this. Do you hear me? Do you hear me? Jesus Christ Almighty, why don't you answer. Answer Answer.'

The young German cowered in the bottom of the hole, trembling like a leaf. Terror had seized him. His face seemed to take on different colour, now white, now red, now grey, as if Death were already in the offing. Saliva trickled down his chin.

These changes of colour in the face seemed to pass across it like gusts of wind. Gusts of fear, terror, despair. Once only he glanced up at the now distorted features of the half crazy Irishman, and made as if to cry out. Once again O'Garra spoke to Elston. Then it was that the English-man opened his eyes, looked across at his mate, and shouted:

'O'Garra! O'Garra. Oh where the funkin' hell are you, O'Garra?'

He stared hard at the Irishman, who, though his lips barely moved, yet uttered sounds:

'In a bloody mad-house. In a shit hole. Can't you smell the rotten dead? Can you hear. Can you hear? You louse, you bloody rat. Pretending to be asleep and all the while your blasted owl's eyes have been glaring at me. Ugh! Ugh!'

'Camerade.'

A sigh came from the youth lying at the bottom of the hole. It was almost flute-like, having a liquidity of tone.

'Ah! uck you,' growled O'Garra. 'You're as much to blame as anybody. Yes. Yes. As much to blame as anybody. Who in the name of Jesus asked you to come here? Haven't I that bastard there to look after. The coward. Didn't I have to drag him across the ground during the advance? Yes. YOU. YOU. YOU.' and O'Garra commenced to kick the prisoner in the face until it resembled a piece of raw beef. The prisoner moaned. As soon as O'Garra saw the stream of blood gush forth from the German's mouth, he burst into tears. Elston too, seemed to have been stirred into action by this furious onslaught on the youth. He kicked the German in the mid-riff, making him scream like a stuck pig. It was this scream that loosed all the springs of action in the Manchester man. It cut him to the heart, this scream. Impotency and futility seemed as ghouls leering at him, goading him, maddening him.

He started to kick the youth in the face too. But now no further sound came from that inert heap. The Englishman dragged himself across to O'Garra. But the Irishman pushed him off.

'Get away. I hate you. Hate you. HIM. Everybody. Hate all. Go away. AWAY.'

'By Jesus I will then,' shouted Elston. 'Think I'm a bloody fool to sit here with two mad-men. I'm going. Don't know where I'll land. But anything is better than this. It's worse than hell.'

He rose to his feet and commenced to climb out of the hole. He looked ahead. Fog. And behind. Fog. Everywhere Fog. No sound. No stir. He made a step forward when O'Garra leaped up and dragged him back. Some reason seemed to have returned to him, for he said:

'Don't go. Stay here. Listen. This state of affairs cannot go on for ever. The fog will lift. Are you listening, and not telling yourself that I am mad? I am not mad. Do you understand? Do you understand. Tell me?'

'Is it day or night, or has day and night vanished,' asked Elston.

'It might well be that the whole bloody universe has been hurled into space. The bugger of it is, my watch has stopped. Sit down here. I want to talk. Do you see now. I want to talk. It's this terrible bloody silence that kills me. Listen now. Can you hear anything. No. You can't. But you can hear me speak. Hear that ucker moaning down there. They are human sounds. And human sounds are everything now. They can save us. So we must talk. All the while. Without resting, without ceasing. Understand. Whilst we are conscious that we are alive, all is well. Do you see now. Do you see now?'

'I thought the bloody Jerry was dead,' muttered Elston.

'Dead my arse. Come! What'll we talk about. Anything. Everything.'

And suddenly Elston laughed, showing his teeth, which were like a horses!

'Remember that crazy house down in Fricourt. Remember that. Just as we started to enter the God-forsaken place, he began to bomb and shell it. Remember? We both went out in the evening, souveniring. Went into that little white house at the back of the hotel. Remember that?'

'Well!'

'Remember young Dollan mounting that old woman. Looked like a bloody witch. I still remember her nearly bald head.'

'Well!'

'And you chucked young Dollan off, and got into bed with her yourself.'

'Was it a long time ago. In this war, d'you mean?'

'Yes. Are you tapped, or what. Course it was in this bloody war. What the funkin' hell are you thinkin' of, you loony.'

For the first time since they had found themselves in this position, they both laughed. And suddenly Elston looked up into his companion's face, laughed again, and said softly:

'Well, by Christ, d'you know that laugh has made me want to do something?'

'Do something?' queried O'Garra.

'Yes,' replied Elston, and standing over the prisoner in the hole, he pissed all over him. Likewise O'Garra, who began to laugh in a shrill sort of way.

There is a peculiar power about rottenness, in that it feeds on itself, borrows from itself, and its tendency is always downward. That very action had seized the polluted imagination of the Irishman. He was helpless. Rottenness called to him; called to him from the pesty frame of Elston. After the action they both laughed again, but this time louder.

'Hell!' exclaimed O'Garra. 'After that I feel relieved. Refreshed. Don't feel tired. Don't feel anything particularly. How do you feel?' he asked.

'The same,' replied Elston. 'But I wish to Christ this soddin' fog would lift.'

This desire, this hope that the fog would lift was something burning in the heart, a ceaseless yearning, the restlessness of waters washing against the flood-gates of the soul. It fired their minds. It became something organic in the brain. Below them the figure stirred slightly.

'Ah!—Ah!—'

'The ucker hasn't kicked the bucket yet,' said Elston. He leaned over and rested his two hands on O'Garra's knees. 'D'you know when I came to examine things; that time I thought you were asleep you know, and you weren't; well I thought hard, and I came to certain conclusions. One of them was this. See that lump of shit in the hole; that Jerry I mean. You do. Well now, he's the cause of everything. Everything. Everything. Don't you think so yourself?'

'Yes I do,' said the Irishman. 'That's damn funny, you know. Here is what I thought. I said to myself: "That bastard lying there is the cause of all this." And piece by piece and thread by thread I gathered up all the inconveniences. All the actions, rebuffs, threats, fatigues, cold nights, lice, toothaches, forced absence from women, nights in trenches up to your knees in mud. Burial parties, mopping-up parties, dead horses, heaps of stale shite, heads, balls, brains, everywhere. All those things. I made the case against him. Now I ask you. Why should he live?'

'Yes,' shouted Elston. 'You're right. Why should he? He is the cause of it all. Only for this bloody German we might not have been here. I know where I should have been anyhow. Only for him the fog might have lifted. We might have got back to our own crowd. Yes. Yes. Only for him. Well there would not have been any barrage, any attack, any bloody war in fact.

'Can't you see it for yourself now? Consider. Here we are, an Englishman, and an Irishman, both sitting here like soft fools. See. And we're not the only ones perhaps. One has to consider everything. Even the wife at home. All the other fellows. All the madness, confusion. Through Germans. And here's one of them.'

'Ah!—'

Elston glared down into the gargoyle of a face now visible to them both, the terrible eyes flaring up at the almost invisible sky.

'Water—Ah!—'

A veritable torrent of words fell from Elston's lips.

'Make the funkin' fog rise and we'll give you anything. Everything. Make the blasted war stop, now, right away. Make all this mud and shite vanish. Will you. You bastards started it. Will you now. See! We are both going mad. We are going to kill ourselves.'

'Kill me—'

'Go and shite. But for the likes of you we wouldn't be here.'

'Water—'

In that moment O'Garra was seized by another fit of madness. Wildly, like some terror-stricken and trapped animal, he looked up and around.

'Fog. Yes fog. FOG. FOG. FOG. FOG. FOG. Jesus sufferin' Christ. FOG. FOG. FOG. HA, HA, HA, HA, HA. In your eyes, in your mouth, on your chest, in your heart. FOG. FOG. Oh hell, we're all going crazy. FOG. FOG.'

'There you are,' screamed Elston into the German's ear, for suddenly seized with panic by the terrific outburst from O'Garra, he had fallen headlong into the hole. The eyes seemed to roll in his head, as he screamed: 'There you are. Can you hear it? You. Can you hear it? You ucker from Muenchen, with your fair hair, and your lovely face that we bashed in for you. Can you hear it? We're trapped here. Through you. Through you and you bloody lot. If only you hadn't come. You baby. You soft stupid little runt. Hey! Hey! Can you hear me?'

The two men now fell upon the prisoner, and with peculiar movements of the hands began to mangle the body. They worried it like mad dogs. The fog had brought about a nearness, that was now driving them to distraction. Elston, on making contact with the youth's soft skin, became almost demented. The velvety touch of the flesh infuriated him. Perhaps it was because Nature had hewn him differently. Had denied him the young German's grace of body, the fair hair, the fine clear eyes that seemed to reflect all the beauty and music and rhythm of the Rhine. Maddened him. O'Garra shouted out:

'PULL his bloody trousers down.'

With a wild movement Elston tore down the prisoner's trousers.

In complete silence O'Garra pulled out his bayonet and stuck it up the youth's anus. The German screamed.

Elston laughed and said: 'I'd like to back-scuttle the bugger.'

'Go ahead,' shouted O'Garra.

'I tell you what,' said Elston. 'Let's stick this horse-hair up his penis.'

So they stuck the horse-hair up his penis. Both laughed shrilly.

A strange silence followed.

'Kill the bugger,' screamed O'Garra.

Suddenly, as if instinctively, both men fell away from the prisoner, who rolled over, emitting a single sigh – Ah—. His face was buried in the soft mud.

'Elston.'

'Well,' was the reply.

'Oh Jesus! Listen. Has the fog risen yet. I have my eyes tight closed. I am afraid.'

'What are you afraid of. Tell me that. There's bugger all here now. This fellow is dead. Feel his bum. Any part you like. Dead. Dead.'

'I am afraid of myself. Listen. I have something to ask you. Will you agree with me now to walk out of it. We can't land any worse place.'

'My *arse* on you,' growled Elston. Where can we walk. You can't see a finger ahead of you. I tell you what. Let's worry each other to death. Isn't that better than this moaning, this sitting here like soft shits. That time I fell asleep I did it in my pants. It made me get mad with that bugger down there.'

'A thing like that,' O'Garra laughed once again.

'Listen,' roared Elston. 'I tell you we can't move. D'you hear. Do you? Shall I tell you why. It's not because there is no ground on which to walk. No. Not that. Its just that we can't move. We're stuck. Stuck fast. Though we have legs, we can't walk. We have both been seized by something, I can't even cry out. I am losing strength. I don't want to do anything. Nothing at all. Everything is useless. Nothing more to do. Let's end it. Let's worry each other like mad dogs. I had the tooth-ache an hour ago. I wish it would come back. I want something to worry me. Worry me.'

'Listen! Did you hear that?'

'Well, its a shell. What did you think it was. A bloody butterfly?'

'It means,' said O'Garra, 'that something is happening, and where something is happening we are safe. Let's go. Now. Now.'

'Are you sure it was a shell?'

'Sure. There's another,' said O'Garra.

'It's your imagination,' said Elston laughing. 'Imagination.'

'Imagination. Well, by Christ. I never thought of that. Imagination. By God, that's it.'

They sat facing each other. Elston leaned forward until his eyes were on a level with those of the Irishman. Then, speaking slowly, he said:

'Just now you said something. D'you know what it was?'

'Yes. Yes. Let's get out of it before we are destroyed.'

'But we're destroyed already,' said Elston, smiling. 'Listen.'

'Don't you remember what you said a moment ago,' continued Elston. 'You don't. Then there's no mistake about it, you are crazy. Why, you soft shite didn't you say we had better talk, talk, talk. About anything. Everything. Nothing. Let us then. What'll we talk about?'

'Nothing. But I know what we must do. Yes, by Jesus I know. D'you remember you said these Germans were the cause of the war. And you kicked that fellow's arse. Well, let's destroy him. Let's bury him.'

'He's dead, you mad bugger. Didn't we kill him before. Didn't I say I felt like back-scuttling him? I knew all along you were crazy. Ugh.'

'Not buried. He's not buried,' shouted O'Garra, 'Are you deaf? Mad yourself, are you?'

The fog was slowly rising, but they were wholly unconscious of its doing so. They were blind. The universe was blotted out. They were conscious only of each other's presence, of that dead heap at the bottom of the hole. Conscious of each other's nearness. Each seemed to have become something gigantic. The one saw the other as a barrier, a wall blotting out everything. They could feel and smell each other. There was something infinite in those moments that held them back from each other's throats.

'Not deaf, but mad like yourself, you big shit-house, can't you see that something has happened. I don't mean outside, but inside this funkin' fog, Savvy?'

'Let's bury this thing. UGH. Everything I look at becomes Him. Everything Him. If we don't destroy him, he'll destroy us, even though he's dead.'

'Let's dance on the bugger and bury him for ever.'

'Yes, that's it,' shouted O'Garra. 'I knew an owld woman named Donaghue whose dog took poison. She danced on the body.'

And both men began to jump up and down upon the corpse. And with each movement, their rage, their hatred seemed to increase. Out of sight, out of mind. Already this mangled body was beginning to disappear beneath the mud. Within their very beings there seemed to burst into flame, all the conglomerated hates, fears, despairs, hopes, horrors. It leaped to the brain for O'Garra screamed out:

'I hate this thing so much now I want to shit on it.'

'O'Garra.'

'Look. Its going down down. Disappearing. Look,' shouted Elston.

'Elston.'

'Let's kill each other. Oh sufferin' Jesus—'

'You went mad long ago but I did not know that—'

'Elston,' called O'Garra.

'There's no way out is there?'

'Uck you. NO.'

'Now.'

'The fog is still thick.'

'Now.'

The bodies hurled against each other, and in that moment it seemed as if this madness had set their minds afire.

Suddenly there was a low whine, whilst they struggled in the hole, all unconscious of the fact that the fog had risen. There was a terrific explosion, a cloud of mud, smoke, and earthy fragments, and when it cleared the tortured features of O'Garra were to be seen. His eyes had been gouged out, whilst beneath his powerful frame lay the remains of Elston. For a moment only they were visible, then slowly they disappeared beneath the sea of mud which oozed over them like the restless tide of an everlasting night.

T. H. WHITE

The Point of Thirty Miles

'Gentlemen,' said Frosty, coughing discreetly, 'and ladies, I ought to have said. It is a hunt with the Scurry and Burstall that I am going to describe to you. The strangest hunt and the longest point that ever I was in. Mr Puffington hunted them in those days, a connection of his late lordship's, in a remote way. His lordship's grandfather married a Jawleyford, and his Great-aunt Amelia Jawleyford married a Puffington; so there was hunting in the family. The original Puffington used to hunt the Mangysterne country in the 'fifties; not a very keen master, by all accounts, but an amazing popular man.

'The old Miss Amelia was never really a fox-hunting woman, and nor was old Puffington a born master. Between them they migrated to London and had a large family in the safety of Belgrave Square. The eldest son went into the city and financed sock-suspenders. It was a paying thing, and the Puffington I am speaking of, the grandson, found himself with a convenient house in the Scurry country and a town house in Pont Street. He took after his grandfather and accepted the mastership of the Burstall. My own father sent me to him, as a second whip, when I was a young lad.

'Those were the days for foxes, as my lady and you gentlemen know, before the modern world was pupped: fat subscriptions, stout foxes, fences kept, and nothing to do but ride all day. It was before the niminy-piminy generation of motor cars to and from the meet, before the day of horse-boxes and bath-salts and changed-for-tea at four o'clock.

'It was my last hunt with the Burstall: because my father was ready to take me back after my apprenticeship, to whip in for the F.H.H., and because nobody would believe the account which I gave when I got home after it. They seemed to think that I had been drinking – as, indeed, I had. I was forced to lie out that night, at a public-house, and after what I'd been through, drinking seemed to be the reasonable solution. But I suppose I ought to begin at the beginning. Mr Puffington was a generous master, mounting his hunt servants in the very best style, and I had a couple of horses for the meet at Wingfield Abbey, in their Saturday country. It was a grand scenting day, a little rain overnight and a cold air to fetch the smell out of the ground in the morning. The going was good; not slippery, for the year had been a mild one; and not holding, for it was early in the season and the summer had been fine. We had a nice dart to begin with; not much of a point, only a mile and a half, in fact, but a good four as hounds ran, and we did it in twenty-five minutes. Just at the end of this I came down at a post and rails. The horse was not really what I should have called a goer, and I fear that Mr Puffington had been done over him. The rails were in a deep bottom, with a good-sized ditch on the landing side. I saw this ditch as I was coming up to it, and put on steam as much as I could. The result was that we hit the top rail, for the horse was blown and never rose as much as he should have done. I have no recollection of what happened on the landing side. Somehow I tore Mr Puffington's flask off my saddle, which he used to like me to carry for him, and had to pick it up whilst the others were waiting to come on. I also split my right hand on something, I thought a hoof, and the horse was going awkwardly in the next field. The kennel huntsman held that he had struck himself behind. Fortunately that fox was rolled over within a hundred yards of his point, in another minute, and this gave me time to shake my head and find out where I was. It must have been about twelve o'clock. There was a bit of a palaver, with people casting up and fussing about, and amongst them came my second horse. I hadn't been intended to change over till late, but after I'd told the groom about my rails and moved the horse about in front of him, we decided to make the change at once. I had scarcely got my leg across the second mount, which was a cob-like chestnut up to Mr Puffington's weight, when they were into a second fox out of Yardley's spinneys. They took him quickly back into the spinneys; and out again, having been brought to their noses, on the far side of a rugged fence with an oxer on the one side and wire on the other. We could see across it perfectly, but it would have been lunacy to jump. The hounds came out of the spinney slowly and well together. They were half into the field, almost under the metaphorical shadow of the wire, when a grey creature that looked like a cross between the Benicia Boy and a bear jumped up amongst them. Personally, the first thing I thought of was a sheep-dog. There was nothing to be done at all. The Master, who was hunting them because the huntsman had asthma, was on the hither side of the wire with the field, and we whips had cleared off round the spinney. The grey creature just went straight away for a windmill on the skyline, and the hounds went after him, within a few yards, as soon as they had recovered from their surprise. The cry was amazing. The field all turned up the fence and went bucketing along for the nearest gate, which proved to be at the farthest corner of a big enclosure. After that there was no hope of stopping hounds.

'Gentlemen, I must not bore you with the details of the run; and in any case I couldn't, because I have forgotten the country. The important things about it were that our quarry ran practically straight and that I was the only person on a fresh horse. I don't suppose that you have ever hunted a wolf. He went away at a tremendous loping pace, a kind of wolf-burst which brought the hounds back to scent within a couple of fields. Then he must have settled to a steadier gait, and he ran like a human being pursued – straight away from his pursuers.

'Like a human being,' repeated Frosty meditatively, and the Professor handed him a cigar.

The Countess said: 'I thought the last British wolf was killed in the eighteenth century, or something.'

'Quite possibly, my lady,' replied the huntsman.

'But, my dear fellow,' said Mr Romford plaintively, 'either yours was a wolf or it wasn't, and I understand you killed it. You really must make up your mind. It makes a great difference, you know.'

'It was difficult,' said Frosty-face, 'to make up one's mind at all. Our quarry took us ten miles towards the North Sea, running parallel with the Thames, before half-past one. I can't pretend that it was a cracking hunt, not after the first half-hour. The hounds simply ran away from us. When we had properly settled down to it, and after I'd had time to think and realize that the sun was behind my back, I took to the roads with the Master and a few others. After a couple of hours, we merely took the nearest road that seemed to lead eastwards and more or less within reported sights of hounds. We went on at these at a goodish pace, but naturally a boring one. There were only five or six in it, and after two hours and a half there was only one objective: to retrieve hounds somehow or other before dark. Every now and then, but very rarely, we had a bit of country and soft going to make up for the eternal trot and canter along the roads. At four o'clock there was only the Master and myself. He was in a temper and couldn't bring his mount to canter. I offered him mine, but he had worked himself into such a fury about the hounds running riot that he wouldn't listen to anything likely to bring him into salutary touch with them. At the same time I had a faint suspicion that he had by now reached the stage when he preferred his home to his hounds. He simply told me to get along as well as I could, and send him a wire from Dover if I caught them. Well, by now I was excited. Anything like a record is apt to excite a young man. So, although it was not enjoyable, and although my horse was beginning to fade, I set out on my travels with a rising heart. To be the only one up with the hounds on a historic run, perhaps on the most historic run of all! And then there was the nature of the quarry: the last wolf in England. I wondered where on earth it had come from, and wished that it might not prove to be a menagerie creature or a pet. It seemed not to be in the best condition, or else, I suppose, it would have beaten us with ease, but he took us thirty miles. Then, just as it was beginning to get dark, the tide turned in our favour. Scent became burning before it faded, the wolf began to pack up, the tired hounds were drawing up to him, and I established contact with the pack for the first time that afternoon. He was still a good way in front of us, gentlemen, but he was beginning to be a tangible identity. I even winded him myself: a whiff of sour bread and stale bananas. I suppose I ought to have stopped the pack; but he seemed just possible, and I was young. The glory of achievement went to my head.'

The huntsman paused to light his cigar with a trembling hand.

'The thing comes back to me very vividly. The love and gratitude which I felt for my broad and striding chestnut; the thrill and fear of the fading quarry and the fading day; the sensation that anything might give at any moment, the horse, the hounds, the wolf or the daylight; the indescribable agony of possibility. Well, everything went; almost within five minutes. First the scent gave out, just as I viewed the wolf. I went mad and lifted the hounds to view, as if I had been doing that sort of thing all my life. And they were as mad as I was, for they rallied to me as if I had always been the Master, and followed where I madly capped them on and shouted. We came to view as the light failed, and the hounds raised a husky cheer just at the moment when my horse gave in. He stood still at a stile which I was trying to put him at, trembled and dropped his head. I left him where he stood, and ran after the hounds like a frantic man, with my spurs biting into my ankles. Then it seemed to get dark almost at a blow, and there was a village with lights in the windows, and a man with a lantern swinging by a barn, and a furious uproar from the hounds, varied by a melancholy cry. I found them by the barn wall, scrumming up against it like a wall game at Eton College, and two hounds seemed to be dead, and a grey leg was cocked upwards above the heaving backs, which drew it to and fro in a terrific worry. The deep-chested savagery of their note was splendid in the lantern-light, terrible, cruel I daresay, but true in kind. They chopped him with an exultant brutality, dragging his entrails, tugging with heads together and heaving shoulders and bloody mouths. But the awful thing, gentlemen, the thing which lost me my place with the Burstall when I reported it, was that the wolf was trying to articulate. Against the background of their full-blooded ferocity there was a thin and guttural note, a human supplication, an enunciation on the borders of the English tongue. The werewolf's leg, gentlemen, that was cocked above the scrummage, turned pink, grew hairless, convulsed itself like a kicking frog's: and Challenger was trotting round the outside of the circus, with a hand of human fingers in his mouth.'

The Professor said, in a hushed voice: 'Well, Frosty, you take the biscuit.'

The huntsman touched his forehead with a pleased smile.

'It isn't,' continued the Professor, 'that I don't know how to loose the arrow a little on the far side myself. I could have told you quite a good story about the Hunt Cup at Cheltenham, in which Mr Siegfried Sassoon ran a horse called Pegasus, that was disqualified because it was found to have wings. But, after a werewolf, what's the use?'

LESLIE HALWARD

Old Sweat

He was over six feet in height, grey-haired, thin as a lath, square-shouldered, with dangling long arms like an ape's. His eyes were bloodshot and his temples sunk in. He kept leaning forward over the table and fixing somebody, anybody, everybody in turn, with the most terrifying expression, as if he hated everybody and would like to kill them all one at a time.

But they all knew he was harmless and took no notice of his expression, only kept laughing and joking among themselves and urging him to sing. Every now and then he laughed, too, about half a minute after somebody had said something he thought funny. Every time somebody said, 'Go on, George, give us one o' the od 'uns,' he said, '*I* can't sing.' Somebody said, 'We know you can't bloody well sing, but you can kick up a row,' and they all laughed at that for a long time.

At last he got to his feet and stood swaying, his long ape's arms dangling, sticking his head forward and looking at first one and then another with that terrifying expression as if he would like to kill them all, and then grinning sheepishly and hanging his head as if affected with modesty, and saying like a shy girl: '*I* can't sing.' They kept saying: 'Go on, George, give us one,' and all at once he began to sing in a thick, drunken voice, running all the words into one and all the notes into each other, so that nobody could tell what the song was about. In the middle of it he stopped and wiped his eyes with the back of his hand and said: '*I* can't sing,' and picked up his pint glass and took three or four great gulps out of it and put it down on the table empty.

But they wouldn't let him sit down, and he stood there swaying and grinning and saying he couldn't sing, and looking at everybody as if he would like to kill them all, and then somebody said: 'How about the wenches in the trenches?' He looked at the speaker for ten seconds, and then laughed and shook his head, and said: 'Ah! The wenches in the trenches! We *had* some!' Somebody said: '*We* musta been in the wrong bloody trenches!' and he laughed and shook his head again and said: 'We *had* some!'

Then somebody who had heard him sing the song before and knew some of it, started to sing it to egg him on, and after a bit he started to sing himself in a quavering voice like a very old man's:

> Oh, the wenches
> In the trenches . . .

and then he stopped and said: 'We *had* some!' and laughed and shook his head again. Somebody said: 'Go on, let's hear the rest on it,' and he said, '*I* can't sing,' and then suddenly started again and sang,

> They stole our wenches
> From us
> In the trenches . . .

and then stopped and wiped his eyes and his face as if somebody had thrown some water over him. And while they were shouting at him to go on, he held his hands in front of him as if he were holding a rifle, and started doing movements as if he were stabbing somebody with a bayonet. He stood in front of one of them, doing these movements, his eyes blood-shot and his head stuck forward and that terrifying expression on his face as if he hated the man who was sitting in front of him, and would like to kill him. He started cursing and raving and shouting orders and saying they were *coming*, and he pranced up and down and sweated and dribbled, and pretended to thrust his bayonet, and said: 'Hold that, you—!' All the other men sat and looked at him with the grins stuck on their faces as if the flesh had frozen. The landlord said, 'Here, see if you can quiet him, Charlie,' and Charlie got up and went to George and said something in his ear, and George pushed him away and shouted they were *coming*, and went on prancing about and pretending to stab the man who sat in front of him. He kept saying; 'Hold that, you—!' Sweat was pouring down his face and dripping off the end of his chin, his mouth was twisted and his eyes were glaring. The man he was pretending to stab was as white as a sheet, and he gripped the edge of the table and didn't take his eyes off George's face. The landlord said, 'Here, we can't have this,' and one of the younger men croaked, 'He's gone bleedin' barmy,' and Charlie said, 'I should think that's about enough,' and he went up to George and hit him on the jaw and knocked him flat on his back. Charlie and another man picked him up and the landlord said: 'You'd better get him home, I should think.' And between them they half-dragged, half-carried him out of the place. And after a bit one of the men said, 'I never seen him go off like that before.' Another said, 'We was only having a bit of fun with him.' And an old gentleman seated at one of the tables blew his nose loudly, and said: 'It's a great pity some fellows haven't the sense to know when they've taken enough.'

JULIAN MACLAREN-ROSS

Death of a Comrade

One of the boys in our battalion died the other day. He got drowned.

Nothing dramatic: he went bathing in the river one Sunday and never came back. Two of his mates were with him, fellows from the signal section; they told me about it in the evening.

'Heard about old Lennox?'

'Lennox,' I said; 'Who's Lennox?'

'You know, Lennox. In our lot. Fair-haired kiddy from Cambridge. He got drowned today.'

'Drowned?'

'They ain't found the body yet.'

'Good lord. How'd it happen?'

They told me. They didn't even notice he was gone, at first; he must have sunk quite suddenly, like a stone. Weeds, the current, cramp; might have been any of them. Down he went, not a trace. Gone.

'Fair shook me, it did,' one of the signallers said, and: 'You hear about this bloke that got drowned?' the orderly sergeant asked me back in the office. 'One of the signals. Went out bathing, drowned himself in the river. Current got him, I reckon. He didn't ought to've done no bathing in there: it's too bleeding deep.'

'Well,' I said, 'it's too late to stop him now.'

'Too bleeding true it is,' the orderly sergeant said.

'Lennox,' I said. 'What was he like?'

'Blowed if I remember.'

'Neither do I.'

And it worried me, not being able to remember. Working in the army

Office I must have seen him scores of times on telephone duty; the signallers had charge of the 'phone.

Lennox, Lennox – I knew the name from typing out nominal rolls, but I couldn't fit it to any face. There were several 'fair-haired kiddies' in the Signal Section, and any of them might have come from Cambridge. Was Lennox the blond, rather tough-looking boy whom I'd last seen at the baths, sitting on a bucket talking about his tart; or was he the other short, cissy-looking one with curly hair, who'd been a barber in civvy street?

Next day the body still hadn't turned up, but a telegram was sent off to Lennox's father, and then, as Company Clerk, I had to compose a letter of condolence, which the Company Commander signed. That night it appeared in orders: 'The Commanding Officer regrets to announce the death . . .' and underneath: 'A Court of Enquiry will assemble as under to determine the cause of death of 6526854 . . .'

The notice announcing the death had a black border typed in around it. I could imagine the orderly room clerk cursing when he had to take out the stencil and re-insert it twice to get the black line level on either side. With wax costing sixpence a sheet you had to be careful not to make a muck of it; it's quite an undertaking. A death gives a lot of trouble, one way and another, in a battalion. Luckily we don't have many; only three in the last year or so. The sergeant who set fire to his tent, the batman who shot himself cleaning a revolver, the bloke who broke his neck on P.T.

The colour sergeant came in with a sack. 'More work,' he said. 'Lennox's personal kit. Give us a hand to sort it out, will you?' – a suit of service dress, civvy shoes, a pack of cards, an old cigarette case with a broken clasp, two photos of naked girls torn from a six-penny magazine, a bundle of letters, a book: *What a Young Husband Ought to Know.*

'Was he getting hitched?'

'Not that I know of.'

'Here's a letter, from his girl'. S.W.A.L.K. on the back of the envelope: *'Dear Dick, why have you not wrote lately. I haven't heard nothing of you for a fortnight now.'*

'Not much good sending 'em that,' the colour sergeant said. He threw it in the salvage bag, the pack of cards and the naked girls followed; they were retrieved later by one of the runners.

'What about, this?'

A pencilled scrawl dated Sunday. He must have been writing it on the river bank just before he dived in.

'*Dear Mum, thank you for the parcel and the P.O. I haven't any news, but I owe you a letter, so I am writing this* . . .'

'What d'you think? Send it?'

'No. Only brings things home more, I reckon.'

'Yeh. No sense in that.' And at last the stuff was sorted out in two piles on the floor, ready to send off.

Did his life flash before him as they say it does when you're drowning, and was this it: the greasy cards, 'Dear Mum', the girl's bare breasts, S.W. A.L.K., *What a Young Husband Ought to know*? ('*I'll* take care of that,' the sergeant-major said, walking out with the book tucked under his arm.)

'What sort of a fellow was Lennox?' I asked the signal sergeant, who'd just come in.

'Lennox? Smart kid. Knew his stuff backwards. But you seen him, surely? On the phone?'

'No,' I said. 'I don't remember.'

It seemed wrong somehow, not to remember a man who'd died like that. Supposing I died myself, would someone say: 'You know him, big tall bloke, used a fag-holder, half-crown voice,' and would the answer be: 'I don't remember'? It seemed to me quite likely.

Service dress and civvy shoes, a bundle of letters, an annoyance to the orderly room clerk, more work for the colour-sergeant; a man dying ought to leave behind him more than that. And so when Lennox's father arrived the next day I tried hard to find in the small, grey-haired man in the dark suit who stood waiting awkwardly downstairs, a raincoat over his arm, some resemblance to a face I must have seen quite often: in the Naffy, or the cookhouse, or in the office, answering a call from the Adjutant. But there was none: he didn't look like anyone I knew.

'Can I see your Commanding Officer?' he said. 'My name's Lennox.'

'If you'll come this way, please,' I said.

He followed me down the long cold stone corridor of the hotel we were billeted in.

'I was very sorry to hear of your loss, Mr Lennox,' I said to him. 'We were all very sorry. We all liked him a lot.'

'Oh, yes,' he said; 'Yes,' absently, and then: 'You knew him?' with sudden interest; 'My son?'

'Of course I knew him,' I said. 'He was a great pal of mine. We used to go about together.'

'He got on all right? With the others?'

'He got on well with everyone.'

'Good,' he said, 'Good. I'm glad. He wasn't a bad lad.'

And I said: 'One of the best.'

The C.O. was in his office, standing with his back to the empty fireplace; the other officers sat round the long table with a crimson cloth on it; the Court of Enquiry had just been concluded.

'Come in.'

'Mr Lennox, sir,' I said, and stood back closing the door as the C.O. came forward with outstretched hand and the correct look of commiseration in his face.

In the Company Office, the signaller on phone duty said: 'That his father?'

'Yes,' I said.

'Poor blighter. They still ain't found the body, y'know.'

And they didn't find it till five days later; it'd floated nearly twenty miles: amazing. The current of that river must have been certainly strong; it's out of bounds to all ranks now.

Then they had the funeral, with all the signallers attending, and the signal corporal and the signal sergeant, and another sergeant to play the Last Post as they lowered the coffin into the grave.

And today I wrote off the last of him, typing a letter and posting a parcel to the Officer i/c Records:

Late 6526854 Pte. Lennox, R., Personal Effects of, forwarded on receipt from Civil Police:
  One black leather diary dated 1941.
  One piece of broken mirror.
  One comb.
  One bronze medallion.
  One key.
  5s. 1d. in cash.

ALUN LEWIS

Private Jones

Dafis the post came down the lane to Siencyn's cottage earlier to-day than usual. He walked his bicycle through the stony muddy ruts, ringing his bell to call them out. Siencyn was still in bed, but Marged, his wife, had been up a couple of hours, feeding the wild chickens that nested in the apple trees and gorse bushes and mixing some swill for Granny the sow.

'It's come, Marged fach, it's come,' Dafis shouted, his excitement at a gleeful pitch. 'Siencyn's notice is come.'

He brandished a small brown envelope.

Marged straightened her heavy body, wiped her wet hands in her sack apron, showed nothing.

'Diw mawr,' she said to herself, thinking that something important was happening inside her.

'Siencyn!' Dafis called, leaning his bicycle with its tied-on parcels against the crumbled wall of the cottage. 'Your calling-up notice I got for you. Look alive, boy.'

Siencyn poked his long head out of the tiny bedroom window, his hair the colour of swedes. He was in his flannel nightshirt.

'Coming now, Dafis,' he said cheerily and withdrew. He pulled his trousers and clogs on, and came downstairs buckling his leather belt across a handful of trousers, very excited.

Dafis opened the letter, Marged looking over his shoulder. She was twice his size.

'Printed matter,' Dafis said. 'There for you. Instructions, look. Railway travel voucher. Free trip, see?'

'In the train?' Siencyn asked.

'Third class,' Dafis said. 'From Cardigan station, Great Western

Railway, to Talcen station, ditto. East Wales Fusiliers it is for you, Siencyn bach, poor dab. Plenty of V.C.'s they got already. Watch out, you.'

'East Wales Fusiliers, is it?' Siencyn repeated. 'Well, well. Third class?'

'When is it?' Marged asked.

'Friday next, 21st inst.,' Dafis said. 'Take your identity card, Siencyn bach, don't forget that, now. Or it's C.B. you'll be right from the word go.'

'Jawch,' said Siencyn, 'there's a lot to remember, Dafis. Where's my identity card, Marged? In the poe in the spare room, is it?'

'And your birth certificate is there,' she said, knowing where to put her hands on things. 'You'll have to find somewhere else to keep your things from now on, Siencyn bach.'

'Aye, that's true,' he said, rubbing his tangled hair. 'Well, I better go round and tell everybody.'

'Don't trouble,' Dafis said. 'I'll tell them on my round. Stay you, my boy. I'll come down to-night and give you a bit of wisdom, see? Four years of it in the last war I had, and no more for me thank you.' He looked at his right hand, from which three fingers were missing. 'German sniper did that,' he said proudly, and then screwed up his red bunioned face into a wink. 'Held it up above the parapet, see, Siencyn, and got a nice little blighty. But there, you don't know what a parapet is yet, I don't doubt.'

'I'll learn,' Siencyn said, with all the good will in the world.

'You will,' Dafis said, speaking with the sardonic finality of experience. 'Solong both.'

'Solong, Dafis, thank you,' Siencyn said.

Dafis pushed his bicycle off, the cycle clips pulling his small trousers up nearly to his knees. He wore a straw boater all the year round, Dafis did.

The third winter of the war was just relaxing its grip on this closed corner of Cardiganshire; six weeks of frost had held up the winter plough-ing and the spring sowing, and Siencyn had been having a soft time of it, lying in bed in the mornings, chopping a bit of firewood, mending a few broken scythes and shafts, patching up the cowsheds of his employer, cutting enough hay for the drayhorses, and a pint or two some nights. He had been medically examined and registered a whole year back, but his call-up was deferred for the summer harvest and the autumn trapping, – Siencyn was the offical trapper of the parish and sent four hundred and thirty-seven rabbits to Cardigan station, Great Western, in five weeks, – and then the winter ploughing. He had got tired of waiting, restless and unable to merge himself in his work and the weather and the requirements of the horses and of Marged. He was a good-natured man, but out of patience with things. He had quarrelled with Marged a lot this winter, beating her once, leaping out of bed on a Sunday morning when the cracked church bell was tolling, and beating her for calling him an idle heathen. And she used her tongue on him for that. Said that people were saying things about them. What things? She shrugged her shoulders. Once he'd cleared out of the way, they were saying, perhaps they'd discover before a year was out whose fault it was there were no babies coming in their house. Well, that wasn't a nice thing to say, and it says a lot for Siencyn's good nature that he only shrugged his shoulders and said pity they hadn't got more important things to think about than that. She didn't use the rough edge of her tongue on him again, but she was very secretive and moody all the winter. He didn't worry about her; he'd go and she'd stay behind; she was his wife; there you are; nobody is indispensable; she wouldn't want to leave the place she'd been born in, whether he went or not. It was different with him. He wanted to see the world. Lots of the boys from round about went into the merchant navy; either the sea or the land it was with all the boys. And he held it a grudge that his widowed mother had kept him home to work at odd jobs instead of letting him go to sea. His father must have been an old soft, too; he wasn't wounded and he wasn't ill in the last war. He just died. Ran home three times from the army, and then died in detention barracks. Heart-broken, his mother said. Well, what a complaint for a man!

Nobody had a bad word for Siencyn, except that he was idle and fond of his drink and irregular as a christian and not reliable for doing a job or fetching you something from market or being prompt at the chapel concert rehearsals. So, when he went round to say solong, everybody was sorry to see him go and genuinely hoped the army would make a man of him before it got him killed. Old Mari Siop, who had a soft spot for anybody in trousers, said she thought strong men like him ought to stay at home in case the Irish attacked us. And he had a real good walk-round, ending up at the Ship hotel, saying good-bye and drinking basin after basin of tea in the cottages and then a pint all round on the house. This was on his last night, and you wouldn't believe the offers he had to knit comforts for him, and old drovers and flannel vests fetched out of the cupboards where they had lain since their wearers had died. He took them all, and all that he didn't drop on the way down from the pub he carried into the kitchen where Marged was sitting doing nothing by the wood fire. She was cross with him for taking them; they'd be saying how she couldn't look after her husband's pants even. She was always seeing the worst side of everything these days. She was almost fit to cry with desperation over a little thing like that.

So they had a bit of bread and milk for supper, not saying anything at all. Then he fetched the money from under the bed upstairs and counted it out, five pounds thirteen and four, and divided it into two piles, three pounds thirteen for her and two pounds for himself. And then he got up and very clumsily and hesitantly smoothed her hair back. She was vexed, and said what a mess she was, all untidy and fat-getting, and she bent her head forward as if she was feeling bad; and she was all white and her eyes were yellow and suffused with watery blood. He was shifting from one foot to the other, uneasy about what to do, and she wouldn't say a thing one way or the other. Dumb she was.

And he was thinking how happy everything and everybody had been when he went round the farms this afternoon, and now Marged spoiling it all. But when she looked up at him, raised her head to him slowly as if there was a millstone round her neck, and then stood up with her arms raised a little, and said that Welsh word to him that she hadn't said since they were courting, then he knew it was a million times better to feel black and torn in pieces like this than to be laughing and drinking tea and saying the Germans wouldn't last long now he was in too. He picked her up, and she wasn't heavy any more; and carried her up the creaking stairs as if she was a young virgin. Only she was better than a virgin, her fine big body which his big shivering hands slowly divested of the red jersey and thick skirt and woollen stocking and flannel vests that she wore on it winter and summer. The moon was out and the river ringing on the stones and the old jollyboy owls crying goodywhoo in the wood, and he knew he'd been waiting for this for a whole year, to say good-bye to Marged like this. And she lay warm and silken and trembling under his huge hands and she heard neither the river nor the owls but only him grunting and breathing in her mouth and in her ears and something gentle at last opening inside her, like a baby begging her to receive it in.

Onions she boiled for his breakfast the next morning, and two hard-boiled eggs and a whole small loaf uncut for his pocket, and off he set, six miles to walk to Cardigan station. Dafis the postman had forgotten to bring him some stamped addressed envelopes, but he had found a letter in the grandfather clock with their address on it. He didn't know how to write the address himself, but somebody would copy it off this old letter for him when he got there, no doubt. So everything was alright. Plenty of wood left for the fire and Marged walking to the crossroads with him, and the weather crisp and young, the cockerels crowing all the way in to Cardigan station, and Dai Pencwm passing him on the road giving him the benediction of the big pew. His heart was like a feather, walking like this through his own countryside, seeing the sea through gates in the sandy hedges, and singing Dr Parry's *Jerusalem* to himself which was this year's test piece at the Eisteddfod, and feeling a free man, as if he owned the place and no need to pick up a shovel nor a scythe nor the handles of the plough . . .

There were other men like him on the train the last part of the journey, from Swansea. But they were different to him, smoking cigarettes and wearing posh navy suits and pointy shoes, with white silk scarves and grease in their hair. He sat a long way from them and he felt hot and uneasy. But when they got there it was all in together and fags out and form up in threes with a soldier showing you how with a silver-knobbed cane, and march through the streets into the barracks. Then he lost direction and control, there were so many things and people. He knew how to sign his name, S. Jones, where they told him, but they wouldn't give him enough time to do it in, and he had to keep on signing in every room they went into, whereas he had never signed his name more than twice a week before, on the dole that was. But he was doing pretty well out of it; same as last night everybody was giving him things – mug, knife, fork, spoon, blankets, bag for straw, khaki suit, leggings, boots, cap, and lots of straps that he didn't know what for. And then a rifle and a bayonet. You didn't take long to become a soldier, for a fact. Then they had a good meal in the cookhouse, with girls in khaki doing for them, and then the most of them went out for a booze, and cursing everything they were when there were no corporals about. But Siencyn didn't open his mouth, and he was frightened a bit because he'd lost count of what was happening, and he wanted to lie down and sleep, being suddenly very weak and shaky and yawning all the time. As for Marged and all them at home, they didn't exist any more. It was all up with them, there was no doubt.

'You're looking buggered, Jack,' a dark man said, sitting on the floor cleaning his rifle in the empty barrack room.

Siencyn, like a frightened animal, watched him suspiciously.

'Yes,' he said. 'Yes.'

'It isn't worth worrying about this lot here,' the man said. 'They don't count in this war. They're all peace-time soldiers. They don't know what the war's about, they only want to stay here and shout on the square and take the tarts out. You keep your head up. Don't pay any attention to them.'

'Yes,' said Siencyn not understanding much except that the man was friendly, 'that is so far a fact.'

The man began cleaning his buttons with a button stick and silvo. 'I'll learn you how to do things,' he said. 'They don't mean anything, all the things they do here, but you might as well do them properly, just to show them there's nothing in it, and then get on out somewhere where there *is* a war.'

'You been a soldier before, is it?' Siencyn asked, friendly with him now, like a dog that barks first, then growls, then wags its tail and sidles up.

'Not in this army, mate. I fought two years in Spain, though. Seen a bit of it then, like.'

'For a living, is it?' Siencyn asked, shifting up, willing to listen.

'No, not for a living,' the man laughed. 'A collier I am for a living, when the pits are open. Collier, stay-in striker, party member, anything's better than keeping a greyhound, chum.'

'Spanish they speak in Spain?' Siencyn asked.

'No, not much now. German and Italian they speak there now. But it doesn't matter much there now.'

'*This* war will do for me alright,' Siencyn said. 'Farm labourer I am, see, and trapper.'

'That's right. You keep to the plough, mate. It's only a knife in your back or a few years in jail or no work and no friends you'll get if you start

93

doing what you believe in. I've never had time to marry a wife, and yet I've never done nothing I can show.'

'I'm married,' Siencyn said. 'It isn't very much of a thing; only down our way you got to get married if you want any peace, see.' The man smiled, and Siencyn smiled back, and then sat thinking of the thing he'd just said.

'No girl in the valleys would take me on,' the man said. 'They want a steady man, see. I'm an anarchist. I won't go and live in two rooms and feed my kids on bread and dripping and make them sell the *Football Echo* and read the race results in the paper and shout hooray in the park on Labour Day.'

Well, well, thought Siencyn, this is a different life to mine, and what it all is I don't know. But I wouldn't like to be on the wrong side of this man, because he is like the prophet Ezekiel, and he can kill people by seizing their wickedness in his hands and squeezing it till they choke.

And Siencyn became devoted to this man, and he wasn't afraid of all the things that happened to him in the next few weeks.

Well, Siencyn became 283749551 Private Jones, S., before you could look round, and the nickname he went by was Timoshenko, which was something like Shenkin, his own name. And the first morning he wore his battledress he had to take it all off and lift his shirt and cough and bare his arm and have a needle in it, all in a whirl, walking round the room with all the others because there was no time to sit down and no furniture, not like waiting for the doctor at home. And then they all walked past a man in a white apron standing on a stool and they had to open their mouths for him and when he looked in Siencyn's mouth, he said 'Christ! Take the lot out. Top and bottom plate for this man. Ever used a toothbrush?' Siencyn said yes, because he'd used one in the infants' school, but he wasn't a kid any more so of course he hadn't used one since. He was a married man now. Jawch!

He was very bad after that, with a big swelling under his arm, and he crawled into his bunk like a sick animal and lay there till he was better, which was a day later. And then he had all his top teeth out, and his new boots were hurting something wicked, and he didn't have a handkerchief to wipe his bleeding mouth which was dripping into the tin of potatoes he was scraping, and the sergeant called him a dirty something and the next morning he was marched into a room and the officer looked fierce at him and said '283749551 Jones, S. Is that your name?' And he was told by the officer to get a shake on and wake his ideas up and not to come back to him again or look out. And Siencyn said he didn't want to come back to him again, not likely, and then he saluted the way he'd seen them do it, and he'd have smiled just to show there was no ill feeling, only his mouth was full of blood. And when he got back to his bunk and they asked him how he got on, he grinned – because he'd spat the blood out on the way back – and said 'The bastard!' And that made everyone laugh and slap his back and say he was a bloody good soldier already, calling the O.C. a bastard like that. And he always called everybody a bastard after that if they said anything rough to him, which was nearly always, and he felt better straight away then.

After he'd been there a fortnight and getting on famous with the boys and not too bad with the sergeants, and knowing how to slope and present, and halt and start up again, and fix bayonets and standing load, and unload, and two weeks wages, ten shillings a time, a telegram came for him, and that made him hot and excited and the centre of every eye, as you might say. But it was only Marged wanting to know if he was alright, because on account of forgetting to bring Dafis's stamped addressed envelopes he hadn't written home, not liking to ask any of the boys to copy the old address out for him; and no news is good news, isn't it? But the O.C. sent for him again and asked him if he had quarrelled with his wife or what, and told him it was bad for civilian morale not to write regularly and tell them you was getting on fine. So he confided to Daniel Evans from Spain and Dan wrote a letter for him in two shakes and addressed it and they posted it together on the way to the Naffy, and Dan said why hadn't he asked him before, it was nothing to him and he'd write Siencyn's letters regular for him. If he wasn't such a good man and a good scholar and knew everything about fighting and mining and unemployed and capitalists, Siencyn would have grabbed him by the waist and wrestled with him the same as they used to do in the country when they was boys in school and big friends.

And at the end of three weeks the whole issue of them was sent off by train to the east coast of England to finish their training in a battalion that was short of men and wanted them handy in case of invasion. And in this new place it was the same as before only worse if anything. They had a new sergeant-major who shouted like a bull and you could smell his breath when he shouted. He came up close and shouted in your face, so you could only *think* he was a bastard, he was too near for you to mutter it. But their sergeant didn't like the sergeant-major and told the boys that he was separated from his wife for stripping her and thinking out dirty things to do to her, and he was only shouting like that because he wanted to keep in with the colonel. So Siencyn didn't bother about the sergeant-major shouting, now he knew there was no religion in him. But some of the boys that you'd have thought wouldn't care a bit – boys always boasting about what they'd done, big breaks in billiards, supper in married women's houses and that – they became like shivering wet rats after a bit and the sergeant-major used to pick on them all the time and shout at them till they shivered all over, only with Siencyn and Spain he never bothered at all. And as for the sergeant, well, he couldn't keep a straight face on parade with Siencyn. And when Siencyn caught a rabbit one day out on an exercise by putting his hand in a hole where he knew a rabbit was, and gave it to the sergeant to give to the grass widow he was always telling them about, the sergeant was always kind to him after that. Siencyn couldn't remember all the names on the Bren gun and the mortar and the 36-grenade and the anti-tank rifle and war gases and all that. So the sergeant never asked him the names when they were being tested.

The only fly in the ointment was the officer in charge of them. Not the young one, he was alright, nobody bothered about him; but the one with the three pips that walked around all day looking at everybody; and when he stopped in front of you on parade he grunted and muttered to himself and then told you what a bloody army you were to be sure. Siencyn didn't like the smell of him, and he didn't feel strong in front of him the same as with the other sergeants and officers.

Everybody was frightened of him, yet they all said he didn't know his job and ought to be sacked. And there were lots of stories about what he did in the nights with his spare time, but still Siencyn couldn't stand up to him. Not even when he found out that the colonel could make the captain shiver like a rat the way the captain did to those under him. And one day, when their training was over and they were taking part in brigade schemes and defending aerodromes and building dannert fences and laughing at the Home Guard like hardened regulars, the captain sent for Siencyn and said 'I hear you're a country bumpkin, Jones.' And Siencyn said 'I live in Penyrheol, Cards, sir.' And the Captain said, 'I hear you were a poacher, Jones?' And Siencyn said 'Trapper, sir.' And the Captain said, 'I'm putting you to work in the Officers' Mess, to catch rabbits and partridges for dinner, and you will be my batman; and if there's any silvo on my uniform or you get caught with a dead partridge trespassing, I'll break your bloody spine, do you understand?' And Siencyn wasn't brave enough to say no, so he said 'Yes, sir.'

So he became a batman for a change, and it was as bad as he feared, because when he woke the captain in the mornings it was like shaking a nest of adders; he always had a liver and a white tongue and never pleased with anything. But sometimes Siencyn got away on his own, three times a week, after rabbits and pheasants, and then he was as happy as could be. When the captain was shouting for him to clean his Sam Browne or fetch some hot water because the hot water had gone lukewarm on account of him not getting up when he was called, Siencyn felt as bitter and cynical as Dan Evans Spain, who was always sneering at the talk in the papers about fighting for freedom and decency and our children's futures. But when he was lying in the ferns watching the way the pheasants went for grubs, or setting a snare in a rabbit's run, then Siencyn really felt as if he were fighting for freedom and the right of a man to live his own life. Anyway, it was no good looking at things the way Dan Evans did. No doubt it was true all he said about the coal owners taking all the profits and the children without a decent pair of boots or a warm coat, and about the men in London exploiting the natives in Africa and India, and about the *Daily Worker* being banned like in a Nazi country; and when he put it to you you did find it queer to wonder why the poor women and babies suffered themselves to be bombed in the slums in Swansea and London when they wasn't getting anything out of it that you could see. Siencyn didn't have anything against the Russians, but all the same he didn't think it much sense wishing you could be one; and it was easy to see that nothing was the way it ought to be these days if you went by what it says in the Bible. But Dan was only making it hard for himself, refusing a stripe and barely civil to the captain and the sergeant-major and both of them with their knives in him, and it was a pity he was always getting daunted by what he read in the papers, or by what he said about the army being unprepared and untrained and unarmed to fight a war with tanks and divebombers like they'll have to. But all the same, if it came to a fight, Siencyn wouldn't think twice whose side he was on. Dan's side he was on. Dan Spain was a man and he'd like anyone to deny it.

Every now and again he got a letter from Penyrheol, written in Dafis the postman's copperplate hand, with bits dictated by Marged in it and grandiloquent flourishes of Dafis's invention embossed on it, giving him the news as it left them at present and hoping he was in the pink. The first two or three letters had nothing abnormal, except that the sow had been up to the boar and was expecting, and the latch had fallen off the back door and she had tied it with string till he came home, and her marriage book had come and she had to walk to the post office every week to draw her twenty-eight shillings, and she was putting some of it by to buy blackout curtains so she could have a light in the house after dark for a change. Then came a different letter, very brief, and not written in Dafis's hand at all, but in pencil by Marged, and it said: 'Siencyn bach, wen coming back are you i am being sick in the mornings and the doctor jest been an sed i am in for a baby hopping you are not angry yewer loving Marged.'

Siencyn sat with this for a long time, and then he began laughing to himself, and got up feeling like the lord of creation, and went to look for Dan Spain to tell him and see what he said. And he didn't want to tell anybody except Dan, although he was just bursting with the news. So he went out of the guard room where he was on guard and across the farmyard and through the sheds looking for Dan. But Dan was out on the cliffs the other side of the wood laying some mines, so Siencyn went after him, forgetting he was supposed to be on guard. And just as he came out of the woods and could see the grey North Sea and the black stubby shapes of a convoy jinking southwards in the middle seas, zoom-woof-scream, down came a big two-engined Dornier 215 for you, straight for the soldiers working in the minefield, straight out of the clouds over the sea. Somebody shouted and a couple made a run for it, and a few more fell on their faces, but most of them just looked up at it. And Siencyn looked at it with great interest, not having seen a Swastika before, and then it opened fire and swept past him only just above his head. One of the boys who was running staggered and clutched his guts and went sprawling, and Siencyn said 'Diw Mawr, too bad,' and ran out of the woods to pick him up. The plane had zoomed up over the trees behind him and was climbing in a great ellipse, going seawards, but Siencyn was only concerned to fetch the boy who was hurted, because he was one of the rest of them, and he was hurted. It was Nick Powell Tonypandy as it happened, and he was a mate of Siencyn's, they'd been on a charge together for putting Naffy buns in their respirators and he was going to get married to a butcher's daughter next leave, so his prospects were too good to waste by a bit of bad luck. And Siencyn picked him up and carried him fireman's lift, like in P.T., to the shelter of the woods. Nick was groaning and cursing healthy enough, so Siencyn told him to be quiet, it wasn't a thing to blaspheme about. And he put Nick against a tree and Nick said 'He's coming again,' only he didn't say it as polite as that. And Siencyn saw the Jerry diving in from the sea again like second house at the pictures and he saw the Bren gun the working party had brought out with them ready loaded by a gorse bush just in front of him in the open; so he said 'Look out, boys bach,' and made a dash for the Bren gun and grabbed hold of it, kneeling, with the butt against his hip. And the Jerry was coming straight for him with spurts of flame coming from the wings and bullets like a little shower of hail sweeping towards Siencyn. And a silvery bomb fell out of the plane as it came to the bottom of its gradual dive and was showing its nose to the climb, just at the sea edge of the minefield. And Siencyn said 'Now!' and pressed the trigger as cool as you like. And nothing happened. Oh Jawch, there's a pity for you, Siencyn thought, what is the matter with the old thing? And the explosion of the bomb knocked him over before he could see whether the safety catch was on Automatic or Safe. And when they brought him round with plenty of cold water and his arm in a sling, Spain was kneeling by him and the captain fidgeting and muttering same as usual, and he remembered he had something to tell Spain about, but for the life of him he couldn't think what it was. And Spain said 'Well done, Siencyn boy. You're a chip off the old block, you are.' And Siencyn said 'Is Nick Powell alright?' And Spain said 'Aye, it was only a flesh wound; he's O.K. for the butchery business, don't worry.' And Siencyn said, 'The gun wouldn't go.' And the captain said 'No wonder, you bloody fool. It was on Safe. What the hell's

the good of wasting khaki and food and training on a cretin like you?'
And Siencyn, although he was on his back with his arm in a sling, suddenly felt immensely stronger than the captain for the first time in his
life, and he looked at him and grinned and said 'You bastard!'

Well, the captain's face was a sight to behold. He pulled at his sagging
cheek and opened his mouth and stood on his toes and didn't say a word.
Then he said to Spain, 'You're a witness, Evans.' And Spain said 'I didn't
hear a thing, sir.' And he looked at the captain with a funny look in his
eyes; he'd killed a tidy few men in Spain, Dan Evans had, and Siencyn
got the wind up and he said, 'Don't do it, Dan bach. Leave him be now.
We're all in the war together so make friends, the two of you.' And the
captain said 'Consider yourselves under arrest, both of you.' And off he
went to fetch the sergeant-major. So Dan sat on his heels like the colliers
do in the back lanes and waited for somebody to come back, and kept on
spitting and spitting and saying he'd give him what for if he dared to
court martial them. He knew very well the colonel would dismiss the case
if he heard what the captain had said to Siencyn when he was knocked
half daft by the bomb; and Dan said he'd get it brought up in Parliament
if they did anything to them; and Siencyn lay against a tree as idle and
as happy as ever he'd been in his life, because he'd called the captain a
bastard and Dan had said 'Well done.'

Siencyn didn't take long to mend; his collar bone wasn't broken, only
bruised; and the colonel praised him in the court of enquiry that sat on
Nick Powell's wound; and nothing was heard of the little difference they'd
had with the captain, and everybody was buying him drinks in the Naffy
for what he'd said. So he had a very placid fortnight on light duties because
of his arm. And then, at the end of the fortnight, two things happened
that demanded a good bit of thinking out.

First there came a letter for him, and it was a very short one, and it
wasn't from Marged and it wasn't signed. Dan read it and said it was an
anonymous letter. And it said that Marged was having a baby in case he
was interested, and who was responsible, this person would like to know?
Funny there'd been no baby in four years when he was living with her,
and now as soon as he'd gone to serve his country she goes and gets in
the family way. And then several names of likely men from the neighbouring farms and a hint that Marged had been seen coming out of the

wood by Twm Gors's cottage late one night. And this person anonymous said it was a shameful sin if nobody could respect a soldier serving his country in her hour of need, and was pleased to sign at the bottom, Sincere Patriot.

Well, whether to ask for compassionate leave or not was the question, but Siencyn wouldn't go and tell the captain all these terrible stories about Marged fooling him, so Dan said why didn't he do a break and hitch-hike home. And he thought yes, he'd do that; but he had no idea at all where Penyrheol was from where they were then, and he'd never find it in a month of Sundays. So he made up a story with Dan that his mother was dead – which was true enough – and Dan wrote it out for him in case the captain asked to see the letter, which he would. And Siencyn was just off to see the sergeant-major to ask for an interview, when the runner came down and said they were both wanted in the company office. So up they went and the sergeant-major had a cunning look in his eyes as if he had them on toast at last, and he showed them into the office, quick march, right wheel, halt, left turn, salute, 'Privates 32 Evans and 51 Jones, sir.' And the captain looked up after a minute as if he was busy, and said, 'You two are on draft for overseas service. Hand in your A.B.64 to the C.Q.M.S. (Siencyn never knew what all the initials meant, but Dan would tell him afterwards), and take your blankets to the stores. Seven days' leave. Any questions?' 'No, sir.' 'March them out, sergeant-major.' About turn, quick march, halt, dismiss.

'That's what comes of calling him a bastard, Siencyn,' Dan said, philosophically tracing the effect to its cause. 'You'll be able to see your missus, anyway, chum.'

They had their pay and ration cards and passes and off to the station, six miles of it, full kit, enjoying every inch of it. Dan said anonymous letters wasn't worth noticing, he'd had plenty in his time; and the best thing to do was to find the sod who wrote it, and not say a word to Marged. Siencyn said he wouldn't put it above Twm Gors, but he would put it above Marged, who was a good wife if trying at times. And so they parted at Paddington the best of friends, with Dan seeing Siencyn was on the right train and telling him to mind he came back and didn't shirk it, because Dan didn't want to go abroad by himself. So Siencyn told him not to worry, solong.

And nothing more to do except stand all the way to Cardiff, and then a seat the rest of the journey, change at Carmarthen and Pencader like Dan told him, and then safe and sound in Cardigan, having had sandwiches from an old lady before they got to Cardiff and cake and biscuits from another younger lady between Swansea and Carmarthen. He wasn't going to spend his pay himself. And he didn't tell anybody he was going overseas because it was information likely to aid the enemy, so he pretended he was nobody special. And so he started walking home along the old roads he knew inside out, singing *Jerusalem* and wondering if the chapel would be holding its Eisteddfod this week, and if so he'd sing *Jerusalem* in his battledress and walk away with the first prize over them in civvies.

And soon enough he was turning down the lane to the sea by the black wood and heard his employer's horses shuffling in the stalls; he stopped to listen to the good sound, and then went into the stable to take their heads in his arm and put his palm against their hot wet nostrils. It was fine, that was, pushing old Deri aside to say good-night and welcome-home to Nansi, and their hooves clashing on the cobbles. It was only round the corner then to his own cottage and he felt as if he'd never been away.

There was a blackout up in the kitchen now, very posh, and when he opened the door slowly Marged was sitting on a sack of meal by the stick fire on the flagstone in the corner. But never such a face did she have before he went away. No red in her cheeks at all, but like a funeral in her black shawl and drooping shoulders. And she looked at him like he was a ghost, never a word, but frightened of him, and then again as if she was finished with him for good. It gave him a bit of a turn; and before he could say 'Well, nghariad, it's Siencyn turned up again,' she began to whimper to herself. Siencyn knew there was a scene going to be, so he took his kit off and knelt down by her with a sack under his knees not to spoil the trousers he'd creased under his bed every night, and then he asked her what was up with her. How they straightened it all out isn't anybody's business except their own. Marged wasn't willing to believe he'd forgotten about her letter owing to being knocked daft by a German plane, but in the end believe it she did, and slowly she began to think differently about him and not with despair and hatred the way she had been since he hadn't replied. And then there was all the old gossip, and a letter in the local paper about it too by someone signed Sincere Patriot; and she knew who it was, it was a certain black-marketing grocer keeping a shop on the top road. And Siencyn said thank God it was a man, anyway, thinking what a pity if it had been a woman he couldn't give a good lamping to. And, to cut a long story short, Marged said she wanted it to be a boy and Siencyn to be his name, and Siencyn showed her his new false teeth and she wouldn't believe he took them out at night, so he said 'Wait and see.' And she rubbed her cheek on his battledress and looked at the shine on his boots and wouldn't believe they were his working boots. And if everything wasn't as smooth as their words made it sound, the rest was only a question of time, for a woman will mend herself with time if so be the man means what he says when he speaks kind to her. So she patched up alright with a bit of praise from Siencyn which was as rare as Cadbury's chocolate to her and every bit as sweet. And Siencyn felt worried and exhausted with pulling her round to his way of seeing it all, and it was worse than driving the old sow up the lane or helping to shoe a young colt, but Jawch, it made all the difference. And next day he went without any malice to the certain grocer's just mentioned and after he'd pasted him good and proper he bore no ill feeling at all. And when they asked him how's the army he said it was alright and nothing to worry about, although his mate Dan Evans said it wasn't much of a concern.

And then, the night before he went back, the chapel held its annual Eisteddfod, which was right in Siencyn's line having a rich tenor a bit loud for volume but very good for tone. And he went in his battledress as clean and straight as a new pin with vaseline on his hair the colour of swedes, and they all cheered when he came up to sing his version of *Jerusalem*. And he never let on to a soul that he was down as a C. of E. in the Army through no fault of his own, having told the clerk when asked his religion 'Christian, sir.' Not that there was any need to say sir to a clerk, but he was new to the game then. And it was fine to be standing there in the whitewashed old chapel with Marged sitting in the pew where he'd carved his initials fifteen years ago, and everybody quiet as the grave except old Twm Morris Cobbler at the harmonium, saying 'One Two Three Four – *Now*.' And off he went with old Twm creaking along just level with him and the faces of the congregation uplifted and swaying slowly as if there was a little breeze going across the pews. And he'd sung it so often in the back of a lorry on exercises in the Army, and in the latrines, and peeling potatoes on jankers, that it came now with all the intimacy and rejoicing of all that had happened to him and not harmed or beaten him. And when he'd finished there was a great silence on them all, and then the men wiped the sweat from under their celluloid collars, and the women sniffed at their hankies and wouldn't look up. And Siencyn walked down and sat by Marged. And then they began to clap, and Siencyn didn't think they were ever going to stop. And although the adjudicator was a conshie in the last war he didn't have any option about giving Siencyn the prize. No money in it of course, not with singing sacred music; it was a different matter from money.

And Siencyn walked home with Marged arm in arm, and he said Dan Spain would write to her regular, but he didn't have the heart to tell her where he was going to, meaning abroad; not yet, because he could only just imagine himself going abroad, and as for coming back again, he couldn't see that at all. But there was nothing to be done about it, only go to bed early and poke his head out of the window to listen to the river and tell the cockerel mind to crow at five thirty to catch the train. And that made Marged laugh for the first time, and Siencyn thought well, it's not so bad so far and no blame attached to me. And Marged promised she'd call the baby Dan as well as Siencyn. And they slept so sound that Jawch if he didn't miss the train. But never mind about that now.

'HENRY GREEN'

The Lull

I

There was a bar in this fire station. On the bar was a case of beer. A fire-man was taking bottles from this case, placing the full bottles onto shelves. He was alone.

Another came in. This one was minus his tunic. He wore a check shirt. The barman began to take him off, without looking up from what he was doing.

'You – you – you fool,' the barman said. The way he spoke you would have thought one or the other stuttered.

'Ten Woodbines, thank you.'

'Ten,' the barman said.

A bell in the cash register. Then silence. These two men stood in silence.

'Cigarette?'

'No, not just yet, thanks all the same, Gerald. I don't smoke such a lot these days.'

'Not like you used to, eh?'

What lay behind this last remark was that Gerald, the man in the check shirt, was echoing an opinion widely held in the station, that this barman often put his sticky fingers, which were of the same length, into the till. But it was said without malice. The barman let it pass. He knew the per-sonnel expected to be robbed, within reason. He lifted another full case onto the bar. After a pause, he said: 'They don't get any lighter. Is there anything on tonight?'

He asked this pleasantly, to get his own back. He was referring to the fact that Gerald, because he did odd jobs carpentering for the officer in charge, was excused the tactical exercises held every evening to keep the men out of bed.

'Not that I know of,' the other replied. His tone of voice was to show, elaborately, that he did not care.

'We want another blitz,' remarked the barman.

'We do,' he was answered.

Neither of these firemen stuttered.

'I saw old Sambo today.'

The other did not make a move.

'Why d'you wear that bloody shirt?' the first man went on. He kept his eyes on the bottles he arranged. 'Has your Mrs got such a number that she can't put your dusters to the proper use? Because we could do with one or two at 'ome. Yes,' he broke off, 'I seen Sam.'

'That fellow with a squint.'

'That's right. Sam Race.'

A short silence.

'You know the last time I seen him?' the barman went on.

'On a working party?' This was a reference to the fact that, because he pleaded he had to check his stock, the barman was excused fatigues.

'On a working party! No! Along Burdett Road the night of that bad blitz.'

'Really?'

'I've not seen 'im since the night Willy Tennant got down under the pump, when old Ted Fowler moved up one. It was surprising it didn't break his leg.'

'The wheel went right over?' the man in the shirt asked, as though enquiring whether the blackbird had got the worm.

'You're telling me. I was there. Yes, from that day until this morning I didn't set eyes on Sam. That's a strange thing, come to look at it.'

They stood, in silence again, leaning each side of the bar. They pondered at the linoleum which covered the counter.

'Sure you couldn't do with a drink?' the barman asked at last.

'Quite sure, thanks.'

At this a third fireman came in.

'Well brother?'

That is to say the barman and the third fireman were both members of the Fire Brigades Union.

'I'll 'ave one of them small light ales, Joe, please. Will you try one?'

'No, thanks all the same. Been out on short leave?' He called it 'leaf'.

'Yes, I 'ad a drop of short.'

A bell in the cash register.

'I was just tellin' Gerald,' the first man went on, 'I seen Sam Race as I was on me way round to the brewer's this morning.'

'Wally Race you mean, Joe.'

'No, Wally Race is the brother.'

'Wally Race 'as no brother,' the third man stuck to his guns.

'What'll you bet me, Gus?'

'Wally Race 'as no brother. 'E's lived at 'ome ever since I can remember. With 'is mother and 'er old man. No, he's an only child, Wally Race is.'

'Come on, Gus, what'll you bet?'

'I wouldn't want to take your money, Joe.'

'What if you do, that's my business! It's my money, ain't it? Come on now, just for a lark, how much?'

'What, on three fourteen and six a week?'

'Some of you chaps just won't 'ave a go. Forgotten what it's like I suppose.'

The barman pretended disgust. He lifted two empty cases down. He began to polish glasses when Gerald, in his check shirt, turned all at once, and hurried out of the room.

'What's 'e making now?' the third man asked.

'Bedside table. Bloody marvellous the work he turns out. You can't see 'is joins, only with a magnifying glass.'

'Yes. The Boy Marvel.'

Silence yet again. Then a fourth man entered.

'Quite busy, thank you, this evenin',' the barman remarked in greeting. He meant it. 'Bloody awful quiet it is in behind this bar sometimes. What can I do for you, brother?'

'Wallop,' the fourth man demanded.

'Now then, Ted, you know there ain't none. We can do you light ale, in quarts or 'alf pints, ditto brown ale, or a nice bottle of Guinness.'

'What, at eightpence 'alfpenny. Not likely.'

They looked at each other, amiably.

'What's become of the Bar Committee?' the fourth man enquired.

'What's become of it?' the barman Joe echoed. 'It's still in existence.'

'Then it's time it 'eld another meeting.'

'These small lights aren't bad, Ted,' the third man said.

'I don't want none o' that. I like it all right, but those lights don't like me. Too gassy.'

'All right then, mate, but make up your mind.' Having said this, the barman began to polish glasses again.

"Ow much a week, now, is this job you've got behind that bar worth to you?' the fourth man went on.

The barman ignored it. Instead he remarked: 'I seen Sam Race this morning.'

'Well, I think I'll risk a brown, Joe. Out of the large bottle.'

'Pronto. Yes, 'e looked very queer, did old Sambo.'

'Sam who?'

'Sam Race. Why you must remember him, Ted.'

'Wally Race you mean.'

'No, Sam.'

'What station?'

"E's moved,' the barman replied, nonplussed for the instant. 'I disremember where exactly,' he went on rather lamely. This attracted the third man's attention, who asked: 'What station was 'e at?'

The barman had pulled himself together. He knew what to say to this.

'Where d'you think, Gus? Up Goldington Road, at 4U of course, with Matty Franks.' He was improvising.

'With 'oo?' the fourth man objected.

'Old Matty Franks,' the barman answered irritably.

A bell in the cash register. A pause.

'Never 'eard of 'im,' the fourth man announced. 'Good 'ealth,' he said.

'God bless,' the third fireman replied.

'Never heard of Matty Franks?' the barman went on. 'The rottenest old bastard in the Service. Up Goldington Road just past the Ploughshare?'

The two men looked at the barman, ruminating. The fourth man was about to object he was not acquainted with a pub of that name up that road when they all heard a sad cry of 'Come and get it,' from below, from the messroom.

'Already?' the fourth man asked aloud. He gulped his down. He left.

The third fireman finished his half pint, and went.

The moment he was alone the barman poured himself out a light from one of the quart bottles.

A bell did not ring in the cash register. Joe had his drinks on the house, when no one was looking.

Silence. He let a lonely belch. He pondered the linoleum which covered the counter.

After five minutes, a kitchen orderly for the day brought the barman up his supper.

'Fred,' the barman said, 'it's getting very slow in this bloody dump.'

'You're telling me,' Fred replied.

'I've 'ad Gus and Ted on about Sam Race.'

'Oo?'

'Sam Race.'

'I don't seem to recollect a Sam Race, Joe.'

'No, nor there ain't never been. There's only the one Wally Race, who squints something 'orrible. Yet they wouldn't 'ave a bet on it. Not one o' them. What a game, eh?'

'You've said it,' Fred replied, uninterested. He went out.

The barman began to eat his supper.

2

Another evening. The same bar. Five or six firemen sat around. Two were without a drink. A fifth man held the floor.

'Yes,' he said, 'a great big woman, my aunt was, twenty-two stone she weighed. And a real wicked old lady. My dad wouldn't allow us kids to have nothing to do with 'er. I'll tell you what she did once. It was a Sunday morning, on the way to church.'

'On the way to church?' another fireman asked.

'Yes, yes, mate, that sort are churchgoers, very often. I'll never forget.

Just as she came up on a sheep she put her umbrella right into it. "Err," she said, "you horrid thing." Went right in, the point did.'

No one accepted this. He realised it. He had to go on.

'Terrible she was. Used to kill cats for the enjoyment. She was well hated. D'you know the manner she used to despatch 'em. By strangilation.'

'Strangled them, eh?' another asked.

'Yes, mate. She put a cord round the neck with a slip knot. Then she'd pass the end through the keyhole. She took the key out first, of course. Then she'd take a turn round her body with the free end. To finish up she just leaned on that door. With all her weight it didn't take more'n a minute.'

'How d'you mean, a turn round 'er body?'

'Well, she'd entice the cat in first, see. After that she'd put a slip knot round its neck,' and this fifth fireman went on into an involved description of the method favoured by his aunt. No one was wiser at the end. In the pause which followed two of the others started a quiet argument between each other as to the performance of a particular towing vehicle.

The fifth man began his last attempt.

'She was hated, real hated she was in the country thereabouts,' he told them. 'My dad always said she'd come unstuck at the finish. And so she did. It was remarkable the way it come about.'

'What was that then, Charley?' someone asked, from politeness.

'The way she died, mate. It was to do with a duck for her supper. Eighty-six years old she was. She couldn't manage to wring this duck's neck. So she got out the old chopper, held the bird down on the block and plonk, the 'ead was gone. Well, this head, it can't 'ave fallen in the basket. When she bent down to pick up the 'ead, she let the carcass fall. And it fell right side up, right side up that bloody carcass fell, on its bloody feet and all. And did it run! Well she must 'ave taken fright. She must 'ave started runnin', with the duck 'ard after. She run out into the garden. The blood from the stump left a trail behind. It followed 'er every turn, that decapitated duck did. Until in the finish she fell down. Dead as mutton she was. 'Eart failure. She'd took a fright. But credit it or not, that duck landed on her arse as she lay there, stretched out. That's where my first cousin, the nephew, came on 'em both. Cold as a stone, she was, already.'

'Damn that for a bloody tale, Charley.'

'You don't believe me, ah? Well, I tell you, it's the bloody truth. It's the nerves or something. You'll see the same with chickens that's had their heads cut off. If it's done sudden they'll run around.'

'Not that distance.'

'I'm sayin' to you, this 'appened just like I told you, Joe. All right, disbelieve me then.'

A game of darts was suggested. All joined in.

3

But it was noticeable that, whenever a stranger came into the bar, these firemen, who had not been on a blitz for eighteen months, would start talking back to what they had seen of the attack on London in 1940. They were seeking to justify the waiting life they lived at present, without fires.

A stranger did not have to join in, his presence alone was enough to stimulate them who felt they no longer had their lives now that they were living again, if life in a fire station can be called living.

These men were passing through a period which may be compared with the experience of changing fast trains. A traveller on the crowded platform cannot be said to command his destiny, who stands, agape, waiting for the next express. It is signalled, he knows that it will be packed, it is down the line. The unseen approach keeps him, as it were, suspended, that is no more than breathing, but more than ready to describe the way he has arrived to a man he does not know, waiting in the same disquiet, at his shoulder.

4

It was an evening session in this bar. They had all had a few beers. The stranger, posted to this station for the night because it was short of riders, stayed bored, expressionless, without a hope of comfort. They were sitting back against the walls, in a rectangle. A silence fell. Then the sixth man began. He asked: 'Joe, remember the night we were called to Jacob's Place?'

'I'll likely never forget that, mate.'

'Nor me.'

Silence. But everyone listened.

'What was that, then?' a seventh man enquired.

'They called us on to Number five Jacob's Place,' he began again, consciously dramatic.

'Number seventeen, Alfred,' the barman said.

'You may be right at that,' the sixth man answered, unwilling to argue because he wanted to get on with his story. 'It's of no consequence,' he added, already beginning to be put out, 'the point is some geezer in the street tells us there's a job in the roof, so of course Joe here an' me gets crackin'. The rest of the crew set in to a hydrant, while the two of us run upstairs with the stirrup pump in case we can put it out easy. It turns out to be one of them houses where there's just a caretaker, like, an' all the furniture is covered with sheets be'ind locked doors. Ghostly. You know the kind, a smashing place, but 'aunted. There must've been fifteen or sixteen rooms. Well there's a lot of cold smoke choking us on the top floor, but we find the old trap-door to the roof all right. It was quite a pleasure to get out in the air again, it certainly was, wasn't it, Joe?'

'It was that,' Joe said back.

'We begin taking a few tiles off,' he went on, 'and we find a place where it's a bit 'ot, but we still 'aven't come on the seat of the fire, we're rummagin' about, like, on top of that bloody roof when all of a sudden there's a bloody blubbering noise up in the sky over'ead, yes, like a dog bloody 'owling in a bass voice, and coming down out of the moon though we couldn't see nothink. Was I scared. I thinks to meself it's another bloody secret weapon. I called out to you, didn't I, mate?'

'You may 'ave done Alf. I was too busy tryin' to get down out of it.'

'Yes, we had a bit of a scramble. Joe 'ere was nearest, so he goes down first. Well, there was no point in that "after you" stunt, was there? Yes, and as I was coming last down through the trap-door, I looks up, and I sees what had put the wind up me to such an extent. Know what it was?'

Everyone in the room, bar the stranger, could have told him. They had heard this story often. And the stranger was not interested.

Alfred answered himself.

'A bloody barrage balloon,' he said. 'The shrapnel had got at it. The blubbering noise is occasioned by the fabric rubbin' together as it comes down, or the gas escapin' out of the envelope, one or the other. I couldn't rightly say. But it didn't half put the wind up me.'

'And me,' said Joe.

Silence fell again. Each man drank sparingly of his beer. Knowing the story had not been a success because it had been told before, Alfred tried to get some response from the stranger.

'What station are you from?' he asked.

This man awoke with a start from a doze of misery. He replied obliquely, saying: 'I'm a CO you know.'

'A conchie? Well, why not,' Alfred generously said.

'I've never been out on a job,' the stranger answered. 'And I don't know if I should put out fires,' he went on, desperate, 'I don't rightly know if I ought.'

A heavier silence followed.

5

Hyde Park on Sunday. It was hot. A fireman in mufti and a young girl were, of an afternoon, by that part of the Serpentine in which fishing is allowed. They had put themselves back from dazzling water, on deck chairs.

A girl of eighteen went slowly by, dressed in pink, a careful inexpensive outfit, one of thousands off a hook. From her deck chair the other said, rapid and sly: 'La petite marquise Osine est toute belle.'

He had been admiring the calves and tender ankles that girl dragged through thin, olive-green grass. He laughed. He was caught out. He turned to his companion.

'Henry,' she went on, bilingual, speaking only a little less fast, 'surely you remember?'

He was sleepy. He shook his head. She recited, quick and low:

> *Oui, certes, il est doux,*
> *Le roman d'un premier amant. L'âme s'essaie,*
> *C'est un jeune coureur à la première haie.*
> *C'est si mignard qu'on croit à peine que c'est mal.*
> *Quelque chose d'étonnamment matutinal.*

He said, 'Yes.' He did not turn away again. He admired her nose, which had caught his eye, as it always did.

'Verlaine?' he asked.

She wondered what he was looking at so particularly about her.

'D'you think my hair's too long?'

'No, I don't,' he replied, 'it's lovely. That was Verlaine, wasn't it?'

She thought, of course, he's the one who likes my nose.

'You know you're the worst-read man I've ever met.'

'Worse than Archie Small?'

'No, not quite. I like Archie because he's not read anything at all. That's probably why he dances so well.'

What lay behind the remark was that this man Henry could not dance. Before he had time to take it up she began again, lying back in the chair, looking at him with half-closed eyes, almost in a sing-song,

> *Ses cheveux, noirs tas sauvage où*
> *Scintille un barbare bijou,*
> *La font reine et la font fantoche.*

She was worried about whether her hair was right.

'Ah,' he said. He stretched. She was wearing an olive-green bow of velvet in it.

She shut her eyes, gated them with eyelashes. It was very hot. After a pause she went on, thinking of his youngest sister, her friend.

> *La femme pense à quelque ancienne compagne,*
> *Laquelle a tout, voiture et maison de campagne,*
> *Tandis que les enfants, leurs poings dans leurs yeux clos,*
> *Ronflant sur leur assiette, imitent des sanglots.*

'Me, with you, I suppose,' he remarked. 'Go on,' he said. He shut his eyes. 'I'm enjoying this.'

She wondered that he could see himself as a child with her, when he was old enough to be her father.

Both were sleepy from a good lunch. After a while she added slowly, in a low voice:

Bien que parfois nous sentions
Battre nos coeurs sous nos mantes
A des pensers clandestins,
En nous sachant les amantes
Futures des libertins.

'Henry,' she said, when there had been another silence. 'You don't know where that comes from, do you?'

He did not open his eyes. 'Verlaine,' he said. He was smiling.

'Yes,' she answered, and shut her eyes. 'It's called "La chanson des Ingénues".

Nous sommes les Ingénues
Aux bandeaux plats, à l'oeil bleu,
Qui vivons, presque inconnues,
Dans les romans qu'on lit peu.

'How sweet,' he said, rather dry. At that moment the syrens sounded. Everyone looked up. It was cloudlessly bare and blue.

'Goodness,' she remarked, without conviction and not moving. 'How worried Mummy will be about me.' They sat on. They did not close their eyes again. It was awkward.

Then he suggested they might go to a film, saying it was waste to spend a leave day in the Park. She jumped at it. They hurried off, arm in arm, to the USA.

6

The ninth fireman said: 'A 'ornet? No, I can't recollect that I ever met with a 'ornet. But crows now. I remember the first time I seen a crow, to really notice, like. Yus. I was out on the allotment. On the previous leave day I'd put me beansticks in just lovely. But this mornin' when I comes to see how the beans was shapin' there's not a bloody beanstick stood in the bloody soil. They was by far too 'eavy for 'em. I couldn't make it out at first. But just as I'm bendin' to 'ave a look, there's a bloody great bloody black think that comes swoop at me out of the sky. I thought it was the blitz all over again for a minute. So then I puts me 'ands up and 'as a peep. There was seven of the buggers in the oak tree there at the bottom, where the road goes along by our allotments. An' can't they 'alf 'oller. Kraa, kraa. A chap come with a gun and killed three. Bloody great things they was. The rest never came back. No, we never seen them no more.'

7

Two firemen were walking back to the station from the factory in which they made shell caps for the two hours during which they were allowed short leave, every second day.

The tenth man said to the eleventh: 'I'm browned off Wal, completely.'

The eleventh answered: 'You're not the only one.'

'Wal, d'you think there'll ever be another blitz?'

'Well, mate, if he doesn't put one on soon we shall all be crackers.'

'You're telling me.'

'And they are going insane, in every station, every day. Have you heard about the patrol man over at 18Y?'

'What was that, Wal?'

'Well it seems that the officer in charge finds something to take him out of his office, and as he comes out he sees no one on guard on the gate. So he looks around, and still he can't spot the patrol man. Till something tells him to look up. And there is the chap that should have been on the gate, sitting across the peak of the roof, hauling on a long line (120 feet of rope) he has between his hands. So he calls to 'im, sarcastic, "'Ow are you gettin' on up there?" And this is the answer he gets: "I've saved five."'

'No.'

'It's as true as I'm here. So this officer in charge he climbs as far as he can get inside the building, till he comes to a window across from where his patrol man is sitting. He's one of those fat bastards, and he's a bit out of breath with the climb, you understand. He doesn't know what to make of it. So he calls out: "You've saved five, 'ave you?"'

' "Yessir. And I'm about done up.'

' " 'Ang on there, then, and I'll be with yer," the officer in charge sings out to him.

'"You can't," is the answer he gets. "I'm surrounded." Surrounded by fire, he meant. In the finish they had to call out the turntable ladders to bring him down. To anyone not acquainted with this job it seems hardly possible, do it?'

'They'll be bringing the plain van any day for me,' the tenth man replied. They walked on, silent.

The passers-by despised them in this uniform that, two years ago, was good in any pub for a drink from a stranger.

SYLVIA TOWNSEND WARNER

The Trumpet Shall Sound

No doubt, thought Mrs Mullen, looking at her niece, no doubt at all, everything was made uncommonly easy for these young ones, not like it was in her time. *Then* you didn't have a death in the house without knowing it.

Rightly speaking, you couldn't call this a death in the house; for poor old Dick, falling over a bicycle in the blackout, had been taken to the hospital, and in the hospital he had died; and from the hospital, no better than a parcel, he had been taken to the undertaker's place to await, no better than a parcel, the day of the funeral.

Flowers c/o Messrs. Kedge, Ring St., Lower Town.

That is why the house felt so queer. No corpse in it, no black weight at its centre to keep it steady. No reason to step softly, no door with silence behind it. Not even the blinds drawn.

The spring sunshine shone full into the front room. There was a fire burning too, the room was very warm. But Cathie kept on shivering and pulling up the collar of her coat. Not tired enough, thought Mrs Mullen. If Dick had been brought home to die the nursing and the running about and the sitting up and one thing and another would have knocked the nerves and the shivers out of her, left her in the right frame of mind to appreciate the repose of a funeral. These young women who thought they were making things so much easier for themselves, small families, bakers' bread, nowadays not even the whites boiled, were making a great mistake. If you'd got to be a woman it was better to be an old-fashioned woman, with plenty of work to keep your mind off it.

Cathie sat on the sofa, and beside her sat Gwennie, Dick's sister-in-law, and Gwennie's girl, Ramona. Ramona yawned incessantly. She was working in munitions, and this week was a night turn.

Soon we shall all be yawning, thought Mrs Mullen. She glanced at the clock. There was still some time to run before the car came for them.

By the window sat Freda, Mrs Mullen's unmarried sister, and Reg, Cathie's husband. He had got leave for his father-in-law's funeral. He sat on a small chair, leaning forward, with his hands dangling between his knees. Beside him stood the boy Alan, staring at his shoulder-badge and corporal's stripes, and slowly drawing them on the air with his forefinger.

'There would have been time for a cup of tea,' said Cathie.

'There's time now,' said Reg. 'I'll go and put on the kettle.'

'Don't trouble for me,' said Freda.

'Nor me, either. Six cups. That wouldn't leave much of Cathie's ration. Ah, you'll miss your poor old dad's ration, won't you, Cath? It'll make a difference.'

'I had a nice cup of tea on my way here,' said Freda. 'Between the buses.'

'How long did it take you to come?'

'Matter of three hours. They've taken off the Kitley bus, so now you have to go round by Swopham. And who do you think I met on the bus, Lottie? Old Mr Tanner, who used to keep the fish-shop. You've never seen a man so changed.'

'Well, he must be getting on, mustn't he?'

'Sixty-seven. You remember how rheumatic he was, and how he always wore a hat because of his face-ache? There he was, strolling into the bus bare-headed, with a potted flower under his arm. Why, Mr Tanner, I said, this war seems to be agreeing with you. And he told me he hasn't had a twinge for the last ten years, and all because of wearing iodine socks. He was right sorry when I told him about poor Dick.'

'Iodine socks? Yes, you do hear of them. All I know is, they never did anything for Florence Gander, Florence Toogood that was. Still, *she's* constitutional. You remember Florence, don't you, Gwennie? One time it looked as though she were going to marry poor old Dick.'

'Didn't she sing, or something?'

'Sing or something?' Mrs Mullen's voice expressed reproachful surprise. 'Why, she played on the violin, and passed examinations for it up in London. That's how Dick took up with your sister. For in the last war Florence went round with a concert-party, all in a bus together, called

The Five Lucky Beans, or something, and Dick, he was in the army, of course, and the first time he came back on leave, "What's become of Florence," he said, and mother said, "Why, haven't the girls told you about her engagement?" meaning the concert-party. But just then the maroons went off and there was that awful Zeppelin, and so Florence went clean out of our heads, and Dick thought she'd taken up with some other boy, and when he came back next he got engaged to your Jessie, and Florence married Nut Gander. Just a misunderstanding, you see. Five children she had, one after another, and not a note of music among them. It's funny how things turn out.'

'Mum,' said the child. 'I think I'll just feed my rabbits.'

'I'll go with him,' said Reg, rising with alacrity.

Cathie looked as though she were about to speak, but said nothing. The three aunts exchanged glances, and then settled down more easily.

'Do you remember Buster, Lottie? And the day he took round the collecting bag at chapel in that blue suit of his? Lord, what a look he gave me as he went up the aisle! Impudent? He was worse than the seven monkeys.'

'And all the time he'd got two wives, one in Chelmsford and the other somewhere in Wales. Well, I don't mind admitting it now, the day that news came out I cried my eyes sore.'

'Yes, and you weren't the only one, either. And it wasn't only us girls that took on about it. Mrs Blandamer, George Blandamer's wife, who got up the whist-drives and socials – well, Julia Kinnear told me that she swallowed half a bottle of disinfectant, and only didn't die of it because they'd happened to eat some bad fish the evening before, and the fish and the disinfectant all came back together.'

'Yes, I heard something about that, too. Well, they do say, Lucky at cards, unlucky in love. What about George, though?'

'Oh, all *he* ever knew of it was the fish.'

Ramona had shut her eyes and begun to breathe heavily. Now she slumped forward. Cathie put an arm about her, and settled the sleeping head on her shoulder. Her face lost its look of nervous strain as the sleeping girl's warmth invaded her.

'I should like a bit of tinned salmon, though. I haven't seen a tin for months,' said Freda.

'Ah, you should have bought it and put it by,' said Lottie Mullen. 'Hoarding or no hoarding, a person's got to keep even with the future. I don't mind telling you, if Lord Woolton were to come along and look under my old double-bed he'd see more than the chamber.'

'In reason, I grant you.' Gwennie eased her scantily-cut black skirt over her knees. 'But the way some people behave, it's a scandal. You know Mrs Mortus, whose Irene works along with our Ramona? Well, last Thursday week I saw her get half a pound of biscuits in a queue, and then go back to the tail of the queue, and take off her glasses, and work her way up and get another half-pound. Well, I said to myself, now I suppose you'll go back again and take out your teeth. Oh, it makes my blood boil!'

'Yes, it makes one want to say something, doesn't it? But talking of bare-faced cheating, what about . . .'

'Mum! Mum!'

The child ran in, flourishing his cap.

'The car's outside, Mum. It's waiting for us.'

'Good Lord! And we were so happy talking over old times, we never heard it. Dear, dear! Poor Dick. Not even brought back for as much as to come in and go out again. It doesn't seem quite reverent, does it, to go out of a house for a funeral with no corpse going before. Where's my gloves?'

The undertaker's car was old and stately, so roomy that it held them all. Reg and the boy sat in front, where Reg and the driver conversed in undertones about double declutching. Cathie and Ramona still clung to each other, and the aunts, ennobled by the deep springing and all the little amber knobs, sat silent and upright, glancing at the shabby streets as though a Jug and Bottle Entrance meant nothing to them.

Outside Mr Kedge's establishment the hearse was waiting, the four mutes standing beside it. As they neared, the mutes scrambled up and it moved off. Another car which had been waiting swung out to follow theirs.

'Well, my goodness, whoever's that? Cathie! Who's in that other car?'

'I didn't see.'

'Well, surely, you ought to know. People don't follow a body uninvited. Here, Gwennie, you're the limberest among us. You watch out of this back window and see who it is.'

'It's the Blackbones. Fred and Mary and old Dodger Blackbones.'

'*The Blackbones?* Well!'

'The Blackbones?'

'Gwennie! Look again. It can't be the Blackbones.'

'Yes, it is. And in mourning, too, as far as one can see.'

'I've never heard of such a thing. After the way Mrs Dodger walked off with our Aunt Mabel's furniture, and Dick never getting as much as a teaspoon, and all of us knowing he was her favourite nephew. Cathie! What are those Blackbones doing at your father's funeral?'

'Well, I suppose they are coming too, Aunt Lot.'

'My word! And is that all you can do about it?'

'Well, what can I do?'

'Did you know they were coming?'

Ramona came stare-eyed and assertive out of her doze.

'Why shouldn't they come, Mrs Mullen? It's Uncle Dick's funeral, I suppose.'

'Hush, Ramona dear.'

'Uncle Dick's funeral? That's just what I'm complaining of. If Dodger wants to go to a funeral, I should think he could pick out some other funeral where he'd be more in keeping. Or wait for his own. Why, it would make Dick turn in his grave.'

Cathie preserved an unassenting silence. Ramona yawned with deliberation. Gwennie, her face mottled with blushes, looked steadily out of the window.

'Well, wouldn't it? After the way Dodger treated your Dad?'

'Dad and Cousin Randall got on all right, Aunt Lot.'

'D'you mean to say . . . ?'

'They used to meet at the Buffaloes, and Cousin Randall was very fond of Dad.'

The car drew up before the church. The coffin was lifted out, the clergyman came from the porch to meet it.

'*I am the Resurrection . . .*'

When he began to speak it was obvious that his teeth were false and didn't fit. On every sibilant he sounded a shrill whistle.

'Who on earth's this awful old parson?' whispered Mrs Mullen, as she and Freda, Cathie, Reg, and the boy, came up from their knees in the front pew. 'Why haven't you got Mr Dacre?'

'He's gone to be an army chaplain, Aunt Lot.'

A little farther down on the opposite side of the aisle sat the Black-bones. Freda, who had no dignity, kept twisting herself to look at them. Mrs Mullen continued to look steadfastly before her, where the coffin, mounted on trestles, seemed irreconcilably large and dominating for anything representing Dick. In the pew just behind, Gwennie was freely and comfortably weeping.

Well, perhaps the coffin was in the right of it. Perhaps her impression of Dick was a false one, after all. For one can't be sure, even about one's own brother. Dick had been reconciled with Dodger. For years he had been meeting Dodger at the Buffaloes, going round to the pub with him afterwards, talking to him of carrier pigeons and tomato blight. Her own brother – and she had never so much as suspected it.

Staring at the coffin, so aloof and so imminent, Mrs Mullen was penetrated by a realisation of the vanity of this world. What's the use, she thought to herself, what's the use of sticking up for one's principles, what's the use of getting up into one's best corsets to attend a funeral, why pay burial insurance, why have wars? There, across the aisle, was Dodger, grown old in wickedness, and here was she, worn out with keeping respectable. And to that whistling clergyman there, not a pin to choose between them. Just two elderly persons who would soon be funerals, and the only odds, which happened to come first.

A lot of good horse-sense would be buried with her. And Dodger, he'd take more knowledge of the world than he was born with down into the grave with him. But nobody would dig for it, nobody wanted the wisdom of the old, any more than they wanted those big mahogany sideboards. That sideboard of Aunt Mabel's, and the dumb waiter, and the eight chairs, so solid you could hardly lift them: Dodger had got them, and Mrs Dodger had dusted them; but young Mrs Fred would sell them as soon as Dodger had hopped it.

'*For the trumpet shwee! — all shwee! — ound . . .*'

But had Saint Paul, thought the Reverend Mr Amwood, foreseen these funeral countenances, blankly unconvinced, glumly polite, amid this funeral incense of dying flowers and mothballs? And with which mourners had Mr Kedge, thriftily complying with the petrol restrictions, ordained that he should ride to the cemetery? Saint Paul, *in watchings often, in fastings often, in stripes above measure, in prisons more frequent, in deaths oft*, had not been required to take over, in his old age, the duty of an industrial parish, under a most energetic and uncongenial Bishop, and on a heavy clay soil.

'*Therefore, my beloved brethren, be ye steadfast, unmovable, always abounding in the work of the Lord, forasmuch as ye know that your labour is not in vain in the Lord.*'

The coffin was lifted and carried from the church. Mr Kedge approached the clergyman.

'Well!' exclaimed Freda. 'If those Blackbones aren't taking the parson with them! What next? I've a good mind to fetch him out again.'

'Do let be, Freda,' said Mrs Mullen. 'And try to remember that this is a funeral, not a remnant sale.'

'Always did fight like cats, those two,' whispered Gwennie to her daughter.

It was a long way to the cemetery, and they drove in silence, except once, when Lottie Mullen, driven to speak her thought aloud, said heavily: 'What's the use?' Then they looked at her enquiringly; but as each left it to the other to take up the question, no one answered.

The cemetery lay on the outskirts of the town, rising above the sad slow river, the countless identical ridges of slate-roofed artisan dwellings, the factories and warehouses. It was a newish cemetery, the farther half of it lay unused, the trees planted by the Town Council still had a youthful tender look. So many of the graves had bunches of daffodils on them that the cemetery appeared to be twinkling with daffodils and responding with yellow flashes to the April sunlight. Two other funerals were taking place. They seemed very small and unimportant among the expanse of completed graves.

Shining, too, in the April sunlight the coffin on its six black legs proceeded like some queer quadruped, turning first right, then left, as though unerringly nosing out its lair. The newly-dug clay, heaped up, was yellow and shiny like the coffin, the walls of the grave had an ochreous glister. The gravedigger was standing a little aloofly behind a neighbouring headstone.

Up shuffled Dodger, his boots creaking. His face was pinched, his few locks of grey hair lifted in the wind. Not long for this world, thought

Mrs Mullen. No wonder he's having a good look. Raising his eyes from the open grave Dodger's glance met hers. Still vibrating to thoughts of mortality she tried to convey by her expression that the past was being overlooked. Dodger blinked once or twice, and turned away.

Up here above the town the wind was blowing quite briskly. White clouds raced over the blue, the daffodils wagged, the clergyman's surplice rustled as he stood waiting while the bearers lifted the wreaths from the coffin, and the mourners took their places. Freda was having trouble with her hat. Once it almost blew off, and Mr Kedge sprang forward, noiseless as a shadow, to retrieve it.

How tiresome Freda was, always a fidget, always coming to bits just like her own parcels. And there was that girl Ramona, looking at her so sarcastically, and Mary Blackbone ostentatiously not noticing. Why must such unpleasantness mar the funeral, just at the most solemn moment, too? But the outdoor part of a funeral usually went wrong, at Hilda's funeral George had had a fit, at George's funeral the wasps were something chronic. If only that clergyman would begin!

He began. Under the heavy rhythm of the burial sentences everything subsided into order and a dreamy majesty, except his own surplice, in which the wind now made a most extraordinary drumming and fluster. Suddenly the grave-digger jumped out from behind his headstone, waving his arms, and shouting:

'Look up there! Look out!'

His voice ripped through the ceremony. They looked. He was pointing to the sky. There, just coming out of a cloud, was something like an enormous pale bird with beating wings. Dangling from it, as the mouse dangles from the claws of the white owl, was a dark object. Now that they looked the noise of the beating parachute, the drumming and flustering, seemed overwhelmingly loud. The noise grew louder, the thing came lower.

Reg seized Alan, and dropped him into the grave. Then he grabbed Cathie, and dropped her in beside the child.

'Jump in, jump in! It's a landmine coming down.'

One after another the mourners got into the grave. The mutes came to the edge, hesitated, seemed inclined to follow. Mr Kedge, with a recalling gesture, pointed them to some bushes. Remembering their position they retired there, and lay down. The clergyman still remained standing. Mr

Kedge touched his elbow, pointed to the grave. The clergyman, on such an occasion, would rank as one of the family. But Mr Amwood shook his head. The parachute came lower, reeling and billowing. It seemed to fill the whole sky. Pursing his lips, Mr Kedge lay down also.

There seemed to be no end to the waiting. Away in the town an engine blew off steam, and one could hear the birds singing. Meanwhile Mr Amwood had knelt down at the graveside and was whistling through the commendatory prayer for the dying. Dodger, pressed close and bony to Lottie Mullen, commented in her ear:

'Bit previous, isn't he, giving us all up for lost like that?'

His pale wrinkled face was lit with an expression of indomitable craft and assurance.

'Amen,' said Mr Amwood rapidly, snatched out his teeth, and cast himself down face forward.

There was a crash that swelled into a long roar. The mourners in the grave were thrown pell-mell against each other. The breath of life seemed to be dragged out of them, they gasped and choked. The air became darkened by a cloud of dust, in which dead leaves, pebbles, twigs, daffodils, clods of earth, shreds of stuff and paper, fragments of wood and stone and metal, were suspended. Glancing into the spattered darkness Mrs Mullen saw two funeral wreaths, her own and Gwennie's, rise up, hang twirling, and fall dishevelled into the grave.

At last, into this darkened air, they saw Mr Amwood erect himself, tall and ghostly-white, saying:

'You may come out now.'

Aided by shoves from Fred and Reg they scrambled out, and looked around. The coffin was lying on its side. Near it was a large fragment of marble, lettered *Also Emma*, and Mr Kedge was holding a bloodstained handkerchief to his ear, and saying it was a near go. Everything was covered with dust and rubble. At the western end of the cemetery a column of dust was still boiling up, and beneath it some small figures were scurrying to and fro.

The funeral proceeded. The coffin was lowered into the grave, earth was scattered on it, and the last prayers were said. Walking rather unsteadily the party turned away. It was then that Dodger went up to Mrs Mullen, remarking affably:

'Hullo, Lot. Looked as though we might be spending the night here, didn't it?'

She gave him an unmoving full-face glare, and walked on.

'Well,' said Gwennie, walking beside her. 'I'll tell you this. I'll be more than thankful to sit down. I never heard any aeroplane, did you?'

Providential, Mrs Mullen was thinking. Providential. If it hadn't been for that landmine, like as not I'd still be forgiving Dodger. And leaving him my best tea-set, I dare say, to show bygones were bygones. And all just because of coming over so soft in church, giving way to the funeral, and thinking *Poor old Dodger*! That's what funerals do, if one's not on one's guard. And Dodger as ready to get round me as a terrier round a rat.

'I heard one thing,' she said, 'and that's what Dodger Blackbone said to me in the grave. All those Blackbones tumbling in without so much as a by-your-leave, and Mr Kedge and that poor old parson left to perish on the brink. Trust Dodger! Trust him to find a safe place to start blaspheming in! Dodger by name, and Dodger by nature.'

'What did Dodger say?'

'I could no more bring myself to forgive it,' said Lottie Mullen, 'than I could bring myself to repeat it. Not if it was my dying hour.'

She strode on firmly towards the cemetery gates.

W. SOMERSET MAUGHAM

Winter Cruise

Captain Erdmann knew Miss Reid very little till the *Friedrich Weber* reached Haiti. She came on board at Plymouth, but by then he had taken on a number of passengers, French, Belgian, and Haitian, many of whom had travelled with him before, and she was placed at the chief engineer's table. The *Friedrich Weber* was a freighter sailing regularly from Hamburg to Cartagena on the Colombian coast and on the way touching at a number of islands in the West Indies. She carried phosphates and cement from Germany and took back coffee and timber; but her owners, the Brothers Weber, were always willing to send her out of her route if a cargo of any sort made it worth their while. The *Friedrich Weber* was prepared to take cattle, mules, potatoes, or anything else that offered the chance of earning an honest penny. She carried passengers. There were six cabins on the upper deck and six below. The accommodation was not luxurious, but the food was good, plain, and abundant, and the fares were cheap. The round trip took nine weeks and was not costing Miss Reid more than forty-five pounds. She looked forward not only to seeing many interesting places, with historical associations, but also to acquiring a great deal of information that would enrich her mind.

The agent had warned her that till the ship reached Port au Prince in Haiti she would have to share a cabin with another woman. Miss Reid did not mind that, she liked company, and when the steward told her that her companion was Madame Bollin she thought at once that it would be a very good opportunity to rub up her French. She was only very slightly disconcerted when she found that Madame Bollin was coal-black. She told herself that one had to accept the rough with the smooth and that it takes all sorts to make a world. Miss Reid was a good sailor, as indeed was only to be expected since her grandfather had been a naval officer, but after a couple of roughish days the weather was fine and in a very short while she knew all her fellow-passengers. She was a good mixer. That was one of the reasons why she had made a success of her business; she owned a tea room at a celebrated beauty spot in the west of England and she always had a smile and a pleasant word for every customer who came in; she closed down in the winter and for the last four years had taken a cruise. You met such interesting people, she said, and you always learnt something. It was true that the passengers on the *Friedrich Weber* weren't of quite so good a class as those she had met the year before on her Mediterranean cruise, but Miss Reid was not a snob, and though the table manners of some of them shocked her somewhat, determined to look upon the bright side of things she decided to make the best of them. She was a great reader and she was glad, on looking at the ship's library, to find that there were a lot of books by Phillips Oppenheim, Edgar Wallace, and Agatha Christie; but with so many people to talk to she had no time for reading and she made up her mind to leave them till the ship emptied herself at Haiti.

'After all,' she said, 'human nature is more important than literature.'

Miss Reid had always had the reputation of being a good talker and she flattered herself that not once during the many days they were at sea had she allowed the conversation at table to languish. She knew how to draw people out, and whenever a topic seemed to be exhausted she had a remark ready to revive it or another topic waiting on the tip of her tongue to set the conversation off again. Her friend Miss Prince, daughter of the late Vicar of Campden, who had come to see her off at Plymouth, for she lived there, had often said to her:

'You know, Venetia, you have a mind like a man. You're never at a loss for something to say.'

'Well, I think if you're interested in everyone, everyone will be interested in you,' Miss Reid answered modestly. 'Practice makes perfect, and I have the infinite capacity for taking pains which Dickens said was genius.'

Miss Reid was not really called Venetia, her name was Alice, but disliking it she had, when still a girl, adopted the poetic name which she felt so much better suited to her personality.

Miss Reid had a great many interesting talks with her fellow-passengers and she was really sorry when the ship at length reached Port au Prince and the last of them disembarked. The *Friedrich Weber* stopped two days there, during which she visited the town and the neighbourhood. When they sailed she was the only passenger. The ship was skirting the coast of the island stopping off at a variety of ports to discharge or to take on cargo.

'I hope you will not feel embarrassed alone with so many men, Miss Reid,' said the captain heartily as they sat down to midday dinner.

She was placed on his right hand and at table besides sat the first mate, the chief engineer, and the doctor.

'I'm a woman of the world, Captain. I always think if a lady is a lady gentlemen will be gentlemen.'

'We're only rough sailor men, madam, you mustn't expect too much.'

'Kind hearts are more than coronets and simple faith than Norman blood, Captain,' answered Miss Reid.

He was a short, thick-set man, with a clean-shaven head and a red, clean-shaven face. He wore a white stengah-shifter, but except at meal-times unbuttoned at the neck and showing his hairy chest. He was a jovial fellow. He could not speak without bellowing. Miss Reid thought him quite an eccentric, but she had a keen sense of humour and was prepared to make allowances for that. She took the conversation in hand. She had learnt a great deal about Haiti on the voyage out and more during the two days she had spent there, but she knew that men liked to talk rather than to listen, so she put them a number of questions to which she already knew the answers; oddly enough they didn't. In the end she found herself obliged to give quite a little lecture, and before dinner was over, *Mittag Essen* they called it in their funny way, she had imparted to them a great deal of interesting information about the history and economic situation of the Republic, the problems that confronted it, and its prospects for the future. She talked rather slowly, in a refined voice, and her vocabulary was extensive.

At nightfall they put in at a small port where they were to load three hundred bags of coffee, and the agent came on board. The captain asked him to stay to supper and ordered cocktails. As the steward brought them Miss Reid swam into the saloon. Her movements were deliberate, elegant, and self-assured. She always said that you could tell at once by the way she walked if a woman was a lady. The captain introduced the agent to her and she sat down.

'What is that you men are drinking?' she asked.

'A cocktail. Will you have one, Miss Reid?'

'I don't mind if I do.'

She drank it and the captain somewhat doubtfully asked her if she would have another.

'Another? Well, just to be matey.'

The agent, much whiter than some, but a good deal darker than many, was the son of a former minister of Haiti to the German court, and having lived for many years in Berlin spoke good German. It was indeed on this account that he had got a job with a German shipping firm. On the strength of this Miss Reid, during supper, told them all about a trip down the Rhine that she had once taken. Afterwards she and the agent, the skipper, the doctor, and the mate sat round a table and drank beer. Miss Reid made it her business to draw the agent out. The fact that they were loading coffee suggested to her that he would be interested in learning how they grew tea in Ceylon, yes, she had been to Ceylon on a cruise, and the fact that his father was a diplomat made it certain that he would be interested in the royal family of England. She had a very pleasant evening. When she at last retired to rest, for she would never have thought of saying she was going to bed, she said to herself:

'There's no doubt that travel is a great education.'

It was really an experience to find herself alone with all those men. How they would laugh when she told them all about it when she got home! They would say that things like that only happened to Venetia. She smiled when she heard the captain on deck singing with that great booming voice of his. Germans were so musical. He had a funny way of strutting up and down on his short legs singing Wagner tunes to words of his own invention. It was *Tannhäuser* he was singing now (that lovely thing about the evening star) but knowing no German Miss Reid could only wonder what absurd words he was putting to it. It was as well.

'Oh, what a bore that woman is, I shall certainly kill her if she goes on much longer.' Then he broke into Siegfried's martial strain. 'She's a bore, she's a bore, she's a bore. I shall throw her into the sea.'

And that of course is what Miss Reid was. She was a crashing, she was a stupendous, she was an excruciating bore. She talked in a steady monotone, and it was no use to interrupt her because then she started again from the beginning. She had an insatiable thirst for information and no casual remark could be thrown across the table without her asking innumerable questions about it. She was a great dreamer and she narrated her dreams at intolerable length. There was no subject upon which she had not something prosy to say. She had a truism for every occasion. She hit on the commonplace like a hammer driving a nail into the wall. She plunged into the obvious like a clown in a circus jumping through a hoop. Silence did not abash her. Those poor men far away from their homes and the patter of little feet, and with Christmas coming on, no wonder they felt low; she redoubled her efforts to interest and amuse them. She was determined to bring a little gaiety into their dull lives. For that was the awful part of it: Miss Reid meant well. She was not only having a good time herself, but she was trying to give all of them a good time. She was convinced that they liked her as much as she liked them. She felt that she was doing her bit to make the party a success and she was naïvely happy to think that she was succeeding. She told them all about her friend Miss Price and how often she had said to her: Venetia, no one ever has a dull moment in your company. It was the captain's duty to be polite to a passenger and however much he would have liked to tell her to hold her silly tongue he could not, but even if he had been free to say what he liked, he knew that he could not have brought himself to hurt her feelings. Nothing stemmed the torrent of her loquacity. It was as irresistible as a force of nature. Once, in desperation, they began talking German, but Miss Reid stopped this at once.

'Now I won't have you saying things I don't understand. You ought all to make the most of your good luck in having me all to yourselves and practise your English.'

'We were talking of technical matters that would only bore you, Miss Reid,' said the captain.

'I'm never bored. That's why, if you won't think me a wee bit conceited to say so, I'm never boring. You see, I like to know things. Everything interests me and you never know when a bit of information won't come in useful.'

The doctor smiled dryly.

'The captain was only saying that because he was embarrassed. In point of fact he was telling a story that was not fit for the ears of a maiden lady.'

'I may be a maiden lady but I'm also a woman of the world, I don't expect sailors to be saints. You need never be afraid of what you say before me, Captain, I shan't be shocked. I should love to hear your story.'

The doctor was a man of sixty with thin grey hair, a grey moustache, and small bright blue eyes. He was a silent bitter man, and however hard Miss Reid tried to bring him into the conversation it was almost impossible to get a word out of him. But she wasn't a woman who would give in without a struggle, and one morning when they were at sea and she saw him sitting on deck with a book, she brought her chair next to his and sat down beside him.

'Are you fond of reading, Doctor?' she said brightly.

'Yes.'

'So am I. And I suppose like all Germans you're musical.'

'I'm fond of music.'

'So am I. The moment I saw you I thought you looked clever.' He gave her a brief look and pursing his lips went on reading. Miss Reid was not disconcerted.

'But of course one can always read. I always prefer a good talk to a good book. Don't you?'

'No.'

'How very interesting. Now do tell me why?'

'I can't give you a reason.'

'That's very strange, isn't it? But then I always think human nature is strange. I'm terribly interested in people, you know. I always like doctors, they know so much about human nature, but I could tell you some things that would surprise even you. You learn a great deal about people if you run a tea-shop like I do, that's to say if you keep your eyes open.'

The doctor got up.

'I must ask you to excuse me, Miss Reid. I have to go and see a patient.'

'Anyhow I've broken the ice now,' she thought, as he walked away. 'I think he was only shy.'

But a day or two later the doctor was not feeling at all well. He had an internal malady that troubled him now and then, but he was used to it and disinclined to talk about it. When he had one of his attacks he only wanted to be left alone. His cabin was small and stuffy, so he settled himself on a long chair on deck and lay with his eyes closed. Miss Reid was walking up and down to get the half-hour's exercise she took morning and evening. He thought that if he pretended to be asleep she would not disturb him. But when she had passed him half a dozen times she stopped in front of him and stood quite still. Though he kept his eyes closed he knew that she was looking at him.

'Is there anything I can do, Doctor?' she said.

He started.

'Why, what should there be?'

He gave her a glance and saw that her eyes were deeply troubled. 'You look dreadfully ill,' she said.

'I'm in great pain.'

'I know. I can see that. Can't something be done?'

'No, it'll pass off presently.'

She hesitated for a moment then went away. Presently she returned.

'You look so uncomfortable with no cushions or anything. I've brought you my own pillow that I always travel with. Do let me put it behind your head.'

He felt at that moment too ill to remonstrate. She lifted his head gently and put the soft pillow behind it. It really did make him feel more comfortable. She passed her hand across his forehead and it was cool and soft.

'Poor dear,' she said. 'I know what doctors are. They haven't the first idea how to take care of themselves.'

She left him, but in a minute or two returned with a chair and a bag. The doctor when he saw her gave a twitch of anguish.

'Now I'm not going to let you talk, I'm just going to sit beside you and knit. I always think it's a comfort when one isn't feeling very well to have someone near.'

She sat down and taking an unfinished muffler out of her bag began busily to ply her needles. She never said a word. And strangely enough the doctor found her company a solace. No one else on board had even noticed that he was ill, he had felt lonely, and the sympathy of that crashing bore was grateful to him. It soothed him to see her silently working and presently he fell asleep. When he awoke she was still working. She gave him a little smile, but did not speak. His pain had left him and he felt much better.

He did not go into the saloon till late in the afternoon. He found the captain and Hans Krause, the mate, having a glass of beer together.

'Sit down, Doctor,' said the captain. 'We're holding a council of war. You know that the day after tomorrow is Sylvester Abend.'

'Of course.'

Sylvester Abend, New Year's Eve, is an occasion that means a great deal to a German, and they had all been looking forward to it. They had brought a Christmas tree all the way from Germany with them.

'At dinner today Miss Reid was more talkative than ever. Hans and I have decided that something must be done about it.'

'She sat with me for two hours this morning in silence. I suppose she was making up for lost time.'

'It's bad enough to be away from one's home and family just now anyway and all we can do is to make the best of a bad job. We want to enjoy our Sylvester Abend, and unless something is done about Miss Reid we haven't a chance.'

'We can't have a good time if she's with us,' said the mate. 'She'll spoil it as sure as eggs is eggs.'

'How do you propose to get rid of her, short of throwing her overboard?' smiled the doctor. 'She's not a bad old soul; all she wants is a lover.'

'At her age?' cried Hans Krause.

'Especially at her age. That inordinate loquacity, that passion for information, the innumerable questions she asks, her prosiness, the way she goes on and on – it is all a sign of her clamouring virginity. A lover would bring her peace. Those jangled nerves of hers would relax. At least for an hour she would have lived. The deep satisfaction which her being demands would travel through those exacerbated centres of speech, and we should have quiet.'

It was always a little difficult to know how much the doctor meant what he said and when he was having a joke at your expense. The captain's blue eyes, however, twinkled mischievously.

'Well, Doctor, I have great confidence in your powers of diagnosis. The remedy you suggest is evidently worth trying, and since you are a bachelor it is clear that it is up to you to apply it.'

'Pardon me, Captain, it is my professional duty to prescribe remedies for the patients under my charge in this ship, but not to administer them personally. Besides, I am sixty.'

'I am a married man with grown-up children,' said the captain. 'I am old and fat and asthmatic, it is obvious that I cannot be expected to undertake a task of this kind. Nature cut me out for the role of a husband and father not for that of a lover.'

'Youth in these matters is essential and good looks are advantageous,' said the doctor gravely.

The captain gave a great bang on the table with his fist.

'You are thinking of Hans. You're quite right. Hans must do it.'

The mate sprang to his feet.

'Me? Never.'

'Hans, you are tall, handsome, strong as a lion, brave, and young. We have twenty-three days more at sea before we reach Hamburg, you wouldn't desert your trusted old captain in an emergency or let down your good friend the doctor?'

'No, Captain, it's asking too much of me. I have been married less than a year and I love my wife. I can hardly wait to get back to Hamburg. She is yearning for me as I am yearning for her. I will not be unfaithful to her, especially with Miss Reid.'

'Miss Reid's not so bad,' said the doctor.

'Some people might call her even nice-looking,' said the captain.

And indeed when you took Miss Reid feature by feature she was not in fact a plain woman. True, she had a long, stupid face, but her brown eyes were large and she had very thick lashes; her brown hair was cut short and curled rather prettily over her neck; she hadn't a bad skin, and she was neither too fat nor too thin. She was not old as people go nowadays, and if she had told you that she was forty you would have been quite willing to believe it. The only thing against her was that she was drab and dull.

'Must I then for twenty-three mortal days endure the prolixity of that tedious woman? Must I for twenty-three mortal days answer her inane questions and listen to her fatuous remarks? Must I, an old man, have my Sylvester Abend, the jolly evening I was looking forward to, ruined by the unwelcome company of that intolerable virgin? And all because no one can be found to show a little gallantry, a little human kindness, a spark of charity to a lonely woman. I shall wreck the ship.'

'There's always the radio-operator,' said Hans.

The captain gave a loud shout.

'Hans, let the ten thousand virgins of Cologne arise and call you blessed. Steward,' he bellowed, 'tell the radio-operator that I want him.'

The radio-operator came into the saloon and smartly clicked his heels together. The three men looked at him in silence. He wondered uneasily whether he had done something for which he was to be hauled over the coals. He was above the middle height, with square shoulders and narrow hips, erect and slender, his tanned, smooth skin looked as though a razor had never touched it, he had large eyes of a startling blue and a mane of curling golden hair. He was a perfect specimen of young Teutonic manhood. He was so healthy, so vigorous, so much alive that even when he stood some way from you, you felt the glow of his vitality.

'Aryan, all right,' said the captain. 'No doubt about that. How old are you, my boy?'

'Twenty-one, sir.'

'Married?'

'No, sir.'

'Engaged?'

The radio-operator chuckled. There was an engaging boyishness in his laugh.

'No, sir.'

'You know that we have a female passenger on board!'

'Yes, sir.'

'Do you know her?'

'I've said good morning to her when I've seen her on deck.' The captain assumed his most official manner. His eyes, which generally twinkled with fun, were stern and he got a sort of bark in to his rich, fruity voice.

'Although this is a cargo-boat and we carry valuable freight, we also take such passengers as we can get, and this is a branch of our business that the company is anxious to encourage. My instructions are to do everything possible to promote the happiness and comfort of the passengers. Miss Reid needs a lover. The doctor and I have come to the conclusion that you are well suited to satisfy Miss Reid's requirements.'

'Me, sir?'

The radio-operator blushed scarlet and then began to giggle, but quickly composed himself when he saw the set faces of the three men who confronted him.

'But she's old enough to be my mother.'

'That at your age is a matter of no consequence. She is a woman of the highest distinction and allied to all the great families of England. If she were German she would be at least a countess. That you should have been chosen for this responsible position is an honour that you should greatly appreciate. Furthermore, your English is halting and this will give you an excellent opportunity to improve it.'

'That of course is something to be thought of,' said the radio-operator. 'I know that I want practice.'

'It is not often in this life that it is possible to combine pleasure with intellectual improvement, and you must congratulate yourself on your good fortune.'

'But if I may be allowed to put the question, sir, why does Miss Reid want a lover?'

'It appears to be an old English custom for unmarried women of exalted rank to submit themselves to the embraces of a lover at this time of year. The company is anxious that Miss Reid should be treated exactly as she would be on an English ship, and we trust that if she is satisfied, with her aristocratic connexions she will be able to persuade many of her friends to take cruises in the line's ships.'

'Sir, I must ask to be excused.'

'It is not a request that I am making, it is an order. You will present yourself to Miss Reid, in her cabin, at eleven o'clock tonight.'

'What shall I do when I get there?'

'Do?' thundered the captain. 'Do? Act naturally.'

With a wave of the hand he dismissed him. The radio-operator clicked his heels, saluted, and went out.

'Now let us have another glass of beer,' said the captain.

At supper that evening Miss Reid was at her best. She was verbose. She was playful. She was refined. There was not a truism that she failed to utter. There was not a commonplace that she forebore to express. She bombarded them with foolish questions. The captain's face grew redder and redder as he sought to contain his fury; he felt that he could not go on being polite to her any longer and if the doctor's remedy did not help, one day he would forget himself and give her, not a piece, but the whole of his mind.

'I shall lose my job,' he thought, 'but I'm not sure that it wouldn't be worth it.'

Next day they were already sitting at table when she came in to dinner.

'Sylvester Abend tomorrow,' she said, brightly. That was the sort of thing she would say. She went on: 'Well, what have you all been up to this morning?'

Since they did exactly the same thing every day, and she knew very well what that was, the question was enraging. The captain's heart sank. He briefly told the doctor what he thought of him.

'Now, no German, please,' said Miss Reid archly. 'You know I don't allow that, and why, Captain, did you give the poor doctor that sour look? It's Christmas time, you know; peace and goodwill to all men. I'm so excited about tomorrow evening, and will there be candles on the Christmas tree?'

'Naturally.'

'How thrilling! I always think a Christmas tree without candles isn't a Christmas tree. Oh, d'you know, I had such a funny experience last night. I can't understand it at all.'

A startled pause. They all looked intently at Miss Reid. For once they hung on her lips.

'Yes,' she went on in that monotonous, rather finicking way of hers, 'I was just getting into bed last night when there was a knock at my door. "Who is it?" I said. "It's the radio-operator," was the answer. "What is it?" I said. "Can I speak to you?" he said.'

They listened with rapt attention. '"Well, I'll just pop on a dressing-gown," I said, "and open the door." So I popped on a dressing-gown and opened the door. The radio-operator said: "Excuse me, miss, but do you want to send a radio?" Well, I did think it was funny his coming at that hour to ask me if I wanted to send a radio, I just laughed in his face, it appealed to my sense of humour if you understand what I mean, but I didn't want to hurt his feelings so I said: "Thank you so much, but I don't think I want to send a radio." He stood there, looking so funny, as if he was quite embarrassed, so I said: "Thank you all the same for asking me," and then I said "Good night, pleasant dreams", and shut the door.'

'The damned fool,' cried the captain.

'He's young, Miss Reid,' the doctor put in. 'It was excess of zeal. I suppose he thought you would want to send a New Year's greeting to your friends and he wished you to get the advantage of the special rate.'

'Oh, I didn't mind at all. I like these queer little things that happen to one when one's travelling. I just get a good laugh out of them.'

As soon as dinner was over and Miss Reid had left them the captain sent for the radio-operator.

'You idiot, what in heaven's name made you ask Miss Reid last night whether she wanted to send a radio?'

'Sir, you told me to act naturally. I am a radio-operator. I thought it natural to ask her if she wanted to send a radio. I didn't know what else to say.'

'God in heaven,' shouted the captain, 'when Siegfried saw Brunhilde lying on her rock and cried: *Das ist kein Mann*' (the captain sang the words, and being pleased with the sound of his voice, repeated the phrase two or three times before he continued), 'did Siegfried when she awoke ask her if she wished to send a radio, to announce to her papa, I suppose, that she was sitting up after her long sleep and taking notice?'

'I beg most respectfully to draw your attention to the fact that Brunhilde was Siegfried's aunt. Miss Reid is a total stranger to me.'

'He did not reflect that she was his aunt. He knew only that she was a beautiful and defenceless woman of obviously good family and he acted as any gentleman would have done. You are young, handsome, Aryan to the tips of your fingers, the honour of Germany is in your hands.'

'Very good, sir. I will do my best.'

That night there was another knock on Miss Reid's door.

'Who is it?'

'The radio-operator. I have a radio for you, Miss Reid.'

'For me?' She was surprised, but it at once occurred to her that one of her fellow-passengers who had got off at Haiti had sent her New Year's greetings. 'How very kind people are,' she thought. 'I'm in bed. Leave it outside the door.'

'It needs an answer. Ten words prepaid.'

Then it couldn't be a New Year's greeting. Her heart stopped beating. It could only mean one thing; her shop had been burned to the ground. She jumped out of bed.

'Slip it under the door and I'll write the answer and slip it back to you.'

The envelope was pushed under the door and as it appeared on the carpet it had really a sinister look. Miss Reid snatched it up and tore the envelope open. The words swam before her eyes and she couldn't for a moment find her spectacles. This is what she read:

'Happy New Year. Stop. Peace and goodwill to all men. Stop. You are very beautiful. Stop. I love you. Stop. I must speak to you. Stop. Signed: Radio-Operator.'

Miss Reid read this through twice. Then she slowly took off her spectacles and hid them under a scarf. She opened the door.

'Come in,' she said.

Next day was New Year's Eve. The officers were cheerful and a little sentimental when they sat down to dinner. The stewards had decorated the saloon with tropical creepers to make up for holly and mistletoe, and the Christmas tree stood on a table with the candles ready to be lit at supper time. Miss Reid did not come in till the officers were seated, and when they bade her good morning she did not speak but merely bowed. They looked at her curiously. She ate a good dinner, but uttered never a word. Her silence was uncanny. At last the captain could stand it no longer, and he said:

'You're very quiet today, Miss Reid.'

'I'm thinking,' she remarked.

'And will you not tell us your thoughts, Miss Reid?' the doctor asked playfully.

She gave him a cool, you might almost have called it a supercilious, look.

'I prefer to keep them to myself, Doctor. I will have a little more of that hash, I've got a very good appetite.'

They finished the meal in a blessed silence. The captain heaved a sigh of relief. That was what meal-time was for, to eat, not to chatter. When they had finished he went up to the doctor and wrung his hand.

'Something has happened, Doctor.'

'It has happened. She's a changed woman.'

'But will it last?'

'One can only hope for the best.'

Miss Reid put on an evening dress for the evening's celebration, a very quiet black dress, with artificial roses at her bosom and a long string of imitation jade round her neck. The lights were dimmed and the candles on the Christmas tree were lit. It felt a little like being in church. The junior officers were supping in the saloon that evening and they looked very smart in their white uniforms. Champagne was served at the company's expense and after supper they had a *Maibowle*. They pulled crackers. They sang songs to the gramophone, *Deutschland, Deutschland über Alles*, *Alt Heidelberg*, and *Auld Lang Syne*. They shouted out the tunes lustily, the captain's voice rising loud above the others, and Miss Reid joining in with a pleasing contralto. The doctor noticed that Miss Reid's eyes from time to time rested on the radio-operator, and in them he read an expression of some bewilderment.

'He's good-looking fellow, isn't he?' said the doctor.

Miss Reid turned round and looked at the doctor coolly.

'Who?'

'The radio-operator. I thought you were looking at him.'

'Which is he?'

'The duplicity of women,' the doctor muttered, but with a smile he answered: 'He's sitting next to the chief engineer.'

'Oh, of course, I recognize him now. You know, I never think it matters what a man looks like. I'm so much more interested in a man's brains than in his looks.'

'Ah,' said the doctor.

They all got a little tight, including Miss Reid, but she did not lose her dignity and when she bade them good night it was in her best manner.

'I've had a very delightful evening. I shall never forget my New Year's Eve on a German boat. It's been very interesting. Quite an experience.'

She walked steadily to the door, and this was something of a triumph, for she had drunk drink for drink with the rest of them through the evening.

They were all somewhat jaded next day. When the captain, the mate, the doctor, and the chief engineer came down to dinner they found Miss

Reid already seated. Before each place was a small parcel tied up in pink ribbon. On each was written: Happy New Year. They gave Miss Reid a questioning glance.

'You've all been so very kind to me I thought I'd like to give each of you a little present. There wasn't much choice at Port au Prince, so you mustn't expect too much.'

There was a pair of briar pipes for the captain, half a dozen silk hand-kerchiefs for the doctor, a cigar-case for the mate, and a couple of ties for the chief engineer. They had dinner and Miss Reid retired to her cabin to rest. The officers looked at one another uncomfortably. The mate fiddled with the cigar-case she had given him.

'I'm a little ashamed of myself,' he said at last.

The captain was pensive and it was plain that he too was a trifle uneasy.

'I wonder if we ought to have played that trick on Miss Reid,' he said. 'She's a good old soul and she's not rich; she's a woman who earns her own living. She must have spent the best part of a hundred marks on these presents. I almost wish we'd left her alone.'

The doctor shrugged his shoulders.

'You wanted her silenced and I've silenced her.'

'When all's said and done, it wouldn't have hurt us to listen to her chatter for three weeks more,' said the mate.

'I'm not happy about her,' added the captain. 'I feel there's something ominous in her quietness.'

She had spoken hardly a word during the meal they had just shared with her. She seemed hardly to listen to what they said.

'Don't you think you ought to ask her if she's feeling quite well, doctor?' suggested the captain.

'Of course she's feeling quite well. She's eating like a wolf. If you want inquiries made you'd much better make them of the radio-operator.'

'You may not be aware of it, Doctor, but I am a man of great delicacy.'

'I am a man of heart myself,' said the doctor.

For the rest of the journey those men spoilt Miss Reid outrageously. They treated her with the consideration they would have shown to some-one who was convalescent after a long and dangerous illness. Though her appetite was excellent they sought to tempt her with new dishes. The doctor ordered wine and insisted on her sharing his bottle with him. They played dominoes with her. They played chess with her. They played bridge with her. They engaged her in conversation. But there was no doubt about it, though she responded to their advances with politeness, she kept herself to herself. She seemed to regard them with something very like disdain; you might almost have thought that she looked upon those men and their efforts to be amiable as pleasantly ridiculous. She seldom spoke unless spoken to. She read detective stories and at night sat on deck looking at the stars. She lived a life of her own.

At last the journey drew to its close. They sailed up the English Channel on a still grey day; they sighted land. Miss Reid packed her trunk. At two o'clock in the afternoon they docked at Plymouth. The captain, the mate, and the doctor came along to say good-bye to her.

'Well, Miss Reid,' said the captain in his jovial way, 'we're sorry to lose you, but I suppose you're glad to be getting home.'

'You've been very kind to me, you've all been very kind to me, I don't know what I've done to deserve it. I've been very happy with you. I shall never forget you.'

She spoke rather shakily, she tried to smile, but her lips quivered, and tears ran down her cheeks. The captain got very red. He smiled awkwardly.

'May I kiss you, Miss Reid?'

She was taller than he by half a head. She bent down and he planted a fat kiss on one wet cheek and a fat kiss on the other. She turned to the mate and the doctor. They both kissed her.

'What an old fool I am,' she said. 'Everybody's so good.'

She dried her eyes and slowly, in her graceful, rather absurd way, walked down the companion. The captain's eyes were wet. When she reached the quay she looked up and waved to someone on the boat deck.

'Who's she waving to?' asked the captain.

'The radio-operator.'

Miss Price was waiting on the quay to welcome her. When they had passed the Customs and got rid of Miss Reid's heavy luggage they went to Miss Price's house and had an early cup of tea. Miss Reid's train did not start till five. Miss Price had much to tell Miss Reid.

'But it's too bad of me to go on like this when you've just come home. I've been looking forward to hearing all about your journey.'

'I'm afraid there's not very much to tell.'

'I can't believe that. Your trip was a success, wasn't it?'

'A distinct success. It was very nice.'

'And you didn't mind being with all those Germans?'

'Of course they're not like English people. One has to get used to their ways. They sometimes do things that – well, that English people wouldn't do, you know. But I always think that one has to take things as they come.'

'What sort of things do you mean?'

Miss Reid looked at her friend calmly. Her long, stupid face had a placid look, and Miss Price never noticed that in the eyes was a strangely mischievous twinkle.

'Things of no importance really. Just funny, unexpected, rather nice things. There's no doubt that travel is a wonderful education.'

ROALD DAHL

Someone Like You

'Beer?'

'Yes, beer.'

I gave the order and the waiter brought the bottles and two glasses. We poured out our own, tipping the glasses and holding the tops of the bottles close to the glass.

'Cheers,' I said.

He nodded. We lifted our glasses and drank.

It was five years since I had seen him, and during that time he had been fighting the war. He had been fighting it right from the beginning up to now and I saw at once how he had changed. From being a young, bouncing boy, he had become someone old and wise and gentle. He had become gentle like a wounded child. He had become old like a tired man of seventy years. He had become so different and he had changed so much that at first it was embarrassing for both of us and it was not easy to know what to say.

He had been flying in France in the early days and he was in Britain during the Battle. He was in the Western Desert when we had nothing and he was in Greece and Crete. He was in Syria and he was at Habbaniya during the rebellion. He was at Alamein. He had been flying in Sicily and in Italy and then he had gone back and flown again from England. Now he was an old man.

He was small, not more than five feet six, and he had a pale, wide-open face which did not hide anything, and a sharp pointed chin. His eyes were bright and dark. They were never still unless they were looking into your own. His hair was black and untidy. There was a wisp of it always hanging down over his forehead; he kept pushing it back with his hand.

For a while we were awkward and did not speak. He was sitting opposite me at the table, leaning forward a little, drawing lines on the dew of the cold beer glass with his finger. He was looking at the glass, pretending to concentrate upon what he was doing, and to me it seemed as though he had something to say, but that he did not know how to say it. I sat there and picked nuts out of the plate and munched them noisily, pretending that I did not care about anything, not even about making a noise while eating.

Then without stopping his drawing on the glass and without looking up, he said quietly and very slowly, 'Oh God, I wish I was a waiter or a whore or something.'

He picked up his glass and drank the beer slowly and all at once, in two swallows. I knew now that there was something on his mind and I knew that he was gathering courage so that he could speak.

'Let's have another,' I said.

'Yes, let's have a whisky.'

'All right, whisky.'

I ordered two double Scotches and some soda, and we poured the soda into the Scotch and drank. He picked up his glass and drank, put it down, picked it up again and drank some more. As he put down the glass the second time, he leaned forward and quite suddenly he began to talk.

'You know,' he said, 'you know I keep thinking during a raid, when we are running over the target, just as we are going to release our bombs, I keep thinking to myself, Shall I just jink a little; shall I swerve a fraction to one side, then my bombs will fall on someone else. I keep thinking, Whom shall I make them fall on; whom shall I kill tonight? Which ten, twenty or a hundred people shall I kill tonight? It is all up to me. And now I think about this every time I go out.'

He had taken a small nut and was splitting it into pieces with his thumb-nail as he spoke, looking down at what he was doing because he was embarrassed by his own talk.

He was speaking very slowly. 'It would just be a gentle pressure with the ball of my foot upon the rudder bar; a pressure so slight that I would hardly know that I was doing it, and it would throw the bombs on to a different house and on to other people. It is all up to me, the whole thing is up to me, and each time that I go out I have to decide which ones shall be killed. I can do it with the gentle pressure of the ball of my foot upon the rudder bar. I can do it so that I don't even notice that it is being done. I just lean a little to one side because I am shifting my sitting position. That is all I am doing, and then I kill a different lot of people.'

Now there was no dew left upon the face of the glass, but he was still running the fingers of his right hand up and down the smooth surface.

'Yes,' he said, 'it is a complicated thought. It is very far-reaching; and when I am bombing I cannot get it out of my mind. You see it is such a gentle pressure with the ball of the foot; just a touch on the rudder bar and the bomb-aimer wouldn't even notice. Each time I go out, I say to myself, Shall it be these or shall it be those? Which ones are the worst? Perhaps if I make a little skid to the left I will get a houseful of lousy women-shooting German soldiers, or perhaps if I make that little skid I will miss getting the soldiers and get an old man in a shelter. How can I know? How can anyone know these things?'

He paused and pushed his empty glass away from him into the middle of the table.

'And so I never jink,' he added, 'at least hardly ever.'

'I jinked once,' I said, 'ground-strafing. I thought I'd kill the ones on the other side of the road instead.'

'Everybody jinks,' he said. 'Shall we have another drink?'

'Yes, let's have another.'

I called the waiter and gave the order, and while we were waiting, we sat looking around the room at the other people. The place was starting to fill up because it was about six o'clock and we sat there looking at the people who were coming in. They were standing around looking for tables, sitting down, laughing and ordering drinks.

'Look at that woman,' I said. 'The one just sitting down over there.'

'What about her?'

'Wonderful figure,' I said. 'Wonderful bosom. Look at her bosom.'

The waiter brought the drinks.

'Did I ever tell you about Stinker?' he said.

'Stinker who?'

'Stinker Sullivan in Malta.'

'No.'

'About Stinker's dog?'

'No.'

'Stinker had a dog, a great big Alsatian, and he loved that dog as though it was his father and his mother and everything else he had, and the dog loved Stinker. It used to follow him around everywhere he went, and when he went on ops it used to sit on the tarmac outside the hangars waiting for him to come back. It was called Smith. Stinker really loved that dog. He loved it like his mother and he used to talk to it all day long.'

'Lousy whisky,' I said.

'Yes, let's have another.'

We got some more whisky.

'Well, anyway,' he went on, 'one day the squadron got orders to fly to Egypt. We had to go at once; not in two hours or later in the day, but at once. And Stinker couldn't find his dog. Couldn't find Smith anywhere. Started running all over the aerodrome yelling for Smith and going mad yelling at everyone asking where he was and yelling, "Smith, Smith," all over the aerodrome. Smith wasn't anywhere.'

'Where was he?' I said.

'He wasn't there and we had to go. Stinker had to go without Smith and he was mad as a hatter. His crew said he kept calling up over the radio asking if they'd found him. All the way to Heliopolis he kept calling up Malta saying, Have you got Smith, and Malta kept saying, No, they hadn't.'

'This whisky is really terrible,' I said.

'Yes. We must have some more.'

We had a waiter who was very quick.

'I was telling you about Stinker,' he said.

'Yes, tell me about Stinker.'

'Well, when we got to Egypt he wouldn't talk about anything except Smith. He used to walk around acting as though the dog was always with him. Damn fool walked around saying, "Come on, Smith, old boy, come on," and he kept looking down and talking to him as he walked along. Kept reaching down and patting the air and stroking this bloody dog that wasn't there.'

'Where was it?'

'Malta, I suppose. Must have been in Malta.'

'Isn't this awful whisky?'

'Terrible. We must have some more when we've finished this.'

'Cheers.'

'Cheers.'

'Waiter. Oh, waiter. Yes; again.'

'So Smith was in Malta.'

'Yes,' he said. 'And this damn fool Stinker Sullivan went on like this right up to the time he was killed.'

'Must have been mad.'

'He was. Mad as a hatter. You know once he walked into the Sporting Club at Alexandria at drinking time.'

'That wasn't so mad.'

'He walked into the big lounge and as he went in he held the door open and started calling his dog. Then when he thought the dog had come in, he closed the door and started walking right down the length of the room, stopping every now and then and looking round and saying, "Come on, Smith, old boy, come on." He kept flipping his fingers. Once he got down under a table where two men and two women were drinking. He got on to his hands and knees and said, "Smith, come on out of there; come here at once," and he put out his hand and started dragging nothing at all from under the table. Then he apologized to the people at the table. "This is the hell of a dog," he said to them. You should have seen their faces. He went on like that all down the room and when he came to the other end he held the door open for the dog to go out and then went out after it.'

'Man was mad.'

'Mad as a hatter. And you should have seen their faces. It was full of people drinking and they didn't know whether it was them who were crazy or whether it was Stinker. They kept looking up at each other to make sure that they weren't the only ones who couldn't see the dog. One man dropped his drink.'

'That was awful.'

'Terrible.'

The waiter came and went. The room was full of people now, all sitting at little tables, talking and drinking and wearing their uniforms. The pilot poked the ice down into his glass with his finger.

'He used to jink too,' he said.

'Who?'

'Stinker. He used to talk about it.'

'Jinking isn't anything,' I said. 'It's like not touching the cracks on the pavement when you're walking along.'

'Balls. That's just personal. Doesn't affect anyone else.'

'Well, it's like car-waiting.'

'I always do it,' I said.

'What is it?'

'Just as you're going to drive off, you sit back and count twenty, then you drive off.'

'You're mad too,' he said. 'You're like Stinker.'

'It's a wonderful way to avoid accidents. I've never had one in a car yet; at least, not a bad one.'

'You're drunk.'

'No, I always do it.'

'Why?'

'Because then if someone was going to have stepped off the kerb in front of your car, you won't hit them because you started later. You were delayed because you counted twenty, and the person who stepped off the kerb whom you would have hit – you missed him.'

'Why?'

'He stepped off the kerb long before you got there because you counted twenty.'

'That's a good idea.'

'I know it's a good idea.'

'It's a bloody marvellous idea.'

'I've saved lots of lives. And you can drive straight across intersections because the car you would have hit has already gone by. It went by just a little earlier because you delayed yourself by counting twenty.'

'Marvellous.'

'Isn't it?'

'But it's like jinking,' he said. 'You never really know what would have happened.'

'I always do it,' I said.

We kept right on drinking.

'Look at that woman,' I said.

'The one with the bosom?'

'Yes, marvellous bosom.'

He said slowly, 'I bet I've killed lots of women more beautiful than that one.'

'Not lots with bosoms like that.'

'I'll bet I have. Shall we have another drink?'

'Yes, one for the road.'

'There aren't any other women with bosoms like that,' I said. 'Not in Germany anyway.'

'Oh yes there are. I've killed lots of them.'

'All right. You've killed lots of women with wonderful bosoms.'

He leaned back and waved his hand around the room. 'See all the people in this room?' he said.

'Yes.'

'Wouldn't there be a bloody row if they were all suddenly dead; if they all suddenly fell off their chairs on to the floor dead?'

'What about it?'

'Wouldn't there be a bloody row?'

'Certainly there'd be a row.'

'If all the waiters got together and put stuff in all the drinks and every-one died.'

'There'd be a godalmighty row.'

'Well, I've done that hundreds of times. I've killed more people than there are in this room hundreds of times. So have you.'

'Lots more,' I said. 'But that's different.'

'Same sort of people. Men and women and waiters. All drinking in a pub.'

'That's different.'

'Like hell it is. Wouldn't there be a bloody row if it happened here?'

'Bloody awful row.'

'But we've done it. Lots of times.'

'Hundreds of times,' I said. 'This is nothing.'

'This is a lousy place.'

'Yes, it's lousy. Let's go somewhere else.'

'Finish our drinks.'

We finished our drinks and we both tried to pay the bill, so we tossed for it and I won. It came to sixteen dollars and twenty-five cents. He gave the waiter a two-dollar tip.

We got up and walked around the tables and over to the door.

'Taxi,' he said.

'Yes, must have a taxi.'

There wasn't a doorman. We stood out on the kerb waiting for a taxi to come along and he said, 'This is a good town.'

'Wonderful town,' I said. I felt fine. It was dark outside, but there were a few street-lamps, and we could see the cars going by and the people walking on the other side of the street. There was a thin, quiet drizzle falling, and the wetness on the black street shone yellow under the lights of the cars and under the street-lamps. The tyres of the cars hissed on the wet surface.

'Let's go to a place which has lots of whisky,' he said. 'Lots of whisky and a man with egg on his beard serving it.'

'Fine.'

'Somewhere where there are no other people but just us and the man with egg on his beard. Either that.'

'Yes,' I said. 'Either that or what?'

'Or a place with a hundred thousand people in it.'

'Yes,' I said. 'OK.'

We stood there waiting and we could see the lights of the cars as they came round the bend over to the left, coming towards us with the tyres swishing on the wet surface and going past us up the road to the bridge which goes over the river. We could see the drizzle falling through the beams of their headlights and we stood there waiting for a taxi.

L. A. G. STRONG

The Rook

A little gathering of rooks, maybe a dozen, sat waiting for the old man to leave his garden. They sat a couple of hundred yards away, some in a tree, some on the fence beneath it, making little guttural noises to one another. It was a fine frosty morning, and the rooks all looked amazingly big and black and glossy in the bright sunshine. One of them, balancing himself on the topmost wire of the fence, kept tilting awkwardly backwards and forwards, revealing a rainbow sheen upon his neck and shoulders. He hung on strongly with his claws, the wire quivering beneath him. Once he tilted so far that he had to use his wings to regain his balance. The flapping seemed to excite his companions: they fidgeted, and broke into a kind of chatter.

Well aware of the rooks' intention, the old man kept looking at them furtively over his shoulder, and muttering to himself. But he did not allow them to interfere with what he was doing: and paused only to rub the side of his nose with his sleeve, and to give an occasional loud sniff. He was an unlovely old man. He had next to no teeth, and his loose lips, pursed wetly up together, made a sort of horrid frill, resting upon the dirty grey frill of his beard, which in its turn was frilled out upon the red woollen muffler wound about his neck.

Straightening himself, with a last malevolent glance at the rooks, he began to hobble stiffly up the path. After a few steps, he paused, resting a hand upon his side, and a bubble of complaint came from him. Then he disappeared into an outhouse at the top of the garden.

Except that they had stopped making noises to one another, there was nothing to show that the rooks had noticed the old man go in. Then, quite casually, the rook on the fence rose, as if he were tired of an uncomfortable position, and flew to the top of the tree. Choosing another insecure perch, a twig hardly strong enough to bear his weight, he settled, and sat swinging gently up and down. There was a few seconds' pause: and then, by one consent, the whole gathering leaned forward and took off without a sound. Obeying some instinct, they swooped close to the ground, flew towards the old man's wall, careening over it, dipping again the moment it was crossed, and made for the place where he had been working. Reaching it, they nullified all their precautions by rising a few feet in the air, and letting themselves slowly settle, with outspread wings. Then instantly they were waddling and nodding hard, making the most of the stolen moments.

For a while there was nothing but sunlight, brown loam, the glossy nodding bodies and clicking beaks of the birds. Then, sharp and wicked, a crack, which put up every bird within a quarter of a mile: and the vengeful figure of the old man, rifle in hand, blinking and chuckling at the outhouse door.

'Did you get them, Da?' called a woman's voice lazily from inside.

'Did I get them! Oh, bedad, I did. Wan of them, anyway. A quare dart, I gev him! A quare dart! The dirty, thievin' divils.'

'Is he in it? Can ye get him?'

'Tcheh! I cannot, then. What do ye think I am? A jack-rabbit, is it, or a retriever dog, to be leppin' fences, an' all? Wha'?'

'It's a pity, now, you couldn't get him. If we were to get one or two of them, we could be putting them in a pie.'

The old man made a furious gesture, shooting out both his arms stiffly, from his sides.

'There ye go again!' he cried. 'There ye go again! Was there ever such a woman! Amn't I after telling ye, this hundred times and more, that it's only the little rooks do be nice in a pie.'

'Well.' The woman appeared at the door, big, still young, wiping a dish and surveyed him good-humouredly. 'Shoot the little ones, then.'

The old man lowered his head, and darted out his frilly lips. He seemed to be collecting all his passion for some venomous retort, when suddenly he tucked his rifle under his arm, and turned off abruptly down the garden.

The ringleader rook had just risen from the ground with a choice morsel, and flown to the top of a stick, when the rifle went off. As his muscles leaped into action, something struck him a terrific blow in the back, knocking him head over heels. For a moment he sprawled and bumped on the ground: then his wings, beating in a panic, pulled him up, and he followed the others. Slow at first, their wings flapping loud and fast, they gathered momentum, soared above the fence, and made for the elms in the wide school playing field a quarter of a mile away. The rook, trying frantically to catch up with them, found with dismay that he could not keep his balance. His legs and the lower part of his back had all gone numb. They trailed behind, dragging down and down, a heavy aching weight. Terrified, he flew harder than ever, and his flight became unsteady and wild. Each fresh effort sent his head and his breast vertically upwards. He rose and dipped, like a bit of black refuse on the surface of a torrent. Next he began to fly crooked, bearing away from the others in a wide arc, to the left of the trees. He did not know, but it was his instinct, realizing that he could not make the height direct, and taking him towards it by a circuit. Even so, he all but failed to reach the tree tops. Flying grew more difficult every second, his body heavier. His wing muscles ached cruelly, and he panted for breath. After little short of a circle, he saw that he was level with the others. A last effort, a sort of unsteady swoop, and he dropped thankfully at a vacant branch – only to fall heavily upon his breast. His paralysed legs refused their hold, and he tumbled down through the branches, flapping wildly, uttering hoarse screams of consternation. For a moment he hung struggling, his left wing caught in a fork, some forty feet above the grass. Then he flapped it loose, and fell, turning helplessly over. It seemed he must crash upon the ground, but somehow, in the last fraction of a second, his wings half gripped the air, and broke his fall.

Feeling the ground thrust up against him, he tried once more to rise, but being unable to stand, he could not get his wings clear of the ground. All he could achieve was a series of agonized flops, which carried him some yards out from the foot of the tree, into the open space of the school playing field.

Except for the black untidy flapping shape, the field was empty.

Exhausted, ceasing his efforts, the rook lay upon his breast, with outspread wings, and considered. The mixture of indignation and fear, which his situation caused him, rose and fell in his mind. He could no longer feel the lower half of his body. A drowsiness came over him, a sense of temporary security. Under its influence he forgot what had happened, till a sick spasm of pain, and the strangeness of the grass pressing up against his breast, woke him to fresh terror. The instinctive reaction to terror would no longer work. He could not rise and fly away from it. He could only struggle a few inches, his wings ignobly scrabbling along on the ground. Soon that effort was too much: he was glad to leave off, and lie quiet, moving his beak from side to side in puzzled, querulous jerks.

In the big hall of the school, two priests were invigilating an examination. There was no real need for both to be there, but they had work to correct, and, as each was technically on duty, it looked better to be there, in case 'His Reverence' should poke his head in the door – as he well might.

One, dark and sturdy, sat frowning leisurely over his corrections. His face was fresh-coloured, with a blue jowl: his eyebrows met in a dark bunch, and he had wide black nostrils. Now and then he sat back, to admire the neatness with which he made a correction in blue pencil.

Presently, out of the corner of his eye, he saw the tall figure of his colleague standing near his desk. This was a younger man, very young in appearance, handsome, spare, with fair hair that looked red in some lights. His nose looked as if the sculptor had given it a firm pinch between finger and thumb, before it had set hard.

The seated priest took no notice. He started another page of corrections, and forgot the figure by his side – or got used to it in his mind. It was a surprise to him when the young priest spoke.

'*Corvus moribundus est*,' he said, little above a whisper. The other looked up.

'What?' he said. Then, taking in the remark, he turned round vaguely in his chair. 'Eh? Where?'

The younger priest nodded out towards the field. Looking, his friend saw first of all the concourse of rooks in the tree, sitting absolutely silent, without movement. Then, on the grass below, he saw the wounded rook.

'Shot?' he asked, looking up.

'Or just dying.'

'Shot, I think.' He paused, making faces in an effort not to sneeze. 'Yes; I heard a shot, just now.'

They both looked at the rook. It moved its head, and every now and then made a sort of gawky flop with its wings. Even from a distance they could see its hurt, bewildered wonder at the sudden unfamiliarity of its world.

As they looked, a man appeared on a bicycle, riding along the drive which cut the big field in two. He too saw the rook, and waved his arm to scare it. The bird, forgetting its plight, tried to rise, and drove its beak hard against the ground. Terrified, it struggled wildly, and its great uninjured wings beat it maybe a yard away from the danger before it collapsed in a sprawling heap, crushed with pain, unable to stir further. It had gained one thing, however: its back was now turned to the man, so that it could no longer see him. He rode on, in too much of a hurry to stop, screwing his face round two or three times over his shoulder, to look at the rook.

'Will I go out and put it out of its agony?' asked the young priest, when the man had disappeared.

The other started, and breathed out loudly through his nose.

'Yes. It would be well to do that.'

'Right. I won't be long.'

'No hurry. I'll have an eye to them.'

The young priest nodded, and went across to his own desk. Opening it a little way only, and leaning back to peer inside, he reached in his hand swiftly and took out a pointer with a thick handle. He slipped it up his sleeve thin end first, made a wry grimace of a smile at his colleague, and went down the hall. A few heads were raised to look at him. One, near the door, continued to watch vacantly after him down the long stone passage.

The priest at the desk saw. Lowering his eyes to his work, he spoke tonelessly, without raising his voice.

'McComas.'

The boy jumped, gaped at the desk, and went on with his work. The priest did not look up. He corrected a paper, pursing up his lips, fingering one side of his close-shaven chin.

But his thoughts were not on the paper, nor on the boys in front of him. All his imagination was now with the doomed rook. Blaming himself, saying that his interest was morbid, he twisted round in his chair. The rook was still in the field, lying on its breast, its wings sprawled out, moving its head in bewildered indignant jerks. There, he thought, there is a live, sentient creature, like myself: in a minute or so it will experience death, and then all its experience will be at an end, while I, who share life with it now, will still be sitting in this chair. In a dreadful sense, he envied the rook: no, perhaps not envied it, but wished for his soul's correction and wisdom, that he could suffer with it and afterwards return to his own person. His mind was always curious after experience, hankering for it, so far as was lawful. So far, that is of course, as was con—

Ah. There was young Kerrigan, walking casually across the grass. At sight of him the rooks in the tree rose in a body and flew away. To the watcher there was something evil in their flight, as though, having gloated over their brother's misery, they now derisively abandoned him to his death.

As he walked, Kerrigan looked about him, and up at the sky, as if he did not see the rook.

It heard his tread, and did its best to escape: but now it was too far exhausted to stir. He bent over it, grasped one wing close to the body, and with a quick movement secured the other. Thus pinioned, the rook could do nothing. It tried to turn its head and peck him, and he saw with compassion that its beak was full of blood.

The watcher from the window saw the young priest pick up the bird and walk off with it in one hand towards the boys' gardens. He admired the decision with which Kerrigan had picked it up. He himself, he knew, would have hesitated lest the bird squawk or flutter. He would have grabbed at it ineffectively, and added to its suffering.

Fascinated, despising himself, he saw Kerrigan reach the gardens, set down his burden, and take the pointer from his sleeve. Forcing his eyes away, he closed them, and muttered a prayer. O Lord, for all suffering things, that must forsake the light . . .

When next he looked, Kerrigan had taken up a fork, and was digging vigorously.

Sighing, the priest looked at the papers before him, and set himself to his work again. But the signs conveyed no meaning to him. He read the same half page three times over, his pencil waving, hesitating what to mark. Pulling himself harshly together, he read the question carefully, and marked it. Then he put the pencil down on the desk, and stared up at the honour boards at the far end of the hall. Somehow, he knew that what had happened was going to affect him all his life; that it had a meaning for him; that he would never be able to forget it.

Twenty minutes after the rook flew into the old man's garden, it lay, still warm, under two feet of dark, wet earth.

T. F. POWYS

The Key of the Field

Uncle Tiddy stood in the road watching the leaves. The leaves spun around him in the wind, for the October frosts had turned them yellow, and the November blasts had shaken them from the trees.

Uncle Tiddy watched the leaves anxiously. He believed they were speaking to him. The yellow leaves were driven here and there; there was no rest for them, for one gust followed another to whirl them about.

Uncle Tiddy remained still and watched the leaves. The wind grew quiet and the driven leaves settled down into the shape of a key. Uncle Tiddy rejoiced. He believed that, one day, he would possess again the key of the field . . .

The field belonged to Squire Jar of Madder Hall. There was no better field in the whole world than this field.

The field consisted of twelve acres of the richest pasture. The grass grew luxuriantly, and in the middle of the field there was a fine oak-tree that gave a welcome shelter to the cows during the hot summer weather.

The field had once – so Neddy, one of the oldest residents in Madder, used to say – been a portion of the Squire's garden, but the Squire – a worthy man who did not wish to keep all the best of everything for himself – built a low wall, and separated the new field from his old garden, hoping that the field would give to one or other of his tenants a lasting happiness.

But, for all the Squire's generosity – he dearly loves those who live upon his lands – Mr Jar was a man who did not like to be too closely looked upon. And, so in order to prevent any other than his chosen tenants from walking too near his pleasure-garden where the choicest fruits and flowers grew, and where his friends were entertained all the year round, the Squire enclosed the field with high palings – the same that are used by noblemen for their deer parks – and also had a strong iron gate built, that was locked by a massive key.

The first tenant of the field, to whom the Squire's steward – a learned man, though somewhat old – handed the key, was Uncle Tiddy.

Uncle Tiddy was a proper man for the field, for, besides being a good husbandman, he was never a one to pry into other people's doings. Also his wife was dead, which may have been a reason – other than Uncle Tiddy's honesty – for choosing him as a tenant. For Squire Jar, as all people know, is a little afraid of women.

He had no objection, however, to Uncle Tiddy's niece, Lily, who was hardly more than a child, being between sixteen and seventeen years old – a girl who could dance and run as well as the best, and could skip better, since she was six years old, than any other maid in the village.

If Lily had a fault – and she was so well-grown and comely a girl that anyone might expect her to wish to be a wanton – it was that her heart was responsive to the slightest touch of love, though she seemed kinder to her uncle than to any other man.

Who then should have been more happy than Uncle Tiddy with kind Lily to tend him, with the Squire's favour, and with the key of the field in his possession?

But even with a field so well worth having, Uncle Tiddy failed to prosper in his business, and old Grandmother Trott, his near neighbour, told a sad story about him, in which she said that Uncle Tiddy was little better than a sinner – indeed, she believed him to be one.

Grandmother Trott lived with her son John – a widower – and her two grandsons, that were as good as grown men; and ever since the new field was made, the garden hedge removed, palings and a gate set up, this family had envied Uncle Tiddy and desired, with all their hearts, to take the key from him and so to have the field.

Even before Uncle Tiddy had the key, the Trotts had hated the Tiddys, and only because the Tiddys had always been looked upon by others as honest, harmless folk, who kept a few good cows, while the Trotts had been but lean farmers, keeping only a sow or two and a few sickly hens, though now, by thieving management – for they stole the corn from

Squire Jar's granary – they grew every day more prosperous, while Uncle Tiddy became every day poorer.

Seeing how affairs were going with Uncle Tiddy, old Grandmother Trott began to be merry, though sometimes she could be glum enough, and she would tell people – even affirming that she had heard the Squire's steward say the very words – that in the long run the good are sure to prosper, but that every sinner will one day or other lose all that he has.

'There be always ways and means to get the better of a man like Uncle Tiddy,' Grandmother Trott told her son John; 'and we have only to mind what we do say, and the field will be ours.'

''Tis a field,' replied John Trott, 'that be too good for Tiddy, for how can his few cows feed off all the rich grass, and they be old too. 'Tis a sin and wickedness that so good a field should be his. I have often seen that when all the grounds elsewhere be burnt by a hot sun as hard as a biscuit, Tiddy's field be still green and flourishing, so that they few cows 'e do still have be always lying down.'

'Oh yes,' replied Mrs Trott angrily, 'they do lie down, while ours be walking all day to get a bellyful, or else raging with tail on end to rid them of stinging flies.'

Neither was it only the goodness of the grass that pleased the Trotts and made them wish for the field. They wished also to be spoken of as trusted people, as a family that was highly thought of by the Squire and his steward, so that at any holiday gathering they might hear folk tell one another: ''Tis they Trotts who have the best field.'

Grandmother Trott was an ill-favoured woman. She moved uncomfortably, hunching up her shoulders as if she were always creeping in under low doorways.

One would have thought that, if the Squire's steward heard any tale of hers repeated to him, he would have doubted her words, but alas! now that he was grown old and his eyesight dim, he was known to listen to all the tittle-tattle of the village, which no just steward ought to do, though he would still speak to the people exactly as the Squire had spoken to him.

One Sunday in May, when all things abroad were lovely and shining under a generous sun, Grandmother Trott found her two grandsons at play at tosspenny in the back parlour at the farm, and went in to them with her head sunk as usual between her shoulders.

'Ah ha!' she said, with a smirking sneer, 'ain't there no soft and young maids in the lanes for ee to tousle and tread, that thee must stay biding here like two worm-eating moles? Lily Tiddy be just tripped into wood to see what flowers she can spy. Thee be pretty men to toss a penny in a parlour! When I were young, a lusty fellow would throw a girl down time you do look at one, and take good heed that Miss did never rise same as she fell.'

George Trott swore loudly. He put his winnings into his pocket and went out.

George was a big handsome fellow, and he hadn't to whisper many words to Lily under the shade of the big trees where she was picking the bluebells, before she willingly permitted him to enjoy her.

As soon as George began to boast at home about what he had done, Grandmother Trott decided what she should do. In a week or two she was noticed walking down the village, as if something pained her. 'Maybe 'tis me back,' she said, and waited beside the well until Uncle Tiddy went by on his way to the field.

'Look,' she said to Mrs Lugg, who washed the steward's silk hood that he wore on state occasions, and so was in his confidence, 'look, there do go Uncle Tiddy! Why, though 'tis summer weather, 'is topcoat be buttoned to 'is chin. That's a-telling folk that he has sins to hide. He don't look happy neither; 'e be got poor and 'tis 'is evil wickedness that won't let 'e thrive.'

Mrs Trott laughed. She thrust out her head at Mrs Lugg and laughed again.

''Twouldn't do,' she whispered, putting her mouth near to Mrs Lugg's ear, ''twouldn't do for Steward to hear what pranks Uncle Tiddy be up to. Uncle Tiddy bain't no honest liver. No one don't ever hear him curse and swear at thik little cunning wench who do bide wi' 'e. No, no, 'tis all loving words and gifts from Uncle Tiddy to she. 'E don't never strike maiden with milking-stool, as a decent man will sometimes. – 'Tis too loving they be for righteous living.'

Lily was both kind and loving – as Grandmother Trott seemed to guess; she was also very simple and innocent, and one evening when George met her in the wood, he begged so hard to be shown one peep of the Squire's pretty flowers over the wall, that Lily, wishing well to one who had pleased her, unlocked the gate and let him into the field.

It was now that Grandmother Trott began to talk indeed. Whenever she went to the well – and the act of pulling up the water suited her stooping shoulders – there would be sure to be someone for her to talk to, and this is how she began:

'Good folk bain't honoured these days,' she said. 'They others do hide wickedness under a thin covering. Some have what they should never have had if Squire Jar knew all. Uncle Tiddy be a loving one to 'is kith and kin, and when a sort of work be begun at home 'tis continued abroad. Squire were deceived in his good man, but Steward, though 'e be near blind, do pry more closely into what be a-doing.'

Mrs Trott had not been talking long about Uncle Tiddy before the Squire's steward heard from Mrs Lugg what was being said, and told the Squire that Uncle Tiddy permitted the gate of the field to be unlocked and that Lily brought men into the field to look at the Squire's garden.

This the Squire, himself, was aware of, for once, when reading beside the pond of water-lilies and watching some pretty children at play, he knew that someone had watched him.

When Squire Jar heard the truth, he was very angry, and said that he did not like to have his quiet, nor yet his rompings and gay jollity, watched by rude strangers – for Squire Jar can be merry at times, as well as grave – and thus it came about that the key of the field was taken from Uncle Tiddy and given to John Trott.

That was a joyful day for John Trott when he received the key of the field.

Mr Jar's trusted steward, who always wore the white robes of his office when anything important was to be done, delivered the key with his own hands to John Trott, in the sight of all people. He also told him – as was proper he should – the Squire's commands, but he hemmed and coughed a little when he said that Uncle Tiddy had disobeyed them in certain matters, for the steward had already forgotten what Uncle Tiddy had done.

As soon as he had finished with his talk, John Trott replied briskly: 'I will never' – he swore on oath – 'look over the Squire's wall. I swear it. I have no wish to watch the Squire, whether he be merry or sad, nor yet to see how his young friends disport themselves. What others do is no business of mine; my only desire is that my family should prosper, and that I should make a fair and honest profit at my trade.'

The reply pleased the steward, who shook John by the hand, and they ate and drank together as the custom is upon such an occasion . . .

Nature works apace, and when Lily walked out one Sunday, she was carrying a baby, and the people – as people will, all the world over – nodded and gossiped.

'Ah yes,' said Mrs Sly, the wife of Nicholas, 'many's the time that I've seen Uncle Tiddy taking in the clothes frozen stiff in winter time for thik lazy maid. And the mats too, that be only straw woons, I've seen 'e shaking. Who does not know that one kindness do lead to another in people's homes?'

Uncle Tiddy was too proud a man to deny these evil tales, though he knew that he was being talked about, but, since he had been deprived of the field, he hardly cared what happened to him.

Troubles do not sleep like quiet, well-pastured cows, and poverty – when once it gets hold – rarely lets go again. Soon Uncle Tiddy had nothing left – no cows, nor even any little pigs, nor cock nor hen. He had always spent more money than he should, and so when the evil days overtook him, he had no savings put away, and Lily was forced to work as a day-servant at the house of the steward.

But, though Uncle Tiddy was now so poor a man as to be obliged to live upon the small wages that Lily brought to him, the Trotts still hated and still wished to torment him.

'There is no trusting to Squire Jar,' Grandmother Trott said crossly, 'and though the good steward makes all things seem easy to us, both here and hereafter, yet that cursed Squire – a man who reaps where he has never sown – may suddenly break into our house, like a thief, and take away the key of the field and give it back again to Uncle Tiddy. Only look how Tiddy troubles us and annoys our brave children. He is for ever standing before the iron gate that leads into the field. He looks through the bars as though the field were still his own, and waits only for the key in order to go in. I have watched him more than once, and he looks so lovingly into the field, as if he tried to draw the field into his own body, and so to deprive us of it.'

Grandmother Trott spoke the truth, for Uncle Tiddy would be always looking through the gate into the field. Any way that he took – for he went out of a morning whether the rain fell or the sun shone – would always bring him to the locked gate of the field.

'You do not know,' he would say to Lily in the evening – for they were alone again, Lily's baby having died of the smallpox: 'You do not know, Lily, how much I long to possess again the key of the field. Will the iron gate be locked against me for ever?'

And Lily would then try, with all the kindness that was in her heart, to console him for the loss.

'Do not sorrow overmuch,' she said, one evening, 'for though the steward seems to command all here, he does not always know his master's mind. And besides, though the key of the field has been given to the Trotts, yet 'tis said that the Squire always keeps a master key at the Manor House, with which he can open, whenever he chooses, any gate upon his land.'

'But the Squire passed me on the hill to-day, and he turned his face away from me,' groaned Uncle Tiddy, 'and unless I can take the key of the field from the Trotts I shall never get in.'

'Alas!' replied Lily, 'I know well enough that the Squire leaves everything nowadays to his steward, an old man who only thinks of the fine house he lives in, the rich clothes he wears, and the ring upon his finger. Besides that, he drinks too much wine. Since I have been a servant within his doors, I have learned to know his ways, and he is a man very easy to deceive. My fellow-servants are always cheating him in one way or the other and they never get found out, for now he grows so blind that he hardly knows the night from the day.'

'Oh, but I long for the field,' said Uncle Tiddy, sadly; 'though I do not want it now for any worldly profit that it gives, I only wish to get again the peace and joy of that field, so green and safe it used to be, so freed from loud noises – a place where only the sound of gentle laughter and the happy voices of the Squire's guests are ever heard.'

'I don't suppose,' said Lily, in a low tone, 'that any of us poor village people could ever get invited into the Squire's garden.'

Uncle Tiddy shook his head.

'No, we cannot go there,' he replied, 'but we may get into the field if we find the key. It's a field to delight in, a rich pasture. I remember how

I used to lie under the oak, while my quiet cows fed near by. I would lie so still that my very life and being seemed to leave me, for the holy stillness of the field entered into me and I lost myself in it. The air was so very still and I lay so contentedly that I hardly knew myself to be alive.'

'But do not go, I beg you,' said Lily, 'always to the gate of the field, for the Trotts are greedy people and are suspicious of what you do. They think that you envy their large red and white cows that feed in the field, and who's to tell that they might not suddenly swing open the gate and crush you?'

Uncle Tiddy hung his head and said no more.

Grandmother Trott had noticed him going to the gate, and she feared that, if the Squire saw him there, he might be let through, and so she wished to harm him again, hoping that he might die of sorrow.

'Surely,' she said to her grandsons, 'thee bain't the ones to let a silly maid stay happy when once she be fallen? Where a hedge be broke 'tis easy climbing, and a second mowing be the greatest pleasure. To her again, my fine boys!'

This time it was James who was sent to do the mischief, and very willingly he went to it. He lay among some tall bushes in wait for Lily, who had to pass along a dark lane on her way home. Seeing her come hurrying by, he laid hold of her and, by means of a blow or two with his fist, he forced her to yield herself to his pleasure.

Lily wept much, but she did not tell her uncle what had happened; and in a few months' time a merry word went about the village that Uncle Tiddy had been at work again, and people said that another child was to be born in his house – which happened as was foretold, only Lily died in childbed, and the babe died too.

Uncle Tiddy was brought before the Squire's steward upon an incestuous charge, for James Trott swore to having seen the act committed beside the field gate before the sun was risen. 'Many a time,' he said, 'he had seen it done.' But the steward who was the chief magistrate in those parts, being a little put out at the necessity of going to the court, had forgotten to drink his bottle that morning, and so could see and hear a little more clearly than usual. This being so, Master Steward had a word or two to say to James Trott, and Uncle Tiddy was allowed to go home.

Lily was buried with her child in a grave near to where her first baby was laid; Uncle Tiddy lived alone, and his wants were relieved by the parish, by order of the Squire's steward . . .

But even now, though anyone would have thought that they had got the better of him and that he was put down, never to arise, the Trotts would not let Uncle Tiddy alone. A new-born calf of theirs happened to die in the field – owing to neglect, for the Trotts took no thought of their beasts when they needed help – and so when this calf died they wished to blame someone for their fault. They blamed Uncle Tiddy, for Grand-mother Trott had seen him look through the gate and bewitch the cows. 'He wrote words in the dust,' she said, 'and then cast the dirt through the gate at the cows. Who can tell what will happen in the future?' cried Grandmother Trott, 'for, as long as Uncle Tiddy do live 'e may one day reach hold of the key. We be all fools to trust to Squire Jar, for Squire bain't never out – except now and again he walks upon Madder Hill. He never looks after his affairs, he is always enjoying himself in his own gar-den, and there bain't no trusting a man who do sit brooding at home. Uncle Tiddy be the one to watch what we be about, and one day, when my son do take a glass wi' Steward, 'e may let fall the key. Folks do tell how Steward do tipple it finely now, and that 'e don't know right from wrong when 'e be drunk. And, maybe, if Uncle Tiddy did steal the key, Steward might think it were his own to hold. We mustn't let Uncle Tiddy have no rest till 'e be dead.'

Grandmother Trott found Mrs Lugg and Mrs Sly beside the well, where they were come to draw water. Mrs Sly had a swollen foot that she was showing to Mrs Lugg.

'I have something to say to 'ee,' said Grandmother Trott, after admiring Mrs Sly's foot, and speaking in a whisper: 'Uncle Tiddy, now 'e bain't got nothing to do, have begun to talk against Squire Jar. He do say that 'tain't 'e alone who have been merry wi' a young maid. 'E do say Squire 'imself have a-done it. Uncle Tiddy do curse and swear how 'tis true what 'e do say. Why, bless us all, 'e did stand beside Farmer Told's barn – where the echo do shout and talk – and damn 'imself to hell if his words weren't true, naming even the village where the maid did live. He said – and swore to it – that Squire did come at his girl in the night-time and over-shadowed her with his black cloak that be like a raven's wings . . .'

The people now began to believe all that Grandmother Trott had to say against Uncle Tiddy, though at first they had not believed her. Uncle Tiddy had been kind to many of them, but even those whom he had once befriended now turned against him, because they knew that he had nothing left to give. The people even forgot how they had once loved Lily, who used to be so merry and playful, and would please even old people by her goodness, for she would talk with old Nicholas Sly, who had a wen as big as a walnut upon his forehead, and was so ugly and foul a man that all the children ran away from him.

Uncle Tiddy was now unable to go out in the day-time, for he could not bear to be treated rudely. Sometimes the village brats would throw dirt after him and spit upon him, so that he was forced to remain indoors until darkness came.

But when the sun went down behind Madder Hill, and the kind darkness of night brought solace to unhappy man, then Uncle Tiddy would go abroad and search diligently for the key of the field.

Perhaps he might have given up all hope of finding it, and used an old cart-rope to end his torment, had it not been that, in loitering by the field gate upon a very still night when all the village was asleep, he thought he heard a voice that he knew well singing some pretty lullaby over the field and in the Squire's garden. The voice he was sure was Lily's, and Uncle Tiddy fancied, as he listened, that infant voices joined in her songs. The sound of their strange singing – though Uncle Tiddy only heard it that once – made him the more eager to get into the field, for he believed that, if he lay down to sleep there, the sound of those voices might come to him again.

And so Uncle Tiddy used to cover himself with a large cloak, and when each evening came, he would set out to search for the key.

The autumn leaves, when they whirled about him and then lay still and silent, told him that the key existed for which he looked. High up in the heavens, upon clear nights, he saw the key – a key of shining stars. Once, when he stood upon the low cliffs and looked into the sea – the waters being all still – he thought he saw, lying very deep in the sea, the key of the field.

At first when Uncle Tiddy began his search, he used to look in the village and usually he would go to the gate itself, hoping that one of the Trotts might have dropped the key when they locked the gate.

After he had searched for a few nights, Uncle Tiddy's troubles and sorrows seemed lighter for him to bear. He even supposed himself to be happier than he had been in the old days, only excepting, of course, those pleasant hours when he used to lay him down to rest in the shelter of the locked field. For, even when Lily had been alive to love him, his troubles and anxieties had often been hard. He had always feared for Lily, knowing how loving she was, and that, for this very reason, she was more likely to become a prey to the spoiler.

In other ways, too, beside the fears he had for Lily, he used to be troubled. He could never understand how the Squire – whom he always believed to be a good man – could allow a steward, who had seldom his ears open to anything but lies, to rule his fine estate. Uncle Tiddy always thought it a very strange thing that this Squire, who owned so many acres of land, should not have found a way – other than the crude methods of his sottish steward who, more often than not, would use the whipping-post as a cure – to protect the simple, the loving, and the kind from horrid outrage.

But now that Uncle Tiddy sought the key so assiduously, his feelings were different. He looked only to the field for comfort.

'Oh,' he would cry out, starting up hurriedly when the darkness drew near, 'oh, that I might find the key! Then would I unlock the gate and, full of joy, enter the field. I would lie down there, but not as I used to lie, for I would never wish, as I used to do, to return again to the village, for I have no hope now left, outside the field . . .'

After a month or two Uncle Tiddy was not content to look only in the village for the key. He thought that he might find it farther away.

Ever since John Trott had possessed the key, that cunning man had prospered finely. The Trotts had even done so well that they had bought land. They owned a large down of near a hundred acres of goodish pasture, that lay behind Madder Hill. And so, Uncle Tiddy thought it not unlikely that while John was looking to his affairs upon the hill, the key might fall out of his pocket and be lost, for Grandmother Trott was too lazy a gossip ever to mend a broken coat.

Besides that chance, there was also the likelihood that one of the sons of John Trott might have the key of the field in his keeping when he walked out upon a Sunday with his young girl, and, indeed, there was hardly a Madder girl that the two young men did not try to lead into evil ways. So Uncle Tiddy thought it not unlikely that, in the excitement of their naughtiness, one or other of them might let fall the key.

As Uncle Tiddy walked about by night, searching carefully upon the hill, often kneeling upon his knees to be nearer to the ground, a curious fancy would sometimes come to him that Lily, whom he had ever loved as a good man loves a child, moved beside him and helped him to look for the key . . .

As time went, on the Trotts – as was proper they should – grew richer and richer, for what the young men spent upon drink or women – they even went into the steward's own house in search of their dainties – they easily made up, or else their father did for them, by cheating someone poorer than themselves in a cunning deal.

Uncle Tiddy was glad that they prospered, for, caring nothing now for any possession in the whole world other than the key of the field, he thought that the Trotts – in order to be rid of his importunity – might yield him that, because having so much land they scarcely seemed to give a thought to the field.

They even began to despise and to hate it, saying that it was too small and too mean, a place of too narrow a compass to yield a man any profit. And besides, being too near the Squire's gardens, they could not drink or sing or lecher there as in other grounds.

One evening about twilight, when the barn owls flutter along the hedgerows, Uncle Tiddy went out, and meeting John Trott, he asked him boldly for the key of the field.

John Trott only laughed loudly and went home laughing, leaving Uncle Tiddy to continue his search for the key. So great now was Uncle Tiddy's hurry and excitement to find what he sought, that he hardly allowed himself time to eat or to sleep. In the day-time he would lay upon his bed and plan in his mind which field to go to when the evening came. If ever he did happen to drop off into a little sleep, a dream would come to him, in which he held the key in his hand, and he would walk along always with a gay step to unlock the gate, though more than once in the dream the key turned in the lock damnable hard.

He had sunk one evening, a little before the time of his going out, into a restless slumber, when all at once he leapt up – the time being near to midnight – out of a strange dream, and putting his cloak over him, he went out into the night.

Uncle Tiddy did not take the path to the downs as he had so often done of late, but turned along the village street and passed the Inn without looking at the ground. This was curious, for he used always to look there when he went by, expecting that John Trott might easily have dropped the key when he walked a little tipsily out of the Inn gate.

But Uncle Tiddy did not hesitate now nor yet look at all; he walked boldy, as if he knew what to do.

Presently he came to the churchyard gate. He opened it and went in.

The time of year was winter. Mournful clouds hung low, while behind them, hidden as by a thick cloak, was the moon. Uncle Tiddy knew the way. He found Lily's grave and knelt beside it.

And now Uncle Tiddy bethought him of one of the rights that belong to those who are born upon Squire Jar's land. For everyone so born is entitled to call boldly upon the Squire for one gift, in the name of a loving one, but that gift must be the last. Uncle Tiddy would not have ventured upon using this right – for he knew the Squire's rules – had he not first asked the steward for the key. But the steward, as Grandmother Trott had foretold, had come to believe the evil stories that were told about Uncle Tiddy, and so, when he asked for the key, wishing only to walk in the field for a little, the steward looked grimly at him and, with an ugly oath, told him he would be locked out for ever.

"Tis the Squire's own words,' said the steward, 'for without are dogs and sorcerers and whoremongers and murderers . . .'

Uncle Tiddy was about to call upon the Squire for the key when his faith failed him. 'Suppose,' he thought, 'that the Squire is a hard man, suppose that were I to call there would be none to answer.'

Uncle Tiddy wept bitterly. He wished a thousand times that he had never been born. Despair held him fast and would have killed him, only that Uncle Tiddy, scarce knowing what he did in his agony, cried out to the Squire for the key, and then lay down as though he were dead.

For a long while he lay there until he knew that Squire Jar had entered the churchyard and was standing beside him.

'I never refuse to anyone a harmless wish,' said the Squire. 'I was walking tonight under the trees in my garden when I heard you call to me for the key of the field.'

Uncle Tiddy endeavoured to rise to greet the Squire, but despair had so trod him down that he could not move.

Then the Squire held out his hand to him and raised him up.

'You have asked me for the key,' said the Squire, kindly; 'do you wish to remain in the field when you have unlocked the gate?'

'Yes, for ever,' replied Uncle Tiddy, 'and I require only the smallest space where a man can lie. I wish to forget.'

'Do you wish to forget Lily?' asked the Squire in a very low tone.

'Where she is, I will be,' said Uncle Tiddy, 'for we have loved much.'

'Then it's true that you have sinned,' said the Squire.

'If to love is to sin, then we have sinned,' replied Uncle Tiddy.

The Squire was silent.

'Give me the key,' cried Uncle Tiddy, 'do not refuse me the key.'

'I give you mine own,' said the Squire, and he handed to Uncle Tiddy a key of gold. 'I will go with you,' said the Squire, 'for John Trott may oppose your entrance into the field.'

The Squire and Uncle Tiddy left the churchyard. On the way to the field Mr Jar talked of the crops and how well he remembered the good hay that Uncle Tiddy had made in former days and how he had sold it to the steward for his master's stables.

They reached the gate of the field and found no one there to prevent their entering, and Uncle Tiddy – having the master key in his hand – easily unlocked the gate and let himself into the field, where, thinking that the Squire had left him, he lay down to sleep. He lay very still and thought that he slept soundly – so soundly that he might have slept for a thousand years. But whether or no he had really slept, he was not sure. He looked up and saw that the Squire was still beside him and the winter's night was the same.

'Come,' said Squire Jar, gently raising Uncle Tiddy from the grass; 'come, we will walk through the field – but do you not hear anything?'

'I hear someone singing,' replied Uncle Tiddy. 'The voice is Lily's; she is singing to her babies in your garden.'

Then Uncle Tiddy grew sad. But he still walked with the Squire, until he came to where he remembered the wall had been.

'Look,' said the Squire, 'for my garden is beautiful, even in winter. The flowers shine like precious stones; the walks are green, and the air is mild and sweet. You have been my tenant for a season: you will now be my guest for ever.'

'We are in your garden,' cried Uncle Tiddy, gladly. 'But where is the Wall?'

'You unlocked the gate of the field with my key,' replied the Squire.

GRAHAM GREENE

The Hint of an Explanation

A long train journey on a late December evening, in this new version of peace, is a dreary experience. I suppose that my fellow traveller and I could consider ourselves lucky to have a compartment to ourselves, even though the heating apparatus was not working, even though the lights went out entirely in the frequent Pennine tunnels and were too dim anyway for us to read our books without straining the eyes, and though there was no restaurant car to give at least a change of scene. It was when we were trying simultaneously to chew the same kind of dry bun bought at the same station buffet that my companion and I came together. Before that we had sat at opposite ends of the carriage, both muffled to the chin in overcoats, both bent low over type we could barely make out, but as I threw the remains of my cake under the seat our eyes met, and he laid his book down.

By the time we were half-way to Bedwell Junction we had found an enormous range of subjects for discussion; starting with buns and the weather, we had gone on to politics, the Government, foreign affairs, the atom bomb, and by an inevitable progression, God. We had not, however, become either shrill or acid. My companion, who now sat opposite me, leaning a little forward, so that our knees nearly touched, gave such an impression of serenity that it would have been impossible to quarrel with him, however much our views differed, and differ they did profoundly.

I had soon realized I was speaking to a Roman Catholic – to someone who believed – how do they put it? – in an omnipotent and omniscient Deity, while I am what is loosely called an agnostic. I have a certain intuition (which I do not trust, founded as it may well be on childish experiences and needs) that a God exists, and I am surprised occasionally into belief by the extraordinary coincidences that beset our path like the traps set for leopards in the jungle, but intellectually I am revolted at the whole notion of such a God who can so abandon his creatures to the enormities of Free Will. I found myself expressing this view to my companion who listened quietly and with respect. He made no attempt to interrupt – he showed none of the impatience or the intellectual arrogance I have grown to expect from Catholics; when the lights of a wayside station flashed across his face which had escaped hitherto the rays of the one globe working in the compartment, I caught a glimpse suddenly of – what? I stopped speaking, so strong was the impression. I was carried back ten years, to the other side of the great useless conflict, to a small town, Gisors in Normandy. I was again, for a moment, walking on the ancient battlements and looking down across the grey roofs, until my eyes for some reason lit on one stony 'back' out of the many, where the face of a middle-aged man was pressed against a window pane (I suppose that face has ceased to exist now, just as perhaps the whole town with its medieval memories has been reduced to rubble). I remembered saying to myself with astonishment, 'That man is happy – completely happy.' I looked across the compartment at my fellow traveller, but his face was already again in shadow. I said weakly, 'When you think what God – if there is a God – allows. It's not merely the physical agonies, but think of the corruption, even of children . . .'

He said, 'Our view is so limited,' and I was disappointed at the conventionality of his reply. He must have been aware of my disappointment (it was as though our thoughts were huddled as closely as ourselves for warmth), for he went on, 'Of course there is no answer here. We catch hints . . .' and then the train roared into another tunnel and the lights again went out. It was the longest tunnel yet; we went rocking down it and the cold seemed to become more intense with the darkness, like an icy fog (when one sense – of sight – is robbed, the others grow more acute). When we emerged into the mere grey of night and the globe lit up once more, I could see that my companion was leaning back on his seat.

I repeated his last word as a question, 'Hints?'

'Oh, they mean very little in cold print – or cold speech,' he said, shivering in his overcoat. 'And they mean nothing at all to another human being than the man who catches them. They are not scientific evidence – or evidence at all for that matter. Events that don't, somehow, turn out as they were intended – by the human actors, I mean, or by the thing behind the human actors.'

'The thing?'

'The word Satan is so anthropomorphic.' I had to lean forward now: I wanted to hear what he had to say. I am – I really am, God knows – open to conviction. He said, 'One's words are so crude, but I sometimes feel pity for that thing. It is so continually finding the right weapon to use against its Enemy and the weapon breaks in its own breast. It sometimes seems to me so – powerless. You said something just now about the corruption of children. It reminded me of something in my own childhood. You are the first person – except for one – that I have thought of telling it to, perhaps because you are anonymous. It's not a very long story, and in a way it's relevant.'

I said, 'I'd like to hear it.'

'You mustn't expect too much meaning. But to me there seems to be a hint. That's all. A hint.'

He went slowly on turning his face to the pane, though he could have seen nothing in the whirling world outside except an occasional signal lamp, a light in a window, a small country station torn backwards by our rush, picking his words with precision. He said, 'When I was a child they taught me to serve at Mass. The church was a small one, for there were very few Catholics where I lived. It was a market town in East Anglia, surrounded by flat chalky fields and ditches – so many ditches. I don't suppose there were fifty Catholics all told, and for some reason there was a tradition of hostility to us. Perhaps it went back to the burning of a Protestant martyr in the sixteenth century – there was a stone marking the place near where the meat stalls stood on Wednesdays. I was only half aware of the enmity, though I knew that my school nickname of Popey Martin had something to do with my religion and I had heard that my father was nearly excluded from the Constitutional Club when he first came to the town.

'Every Sunday I had to dress up in my surplice and serve Mass. I hated it – I have always hated dressing up in any way (which is funny when you come to think of it), and I never ceased to be afraid of losing my place in the service and doing something which would put me to ridicule. Our

178

services were at a different hour from the Anglican, and as our small, far-from-select band trudged out of the hideous chapel the whole of the townsfolk seemed to be on the way past to the proper church – I always thought of it as the proper church. We had to pass the parade of their eyes, indifferent, supercilious, mocking; you can't imagine how seriously religion can be taken in a small town – if only for social reasons.

'There was one man in particular; he was one of the two bakers in the town, the one my family did not patronize. I don't think any of the Catholics patronized him because he was called a free-thinker – an odd title, for, poor man, no one's thoughts were less free than his. He was hemmed in by his hatred – his hatred of us. He was very ugly to look at, with one wall-eye and a head the shape of a turnip, with the hair gone on the crown, and he was unmarried. He had no interests, apparently, but his baking and his hatred, though now that I am older I begin to see other sides to his nature – it did contain, perhaps, a certain furtive love. One would come across him suddenly, sometimes, on a country walk, especially if one was alone and it was Sunday. It was as though he rose from the ditches and the chalk smear on his clothes reminded one of the flour on his working overalls. He would have a stick in his hand and stab at the hedges, and if his mood were very black he would call out after you strange abrupt words that were like a foreign tongue – I know the meaning of those words, of course, now. Once the police went to his house because of what a boy said he had seen, but nothing came of it except that the hate shackled him closer. His name was Blacker, and he terrified me.

'I think he had a particular hatred of my father – I don't know why. My father was manager of the Midland Bank, and it's possible that at some time Blacker may have had unsatisfactory dealings with the bank – my father was a very cautious man who suffered all his life from anxiety about money – his own and other people's. If I try to picture Blacker now I see him walking along a narrowing path between high windowless walls, and at the end of the path stands a small boy of ten – me. I don't know whether it's a symbolic picture or the memory of one of our encounters – our encounters somehow got more and more frequent. You talked just now about the corruption of children. That poor man was preparing to revenge himself on everything he hated – my father, the Catholics, the

God whom people persisted in crediting – by corrupting me. He had evolved a horrible and ingenious plan.

'I remember the first time I had a friendly word from him. I was passing his shop as rapidly as I could when I heard his voice call out with a kind of sly subservience as though he were an under-servant. "Master David," he called, "Master David," and I hurried on. But the next time I passed that way he was at his door (he must have seen me coming) with one of those curly cakes in his hand that we called Chelsea buns. I didn't want to take it, but he made me, and then I couldn't be other than polite when he asked me to come into his parlour behind the shop and see something very special.

'It was a small electric railway – a rare sight in those days, and he insisted on showing me how it worked. He made me turn the switches and stop and start it, and he told me that I could come in any morning and have a game with it. He used the word "game" as though it were something secret, and it's true that I never told my family of this invitation and of how, perhaps twice a week those holidays, the desire to control that little railway became overpowering, and looking up and down the street to see if I were observed, I would dive into the shop.'

Our larger, dirtier, adult train drove into a tunnel and the light went out. We sat in darkness and silence, with the noise of the train blocking our ears like wax. When we were through we didn't speak at once and I had to prick him into continuing.

'An elaborate seduction,' I said.

'Don't think his plans were as simple as that,' my companion said, 'or as crude. There was much more hate than love, poor man, in his make-up. Can you hate something you don't believe in? And yet he called himself a free-thinker. What an impossible paradox, to be free and to be so obsessed. Day by day all through those holidays his obsession must have grown, but he kept a grip; he bided his time. Perhaps that thing I spoke of gave him the strength and the wisdom. It was only a week from the end of the holidays that he spoke to me of what concerned him so deeply.

'I heard him behind me as I knelt on the floor, coupling two coaches. He said, "You won't be able to do this, Master David, when school starts." It wasn't a sentence that needed any comment from me any more than the one that followed, "You ought to have it for your own, you ought," but how skilfully and unemphatically he had sowed the longing, the idea of a possibility . . . I was coming to his parlour every day now; you see I had to cram every opportunity in before the hated term started again, and I suppose I was becoming accustomed to Blacker, to that wall eye, that turnip head, that nauseating subservience. The Pope, you know, describes himself as "The servant of the servants of God", and Blacker – I sometimes think, that Blacker was "the servant of the servants of . . ." well, let it be.

'The very next day, standing in the doorway watching me play, he began to talk to me about religion. He said, with what untruth even I recognized, how much he admired the Catholics; he wished he could believe like that, but how could a baker believe? He accented "a baker" as one might say a biologist, and the tiny train spun round the gauge O track. He said, "I can bake the things you eat just as well as any Catholic can," and disappeared into his shop. I hadn't the faintest idea what he meant. Presently he emerged again, holding in his hand a little wafer. "Here," he said, "eat that and tell me . . ." When I put it in my mouth I could tell that it was made in the same way as our wafers for communion – he had got the shape a little wrong, that was all, and I felt guilty and irrationally scared. "Tell me," he said, "what's the difference?"

'"Difference?" I asked.

'"Isn't that just the same as you eat in church?"

'I said smugly, "It hasn't been consecrated."

'He said, "Do you think if I put the two of them under a microscope, you could tell the difference?" But even at ten I had the answer to that question. "No," I said, "the – accidents don't change," stumbling a little on the word "accidents" which had suddenly conveyed to me the idea of death and wounds.

'Blacker said with sudden intensity, "How I'd like to get one of your ones in my mouth – just to see . . ."

'It may seem odd to you, but this was the first time that the idea of transubstantiation really lodged in my mind. I had learnt it all by rote; I had grown up with the idea. The Mass was as lifeless to me as the sentences in *De Bello Gallico*, communion a routine like drill in the school-yard, but here suddenly I was in the presence of a man who took it seriously, as seriously as the priest whom naturally one didn't count – it was his job. I felt more scared than ever.

'He said, "It's all nonsense, but I'd just like to have it in my mouth."

'"You could if you were a Catholic," I said naïvely. He gazed at me with his one good eye like a Cyclops. He said, "You serve at Mass, don't you? It would be easy for you to get at one of those things. I tell you what I'd do – I'd swap this electric train set for one of your wafers – consecrated, mind. It's got to be consecrated."

'"I could get you one out of the box," I said. I think I still imagined that his interest was a baker's interest – to see how they were made.

'"Oh, no," he said. "I want to see what your God tastes like."

'"I couldn't do that."

'"Not for a whole electric train, just for yourself? You wouldn't have any trouble at home. I'd pack it up and put a label inside that your Dad could see – 'For my bank manager's little boy from a grateful client.' He'd be pleased as Punch with that."

'Now that we are grown men it seems a trivial temptation, doesn't it? But try to think back to your own childhood. There was a whole circuit of rails on the floor at our feet, straight rails and curved rails, and a little station with porters and passengers, a tunnel, a foot-bridge, a level crossing, two signals, buffers, of course – and above all, a turntable. The tears of longing came into my eyes when I looked at the turntable. It was my favourite piece – it looked so ugly and practical and true. I said weakly, "I wouldn't know how."

'How carefully he had been studying the ground. He must have slipped several times into Mass at the back of the church. It would have been no good, you understand, in a little town like that, presenting himself for communion. Everybody there knew him for what he was. He said to me, "When you've been given communion you could just put it under your tongue a moment. He serves you and the other boy first, and I saw you once go out behind the curtain straight afterwards. You'd forgotten one of those little bottles."

'"The cruet," I said.

'"Pepper and salt." He grinned at me jovially, and I – well, I looked at the little railway which I could no longer come and play with when term started. I said, "You'd just swallow it, wouldn't you?"

'"Oh, yes," he said, "I'd just swallow it."

'Somehow I didn't want to play with the train any more that day. I got up and made for the door, but he detained me, gripping my lapel. He said, "This will be a secret between you and me. Tomorrow's Sunday. You come along here in the afternoon. Put it in an envelope and post it in. Monday morning the train will be delivered bright and early."

'"Not tomorrow," I implored him.

'"I'm not interested in any other Sunday," he said. "It's your only chance." He shook me gently backwards and forwards. "It will always have to be a secret between you and me," he said. "Why, if anyone knew they'd take away the train and there'd be me to reckon with. I'd bleed you something awful. You know how I'm always about on Sunday walks. You can't avoid a man like me. I crop up. You wouldn't even be safe in your own house. I know ways to get into houses when people are asleep." He pulled me into the shop after him and opened a drawer. In the drawer was an odd-looking key and a cut-throat razor. He said, "That's a master key that opens all locks and that – that's what I bleed people with." Then he patted my cheek with his plump floury fingers and said, "Forget it. You and me are friends."

'That Sunday Mass stays in my head, every detail of it, as though it had happened only a week ago. From the moment of the Confession to the moment of Consecration it had a terrible importance; only one other Mass has ever been so important to me – perhaps not even one, for this was a solitary Mass which could never happen again. It seemed as final as the last Sacrament, when the priest bent down and put the wafer in my mouth where I knelt before the altar with my fellow server.

'I suppose I had made up my mind to commit this awful act – for, you know, to us it must always seem an awful act – from the moment when I saw Blacker watching from the back of the church. He had put on his best Sunday clothes, and as though he could never quite escape the smear of his profession, he had a dab of dried talcum on his cheek, which he had presumably applied after using that cut-throat of his. He was watching me closely all the time, and I think it was fear – fear of that terrible undefined thing called bleeding – as much as covetousness that drove me to carry out my instructions.

'My fellow server got briskly up and taking the communion plate preceded Father Carey to the altar rail where the other Communicants knelt. I had the Host lodged under my tongue: it felt like a blister. I got up and made for the curtain to get the cruet that I had purposely left in the sacristy. When I was there I looked quickly round for a hiding-place and saw an old copy of the *Universe* lying on a chair. I took the Host from my mouth and inserted it between two sheets – a little damp mess of pulp. Then I thought: perhaps Father Carey has put the paper out for a particular purpose and he will find the Host before I have time to remove it, and the enormity of my act began to come home to me when I tried to imagine what punishment I should incur. Murder is sufficiently trivial to have its appropriate punishment, but for this act the mind boggled at the thought of any retribution at all. I tried to remove the Host, but it had stuck clammily between the pages and in desperation I tore out a piece of the newspaper and screwing the whole thing up, stuck it in my trouser pocket. When I came back through the curtain carrying the cruet my eyes met Blacker's. He gave me a grin of encouragement and unhappiness – yes, I am sure, unhappiness. Was it perhaps that the poor man was all the time seeking something incorruptible?

'I can remember little more of that day. I think my mind was shocked and stunned and I was caught up too in the family bustle of Sunday. Sunday in a provincial town is the day for relations. All the family are at home and unfamiliar cousins and uncles are apt to arrive packed in the back seats of other people's cars. I remember that some crowd of that kind descended on us and pushed Blacker temporarily out of the foreground of my mind. There was somebody called Aunt Lucy with a loud hollow laugh that filled the house with mechanical merriment like the sound of recorded laughter from inside a hall of mirrors, and I had no opportunity to go out alone even if I had wished to. When six o'clock came and Aunt Lucy and the cousins departed and peace returned, it was too late to go to Blacker's and at eight it was my own bed-time.

'I think I had half forgotten what I had in my pocket. As I emptied my pocket the little screw of newspaper brought quickly back the Mass, the priest bending over me, Blacker's grin. I laid the packet on the chair by my bed and tried to go to sleep, but I was haunted by the shadows on the wall where the curtains blew, the squeak of furniture, the rustle in the chimney, haunted by the presence of God there on the chair. The Host had always been to me – well, the Host. I knew theoretically, as I have said, what I had to believe, but suddenly, as someone whistled in the road outside, whistled secretively, knowingly, to me, I knew that this which I had beside my bed was something of infinite value – something a man would pay for with his whole peace of mind, something that was so hated one could love it as one loves an outcast or a bullied child. These are adult words and it was a child of ten who lay scared in bed, listening to the whistle from the road, Blacker's whistle, but I think he felt fairly clearly what I am describing now. That is what I meant when I said this Thing, whatever it is, that seizes every possible weapon against God, is always, everywhere, disappointed at the moment of success. It must have felt as certain of me as Blacker did. It must have felt certain, too, of Blacker. But I wonder, if one knew what happened later to that poor man, whether one would not find again that the weapon had been turned against its own breast.

'At last I couldn't bear that whistle any more and got out of bed. I opened the curtains a little way, and there right under my window, the moonlight on his face, was Blacker. If I had stretched my hand down, his fingers reaching up could almost have touched mine. He looked up at me, flashing the one good eye, with hunger – I realize now that near-success must have developed his obsession almost to the point of madness. Desperation had driven him to the house. He whispered up at me, "David, where is it?"

'I jerked my head back at the room. "Give it me," he said, "quick. You shall have the train in the morning."

'I shook my head. He said, "I've got the bleeder here, and the key. You'd better toss it down."

'"Go away," I said, but I could hardly speak with fear.

'"I'll bleed you first and then I'll have it just the same."

'"Oh no, you won't," I said. I went to the chair and picked it – Him – up. There was only one place where He was safe. I couldn't separate the Host from the paper, so I swallowed both. The newsprint stuck like a prune to the back of my throat, but I rinsed it down with water from the ewer. Then I went back to the window and looked down at Blacker. He began to wheedle me. "What have you done with it, David? What's the fuss? It's only a bit of bread," looking so longingly and pleadingly up at me that even as a child I wondered whether he could really think that, and yet desire it so much.

'"I swallowed it," I said.

'"Swallowed it?"

'"Yes," I said. "Go away." Then something happened which seems to me now more terrible than his desire to corrupt or my thoughtless act: he began to weep – the tears ran lopsidedly out of the one good eye and his shoulders shook. I only saw his face for a moment before he bent his head and strode off, the bald turnip head shaking, into the dark. When I think of it now, it's almost as if I had seen that Thing weeping for its inevitable defeat. It had tried to use me as a weapon and now I had broken in its hands and it wept its hopeless tears through one of Blacker's eyes.'

The black furnaces of Bedwell Junction gathered around the line. The points switched and we were tossed from one set of rails to another. A spray of sparks, a signal light changed to red, tall chimneys jetting into the grey night sky, the fumes of steam from stationary engines – half the cold journey was over and now remained the long wait for the slow cross-country train. I said, 'It's an interesting story. I think I should have given Blacker what he wanted. I wonder what he would have done with it.'

'I really believe,' my companion said, 'that he would first of all have put it under his microscope – before he did all the other things I expect he had planned.'

'And the hint?' I said. 'I don't quite see what you mean by that.'

'Oh, well,' he said vaguely, 'you know for me it was an odd beginning, that affair, when you come to think of it,' but I should never have known what he meant had not his coat, when he rose to take his bag from the rack, come open and disclosed the collar of a priest.

I said, 'I suppose you think you owe a lot to Blacker.'

'Yes,' he said. 'You see, I am a very happy man.'

G. F. GREEN

A Wedding

How but in custom and in ceremony are innocence and beauty born?

The light in his bedroom was of a new June day. It fell redolent of fields, woods, by the curtains, broad floor boards, to lose in faded stripes of white damp blurred walls – as for days past. But Tom, dressing, did not take it in. He reached for the new-bought shirt. It was his father's wedding day; not his day. He put the shirt on. His body was small, his gestures wooden, a puppet's. The room was empty, not his; not the room he went from onto the farm, by his father; but ante-room to an event, in the midst of this June day, which he did not think of, not understanding; and where he must dress. He tied the tie. Sun did not warm his chill hand. It was visitor like, not an inhabiter. 'Call me Phyllis, not Mother,' Miss Howland said. She had flax hair, black lashes separate as flies' legs, round blue eyes. 'Yes.' He would see a lot of her he knew. He went for his brushes, but glanced to the window. The great tree edge to the field, line of lake to the right was dry as cardboard – a toy theatre at his grandfather's near Marlden was long discarded – meant nothing to him: isolated, of different material. He put on a new flannel jacket. His dislike of not being part of the day, did not make him think. He got ready and went down.

He went down the stairs; a boy of twelve, sturdy, but calm faced, his hair neatly done. His hand slid on the flat-topped banister. The cool, stone and cleaned pan smell closed him, dark in his grey suit, from the hot day. Annie was in the hall. He came down.

'Where's Father?' he said.

'Let's see,' Annie turned on him. 'That'll do. Your father's busy. You're to go straight to the church with Don in the trap.'

She shifted a bowl of flowers on the chest, moved some papers and books.

'Their lot'll take you on in a car. So be sharp.'

She bustled, fat, to the kitchen. Tom walked in to the living room. The buff blinds, half down, diffused light in the chintz chairs, new vases of flowers, and the ornaments. No one was in the room. His mother's photograph was on the cabinet. He moved round. One of Phyllis in a silver frame stood on the piano. His father was not there. He went out, and down the passage by the kitchens, to find Don in the yard.

It was hot driving to church in the trap. His new suit creased on him. May in the hedges was like dust, the sky and birds' song toneless. He saw their fluttered, town-smart crowd on the steps. He got out; went, cramped and soiled, to join them; but relieved to be in the church.

The small church was quiet and cool. He stood with the few guests of his father that he knew. His skin sallowed, his eyes grave, his hands were bare and lithe on the pew top, by the solemnity. A man held Phyllis who leant – soft blue, a huge hung reddish fur, a pink bouquet, her face done white to round spider eyes, her loose hair. 'Her' people across the aisle – a flurry of blouse, dark-cut skirt, wide hats – stared on his father's group, raised the prayer books, the small clasped reticules: did each perhaps hold money? The plain, arc-topped windows were behind them. Near, Ned Ellis, in his serge with leggings, muddled a gold ring; nods, sudden amens breaking his red, cracked face: was he drunk again? A lady, big amber beads on her breast, watched him. Tom's eyes, dark, reflected pain. Prayer, like a net closed on them at the altar, and about the church – warmer. He glanced about him for release.

His grandfather was in front. His tall, long-coated back to him, the grey hand on the pew. His head, the clipped white beard, sharp eyes, fixed them in the church. He had watched rigid, his hand on a dark stick, a dog cease worrying his sheep, on the fells once. Tom eyed him, sought refuge in his control. They all knelt. He shut his eyes. The frilly satin gathering, money, the Howlands' Phyllis, fell from the stern shoulders, that gave: the farm and the owned day. They prayed. Then all rose. He filed out with them onto the sunlit steps; at the base the cars waited.

He sat small in a car with some three ladies. Sunlight mixed with perfume, powder – and new gloves-smell. It drove on.

'Such a quaint church. Like an old-fashioned police court.'

Houses passed – laburnums – painted gates. It was very light. He looked out, bare eyed. The lamp posts and shrubberies. *The Firs*.

'Here we are.'

It slowed up, stopped. They got out and went up the gravelled drive.

He entered the room, where the guests already were, sipping, nibbled biscuits, chatted. He was unnoticed. Smell of paste, scribbled-pink white wallpaper touched him, from shut windows to pink upholstery. Phyllis bent at an iced cake; the laid buffet held flowers in silver vases. His father was beyond. A man came and offered him drink. He took it.

'Champagne,' the man said, 'not for every day, eh?'

He drank. The foul stuff split his nose and throat. He backed from the man, thick-faced, heavy over him: and saw his grandfather. He went brief through the crowd up to him.

He spoke rapidly and wildly. His grandfather looked down at him, answered him briefly. His face was flushed, his eyes clear bright by excitement, he moved his hands, was exaggerated. He chattered, as if he would gain something, be even with him. His hands sought once in a smoke-scented cupboard at Marlden. People were beginning to go, round them. Sudden, he took his grandfather's hand.

'Good-bye, Grandfather,' he said.

His grandfather gazed steady at the cowed boy who held his hand.

'Good-bye, Son.'

Many people had gone. Phyllis had left. He went back to his glass.

He picked it up. Few remained in the warm, now disordered, room. But the man came to him; he glanced up.

'Forgettin' you? It's not cheap stuff, this – keep you alive, sonnie.'

He filled up his glass. Tom saw beyond him. The amber bead lady going to the door, made one less. He drank. A woman's hand, gold worn ring, had touched his face, a night dark with trees: his mother's.

'I must go,' he said, 'to see them off.'

He was at the gate. He saw Phyllis, white-powdered in blue, stoop into a car at his father's side. One threw confetti. They all waved. The car drew off in the road.

He went to his car, but turned where his grandfather stood dark by the brick wall. He held out his hand, speaking quickly.

'Good-bye, Grandfather.'

The man stood, ignored his hand. The boy's eyes shifted, his face hot with sweat, his hand and mouth unstill.

'You've said that once, boy,' he said. 'What do you want.'

'Nothing.'

He turned quickly. The last guests got into their cars. He knew. Sun struck him from the cars and road. His grandfather believed he cadged for a tip. His legs weakened – for money – taking him to his car.

He sat in the back, sun and dust scattered by him. It bumped him down roads, away from the smart people at the cars, the sun hot road, his grandfather at the brick wall. He held the glossed leather seat. But he scarce saw the passed countryside. Glazed windows shut his stung throat, eyes, his throbbing head, within the close car. His flannel suit ached on him, as he waited. At length the car drew in to the yard: he got out to quiet afternoon.

It was still in his bedroom. The light hung in view of great trees and field. He quickly undressed. Air, alone from woods of shade and water, touched him. He took an open shirt and cord breeches. As he dressed, his hands felt his own clothes; met, too, things about the farm, field things, the fences, and boat tether at the lake: tried the known limits of his world. He tied loosely the knee laces. But he bent in a world made his, by a near, perpetual woman, her soft dresses, quiet, straight hands; by an other day. He put on his shoes. His way was easy as days before. He went out, and down the wide staircase.

He took his rod in the hall, and went through the fields, to the lake. The boat was tethered in a tree's shade. He stooped to free it, grass lush at his half-tied knees. He threw in the rope, followed it. For a time he rowed quickly, then sank the oars. He fixed the bait, threw and dropped it in. He sat in the boat; his hand crept on a brass ring in the rod's haft; his serious eyes watched intently. Water's light lipped on his still face, the clothes, and the boat; spit gold in the huge trees' gloom behind.

ANGUS WILSON

The Wrong Set

Just before the club closed, Mrs Lippiatt asked very specially for a medley of old numbers. Mr Pontresoli himself came over and told Terry. 'It's for your bundle of charms' he said 'so don't blame me.' Vi wanted to refuse when Terry asked her – she had a filthy headache and anyway she was sick of being kept late. 'Tell the old cow to go and . . .' she was saying, when Terry put a finger on her lips. 'Do it for me, dear' he said. 'Remember without her I don't eat.' Poor Kid! thought Vi, having to do it with an old trout like that, old enough to be his grandmother – still she stank of money, he was on to a good thing if he could keep it. So she put on a special sweet smile and waved at Mrs Lippiatt. 'Here's wishing you all you wish yourself, dear' she called. Then she smiled at Mr Pontresoli, just to show him how hard she worked for his lousy club – might as well kill two birds with one stone. 'Let it go, Terry' she called and the two pianos jazzed out the old duet routine – Souvenirs, Paper Doll, Some of these Days, Blue Again, everything nice and corney. It was while they were playing 'The Sheik of Araby' that she noticed Mrs Lippiatt's face – all lit up with memories. Christ! she must be old if she goes back to that, thought Vi, and then she said to herself 'Poor old bitch, she must have been pretty once, but, there you are, that's life, makes you hard.' At least she'd got a nice bit of stuff in Terry, best looking boy in the place; not that she didn't prefer something a bit nearer her own age herself, and she gazed proudly over at Trevor, with his wavy grey hair and soldier's moustache, talking to Mr Pontresoli. Funny how class told. Old Pontresoli could have bought Trevor up any day, but there he was, respectful as anything, listening to what Trevor had to say. She could hear Trevor's voice above the music 'My dear old Ponto, you'll never change that sort of thing in this country till you clear out the Yids.' If Mr Pontresoli knew what Trevor really thought of him! 'Filthy wop' he'd said, but he'd agreed to be nice, because of Vi's piano act and until he got a job they needed all the money she could earn.

After closing time she had a drink with Terry and Mrs Lippiatt. Mrs Lippiatt said what was the good of having money, there was nothing to spend it on. Vi thought to herself what she would like was to have some money to spend, but aloud she said in her smart voice 'Yes, isn't it awful? With this government you have to be grateful for the air you breathe. Look at the things we can't have – food, clothes, foreign travel.' 'Ah, yes, foreign travel' said Mrs Lippiatt, though she knew damned well Vi had never been abroad. 'It's bad enough for you and me, Mrs Cawston, but think of this poor boy' and she put her fat, beringed hand on Terry's knee '*he's* never been out of England. Never mind, darling, you shall have your trip to Nice the day we get a proper government back.' Mr Pontresoli and Trevor joined them. Trevor was the real public schoolboy with his monocle and calling Mrs Lippiatt 'my dear lady', Vi could see that Terry was worried – he was frightened that Trevor was muscling in; but that was just Trevor's natural way with women – he had perfect manners. Later in the evening he asked Vi who the hell the old trout was.

'The Major's got a good one about Attlee' said Mr Pontresoli in his thick, adenoidal Italian cockney, his series of blue stubbed chins wobbling as he spoke.

'It's impossible to be as funny about this government as they are themselves' said Trevor. He had *such* a quiet sense of humour. 'They're a regular Fred Karno show.' But they all begged to hear the story, so he gave it to them. 'An empty taxi drove up to No. 10,' he said 'and Mr Attlee got out.' Beautifully told it was, with his monocle taken out of his eye and polished just at the right moment.

'Well Sir Stafford gives me the creeps' said Terry. No one thought that very funny except Mrs Lippiatt and she roared.

'Are you ready, young woman?' Trevor said to Vi with mock severity 'because I'm not waiting all night.' As she was coming out of the ladies', Vi met Mona and her girl friend. She stopped and talked to them for a minute although she knew Trevor would disapprove. It was true, of course, that that sort of thing was on the increase and Trevor said it was the ruin of England, but then he said that about so many things – Jews and foreigners, the Labour Government and the Ballet. Anyhow Mona's crowd had been very kind to her in the old days when she was down to her last sausage, and when they'd found she wasn't their sort there'd never been so much as a word to upset her.

'For Christ's sake, Kiddie' said Trevor 'I wish you wouldn't talk to those Lizzies.'

On the stairs they met young Mr Solomons. Vi *had* to talk to him, whatever Trevor said. First of all he was important at the club, and then his smile always got her – nice and warm somehow like a cat purring, but that was what she felt about a lot of Jews. 'She's stood me up, Vi' he said, his eyes round with pretended dismay 'left me in the lurch. Ah! I ought to have stuck to nice girls like you.' Vi couldn't help laughing, but Trevor was wild with anger. He stood quite still for a moment in Denman Street under the electric sign which read 'Passion Fruit Club.' 'If I catch that lousy Yid hanging around you again, girlie', he said 'I'll knock his ruddy block off.' All the way in the tube to Earls Court he was in a rage. Vi wanted to tell him that she was going to visit her nephew Norman tomorrow, but she feared his reception of the news. Trevor had talked big about helping Norman, when she told him the boy had won a scholarship at London University and was coming to live with them. But somehow her sister Ivy had got word that she wasn't really married to Trevor and they'd sent the boy elsewhere. She and Trevor had taken him out to dinner once in the West End – a funny boy with tousled black hair and thick spectacles who never said a word, though he'd eaten a hearty enough meal and laughed fit to split at the Palladium. Trevor said he wasn't all there and the less they saw of him the better, but Vi thought of him as her only relative in London and after all Ivy *was* her sister, even if she was so narrow.

'I'm going to see Norman tomorrow' Vi said timidly, as they crossed the Earls Court Road.

'Good God' cried Trevor, 'What on earth for, girlie?'

'I've written once or twice to that Hampstead address and had no reply.'

'Well, let the little swine stew in his own juice if he hasn't the decency to answer' said Trevor.

'Blood's blood after all' countered Vi, and so they argued until they were back in their bed-sitting room. Vi put on a kimono and feathered mules, washed off her make-up and covered her face in cream until it shone with highlights. Then she sat plucking her eyebrows. Trevor put his trousers to press under the mattress, gave himself a whisky in the toothglass, refilled it with Milton and water and put in his dentures. Then he sat in his pants, suspenders and socks squeezing blackheads from his nose in front of a mirror. All this time they kept on rowing. At last Vi cried out 'Alright, alright, Trevor Cawston, but I'm *still* going.' 'O.K.' said Trevor 'how's about a little loving?' So then they broke into the old routine.

When the time came to visit Norman, Vi was in quite a quandary about what to wear. She didn't want the people he lived with to put her down as tarty – there'd probably been quite enough of that sort of talk already – on the other hand she wasn't going to look a frump for anyone. She compromised with her black suit, white lace jabot and gold pocket seal, with coral nail varnish instead of scarlet.

The house when she got there wasn't in Hampstead at all, but in Kilburn. Respectable, she decided, but a bit poor looking.

'Norman's out at the demo,' said Mrs Thursby 'but he should be back any time now. You'll come in and have a cup of tea, won't you?' Vi said she thought she would. She hadn't quite understood where her nephew was, but if he was coming back soon, she might as well wait. The parlour into which she was ushered brought her home in Leicester back to her – all that plush, and the tassels and the china with crests on it got her down properly now. One thing they wouldn't have had at home though and that was all those books, cases full of them, and stacks of newspapers and magazines piled on the floor, and then there was a typewriter – probably a studious home, she decided. She did wish the little dowdy, bright-eyed woman with the bobbed hair would sit down instead of hopping about like a bird. But Mrs Thursby had heard something about Vi, and she was at once nervous and hostile; she stood making little plucking gestures at her necklace and her sleeve ends and shooting staccato inquiries at Vi in a chirping voice that had an undertone of sarcasm.

'Mrs . . . Mrs Cawston, is it?'

'That's right' said Vi.

'Oh yes. I wasn't quite sure. It's so difficult to know sometimes these days, isn't it? with . . .' and Mrs Thursby's voice trailed away.

Vi felt she was being got at. But Mrs Thursby went on talking.

'Oh! The man *will* be sorry you came when he was out.' By calling Norman 'The man' she seemed to be claiming a greater relationship to him than that of a mere aunt. 'He's talked of you' and she paused, then added drily 'a certain amount. I won't say a great deal, but then he's not a great talker.'

'Where did you say he was?' asked Vi.

'At Trafalgar Square' said Mrs Thursby. 'They're rallying there to hear Pollitt or one of those people. My two went, they're both C.P., and Norman's gone with them. Though I'm glad to say he's had the good sense not to join up completely, he's just a fellow traveller as they call them.'

Vi was too bemused to say much, but she managed to ask for what purpose they were rallying.

'To make trouble for the Government they put into power' said Mrs Thursby drily. 'It makes me very angry sometimes. It's taken us forty years to get a real Labour Government and then just because they don't move fast enough for these young people, it's criticism, criticism all the time. But, there it is, I've always said the same, there's no fool like a young fool' and she closed her tight, little mouth with relish 'they'll come round in time. Hilda, that's my girl, was just the same about the chapel, but now it seems they've agreed to the worship of God. Very kind of them I'm sure. I expect you feel the same as I do, Mrs Cawston.'

Vi wasn't quite sure exactly what Mrs Thursby did feel, but she *was* sure that she didn't agree, so she said defiantly 'I'm conservative.'

'Lena' said Mrs Thursby in a dry, abrupt voice to a tall, middle-aged woman who was bringing in the tea-tray 'We've got a Tory in the house. The first for many a day.'

'Oh no!' said Lena, and everything about her was charming and gemütlich from her foreign accent to her smile of welcome. 'I am so pleased to meet you but it is terrible that you are a Tory.'

'Miss Untermayer teaches the man German' said Mrs Thursby. 'Mrs Cawston is Norman's aunt.'

'Oh!' cried Miss Untermayer, her gaunt features lit up with almost girlish pleasure 'Then I congratulate you. You have a very clever nephew.'

Vi said she was sure she was pleased to hear that, but she didn't quite like the sound of these rallies.

'Oh! that' said Miss Untermayer 'He will grow out of that. All this processions and violence, it is for children. But Norman is a very spiritual boy, I am sure that he is a true pacifist.'

'I'm sure I hope not' said Vi who was getting really angry. 'I've never had anything to do with conchies.'

'Then you've missed contact with a very fine body of men' said Mrs Thursby 'Mr Thursby was an objector.'

'I'm sorry, I'm sure' said Vi. 'Major Cawston was right through the war.'

'The important thing is that he came out the other side' remarked Mrs Thursby drily.

'There are so many kinds of bravery, so many kinds of courage. I think we must respect them all.' Miss Untermayer's years as a refugee had made her an adept at glossing over divisions of opinion. All the same she gave a sigh of relief when Norman's voice was heard in the hall, at least the responsibility would not be on *her* any more.

'Hilda and Jack have gone on to a meeting' he shouted 'I'd have gone too but I've got to get on with this essay.'

'You aunt's come to see you' shouted back Mrs Thursby.

Norman came into the room sideways like a crab, he was overcome with confusion at the sight of Vi and he stood, running his hands through his hair and blinking behind his spectacles.

'You were such a long time answering my letters that I thought I'd better come down and see what sort of mischief you'd got into' said Vi 'and I have' she added bitterly. 'Demonstrations indeed. I'd like to know what your mother would say, Norman Hackett?'

Norman's face was scarlet as he looked up, but he answered firmly. 'I don't think Mum would disapprove, not if she understood. And even if she did, it couldn't make any difference.'

'Not make any difference what your mother said. I'm ashamed of you, Norman, mixing up with a lot of reds and Jews.'

'That's enough of that' cried Mrs Thursby. 'We'll not have any talk against Jews in this house. No, not even from Rahab herself.'

Vi's face flushed purple underneath her makeup. 'You ought to be ashamed' she cried 'an old woman like you to let a boy of Norman's age mix up with all this trash.'

'You've no right to say that . . .' began Norman, but Mrs Thursby interrupted him. 'Oh let the woman say her say, Norman. I've had a windful of Tory talk before now and it hasn't killed me. If Father and I have taught the man to stand up for his own class, we're proud of it. And now, Mrs Cawston, if you've nothing more to say to Norman, I think you'd better go.'

Vi arrived at the Unicorn sharp at opening time that evening. She'd got over most of her indignation, after all Ivy didn't think much about *her*, and if the boy wanted to go to pot, good riddance. She had a couple of gins and lime as she waited for Trevor.

Mr Pontresoli came across the saloon bar. 'Hullo, Vi' he said in his thick voice 'Have you heard the news about Solomons? Dreadful, isn't it?'

It really gave Vi quite a shock to hear that they'd charged young Mr Solomons – something to do with clothing coupons. She had felt quite guilty towards him after speaking out like that against the Jews, and now to hear of this, it made you wonder what sort of a government we *had* got. As Mr Pontresoli said 'It's getting to be the end of liberty, you mark my words.'

'Trevor'll have something to say about this, Mr Pontresoli' Vi said, and then she remembered what Trevor said about the Jews, it was all too difficult, one could never tell. Mr Pontresoli offered her another gin, so she said yes. 'I'll tell you what' said Mr Pontresoli. 'It's going to make a difference to me financially. Solomons was one of my best backers at the club. It may mean cutting down a bit. We shan't be needing two pianos.'

What with the gin – will you have another? said Mr Pontresoli, and yes said Vi – and the tiring day she'd had, Vi felt quite cast down as she thought of Terry out of a job. A nice boy like that. But then he'd got Mrs Lippiatt.

'Poor Terry, Mr Pontresoli' she said, her eyes filling with tears 'We *shall* miss him at the club. Here's wishing him more Mrs Lippiatts' and she drained her glass. 'This one's on me, Mr Pontresoli' she said, and Mr Pontresoli agreed.

'We couldn't afford to let Terry go' said Mr Pontresoli 'that's certain. Mrs Lippiatt says he draws all the women, and she ought to know, she spends so much money.'

Vi worked all this out and it seemed to come round to her. This made her angry. 'Why that's nonsense, Mr Pontresoli' she said, and she smiled broadmindedly 'surely you know Terry's a pansy.'

Mr Pontresoli's fat, cheerful, face only winked. 'That gets 'em all ways' he said and walked out of the saloon bar.

Vi felt quite desperate. She couldn't think where Trevor had got to. 'Have you seen my husband Major Cawston, Gertie?' she asked the barmaid. No one could say I haven't got dignity when I want it, she thought. Gertie hadn't seen Trevor, but Mona's girl friend said she had, twenty minutes ago at the George *and* stinking. No job and Trevor stinking. It all made Vi feel very low. Life was hell anyhow, and with all those Reds, she'd go after Trevor and fetch Norman back. She was about to get down from the high stool, when she noticed that Mona's girl friend's eyes were red. 'What's the matter, dear?' she asked.

'Mona's gone off with that Bretonne bitch' said the girl. 'Oh dear' said Vi solemnly 'That's very bad.' So they both had another drink to help them on. Vi was in battling mood. 'Go out and fetch Mona back' she cried. 'You won't get anywhere sitting still.' 'You do talk silly sometimes' said the girl 'What can I do against a Bretonne, they're so passionate.'

The sadness of it all overcame Vi, it was all so true and so sad and so true – all those Bretonnes and Reds and passionates, and Trevor going off to demos, no, Norman going off to demos, and Mr Solomons in the hands of the Government, and her nephew in the hands of the Reds. Yes, that was the chief thing.

'I must let my sister know that her son's in trouble' she said. 'How can I tell her?'

'Ring her up' suggested Mona's friend, but Vi told her Ivy had no 'phone. 'Send a telegram, dear, that's what I should do' said Gertie. 'You can use the 'phone at the back of the bar. Just dial TEL.'

It took Vi some time to get through to Telegrams, the telephone at the Unicorn seemed to be such a difficult one. I mustn't let Ivy know that I'm in this condition, she thought, she was always the grand lady with Ivy, so holding herself erect and drawling slightly, she said 'I want to send a telegram to my sister, please. The name is Hackett – 44 Guybourne Road, Leicester. Terribly worried.' It sounded very Mayfair and she repeated it 'Terribly worried. Norman in the Wrong Set. Vi.' 'I feel much better now, Gertie' she said as she stumbled back to the bar. 'I've done my duty.'

RHYS DAVIES

A Human Condition

Having done the errand at the Post Office, which he had timed with a beautiful precision that he imagined completely hoodwinked those left at home, Mr Arnold crossed the Market Square just as the doors of the Spreadeagle inn were opened.

This morning he was in lamentable condition. He felt he would never get through the day without aid. Never, never, never. Deep inside him was a curious dead sensation of which he was frightened. It lay in the pit of his stomach like some coiled serpent fast asleep, and he was fearful that at any moment the thing would waken and writhe up in unholy destructive fury. And ultimately *he* would be destroyed. Not his critics, today collected in dark possession of his home.

He sailed into the pub with his ample, slightly rolling strut, a man of substance handsomely ripe of body and face, his attire as conservative as a psalm to godliness; no one could say Mr Arnold neglected his person. Of the town's few pubs the Spreadeagle was his favourite haunt. It was cosily shut in on itself and dark with shadows; it had low, black-beamed ceilings, copper gleams, honest smells, and morose windows hostile to light. In the hall a torpid spaniel bitch looked at him with the heavily drooping eyes of a *passée* actress; she knew Mr Arnold, and there was no necessity for even a languid wag of her tail. Always the first customer, he stepped into the bar parlour with his usual opening-time briskness. But Mrs Watson, polishing glasses behind the bar, looked at him with a start. 'Well!' she seemed about to exclaim, but only pursed her lips.

'A whisky,' he said; 'a double.'

'A double?' Something was concealed in her tone.

'Yes, for God's sake.' The false briskness was suddenly deflated. 'And pour another for me while you're about it.'

'*No*, Mr Arnold,' she said, flat; 'no. Not *two* doubles . . . It isn't right,' she bridled; 'not today. Good heavens! Don't forget you've got to be there sober at two o'clock. *No*, Mr Arnold.'

'Hell!' he muttered. He looked over his shoulder with child-blue eyes round in fear. 'Where's Alec?' A man would understand, must surely understand, what that day really meant. Women were incalculable in the domain of the affections, could run so drastically from the extremes of loving solicitude to the bleakest savagery. 'Where's Alec?' he peered.

'Gone to London for the day,' his wife said. 'Gone to buy me a budgerigar.'

'Gone to London,' he mumbled, preoccupied.

'They can chirp ever so sweet,' she said tightly, 'and intelligent, my goodness! – my sister had one that would hop on the table when she was making cake and stone the raisins for her.'

'What?' He started from his glassy preoccupation.

'The budgerigar she had. With its beak. Intelligent, my stars! . . . I've known many a human being,' she said forbiddingly, 'that could do with their brains and feelings.'

Both the Malt Shovel and the Bleeding Horse, which were on his way home, were only beer houses. No licence for spirits. But there was plenty of time. He would climb to Cuckoo Ridge, up to the Self Defence. Its landlord, whose wife had been in an asylum for years, would understand. There was the Unicorn too, nearer, but repellent with its horrible modern cocktail bar, its café look, and its dirty waiters.

Mrs Watson, solicited with flattery and whining, allowed him a single whisky more. She asked him what would be said in the town if she allowed him to have all he wanted on that morning of all mornings. He left the house with dignity, part of him pre-occupied with feeling offended, but the greater part obeying a huge desolate urge to complete the scarcely begun journey into that powerful state where he would feel secure, a captain of his fate, if a melancholy one. He had never been able to take to drinking at home. Besides, Susan never encouraged it. Never a bottle of whisky in the house.

In the shopping street, those people who knew Mr Arnold – and they were many, for by now he was a local celebrity – looked at him with their cheerfulness, due to the brilliant day, wiped momentarily from their faces. But he encouraged no one to pass a few words with him; time must not be wasted. He took a side turning and began to climb among loaded apple and pear trees spread over garden walls. The whole fragrantly warm little town was fat with sunlight, fruit and flowers. Mr Arnold began to pant and lean on his expensive malacca stick.

Above, on the bright emerald slopes with their small well-groomed fields, cows stood like shiny china ornaments. The short local train from London puffed a plume of snowy cotton-wool. It was toy countryside, and Mr Arnold felt obliged to admire its prettiness; it had been Susan's idea to live here on his retirement from his highly successful career in the City lanes near Tower Bridge, where scores of important men knew him. He liked to feel that London was still near, he liked to see, on Sundays and Bank Holidays, clumps of pallid cockney youths and girls in cycling knickers dotting those slopes like mushrooms. The high air, clear as mineral waters, was supposed to be good for one. Susan said it eased her chest, and she had become a leading voice in the Women's Institute . . . Ah, Susan, Susan! Her husband panted in sore distress, climbing.

On Cuckoo Ridge the landlord of the Self Defence greeted him, after a slight pause, courteously. But Mr Arnold saw at once that he was in the know. Rapidly he asked for a second double. The landlord, a stout, placid man in braces, looked at him. Perhaps he saw a man in agony of spirit; he served the drink. Mr Arnold thought he felt deep sympathy flowing from this man whose own wife had been shut away from him for several years already. He asked for a third double.

The landlord mournfully shook his head. 'Best not, Mr Arnold.'

'One more,' panted Mr Arnold. 'Only one. I've got a day in front of me.' In the pit of his stomach was a stirring of fear, as if the sleeping coil shuddered. 'Never be able to face it,' he whimpered.

The landlord shook his head in slow, heavy decision. 'There's the circumstances to consider,' he said.

Mr Arnold attempted a hollow truculence. 'My money's as good as anyone's—'

'Now, sir,' said the landlord distantly, 'best be on your way.' And, solemnly: 'You've got a job to do, Mr Arnold.'

Mr Arnold walked out with deliberate steadiness. A clock had struck twelve-thirty. It would have to be the Unicorn, and time was pressing now. Actually he had already taken his morning allowance, but today . . . today . . . He descended from the Ridge with a careful step, crossed the watercress beds into the London road, and looked sourly at the gimcrack modern façade of the Unicorn, a rebuilt house done up for motoring whipper-snappers and their silly grinning dolls. He went in like an aggressive magistrate with power to deprive the place of its licence. But he cast himself into a bony scarlet-and-nickel chair with a groan, wiping his brow. A white presence slid up to his chair.

'Double whisky,' he said.

'Yes, Mr Arnold,' said the waiter.

He cocked up his eye sharply. Known here too! In a blurred way, the grave young face looking down at him was familiar. Ha, it was Henry, who used to come with his father to do the garden! Quickly Mr Arnold assumed the censorious glare of a boss of substance. 'And mind it's genuine Scotch, Henry,' he said. He did not like the boy's solicitous look as he withdrew to the blonde cinema star serving behind the jazzy zigzagged corner counter. He took out his big presentation gold watch and looked at it importantly. Was there a pausing at the bar, a whispering? Surely he, who had been a guest at Lord Mayors' banquets in the Mansion House, was not going to be dictated to in a shoddy hole like this? Henry brought the double. 'Get me another, my boy,' Mr Arnold said. Henry hesitated, but withdrew; came back – 'Sir,' he said awkwardly, 'sir, there's no more except this single. Our supplies haven't arrived; they'll be here by tonight.'

Was everybody his enemy that day? Was there a plot against him? After that long walk, to be allowed only this! Mr Arnold pushed back his chair, made an effort to collect his forces for dire protest. But somehow – was it because of guilt or the heat? – they would not assemble. He could only gaze fixedly at Henry in silent reproach, anger, and finally, entreaty. 'Very sorry, sir,' mumbled Henry from far away. 'Can I call up the garage for a taxi, sir?'

'A taxi? Certainly not.' He swallowed the single, tipped lavishly, rose like an offended emperor, sat down, and rose again, thunderous yet dignified.

'Your stick, Mr Arnold.' Henry handed it.

He needed it now. Outside, his eyes could focus neither on the shifting ground nor the burning pansy-coloured sky. The soft amateur hills ran into each other like blobs of water-colours imperfectly handled. But he would walk, he would walk. Anything rather than be in the house before it was quite essential. Not with *them* there . . . The town hall clock, its notes gently without chiding, struck the quarter after one. Yet those chimes were like knells bringing grief. Grief, grief. A sensation of burning grief, physical and staggering, pierced him. He sat gasping on the low roadside wall. The day was no longer brilliant, crackling with sun. The desolation of what awaited his presence swept down on him in gusts of black depression. God above, he could never face it. Not without—. He rose with remarkable celerity.

Fool, fool! Why had he forgotten the Adam and Eve? He walked rapidly, a man refreshed, stick striking the road almost evenly . . . But outside the Adam and Eve, a sixteenth-century house sagging in a dark medieval alley hidden in the town, he paused to arrange himself into the aspect of a man with a grip on himself, and he rolled into the pub with a lordly assurance.

The poky, cool bar parlour was deserted except for a cat enormously asleep on the counter. Mr Arnold called: 'Hey! Customer here!' He banged the counter with his stick. No one appeared. Not a sound shifted into the stagnant air. He gave the cat a sharp dig with his stick; it did not stir or open an eye. He shouted, thumped the counter. A dead petal of plaster fell from the ceiling. But no one came. The silence closed impervious over his shouts of anguish. No one passed in the shadowed alley outside. His stick rang frenziedly on the counter. He had the feeling he was in a dream in which a ghostly, senseless frustration dogs one's every move. The cat slept. The hands of a dusty old clock remained neatly and for ever together at twelve o'clock. The bottles on the shelves looked as if they were never opened. He jabbed at the cat again; it did not move out of its primeval sleep.

Mr Arnold whimpered. He lurched over to the door in the crooked bellied-out wall and lifted the old-fashioned latch. But the door wouldn't open. Had it been locked behind him? Was he being imprisoned? 'Who's there?' he screamed, banging his stick furiously against the rickety panel. The after-silence did not budge. He tore madly at the latch. Suddenly the door flew open; it had jammed in the ancient frame. Raging, Mr Arnold stamped down the passage, threw back another door.

A dazzle of pink interior light struck into his eyes. He stepped into a hot living-room with a huge window and an opened door leading to a garden blazing with snapdragons, roses and hollyhocks. A blue-gowned woman, immensely fat, was pegging out washing over the gush of flowers. Mr Arnold all but sobbed with relief. 'Customer!' he yelled.

'Be there in a minute,' she called affably. 'It's a beautiful drying day.'

'Got a train to catch,' he bellowed. 'I want a double Scotch.'

'All right, all right.' Smooth and brown-faced as an egg, and with a dewlap of Turkish chins, she indolently left her basket, saying: 'No need to be crotchety. Where there's one train there's another; they've got the extra summer service now to London. I'm going up myself on Thursday; my daughter's going to be examined . . . Why, it's Mr Arnold!' She paused, in pastoral caution. 'Are they taking her by train, then? I didn't know.' As if this settled her doubt, she hurried into the bar.

Mr Arnold said nothing. He drank the double in two gulps and asked for another, saying quickly: 'Then I've got to hurry.' The woman talked of her daughter with soft, unstressed tact. He paused uncertainly after the second double.

'No, Mr Arnold,' she decided for him, 'I can't give you any more.'

'Mrs Busby,' he said grandly, grasping his stick as for a march, 'I know when to stop.'

'Gents always do.' She nodded approval. 'God bless you.'

Now he felt translated into the desired sphere, where he could survey his kingdom without lamentations. Power radiated in him. As in the old days of his office fame, he could have settled a ledger page of complicated figures in a twinkling. And that menacing dead weight in the pit of his stomach had vanished. He felt himself walking erect and proud though the luncheon-quiet town. He required no one's compassion. This heady brilliance lasted him all the way home. And he would not be late; a fixed stare at his watch testified to that. He congratulated himself on the efficient way he had handled his time. *They* would not be able to rebuke him for being late, on this day of all days.

Yet sight of his well-kept villa at the edge of the town struck a note in his soul like a buried knell. The garden, green-lawned and arched with trellises of roses, was trim beyond reproach – the packet he spent on it every year! And the house was cleanly white as a wedding cake. But quite suddenly now he felt that its walls and contents, its deeds and insurance policies, no longer interested or concerned him. At the gate he paused in panic. Was this the first faint rising of the horror he thought was obliterated from his being? . . . But almost at once this fear became blurred. His stick decisively tapping the crazy paving, he rolled up under the arches of roses with an air of having unfortunate business to transact.

The white-porched door was wide open. He entered bustlingly. Out of the drawing-room came Miriam, his elder sister-in-law; the woman in charge now, and his enemy. She looked at him and shrank. 'We waited lunch as long as we could,' she said, in her hard, gritty way. Her husband hovered behind her, thick horn glasses observant. 'I wanted George to go into the town and look for you—' she said hopelessly.

'Food!' Mr Arnold said, in high rebuke. 'You didn't expect me to eat lunch *today*?'

They all advanced out of the drawing-room into the hall, looking at him sideways. Ellen, the younger sister-in-law, and her husband, the dentist's assistant; their grown-up daughter; and Miriam's adolescent son. Alert but careful, visitors and yet that day not visitors, they were all dressed up and important, as if they were going to be photographed. Mr Arnold stretched his hat to a peg on the stand but miscalculated its position – 'Cursed thing,' he remarked solemnly to the fallen hat. He sat heavily in the hard oak hall chair and wiped his brow. 'In good time,' he observed. 'Five minutes yet . . . What . . . what you all standing there for?' He jerked up his head despotically. He saw tears streaming down Ellen's face before she turned, and hurrying into the drawing-room, moaned: 'I shall be ashamed to go. He's ruined the day. Something must be done. Henry—' she motioned to her husband. But Miriam, stark and glaring, stood like judgment.

'They're coming,' called her son, who had gone to the open door and was keeping a watch on the lane.

'Two o'clock!' said Mr Arnold in a solemn but strangely forlorn voice. 'Two o'clock!' Still collapsed in the chair, he groaned; his glassy eyes rolled, then stonily looked forth like tortoise eyes.

Henry and Ellen came back and whispered to Miriam's husband; they advanced briskly to Mr Arnold. 'Look, old boy,' George attempted male understanding. 'We think you'd better not go with us. We will see to everything. Take it easy and have a rest.' Enticingly he laid his hand under Mr Arnold's armpit, while Henry gripped the other arm. 'They're here; come upstairs,' he coaxed. The two sisters watched in pale, angry withdrawal.

Mr Arnold, shaking away the possessive hands, rose from the chair tremendously. 'What!' he panted. 'Better not go!' Masterfully he drew himself up. 'Me! *Me!*'

'*You are drunk*,' pronounced Miriam in icy rage. 'You are blind drunk. It's shameful.' Ellen wilted with a bitter sob against the wall.

Mr Arnold's eyes bulged. Their devilish shine enveloped Miriam with a terrible contempt, restrained for many years. 'This,' said Mr Arnold, '*this* is no time for insults. The pack of you can clear out now if you like. *I will go alone*,' he said defiantly.

'Now look here—' George began, conciliatory but aghast.

At that moment four men loomed at the open doorway. Four tall men, sleek and black-garbed, leanly efficient of aspect. With everyone in the hall black-clothed, too, the fair summer day seemed turned to shadow. The drawing-room clock struck two dainty *pings*. At the sound the four men entered, admirably prompt. There was something purifying in their sinewy impersonality. 'Upstairs,' Mr Arnold, steady as a stout column, told them, 'in the dark room.' The black quartet filed up the staircase. Out of the kitchen came Mrs Wills, her apron removed, and stood apart with her kind cook's fist under an eye.

'Have you decided to risk it?' Henry muttered to the women, while Mr Arnold reached down with glacial but careful dignity for his black hat. There was whispering, a furtive watching of him.

Down the staircase came the four men with the coffin tilted on their shoulders. The severn mourners stood back. Mr Arnold's face was stonily set again. He followed the quartet out with a stern and stiff gait. George and Henry, watchful, went close behind him. After them, in ceremonious orderliness, the others. But the two sisters, under their fashionably crisp black hats bought especially for the journey, crept forward with heads bowed very low, asking pardon of the world for this disgrace.

Mr Arnold negotiated half the length of the crazy paving with masterful ease. Then he began to sway. A hand grasped the trellis of an arch, and a shower of pink and white petals fell on his head and shoulders; his hat dropped out of his hand. The two men took his elbows, and now he submitted to their aid. Ellen sobbed anew; and Miriam moaned: 'We can only hope people will think it's grief.' Then she hissed frantically: 'Brush those petals off him, George; he looks as if he's getting married.'

The hearse contained its burden, the three limousines behind were elegant. 'Four wreaths,' said the supported Mr Arnold, hanging out his head like a bull. While the impersonal mutes went back to the house, the mourners disposed themselves in the cars. Though the two sisters had planned to occupy the first car with Mr Arnold, their husbands went in with him instead. 'There, take it easy, old boy,' said George, over-friendly now. Mr Arnold was well off and a triumphant example of industrious rectitude in the City.

'Eh? . . . eh?' said Mr Arnold vacantly. And, sunk between the two men into luxurious cushions, he straightway went into a doze. The car began its two-mile journey with a silent, soft glide.

'We mustn't let him go right off,' Henry worried. 'Hey! Mr Arnold, hey!'

Mr Arnold opened his eyes ferociously. 'The best wife a man ever had,' he groaned. 'Susan, Susan!' he called wildly. The driver turned his head for a moment. 'Ha, shameful, am I! . . . That woman hasn't got the intelligence of a . . . of a . . . budgerigar! And no more Christian feeling than a trout. Who'd have thought she and Susan were sisters! . . . And that other one,' he grunted, 'what's her name . . . Ellen, always grizzling and telling Susan she was hard up and her husband kept her short – pah! . . . A depressing lot,' summed up Mr Arnold, staring rigidly into space. Then again he called in loud anguish: 'Susan, Susan, what will I do now?'

Beads of perspiration stood on Henry's forehead. But George remained cool; despite the abuse of his wife, he even sounded affectionate – 'Never mind, old chap,' he comforted the bereaved, 'it'll be over soon. But keep awake, don't let down the whole family.'

'What family?' asked Mr Arnold. 'Got none.' And, sunk down and torpid, he seemed a secret being gathered eternally into loneliness. The two other men glanced at each other. 'Susan,' whispered Mr Arnold, chin on chest, 'Susan . . . God above!' he wailed again, 'what will I do now?' They were going through the full shopping street; people stopped to look, with arrested eyes. 'The only one of the bunch to keep her sweetness,' muttered Mr Arnold. 'Coming here in their showy hats!' he chuckled. 'But they couldn't make a man feel proud like Susan did. That time I took her to the Mansion House banquet—' But wild grief engulfed him anew. 'Susan, Susan,' he called, 'what'll I do now?'

'Here, pull yourself together,' Henry protested sharply at last, and, perhaps feeling Mr Arnold had gone far enough in insults, 'We're coming to the cemetery.'

Mr Arnold heaved into physical alertness for the ordeal. In a minute or two the car slid to a delicate standstill. Inside the cemetery gates was a group of half-a-dozen women, representatives of the institute for which Susan had organised many an event. Out of the lodge came the surpliced vicar, prayer-book in hand. Henry got out first and, red-faced, offered a hand to Mr Arnold, who ignored it and alighted without mishap. But for an awful moment the widower's legs seemed boneless. Then he drew himself up nobly, stood rock-like in ruminative strength, while the coffin was drawn out and borne ahead.

The two sisters stood in helplessness, hiding their faces, but peering like rabbits. The procession began to form. The vicar turned the pages of his book in mild abstraction. George and Henry sidled up beside Mr Arnold. 'I'll walk alone,' hissed Mr Arnold, and he reminded them fiercely that Miriam and Ellen were entitled to follow immediately behind him. He insisted on that being arranged. The institute women, who seemed unaware of anything unusual, took their places in the rear. The cortège moved.

The cemetery was cut out of a steepish slope, and the newly acquired section was at the top. It was quite a climb for elderly mourners; a discussion had waged in the local paper about the lack of foresight in not making a carriage road through the place. Mr Arnold, close behind the coffin and without his well-known stick, negotiated the climb with an occasional lapsing of his knees, a straightening of his back, or a rigid turning and jerking of his head, like a man doing physical exercises. But he achieved it victoriously. Behind him Ellen wept and Miriam stared in blank fear.

It was not until all were assembled before the graveside and the service had begun that Mr Arnold began to display signs of collapse. He vaguely swayed; his head lolled. George and Henry took a step nearer him. The abstract vicar droned unseeing; the institute women remained tactful behind the chief mourners. The attendants took up the roped coffin; it disappeared; a handful of earth was thrown in after it. Presently the vicar's voice stopped. George and Henry took Mr Arnold's elbows to assist him for the last look.

'Leave me alone,' Mr Arnold muttered, drawing his elbows angrily away. What had these to do with him! He advanced with renewed dignity to the brink of the grave. Looked in as if into an abyss of black tremendous loneliness. Stood there staring down in concentrated intentness, prolonged, fascinated. The vicar waited in faint surprise at the mourner's lengthy scrutiny.

George and Henry darted forward. Too late. While a single hysterical woman's cry shot up, Mr Arnold shot down, falling clumsily, arms flapping out, his disappearing face looking briefly astonished, the mouth wide open and showing all his artificial teeth. There was a moment's hesitation of unbelieving dismay. Then the bustling began. Mr Arnold lay down there on his stomach across the coffin. An upper denture gleamed out in the clay beside him.

'I knew it,' said Miriam, later, 'I felt it in my bones when you two allowed him to walk alone to the graveside. Thank heaven we don't live here.' They were in the villa in conference. Mr Arnold had been taken to the county hospital with a fractured leg.

He stayed there two months. The first patient to be received out of a grave, he was the talk and pet of the hospital; as the night sister remarked: 'He must have been a devoted husband to throw himself into his wife's grave like that! I've never known a man grieve so much. How he calls out in the night for his Susan!' . . . Cantankerous at first, he became astonishingly meek. The doctor allowed him a certain amount of whisky. The night sister, perhaps because she was shortly due for retirement, secretly allowed him a little more. She took quite a fancy to him, and some months later, thinking he had detected in her a flavour of Susan's character, Mr Arnold married her.

FRANCIS KING

The Mouse

Vernon Thurible loved his wife, Stella, as much as their daughter, Mavis, loved the white mouse which they gave her for her seventh birthday. Mavis had herself asked for the mouse, insisting that it was one mouse only, and not a pair, that she wanted: 'It won't be lonely,' she said, 'because, you see, it will always have me for its friend. I don't want it to have other friends,' she added. Vernon and Stella thought this explanation charming, and they repeated it widely in their Blackheath circle. They both adored their child.

On the day when they bought the mouse in the pet department of a large London store, they had one of their many quarrels; and, as usual, money was the cause. For a man who affected to despise money, Vernon spent an inordinate amount of time thinking how he could make it, or make his wife borrow it. It was when they came to pay for the mouse (it was handed to them in a small wicker cage which was wrapped in brown paper) that Vernon had to face the disagreeable discovery that Stella had nothing but a single ten-shilling note in her bag; so that, as they walked to the underground, he spent the time either chiding her for having spent so much that week or urging her to ask her mother for more. Vernon despised Stella's relatives, who were in business, while his were in trade. 'You were always talking about your rich uncles and aunts before we got married. But now, when it's a question either of keeping your pride or of letting your child starve, you prefer to keep your pride.'

'You know it's not that, Vernon darling.' Stella, who was small and thin, with a delicate pink and white colouring and prettily weak features, slipped her arm through her husband's. 'But it's so awful to have to ask and ask and ask. And we still owe Mummy that fifty pounds we borrowed last year.'

'If she'd had any generosity, she'd have made it a gift. She's supposed to be so fond of Mavis, isn't she? And yet if it comes to helping us over a bad patch, she won't lift a finger.' The life of the Thuribles was made up of 'bad patches'.

So Vernon continued to nag; but the curious thing was that, as he did so, his voice was never anything but friendly and reasonable, and his intelligent, humorously vivid face never ceased to smile. But for Stella's look of distress any passer-by would have assumed that they were at that moment on the best of terms.

The Thuribles were now standing on the platform, and Vernon was saying: 'Oh, I'm sick of this endless living from hand to mouth. No wonder I can't write music, when I have to worry about money day after day after day. Little did I guess what a millstone I was putting round my neck that evening I proposed to you.' When he saw the tears in Stella's eyes, he gave a good-natured laugh, to show that he was joking: no one could say that Vernon was lacking in a sense of humour. 'How wonderful it would be to have my freedom again! Do you remember how you used to say that two could live as cheaply as one? You've never been much good at addition, have you?' He swung the cage back and forth, apparently forgetful of the terrified animal that was being rolled from side to side with feebly convulsive claws that scratched on the wicker. 'Really, one day I think I shall have to get rid of you.' Stella, head lowered, was blinking away the tears with her long, flaxen eye-lashes. He came up behind her: 'Just one push' – his hands were on her shoulders – 'gently – like this.' His green eyes were flashing with merriment, and as he spoke he laughed; but Stella (who tended, as Vernon often said, to hysteria) wrenched herself free and shot through the tunnel to the opposite platform from which trains went north, instead of south. There was a train just leaving, and she was able to squeeze herself in before the doors closed on Vernon's outraged face.

At the next stop, Stella got out, and caught the bus to Blackheath; and there at the bus stop, waiting as if she had told him how she would come, Vernon was standing, with the mouse's cage still in his hand. Stella laughed as she climbed off the bus and Vernon laughed too, putting an arm round her shoulder.

Mavis was delighted with her present, and next day, at her birthday party, she amused her seven little friends by taking the mouse out of its cage and making it run up and down the sofa by prodding it with a pencil. But when a little boy attempted to prod it with his own stubby finger, she gave him a kick. She was devoted to her mouse, and wouldn't have anyone else tease it. At tea she fed it on cake crumbs and made it say 'Thank you' by pinching it between her thumb and her forefinger. She was a child with all her father's looks and good humour.

The mothers who were present were charmed by Vernon and decided that any talk of noisy quarrels or even of 'differences' must have been malicious gossip. They noticed, in particular, how lovingly Vernon stroked Stella's ash-blonde hair as he perched on the arm of the sofa beside her, and they agreed that any man who could dress so elegantly and offer them glasses of sherry at six o'clock, could not really be as badly off as their husbands maintained.

But the day after this successful tea party Vernon felt ill; he always said that the mere thought of money made him feel ill, and perhaps it was indeed this that sent him to his bed with a couple of aspirins. It was, as he pointed out to Stella, particularly unfortunate that he should be indisposed at this moment, as a music publisher had sent him a book for which an index had to be prepared by the end of the week. 'He'll never send me anything again.' Vernon groaned, and added: 'Oh, do draw those curtains. The light hurts my eyes.'

'Couldn't I do it for you?'

'The index? You, darling?' He gripped her small hand in his own large one; one would have thought that with a single squeeze he would be able to crush those fragile fingers. But Vernon was always gentle. 'How can you? You know you hate that sort of thing.'

'But we do need the money, don't we?'

'Oh, the money!' He sighed deeply and covered his face with his hands. 'Yes, we certainly need that.'

'Then don't worry. I'll do what I can with the index.'

Mavis had come in during this conversation and had thrown herself on the bed; the mouse was inside the sleeve of her cardigan and from time to time she peered down to see if all went well.

'You are angelic, darling. I don't know what I would do without you.'

But really, Vernon decided, as Stella came back and back to him with her fatuous, uncomprehending questions about the index, it would have been far simpler to do it oneself. Mavis was playing on the floor of the bedroom, and he liked to lie and watch her, as she urged the mouse up and down a staircase she had made for it out of matchboxes; but how could he be at peace and get well if Stella kept coming in to ask what should be included in the index and what left out? Not that he wanted to hurt her feelings – in fact, when she began to cry because he pointed out to her (in an entirely friendly manner, of course) that he had already explained the same point to her at least three times, he at once pulled her down on to the bed and began to kiss her neck. But, oh, he did so wish that he had married a woman of some intelligence! . . . However, she *did* persevere, there was no doubt of that; so that somehow, by staying up late for a week, she managed to complete the work, and cash a cheque for fifteen pounds with which Vernon was able to buy, among other things, the claret which the doctor had recommended so strongly for his health.

Meanwhile, by the end of that same week, Mavis had taught her mouse to scuttle up and down the matchboxes, for the reward of a piece of cheese rind. 'He's really awfully clever,' she said to her father. 'I think I could teach him anything.'

But still they needed money; soon the publisher's fifteen pounds had been spent on what Vernon would call 'the bare necessities of life' and inexplicably none of Stella's relatives would help them with a loan. Even Stella's mother, usually so generous, would do no more than treat Stella and Mavis to tea at Harrods and buy Mavis a new cage, of silver wire, for her mouse. Vernon was in despair. How could he write music? he would demand. Oh, he was sick of this life. For four years he had laboured at his symphony and now, for lack of bread, he would never get it finished. He would have to take a job. But of course, he hastened to add kindly, he didn't blame Stella.

Fortunately, however, his symphony was saved by the arrival in the flat below of a retired prep-schoolmaster. This man, who had suffered a slight stroke after his wife's death, needed someone to help with his cooking and cleaning, and Vernon put it to Stella that it would be an act of charity to help the poor old boy in his hour of distress. Stella received, of course, a token payment; for the man was not poor, and as Vernon pointed out, 'He'd probably much rather keep his independence. One must think of such things.'

The arrangement was not, however, wholly satisfactory. Often when Vernon needed Stella to copy music for him, to run an errand or to make him a cup of tea, she would be downstairs. He began to feel that the old man imposed on her; and it was no use Stella saying that he was really most kind and paid her extra if she stayed for more than the hour, for Vernon would only answer: 'You are a sweet-natured little thing. Anyone can get the better of you.'

Mr Errin (for that was his name) also had a dog, of indeterminate breed and sex, which was so old that it spent its whole day stretched out asleep on one of the flower-beds of the garden which was shared by the two flats; the poor creature appeared to like the warm moisture of the earth. Vernon himself did not work in the garden – it brought on his fibrositis – but Stella did, and it upset him to see the dog crush the flowers which she had planted with so much care. More than once he had to complain (of course in his usual friendly fashion) to old Mr Errin. Mavis also disliked the dog, being afraid it would eat her mouse; though on the rare occasions when, by accident, the animals came face to face, they appeared to feel nothing but a mild curiosity towards each other.

'Do you really *like* the old chap?' Vernon asked Stella.

'Yes, of course I do. He's awfully sweet and kind . . . By the way, he said he would lend us that twenty pounds for the rent.'

'You didn't ask him, did you?' Vernon said, horrified.

'Well – yes . . . I did.'

'Have you no pride?'

'But I thought . . . you said . . . As we were going to be turned out of the flat if we couldn't pay.'

Vernon ran his fingers through Stella's luxuriant hair: 'Silly!' he said. 'No one minds borrowing off relations. That's what relations are for. But from someone we hardly know—'

'Oh, Mr Errin's a real friend,' Stella protested. She saw the smile fade from her husband's face, and she added with a note of fearfulness in her voice: 'Isn't he?' Vernon's fingers tightened in her hair, so that it felt as if an electric current were shooting among the roots.

A week later Vernon was going to have lunch with a publisher; he was already late, as he had had to talk to Mavis severely about not teasing her mouse (she loved it, of course, and didn't mean to hurt it; but he couldn't bear to see her pulling it along by its tail, or pinching it between her fingers until it emitted its shrill, frightened squeaks) and now he found that a button was missing from the suit he wanted to wear. It was a suit barely three months old and he felt angry with the Savile Row tailors who had made it for him, and even more angry with Stella for not having noticed that the button needed sewing, when she put the suit away for him. 'Stella, old thing!' he had shouted amiably. But Stella was not in the flat.

He looked at his watch and saw that it was ten past twelve; Stella was supposed to finish her work for Mr Errin at twelve o'clock precisely. So he went down in his dressing-gown and rang at their neighbour's bell. 'Oh, Mr Thurible!' Mr Errin exclaimed. 'Do come in, won't you? Stella – your wife' – as Mr Errin corrected himself, he blushed like a schoolboy – 'that is – we are just drinking a cup of coffee together. Won't you come in and join us?'

Vernon gave his frank and charming smile. 'It's awfully decent of you, but I'm afraid it'll have to be another time. I'm dashing out to meet my publisher, and the button has come off my one and only suit. I don't want to hurry Stella, but if she *could* sew it on for me—'

'But of course, darling!' Stella had overheard the conversation and now rushed out of the sitting-room, in an overall and with her hair bound up in a scarf. 'I'm so sorry. I couldn't have noticed when I put it away.'

The Thuribles both thanked Mr Errin for his offer of the coffee and apologized for leaving so hurriedly. Vernon put his arm round Stella's waist and squeezed her as they went upstairs: but (no doubt from the haste with which he had dressed) he was trembling from head to foot.

'You look just like a little charwoman,' he teased.

'Do I, darling?'

'Which, of course, is what you are now!' They both laughed together.

When they had shut the door of their flat, Vernon said, 'I'm going to be at least half an hour late. I'd better call the whole thing off. It'll look better than keeping him waiting all that time.'

'Oh, darling!' Stella looked at him in horror. 'But I thought you were hoping to persuade him to give you an advance.'

'Well, I shall have to persuade him to do that some other time. It'll take you at least five minutes to sew on that button. You're not exactly a needlewoman, are you, poor dear?' He kissed her on the forehead.

'Couldn't – couldn't you wear another suit?' Stella suggested timidly.

'You talk as if I had a dozen to choose from.'

'Well, you have got the grey flannel—'

'*Light* grey flannel at the Athenaeum!' He laughed indulgently. 'And I can't wear the blue, it needs pressing. You remember I asked you to take it—'

'Oh, dear!' She remembered, appalled. 'I've been so busy.'

'Yes, I know. That's why I really think you'd better stop working for Mr Errin. I've noticed that you've been looking awfully run down and seedy just these last few days, and obviously the whole thing is becoming far too much for you.'

'But I *enjoy* going,' Stella protested; and at once, from the tightening of Vernon's mouth, she noticed her mistake.

'Oh, I've no doubt you do. But that doesn't alter the fact that you can't hope to run two households at one and the same time. However much you *enjoy it*.' He gave the last two words the faintest and most subtle of emphases. 'I don't like to think of Mavis being neglected – and particularly neglected for an old bore like Errin. He'll have to find himself a daily woman.'

'But I don't look on him as an employer, he's a—' she broke off.

'Yes, my dear?' She was silent. 'Well, what is he?' Stella made no answer; her large blue eyes were filling with tears. Vernon once more put his arm round her: 'Anyway we can discuss all this later – when we're a little calmer, eh?' He gave the smile which the wives of their little circle found so irresistible. 'The immediate problem is this damned lunch party. Would you ring up the old man and tell him that I've got another of my migraines? I expect he's still at his office – otherwise leave a message at the Athenaeum.'

'Oh, Vernon! Couldn't you possibly – if you take a taxi—?'

'Look, my sweet, do let me decide what I should, or should not do.' He picked up the telephone receiver and handed it to her, himself dialling the number. Stella, who had been well rehearsed in such falsehoods, told his lie for him in the tone of worried innocence which she usually adopted on such occasions. Then she put back the receiver and burst into tears.

'Now what's the matter?' Vernon asked, surprised.

Stella sobbed loudly, making strange gulping noises in the back of her throat. 'Oh, for God's sake!' Vernon said rather than shouted. 'Darling!' Now he was putting his arm again about her. 'What on earth is the matter?'

'Oh, I'm so hopeless – so useless –! I know it's all my fault.'

'It's just your kindness,' Vernon said. 'That's all it is, darling – that excessive kindness of yours. I know it's simply that you feel sorry for Mr Errin, and that of *course* there's nothing else – on your side, at least. Oh, darling – please!' Stella was now howling. 'Darling! For God's sake, be quiet! You know that I hate scenes.'

At last he picked up the latest number of the *Connoisseur* from his bureau and decided to go to the garden; one's nerves could stand just so much, and then no more. 'Darling!' he remonstrated once again as he passed out of the door. But Stella either did not, or would not, hear him. Really, she was so emotional, he told himself, as he took the stairs in twos. And a scene like this quite ruined one's appetite for lunch – apart from making it impossible for one to work.

But in the garden there was no peace either. Mavis was sobbing hysterically and battering some object, again and again, with a stone from the rock garden. Vernon went across: 'What on earth are you doing?'

Mavis continued to beat the stone wildly on the earth while the old dog, his mangy head raised, blinked glassy eyes at her from the neighbouring flower-bed.

'My God! It's – it's your mouse,' Vernon said.

'I told it – and told it – and told it,' Mavis cried between each stroke. 'I said it was not to go near the dog.' Her hair was falling about her face, and there was blood on her pinafore. Then suddenly she looked up at Vernon with a glance so cold and so penetrating that he found that he could not hold it.

'Where's Mummy?' she asked.

WILLIAM SANSOM

A Contest of Ladies

Fred Morley might easily have been mistaken for something of an eccentric. He was a 'bachelor', he was 'wealthy', he was 'retired from the stage'. It was not held unusual for such a man to be somewhat out of line with the rest of the world.

Nor, because he was a bachelor, was it unusual that a certain July evening found him in his bedroom wandering from door to window, from bed to fireplace, wondering what to do. Many evenings found him so – with the warm nights and in the dangerous flush of middle-age.

He looked at the metal plaque of bells by his bed. 'Chambermaid'. 'Waiter'. But he knew that if he rang, neither would come. His eye dropped to the telephone beneath – there were buttons which led to 'Reception' and 'Restaurant' and 'Toilet Saloon': again he knew there would be no response. He wondered – as he had done so very often in the past – whether he really would have liked a response, had this been possible. But he quickly put that old idea from his mind, he was much happier as things were.

Up on the pink satin wall-paper, in a discreet position, was inset a white celluloid notice: a scramble of black lettering begged visitors to do this or not to do that. Morley's empty mind passed to all the other empty rooms around and above him, all with the same small notice bowing and begging – for the wording of these notices was polite and obsequious, a cut above the terse commercial command – by each closed door.

Downstairs the lounge would be empty. Magazines would be arranged neatly on a central table – *Country Life*, *The Gas Times*, *The Tatler* – and the curtains would be still undrawn to let a blue evening light through on to a great splay of fresh-bought lupins. Across from the empty lounge the bar would stand open and brightly polished – and empty too. At this thought old Morley brightened. Thank goodness – no one in the best chair, no chattering gin-groups, no idle guests to be sauntered into. No porter on the doorstep to mar the evening with a 'Good evening' and a searching eye. Fred Morley knew he could stand alone on the step and survey what he wished, undisturbed and in silence. He brightened. Such people might have meant company. But was such company preferable to his own selected privacy? By all means no.

By what means? What sort of hotel was this – all trim and in working order, yet absolutely empty of people? Not empty as death, not dust-covered and cobweb-hung – but fresh-swept, with the feeling that a dozen servants had only a moment before left. It was as one might imagine a live hotel struck by plague, or conjured up in some ghost-tale, or in some unknown way emptied yet sailing equipped on its course like the maddening *Mary Celeste*.

A hotel bought by Morley? A hotel occupied entirely by Morley?

Almost. But in fact it was not a hotel at all. It was Morley's private house – decorated, in many of its more obvious features, like a hotel. This was Morley's 'eccentricity'. But was it, on closer consideration, so very eccentric? It is commonly a habit of furnishers and decorators to make things appear what they are not. Rooms – particularly of the well-to-do – have become escapes. The *chinoiserie* of Chippendale, sea-shell lairs of the rococo nymph, even the Greek revival – all have succeeded to make rooms what they are not. There have been Tudor cocktail-bars and Elizabethan garages, ship's-cabin beer-houses land-locked in a city street, chintzy cottage-rooms whose spinning-wheels shudder as the underground trains worm their way beneath. All of them studios of desire, each room an escape from four walls.

Morley's fancy to make his house look like a hotel was in fact less exotic than these. He had no vague wish to be different, it was a practical planned escape. A deep disaffection in him – the same that had left him a bachelor – had revolted against the idea of house-and-home. Given a homely looking home he would feel home-bound, anchored, done. But hotels! These he loved – he felt in them adventure, the passage of possibility, a lovely rootless going and coming, excitement stalking the corridors, sin lurking in the shadows of the fire extinguishers. They reminded him, too, of his touring days in the theatre. But against this stood the truth that hotels were in fact dreadfully uncomfortable: and homes were not. Hence – most reasonably – the transposition. He had dressed his seven-bedroomed mansion on the front of this rakish Channel seaside resort in a glamorous nostalgia for no-home.

Thus at six-thirty he sat and gazed his handsome eyes about the room and wondered what to do. Six-thirty is a bad hour. Hour of sundowners. Hour when the human beast, old moon-monkey, awakes to the idea of night. Hour of day's death and dark's beginning, uneasy hour of change. Bedrooms stalk with people changing clothes, drinks are drunk, high teas eaten, limbs washed fresh of used daylight. No wonder Fred Morley wondered, like millions around him, what to do. A stall at the Hippodrome? A sole at the Ship? Oysters at Macey's? A glass with old Burgess? A stroll by the Band – strains of the *Rosenkavalier* across green breakwaters, the dying sands? A tinkle to Mrs Vereker – though it wasn't really His Night?

But none of these appealed. So, old bachelor that he was, he decided to pamper himself. His hand, strong, freckled, mildly arthritic, flashed its opal ring round the telephone dial. To a waiter at a real hotel some doors away his actor's accent, from between handsome curling lips and through teeth white and strong, ordered oysters and mulligatawny soup and what – oh, pigeon pie? Excellent. And a good dollop of Stilton, thank you. Wine he had, and plenty of port. Down went the receiver – above his clean square jaws the lips silently smacked – and with erect leisurely stride his legs took him over to the bathroom. A good hot bath, plenty of lather. Then, in grace to a good quiet evening at home, the raisin-red frogged smoking jacket.

Morley had played the romantic lead in most of the more robust musical comedies. He had toured for twenty years the length and breadth of the Isles in the boots of a Hussar, the breeches of a Desert Hero, the golden robes of Baghdad. He had made his money, saved it, and retired. Now as he strode his ample carpets he was still every inch a baritone. The theatrical years had stylized every manly gesture, incised surety into every feature of his square strong face, greyed not at all the good brown curly hair brushed suavely back and half sideways. And now as he undid his stays the deep and tuneful voice that had quickened hearths throughout the land broke into satisfied strains that declared how Maud was to come into the garden since the Black Bat Night had flown.

But, of course, the Black Bat Night was really at that time flying in: and with it, on the evening train, there had flown in six ladies new to the town – a Miss Clermont-Ferrand, the Misses Amsterdam and Rotterdam, Miss Sauerkraut of Nuremburg, Miss Civitavecchia and Miss Great-Belt of Denmark. Every summer the Town Corporation organized a Contest of Beauty. This year, spreading its festive wings, it had decided to make the Contest international. Invitations had been despatched. In some cases accepted. Part of the result, who had been rallied in London by their various agencies, had been sent down by the evening train.

Now they stood in the Railway Buffet studying little lists of recommended hotels and sipping, with wonder and weary enthusiasm, their watery-milked sweet cups of railway tea. The names of the hotels stared up at them with promise but nonentity. There were no Ritzes, no Savoys, none of the ordinary run. There were Ships and Crescents and Royals and many lesser establishments, listed as Boarding Houses, with Gaelic, Celtic and sometimes Malayan names. All the ladies had different ideas and different purses, and all talked at once.

A group of local gentlemen sat drinking whisky and listening. These were a convivial lot, mixed commercials and retired front-walkers, black trilbies or stiff-collar tweeds. They spent most of the time ponderously pulling each other's legs; but now, with such a sudden advent of beautiful ladies, they went further. They went a bit silly. They giggled, they whispered, they mouthed and winked – the ladies, accompanied by the whisky, went straight to their heads.

Thus it was inevitable that sooner or later a sally would arch itself out at the ladies. It came very soon: an idea not indeed original, for it involved a well-tried local joke, flashed through the black trilby, the hair-grease, the hair and into the little grey cells of one of the fat red-faced commercials.

Lifting his hat, he sweated towards the ladies:

'Excuse my intruding upon yourselves, ladies – but I cannot help but see where you're not fixed up with your hotel. Now if you was to ask me – that is as I am the local man, I've lived here thirty years now – I wonder if you'd know where I'd say you'd be as best fixed up?'

He paused and looked from one to the other of those girls, eyebrows raised in huge surprise. These various girls winced, or looked away, or primped fascinated at him. He then said, sharply, with lips terse to keep a straight face:

'I'd say you'd best go to Morley's.'

A gasp, quickly suppressed, from the other men. They were adept at the grave concealing face.

The ladies looked from one to the other, then at their lists. They said there was no mention of Morley's.

The man in the trilby rose instantly to this:

'And that's where you ladies hit the nail on its head. Morley's you won't find on no list. Morley's is more . . .' he waved his hands, screwing up his eyes and searching for just that one word which would do justice to the exquisition he proposed ' . . . more what you call *select*.'

One of the tweeded gentlemen, removing his pipe from his mouth like a stopper, said gravely: 'Morley's is a *private* hotel.'

'Number Thirty-two, Marine Parade,' another said. 'Not five minutes.'

Those jolly men then fell to in earnest. Morley's was this, Morley's was that. Once warmed up they discovered subtleties of compliment one would never have suspected; they even began to argue among themselves. In short, the ladies were at length convinced, a street-plan was quickly sketched showing the way to Number Thirty-two, and, gamely swallowing their tea, they left for Fred Morley's house.

One or two, Miss Great-Belt for one, wished inwardly to show her personal superiority by choosing a more grandly named hotel (there was indeed a Bristol, a name as hallowed as the Ritz), but on practical thought it seemed wiser in a strange land at first to stick together.

One of the gentlemen started up to escort them: but was quickly dissuaded by a furtive shake of the head from the ringleader. Let matters take their course. It might be tempting to watch old Fred Morley's face; but if any one of them were seen the game would be given away.

Such was the preposterous situation when those six Beauty Queens rang the bell of Mr Morley's house. That fact is stranger than fiction has been often observed – but seldom believed. We like the ordinary, it is more restful, and liking it tend to close our eyes to the bewilderment of chance and coincidence that otherwise would strike us every minute of the day.

In the case of these six Beauty Queens, the glove of coincidence might have fitted all the more neatly if, for instance, the waiter who had brought Fred Morley's supper had just at that moment been about to leave the house. A uniformed servant would have perfected an otherwise passable illusion. But in fact that waiter had not even arrived by the time those girls pulled the bell. And it was Morley himself, in his raisin-red smoking jacket, who finally opened the door.

'*Come* into the gar – den M—' he still sang, and then stood stupefied.

'We would like some rooms,' said Miss Great-Belt, who like many Danes spoke English well. 'Have you any to spare?'

Since those girls were Beauty Queens, they were passably beautiful. To Fred Morley the vision of their six faces framed in his doorway like singers at some strange summer carol-feast both bewildered him and set his mind working at an unusual rate.

The Misses Amsterdam and Rotterdam, and the two Latins Civitavecchia and Clermont-Ferrand, now followed by saying in many mixed words that for their part double rooms would do. Morley had a further second's freedom for thought. It did not occur to him that these girls were part of a joke that had in fact been played once or twice before. Beauty seldom suggests fun. His mind instead remembered that the town was full, that these girls were probably tramping from door to door hoping for rooms in a private house, that this was difficult since they were so large a party, that it was pitiable that people should be in such a predicament, that it was the more so since they were beautiful people, that he had a large house, that it was largely empty, and . . . why not?

He bowed and opened the door wider for the ladies to pass:

'Certainly, Madame,' he said, wondering what the plural could be, ' . . . I should be delighted to accommodate you.'

They scarcely bothered to thank him, but moved brusquely into what was patently the vestibule of a hotel. In fact, that eccentric decoration hardly mattered. As foreign visitors they would never have questioned an ordinary homely hall: it would simply have looked part of the mad English scene.

'La fiche?' asked Miss Clermont-Ferrand.

'Ah, oui,' Morley smiled, having no idea what this could mean. And added, as a pleasantry: 'Sanfaryan.'

'Vraiement?' smiled back Miss Clermont-Ferrand, impressed by such liberty.

But Morley then thought: By Jiminy I'll have to get moving. And raised his hand to command attention, and asked them kindly to wait a moment, and scuttled upstairs. He ran – striding now no longer – to the telephone by his bed and breathlessly called the restaurant to order not one but seven dinners. In half an hour. And then raced round the bedrooms. Fortunately these were kept made up: two double rooms, a good single room and a single dressing-room. One of these had already been slept in by guests on the previous weekend. He pulled the sheets back, smoothed out a crease or two, decided to risk it. But airing? Six hot-water bottles? Impossible. He ran round lighting with little pops gas-fire after gas-fire. Then he thought: Bathrooms! And banged open the door of the second bathroom, removing his rowing machine, a Hoover, some dirty linen and his golf-clubs: then rushed to his own to wipe off the comfortable soap-ring left only half an hour before.

In that fine old actor's frame there coursed a sort of boyish exaltation. For nearly nothing would he have disturbed the repose of his calm dinner alone: but for such a six . . . well, it hardly happened every night. He had no designs. He was simply exhilarated, flowing with the good red blush of boyishness. He felt chivalrous, too. No snake of desire but simply the flushes of virtue filled him.

He descended to take the ladies up to their rooms.

The oysters were laid out on seven plates, the ladies had been allocated their seats round the large table in the dining-room, and he himself, having seen that seven portions of pigeon pie were keeping hot in the kitchen, was at last on the point of sitting himself down – when, in the general delight at the sight of oysters, Miss Great-Belt spoke out:

'Oysters! This is very good!' she said, wondering at the same time what the charges of so considerable a hotel might be. 'But it was good luck indeed those gentlemen recommended us such a hotel!'

Morley's hand was actually on his chair to pull it back. Instead, he pulled back his hand.

'Recommended? Hotel?'

A sudden spasm gripped him where a moment before the gastric juices had begun to play.

'Surely yes,' Miss Great-Belt smiled. 'Some gentlemen in the railway bar. They said this is the best hotel we can have.' Then she added with a knowing smile, a condescension to the servant standing above her, 'But they will come quick enough for their percentage, no?'

'No?' Morley stuttered. 'Oh, yes, yes.'

The old joke! This time it had come off? His chivalry blew away like old hot air. He saw suddenly that he was in a very difficult position – he was a fraud. These ladies were deceived. They might be very angry. And more. He was a bachelor. Alone in his house, he had induced them to come inside. What would the world make of *that?* What would the neighbours, what would the Town Council, what would even the Court of Law think? Was it legal? Were there seduction laws? Certainly there were Boarding House Licences.

These and more terrors mounted in his mind. With regret he let his hand fall absolutely from the chair, then sculpted it round towards his plate of oysters, already beginning to act the part of a real hotel employee. He muttered that he did not know why an extra place had been laid and began to withdraw the oysters to take and to eat them in the sanctity of the kitchen, in what now must be his right and proper place. For he had decided to play the rôle out. For the moment it was the only thing to do. At all costs avert suspicion, a scene, the full fury of these now formidable girls.

His hand was about to grasp the plate – but Miss Civitavecchia's, lizard-like, was quicker:

'Piacere – do not trouble. It is plain,' she said, smiling round at the others, 'that we can eat some more?'

'Please place this on the bill,' she added.

Morley tried to smile and withdrew, oysterless, to the empty kitchen. Some minutes later he took care to bring only six soup-platesful of mulligatawny into the dining-room.

The dining-table had been laid with only one pepper-pot, one salt-cellar. The ladies required more. Morley, his soup and now his lonely pigeon growing cold, had to search for, fill, and serve others. Vinegar was required. And oil. And in the matter of drinks there was white wine, red wine, beer and water to be found for different tastes. Morley was run off his feet. His hurriedly gulped pigeon flew instantly back at him. And on top of all this he found it necessary, on being questioned, to invent excuses for the quietness of the 'hotel' and for the non-appearance of other servants.

Only later, when at last he had seen the last of the ladies mount the stairs – tired from their travels, they all went up early – only later when the front door was locked and with waiter-tired feet he lay in bed, did he allow himself at last a great retrogressive chuckle.

He saw suddenly how he lay there on his back like a dear old daddy-keeper, with his six young charges all tucked safely up sleeping blissfully on their six pillows. Six sudden beautiful girls at first look all of a piece. Only after a while, when the first endazzlement is over, can one distinguish between them. Now still to Morley they were banded indistinguishable, six little beauties all in a row, as if that beauty itself served the uniform purpose of a school hat and a gym frock.

And so there he lay, hoary old guardian of his exquisite crocodile, and chuckled, and gradually – not knowing what might happen in the morning, too tired now to care – fell asleep.

In the morning, reason asserted itself. Such a fantastic situation could not be allowed to continue. He considered for a moment applying for a boarding-house licence, hiring servants: but this was plainly too much trouble. And plainly it extended the falsity of the situation.

His daily housekeeper supplied the answer. He rose early to intercept her. He explained that he had given sanctuary the night before to six roofless ladies. The housekeeper froze. Morley pretended not to notice and asked her to prepare six breakfasts. The housekeeper pressed her lips together. Morley acted a laugh.

'An – er – equivocal position for an old bachelor, eh, Mrs Laidlaw?' his lips laughed. 'But safety in numbers, Mrs L., safety in numbers.'

This simple remark had a far greater effect than Morley could have hoped for. The word 'equivocal' put Mrs Laidlaw momentarily off her balance, it rescued Morley again into the status of the Master. But then that 'safety in numbers' in its turn saved her own comfort of mind, it sank her happily to earth, it was comfortable and what it said was what other people said all the world over. She served the breakfasts, hypnotized by the saying, muttering it over and over to herself. Only some hours later, when she had digested the good looks and the alien chic of the ladies' clothes, whorish to her woollen eyes, did she give notice.

But long before that Morley had waylaid Miss Amsterdam, who was first down. Miss Amsterdam was a dark-haired Hollander, possibly a descendant of the Spanish occupation. Most of her was covered with long dark hairs – but her face shone out from among the cropping like a lovely pale brown moon. She came hurrying down the stairs, and was already across the hall, between the ever-open cocktail-bar and the ever-empty lounge, almost to the door, handbag swinging like a third buttock, before Morley could stop her. But he came striding on with great actor's strides, calling: 'Excuse me! Miss . . . Miss . . . ?'

'Call me Amsterdam.'

'Oh? . . . Well, by all means . . .'

Leading her aside into the lupined lounge, he made an unclean breast of it all. The word 'roofless' that he had by chance brought up to thaw Mrs Laidlaw provided his key to a happy simulation of the truth. It conjured the pitiful idea of 'roofless' ladies, it implied an open door and an open heart to all the travel-stained abroad in the night in this his native country. He explained the hotel furnishings as mementoes of his own travels, his tours – off-handedly stressing, as a condiment of glamour, his place in the theatre – and finally begged Miss Amsterdam to excuse this whole misunderstanding that might so easily be taken as an impertinence on his, a bachelor's part. Would she convey this to the other ladies, would they understand?

Miss Amsterdam's brown round lovely face went this way and that, it made shapes of surprise and petulance and tenderness and excitement – then finally all broke up into a wild pudding of laughter. Brown pudge of cheeks crinkling, eyes gone, brows ridged, red mouth neighing never-seen underteeth – no more now than a big brown baby howling agonies of wind.

Slapping one hand across that mouth, and the other over her stomach, she tripped her lovely legs upstairs. And Fred Morley was left waiting – for was this laughter or hysteria? – on his uneasy tenterhooks.

From upstairs silence.

A long silence. A silence in a lonely downstairs when the upstairs is full but behind closed doors. Creaks of silence, rafters loaded with words.

But – ten minutes later all was over. On the landing a door burst open and laughter, like water from a thirsty tap, laved out and down the stairs. Morley heaved a long and blessed relief.

With the laughter came the ladies – all six, all smiles. They milled in and stood in a semicricle round old Fred Morley, who rose and gravely bowed. Miss Amsterdam broke instantly.

'Mr Morley – I have told all the girls all you have told me and all of us girls have agreed together you are a kind and a big sweet.'

'We thank you,' dimpled Miss Rotterdam, a round blonde cheese of a girl.

'Comme c'est infiniment drôle . . .' giggled Clermont-Ferrand, who, in trousers and a checked shirt, but with a wicked fringe and a golden anklet, appeared to be a woman on two levels or layers – a check-shirt cowgirl of St Germain enclosing a Nana of more liberal boulevards.

'Such a dinner!' sighed with wondering shakes of her head the practical Miss Nuremburg. This one, who held the annual title, comic to the English but a beautiful reality to the German, of Miss Sauerkraut, had in her pallid tall glory exactly the texture of that well-prepared vegetable. A dab of rotkohl would not have harmed her cheeks.

Miss Civitavecchia took a deep breath and began, palms outstretched: 'Ma – ma Mi – a!' And went on, for a long time, expending in a tumult of Italian the full breath of her bosom. On the solid foundations of a Roman body she carried the small head of a snake: it was as if some Laocoon had been fused with the bust – the bust is meant – of a great – and great is intended – Roman Empress.

So Fred Morley stood overwhelmed by this crescent before him of beauty, smiles and gratitude. He felt, and for the moment was, loved. A pleasant sensation. But, as an Englishman, he was embarrassed . . . and through the glow of pleasure his instinct was to escape by offering them all a drink. This last was on his lips – when Miss Great-Belt at last spoke up.

Miss Great-Belt was plainly the most beautiful of all. Her present title embraced that royal reach of sea separating the Danish islands of Fünen and Zealand, and no dimension of her own. She was a dark red-head. Her skin white over lilac. Her eyes deep dark blue. Her whole face the face of a cat – round high cheekbones, nearly no nose, many small teeth curving in a long smile like the dream of a bite: yet all squared into the face of a girl. How could she have become so? Copenhagen is a great seaport through which have passed many strange fathers. Whatever . . . there she was, a brilliant cat-faced red-head, who might bite, who might smile, and who now was the only one to say a disaffected word:

'How much do we owe?' she said.

Practical? Or battle-cry? Fred Morley's interest quickened. Confused by the compliments of the others, which made those ladies into no more than lovely willing sisters, his well-tried nose sniffed Woman. For the first time one among those beauties stood out separate.

'I had hoped,' he instantly said, 'that in the circumstances you would accept my hospitality?'

Miss Great-Belt looked him calmly in the eye.

'Thank you,' she said, serene and ominously composed, 'but that is impossible. Would you please be so kind as to tell us the charge?'

Of course, all the others had now to agree with her. All their various voices rose to insist. They chattered to each other and at Morley and he could not say a word. But he kept his eye on Miss Great-Belt. She had taken out her powder-puff and with aggravated unconcern dabbed her nose: he noticed with rising spirits that she used no mirror. It was a gesture. It meant war.

Finally it was settled that the ladies paid Morley a reasonable sum per day. Later he telephoned the Town Hall to ask whether he might take in paying-guests. The clerks, for the town was overcrowded, were delighted. He arranged for service and food – after all, he said to himself, it would only be for two or three days. Then, much later, when all this was fixed, asked Miss Great-Belt personally whether he might escort her round the town.

'No,' was the answer. With a straight look between the eyes.

All that was on the Thursday. The Contest was scheduled for the Saturday. For three in the afternoon at the Pier Aquadrome.

Thus, for these girls, there was much to be done. Much final furbishing. Polishing, paring, depilating and all the other many measures of massage and exercise necessary to bring tissues of flesh and hair – Fred Morley was heard with a weary chuckle later to say – to scratch. For in the course of these operations old Morley's eyes were opened.

Overnight the calm of his bachelor ménage was transformed. Those girls worked themselves hard. The rooms, the corridors, the bathrooms drifted in a dry flood of cosmetic cartons: balls of cotton-wool and paper tissues mated with blonde, brunette and auburn curlings in every corner: powder flew everywhere, made solid marble shafts of the sunbeams: oil and cream made each empty surface – every table, every shelf – a viscous adventure.

Masseuses and masseurs – brisk women and strange men – came and went: Morley, to lighten the load on his new temporary staff, and because he spent much time nervously wandering and waiting downstairs, answered the door to a ceaseless stream of such visitors and the slick peremptory drivers of delivery vans. He tried as far as possible to avoid going upstairs. Things upstairs were too strange. He had found Miss Clermond-Ferrand sitting with her head in her beautiful hands and each elbow cupped in the half of a lemon. Across the landing there had whisked a blue kimono topped by a face plastered livid dry pink, with hollows it seemed where the eyes might be and naked lips huge now as a clown's, a face terribly faceless – too late he had seen that this might be Miss Great-Belt. Then Miss Rotterdam, in a bathing-dress, had come bumping across the landing on her bottom, and vanished into the bathroom: no hands nor legs, she had explained *en route* – a question of stomach muscles. Miss Sauerkraut liked to lie on the balcony on half a ping-pong table, head-downwards. Miss Civitavecchia he had found carefully combing the long black beards that hung from her armpits, a peninsular speciality: unlike Miss Amsterdam, who took no such Latin pride in the strong growth of dark hair that covered most of her – it seemed that whenever he asked for her the answer came: 'Upstairs shaving.'

So Morley remained downstairs.

He sat there with a whisky and soda, half impatient, half-amused, but more simply apprehensive of what else might come. He sat listening, cocking his head anxiously at the bumps and scufflings that came from above, and answering the doorbell.

But above all the question of Miss Great-Belt lightly, but persistently, tormented him. He was quite conscious of his middle years, and of her youth – yet after all was he not Frederick Morley, the idol of a thousand hearts? He felt affronted: a smile perhaps, a gracious gesture would have been enough to appease him. But this – what was it called – *snootiness*!

Beyond the Fred Morley in him, the male rose in combat. Something must be done.

Yet was this attitude of hers exactly *snooty*? He wondered whether it might run deeper. It lacked the proper coquetry. It was the result, perhaps, more of a solid and almost matronly composure unusual in a so strikingly beautiful young girl. She had an air of remarkable self-containedness. When she walked, it was always with a sense of destination: she knew where she was going. When she carried parcels, one felt those parcels would never be undone in a flurry but would each await its proper time. There was a feeling of unhurried *process* about her. Though she bore the fiercely beautiful face of a cat, she was phlegmatic – but then perhaps a cat is, despite some appearances, the most phlegmatic of animals?

Later that evening – it had been a beautiful, if indeed a long day – he watched her leave the house arm-in-arm with Miss Sauerkraut. Their summer dresses clung coolly in the evening air to what must have been naked bodies, and the tall swanlike Sauerkraut served only to emphasize Miss Great-Belt's warm pliabilities. The two paused outside the door, then turned one way down the westering front. Two youths in padded flannels detached themselves from the group that lounged now always discreetly over the road from his front door, and at a suitable distance followed, eyes intent, mouths whetting for the whistles that would come.

The cavalier rose in Morley; but he quieted it. Then, pair by pair, he watched the others go. Each was followed by two, sometimes three, of the watching gentlemen. And then he was left alone in the house. At last – peace. He breathed a great sigh of peace. But to himself, and for himself. It was a false sigh. He knew that in a very few minutes the house would feel too empty. And so it did. He wandered for some time from room to room fingering things, sitting for a while here and then there. But he kept thinking of all those who had left, so young and expectant, to enjoy the evening – and he began to feel his years. That would never do. His bachelordom had taught him all about self-commiseration – and it was his custom to guard against it. He selected a hat, a curl-brimmed panama, pale but not too pale for evening wear, and left for the Club. The stolid usuality, the pot-belly of male companionship was what he needed.

*

The Yacht Club was not much frequented by yachtsmen. A few faded photographs of old racing-cutters spinnakered across the cream-painted, nautically planked walls. Well-polished brass shone here and there, and to seaward one wall of the lounge was given to good white-framed observatory glass. However, it was now a place mostly of comfortable horsehair where members, the elect of the town, might come and drink.

The warm fruity smell of gentlemen at ease greeted Fred Morley as he entered the lounge: tobacco smoke, fumes of whisky and port, horsehair and something else – starch, red flesh, woollen underpants? – ballooned out its bouquet of security across the Turkey carpet. Here at last was escape from all feminine essences! He rang the bell for a drink and, giving a wink or a nod to various members couched in the horsehair, joined a group at the further end.

'Why if it isn't Fred!'

'Come in, Fred – we was just about to 'ave a round of Kiss-in-the-Ring.'

For it had already got about that Fred Morley had some young ladies staying in his house. Young ladies of the theatrical profession, it was presumed.

Those who now addressed Fred were a mixed bag of the livelier, wealthier citizens of the town – a couple of aldermen, a big butcher, a retired military man well-invested in beach and fairground concessions, the local brewer's brother-in-law. They were an affable, energetic, powerful lot. As far as they were allowed, they ran the town – not too unfairly. Mixed of the professional and tradesmen's classes, they forgot such differences in a close-masonry of well-to-do malehood; they even included some of the now not so well-to-do, on grounds that they had once been so – those only were excluded who had not yet come solidly up in the world. They were a cut above those other bantering gentlemen who in the first place had sent his six guests to Morley – yet they too always affected a jovial banter among themselves.

For some time Fred Morley sipped his whisky and warmed his marrow at the hands of these gentlemen. Then a Mr Everett Evans came in. Everett Evans, since he was an alderman, a prosperous draper and a local bright spark, had been appointed chairman of the judicial committee that was to sit upon the Beauty Queens. Conversation had already turned upon this coming event. Morley had kept his mouth immaculately shut. But now Evans himself had come in.

'Hallo, hallo – look who comes here!' called this group of men.

'What you having, Everett?' they then said.

'Large bicarbonate and soda, thank you,' answered Mr Evans.

'For Evans' sake!'

'That's just what. For the sake of poor Evans's poor belly, that's what.' He paused and looked mystified. Then: 'Know what I've been drinking last twenty-four hours?'

They had fallen into amused, expectant silence. Evans's chin went out, he looked at each of them accusingly, then let his eyes bulge as he blurted:

'Barium.'

'Barium?'

'No lie. Barium. Little white glassfuls of bloody barium.'

'What the hell . . . ?'

'First they strip you. Then they put you in a kind of a smock affair, apron you might call it – with bloody lacing up the back. They let you keep your socks on – but them laces! Bows all down the back, bows all over your arse come to that.' He paused for breath, the others were looking startled.

And then he went on: 'That's the start of it. So you're left there all buttons and bows reading your old copy of *Punch*. Then they say come in, and in you go in a big dark black room and then you get your barium. Whole glassful. First thing down your gullet for twelve hours. Metal, it is. Tastes like ice-cream carton.'

Another breath:

'Then they do you.'

'Do you?' The gentlemen leaned forward, uneasy. '*Do* you?'

'Take your photo. The old X-ray.'

Now breaths of relief, tittering. But Evans raised his hand.

'No laughing matter, I tell you. Ulcers, that's what I've got. Stomach ulcers. You know when I've been feeling bad these last months – since Christmas like? The old sawbones says he's worried I might have something proper dicky down below and sends me along to this hospital for the photo. Well, they found 'em all right. Ulcers. No lie.

'And what's more I got more photos to be took – taken like. And 'ow the 'ell I'm going to look all these bathing bellies in the face I don't know.'

Everett Evans looked down sadly into his glass of soda. Little bubbles raced up at him, burst at him.

'Day after tomorrow it is. I can't do it. Someone'll 'ave to stand in for me.'

He looked up suddenly and glared round the company.

'Well?' he said vicious, 'any offers?'

All those men now looked at each other nervously. They simpered. Not one but secretly would have loved being up lording it over so many Beauties. But there had been too many jokes about the 'Bellies' already, each man saw himself up there on the platform blushing and being laughed at. So now all began rapidly to mumble excuses – jolly excuses, for seriousness would be suspect. 'The old woman'd never forgive me.' 'What – me with a grown-up daughter?' 'Think of my poor old heart.'

Except for Morley. Through Morley's mind there flashed a sudden sunlight. Here it was – on a platter! Here was the prize for Miss Great-Belt! And he – with a courteous smile – presenting it! She'd eat out of his hand! He gave a great cough.

They all looked at him. He said nothing, coughed again, looked particularly at no one and nothing.

It worked.

'The very man! Why did no one think?'

'Love's young dream! Be like falling off a log, eh, Fred? Busman's holiday.'

Everett frowned at him, the only one severe: 'Well, Fred – how about it? I can fix it—'

'Mm,' Fred said, looking out through the big marine windows. The sea was dotted here and there with little boats. Their sails took the last evening sun. He did not see them. 'I don't know that I'm doing anything that afternoon, nothing special . . .'

'I'll fix it then, Fred.' Everett pressed his lips, fixing, together.

'We–ell—,' mused Fred.

'*But*,' said the one man there who knew, 'is this right? With some of them staying there in his house?'

'What!' This was news. They all dug him in the ribs – with their eyes, their great laughing teeth. 'Old rascal!' 'There's a dark horse!'

'Yes,' Fred sighed, more than ever casual, 'I've got six of them.'

'Safety in numbers then,' hissed Everett Evans, 'that fixes it.'

'*But*,' said that one man again.

'Now look 'ere,' Evans exploded, 'Fred's had more skirt in 'is life than you've 'ad 'ot dinners. Think six little bellies mean a thing to Fred? You're off your rocker! I tell you I can fix this easy.'

In any case those other men, accustomed to the pulling of wires, were hardly worried by prospects of collusion. This now suited them. It made things easy. Fred was the man. They all agreed.

'Well, Fred, shall I fix it?' said Everett.

Morley made one final hesitation, for form's sake. He pursed his lips, ruminated, then suddenly sharply nodded. 'All right then. I'll do it.'

'Good boy,' rose ulcerous Evans. 'Lead me to the blower. This needs fixing right now.'

And so it was fixed.

It was a different Fred Morley who sat downstairs the next morning in deference to the upstairs pandemonium. From bar to lounge to front door he walked – but this time with a glint in his eye, a chuckling of hands together, sometimes the tum-tumty-tum of a little song. She may touch her toes and waggle herself and knead herself like dough, he thought – ha, *knead* herself, who'll she be needing next, eh? He blew a kiss upstairs to the invisibly exercising Great-Belt. Old Fred Morley and none other! Tum-ti-tumty-tum. And outside it was a beautiful morning, the sun shone. Old Fred Morley? Old me Aunt Fanny! Forty-eight if a day. Middle-age. And no spread.

Nor was it quite the same upstairs that morning as the day before. Those girls had had their bikinis delivered: some were too big, some too small. Tall pale Sauerkraut became too huge a goddess in hers too big: Miss Amsterdam, her brown skin cooing against the new white slips ordained by the Council but also too small, went into a corner and attached with the vigour of a true Hollander various appealing frills of her own – and of course there was a row about that. And of course the girls had by now survived their first affability – they were getting each other's measure. Some had seen others at something, others had heard some say this or that. Sides were taken, embattlements formed. But between squalls and bickering a sense of dignity prevailed. No one actually touched anyone else.

Meanwhile out on the front, on the sea – all was plain sailing. It was lovely weather and the sea lay smoothly sparkling blue. White paint of pier and railing stood freshly deadly clean against all that blue and the colours of people, boats, cars, kites – and Fred Morley had an idea. He sent, by the new and overpaid and delighted maid, messages up to the ladies Rotterdam and Clermont-Ferrand. Would they do him the honour of a stroll and an apéritif before luncheon?

All he thought was: 'They're nice girls. I'd like a stroll. I've better plans for the Danish lass, let her bide (and it'll perhaps do her good).'

Rotterdam and Clermont-Ferrand – the one butterflying her arms to raise further her already sturdy breasts, the other sitting in front of a mirror practising 'facial yoga' – that is making grotesque narcissist kisses at herself to exercise the mouth, then pecking her head forward twenty times a minute like a little hen on her bright young egg – read their messages with approval and half an hour later those two were one on each of Fred Morley's arms strolling the Front. Morley in a fault-lessly raffish suit of biscuit tussore, with a high stiff collar, a pin in his tie and a curl to his hat: Miss Rotterdam blonde in flowered silk that wisped round her so closely in the breeze that those following could see not only the lovely knobbles of her vertebrae but the knobbles of her suspender-belt too: Miss Clermont-Ferrand in high white shoes and a strange white belt almost taller than its breadth round her no-waist, black hair flowing, black silk buttocks a-swing, preposterously and magnifi-cently French.

Rotterdam in her friendly Dutch way, which concealed heaven knew what guile, had taken Morley's arm to draw his attention to a group of young men playing cricket on the sands below. 'You English,' she had laughed, pressing her round lips back on to her teeth, making enormous dimples, and giving Morley's arm a niecely squeeze. All of which Clermont-Ferrand immediately, and fiercely, noticed – so that not to be outdone she had taken the other arm, pulling Fred's interest towards a sombre green-painted glass wind shelter: 'Why do you have autobus shel-ters,' she asked, in innocence of the normal weather prevailing on such a parade, 'when you have no autobuses?' And panted up a charming little laugh to him that also implied 'Oh, you dear mad Englishman.' But at the same time panted her mouth itself, open and eager, red-lipped and wetly pink inside, teeth laughing wide and tongue-tip pointing right out at him very close to his startled eyes.

So Fred had them both hugged on his arms. He puffed his chest with a deep breath of the good clear sea-air of morning and felt, there in the sunlight with sea to the left and bright traffic to the right, with the Cliff Memorial Gardens pine-green ahead and the white pier-dome flashing all holiday joy, good to be alive.

It was in such style that he was observed, a little further on, by those same local gentlemen who had first sent him the girls. These locals moved in a group: just then they had moved that group, bellies eased and jolly with good morning beer, from the brass-flashing doors of a near-by saloon to take a breather of sea-air before the next. But when they saw Fred they gaped, their spirits gravened and sank. For they were in that least enviable of situations – that of the practical joker who slips on his own banana-skin, that of him who is laughed at last. Yes, it had gone wrong all right. There was Fred sitting pretty, with *two*, with a blondie and a blackie, one of each kind, one to suit whatever his fancy was, turn and turn about – and they had put this in his way! They had actually been such damned idiots as to send him that choice handful he had there! Not thinking, not dreaming to keep the handful for themselves, and send it somewhere quiet round the corner where they might call later to pass the time of day . . . Oh well, they supposed it was the booze again, that's what it was. Can't have everything. But – that it should be Fred! Fred whom always secretly they had envied, Fred who'd had it on a platter all his life, bags of it, oodles of it there on his stage-doorstep whichever way he might turn . . . while *they* . . .

Now to Fred passing with a beauty on each arm they raised their hats and gave grim fixed smiles, new white teeth and old yellow ones flashing in the sun: to which Fred Morley, deeply satisfied, bowed and passed on his triumphant way.

Yet those gentlemen would not have been so discomforted had they seen him an hour hence. For matters did not continue so well. In the first place, those girls were young and active, they were out to enjoy themselves and not content at all simply to take the morning air. Also, as foreigners, they were inquisitive, they wanted to taste the oddities of this strange new country. So that soon Clermont-Ferrand had dragged them to a fish-and-chip booth that lay just below down some steps: and she walked now with newspaper in one hand and a chip in the other, fish-oil lustrous all over her lipstick and powdered chin. And Rotterdam had asked for a small propeller on a coloured stick, which she waved fluttering high, while firmly her other fist clasped a long thick truncheon of pink peppermint rock. They giggled bending, pointing, nudging, giving high shrieks of awe and shock at so many strange things to see. With rock and fish-and-chips they had settled their feminine differences, now they were all for fun. And having discovered the livelier scenes of stalls and crowds beneath the arches of the Parade they dragged Morley from sweet-shop to pin-table, from whelk to winkle stand, from jellied-eel to ice-cream barrow. They took him on the Dodgem cars and they had him photographed with them in sailor hats standing in front of a huge cardboard fishing-smack. (The photographer, giving his rump a resounding whack, had cried: 'Another good smack gone to the bottom!') Loudly as Morley protested, the louder they laughed and the further they dragged him. They thought these were no more than the coy protestations of an elderly man enjoying himself.

Fred Morley had planned an apéritif on the terrace of the best hotel in the town, a terrace just overlooking the street and readily seen from there: he would have sat with his two beautiful guests and from that eminence with a drink in hand and a naughty glint in his eye enjoyed the envy of passers-by for the half-hour until luncheon. And then luncheon. Cold salmon, a bottle of the best, the white clean cloth, the silver and the laughter of these two pairs of lovely red lips. This had all gone wrong. Those girls had no time for luncheon. He was tired, jolted, hungry, thirsty. And he did not wish to be seen even up on the Marine Parade itself with two such high-spirited girls – who now wore each a hat with a large motto printed on it. Yet of course, when they had had enough of the beach, up they had to go.

And there, to cap everything, he saw approaching him Miss Great-Belt. Miss Great-Belt with her fine red hair and in an orange dress holding in one hand a towering stick of electric pink candy-floss, a wild mane of strident sugar which every so often she kissed with her bright carmine lips. In the other hand – and still she managed all this with no lessening of self-composure – she held the arm of a sleek young giant in a shirt of flowered American silk.

He nearly hated her. And it was then, at a moment of shame and dislike, that she made towards him her first affable gesture. She waved her great pink floss-stick with the benign gesture of passing royalty – then gave him a huge, long, tranquil wink! And passed on.

When at last he was safely home, and when thus in comfort and at ease his temper had subsided – he still remembered that wink, reviewed it in a more benevolent light, and began to build up implications for it. Hope flowered. Wish welcomed fulfilment. It was plain her mood had turned, she had completed her feminine duties – the period of cat-and-mouse play laid down in the rules – and now she was blossomed and waiting. It only remained for him to pluck her.

So that an hour later, when he met her in the hall, he mentioned that he had a box at the Hippodrome that night. And she charmingly agreed to be his guest. At the theatre? At seven-thirty? Most kind. And supper afterwards. Delightful.

But at seven-thirty she was not at the theatre, nor at eight-thirty. He telephoned home. No, she was not in. She had gone out – to what? *What*? To a *dance*?

He slammed down the receiver and left, furious.

When she came in that night he was waiting for her. She came in early – for the next day was the day of the Contest, and she had to enjoy a long night's sleep – she came in a little breathless, her lovely red hair ablaze in the light, now with no pink candyfloss but in an evening dress the colour of the night sky. For a second when she saw him she hesitated: but instantly then gathered herself and came flouncing, almost on those tall legs bouncing, along the hall, unperturbed as usual, a glint of disdain in her navy eyes, but her lips pouted to smile. And as she came up to him she did smile.

'Good evening.'

Now it was he who played with composure.

'Good evening,' he said coldly. 'I missed you at the theatre.'

'The theatre? Of course – I'm so sorry. But you know – I really felt I could not come. To sit about all evening in a stuffy box! I needed exercise, you know. The great day tomorrow!'

'Indeed? And it was nothing that I waited a full hour for you?'

'I've said I am sorry.'

'And that is all?'

She said nothing. But looked at him curiously.

Then she asked: 'You really expected me?'

He looked surprised. 'Naturally.'

'Well *really*. You spend the morning with not one but *two* of these . . . these *women* upstairs. And then you expect to spend the evening with *me*? What do you think I am? What next? Shall I tell you what *you* are – you're an old satyr, that is what. A wolf! With pointed ears! With *hoofs*!'

She had raised her voice – he was so surprised he put up a hand to feel his ears – and then, having reached her climax with the word 'hoofs', which she blew at him with a mouth shaped for whoofing whole houses down, she was gone.

He stood there a moment amazed. Then his lips snapped shut. 'The Great Day tomorrow?' he said to himself. 'So be it.'

The Great Day dawned differently to those preceding. In the early hours, as from nowhere, big clouds blacker than the night had loomed up, flashed into fire, burst into water. Straight down, as if some celestial bucket had slopped over, the rains had fallen. Summer hails had swept the front. The temperature had fallen a swift ten degrees: then more. A wind had sprung up, gathering into a light steady gale. Until when dawn finally broke the Marine Parade lay drenched and grey, chilled and windy and drizzled, deserted and to remain so throughout a long wet cold day.

Morley had awoken in the night to hear the hailstones drumming and booming on the glass verandah roof below his window: and when at nine o'clock he went downstairs not at all well-slept, the house was grey and dead, no shafts of summer light livened the rooms, the blue lupins sat dusty like drab flowers in the corner of a dull boarding-house. Which this is, he savagely thought.

Yet it was hardly dull – for throughout the morning the sounds upstairs rose to a climax. Most of the girls were now not speaking to each other. But those who did yelled at the tops of their voices. Their frenzy in these last hours of preparation rose to new and furious levels. By twelve o'clock Morley could bear it no longer, he took his mackintosh off the peg and went out.

The air on the Parade was pleasanter than he had supposed. Forlorn, perhaps, the look of things – but there was a stimulating clarity abroad, a briskness of new air blown in from the sea. He looked across at the scudding waves, took deep breaths, and in between puddles stepped out briskly. Rain-soaked boats lay about the deserted beach like wrecks, a solitary figure in a mackintosh came swept by the wind down one street and disappeared up another.

This was exactly what Morley needed. He needed a change, he needed a breath of air. He was no longer angry with that Miss Great-Belt – he had lived too long to stay too deeply perturbed by such events – but only irritated: and that irritation included Miss Rotterdam and Miss Clermont-Ferrand as well, in fact the whole lot of them. He wanted his peace back. And now as he stepped out against the rain he reflected with pleasure that in a few hours it would in fact be all over. The Contest would be done and won. Not won by Miss Great-Belt, though – and a sense of justice rather than rancour filled him as he made this reservation. Yet after the Contest would they really leave? Probably – they were mostly subsidized. And certainly – if the weather held. 'Blow, blow, thou winter wind—' he hummed more cheerfully to himself as he paced along.

He went to the Club and refreshed himself. Everett Evans wished him a gloomy 'best of luck' for the afternoon – but left before the eating. Morley then had a good luncheon in the company of his fellows.

The Contest had been scheduled to take place in the open-air salt-water pool – the Pier Aquadrome, a place of civic pride. Now it had to be removed inside, into the Aquadrome's Winter Garden. This was a large white concrete modern building set like a plate-glassy liner, all decks and terraces, astern the paddle-boat old Pier.

By half-past two, in spite of the weather, quite a queue had assembled. Most of those that formed it, men and women alike, wore pixie-hoods. Tall-pointed heads leaned this way and that, chattering like a troop of fairies drenched with harebell dew – the women like wet narcissus petals in their grey-white plastics, the men in duffle-hoods like hairy great gnomes. All these were admitted slowly into a bare concrete hall brilliantly shadowed by mauve strip-lighting.

This ominous form of illumination has been called 'daylight' lighting. Yes – but it is the light of the worst day of the worst month of the year, the lilac light of a raw February afternoon. Faces everywhere lost their colour, lips turned purple-black and skins took on the pallor of long illness. Nevertheless, though soaked and drained of colour, the audience managed a certain cheerfulness: it was the cheerfulness particular to a wet seaside afternoon, when spirits soaked by the rain dribbling down windows of boarding-houses and hotels eventually make a burst for freedom – to batter along against rain and sea-wind, and thence to commingle at some echoing hall of entertainment with a cluttering of umbrellas, a thumping of boots, a wet rubber smell, a draughty gusto of raised voices.

So that now, sodden but heady with relief to be taken out of themselves on this stolen day of their holiday, the pixie audience gradually massed into seats set in amphitheatrical style round a semi-circular raised platform. On this the Beauties were to parade. And on its straight side there were ranged the judges' chairs, and their long table draped with Union Jacks.

A roar of laughter went up as Fred Morley and his four fellow-adjudicators entered. They were a great joke. Five portly gentlemen, wrested from their everyday dignities and their all-embracing wives, put to the task of examining pretty girls with hardly anything on! . . . Watch that professional eye glaze over. Watch blood pressures rise and pulses quicken! Five fat ruddy genial lambs up there on their altar . . . it was slaughter, it was murder, it was *killing*! 'Hooooo,' roared the crowd.

Dressed in their best suits, the judges simpered and blushed, dug each other in their ribs and whispered wicked chuckles in each other's ears as they settled down. One made an over-courtly gesture ushering his neighbour to his chair; another made for a brief two steps the motion so beloved of hefty hearties in their cups, he put one hand on a hip and lumbered along mincing like what he thought was a lady. Only old Fred, who was accustomed to an audience, retained his composure. He contented himself with a short, but most telling, twirl of his silken moustache-end.

Then the uniformed Silver Band at the other end of the hall struck up – what but *A Pretty Girl is like a Melody*? – and a door opened at one side and up a long inclined gang-plank came the girls.

They came first jostling, then as they reached the raised parade spaced themselves out – a plump, slender, tall, short, round forty of them. In slow measure, with short proud steps, pausing almost at each step, hesitating just as heel touched passing heel, like primping prancing two-legged ponies they passed round the ring.

All wore the same small costume. That had been one of the rules. It had been adopted because it was time the proposer had one of his ideas accepted, so that he might remain quiet in other matters. The Contest Organization bore the cost, which in terms of the area of material needed had been slight. White rayon had been chosen – a remnant from Everett Evans's Drapery Store. Now each girl wore at her loins a close-fitting triangle, and at her breasts two discreetly billowing moons. No more. And, for sure, no less.

Each carried in her hand a card with a number. Only their shoes were their own, and these were in every case the highest they had – from great clobbering wedges to elegancies of the white summer, from shoes tasselled and curiously strapped to patent black evening shoes that quarrelled painfully with the naked flesh pressed into them. One girl, hard put, had come in a pair of tennis plimsolls: she went round balancing avidly on her toes, a Shetland among the Shires.

The five judges leaned forward or sat back, pretending thus either keen judicial interest or recessive judicial wisdom. At first they were simply bewildered by so much sudden beauty. They sat in a fog of arms, legs, eyes, teeth, hair and all else. From bubble-bath and mud-tub, from pummelling-board and rubber roller came those fleshlings shining and smiling. Some had enclosed their legs in whole sheets of hot wax, from which they came hairless as ivory; others had forgone the luxuriance of mascara and instead brushed their eye-lashes with black boot polish to get a stronger set, a more lustrous shine. All smiled largely – though some by lowering their eyes achieved a sort of modesty at the same time, a redoubtable feat. All seemed not only to be following in each other's footsteps but in their own as well – this because their high heels forced their knees forward, so that they hung back on themselves, as if searching out the ground before the main upperwork should follow: bended knees, mad knees stealing on tiptoe to unheard-of larders.

Miss Great-Belt hung just behind such knees when she first passed the judges' stand. Then she saw Frederick Morley – and nearly fell on them. For a second she lost her composure. Her face had been stretched into a design of radiant happy loveliness – eyes stretched wide yet with slightly lowered lids, lips stretched ovalling round their last liquid teeth. Now as she saw Morley there, Morley whom she had never expected, Morley whom she had told off only the night before, that expression did not leave her face – but in every feature it contracted, it grew smaller for a moment into an exactly reduced replica of itself. Heavens, her first thought was, what a stupid girl I am! Never to have known! (It never occurred to her how she could ever have known, she instantly blamed herself.) . . . But what a monster he is not to have told me! Then, as she transferred the blame to him, her self-esteem came flooding back, the eyes and lips opened again like the flesh of a startled anemone flowering for the attack, and never having really faltered and now with new aplomb she passed on. He would be feeling sorry, she thought, and wish to expiate his deception. Besides, deep down he's fallen for me. Besides, there are four other judges. Besides, whatever the odds I'm good enough to beat the lot of them.

As she passed him and for a moment their eyes met, Morley was able to look as though he was looking right through her.

And then round and round the girls paraded. Sometimes the band changed its tune, broke into a dreamy waltz, and then all the girls broke step, bewildered in their dancing blood by the change of tempo: they quickly regained themselves and went kneeing on.

The vast hall echoed to laughter, catcalls, whistles and sighs from the crowd. 'Irene!' some called: 'Doreen!' others. 'Git up them stairs,' yelled the lustier members, and one man throughout the long parade repeated over and over again, at most regular intervals, and on a note of despair: 'Roll me over.'

But despite such convivialities – how misfortunate those girls were! It was cold there in that hall. They shivered, and many arms and legs so smoothly cared for now erupted into gooseflesh. In the changing room the six foreign girls had shivered with cold – and with anger. They had combined in wholehearted vituperation of the English weather, and finally all things English. When they had exhausted everything else – food, clothes, weather and so on – Miss Clermont-Ferrand had summed the matter up with the irrelevant, but emphatic and somehow damning words: 'Double-decker Buses!'

Not only was it cold, but it looked cold. That hard mauve light stared down from the ceiling with the glare of arc-lamps on arterial concrete, rinsing all in varying shades of its mauve, killing all other colour. Lilac flesh, lavender crannies, purple lips, night-shade eyes – it became a circumambulation of the dead: corpsy smiles luked the way, rigor mortis was on the move, it was a dream parade of maidens killed before their time. And far away, like an old grey wardress, Life still drizzled a dustbin blessing from the windowed world outside.

The judges, first dazzled, then surfeited, had now become so used to the bodies before them that their minds, obeying the laws of curiosity and creation, began to work on them afresh. Their eyes searched those bodies as a prisoner may search his cell and find in such bareness a new world of hidden detail. Thus they began to notice that where the spine of one girl snuggled like a long and lovely dimple, the next protruded in a sweet and charming ladder of little knobs. Where one naked torso showed a broad squarish form moulded like Greek armour, the next was softly shapeless as the ribless tube of an odalisque.

Moles took on a new presence, they grew insistent as flies on a bare ceiling. Bruises – wide brown smudges and little purple nips – showed clearer and clearer, freckles came into their own, and in that light the yellowing of armpits took on a new and virulent lilac life. So too the flushed pork-crackling, the armadillo flesh at the backs of heels – this turned deep purple, so that sometimes it looked as if a girl wore the kind of stocking that had a dark reinforcement above the back of her shoe. And the light made Miss Sauerkraut's ears, which with her blonde pallor were normally bright red, black.

The veins of auburn girls stood out like nests of rivers on maps and the lines that others wore from navel to pudenda split like cheese-wire. But the navels themselves were a study on their own – dear little buttons, wicked forget-me-knots like cropped pink piglet tails, fingertip holes and penny-size pits and sometimes none at all but simply a recessive folding of modest flesh: one alderman, who had a compulsion complex, who normally had to walk between the lines of pavement stones or make countings of objects in rooms, found himself muttering a kind of permutation gamble to himself as the navels passed: 'Button-Putton. Holey-Poley. Button-Put – no, damn, Holey-Poley . . .'

And there were the operation scars, the appendix marks. And the vaccination marks, brown cornflowers on arm and thigh. And where some had taken the sun, the criss-cross of bathing-costume straps white on brown; and the cabalist label on the wrist where a watch and strap had been. And then all the other little marks, the little creases, and the wobbling and swinging of this and of that – all of these and so much more came to the fascinated eyes of the five startled gentlemen as that blanched and black-lipped procession passed before them.

(Yet how much more startled they would have been had their ears grown as alert as their eyes – for then they would have heard the ceaseless silent song whispered on the lips of every one of those priestesses as they marched, a song of one word only, the lip-stretched litany: 'Cheese.')

Even Fred Morley, accustomed to rub shoulders with so many ladies of the chorus, was surprised. In the theatre the light was kinder, and there was powder and paint. Here, he found himself thinking, they were like medical samples, girls in bottles, selected picklings.

Finally the moment for judgment arrived. The judges whispered to each other, passed little scraps of paper. The band stopped playing. The great hall was hushed – a murmur of whispering and tittering only, the sound of a hive of waiting bees. The girls stood in a long line in front of the judges, their hands to their sides, defenceless, offered.

Three of Morley's co-judges elected immediately and unreservedly for Miss Great-Belt. It took him some time to disenchant them. But he did. To them he stood as something of an expert, a professional man: he played on this, ironically arguing their lack of taste, making them feel silly. But instantly he raised their esteem by congratulating them on their second and third choices – with raised eyebrows and a knowing wink: 'Ho, I see you *do* know a thing or two!'

Finally a decision was taken.

Miss Amsterdam was awarded the first prize. A local lady, a blonde Miss Browne, came second, and long pale Miss Sauerkraut romped in third. Miss Great-Belt came nowhere at all.

The crowd cheered and booed, cheered for Miss Browne, and booed for Miss Great-Belt. But the judges' decision was final. There was no going back. And now Fred Morley rose to present the prizes.

A fine crocodile dressing-case for Number One, a portable wireless for Number Two, and oddly a set of pressure cookers for Miss Sauerkraut.

And cheques for all. And for everybody present a few words from Frederick Morley.

'Ladies,' he began, and gave a great sigh, rolling his eyes. Roars of laughter.

'And Gentlemen,' he continued, with a sniff, as though he disbelieved in the presence of these. Redoubled laughter.

But then he silenced the laughter with measured and grave opening words. He made one of those speeches that keep the audience well on their toes – as soon as he got them uncomfortable and guilty with a passage of great gravity, he let fall a howling joke (and he was careful to make it a howler, not to serve wit in that most mixed hall). And as soon as they were howling, down he came on them hard with a passage of such stony grandeur that the air echoed a susurrus of shoe shufflings and coughs as presenceful as the laughter itself.

He had prepared this. And the reason he had taken so much trouble was to introduce a more personal condiment addressed to Miss Great-Belt. It was an address of omission. He made particular reference to the other international visitors – but not to her: and to make this the more striking he made it the less pointed by omitting one of the others, Miss Rotterdam, as well. He expressed on behalf of all present his gratitude to these ladies of lands across the sea for the honour of their visit – and then brought out some personal whoppers: of the lady from Rome's seaside, 'all roads lead to Miss Civitavecchia'; of Miss Sauerkraut, 'my little cabbage – and not so sour at that'; of the first prize-winner, 'not only a fair damsel but a veritable *Amster*-damsel', and so on, whoppers that issuing from his presidential mouth achieved an arch and fearful force.

And that, all but the shouting, was that. There was nothing left but to go off into the drizzle.

Except – for a brief moment, but a moment which was to have great repercussion – for Miss Great-Belt.

Miss Great-Belt had her place, like all the others, in the line of girls listening to Morley's speech. But with a difference – she was the only one who somehow appeared thoroughly and properly dressed. It was as usual – her self-containedness at its magic work again. There she stood in her little triangle and her two small moons, nothing else, with her hands to her sides. She should have stood as sacrificially slavishly offered as all the others. Instead she remained composed and remote. She stood on her own legs, in her own right, occupied only by herself.

But when the speech ended, and the line of girls broke up, she simply stood on.

For only a few seconds – yet seconds at such a time that stretched in the eyes of the onlookers into statuesque minutes – she stood alone exactly as she had stood for the previous quarter-hour, her eyes fixed vaguely on the platform of judges.

Then her eyes woke up, startled. She looked around her. For a moment she hesitated. She seemed even to totter, not knowing which way she had to go. Then she saw, regained herself, turned and walked with all composure down the gangplank.

Miss Great-Belt had been thinking.

That moment of action, or of inaction, had not gone unperceived by Fred Morley. He had noticed it from the corner of his eye, not then wishing to turn his full face upon her, and had triumphantly noted it as an expression of her discomfort at losing the prize. But intuition is not a monopoly of the feminine, and far back and vaguely through his jubilation a bell of unease had tolled. An intuitive woman, in his place, would have sought for an immediate solution, right or wrong, to such a problematic sound; but Fred Morley had preferred to shut his ears to it, it was uncomfortable, he had done a good day's work and wished to relax upon his laurels.

Relaxation took the form of a visit to the Yacht Club. There, again in manly company, again among the chaffing and congratulations of his fellows, there was every hope of a pleasant end to a perfect day. But the opposite occurred. As the conviviality compounded, so did the tolling of that small bell of unease. It rang louder and louder. He tried to be, but he could not remain, deaf to it. And as the sound grew louder it took shape – from a vague unease it invented form. What – he began to consider – would be her real reaction to the afternoon's happening? How on earth could – he thought between drinks and digs in the ribs – a strong woman like that take such treatment lying down?

In the end he grew certain she would have her revenge. He remembered that women are said to like the last word: he considered this afresh, and began to believe it. He remembered the adage about he who laughs last laughing longest: he believed that too. And when he mixed the two ideas, substituting a 'she' for a 'he', the significance grew appalling.

But what form could such revenge take? Whichever way he looked at it, his apprehension grew. He knew that the ways of women were profound and unpredictable, their veiled wiles a labyrinth, their capacity for innuendo prodigious. Yet on the other hand there was the fact that when women fought, when the battle-cry was really raised, then they fought with the gloves off. His mind grew confused with visions of the Wives of Kings and Fishwives with Arms Akimbo. But since his own capacities for innuendo were small, his mind attached itself to, and enlarged upon, the latter conception.

She would slap his face in public! She would tear the house down – shatter the windows, slash the furniture, flood the baths, fire the curtains! (If that were only all . . . !) But what among these oversize visions he really feared was that she would invent a story against him, perhaps make some appalling charge. Assault. Rape. Or what was that word even worse? . . . Interference! She would say he had Interfered with Her. No proof, no witnesses? No such luck – he knew that two women can get together, and that there would be one or two others dissatisfied with the result of the Contest.

He became overwrought. He dared not go home: but nor could he bear the anticipation.

Finally, less from courage than from a simpler impulse to 'go and see what it's all about', he excused himself from Evans and the others ('Ho, the Homing Pigeon!' 'Bye Bye, Bluebeard! Love to the Misses!') and made his way home. Less certainly from courage, for he made his way in by the back door.

Excusing himself round the maid in the kitchen, who looked at him with surprise and suspicion mixed (another black mark? 'Miss Abercrombie, a temporary domestic in the employ of the accused, was called to the witness stand'), he tiptoed into the hall and listened.

No one downstairs.

Upstairs, sounds that might have meant packing.

What voices he now heard spoke in their own languages. No more need of a common language? Getting into groups? Not too good.

Then suddenly down the stairs the sounds of running rustling skirts, heels! In panic he looked each way – impossible to return to the kitchen, no time to cross to the lounge! He was cornered! However, thank Heavens, it was only one of them – Miss Amsterdam, first prize-winner, a friend!

She gave a cry of delight, flung her arms round him and kissed him.

'Oh you dear good kind man,' she cried, hugging him, 'thank you, thank you, *thank* you!'

If anyone comes in now, Morley thought, then Evidence, Witnesses, Deeper than Ever . . . gently and quickly he disengaged himself, more formally congratulating her.

'But I am so glad you're here,' she went on to say, 'we've been looking all over for you! Now I must tell you . . .' And she went into details of how some girls would leave on the morrow, by what trains, and the rest on the following day. She made no mention of Miss Great-Belt's intention. But as an afterthought, turning her head back from the front-door: 'Oh by the way, that Danish girl wants to see you – urgently, she said.'

He was left alone with this. He went on standing in the hall, too centrally for simply standing. The maid came in to ring the gong. He threw out a hand, giving the barometer a great thud, nearly knocking it from the wall. Simultaneously as he went on pounding that thing, the old brass gong rang out. The house echoed with huge sudden noise. And for once, all at once, all the girls seemed to pile out of their rooms together. They came tripping down the stairs at him.

He was cornered with greetings. He could not opt but to go into dinner with them.

Miss Great-Belt nearly forced Miss Sauerkraut out of her chair in order to sit next to him. And of all others her smile was the most welcoming, throughout dinner she was charming.

Naturally, he made himself most gracious to her in return. But he distrusted her, he distrusted every flutter of her lovely eyelids. It must all be a cover for something terrible to come.

And after dinner, after all valedictory speeches had been made, Miss Great-Belt went so far as to suggest that he take her out for some coffee, perhaps even to dance. 'But I know dancing must be a sore question between us,' she went on to say, 'I know it was uncivil of me to go dancing that night you invited me to the theatre. But I *do* apologize. Let's say bygones are bygones? Shall we?'

At that moment Fred Morley could easily have excused himself. His better judgment advised him to. But two other voices spoke inside him. One said that a dance-floor in a hotel was public and therefore safe; the second whispered that perhaps she really was, after all, making her peace with him. The latter voice, though in a whisper, spoke the louder. In fact, engaged again by her charms and never at a loss for respect of his own, he had already begun to believe that she was finally expressing a real attraction towards him.

They took coffee together at Morley's favourite hotel – the very terrace, glass-shaded, where once he had foreseen himself with the Misses Rotterdam and Clermont-Ferrand – and later went in to dance. He took care to act with the greatest propriety and even introduced her to his friend the head-waiter as a professional lady from Denmark, who, with her colleagues, had been billeted by the Town Hall on his house. This would put to rest any wilder speculations as to the nature of his strange and beautiful guest. The bush-telegraph would tap round the room a rational and respectable tune.

As for Miss Great-Belt, she continued to be soft, sweet, charming. All her past animosity had vanished. She seemed to throw open that invisible veil that had hitherto made her so unattainable, so much the woman of 'process', and now welcomed him without question into the privacy of her composure. A woman so self-contained is ordinarily an uneasy companion. But when such a woman decides to invite one into her private sympathies, to give exactly her laughter and her confidence in the measure one knows it is withheld from others – then she becomes overwhelming. Without indulgence, with no condescension, but purely and simply, Miss Great Belt welcomed Morley to herself. He was bowled over.

Quite early in the evening she made one point clear. 'Now I do want to say once and for all,' she said, opening her great eyes wide for frankness, leaning towards him like a large dark red cat, 'that I congratulate you on your decision this afternoon. In my view you were absolutely right. That sweet Dutch girl was obviously the winner. I can see that one of the prizes had to go to an English girl – politics are politics. And there was every reason for poor Nuremburg – she looks so pale, doesn't she? A sick woman, yes she needs encouragement, it was very kind – taking third prize. Who wants to be third anyhow? No, I know you'll suspect I'm jealous – but honestly I'm not. With me justice counts before – whatever is the word? – *self*.'

She said this with great content, purring over her sacrifice, her frank good nature. He did not notice this. His instinct rose to protect a lady in distress. He began instantly to lie that he himself had voted for her for first prize – but what could he do against so many others?

He was surprised to notice that this was not received well. She looked, he thought, even a trifle offended. Why? Ah! . . . And he went straight on to point out that it was exactly because of this out-voting that, momentarily piqued, he simply could not bear to mention so much as her name in his presidential address.

As he stumbled through these paces, Miss Great-Belt watched him keenly. She saw that he was lying, and was satisfied. They finished the evening in high spirit with each other.

When the other ladies left during the next days, Miss Great-Belt stayed on. For propriety's sake she removed to the near-by hotel but she stayed on in the town. She and Morely saw each other every day. They went to the theatre, they dined together, they took motor-trips into the country and they went sailing on the sea.

The weather continued fine, it was a memorable month. Miss Great-Belt wrote to her father and begged permission to remain a few weeks more. Morley was in heaven. Now he avoided the Yacht Club altogether: he spent all his time with his new and lovely companion in places where they might be admired by more discriminating eyes.

It was for him a flirtation *de luxe*. It complimented his years, it redounded satisfactorily to his prowess. Finally, he told himself, he had won the day. Trust an old bachelor! Sometimes, when he thought of it all, he remembered with a reproving chuckle the first days, the very first days when he had unfolded every charm to entice her, when he had sacrificed every self-respect. How had he not realized that it was the exact opposite which would win her? Why – in a dozen musical shows this very process nightly comprised the whole plot! He had played it out himself night after night, year after year – it was the very stuff of life? Why had he never realized . . . ? But then why, damn our eyes, do we all spend our lives delighting in the wisdom of paradox – yet hesitate to apply the risks to ourselves?

He laughed and wagged his doggy head. Silly old fool! But then – hadn't that same silly old fool come through with flying colours? In the end? It took perseverance. He smiled, a little in love with her and himself and with everything else. 'He who laughs last,' he chuckled.

But then she married him.

SAMUEL SELVON

Knock On Wood

The last time I see Jupsingh, he had a piece of a broomstick handle up in the lining of his coat. He say that he have that there because a Chinese fellar in Bayswater want to beat him, and he only waiting to crack this Chinese fellar head wide open with the handle.

But I feel Jup have that broomstick there because he like to knock wood for luck. In point of fact, Jarvis and myself see him lift the coat and take a little knock while we was talking to him, and at the same time he sort of make a half turn and kiss a cross that he have pin on his chest.

The first time I meet this test was one night Jarvis and me combing the Bayswater Road late to see if we could pick up a little thing to pass the time away. Same time, who should be coming down the road but Jupsingh, with a sharp thing holding on to his arm, a real chic chick.

'Oh God!' Jarvis say. 'Boy, look Jupsingh. He is a real depressor, always bawling. He come from Trinidad. Listen to him when he come.'

'What happening, what happening, man?' Jupsingh come up and hold Jarvis' shoulder. 'Meet my new fiancée, Pat.'

The thing shake hands with we. She had a babydoll face and it look like butter won't melt in she mouth. Jupsingh have on a colin-wilson and he keep pulling the long sleeves down to cover his fingers, like gloves. He have a bottle of South African sherry in his hand.

Jarvis haul him to one side and whisper, 'Which part you get that piece of skin, Jupsingh?'

'Listen, man, I in a jam,' the old Jup say. 'I bring this thing with me up from Woking and I ain't have no place to take she. What you think, boy? You think she all right? You think I could sleep with she tonight?'

'Well, you can't come by me,' Jarvis say, 'but I will ask my friend, he have a big room.'

Jarvis ask me and I say all right, that at least we could polish off the bottle of sherry.

Up in my room Jupsingh anxious and restless as if he rusty and thirsty to hit one. Now and then, while Jarvis old-talking with Pat, he putting his hand to his face and saying Jesus Christ, and kissing a sign of the cross what he have pin on to the front of the colin-wilson. And he knocking wood. He knocking chair, table, floor – anything make out of wood in my room.

Meanwhile Jarvis talking with Pat and asking she which part she come from, and if she like London, and how she hurt her ankle, and Pat saying she come from Ireland, that she don't like London, and that she fall off a bicycle and hurt her foot.

I open the sherry and we finish off the bottle, with Jupsingh trying to force Pat to have more, but she won't. He ask she if she playing shy, and Pat smile and hang her head. You could see that the girl innocent and young, and only the good lord know how a evil test like Jupsingh manage to inveigle she to come up to London.

Well, whenever he get a chance Jupsingh asking either Jarvis or myself if we think the thing nice, and if we think she would spend the night with him, and the both of we telling him yes, yes, to keep him easy, because he restless like a racehorse at the starting line.

Pat begin to say it getting late and they have to catch the last train, but old Jup telling she to take it easy and relax, and he trying to cuddle her, but she pushing him off.

'If is anything, we could always sleep here,' Jupsingh say, looking at me and winking.

'You can't sleep here,' I say. 'It have plenty hotels in the Water.'

'You think I could get a room, boy?'

'Yes, man,' Jarvis say.

Well, the four of we old-talk till it was late, then all of we went out to look and try and get a room for Jupsingh.

Outside in the road, Pat ask Jupsingh: 'What are you going to do?'

'I will get a room, don't worry,' he say.

You could see like he want to knock wood bad, and it chance to have some plane trees in the road where we was, and my boy went and knock the trunk of one and come back rubbing his face and saying Jesus Christ, and bending his head down and kissing the cross.

'I am not staying in a room together with you,' Pat say.

'What happen to this girl at all?' Jupsingh say.

A big argument start up in the road. Pat have she hands folded and she cool as a cucumber, and you could see that she make up her mind that whatever happen she ain't going to bed down with my boy for the night. And the old Jup as if he in a kind of panic, he turning his back to kiss the cross and all the time he only asking Jarvis, 'So what you think, what you think,' like a recurring decimal.

'Well, let Pat go in the hotel and ask,' Jarvis say. 'You know how it is, they mightn't give you a room even if they have.'

'How much hotel is around here?' My boy start to check up on how much money he have.

'This is a posh area, only aristocrats live here,' Jarvis say, 'but you might get one for one fifteen.'

'Come on then, Pat, you coming?' Jupsingh holding the girl hand and pulling.

Eventually the two of them reach the entrance, but Pat stop and stand up and they argue a little, then Jupsingh breeze in alone.

Me and Jarvis stand up on the other side watching she.

'That man crazy,' I say, 'he can't see the girl don't want to sleep with him? What he believe? This is London, man.'

'Look how she stand up there alone,' Jarvis say.

'It look bad,' I say. 'Call she.'

Jarvis call she with his hand and she cross the road.

'What is he trying to do?' Pat ask.

'Well you see,' Jarvis say, trying to pacify the situation, 'he gone to get a room for you.'

'And where is he going to sleep?'

'With you.'

'Oh no.' The way Pat say that, any man but Jupsingh would throw in the sponge.

Jupsingh fly back out the hotel, rubbing his face and muttering Jesus Christ.

'No rooms, man, no rooms. Which part again we could try?'

'It have some other hotels in the next street,' Jarvis say.

'Come on then.' Jupsingh hold Pat and take off.

In the next street had a posh-looking hotel, and it had some people going in. Like they just come from theatre or something, with fur coat and bow tie and evening suit.

'It don't look like I would get a room there,' Jup say uneasily. 'You want to try, Pat?'

But the way Jupsingh thirst, he would of tried to get in the Savoy that night. He went in, but is either they dish him up quick or else he don't trust leaving Pat too long with we outside, because he come back in a hurry.

After that we start combing all over the Water for a hotel, but as if a hoodoo on the old Jup that night, he can't make a note. He only flying in and flying out, and sweating and smoking, and kissing the cross every chance he get, and now and then pulling Jarvis to one side and saying, 'So what you think, boy? You think she will sleep with me? You think I stand a chance?'

By this time we reach down by Westbourne Grove and it had a taxi rank there, and Jarvis tell Jup to try the drivers, that they does know of places. But when Jup went, I don't know what the taxi fellar tell him, only thing he come back cursing and calling them bastards. And he vex too bad. He try to cuddle Pat and she turn away.

'I bet I slap you up here tonight!' Jup say. 'I bet I start to get on ignorant!'

Poor Pat just stay quiet.

Jarvis say, 'Man Jupsingh, you surprise me, man. You shouldn't tell the girl a thing like that. You letting me down. You from good family, man.'

'I apologise,' Jup say, coming quiet and turning and kissing the cross. 'I apologise, Jarvis. Sorry, man.'

We stand up there on the pavement, and I wondering at the arse I put myself in for this night.

'I know three fellars from Barbados living by Tottenham Court-road,' Jup say. 'We could go there and sleep. They have three bed.'

'Where will I sleep?' Pat ask.

'With me, darling,' Jup say.

'No,' Pat say, and you could see she ain't weakening. As a matter of fact as the night wearing away so she getting stronger with the negatives.

'Jesus Christ,' Jup say, looking around desperately for wood to knock, 'I will sleep alone on the floor, and you have a bed to yourself. What happen, you don't trust me?'

'Listen, man,' Jarvis say, 'let we go up by Paddington, it have a lot of places there, we bound to get one.'

So we start to walk up the road, and on the way we pass a wooden fence and Jup seize the opportunity to knock lightly as he pass.

We come up in a side street near to the station where it have some evil-looking joints where Londoners does go late in the night to make a stroke. Some frowsy-looking things going in, as if they just off a beat on the Bayswater Road, and some coming out, and one of them in a red dress scratching she thigh and chewing gum.

Another set of big argument start up as we stand up opposite a hotel with a neon sign. Pat won't go in with Jup, and we there arguing and flinging hands in the air and getting no place at all. To make things worse a police car making a rounds and coming up the road.

'Stop leaning on the wall like that, man!' Jup tell Pat. 'You don't see the police coming? You want them to think we is criminals?'

Pat lean off the wall.

The police make a rounds, and they give we a look, but they drive on up the road.

Well, after about fifteen minutes of yes and no and kiss-the-cross Jup and Pat went inside the hotel, and me and Jarvis stand up outside waiting. We run out of cigarettes and I went up by the station to look for a machine. When I come back I see Pat there with Jarvis.

'What happen?' I say.

'I am not staying in that hotel with him,' Pat say.

A minute after, the old Jup come out.

'I get the room,' he say. 'Is all right? The fellar waiting for we to make up we mind. What you say, Pat?'

'No,' Pat say.

'Oh, Jesus Christ!' Jupsingh start up again. 'You say you want to meet coloured people, and I take you around. Now you doing as if I is a criminal. I should of let you go with some of them damn' Jamaican and let them rough you up! What you think, eh? I sure if it was a white man you would of come!'

'It would not have made any difference,' Pat say, and though she kind of uneasy about everything me and Jarvis had was to admire the consistency of the negatives she throwing at Jup.

'You shouldn't tell the girl such things, man,' Jarvis say. 'You shouldn't treat the girl like that.'

Well, I don't know what would of happened there that night, the way things was going. The three of them argue and argue, and I draw to one side and every now and then I telling Jarvis, 'I going home, eh,' and Jarvis only waving his hand and telling me to wait for him, and Jup kissing the cross now without trying to hide, and rubbing his face and saying, 'Jesus Christ!'

People come out of the hotel to watch the bacchanal, and Jup pointing to them and telling Pat look the man waiting on us.

At last, after about half an hour, it look like my boy cool off and reconcile to the situation.

He turn to me. 'Boy, I could sleep by you tonight?'

Now I frighten from what I see that this man run basic in my room, because I staying in a respectable house and I don't want no contention at this hour of the night, so I hesitating and hemming and hawing.

'Oh God, old man, we is Indian together, from the same island, man,' he say.

It look as if the only way to settle the business is to say yes, so I say yes, and Jup throw his hand around my shoulder and repeating the song about how we is Indian together.

Well, it decided that Pat should stay in the hotel, Jup by me, and in the morning early please God he would come and meet she and the both of them would catch train go back to Woking.

We left Pat going in the hotel and start to walk back to the Water.

'What you think, boy? You think them fellars in the hotel would rape she? I tell she to shut the door and lock it. So what you think, boy? You think she good for me? She all right?'

The old Jup start up again, and only looking over his shoulder as if he mad to turn back and go to the hotel.

'Is all right, man, is all right,' Jarvis pacifying him. 'Take it easy. You have a place to sleep, and Pat have a place to sleep.'

'Oh God!' Jup say suddenly, feeling in his pocket. 'I forget to bring my sun-shades!'

'What the arse your sun-shades have to do with the position?' Jarvis want to know.

'Suppose sun shine bright tomorrow?' Jup want to know.

All the time we going, Jarvis telling Jup to look at the road good, so he won't get lost when he coming in the morning.

We break up when we reach the Water and Jup and me gone up in my room. I did tired and want to sleep, but Jup keep behind me all the time, asking me if I think Pat safe in the hotel, if he should go back and look after she.

When both of we in the bed he talking in a hoarse whisper, but every now and then as if his voice break and he talking naturally, and then as if he realise it sounding loud he fall back to whispering.

I was just falling asleep when I hear a knocking. I think perhaps the neighbour feel we making too much noise and I tell Jup to keep quiet and go to sleep. But the knocking still going on. When I look to see what it was, I see my boy leaning off the bed and lifting up the carpet to knock wood.

I start to get vex. 'You best hads go and sleep in the chair if you can't sleep, man,' I tell him.

'I can't sleep, man, this clock making too much noise. Put it under the bed. You set it to alarm at six in the morning?'

'Yes,' I say, 'and is nearly six already.'

He keep quiet for five minutes then he start to cough. He start to cough some big cough that rattling the bed. Cough that coming from deep down as if the man dead and 'fraid to lay down. When at last he fall asleep he start to snore like a character in a animated cartoon.

Jupsingh wake up before the alarm went off. He knock wood and shake me at the same time.

'The alarm didn't go, man!' he saying.

'Is not time yet,' I tell him.

'Well, I better get up anyway. You have any coffee?'

'It have some in the saucepan.'

'Thank you, man, thank you.'

He get up. I turn over and try to go back to sleep, but as if I hear a muttering. I look up and I see Jup kneeling by the side of the bed.

'Hail Mary . . . forgive us our sins . . . blessed is Mary child of God . . .'

He finish prayers and kiss the cross. He knock wood and went and drink the coffee cold from the saucepan. He get dress and come back by the bed.

'Thanks a lot, boy, God bless. Both of we is Indian together, boy. You is a real friend. Cheerio, boy.'

Now this is a true ballad – if I lie I die – and it ain't have no fancy ending to end up with. In fact, it have some more to sing.

Who me and Jarvis should see breezing in the Water that weekend but my boy and Pat.

'I just went round by you, man!' Jup tell me after greetings.

'I don't live there any more,' I say, because I want nothing more to do with this man. 'I living in Camberwell now, I just come up here to see Jarvis.'

Jup say that Pat hungry and he ask Jarvis if it have any good restaurants in the Water, and Jarvis send him down by one in Westbourne Grove.

'I didn't think she would ever go out with that test again,' I tell Jarvis after they gone.

'It look as if she really like him,' Jarvis say.

Well, about midnight that night my bell ring and I went downstairs, thinking that Jarvis was on a late lime and wanted some company. But when I open the door who I should see but my boy.

'I tell you I ain't living here any more, man,' I say, pushing the door to close it.

'Listen, man, Jarvis outside, he want to see you. Jesus Christ, boy, if you know what happen to me!'

I went outside and see Jarvis.

'My boy have a piece of wood in his coat lining,' Jarvis tell me before Jup could come up. 'He have a piece of broom handle and he knocking it all the time!'

'Yes, but why you-all ringing my bell at this hour, man?' is what I want to find out.

'Boy,' Jupsingh begin, 'if you know what happen! You really can't trust these Nordic women. Today I take Pat round by my uncle. And all the time the man only sending me out to buy wine. Two-three times he send me. The last time I say, "But a-a, why this man sending me out so all the time?" And I open the door quiet. Man, Pat laying down on the bed with my uncle! But my uncle right, you know. He tell me that she no good.'

Jup haul up his coat and knock the broom handle.

'What the arse you doing with that broomstick?' I want to know.

'A Chinee fellar want to beat me, but I carrying this for protection.'

'So you left Pat?' Jarvis ask him.

'I take she to the station and I give she three-four slap and left she.' He turn to me. 'Listen, man, you could put me up tonight? I ain't have no place to sleep. You have anything to eat? Boy, all of we is Indian together, boy.'

'Don't worry with that line, old man,' I say. 'I done tell you I don't live here any more. I only come to get my clothes and thing.'

Jup hold on to me as I make to go. 'At least give me two shillings to buy a train fare,' he say. 'I spend all my money on that girl and I ain't have a cent – if you stick me with a pin you wouldn't draw blood.'

'You better ask Jarvis,' I say. 'I going. See you sometime.'

When I turn to close the door I see Jup making a kiss of the cross that he have pin on under his tie. He and Jarvis start to walk up the road arguing.

MURIEL SPARK

Bang-Bang You're Dead

At that time many of the men looked like Rupert Brooke, whose portrait still hung in everyone's imagination. It was that clear-cut, 'typically English' face which is seldom seen on the actual soil of England but proliferates in the African Colonies.

'I must say,' said Sybil's hostess, 'the men look charming.'

These men were all charming, Sybil had decided at the time, until you got to know them. She sat in the dark room watching the eighteen-year-old film unrolling on the screen as if the particular memory had solidified under the effect of some intense heat coming out of the projector. She told herself, I was young, I demanded nothing short of perfection. But then, she thought, that is not quite the case. But it comes to the same thing; to me, the men were not charming for long.

The first reel came to an end. Someone switched on the light. Her host picked the next film out of its tropical packing.

'It must be an interesting experience,' said her hostess, 'seeing yourself after all those years.'

'Hasn't Sybil seen these films before?' said a latecomer.

'No, never – have you, Sybil?'

'No, never.'

'If they had been my films,' said her hostess, 'my curiosity could not have waited eighteen years.'

The Kodachrome reels had lain in their boxes in the dark of Sybil's cabin trunk. Why bother, when one's memory was clear?

'Sybil didn't know anyone who had a projector,' said her hostess, 'until we got ours.'

'It was delightful,' said the latecomer, an elderly lady, 'what I saw of it. Are the others as good?'

Sybil thought for a moment. 'The photography is probably good,' she said. 'There was a cook behind the camera.'

'A cook! How priceless; whatever do you mean?' said her hostess.

'The cook-boy,' said Sybil, 'was trained up to use the camera.'

'He managed it well,' said her host, who was adjusting the new reel.

'Wonderful colours,' said her hostess. 'Oh, I'm so glad you dug them out. How healthy and tanned and open-necked everyone looks. And those adorable shiny natives all over the place.'

The elderly lady said, 'I liked the bit where you came out on the veranda in your shorts carrying the gun.'

'Ready?' said Sybil's host. The new reel was fixed. 'Put out the lights,' he said.

It was the stoep again. Through the french windows came a dark girl in shorts followed by a frisky young Alsatian.

'Lovely dog,' commented Sybil's host. 'He seems to be asking Sybil for a game.'

'That is someone else,' Sybil said very quickly.

'The girl there, with the dog?'

'Yes, of course. Don't you see me walking across the lawn by the trees?'

'Oh, of course, of course. She did look like you, Sybil, that girl with the dog. Wasn't she like Sybil? I mean, just as she came out on the veranda.'

'Yes, *I* thought it was Sybil for a moment until I saw Sybil in the background. But you can see the difference now. See, as she turns round. That girl isn't really like Sybil, it must be the shorts.'

'There was a slight resemblance between us,' Sybil remarked.

The projector purred on.

'Look, there's a little girl rather like you, Sybil.' Sybil, walking between her mother and father, one hand in each, had already craned round. The other child, likewise being walked along, had looked back too.

The other child wore a black velour hat turned up all round, a fawn coat of covert-coating, and at her neck a narrow white ermine tie. She wore white silk gloves. Sybil was dressed identically, and though this in

itself was nothing to marvel at, since numerous small girls wore this
ensemble when they were walked out in the parks and public gardens of
cathedral towns in 1923, it did fortify the striking resemblance in features,
build, and height, between the two children. Sybil suddenly felt she was
walking past her own reflection in the long looking-glass. There was her
peak chin, her black bobbed hair under her hat, with its fringe almost
touching her eyebrows. Her wide-spaced eyes, her nose very small like a
cat's. 'Stop staring, Sybil,' whispered her mother. Sybil had time to snatch
the gleam of white socks and black patent leather button shoes. Her own
socks were white but her shoes were brown, with laces. At first she felt
this one discrepancy was wrong, in the sense that it was wrong to step on
one of the cracks in the pavement. Then she felt it was right that there
should be a difference.

'The Colemans,' Sybil's mother remarked to her father. 'They keep that
hotel at Hillend. The child must be about Sybil's age. Very alike, aren't
they? And I suppose,' she continued for Sybil's benefit, 'she's a good little
girl like Sybil.' Quick-witted Sybil thought poorly of the last remark with
its subtle counsel of perfection.

On other occasions, too, they passed the Coleman child on a Sunday
walk. In summer time the children wore panama hats and tussore silk
frocks discreetly adorned with drawn-thread work. Sometimes the Coleman child was accompanied by a young maid-servant in grey dress and
black stockings. Sybil noted this one difference between her own entourage
and the other girl's. 'Don't turn round and stare,' whispered her mother.

It was not till she went to school that she found Désirée Coleman to
be a year older than herself. Désirée was in a higher class but sometimes,
when the whole school was assembled on the lawn or in the gym, Sybil
would be, for a few moments, mistaken for Désirée. In the late warm
spring the classes sat in separate groups under the plane trees until, as by
simultaneous instinct, the teachers would indicate time for break. The
groups would mingle, and 'Sybil, dear, your shoe-lace,' a teacher might
call out; and then, as Sybil regarded her neat-laced shoes, 'Oh no, not
Sybil, I mean Désirée.' In the percussion band Sybil banged her triangle
triumphantly when the teacher declared, '*Much* better than yesterday,
Sybil.' But she added, 'I mean Désirée.'

Only the grown-ups mistook one child for another at odd moments.

None of her small companions made this mistake. After the school concert Sybil's mother said, 'For a second I thought you were Désirée in the choir. It's strange you are so alike. I'm not a bit like Mrs Coleman and your daddy doesn't resemble *him* in the least.'

Sybil found Désirée unsatisfactory as a playmate. Sybil was precocious, her brain was like a blade. She had discovered that dull children were apt to be spiteful. Désirée would sit innocently cross-legged beside you at a party, watching the conjurer, then suddenly, for no apparent reason, jab at you viciously with her elbow.

By the time Sybil was eight and Désirée nine it was seldom that anyone, even strangers and new teachers, mixed them up. Sybil's nose became more sharp and pronounced while Désirée's seemed to sink into her plump cheeks like a painted-on nose. Only on a few occasions, and only on dark winter afternoons between the last of three o'clock daylight and the coming on of lights all over the school, was Sybil mistaken for Désirée.

Between Sybil's ninth year and her tenth Désirée's family came to live in her square. The residents' children were taken to the gardens of the square after school by mothers and nursemaids, and were bidden to play with each other nicely. Sybil regarded the intrusion of Désirée sulkily, and said she preferred her book. She cheered up, however, when a few weeks later the Dobell boys came to live in the square. The two Dobells had dusky-rose skins and fine dark eyes. It appeared the father was half Indian.

How Sybil adored the Dobells! They were a new type of playmate in her experience, so jumping and agile, and yet so gentle, so unusually courteous. Their dark skins were never dirty, a fact which Sybil obscurely approved. She did not then mind Désirée joining in their games; the Dobell boys were a kind of charm against despair, for they did not understand stupidity and so did not notice Désirée's.

The girl lacked mental stamina, could not keep up an imaginative game for long, was shrill and apt to kick her playmates unaccountably and on the sly; the Dobells reacted to this with a simple resignation. Perhaps the lack of opposition was the reason that Désirée continually shot Sybil dead, contrary to the rules, whenever she felt like it.

Sybil resented with the utmost passion the repeated daily massacre of herself before the time was ripe. It was useless for Jon Dobell to explain,

'Not yet, Désirée. Wait, wait, Désirée. She's not to be shot down yet. She hasn't crossed the bridge yet, and you can't shoot her from there, anyway – there's a big boulder between you and her. You have to creep round it, and Hugh has a shot at you first, and he thinks he's got you, but only your hat. And . . .'

It was no use. Each day before the game started, the four sat in conference on the short dry prickly grass. The proceedings were agreed. The game was on. 'Got it all clear, Désirée?' 'Yes,' she said, every day. Désirée shouted and got herself excited, she made foolish sounds even when supposed to be stalking the bandits through the silent forest. A few high screams and then, 'Bang-bang,' she yelled, aiming at Sybil, 'you're dead.' Sybil obediently rolled over, protesting none the less that the game had only begun, while the Dobells sighed, 'Oh, *Désirée!*'

Sybil vowed to herself each night, I will do the same to her. Next time – tomorrow if it isn't raining – I will bang-bang her before she has a chance to hang her panama on the bough as a decoy. I will say bang-bang on her out of turn, and I will do her dead before her time.

But on no succeeding tomorrow did Sybil bring herself to do this. Her pride before the Dobells was more valuable than the success of the game. Instead, with her cleverness, Sybil set herself to avoid Désirée's range for as long as possible. She dodged behind the laurels and threw out a running commentary as if to a mental defective, such as, 'I'm in disguise, all in green, and no one can see me among the trees.' But still Désirée saw her. Désirée's eyes insisted on penetrating solid mountains. 'I'm half a mile away from everyone,' Sybil cried as Désirée's gun swivelled relentlessly upon her.

I shall refuse to be dead, Sybil promised herself. I'll break the rule. If it doesn't count with her why should it count with me? I won't roll over any more when she bangs you're dead to me. Next time, tomorrow if it isn't raining . . .

But Sybil simply did roll over. When Jon and Hugh Dobell called out to her that Désirée's bang-bang did not count she started hopefully to resurrect herself; but 'It does count, it *does*. That's the rule,' Désirée counter-screeched. And Sybil dropped back flat, knowing utterly that this was final.

And so the girl continued to deal premature death to Sybil, losing her head, but never so much that she aimed at one of the boys. For some reason which Sybil did not consider until she was years and years older, it was always herself who had to die.

One day, when Désirée was late in arriving for play, Sybil put it to the boys that Désirée should be left out of the game in future. 'She only spoils it.'

'But,' said Jon, 'you need four people for the game.'

'You need four,' said Hugh.

'No, you can do it with three.' As she spoke she was inventing the game with three. She explained to them what was in her mind's eye. But neither boy could grasp the idea, having got used to Bandits and Riders with two on each side. 'I am the lone Rider, you see,' said Sybil. 'Or,' she wheedled, 'the cherry tree can be a Rider.' She was talking to stone, inoffensive but uncomprehending. All at once she realized, without articulating the idea, that her intelligence was superior to theirs, and she felt lonely.

'Could we play rounders instead?' ventured Jon.

Sybil brought a book every day after that, and sat reading beside her mother, who was glad, on the whole, that Sybil had grown tired of rowdy games.

'They were preparing,' said Sybil, 'to go on a shoot.'

Sybil's host was changing the reel.

'I get quite a new vision of Sybil,' said her hostess, 'seeing her in such a . . . such a *social* environment. Were any of these people intellectuals, Sybil?'

'No, but lots of poets.'

'Oh, *no*. Did they all write poetry?'

'Quite a lot of them,' said Sybil, 'did.'

'Who *were* they all? Who was that blond fellow who was standing by the van with you?'

'He was the manager of the estate. They grew passion-fruit and manufactured the juice.'

'Passion-fruit – how killing. Did *he* write poetry?'

'Oh, yes.'

'And who was the girl, the one I thought was you?'

'Oh, I had known her as a child and we met again in the Colony. The short man was her husband.'

'And were you all off on safari that morning? I simply can't imagine you shooting anything, Sybil, somehow.'

'On this occasion,' said Sybil, 'I didn't go. I just held the gun for effect.'

Everyone laughed.

'Do you still keep up with these people? I've heard that colonials are great letter-writers, it keeps them in touch with—'

'No.' And she added, 'Three of them are dead. The girl and her husband, and the fair fellow.'

'Really? What happened to them? Don't tell me *they* were mixed up in shooting affairs.'

'They were mixed up in shooting affairs,' said Sybil.

'Oh, these colonials,' said the elderly woman, 'and their shooting affairs!'

'Number three,' said Sybil's host. 'Ready? Lights out, please.'

'Don't get eaten by lions. I say, Sybil, don't get mixed up in a shooting affair.' The party at the railway station were unaware of the noise they were making for they were inside the noise. As the time of departure drew near Donald's relatives tended to herd themselves apart while Sybil's clustered round the couple.

'Two years – it will be an interesting experience for them.'

'Mind out for the shooting affairs. Don't let Donald have a gun.'

There had been an outbreak of popular headlines about the shooting affairs in the Colony. Much had been blared forth about the effect, on the minds of young settlers, of the climate, the hard drinking, the shortage of white women. The Colony was a place where lovers shot husbands, or shot themselves, where husbands shot natives who spied through bedroom windows. Letters to *The Times* arrived belatedly from respectable colonists, refuting the scandals with sober statistics. The recent incidents, they said, did not represent the habits of the peaceable majority. The Governor told the press that everything had been highly exaggerated. By the time Sybil and Donald left for the Colony the music-hall comics had already exhausted the entertainment value of colonial shooting affairs.

'Don't make pets of snakes or crocs. Mind out for the lions. Don't forget to write.'

It was almost a surprise to them to find that shooting affairs in the Colony were not entirely a music-hall myth. They occurred in waves. For three months at a time the gun-murders and suicides were reported weekly. The old colonists with their very blue eyes sat beside their whisky bottles and remarked that another young rotter had shot himself. Then the rains would break and the shootings would cease for a long season.

Eighteen months after their marriage Donald was mauled by a lioness and died on the long stretcher journey back to the station. He was one of a party of eight. No one could really say how it happened; it was done in a flash. The natives had lost their wits, and, instead of shooting the beast, had come calling 'Ah-ah-ah,' and pointing to the spot. A few strides, shouldering the grass aside, and Donald's friends got the lioness as she reared from his body.

His friends in the archaeological team to which he belonged urged Sybil to remain in the Colony for the remaining six months, and return to England with them. Still undecided, she went on a sight-seeing tour. But before their time was up the archaeologists had been recalled. War had been declared. Civilians were not permitted to leave the continent, and Sybil was caught, like Donald under the lioness.

She wished he had lived to enjoy a life of his own, as she intended to do. It was plain to her that they must have separated had he lived. There had been no disagreement but, thought Sybil, given another two years there would have been disagreements. Donald had shown signs of becoming a bore. By the last, the twenty-seventh, year of his life, his mind had ceased to inquire. Archaeology, that thrilling subject, had become Donald's job, merely. He began to talk as if all archaeological methods and theories had ceased to evolve on the day he obtained his degree; it was now only a matter of applying his knowledge to field-work for a limited period. Archaeological papers came out from England. The usual crank literature on roneo foolscap followed them from one postal address to another. 'Donald, aren't you going to look through them?' Sybil said, as the journals and papers piled up. 'No, really, I don't see it's necessary.' It was not necessary because his future was fixed; two years in the field and then a lectureship. If it were my subject, she thought, these papers would be necessary to me. Even the crackpot ones, rightly read, would be, to me, enlarging.

Sybil lay in bed in the mornings reading the translation of Kierkegaard's *Journals*, newly arrived from England in their first, revelatory month of publication. She felt like a desert which had not realized its own aridity till the rain began to fall upon it. When Donald came home in the late afternoons she had less and less to say to him.

'There has been another shooting affair,' Donald said, 'across the valley. The chap came home unexpectedly and found his wife with another man. He shot them both.'

'In this place, one is never far from the jungle,' Sybil said.

'What are you talking about? We are eight hundred miles from the jungle.'

When he had gone on his first big shoot, eight hundred miles away in the jungle, she had reflected, there is no sign of a living mind in him, it is like a landed fish which has ceased to palpitate. But, she thought, another woman would never notice it. Other women do not wish to be married to a Mind. Yet I do, she thought, and I am a freak and should not have married. In fact I am not the marrying type. Perhaps that is why he does not explore my personality, any more than he reads the journals. It might make him think, and that would be hurtful.

After his death she wished he had lived to enjoy a life of his own, whatever that might have been. She took a job in a private school for girls and cultivated a few friends for diversion until the war should be over. Charming friends need not possess minds.

Their motor launch was rocking up the Zambezi. Sybil was leaning over the rail mouthing something to a startled native in a canoe. Now Sybil was pointing across the river.

'I think I was asking him,' Sybil commented to her friends in the darkness, 'about the hippo. There was a school of hippo some distance away, and we wanted to see them better. But the native said we shouldn't go too near – that's why he's looking so frightened – because the hippo often upset a boat, and then the crocs quickly slither into the water. There, look! We got a long shot of the hippo – those bumps in the water, like submarines, those are the snouts of hippo.'

The film rocked with the boat as it proceeded up the river. The screen went white.

'Something's happened,' said Sybil's hostess.

'Put on the light,' said Sybil's host. He fiddled with the projector and a young man, their lodger from upstairs, went to help him.

'I loved those tiny monkeys on the island,' said her hostess. 'Do hurry, Ted. What's gone wrong?'

'Shut up a minute,' he said.

'Sybil, you know you haven't changed much since you were a girl.'

'Thank you, Ella. I haven't changed at all so far as I still think charming friends need not possess minds.'

'I expect this will revive your memories, Sybil. The details, I mean. One is bound to forget so much.'

'Oh yes,' Sybil said, and she added, 'but I recall quite a lot of details, you know.'

'Do you *really*, Sybil?'

I wish, she thought, they wouldn't cling to my least word.

The young man turned from the projector with several feet of the film-strip looped between his widespread hands. 'Is the fair chap your husband, Mrs Greeves?' he said to Sybil.

'Sybil lost her husband very early on,' her hostess informed him in a low and sacred voice.

'Oh, I *am* sorry.'

Sybil's hostess replenished the drinks of her three guests. Her host turned from the projector, finished his drink, and passed his glass to be refilled, all in one movement. Everything they do seems large and important, thought Sybil, but I must not let it be so. We are only looking at old films.

She overheard a sibilant 'Whish-sh-sh?' from the elderly woman in which she discerned, 'Who is she?'

'Sybil Greeves,' her hostess breathed back, 'a distant cousin of Ted's through marriage.'

'Oh yes?' The low tones were puzzled as if all had not been explained.

'She's quite famous, of course.'

'Oh, I didn't know that.'

'Very few people know it,' said Sybil's hostess with a little arrogance.

'OK,' said Ted, 'lights out.'

'I must say,' said his wife, 'the colours are marvellous.'

All the time she was in the Colony Sybil longed for the inexplicable colourings of her native land. The flamboyants were too rowdy, the birds, the native women with their heads bound in cloth of piercing pink, their blinding black skin and white teeth, the baskets full of bright tough flowers or oranges on their heads, the sight of which everyone else admired ('How I wish I could paint all this!') distressed Sybil, it bored her.

She rented a house, sharing it with a girl whose husband was fighting in the north. She was twenty-two. To safeguard her privacy absolutely, she had a plywood partition put up in the sitting-room, for it was another ten years before she had learnt those arts of leading a double life and listening to people ambiguously, which enabled her to mix without losing identity, and to listen without boredom.

On the other side of the partition Ariadne Lewis decorously entertained her friends, most of whom were men on leave. On a few occasions Sybil attended these parties, working herself, as in a frenzy of self-discipline, into a state of carnal excitement over the men. She managed to do this only by an effortful sealing-off of all her critical faculties except those which assessed a good male voice and appearance. The hangovers were frightful.

The scarcity of white girls made it easy for any one of them to keep a number of men in perpetual attendance. Ariadne had many boyfriends but no love affairs. Sybil had three affairs in the space of two years, to put herself to the test. They started at private dances, in the magnolia-filled gardens that smelt like a scent factory, under the Milky Way which looked like an overcrowded jeweller's window. The affairs ended when she succumbed to one of her attacks of tropical flu, and lay in a twilight of the senses on a bed which had been set on the stone stoep and overhung with a white mosquito net like something bridal. With damp shaky hands she would write a final letter to the man and give it to her half-caste maid to post. He would telephone next morning, and would be put off by the house-boy, who was quite intelligent.

For some years she had been thinking she was not much inclined towards sex. After the third affair, this dawned and rose within her as a whole realization, as if in the past, when she had told herself, 'I am not predominantly a sexual being,' or 'I'm rather a frigid freak, I suppose,' these were the sayings of an illiterate, never quite rational and known until now, but after the third affair the notion was so intensely conceived as to be almost new. It appalled her. She lay on the shady stoep, her fever subsiding, and examined her relations with men. She thought, what if I married again? She shivered under the hot sheet. Can it be, she thought, that I have a suppressed tendency towards women? She lay still and let the idea probe round in imagination. She surveyed, with a stony inward eye, all the women she had known, prim little academicians with cream peter-pan collars on their dresses, large dominant women, a number of beauties, conventional nitwits like Ariadne. No, really, she thought; neither men nor women. It is a not caring for sexual relations. It is not merely a lack of pleasure in sex, it is dislike of the excitement. And it is not merely dislike, it is worse, it is boredom.

She felt a lonely emotion near to guilt. The three love affairs took on heroic aspects in her mind. They were an attempt, thought Sybil, to do the normal thing. Perhaps I may try again. Perhaps, if I should meet the right man . . . But at the idea 'right man' she felt a sense of intolerable desolation and could not stop shivering. She raised the mosquito net and reached for the lemon juice, splashing it jerkily into the glass. She sipped. The juice had grown warm and had been made too sweet, but she let it linger on her sore throat and peered through the net at the backs of houses and the yellow veldt beyond them.

Ariadne said one morning, 'I met a girl last night, it was funny. I thought it was you at first and called over to her. But she wasn't really like you close up, it was just an impression. As a matter of fact, she knows you. I've asked her to tea. I forget her name.'

'I don't,' said Sybil.

But when Désirée arrived they greeted each other with exaggerated warmth, wholly felt at the time, as acquaintances do when they meet in another hemisphere. Sybil had last seen Désirée at a dance in Hampstead, and there had merely said, 'Oh, hallo.'

'We were at our first school together,' Désirée explained to Ariadne, still holding Sybil's hand.

Already Sybil wished to withdraw. 'It's strange,' she remarked, 'how, sooner or later, everyone in the Colony meets someone they have known, or their parents knew, at home.'

Désirée and her husband, Barry Weston, were settled in a remote part of the Colony. Sybil had heard of Weston, unaware that Désirée was his wife. He was much talked of as an enterprising planter. Some years ago he had got the idea of manufacturing passion-fruit juice, had planted orchards and set up a factory. The business was now expanding wonderfully. Barry Weston also wrote poetry, a volume of which, entitled *Home Thoughts*, he had published and sold with great success within the confines of the Colony. His first wife had died of blackwater fever. On one of his visits to England he had met and married Désirée, who was twelve years his junior.

'You *must* come and see us,' said Désirée to Sybil; and to Ariadne she explained again, 'We were at our first little private school together.' And she said, 'Oh, Sybil, do you remember Trotsky? Do you remember Minnie Mouse, what a hell of a life we gave her? I shall never forget that day when . . .'

The school where Sybil taught was shortly to break up for holidays; Ariadne was to visit her husband in Cairo at that time. Sybil promised a visit to the Westons. When Désirée, beautifully dressed in linen suiting, had departed, Ariadne said, 'I'm so glad you're going to stay with them. I hated the thought of your being all alone for the next few weeks.'

'Do you know,' Sybil said, 'I don't think I shall go to stay with them after all. I'll make an excuse.'

'Oh, why not? Oh, Sybil, it's such a lovely place, and it will be fun for you. He's a poet, too.' Sybil could sense exasperation, could hear Ariadne telling her friends, 'There's something wrong with Sybil. You never know a person till you live with them. Now Sybil will say one thing one minute, and the next . . . Something wrong with her sex-life, perhaps . . . odd . . .'

At home, thought Sybil, it would not be such a slur. Her final appeal for a permit to travel to England had just been dismissed. The environment mauled her weakness. 'I think I'm going to have a cold,' she said, shivering.

'Go straight to bed, dear.' Ariadne called for black Elijah and bade him prepare some lemon juice. But the cold did not materialize.

She returned with flu, however, from her first visit to the Westons. Her 1936 Ford V8 had broken down on the road and she had waited three chilly hours before another car had appeared.

'You must get a decent car,' said the chemist's wife, who came to console her. 'These old crocks simply won't stand up to the roads out here.'

Sybil shivered and held her peace. Nevertheless, she returned to the Westons at mid-term.

*

Désirée's invitations were pressing, almost desperate. Again and again Sybil went in obedience to them. The Westons were a magnetic field.

There was a routine attached to her arrival. The elegant wicker chair was always set for her in the same position on the stoep. The same cushions, it seemed, were always piled in exactly the same way.

'What will you drink, Sybil? Are you comfy there, Sybil? We're going to give you a wonderful time, Sybil.' She was their little orphan, she supposed. She sat, with very dark glasses, contemplating the couple. 'We've planned – haven't we, Barry? – a surprise for you, Sybil.' 'We've planned – haven't we, Désirée? – a marvellous trip . . . a croc hunt . . . hippo . . .'

Sybil sips her gin and lime. Facing her on the wicker sofa, Désirée and her husband sit side by side. They gaze at Sybil affectionately, 'Take off your smoked glasses, Sybil, the sun's nearly gone.' Sybil takes them off. The couple hold hands. They peck kisses at each other, and presently, outrageously, they are entwined in a long erotic embrace in the course of which Barry once or twice regards Sybil from the corner of his eye. Barry disengages himself and sits with his arm about his wife; she snuggles up to him. Why, thinks Sybil, is this performance being staged? 'Sybil is shocked,' Barry remarks. She sips her drink, and reflects that a public display between man and wife somehow is more shocking than are courting couples in parks and doorways. 'We're very much in love with each other,' Barry explains, squeezing his wife. And Sybil wonders what is wrong with their marriage since obviously something is wrong. The couple kiss again. Am I dreaming this? Sybil asks herself.

Even on her first visit Sybil knew definitely there was something wrong with the marriage. She thought of herself, at first, as an objective observer, and was even amused when she understood they had chosen her to be their sort of Victim of Expiation. On occasions when other guests were present she noted that the love scenes did not take place. Instead, the couple tended to snub Sybil before their friends. 'Poor little Sybil, she lives all alone and is a teacher, and hasn't many friends. We have her here to stay as often as possible.' The people would look uneasily at Sybil, and would smile. 'But you must have *heaps* of friends,' they would say politely. Sybil came to realize she was an object of the Westons' resentment, and that, nevertheless, they found her indispensable.

Ariadne returned from Cairo. 'You always look washed out when you've been staying at the Westons',' she told Sybil eventually. 'I suppose it's due to the late parties and lots of drinks.'

'I suppose so.'

Désirée wrote continually. 'Do come, Barry needs you. He needs your advice about some sonnets.' Sybil tore up these letters quickly, but usually went. Not because her discomfort was necessary to their wellbeing, but because it was somehow necessary to her own. The act of visiting the Westons alleviated her sense of guilt.

I believe, she thought, they must discern my abnormality. How could they have guessed? She was always cautious when they dropped questions about her private life. But one's closest secrets have a subtle way of communicating themselves to the resentful vigilance of opposite types. I do believe, she thought, that heart speaks unto heart, and deep calleth unto deep. But rarely in clear language. There is a misunderstanding here. They imagine their demonstrations of erotic bliss will torment my frigid soul, and so far they are right. But the reason for my pain is not envy. Really, it is boredom.

Her Ford V8 rattled across country. How bored, she thought, I am going to be by their married tableau! How pleased, exultant, they will be! These thoughts consoled her, they were an offering to the gods.

'Are you comfy, Sybil?'

She sipped her gin and lime. 'Yes, thanks.'

His pet name for Désirée was Dearie. 'Kiss me, Dearie,' he said.

'There, Baddy,' his wife said to Barry, snuggling close to him and squinting at Sybil.

'I say, Sybil,' Barry said as he smoothed down his hair, 'you ought to get married again. You're missing such a lot.'

'Yes, Sybil,' said Désirée, 'you should either marry or enter a convent, one or the other.'

'I don't see why,' Sybil said, 'I should fit into a tidy category.'

'Well, you're neither one thing nor another – is she, honeybunch?'

True enough, thought Sybil, and that is why I'm laid out on the altar of boredom.

'Or get yourself a boyfriend,' said Désirée. 'It would be good for you.'

'You're wasting your best years,' said Barry.

'Are you comfy there, Sybil? . . . We want you to enjoy yourself

here. Any time you want to bring a boyfriend, we're broadminded – aren't
we, Baddy?'

'Kiss me, Dearie,' he said.

Désirée took his handkerchief from his pocket and rubbed lipstick from
his mouth. He jerked his head away and said to Sybil, 'Pass your glass.'

Désirée looked at her reflection in the glass of the french windows and
said, 'Sybil's too intellectual, that's her trouble.' She patted her hair, then
looked at Sybil with an old childish enmity.

After dinner Barry would read his poems. Usually, he said, 'I'm not
going to be an egotist tonight. I'm not going to read my poems.' And
usually Désirée would cry, 'Oh do, Barry, do.' Always, eventually, he did.
'Marvellous,' Désirée would comment, 'wonderful.' By the third night of
her visits, the farcical aspect of it all would lose its fascination for Sybil,
and boredom would fill her near to bursting point, like gas in a balloon.
To relieve the strain, she would sigh deeply from time to time. Barry was
too engrossed in his own voice to notice this, but Désirée was watching.
At first Sybil worded her comments tactfully. 'I think you should devote
more of your time to your verses,' she said. And, since he looked puzzled,
added, 'You owe it to poetry if you write it.'

'Nonsense,' said Désirée, 'he often writes a marvellous sonnet before
shaving in the morning.'

'Sybil may be right,' said Barry. 'I owe poetry all the time I can give.'

'Are you tired, Sybil?' said Désirée. 'Why are you sighing like that; are
you all right?'

Later, Sybil gave up the struggle and wearily said, 'Very good,' or 'Nice
rhythm' after each poem. And even the guilt of condoning Désirée's
'marvellous . . . wonderful' was less than the guilt of her isolated mind.
She did not know then that the price of allowing false opinions was
the gradual loss of one's capacity for forming true ones.

Not every morning, but at least twice during each visit Sybil would
wake to hear the row in progress. The nanny, who brought her early tea,
made large eyes and tiptoed warily. Sybil would have her bath, splashing
a lot to drown the noise of the quarrel. Downstairs, the battle of voices
descended, filled every room and corridor. When, on the worst occasions,
the sound of shattering glass broke through the storm, Sybil would know
that Barry was smashing up Désirée's dressing-table; and would wonder

how Désirée always managed to replace her crystal bowls, since goods of that type were now scarce, and why she bothered to do so. Sybil would always find the two girls of Barry's former marriage standing side by side on the lawn frankly gazing up at the violent bedroom window. The nanny would cart off Désirée's baby for a far-away walk. Sybil would likewise disappear for the morning.

The first time this happened, Désirée told her later, 'I'm afraid you unsettle Barry.'

'What do you mean?' said Sybil.

Désirée dabbed her watery eyes and blew her nose. 'Well, of *course*, it stands to reason, Sybil, you're out to attract Barry. And he's only a man. I know you do it *unconsciously*, but . . .'

'I can't stand this sort of thing. I shall leave right away,' Sybil said.

'No, Sybil, no. Don't make a *thing* of it. Barry needs you. You're the only person in the Colony who can really talk to him about his poetry.'

'Understand,' said Sybil on that first occasion, 'I am not at all interested in your husband. I think he's an all-round third-rater. That is my opinion.'

Désirée looked savage. 'Barry,' she shouted, 'has made a fortune out of passion-fruit juice in eight years. He has sold four thousand copies of *Home Thoughts* on his own initiative.'

It was like a game for three players. According to the rules, she was to be in love, unconsciously, with Barry, and tortured by the contemplation of Désirée's married bliss. She felt too old to join in, just at that moment.

Barry came to her room while she was packing. 'Don't go,' he said. 'We need you. And after all, we are only human. What's a row? These quarrels only happen in the best marriages. And I can't for the life of me think how it started.'

'What a beautiful house. What a magnificent estate,' said Sybil's hostess.

'Yes,' said Sybil, 'it was the grandest in the Colony.'

'Were the owners frightfully grand?'

'Well, they were rich, of course.'

'I can see that. What a beautiful interior. I adore those lovely old oil lamps. I suppose you didn't have electricity?'

'Yes, there was electric light in all the rooms. But my friends preferred the oil-lamp tradition for the dining-room. You see, it was a copy of an old Dutch house.'

'Absolutely charming.'

The reel came to an end. The lights went up and everyone shifted in their chairs.

'What were those large red flowers?' said the elderly lady.

'Flamboyants.'

'Magnificent,' said her hostess. 'Don't you miss the colours, Sybil?'

'No, I don't, actually. There was too much of it for me.'

'You didn't care for the bright colours?' said the young man, leaning forward eagerly.

Sybil smiled at him.

'I liked the bit where those little lizards were playing among the stones. That was an excellent shot,' said her host. He was adjusting the last spool.

'I rather *liked* that handsome blond fellow,' said her hostess, as if the point had been in debate. 'Was he the passion-fruiter?'

'He was the manager,' said Sybil.

'Oh yes, you told me. He was in a shooting affair, did you say?'

'Yes, it was unfortunate.'

'Poor young man. It sounds quite a dangerous place. I suppose the sun and everything . . .'

'It was dangerous for some people. It depended.'

'The blacks look happy enough. Did you have any trouble with them in those days?'

'No,' said Sybil, 'only with the whites.'

Everyone laughed.

'Right,' said her host. 'Lights out, please.'

Sybil soon perceived the real cause of the Westons' quarrels. It differed from their explanations: they were both, they said, so much in love, so jealous of each other's relations with the opposite sex.

'Barry was furious,' said Désirée one day, '– weren't you, Barry? – because I smiled, merely smiled, at Carter.'

'I'll have it out with Carter,' muttered Barry. 'He's always hanging round Désirée.'

David Carter was their manager. Sybil was so foolish as once to say, 'Oh surely David wouldn't—'

'Oh wouldn't he?' said Désirée.

'Oh wouldn't he?' said Barry.

Possibly they did not themselves know the real cause of their quarrels. These occurred on mornings when Barry had decided to lounge in bed and write poetry. Désirée, anxious that the passion-fruit business should continue to expand, longed for him to be at his office in the factory at eight o'clock each morning, by which time all other enterprising men in the Colony were at work. But Barry spoke more and more of retiring and devoting his time to his poems. When he lay abed, pen in hand, worrying a sonnet, Désirée would sulk and bang doors. The household knew that the row was on. 'Quiet! Don't you see I'm trying to think,' he would shout. '*I* suggest,' she would reply, 'you go to the library if you want to write.' It was evident that her greed and his vanity, facing each other in growling antipathy, were too terrible for either to face. Instead, the names of David Carter and Sybil would fly between them, consoling them, pepping-up and propagating the myth of their mutual attraction.

'Rolling your eyes at Carter in the orchard. Don't think I didn't notice.'

'Carter? That's funny. I can easily keep Carter in his place. But while we're on the subject, what about you with Sybil? You sat up late enough with her last night after I'd gone to bed.'

Sometimes he not only smashed the crystal bowls, he hurled them through the window.

In the exhausted afternoon Barry would explain, 'Désirée was upset – weren't you, Désirée? – because of you, Sybil. It's understandable. We shouldn't stay up late talking after Désirée has gone to bed. You're a little devil in your way, Sybil.'

'Oh well,' said Sybil obligingly, 'that's how it is.'

She became tired of the game. When, in the evenings, Barry's voice boomed forth with sonorous significance as befits a hallowed subject, she no longer thought of herself as an objective observer. She had tired of the game because she was now more than nominally committed to it. She ceased to be bored by the Westons; she began to hate them.

'What I don't understand,' said Barry, 'is why my poems are ignored back in England. I've sold over four thousand of the book out here. Feature articles about me have appeared in all the papers out here; remind me to show you them. But I can't get a single notice in London. When I send a poem to any of the magazines I don't even get a reply.'

'They are engaged in a war,' Sybil said.

'But they still publish poetry. Poetry so-called. Utter rubbish, all of it. You can't understand the stuff.'

'Yours is too good for them,' said Sybil. To a delicate ear her tone might have resembled the stab of a pin stuck into a waxen image.

'That's a fact, between ourselves,' said Barry. 'I shouldn't say it, but that's the answer.'

Barry was overweight, square and dark. His face had lines, as of anxiety or stomach trouble. David Carter, when he passed, cool and fair through the house, was quite a change.

'England is finished,' said Barry. 'It's degenerate.'

'I wonder,' said Sybil, 'you have the heart to go on writing so cheerily about the English towns and countryside.' Now, now, Sybil, she thought; business is business, and the nostalgic English scene is what the colonists want. This visit must be my last. I shall not come again.

'Ah, that,' Barry was saying, 'was the England I remember. The good old country. But now, I'm afraid, it's decadent. After the war it will be no more than . . .'

Désirée would have the servants into the drawing-room every morning to give them their orders for the day. 'I believe in keeping up home standards,' said Désirée, whose parents were hotel managers. Sybil was not sure where Désirée had got the idea of herding all the domestics into her presence each morning. Perhaps it was some family-prayer assembly in her ancestral memory, or possibly it had been some hotel-staff custom which prompted her to 'have in the servants' and instruct them beyond their capacity. These half-domesticated peasants and erstwhile small-farmers stood, bare-footed and woolly-cropped, in clumsy postures on Désirée's carpet. In pidgin dialect which they largely failed to comprehend, she enunciated the duties of each one. Only Sybil and David Carter knew that the natives' name for Désirée was, translated, 'Bad Hen'. Désirée complained much about their stupidity, but she enjoyed this morning palaver as Barry relished his poetry.

'Carter writes poetry too,' said Barry with a laugh one day.

Désirée shrieked. 'Poetry! Oh, Barry, you can't call that stuff *poetry.*'

'It is frightful,' Barry said, 'but the poor fellow doesn't know it.'

'I should like to see it,' Sybil said.

'You aren't interested in Carter by any chance, Sybil?' said Désirée.

'How do you mean?'

'Personally, I mean.'

'Well, I think he's all right.'

'Be honest, Sybil,' said Barry. Sybil felt extremely irritated. He so often appealed for frankness in others, as if by right; was so dishonest with himself. 'Be honest, Sybil – you're after David Carter.'

'He's handsome,' Sybil said.

'You haven't a chance,' said Barry. 'He's mad keen on Désirée. And anyway, Sybil, you don't want a beginner.'

'You want a mature man in a good position,' said Désirée. 'The life you're living isn't natural for a girl. I've been noticing,' she said, 'you and Carter being matey together out on the farm.'

Towards the end of her stay David Carter produced his verses for Sybil to read. She thought them interesting but unpractised. She told him so, and was disappointed that he did not take this as a reasonable criticism. He was very angry. 'Of course,' she said, 'your poetry is far better than Barry's.' This failed to appease David. After a while, when she was meeting him in the town where she lived, she began to praise his poems, persuading herself that he was fairly talented.

She met him whenever he could get away. She sent excuses in answer to Désirée's pressing invitations. For different reasons, both Sybil and David were anxious to keep their meetings secret from the Westons. Sybil did not want the affair mythologized and gossiped about. For David's part, he valued his job in the flourishing passion-fruit concern. He had confided to Sybil his hope, one day, to have the whole business under his control. He might even buy Barry out. 'I know far more about it than he does. He's getting more and more bound up with his poetry, and paying next to no attention to the business. I'm just waiting.' He is, Sybil remarked to herself on hearing this, a true poet all right.

David reported that the quarrels between Désirée and Barry were becoming more violent, that the possibility of Barry's resigning from business to devote his time to poetry was haunting Désirée. 'Why don't you come,' Désirée wrote, 'and talk to Barry about his poetry? Why don't you come and see us now? What have we done? Poor Sybil, all alone in the world, you ought to be married. David Carter follows me all over the place, it's most embarrassing, you know how furious Barry gets. Well, I suppose that's the cost of having a devoted husband.' Perhaps, thought Sybil, she senses that David is my lover.

One day she went down with flu. David turned up unexpectedly and proposed marriage. He clung to her with violent, large hands. She alone, he said, understood his ambitions, his art, himself. Within a year or two they could, together, take over the passion-fruit plantation.

'Sh-sh, Ariadne will hear you.' Ariadne was out, in fact. David looked at her somewhat wildly. 'We must be married,' he said.

Sybil's affair with David Carter was over, from her point of view, almost before it had started. She had engaged in it as an act of virtue done against the grain, and for a brief time it had absolved her from the reproach of her sexlessness.

'I'm waiting for an answer.' By his tone, he seemed to suspect what the answer would be.

'Oh, David, I was just about to write to you. We really must put an end to this. As for marriage, well, I'm not cut out for it at all.'

He stooped over her bed and clung to her. 'You'll catch my flu,' she said. 'I'll think about it,' she said, to get rid of him.

When he had gone she wrote him her letter, sipping lemon juice to ease her throat. She noticed he had brought for her, and left on the floor of the stoep, six bottles of Weston's Passion-fruit Juice. He will soon get over the affair, she thought, he has still got his obsession with the passion-fruit business.

But in response to her letter David forced his way into the house. Sybil was alarmed. None of her previous lovers had persisted in this way.

'It's your duty to marry me.'

'Really, what next?'

'It's your duty to me as a man and a poet.' She did not like his eyes.

'As a poet,' she said, 'I think you're a third-rater.' She felt relieved to hear her own voice uttering the words.

He stiffened up in a comical melodramatic style, looking such a clean-cut settler with his golden hair and tropical suiting.

'David Carter,' wrote Désirée, 'has gone on the bottle. I think he's bats, myself. It's because I keep giving him the brush-off. Isn't it all silly? The estate will go to ruin if Barry doesn't get rid of him. Barry has sent him away on leave for a month, but if he hasn't improved on his return we shall have to make a change. When are you coming? Barry needs to talk to you.'

Sybil went the following week, urged on by her old self-despising; driving her Ford V8 against the current of pleasure, yet compelled to expiate her abnormal nature by contact with the Westons' sexuality, which she knew, none the less, would bore her.

They twisted the knife within an hour of her arrival.

'Haven't you found a man yet?' said Barry.

'You ought to try a love affair,' said Désirée. 'We've been saying – haven't we, Barry? – you ought to, Sybil. It would be good for you. It isn't healthy, the life you lead. That's why you get flu so often. It's psychological.'

'Come out on the lawn,' Barry had said when she first arrived. 'We've got the ciné camera out. Come and be filmed.'

Désirée said, 'Carter came back this morning.'

'Oh, is he here? I thought he was away for a month.'

'So did we. But he turned up this morning.'

'He's moping,' Barry said, 'about Désirée. She snubs him so badly.'

'He's psychological,' said Désirée.

'I love that striped awning,' said Sybil's hostess. 'It puts the finishing touch on the whole scene. How carefree you all look – don't they, Ted?'

'*That* chap looks miserable,' Ted observed. He referred to a shot of David Carter who had just ambled within range of the camera.

Everyone laughed, for David looked exceedingly grim.

'He was caught in an off-moment there,' said Sybil's hostess. 'Oh, there goes Sybil. I thought you looked a little sad just then, Sybil. There's that other girl again, and the lovely dog.'

'Was this a *typical* afternoon in the Colony?' inquired the young man.

'It was and it wasn't,' Sybil said.

Whenever they had the camera out life changed at the Westons'. Everyone, including the children, had to look very happy. The house natives were arranged to appear in the background wearing their best whites.

Sometimes Barry would have everyone dancing in a ring with the children, and the natives had to clap time.

Or, as on the last occasion, he would stage an effect of gracious living. The head cook-boy, who had a good knowledge of photography, was placed at his post.

'Ready,' said Barry to the cook, 'shoot.'

Désirée came out, followed by the dog.

'Look frisky, Barker,' said Barry. The Alsatian looked frisky.

Barry put one arm round Désirée and his other arm through Sybil's that late afternoon, walking them slowly across the camera range. He chatted with amiability and with an actor's lift of the head. He would accentuate his laughter, tossing back his head. A sound track would, however, have reproduced the words, 'Smile, Sybil. Walk slowly. Look as if you're enjoying it. You'll be able to see yourself in later years, having the time of your life.'

Sybil giggled.

Just then David was seen to be securing the little lake boat between the trees. 'He must have come across the lake,' said Barry. 'I wonder if he's been drinking again?'

But David's walk was quite steady. He did not realize he was being photographed as he crossed the long lawn. He stood for a moment staring at Sybil. She said, 'Oh hallo, David.' He turned and walked aimlessly face-on towards the camera.

'Hold it a minute,' Barry called out to the cook.

The boy obeyed at the moment David realized he had been filmed.

'OK,' shouted Barry, when David was out of range. 'Fire ahead.'

It was then Barry said to Sybil, 'Haven't you found a man yet . . . ?' and Désirée said, 'You ought to try a love affair . . .'

'We've made Sybil unhappy,' said Désirée.

'Oh, I'm quite happy.'

'Well, cheer up in front of the camera,' said Barry.

The sun was setting fast, the camera was folded away, and everyone had gone to change. Sybil came down and sat on the stoep outside the open french windows of the dining-room. Presently, Désirée was indoors behind her, adjusting the oil lamps which one of the house-boys had set too high. Désirée put her head round the glass door and remarked to Sybil, 'That

Benjamin's a fool, I shall speak to him in the morning. He simply will not take care with these lamps. One day we'll have a real smoke-out.'

Sybil said, 'Oh, I expect they are all so used to electricity these days . . .'

'That's the trouble,' said Désirée, and turned back into the room.

Sybil was feeling disturbed by David's presence in the place. She wondered if he would come in to dinner. Thinking of his sullen staring at her on the lawn, she felt he might make a scene. She heard a gasp from the dining-room behind her.

She looked round, but in the same second it was over. A deafening crack from the pistol and Désirée crumpled up. A movement by the inner door and David held the gun to his head. Sybil screamed, and was aware of running footsteps upstairs. The gun exploded again and David's body dropped sideways.

With Barry and the natives she went round to the dining-room. Désirée was dead. David lingered a moment enough to roll his eyes in Sybil's direction as she rose from Désirée's body. He knows, thought Sybil quite lucidly, that he got the wrong woman.

'What I can't understand,' said Barry when he called on Sybil a few weeks later, 'is why he did it.'

'He was mad,' said Sybil.

'Not all that mad,' said Barry. 'And everyone thinks, of course, that there was an affair between them. That's what I can't bear.'

'Quite,' said Sybil. 'But of course he was keen on Désirée. You always said so. Those rows you used to have . . . You always made out you were jealous of David.'

'Do you know,' he said, 'I wasn't, really. It was a sort of . . . a sort of . . .'

'Play-act,' said Sybil.

'Sort of. You see, there was nothing between them,' he said. 'And honestly, Carter wasn't a bit interested in Désirée. And the question is *why* he did it. I can't bear people to think . . .'

The damage to his pride, Sybil saw, outweighed his grief. The sun was setting and she rose to put on the stoep light.

'Stop!' he said. 'Turn round. My God, you did look like Désirée for a moment.'

'You're nervy,' she said, and switched on the light.

'In some ways you *do* look a little like Désirée,' he said. 'In some lights,' he said reflectively.

I must say something, thought Sybil, to blot this notion from his mind. I must make this occasion unmemorable, distasteful to him.

'At all events,' she said, 'you've still got your poetry.'

'That's the great thing,' he said, 'I've still got that. It means everything to me, a great consolation. I'm selling up the estate and joining up. The kids are going into a convent and I'm going up north. What we need is some good war poetry. There hasn't been any war poetry.'

'You'll make a better soldier,' she said, 'than a poet.'

'What do you say?'

She repeated her words fairly slowly, and with a sense of relief, almost of absolution. The season of falsity had formed a scab, soon to fall away altogether. There is no health, she thought, for me, outside of honesty.

'You've always,' he said, 'thought my poetry was wonderful.'

'I have said so,' she said, 'but it was a sort of play-act. Of course, it's only my opinion, but I think you're a third-rater poet.'

'You're upset, my dear,' he said.

He sent her the four reels of film from Cairo a month before he was killed in action. 'It will be nice in later years,' he wrote, 'for you to recall those good times we used to have.'

'It has been delightful,' said her hostess. 'You haven't changed a bit. Do you *feel* any different?'

'Well yes, I feel rather differently about everything, of course.' One learns to accept oneself.

'A hundred feet of one's past life!' said the young man. 'If they were mine, I'm sure I should be shattered. I should be calling "Lights! Lights!" like Hamlet's uncle.'

Sybil smiled at him. He looked back, suddenly solemn and shrewd.

'How tragic, those people being killed in shooting affairs,' said the elderly woman.

'The last reel was the best,' said her hostess. 'The garden was entrancing. I should like to see that one again; what about you, Ted?'

'Yes, I liked those nature-study shots. I feel I missed a lot of it,' said her husband.

'Hark at him – nature-study shots!'

'Well, those close-ups of tropical plants.'

Everyone wanted the last one again.

'How about you, Sybil?'

Am I a woman, she thought calmly, or an intellectual monster? She was so accustomed to this question within herself that it needed no answer. She said, 'Yes, I should like to see it again. It's an interesting experience.'

ROBERT AICKMAN

Bind Your Hair

No one seemed able to fathom Clarinda Hartley. She had a small but fastidious flat near Church Street, Kensington; and a responsible job in a large noncommittal commercial organisation. No one who knew her now had ever known her in any other residence or any other job. She entertained a little, never more nor less over the years; went out not infrequently with men; and for her holidays simply disappeared, returning with brief references to foreign parts. No one seemed to know her really well; and in the course of time there came to be wide differences of opinion about her age, and recurrent speculation about her emotional life. The latter topic was not made less urgent by a certain distinction in her appearance, and also in her manner. She was very tall (a great handicap, of course, in the opinion of many) and well-shaped; she had very fair, very fine, very abundant hair, to which plainly she gave much attention; her face had interesting planes (for those who could appreciate them), but also soft curves, which went with her hair. She had a memorable voice: high-pitched, but gentle. She was, in fact, thirty-two. Everyone was greatly surprised when she announced her engagement to Dudley Carstairs.

Or rather it was Carstairs who announced it. He could not keep it to himself as long as there was anyone within earshot who was ignorant of it; and well might he be elated, because his capture followed a campaign of several years' continuance, and supported by few sweeping advantages. He worked in the same office as Clarinda, and in a not unsatisfactory position for his thirty years; and was in every way a thoroughly presentable person: but even in the office there were a number of others like him, and it would have seemed possible that Clarinda could have further extended her range of choice by going outside.

The weekend after the engagement Dudley arranged for her to spend with him and his parents in Northamptonshire. Mr Carstairs, Senior, had held an important position on the administrative side of the Northampton boot and shoe industry; and when he retired upon a fair pension had settled in a small but comfortable house in one of the remote parts of a county where the remote parts are surprisingly many and extensive. Mr Carstairs had been a pioneer in this particular, because others similarly placed had tended upon retirement to emigrate to the Sussex coast or the New Forest; but his initiative, as often happens in such cases, had been imitated, until the little village in which he had settled was now largely populated by retired industrial executives and portions of their families.

Clarinda would have been grateful for more time in which to adjust herself to Dudley in the capacity of accepted lover; but Dudley somehow did not seem to see himself in that capacity, and to be reluctant in any way to defer Clarinda's full involvement with her new family position. Clarinda, having said yes to what was believed to be the major question, smiled slightly and said yes to the minor.

Mr Carstairs, Senior, met them at Roade station.

'Hullo, Dad.' The two men gazed at one another's shoes, not wanting to embrace and hesitating to shake hands. Mr Carstairs was smiling, benignly expectant. Plainly he was one who considered that life had treated him well. Almost, one believed, he was ready to accept his son's choice of a bride as, for him, joy's crown of joy.

'Dad. This is Clarinda.'

'I *say*, my boy . . .'

Outside the station was a grey Standard, in which Mr Carstairs drove them many miles to the west. Already the sun was sinking. Soon after they arrived they had settled down, with Mrs Carstairs and Dudley's sister Elizabeth, to crumpets in the long winter dusk. Elizabeth had a secretarial position in Leamington, and bicycled there and back every day. All of them were charmed with Clarinda. She exceeded their highest, and perhaps not very confident, hopes.

Clarinda responded to their happy approval of her, and smiled at Dudley's extreme pleasure at being home. An iced cake had been baked for her specially, and she wondered whether these particular gilt-edged cups were in daily use. They neither asked her questions nor talked mainly about themselves: they all made a warm-hearted, not unskilful effort to make her feel completely one with them from the outset. She and Elizabeth discovered a common interest in the theatre (shared only in a lesser degree by Dudley).

'But Leamington's so stuffy that no one's ever made a theatre pay there.'

'Not since the war,' said Mr Carstairs in affectionate qualification.

'Not since the *first* war,' said Elizabeth.

'Is Leamington the nearest town?' asked Clarinda.

'It's the nearest as the crow flies, or as Elizabeth cycles,' said Dudley, 'but it's not the quickest when you're coming from London. Narrow lanes all the way.'

'Fortunately we've got our own friends by now in the village,' said Mrs Carstairs. 'I've asked some of them in for drinks, so that you can meet them at once.'

And indeed, almost immediately the bell rang, and the first of the visitors was upon them. Mr Carstairs went round the room putting on lights and drawing the curtains. Every now and then he gave some jocular direction to Dudley, who was complementarily engaged. A domestic servant of some kind, referred to by Mrs Carstairs as 'our local woman', had removed the remains of tea; and by the time Elizabeth had borne in a tray of drinks, three more visitors had added themselves to the first two.

'Can I help?' Clarinda had said.

'No,' the Carstairs family had replied. 'Certainly not. Not *yet.*'

Altogether there were eleven visitors, only two of whom were under forty. All eleven of them Clarinda liked very much less than she liked the Carstairs family. Then just as several of them were showing signs of departure, a twelfth arrived; who made a considerable change. A woman of medium height and in early middle age, she had a lined and sallow face, but an alert expression and large, deeply set black eyes. She had untidy, shoulder-length black hair which tended to separate itself into distinct compact strands. Her only make-up appeared to be an exceptionally vivid lipstick, abundantly applied to her large square mouth. She entered in a luxuriant fur coat, but at once cast it off, so that it lay on the floor, and appeared in a black corduroy skirt and a black silk blouse, cut low, and with long tight sleeves. On her feet were heel-less golden slippers.

'I've been so *busy.*' She seized both of Mrs Carstairs's hands. Her voice was very deep and melodious, but marred by a certain hoarseness, or uncertainty of timbre. 'Where is she?'

Mrs Carstairs was smiling amiably as ever; but all conversation in the room had stopped.

'Do go on talking.' The newcomer addressed the party at random. She had now observed Clarinda. 'Introduce me,' she said to Mrs Carstairs, as if her hostess were being a little slow with her duties. 'Or am I too late?' Her sudden quick smile was possibly artificial but certainly bewitching. For a second, various men in the room missed the thread of their resumed conversations.

'Of course you're not too late,' said Mrs Carstairs. Then she made the introduction. 'Clarinda Hartley. Mrs Pagani.'

'Nothing whatever to do with the restaurant,' said Mrs Pagani.

'How do you do?' said Clarinda.

Mrs Pagani had a firm and even but somewhat bony handshake. She was wearing several large rings, with heavy stones in them, and round her neck a big fat locket on a thick golden chain.

By now Mrs Carstairs had brought Mrs Pagani a drink. 'Here's to the future,' said Mrs Pagani, looking into Clarinda's eyes, and as soon as Mrs Carstairs had turned away, drained the glass.

'Thank you,' said Clarinda.

'Do sit down,' said Mrs Pagani, as if the house were hers.

'Thank you,' said Clarinda, falling in with the illusion.

Mrs Pagani stretched out an arm (Clarinda noticed that her arms, in their tight black sleeves, were uncommonly long) and pulled up a chair, upon which she sat. Clarinda noticed also that when she was seated, her hips too looked bony and obtrusive. Altogether Mrs Pagani gave an impression of unusual physical power, only partly concealed by her conventional clothes. It was as if suddenly she might arise and tear down the house.

'You cannot imagine,' said Mrs Pagani, 'how much it means to me to have someone new in the village, especially someone more or less my own age. Or perhaps you can?'

'But I'm not going to *live* here,' said Clarinda, clutching hold of the main point.

'Well, of course not. But there'll be frequent weekends. Whatever else may be said for or against Dudley, he's devoted to his home.'

Clarinda nodded thoughtfully. She was aware that everyone's eyes were upon them, and realised that Mrs Pagani had so far acknowledged the presence of none of the other guests, well though she must presumably know them.

'Who would want to know any of these people?' enquired Mrs Pagani in a husky, telepathic undertone.

One trouble was that Clarinda rather agreed with her.

'Why do *you* live here?'

'I can't live in towns. And in the country people are the same wherever you go. Most people, I mean. You don't live in the country for the local society.'

Clarinda failed to ask why you did live in the country.

Elizabeth came up with more drinks.

'Hullo, Elizabeth,' said Mrs Pagani.

For some reason Elizabeth went very red.

'Hullo, Mrs Pagani.' She left two drinks with them, and hurried away on her errand of hospitality. Mrs Pagani's eyes followed her for a few seconds. Then she turned back to Clarinda, and said: 'We two will be seeing a lot of one another.'

Again Clarinda could only nod.

'I needn't tell you that you're not what I expected. Do you know where I live?'

Clarinda, still silent, shook her head.

'Have you been round the village yet?'

'No.'

'Not seen the church?'

'It was getting dark when I arrived.'

'I live in the churchyard.' Mrs Pagani suddenly shouted with laughter. 'It always surprises people.' She placed her long bony left hand on Clarinda's knee. 'There used to be a chapel in the churchyard, with a room over it. This is a thinly populated district, and they brought the corpses from the farmhouses and cottages, often a long slow journey, and left the coffin in the chapel waiting for the funeral the next day. And the mourners passed the night upstairs, watching and, of course, drinking. When all this became unnecessary, the chapel fell into ruin. The parish council was glad to sell it to me. The vicar's a hundred and one anyway. I restored it and I live in it. The ground had to be specially deconsecrated for me.' Mrs Pagani removed her hand and picked up her glass. 'Come and see me.' For the second time she toasted Clarinda. 'I call it the Charnel House. Not quite correct, of course: a charnel house is where the dead lie *after* the funeral. But I thought the name rather suited me.' Suddenly her attention was distracted. Without moving her eyes, she inclined her head slightly sideways. 'Just look at Mr Appleby. Used to be managing director of an important company. Appleby's Arterial Bootlaces.'

Clarinda could not see that Mr Appleby, with whom she had been talking before Mrs Pagani's arrival, was doing anything much out of the ordinary. He seemed simply to be telling stories to two or three other guests, who admittedly seemed less interested than he was. But Clarinda was unaccustomed to making twelve or fifteen intimate acquaintances for life en bloc; and all coming within the, at best, uncertain category of friends' friends.

Again Mrs Pagani had drained her glass. 'I must be going. I only looked in for a minute. I have a lot to do tonight.' She rose and held out her hand. 'Tomorrow then?'

'Thank you very much, but I'm not quite sure. I expect Mr and Mrs Carstairs have some plans for me.'

Mrs Pagani looked her in the eyes, then nodded. 'Yes. You mustn't quarrel with them. That's very important. Well: come if you can.'

'Thank you, I'd like to.'

Mrs Pagani was resuming her expensive sable coat, and saying good-bye to Mrs Carstairs.

'You've nothing to worry about,' Clarinda heard her say, 'Dudley's chosen well.'

'Darling.' It was Dudley standing behind Clarinda's chair. He kissed the top of her head. 'Don't mind her. She's far round the bend, of course, but good-hearted at bottom. Anyway she's the only one of her kind in the village. Pots of money too.'

'What makes you think that, Dudley?' asked the marzipan voice of Mr Appleby. Conversation about Mrs Pagani was now general.

'Couldn't behave as she does if she hadn't, Mr Appleby,' replied Dudley. That seemed to be the consensus of opinion.

When everyone had gone, they listened to the radio. Then they had supper, and Clarinda was permitted, after strenuous application, to participate in the washing up. As they retired in a warm mist of gently affectionate demonstrativeness, the thought crossed Clarinda's mind that she might like to sleep with Dudley. It was still not an urgent wish, only a thought; but in Dudley there was no evidence that it was even a thought. For him the fateful outer wall of the fortress had been successfully battered down after a long siege; the course of time would bring the later degrees of capitulation.

The next morning Clarinda had to admit to herself that she was very depressed. As she lay in bed watching wisps of late-autumn fog drift and swirl past her window, she felt that inside the house was a warm and cosy emptiness in which she was about to be lost. She saw herself, her real self, for ever suspended in blackness, howling in the lonely dark, miserable and unheard; while her other, outer self went smiling through an endless purposeless routine of love for and compliance with a family and a community of friends which, however excellent, were exceedingly unlike her, in some way that she did not fully understand. Elizabeth might bill and coo about the theatre, but it could hardly be said that any one of them had a sense of drama. They lived in the depths of the country, but had no idea of the wilderness. They were constantly together, but knew one another too well to be able to converse. Individuality had been eroded from all of them by the tides of common sentiment. Love me, said Dudley in effect, his eyes softly glowing; love mine. His London personality seemed merely a bait with which to entice her into the capacious family lobster pot. Mrs Pagani was certainly different from the rest of them; but Clarinda was far from sure that Mrs Pagani was her idea of an ally.

Then she got up, turned on the big electric heater, and felt that her thoughts had been the morbid product of lying too long abed. Moreover, the flying swathes of fog were most beautiful. She stood in her nightdress by the window looking at them; with the heater behind her sending ripples of warmth up her back. It was an old sash window with the original well-proportioned glazing bars. The new white paint covered numerous under-currents in the surface of earlier coats. Clarinda liked such details in the house; always kept neat and spruce, like an old dandy whom people still cared about.

But from breakfast onwards her spirits once more began to sink. One trouble was that the Carstairs family, in fact, had no plans for her whatever, and nor had Dudley individually. There was a half-hearted suggestion of church, which no one seemed wishful to keep alive; and after that a sequence of minor interruptions and involved jobs which Clarinda felt could be much better organised, but which everyone else seemed quietly to enjoy as they were. The whole family, Dudley included, seemed to like even the most pointless chores simply because they were being undertaken collectively. The four of them did all they could to give Clarinda a place in the various undertakings; and Clarinda hated the perverse barrier which seemed more and more to isolate her from their kindness. But when by the middle of the afternoon (Sunday luncheon was a substantial reaping of the morning's seedtime) no one had even suggested a walk, she did something precipitate. Without speaking to Dudley, who was helping his father in the garden, she went up to her bedroom, changed into a pair of trousers and a sweater, donned her mackintosh, wrote on the inside of a cigarette box 'Gone for a walk. Back soon', and quietly left the house.

The swathes of fog were still sweeping before the wind, but, though damp, it was not a cold wind nor unfriendly. Immediately she was away from the house, Clarinda felt alive again. After walking a few hundred yards rather furtively, she ascended a roadside bank from which the grass had recently been sickled, and looked about her. She was looking for the church; and when, through a break in the mist, she saw the battlemented top of the yellow stone tower, with a jutting gargoyle at each corner, she knew which way she would go. She turned her back on the church, and walked away from the few cottages which made up the village. Mrs Pagani had possibly served a purpose as serio-comic relief the previous evening, but Clarinda had no wish to enlarge the acquaintanceship.

The patches of cloud and fog drifted and lifted, making constant changes of scene. There was no hope of sunshine, but the mist was uncharged with smoke, and served to melt the sharp air of winter and to enclose Clarinda with an advancing tent of invisibility. Other than Clarinda's light, quick step on the granite chips of the old-fashioned narrow road, the only sound was the dripping of water from the trees, the hedges, the occasional gates. At the tip of every leaf was a fat pearl about to drop and vanish. Clarinda realised that her hair was becoming damp. She bundled it on to the top of her head, soaking her hands in the process; then drew a long black scarf from her mackintosh pocket, and twisted it into a tight turban. The road seemed to be lined with dripping trees, which appeared dimly one at a time, grew into a fullness of detail which had seemed impossible a minute before, and then dissolved away, even from the backward glance; but the air also was itself heavy with soft wetness. Soft and wet, but good on the face . . . 'Let there be wet,' quoted Clarinda to herself in her clear gentle voice. 'Oh let there be wet.'

She had seen no one in the village, and if there were animals in the fields, the mist cut off sight and hearing of them. Clarinda was aware that she might have some difficult personal problems almost immediately ahead of her; but she thought nothing of them as the renewal of contact with the country, the adventurous loneliness of her walk, suffused her with their first freshness. Out of the mist advanced a small square notice-board, lopsided on top of a sloping wooden pole: 'No Rite of Way,' read Clarinda. 'Persons Proceed Beyond This Point By Favour Only.'

It was perhaps an unusual announcement, and not made more convincing by the misspelling, and by the crudeness of the erection; but Clarinda had heard of landowners who close gates on one day each year in order to prevent the establishment of an easement, and there seemed to be no change whatever in the nature or surface of the road, at least in the short distance ahead which was visible. Clarinda continued her walk.

No one, however, is entirely unaffected, either towards carefulness, or towards challenge, by passing such a notice; and in due course Clarinda realised that she was walking more slowly. Then she perceived that the road itself had for some time been rising slightly but continuously. It also seemed narrower, and the hedges higher. Clarinda stopped and looked at her watch. Despite the muffling mist, she could hear its ticking with extreme clarity, so silent were the hidden pastures around her. It had been something before three o'clock when she had crept out of the house; it was now something after half past. She had possibly another hour of daylight. If she went on for a quarter of that hour, there would be as much time in which to return as she had taken upon the outward journey, and the way back was along a known road, and one which inclined downhill.

Moreover, there had not been a single cross-roads or doubtful turning. And in any case Clarinda liked walking in the dark. Certainly neither her mind nor her stomach was inclined to a cosy crumpet tea with the Carstairs family, or to a further session bound, like Catherine upon her wheel, to the mark of interrogation which Dudley remained for her. Again, therefore, she continued her walk.

The gradient increased, but the trees came more quickly, imperceptibly losing, tree by tree, the moment of clear detail which had previously characterised each of them. The road had begun to wind steeply upwards through a wood. Now the hedges, lately so high, had ceased, but the road, although the antique metalling seemed more and more lost in the damp loamy soil, remained distinct. Intermittently, the going had become a little muddy, but the softness underfoot made a change from the angular granite. The trees had now become dim and uniform shapes which passed so quickly and monotonously that sometimes they seemed almost to move, as in a very early cinematograph.

Then, unmistakably, something else was moving. From among the tall, thin trees, and out of the veiling mist, came a small animal. It crossed the track ten or twelve feet in front of Clarinda, and disappeared again almost at once. It neither walked nor ran, but slowly ambled. It was not quite silent, but the atmosphere made the sound of its passage seem insufficient; it whispered and sighed its way through the undergrowth. Clarinda could not think what animal it was. Probably a dog which the mist had misshaped. She checked for a moment, then went on.

Swiftly and momentarily the mist cleared a larger area around her, as she had seen it do several times before. She could see many trees, and could now perceive also that they were beeches. Dotted about the bare earth which surrounds beech trees even in a thick wood were many more of the animals. They were pigs.

Each of the pigs seemed very intent about its business, softly snuffling after unknown sweets in the naked soil. None grunted or squeaked; but the dead, brown-paper leaves rustled slightly as the herd rooted. The pigs were on both sides of the track, and again Clarinda hesitated briefly before advancing through the midst of them.

At first they took no notice of her, perhaps, she thought, unafraid of man because little knowing him; and the tent of mist, temporarily a marquee, advanced with her on to the wooded heights ahead. Then, most unexpectedly, there came from the obscurity thirty yards away on Clarinda's right a shattering animal shriek, short but so loud and high as to pain the ear. All the pigs looked up, stood motionless for a second, then massed together in the direction the sound had come from, some of them crossing the track behind and ahead of her for the purpose. Again they stood, an indistinct agglomeration on the edge of the mist; then suddenly swept back the way they had come. The whole herd, packed tightly together, charged across the track and disappeared into the mist on the left. The pigs had passed no more than five or six feet in front of Clarinda; who was able to observe that in the very middle of the throng was a creature much larger than the rest, a bristling, long-snouted boar, with large curving bluish-white tusks. He it was, she suspected, that had cried from the enveloping mist. She had never before seen such a creature, and was slightly alarmed.

The scampering flight of the pigs could be heard for a few seconds after the fog had surrounded them. Then the wood was silent again. It was as if the pigs had been the last creatures left alive in it. The fog had now closed up again, scudding across the track on a wind which seemed colder and stronger than it had been in the village at the beginning of Clarinda's walk. But the track was now rising steeply, and the extra exertion kept her warm. The long-drawn-out winter dusk must have begun, because not until she was right upon them did Clarinda notice two figures on the path.

They were children. They did not seem to be either ascending or descending, but to be quietly waiting by the side of the track for someone to pass. They were identically dressed in one-piece waterproof garments, like small, trim diving suits, bright blue in colour, and provided with hoods. One child had its hood over its head, but the other was bareheaded and displayed a curly mass of silky flaxen hair, much the colour of Clarinda's own in childhood. The bareheaded child had blue eyes very widely spaced, and a pale skin. The face of the other child was shadowed by its hood, and from Clarinda's altitude amounted to little more than a long red mouth. Both children, Clarinda noticed, had long red mouths. She was unable to determine their sex.

'Excuse me,' said the bareheaded child, very politely. Clarinda decided it was a girl. The girl spoke well.

Clarinda stopped.

The little girl smiled charmingly. 'Have you seen the pigs?' She spoke as if the pigs were a matter of common interest to them, and automatically identifiable; as if a straggler from a hunt had asked, Had she seen the hounds?

'Yes,' said Clarinda. 'Are they your pigs?'

'How long ago?' asked the child, with a child's disregard of side issues.

'About five minutes ago.' Clarinda looked at her watch. Quarter to four. Time to go back. 'As a matter of fact, I'm afraid I frightened them.'

'Silly old pigs,' said the child, fortunately taking Clarinda's side. 'Which way did they go? *This way*? Or *that* way?' She indicated up the hill or down. Clarinda thought that she was about eight.

'That way, I'm afraid,' said Clarinda, pointing vaguely into the mist. 'I hope they'll not get lost in the fog.'

'There's always a fog,' said the child.

Clarinda let that one go.

'What happens if I get to the top?' she asked.

The hooded child, who had said nothing, suddenly made an odd movement. It raised one foot and stamped on the ground. It was as if its whole small body were swept by a spasm. The movement reminded Clarinda of an animal which had been startled and pawed the earth: a large animal, moreover. In the child seemed to be a disproportionate strength. Clarinda was really frightened by it.

'There's a lovely view some days,' said the bareheaded child helpfully.

'Not much good this evening.'

The child shook its head, smiling politely. The hooded child snatched at the bareheaded child's sleeve and pulled it sharply.

'There's a maze.' The bareheaded child was showing off slightly but meaning to help also.

'What kind of maze? With hedges? I don't believe it.' To Clarinda a maze meant Hampton Court.

'An ordinary maze. You have to look for it though.'

'How far away?'

'Quite near.'

'Where do I look?' Clearly the child was speaking the truth, and Clarinda was interested.

'In among the bushes. There's a little path.'

Clarinda noticed that the second child had cocked up its head and was looking at her. It seemed to have sharp, sallow features, and big eyes. In its hood it was not unlike a falcon.

'Shall I get lost in the maze?'

The bareheaded child appeared unable to understand this question and looked at Clarinda disappointedly.

'Well that's up to me,' said Clarinda, coming to the rescue.

The child nodded. She had still not understood. 'Thank you for telling us about the pigs.'

'Thank you for telling me about the maze.'

The little girl smiled her pretty smile. Really I never saw such a beautiful child, thought Clarinda. The children departed quickly down the hill. In a moment they had vanished.

Clarinda again looked at her watch. Three-fifty. She decided that she would give fifteen minutes to looking for the child's maze, and that even then she would be back soon after five.

Before long she reached a gate. It was at the edge of the wood and the end of the track. Outside the wood was short, downlike grass, mossy with moisture. Clarinda's feet sank into it, as into very soft rubber. There were frequent, irregularly placed clumps of thorny scrub, and no sign of even the sketchiest path. The wind was still growing chillier, and the mist was darkening all the time. Clarinda had not gone fifty yards from the gate when she decided to return. The question of whether or not it would be worth looking for the maze did not arise. On top of the hill it would be easy to lose oneself without entering a maze.

In the dim light she perceived that a man was leaning against the gate and facing her. He had red curly hair which had receded slightly at the sides, and a prominent nose. He wore pale-hued riding breeches and dark boots. Across his shoulders was a fur cape, which Clarinda vaguely connected with the idea of aviation. As Clarinda approached, he neither spoke nor moved. She saw that in his right hand he held a long thick shepherd's crook. It was black, and reached from the ground to his shoulder.

Clarinda put her hand on the wooden drawbar of the gate. She assumed that this action would make the man move. But he continued leaning on the gate and regarding her. If she opened the gate, he would fall.

'I want to go through.' It was not an occasion for undue politeness.

Without change of expression, the man swiftly placed his left hand on the other end of the drawbar. Clarinda pushed at it, but it would not give. Not given to panic, Clarinda momentarily considered the situation, and began to climb the gate.

'*Hullo,*' said a voice behind her. 'Rufo! What do you suppose you're doing?' Unmistakably it was the voice of Mrs Pagani.

Clarinda stepped down. Mrs Pagani was also wearing high boots, and her head was enveloped like Clarinda's in a dark scarf; but, strangely, she was wearing the capacious and opulent fur coat in which Clarinda had first seen her. The top of her boots were hidden beneath it.

'Rufo!' Mrs Pagani spoke to the man by the gate as if she were calling off a foolish and over-demonstrative dog. The man said something in a strange language. It was so unlike any language Clarinda had heard that at first she thought he had a defect in his speech.

Mrs Pagani, however, replied to him in what was presumably the same tongue. In her mouth it sounded less unfamiliar because she lacked his oddly throaty delivery. Clarinda wondered whether this might be Romany.

The man was remonstrating against Mrs Pagani's reproof. Her reply was curious: she was fluently pantomimic, and Clarinda could not but gather that Rufo was being told that she, Clarinda, was to be admitted where others were to be denied. The man scowled, and leered, then shuffled off. Although young and apparently strong, he stumbled in his gait and leaned on his crook. There was now very little light, but after he had gone a few paces, he appeared to draw his fur cape high over the back of his head.

'What can you think of Rufo?'

Clarinda often found Mrs Pagani's remarks difficult to answer.

'Will you forgive him? And me?'

'There's nothing to forgive. I didn't know he couldn't speak English.'

'How could you?' Clarinda got the impression that the tone of this was not apologetic, but amicably ironical. Not for the first time she thought that Mrs Pagani implied some understanding between them which did not exist.

'And *will* you come back?'

It was ridiculous. But Mrs Pagani had saved her from a menacing situation, and she had to say something.

'When should I come back?'

'Tonight.' The intonation made it plain that no other time could be in question.

'Here?'

Mrs Pagani said nothing, but dropped her head to one side and smiled.

It was almost impossible after that to seek a reason.

Moreover, Mrs Pagani left no time.

'You've bound your hair very well.'

Clarinda had been noticing how carefully Mrs Pagani's own thick locks had been turbanned.

'It was getting wet.'

Mrs Pagani nodded and smiled. She was looking Clarinda over.

'Au revoir.'

Clarinda had not expected that either.

'Good-bye. Thank you for rescuing me.'

'My dear, we wouldn't lose *you*.' Mrs Pagani strode off. The plural was a new mystery, for Clarinda felt that it could not refer to Rufo.

Although by now it was night, Clarinda leaped and ran down the dark track. At one time she thought she heard the pigs softly rooting in the invisible undergrowth. But she did not stop to listen, and duly reached the house only a few minutes after five.

Dudley seemed to take her escapade for granted (although she provided no details). Clarinda wondered whether this suggested that already he was growing accustomed to her, or whether it was evidence that he would be a good and unexacting husband, prepared to allow her due liberty and no questions asked. She certainly valued his success in persuading his family to adopt the same attitude.

'Out at night in winter,' said Mrs Carstairs, 'when you don't have to be!' And upon her gentle mark of exclamation, the matter dropped and tea began. Clarinda wondered whether their surprising equanimity was a product of Dudley's leadership in a full discussion during her absence. She liked Dudley for not fussing, whatever his reasons.

Elizabeth had got out a quantity of clothes and ranged them round the room for inspection and comparison by Clarinda. This was a lengthy undertaking. In the end there was a knock at the door.

'Liz.' It was Dudley's voice outside.

'One moment.' Elizabeth drew on a sweater. 'Now.'

Dudley entered. 'I've been sent up to fetch you both downstairs.' He smiled fraternally.

'We're ready,' said Elizabeth, looking at Clarinda as woman to woman.

On the dark landing outside, Dudley held Clarinda back for a moment and embraced her. 'Go on, Liz, you fool.' Elizabeth went on. 'You understand?' said Dudley to Clarinda. 'At least I hope you do. I've been trying to keep out of sight as far as possible so that you can get to know the family. That walk of yours. I've been wondering.'

Clarinda squeezed his hand.

'It's all right? And you do like them?'

'Of course it's all right. And I like them very much.'

Every Sunday evening, Clarinda understood, Mr Carstairs read aloud from about half past six until they had supper at eight. Tonight the start had been delayed by her walk and by the discussion in Elizabeth's bedroom; but still there was time for four chapters of *Persuasion*. Mr Carstairs read well, Clarinda thought; and the book was new to her.

Dudley, who could be convincing in such matters, had somehow contrived to arrange that both of them could arrive late at the office the next day: otherwise they would have had to return to London that same night. Soon after supper Elizabeth had disappeared upstairs, saying she had some letters to write, and that she probably would not be coming down again. She bade Clarinda goodnight, and kissed her affectionately on the cheekbone. About half an hour later, Mr and Mrs Carstairs also withdrew. Dudley went to assist his father with stoking up the boiler for the night. The clock struck half past nine. Otherwise the house was very quiet. Clarinda supposed that she and Dudley were being purposefully left to themselves.

'I wish *we* could live in the country,' said Dudley when he reappeared.

'I expect we could.'

'Not the real country. Not unless I get another job.'

'Where does the real country begin?'

'About Berkhamstead. Or perhaps Tring. Nowadays, that is.'

'The country stretches in this direction only.' Clarinda smiled at him.

'For me it does, darling.' She had not yet got into the habit of his calling her 'darling'. 'I *belong* around here.'

'But surely until recently you lived in a town? Northampton is a town isn't it?' She really wasn't quite sure.

'Yes, but I was always out and about.'

Clarinda had observed that every normal English male believes that he wants to live in the country, and said no more.

Dudley talked for some time about the advantages of the arrangement. Then he stopped, and Clarinda perceived that he was waiting for her assent. There was a slight pause.

'Dudley,' said Clarinda. 'How well do your father and mother know Mrs Pagani?'

'Not very well,' said Dudley, faintly disappointed. 'What you would call a bare acquaintanceship. Why?'

'They asked her to the party.'

'Actually they didn't. She heard about it and just came. Not the first time she's done it, either. But you can't put on side in a small village, and she's not a bad old bird really.'

'How do you know?'

'I don't,' said Dudley, grinning at her earnestness. 'So what?'

'What does she do with herself? Live on, I mean?'

'I don't know what she lives on, darling. Little children, I expect, like Red Riding Hood's grandmother. You know she occupies an old ruin in the churchyard?'

'So she told me. I should like to go and see it.'

'What, *now*?'

'Will you come with me?'

'It's a bit late for calls in the country.'

'I'm not suggesting a call. I just want to have a look round.'

'She might think that a trifle nosey, mightn't she?'

Clarinda nodded. 'Of course, you know Mrs Pagani better than I do.' She suddenly remembered a nocturnal stroll in Marseilles with a fellow tourist, who had proved unexpectedly delightful.

'Tell you what I'll do,' said Dudley, 'I'll whistle you round before we push off to Roade tomorrow.'

'We mustn't miss the train.'

'Never missed a train in my life.'

Clarinda's second night was worse than her first, because now she couldn't sleep at all. Dudley had considered that they should go their separate ways soon after eleven, in order, as he said, not to disturb Mr and Mrs Carstairs; and when the church clock, brooding over Mrs Pagani's romantic residence, struck one, Clarinda was still tense and tumultuous in the prickly dark. Without switching on the light she got out of bed and crossed to the window. She hoped that the sudden chill would numb her writhing nerves. When, an hour and a half before, she had drawn back the curtains, and opened the window at top and bottom, she had noticed that the mist seemed at last to have vanished, although it was so black that it was hard to be sure. Now the moon was rising, low and enormous, as if at the horizon the bottom edge of it dragged against the earth, and Clarinda saw that indeed all was clear, the sky starry, and the mist withdrawn to the distant shadowy hills. In the foreground there was nothing to be seen but the silent fields and naked trees.

Swiftly a bat loomed against the night and flew smack against the outer sash. Another two feet higher or two feet lower and he would have been in. Clarinda softly shivered for a moment, then watched the bat skid into invisibility. The silver-gilt autumn night was somehow warmer and more welcoming than Clarinda's unadventurous bed; fellow-bed, twin-bed to a thousand others in a thousand well-ordered houses. The grave self-sufficiency of the night was seeping into Clarinda's bloodstream, renewing her audacity, inflaming her curiosity; and its moonlit beauty agitating her heart. By the light of the big moon she began to dress.

When, upon her return from the woods, she had taken off her walking shoes, she had thought them very wet; but now they seemed dried, as if by the moon's rays. She opened the door of her room. Again a bat struck the window at the end of the passage outside. There was no other sound but that of disturbed breathing; which, however, seemed all around her. The other occupants of the house slept, but, as it appeared, uneasily. She descended the stairs and creaked into her mackintosh before trying the door. She expected difficulty here, but it opened at a touch. Doubtless it would be side to lock one's doors in a village.

The moon shone on the gate and on the lane beyond; but the long path from the front door was in darkness. With the moon so low the house cast a disproportionate shadow. As Clarinda walked down the narrow strip of paving, a hare scuttered across her feet. She could feel his warmth on her ankles as he nearly tripped her. The gate had a patent catch which had caused her trouble before, and she had to stand for half a minute fumbling.

As she walked along the road, passed the 'By Favour Only' notice, and began to ascend into the wood, she never doubted that at the top of the hill would be some remarkable warrant for her efforts; and she was resolved to find out what it was. Now the regular roadside trees were as clear-cut and trim as a guard of honour, and the owls seemed to be passing a message ahead of her into the thickets. Once or twice, when entering a straighter part of the road, she thought she saw a shambling figure rounding the distant corner ahead, but she decided that it was probably only a shadow. The bats were everywhere, hurtling in and out of the dark patches, and fluting their strange cries, which Clarinda was always so glad that she was among those who are privileged to hear. There were even some surviving or revitalised moths; and a steadily rising perfume of moisture and decay.

The gate at the hilltop was shut. But as soon as Clarinda drew near, she saw the little blue girl standing by it.

'Hullo.'

'Hullo,' said Clarinda.

'You're rather late.'

'I'm very sorry. I didn't know.'

'It's important to be punctual.' The child spoke in a tone of earnest helpfulness.

'I'll try to remember,' said Clarinda humbly.

The child had opened the gate and was leaning back against the end of it, her chin stuck in her neck and her feet in the ground, holding it for Clarinda.

Clarinda passed through. The moon was now higher, and the soft grass glistened and gleamed. Even in the almost bright light there was no sign of a continuing path.

'I shall get my feet wet.'

'Yes, you will. You should wear boots.' Clarinda observed the legs of the child's blue garment were stuck into close-fitting black wellingtons. Also its hood was now over its head.

There was no sign of the other child.

The little girl had carefully shut the gate. She stood looking ruefully at Clarinda's feet. Then apparently deciding there was nothing to be done about them, she said very politely, 'Shall I show you where you change?'

'Can I change my shoes?' asked Clarinda, humouring her.

'No, I don't think you can change your shoes,' said the child very seriously. 'Only everything else.'

'I don't want to change anything else.'

The child regarded her, all at sea. Then, perhaps considering that she must have misunderstood, said, 'It's over there. Follow me. And do take care of your feet.'

It certainly was very wet, but the grass proved to be tussocky, and Clarinda did her best to keep dry by striding from tussock to tussock in the moonlight.

'Rufo's in there already,' said the child conversationally. 'You see you're the last.'

'I've said I'm sorry.'

'It doesn't matter.' This was uttered with that special magnanimity only found in the very young.

The little girl waded on, and Clarinda struggled after her. There was no sign of anyone else: indeed, the place looked a hilltop of the dead. The lumpy, saturated grass and the rank and stunted vegetation compared most unfavourably with the handsome trees behind.

There was one place where the briars and ragged bushes were particularly dense and abundant, constituting a small prickly copse. Round the outskirts of this copse, the child led the way until Clarinda saw that embedded in its perimeter was a rickety shed. Possibly constructed for some agricultural purpose but long abandoned by its maker, it drooped and sagged into the ground. From it came a penetrating and repugnant odour, like all the bad smells of nature and the stockyard merged together.

'That's it,' said the little girl pointing. They were still some yards off, but the feral odour from the shed was already making Clarinda feel sick.

'I don't think I want to go in there.'

'But you *must*. Rufo's in there. All the others changed long ago.'

Apart from other considerations, the shed seemed too small to house many; and Clarinda could now see that the approach to it was thick with mud, which added its smell to the rest. She was sure that the floor of the shed was muddy almost to the knees.

The child's face was puckered with puzzlement.

'I'm sorry,' said Clarinda, 'but you know I don't want to change at all.'

Clearly she was behaving in quite the wrong way. But the child took a grip on the situation and said, 'Wait here. I'll go and ask.'

'All right,' said Clarinda. 'But I'll wait over there, if you don't mind.' The child seemed not to notice the awful smell, but Clarinda was not going to be the first to mention it.

'*There*,' said the child, pointing to an exact spot. Clarinda took up her stance upon it. 'Mind you don't move.'

'Not if you hurry.' The smell was still very detectable.

'Quite still,' insisted the child.

'Quite still,' said Clarinda.

Swiftly the child ran three times round Clarinda in a large circle. The light was so clear that Clarinda could see the drops of water flying up from her feet.

'*Hurry*,' urged Clarinda; and, the third circle complete, the child darted away round the edge of the copse in the direction from which they had come.

Left alone in the still moonlight, Clarinda wondered whether this were not her great chance to return home to safety and certainty. Then she saw a figure emerging from the dilapidated hut.

The figure walked upright, but otherwise appeared to be a large furry animal, such as a bear or ape. From its distinctive staggering uncertainty of gait, Clarinda would have recognised Rufo, even without the statements of the little girl. Moreover, he was still leaning upon his long crook, which stuck in the mud and had to be dragged out at every step. He too was going back round the edge of the copse, the same way as the child. Although he showed no sign of intending to molest Clarinda, she found him a horrifying sight, and decided upon retreat. Then she became really frightened; because she found she could not move.

The hairy slouching figure drew slowly nearer, and with him came an intensification of the dreadful smell, sweet and putrid and commingled.

The animal skin was thick and wrinkled about his neck and almost covered his face, but Clarinda saw his huge nose and expressionless eyes. Then he was past, and the child had reappeared.

'I ran all the way.' Indeed it seemed as if she had been gone only an instant. 'You're not to bother about changing because it's too late anyway.' Clearly she was repeating words spoken by an adult. 'You're to come at once, although of course you'll have to be hidden. But it's all right,' she added reassuringly. 'There've been people before who've had to be hidden.' She spoke as if the period covered by her words were at least a generation. 'But you'd better be quick.'

Clarinda found that she could move once more. Rufo, moreover, had disappeared from sight.

'Where do I hide?'

'I'll show you. I've often done it.' Again she was showing off slightly. 'Bind your hair.'

'What?'

'Bind your hair. Do be quick.' The little girl was peremptory but not unsympathetic. She was like a mother addressing an unusually slow child she was none the less rather fond of. 'Haven't you got that thing you had before?'

'It was raining then.' But Clarinda in fact had replaced the black scarf in her mackintosh pocket after drying it before the Carstairs' kitchen fire. Now, without knowing why, she drew it out.

'Go *on*.' Clarinda's sluggishness was making the child frantic.

But Clarinda refused to be rattled. With careful grace she went through the moonlit ritual of twisting the scarf round her head and enveloping her abundant soft hair.

The child led her back halfway round the copse to where there was a tiny path between the bushes. This path also was exceedingly muddy; ploughed up, as Clarinda could plainly see, by innumerable hoofmarks.

'I'd better go first,' said the little girl; adding with her customary good manners, 'I'm afraid it's rather spiky.'

It was indeed. The little girl, being little, appeared to advance unscathed; but Clarinda, being tall, found that her clothes were torn to pieces, and her face and hands lacerated. The radiance of the moon had sufficed outside, but in here failed to give warning of the thick tangled briars and rank whipcord suckers. Everywhere was a vapour of ancient cobwebs, clinging and greasy, amid which strange night insects flapped and flopped.

'We're nearly there,' said the little girl. 'You'd better be rather quiet.'

It was impossible to be quiet, and Clarinda was almost in tears with the discomfort.

'*Quieter*,' said the little girl; and Clarinda did not dare to answer back.

The slender muddy trail, matted with half-unearthed roots, wriggled on for another minute or two; and then the little girl whispered, 'Under here.'

She was making a gap in the foliage of a tall round bush. Clarinda pushed in. 'Ssh,' said the little girl.

Inside it was like a small native hut. The foliage hung all round, but there was room to stand up and dry ground beneath the feet.

'Stand on this,' whispered the little girl, pointing to a round, sawn section of tree, about two feet high and four in diameter. 'I call it my fairy dinner table.'

'What about you?'

'I'm all right, thank you. I'm always here.'

Clarinda climbed on to the section of tree, and made a cautious aperture in the boscage before her.

The sight beyond was one which she would not easily forget.

Clearly, to begin with, this was the maze, although Clarinda had never seen or heard of such a maze before. It filled a clearing in the copse about twenty or thirty yards wide and consisted in a labyrinth of little ridges, all about nine inches high. The general pattern of the labyrinth was circular, with involved inner convolutions everywhere, and at some points flourishes curving beyond the main outer boundary, as if they had once erupted like boils or volcanic blow-holes. In the valleys between the ridges, grass grew, but the ridges themselves were trodden bare. At the centre of the maze was a hewn block of stone, which put Clarinda in mind of the Stone of Scone.

Little of this, however, had much immediate significance for Clarinda; because all over the maze, under the moon, writhed and slithered and sprawled the smooth white bodies of men and women. There were scores of them; all apparently well-shaped and comely; all (perhaps for that reason) weirdly impersonal; all recumbent and reptilian, as in a picture

Clarinda remembered having seen; all completely and impossibly silent beneath the silent night. Clarinda saw that all round the maze were heaps of furry skins. She then noticed that the heads of all the women were bound in black fillets.

At the points where the coils of the maze surged out beyond the main perimeter were other, different figures. Still wrapped in furs, which distorted and made horrible the outlines of their bodies, they clung together as if locked in death. Down to the maze the ground fell away a few feet from Clarinda's hiding place. Immediately below her was one of these groups, silent as all the rest. By one of the shapeless figures she noticed a long thick staff. Then the figure soundlessly shifted, and the white moonlight fell upon the face of the equally shapeless figure in its arms. The eyes were blank and staring, the nostrils stretched like a running deer, and the red lips not so much parted as drawn back to the gums: but Clarinda recognised the face of Mrs Pagani.

Suddenly there was a rustling in the hiding-place. Though soft, it was the first sound of any kind since Clarinda had looked out on the maze.

'Go away, you silly little boy,' muttered the little girl.

Clarinda looked over her shoulder.

Inside the bower, the moonlight, filtered through the veil of foliage, was dim and deceitful; but she could see the big eyes and bird-of-prey mien of the other child. He was still wearing his bright blue hooded garment; but now the idea occurred to Clarinda that he might not be a child at all, but a well-proportioned dwarf. She looked at the black ground before stepping down from the tree trunk; and instantly he leapt at her. She felt a sharp, indefinite pain in her ankle and saw one of the creature's hands yellow and clawlike where a moonbeam through the hole above fell on the pale wood of the cut tree. Then in the murk the little girl did something which Clarinda could not see at all, and the hand jerked into passivity. The little girl was crying.

Clarinda touched her torn ankle, and stretched her hand into the beam of light. There was duly a mess of blood.

The little girl clutched at Clarinda's wrist. 'Don't let them see,' she whispered beseechingly through her tears. 'Oh please don't let them see.' Then she added with passionate fury, 'He always spoils *everything*. I hate him. I hate him. I hate him.'

Clarinda's ankle hurt badly, and there was palpable danger of blood poisoning, but otherwise the injury was not severe.

'Shall I be all right if I go?'

'Yes. But I think you'd better run.'

'That may not be so easy.'

The little girl seemed desolated with grief.

'Never mind,' said Clarinda. 'And thank you.'

The little girl stopped sobbing for a moment. 'You *will* come back?'

'I don't think so,' said Clarinda.

The sobbing recommenced. It was very quiet and despairing.

'Well,' said Clarinda, 'I'll see.'

'Punctually? That makes all the difference, you know.'

'Of course,' said Clarinda.

The child smiled at her in the faint moonlight. She was being brave. She was remembering her manners.

'Shall I come with you?'

'No need,' said Clarinda rather hastily.

'I mean to the end of the little path.'

'Still no need,' said Clarinda. 'Thank you again though. Good-bye.'

'Good-bye,' said the little girl. 'Don't forget. Punctual.'

Clarinda crept along the involved muddy path: then she sped across the soft wet sward, which she spotted with her blood; through the gate where she had seen Rufo, and down the hill where she had seen the pigs; past the ill-spelled notice; and home. As she fumbled with the patent catch, the church clock which kept ward over Mrs Pagani's abode struck three. The mist was rising again everywhere; but, in what remained of the moonlight, Clarinda, before entering the house, unwound the black scarf from her head and shook her soft abundant locks.

The question of Mrs Pagani's unusual dwelling-place arose, of course, the next morning, as they hurriedly ate the generously over-large breakfast which Mrs Carstairs, convinced that London meant starvation, pressed upon them.

'Please not,' said Clarinda, her mouth full of golden syrup. She was wearing ankle socks to conceal her careful bandage. 'I just don't want to go.'

The family looked at her; but only Dudley spoke. 'Whatever you wish, darling.'

There was a pause; after which Mr Carstairs remarked that he supposed the good lady would still be in bed anyway.

But here, most unusually, Mr Carstairs was wrong. As Dudley and Clarinda drove away, they saw the back of Mrs Pagani walking towards the church and not a couple of hundred yards from their own gate. She wore high, stout boots, caked with country mud, and an enveloping fur coat against the sharpness of the morning. Her step was springy, and her thick black hair flew in the wind like a dusky gonfalon.

As they overtook her, Dudley slowed. 'Good morning,' he shouted. 'Back to the grindstone.'

Mrs Pagani smiled affectionately.

'Don't be late,' she cried, and kissed her hand to them.

V. S. NAIPAUL

The Perfect Tenants

We heard about the Dakins before they arrived. 'They're the perfect tenants,' Mrs Cooksey, the landlady, said. 'Their landlady brought them to me personally. She says she's sorry to lose them, but she's leaving London and taking over a hotel in Benson.'

The Dakins moved in so quietly it was some days before I realized they were in the house. On Saturday and Sunday I heard sounds of washing and scrubbing and carpet-sweeping from the flat above. On Monday there was silence again.

Once or twice that week I saw them on the steps. Mrs Dakin was about forty, tall and thin, with a sweet smile. 'She used to be a policewoman,' Mrs Cooksey said. 'Sergeant, I think.' Mr Dakin was as old as his wife and looked as athletic. But his rough, handsome face was humourless. His greetings were brief and firm and didn't encourage conversation.

Their behaviour was exemplary. They never had visitors. They never had telephone calls. Their cooking never smelled. They never allowed their milk bottles to accumulate and at the same time they never left an empty milk bottle on the doorstep in daylight. And they were silent. They had no radio. The only sounds were of scrubbing brush, broom and carpet-sweeper. Sometimes at night, when the street fell silent, I heard them in their bedroom: a low whine punctuated infrequently with brief bass rumbles.

'There's respectable people in every class,' Mrs Cooksey said. 'The trouble these days is that you never know where you are. Look at the Seymours. Creeping up late at night to the bathroom and splashing about together. You can't even trust the BBC people. Remember that Arab.'

The Dakins quickly became the favourite tenants. Mr Cooksey invited Mr Dakin down to 'cocktails'. Mrs Dakin had Mrs Cooksey up to tea and Mrs Cooksey told us that she was satisfied with the appearance of the flat. 'They're very fussy,' Mrs Cooksey said. She knew no higher praise, and we all felt reproached.

It was from Mrs Cooksey that I learned with disappointment that the Dakins had their troubles. 'He fell off a ladder and broke his arm, but they won't pay any compensation. The arm's bent and he can't even go to the seaside. What's more, he can't do his job properly. He's an electrician, and you know how they're always climbing. But there you are, d'you see. *They* don't care. What's three hundred pounds to *them*? But will they give it? Do you know the foreman actually burned the ladder?'

I hadn't noticed any disfigurement about Mr Dakin. He had struck me as a man of forbidding vigour, but now I looked on him with greater interest and respect for putting up so silently with his misfortune. We often passed on the stairs but never did more than exchange greetings, and so it might have gone on had it not been for the Cookseys' New Year's Eve party.

At that time I was out of favour with the Cookseys. I had left a hoard of about fifteen milk bottles on the doorstep and the milkman had refused to take them all at once. For a whole day six partly washed milk bottles had remained on the doorstep, lowering Mrs Cooksey's house. Some unpleasantness between Mrs Cooksey and the milkman had followed and quickly been passed on to me.

When I came in that evening the door of the Cookseys' sitting-room was open and through it came laughter, stamping and television music. Mr Cooksey, coming from the kitchen with a tray, looked at me in embarrassment. He brought his lips rapidly over his false teeth and made a popping sound.

'*Pop-pop*. Come in,' he said. 'Drink. Cocktail.'

I went in. Mrs Cooksey was sober but gay. The laughter and the stamping came from the Dakins alone. They were dancing. Mrs Dakin shrieked whenever Mr Dakin spun her around, and for a man whose left arm was permanently damaged he was doing it quite well. When she saw me Mrs Dakin shrieked, and Mrs Cooksey giggled, as though it was her duty to cheer the Dakins up. The couple from the flat below mine were there too, she on the seat of an armchair, he on the arm. They were dressed in their usual sub-county manner and looked constrained and unhappy. I thought of this couple as the Knitmaster and the Knitmistress. They had innumerable minor possessions: contemporary coffee tables and lampstands, a Cona coffee machine, a record-player, a portable television-and-VHF set, a 1946 Anglia which at the appropriate season carried a sticker: FREE LIFT TO GLYNDEBOURNE AT YOUR OWN RISK, and a Knitmaster machine which was never idle for long.

The music stopped, Mrs Dakin pretended to swoon into her husband's injured arms, and Mrs Cooksey clapped.

"Elp yourself, 'elp yourself,' Mr Cooksey shouted.

'Another drink, darling?' the Knitmaster whispered to his wife.

'Yes, yes,' Mrs Dakin cried.

The Knitmistress smiled malevolently at Mrs Dakin.

'Whisky?' said Mr Cooksey. 'Beer? Sherry? Guinness?'

'Give her the cocktail,' Mrs Cooksey said.

Mr Cooksey's cocktails were well known to his older tenants. He had a responsible position in an important public corporation – he said he had thirty-four cleaners under him – and the origin and blend of his cocktails were suspect.

The Knitmistress took the cocktail and sipped without enthusiasm.

'And you?' Mr Cooksey asked.

'Guinness,' I said.

'Guinness!' Mr Dakin exclaimed, looking at me for the first time with interest and kindliness. 'Where did you learn to drink Guinness?'

We drew closer and talked about Guinness.

'Of course it's best in Ireland,' he said. 'Thick and creamy. What's it like where you come from?'

'I can't drink it there. It's too warm.'

Mr Dakin shook his head. 'It isn't the climate. It's the Guinness. It can't travel. It gets sick.'

Soon it was time to sing Auld Lang Syne.

The next day the Dakins reverted to their exemplary behaviour, but now when we met we stopped to have a word about the weather.

*

One evening, about four weeks later, I heard something like a commotion in the flat above. Footsteps pounded down the stairs, there was a banging on my door, and Mrs Dakin rushed in and cried, 'It's my 'usband! 'E's rollin' in agony.'

Before I could say anything she ran out and raced down to the Knitmasters.

'My husband's rollin' in agony.'

The whirring of the Knitmaster machine stopped and I heard the Knitmistress making sympathetic sounds.

The Knitmaster said, 'Telephone for the doctor.'

I went and stood on the landing as a sympathetic gesture. Mrs Dakin roused the Cookseys, there were more exclamations, then I heard the telephone being dialled. I went back to my room. After some thought I left my door wide open: another gesture of sympathy.

Mrs Dakin, Mrs Cooksey and Mr Cooksey hurried up the stairs.

The Knitmaster machine was whirring again.

Presently there was a knock on my door and Mr Cooksey came in. '*Pop-pop*. It's as hot as a bloomin' oven up there.' He puffed out his cheeks. 'No wonder he's ill.'

I asked after Mr Dakin.

'A touch of indigestion, if you ask me.' Then, like a man used to more momentous events, he added, 'One of my cleaners took ill sudden last week. Brain tumour.'

The doctor came and the Dakins' flat was full of footsteps and conversation. Mr Cooksey ran up and down the steps, panting and pop-popping. Mrs Dakin was sobbing and Mrs Cooksey was comforting her. An ambulance bell rang in the street and soon Mr Dakin, Mrs Dakin and the doctor left.

'Appendix,' Mr Cooksey told me.

The Knitmaster opened his door

'Appendix,' Mr Cooksey shouted down. 'It was like an oven up there.'

'He was cold,' Mrs Cooksey said.

'Pah!'

Mrs Cooksey looked anxious.

'Nothing to it, Bess,' Mr Cooksey said. ''Itler had the appendix took out of all his soldiers.'

319

The Knitmaster said, 'I had mine out two years ago. Small scar.' He measured off the top of his forefinger. 'About that long. It's a nervous thing really. You get it when you are depressed or worried. My wife had to have hers out just before we went to France.'

The Knitmistress came out and smiled her terrible smile, baring short square teeth and tall gums, and screwing up her small eyes. She said, 'Hallo,' and pulled on woollen gloves, which perhaps she had just knitted on her machine. She wore a tweed skirt, a red sweater, a brown velveteen jacket and a red-and-white beret.

'Appendix,' Mr Cooksey said.

The Knitmistress only smiled again, and followed her husband downstairs to the 1946 Anglia.

'A terrible thing,' I said to Mrs Cooksey tentatively.

'*Pop-pop.*' Mr Cooksey looked at his wife.

'Terrible thing,' Mrs Cooksey said.

Our quarrel over the milk bottles was over.

Mr Cooksey became animated. 'Nothing to it, Bess. Just a lot of fuss for nothing at all. Gosh, they kept that room like an oven.'

Mrs Dakin came back at about eleven. Her eyes were red but she was composed. She spoke about the kindness of the nurses. And then, to round off an unusual evening, I heard – at midnight on a weekday – the sound of the carpet-sweeper upstairs. The Knitmistress complained in her usual way. She opened her door and talked loudly to her husband about the nuisance.

Next morning Mrs Dakin went again to the hospital. She returned just before midday and as soon as she got into the hall she began to sob so loudly that I heard her on the second floor.

I found her in Mrs Cooksey's arms when I went down. Mrs Cooksey was pale and her eyes were moist.

'What's happened?' I whispered.

Mrs Cooksey shook her head.

Mrs Dakin leaned against Mrs Cooksey, who was much smaller.

'And my brother is getting married tomorrow!' Mrs Dakin burst out.

'Come now, Eva,' Mrs Cooksey said firmly. 'Tell me what happened at the hospital.'

'They're feeding him through a glass tube. They've put him on the danger list. And – his bed is near the door!'

'That doesn't mean anything, Eva.'

'It does! It does!'

'Nonsense, Eva.'

'They've got him screened round.'

'You must be brave, Eva.'

We led Mrs Dakin to Mrs Cooksey's sittingroom, made her sit down and watched her cry.

'It burst inside 'im.' Mrs Dakin made a wild gesture across her body. 'They had to cut him clean open, and – *scrape* it out.' Having uttered this terrible word, she abandoned herself to her despair.

'Come now, Eva,' Mrs Cooksey said. 'He wouldn't like you to behave like this.'

We all took turns to look after Mrs Dakin between her trips to the hospital. The news didn't get better. Mrs Dakin had tea with the Cookseys. She had tea with the Knitmistress. She had tea with me. We talked gaily about everything except the sick man, and Mrs Dakin was very brave. She even related some of her adventures in the police force. She also complained.

'The first thing Mr Cooksey said when he came up that evening was that the room was like an oven. But I couldn't help that. My husband was cold. Fancy coming up and saying a thing like that!'

I gave Mrs Dakin many of the magazines which had been piling up on the enormous Victorian dresser in my kitchen. The Knitmistress, I noticed, was doing the same thing.

Mr Cooksey allowed himself to grow a little grave. He discussed the operation in a sad but clinical way. 'When it bursts inside 'em, you see, it poisons the whole system. That's why they had to cut 'im open. Clean it out. They hardly ever live afterwards.'

Mrs Cooksey said, 'He was such a nice man. I am so glad now we enjoyed ourselves on New Year's Eve. It's her I'm really sorry for. He was her second, you know.'

'Aah,' Mr Cooksey said. 'There are women like that.'

I told the Knitmistress, 'And he was such a nice man.'

'Wasn't he?'

I heard Mrs Dakin sobbing in everybody's rooms. I heard her sobbing on the staircase.

Mrs Cooksey said, 'It's all so terrible. Her brother got married yesterday, but she couldn't go to the wedding. She had to send a telegram. They are coming up to see Mr Dakin. What a thing to happen on anybody's honeymoon!'

Mrs Dakin's brother and his bride came up from Wales on a motorbike. Mrs Dakin was at the hospital when they came and Mrs Cooksey gave them tea.

I didn't see Mrs Dakin that evening, but late that night I saw the honeymoon couple running upstairs with bottles wrapped in tissue paper. He was a huge man – a footballer, Mrs Cooksey said – and when he ran up the steps you heard it all over the house. His bride was small, countrified and gay. They stayed awake for some time.

Next morning, when I went down to get the paper, I saw the footballer's motorbike on the doorstep. It had leaked a lot of oil.

Again that day Mrs Dakin didn't come to our rooms. And that evening there was another party in the flat above. We heard the footballer's heavy footsteps, his shouts, his wife's giggles, Mrs Dakin's whine.

Mrs Dakin had ceased to need our solace. It was left to us to ask how Mr Dakin was getting on, whether he had liked the magazines we had sent, whether he wanted any more. Then, as though reminded of some sadness bravely forgotten, Mrs Dakin would say yes, Mr Dakin thanked us.

Mrs Cooksey didn't like the new reticence. Nor did the rest of us. For some time, though, the Knitmaster persevered and he had his reward when two days later Mrs Dakin said, 'I told 'im what you said about the nervousness, and he wondered how you ever knew.' And she repeated the story about the fall from the defective ladder, the bent arm, the foreman burning the ladder.

We were astonished. It was our first indication that the Dakins were taking an interest in the world outside the hospital.

'Well, really!' Mrs Cooksey said.

The Knitmistress began to complain about the noise in the evenings.

'Pah!' Mr Cooksey said. 'It *couldn't* 'ave burst inside him. Feeding through a glass tube!'

We heard the honeymoon couple bounding down the stairs. The front door slammed, then we heard the thunderous stutter of the motorbike.

'He could be had up,' Mr Cooksey said. 'No silencer.'

'Well!' Mrs Cooksey said. 'I am glad *somebody's* having a nice time. So cheap too. Where do you think they're off to?'

'Not the hospital,' Mr Cooksey said. 'Football, more likely.'

This reminded him. The curtains were drawn, the tiny television set turned on. We watched horse-racing, then part of the football match. Mrs Cooksey gave me tea. Mr Cooksey offered me a cigarette. I was back in favour.

The next day, eight days after Mr Dakin had gone to the hospital, I met Mrs Dakin outside the tobacconist's. She was shopping and her bulging bag reflected the gaiety on her face.

'He's coming back tomorrow,' she said.

I hadn't expected such a rapid recovery.

'Everybody at the hospital was surprised,' Mrs Dakin said. 'But it's because he's so strong, you see.' She opened her shopping bag. 'I've got some sherry and whisky and' – she laughed – 'some Guinness of course. And I'm buying a duck, to have with apple sauce. He loves apple sauce. He says the apple sauce helps the duck to go down.'

I smiled at the little family joke. Then Mrs Dakin asked me, 'Guess who went to the hospital yesterday.'

'Your brother and his wife.'

She shook her head. 'The foreman!'

'The one who burned the ladder?'

'Oh, and he was ever so nice. He brought grapes and magazines and told my husband he wasn't to worry about anything. They're frightened now all right. As soon as my husband went to hospital my solicitor wrote them a letter. And my solicitor says we stand a good chance of getting more than three hundred pounds now.'

I saw the Knitmaster on the landing that evening and told him about Mr Dakin's recovery.

'Complications couldn't have been serious,' he said. 'But it's a nervous thing. A nervous thing.'

The Knitmistress opened the kitchen door.

'He's coming back tomorrow,' the Knitmaster said.

The Knitmistress gave me one of her terrible smiles.

'Five hundred pounds for falling off a ladder,' Mr Cooksey said. 'Ha! It's as easy as falling off a log, ain't it, Bess?'

Mrs Cooksey sighed. 'That's what the Labour has done to this country. They didn't do a thing for the middle class.'

'Bent arm! Can't go to the seaside! Pamperin', that's what it is. You wouldn't've found 'Itler pampering that lot.'

A motorbike lacerated the silence.

'Our happy honeymooners,' Mr Cooksey said.

'They'll soon be leaving,' Mrs Cooksey said, and went out to meet them in the hall.

'Whose key are you using?'

'Eva's,' the footballer said, running up the stairs.

'We'll see about that,' Mrs Cooksey called.

Mrs Dakin said: 'I went down to Mrs Cooksey and I said, "Mrs Cooksey, what do you mean by insulting my guests? It's bad enough for them having their honeymoon spoilt without being insulted." And she said she'd let the flat to me and my 'usband and not to my brother and his wife and they'd have to go. And I told her that they were leaving tomorrow anyway because my husband's coming back tomorrow. And I told her I hoped she was satisfied that she'd spoiled their honeymoon, which comes only once in a lifetime. And she said some people managed to have two, which I took as a reference to myself because, as you know, my first husband died during the war. And then I told her that if that was the way she was going to behave then I could have nothing more to say to her. And she said she hoped I would have the oil from my brother's bike cleaned up. And I said that if it wasn't for my husband being so ill I would've given notice then and there. And she said it was *because* my husband was ill that she didn't give me notice, which any other landlady would've done.' Three things happened the next day. The footballer and his wife left. Mrs Dakin told me that the firm had given her husband four hundred pounds. And

Mr Dakin returned from hospital, no more noticed by the rest of the house than if he had returned from a day's work. No sounds came from the Dakins' flat that evening except for the whine and rumble of conversation.

Two days later I heard Mrs Dakin racing down to my flat. She knocked and entered at the same time. 'The telly's coming today,' she said.

Mr Dakin was going to put up the aerial himself. I wondered whether he was as yet strong enough to go climbing about the roof.

'They wanted ten pounds to do it. But my husband's an electrician and he can do it himself. You must come up tonight. We're going to celebrate.'

I went up. A chromium-plated aeroplane and a white doily had been placed on the television set. It looked startlingly new.

Mrs Dakin emptied a bottle of Tio Pepe into three tumblers.

'To good 'ealth,' she said, and we drank to that.

Mr Dakin looked thin and fatigued. But his fatigue was tinged with a certain quiet contentment. We watched a play about a 400-year-old man who took certain drugs and looked no more than twenty. From time to time Mrs Dakin gave little cries of pleasure, at the play, the television set, and the quality of the sherry.

Mr Dakin languidly took up the empty bottle and studied the label. '*Spanish* sherry,' he said.

Mr Cooksey waylaid me the following day. 'Big telly they've got.'

'Eighteen inch.'

'Those big ones hurt the eyes, don't you find?'

'They do.'

'Come in and have a drink. BBC and Commercial?'

I nodded.

'Never did hold with those commercials. Ruining the country. We're not going to have ours adapted.'

'We're waiting for the colour,' Mrs Cooksey said.

Mrs Cooksey loved a battle. She lived for her house alone. She had no relations or friends, and little happened to her or her husband. Once, shortly after Hess had landed in Scotland, Mr Cooksey had been mistaken by a hostile crowd at Victoria Station for Mussolini, but for the most part Mrs Cooksey's conversation was about her victories over tenants. In her battles with them she stuck to the rules. *The Law of Land-lord and Tenant* was one of the few books among the many china animals in the large bookcase in her sittingroom. And Mrs Cooksey had her own idea of victory. She never gave anyone notice. That was almost an admission of defeat. Mrs Cooksey asked me, 'You didn't throw a loaf of stale bread into the garden, did you?'

I said I hadn't.

'I didn't think you had. That's what the other people in this street do, you know. It's a fight to keep this house the way it is, I can tell you. There's the mice, d'you see. You haven't any mice up here, have you?'

'As a matter of fact I had one yesterday.'

'I knew it. The moment you let up these things start happening. All the other houses in this street have mice. That's what the sanitary inspector told me. He said this was the cleanest house in the whole street. But the moment you start throwing food about you're bound to get mice.'

That evening I heard Mrs Dakin complaining loudly. She was doing it the way the Knitmistress did: talking loudly to her husband through an open door.

'Coming up here and asking if I had thrown a loaf of bread into 'er 'orrible little garden. And talking about people having too much to eat these days. Well, if it's one thing I like, it is a warm room. I don't wrap myself up in a blanket and *'uddle* in front of cinders and then come and say that somebody else's room is like an oven.'

Mrs Dakin left her kitchen door open and did the washing up with many bangs, jangles, and clatters. The television sound was turned up and in my room I could hear every commercial, every song, every scrap of dialogue. The carpetsweeper was brought into action; I heard it banging against walls and furniture.

The next day Mrs Cooksey continued her mice hunt. She went into all the flats and took up the linoleum and put wads of newspaper in the gaps between the floorboards. She also emptied Mrs Dakin's dustbin. 'To keep away the mice,' she told us.

I heard the Dakins' television again that night.

The next morning there was a large notice in the hall. I recognized Mr Cooksey's handwriting and style: WILL THE PERSON OR PERSONS RESPONSIBLE SEE ABOUT THE IMMEDIATE REMOVAL OF THE OIL

STAINS ON THE FRONT STEPS. In the bathroom there was a notice tied to the pipe that led to the geyser: WILL THE PERSON OR PERSONS WHO HAVE BEEN TAMPERING WITH THIS TAP PLEASE STOP IT. And in the lavatory: WE NEVER THOUGHT WE WOULD HAVE TO MAKE THIS REQUEST BUT WILL THE PERSON OR PERSONS RESPONSIBLE PLEASE LEAVE THESE OFFICES AS THEY WOULD LIKE TO FIND THEM.

The Dakins retaliated at once. Four unwashed milk bottles were placed on the stains on the steps. An empty whisky bottle was placed, label outwards, next to the dustbin.

I felt the Dakins had won that round.

'Liquor and football pools,' Mr Cooksey said. 'That's all that class spends its money on. Pamperin'! You mustn't upset yourself, Bess. We're giving them enough rope to hang themselves.'

The television boomed through the house that evening. The washing-up was done noisily, the carpet-sweeper banged against walls and furniture, and Mrs Dakin sang loudly. Presently I heard scuffling sounds and shrieks. The Dakins were dancing. This went on for a short time. Then I heard a bath being run.

There was a soft knock on my door and Mrs Cooksey came in. 'I just wanted to find out who was having the bath,' she said.

For some moments after she left the bath continued to run. Then there was a sharper sound of running water, hissing and metallic. And soon the bath was silent.

There was no cistern to feed the geyser ('Unhygienic things, cisterns,' Mr Cooksey said) and the flow of water to it depended on the taps in the house. By turning on a tap in your kitchen you could lessen the flow and the heat of the water from the geyser. The hissing sound indicated that a tap had been turned full on downstairs, rendering the geyser futile.

From the silent bathroom I heard occasional splashes. The hissing sound continued. Then Mr Dakin sneezed.

The bathroom door opened and was closed with a bang. Mr Dakin sneezed again and Mrs Dakin said, 'If you catch pneumonia, I know who your solicitor will have to be writing to next.'

And all they could do was to smash the gas mantle in the bathroom.

It seemed that they had accepted defeat, for they did nothing further the next day. I was with the Cookseys when the Dakins came in from work that afternoon. In a few minutes they had left the house again. The light in the Cookseys' sitting room had not been turned on and we stared at them through the lace curtains. They walked arm in arm.

'Going to look for a new place, I suppose.' Mrs Cooksey said.

There was a knock and the Knitmistress came in, her smile brilliant and terrible even in the gloom. She said, 'Hullo.' Then she addressed Mrs Cooksey: 'Our lights have gone.'

'Power failure,' Mr Cooksey said. But the street lights were on. The light in the Cookseys' room was turned on but nothing happened.

Mrs Cooksey's face fell.

'Fuse,' Mr Cooksey said briskly. He regarded himself as an electrical expert. With the help of a candle he selected fuse wire, went down to the fuse box, urged us to turn off all lights and fires and stoves, and set to work. The wire fused again. And again.

'He's been *up* to something,' Mr Cooksey said.

But we couldn't find out what that was. The Dakins had secured their rooms with new Yale locks.

The Knitmistress complained.

'It's no use, Bess,' Mr Cooksey said. 'You'll just have to give them notice. Never *did* hold with that class of people anyway.'

And defeat was made even more bitter because it turned out that victory had been very close. After Mrs Cooksey asked them to leave, the Dakins announced that they had used part of the compensation money to pay down on a house and were just about to give notice themselves. They packed and left without saying goodbye.

Three weeks later the Dakins' flat was taken over by a middle-aged lady with a fat shining dachshund called Nicky. Her letters were posted on from a ladies' club whose terrifying interiors I had often glimpsed from the top of a number sixteen bus.

J. G. BALLARD

The Cloud-Sculptors of Coral D

All summer the cloud-sculptors would come from Vermilion Sands and sail their painted gliders above the coral towers that rose like white pagodas beside the highway to Lagoon West. The tallest of the towers was Coral D, and here the rising air above the sand-reefs was topped by swan-like clumps of fair-weather cumulus. Lifted on the shoulders of the air above the crown of Coral D, we would carve seahorses and unicorns, the portraits of presidents and film stars, lizards and exotic birds. As the crowd watched from their cars, a cool rain would fall on to the dusty roofs, weeping from the sculptured clouds as they sailed across the desert floor towards the sun.

Of all the cloud-sculptures we were to carve, the strangest were the portraits of Leonora Chanel. As I look back to that afternoon last summer when she first came in her white limousine to watch the cloud-sculptors of Coral D, I know we barely realized how seriously this beautiful but insane woman regarded the sculptures floating above her in that calm sky. Later her portraits, carved in the whirlwind, were to weep their storm-rain upon the corpses of their sculptors.

I had arrived in Vermilion Sands three months earlier. A retired pilot, I was painfully coming to terms with a broken leg and the prospect of never flying again. Driving into the desert one day, I stopped near the coral towers on the highway to Lagoon West. As I gazed at these immense pagodas stranded on the floor of this fossil sea, I heard music coming from a sand-reef two hundred yards away. Swinging on my crutches across the sliding sand, I found a shallow basin among the dunes where sonic statues had run to seed beside a ruined studio. The owner had gone, abandoning the hangar-like building to the sand-rays and the desert, and on some half-formed impulse I began to drive out each afternoon. From the lathes and joists left behind I built my first giant kites and, later, gliders with cockpits. Tethered by their cables, they would hang above me in the afternoon air like amiable ciphers.

One evening, as I wound the gliders down on to the winch, a sudden gale rose over the crest of Coral D. While I grappled with the whirling handle, trying to anchor my crutches in the sand, two figures approached across the desert floor. One was a small hunchback with a child's over-lit eyes and a deformed jaw twisted like an anchor barb to one side. He scuttled over to the winch and wound the tattered gliders towards the ground, his powerful shoulders pushing me aside. He helped me on to my crutch and peered into the hangar. Here my most ambitious glider to date, no longer a kite but a sail-plane with elevators and control lines, was taking shape on the bench.

He spread a large hand over his chest. 'Petit Manuel – acrobat and weight-lifter. Nolan!' he bellowed. 'Look at this!' His companion was squatting by the sonic statues, twisting their helixes so that their voices became more resonant. 'Nolan's an artist,' the hunchback confided to me. 'He'll build you gliders like condors.'

The tall man was wandering among the gliders, touching their wings with a sculptor's hand. His morose eyes were set in a face like a bored boxer's. He glanced at the plaster on my leg and my faded flying-jacket, and gestured at the gliders. 'You've given cockpits to them, major.' The remark contained a complete understanding of my motives. He pointed to the coral towers rising above us into the evening sky. 'With silver iodide we could carve the clouds.'

The hunchback nodded encouragingly to me, his eyes lit by an astronomy of dreams.

So were formed the cloud-sculptors of Coral D. Although I considered myself one of them, I never flew the gliders, but taught Nolan and little Manuel to fly, and later, when he joined us, Charles Van Eyck. Nolan had found this blond-haired pirate of the café terraces in Vermilion Sands, a laconic Teuton with hard eyes and a weak mouth, and brought him out to Coral D when the season ended and the well-to-do tourists and their nubile daughters returned to Red Beach. 'Major Parker – Charles Van Eyck. He's a headhunter,' Nolan commented with cold humour,

'– maidenheads.' Despite their uneasy rivalry I realized that Van Eyck would give our group a useful dimension of glamour.

From the first I suspected that the studio in the desert was Nolan's, and that we were all serving some private whim of this dark-haired solitary. At the time, however, I was more concerned with teaching them to fly – first on cable, mastering the updraughts that swept the stunted turret of Coral A, smallest of the towers, then the steeper slopes of B and C, and finally the powerful currents of Coral D. Late one afternoon, when I began to wind them in, Nolan cut away his line. The glider plummeted on to its back, diving down to impale itself on the rock spires. I flung myself to the ground as the cable whipped across my car, shattering the windshield. When I looked up, Nolan was soaring high in the tinted air above Coral D. The wind, guardian of the coral towers, carried him through the islands of cumulus that veiled the evening light.

As I ran to the winch the second cable went, and little Manuel swerved away to join Nolan. Ugly crab on the ground, in the air the hunchback became a bird with immense wings, outflying both Nolan and Van Eyck. I watched them as they circled the coral towers, and then swept down together over the desert floor, stirring the sand-rays into soot-like clouds. Petit Manuel was jubilant. He strutted around me like a pocket Napoleon, contemptuous of my broken leg, scooping up handfuls of broken glass and tossing them over his head like bouquets to the air.

Two months later, as we drove out to Coral D on the day we were to meet Leonora Chanel, something of this first feeling of exhilaration had faded. Now that the season had ended few tourists travelled to Lagoon West, and often we would perform our cloud-sculpture to the empty highway. Sometimes Nolan would remain behind in his hotel, drinking by himself on the bed, or Van Eyck would disappear for several days with some widow or divorcée, and Petit Manuel and I would go out alone.

None the less, as the four of us drove out in my car that afternoon and I saw the clouds waiting for us above the spire of Coral D, all my depression and fatigue vanished. Ten minutes later, the three cloud gliders rose into the air and the first cars began to stop on the highway. Nolan was in the lead in his black-winged glider, climbing straight to the crown of Coral D two hundred feet above, while Van Eyck soared to and fro below, showing his blond mane to a middle-aged woman in a topaz convertible. Behind them came little Manuel, his candy-striped wings slipping and churning in the disturbed air. Shouting happy obscenities, he flew with his twisted knees, huge arms gesticulating out of the cockpit.

The three gliders, brilliant painted toys, revolved like lazing birds above Coral D, waiting for the first clouds to pass overhead. Van Eyck moved away to take a cloud. He sailed around its white pillow, spraying the sides with iodide crystals and cutting away the flock-like tissue. The steaming shards fell towards us like crumbling ice-drifts. As the drops of condensing spray fell on my face I could see Van Eyck shaping an immense horse's head. He sailed up and down the long forehead and chiselled out the eyes and ears.

As always, the people watching from their cars seemed to enjoy this piece of aerial marzipan. It sailed overhead, carried away on the wind from Coral D. Van Eyck followed it down, wings lazing around the equine head. Meanwhile Petit Manuel worked away at the next cloud. As he sprayed its sides a familiar human head appeared through the tumbling mist. The high wavy mane, strong jaw but slipped mouth Manuel caricatured from the cloud with a series of deft passes, wingtips almost touching each other as he dived in and out of the portrait.

The glossy white head, an unmistakable parody of Van Eyck in his own worst style, crossed the highway towards Vermilion Sands. Manuel slid out of the air, stalling his glider to a landing beside my car as Van Eyck stepped from his cockpit with a forced smile.

We waited for the third display. A cloud formed over Coral D and within a few minutes had blossomed into a pristine fair-weather cumulus. As it hung there Nolan's black-winged glider plunged out of the sun. He soared around the cloud, cutting away its tissues. The soft fleece fell towards us in a cool rain.

There was a shout from one of the cars. Nolan turned from the cloud, his wings slipping as if unveiling his handiwork. Illuminated by the afternoon sun was the serene face of a three-year-old child. Its wide cheeks framed a placid mouth and plump chin. As one or two people clapped, Nolan sailed over the cloud and rippled the roof into ribbons and curls.

However, I knew that the real climax was yet to come. Cursed by some malignant virus, Nolan seemed unable to accept his own handiwork, always destroying it with the same cold humour. Petit Manuel had thrown away his cigarette, and even Van Eyck had turned his attention from the women in the cars.

Nolan soared above the child's face, following like a matador waiting for the moment of the kill. There was silence for a minute as he worked away at the cloud, and then someone slammed a car door in disgust.

Hanging above us was the white image of a skull.

The child's face, converted by a few strokes, had vanished, but in the notched teeth and gaping orbits, large enough to hold a car, we could still see an echo of its infant features. The spectre moved past us, the spectators frowning at this weeping skull whose rain fell upon their faces.

Half-heartedly I picked my old flying helmet off the back seat and began to carry it around the cars. Two of the spectators drove off before I could reach them. As I hovered about uncertainly, wondering why on earth a retired and well-to-do air-force officer should be trying to collect these few dollar bills, Van Eyck stepped behind me and took the helmet from my hand.

'Not now, major. Look at what arrives – my apocalypse . . .'

A white Rolls-Royce, driven by a chauffeur in braided cream livery, had turned off the highway. Through the tinted communication window a young woman in a secretary's day suit spoke to the chauffeur. Beside her, a gloved hand still holding the window strap, a white-haired woman with jewelled eyes gazed up at the circling wings of the cloud-glider. Her strong and elegant face seemed sealed within the dark glass of the limousine like the enigmatic madonna of some marine grotto.

Van Eyck's glider rose into the air, soaring upwards to the cloud that hung above Coral D. I walked back to my car, searching the sky for Nolan. Above, Van Eyck was producing a pastiche Mona Lisa, a picture-postcard Gioconda as authentic as a plaster virgin. Its glossy finish shone in the over-bright sunlight as if enamelled together out of some cosmetic foam.

Then Nolan dived from the sun behind Van Eyck. Rolling his black-winged glider past Van Eyck's, he drove through the neck of the Gioconda, and with the flick of a wing toppled the broad-cheeked head. It fell towards the cars below. The features disintegrated into a flaccid mess, sections of the nose and jaw tumbling through the steam. Then wings brushed. Van Eyck fired his spray gun at Nolan, and there was a flurry of torn fabric. Van Eyck fell from the air, steering his glider down to a broken landing.

I ran over to him. 'Charles, do you have to play von Richthofen? For God's sake, leave each other alone!'

Van Eyck waved me away. 'Talk to Nolan, major. I'm not responsible for his air piracy.' He stood in the cockpit, gazing over the cars as the shreds of fabric fell around him.

I walked back to my car, deciding that the time had come to disband the cloud-sculptors of Coral D. Fifty yards away the young secretary in the Rolls-Royce had stepped from the car and beckoned to me. Through the open door her mistress watched me with her jewelled eyes. Her white hair lay in a coil over one shoulder like a nacreous serpent.

I carried my flying helmet down to the young woman. Above a high forehead her auburn hair was swept back in a defensive bun, as if she were deliberately concealing part of herself. She stared with puzzled eyes at the helmet held out in front of her.

'I don't want to fly – what is it?'

'A grace,' I explained. 'For the repose of Michelangelo, Ed Kienholz and the cloud-sculptors of Coral D.'

'Oh, my God. I think the chauffeur's the only one with any *money*. Look, do you perform anywhere else?'

'Perform?' I glanced from this pretty and agreeable young woman to the pale chimera with jewelled eyes in the dim compartment of the Rolls. She was watching the headless figure of the Mona Lisa as it moved across the desert floor towards Vermilion Sands. 'We're not a professional troupe, as you've probably guessed. And obviously we'd need some fair-weather cloud. Where, exactly?'

'At Lagoon West.' She took a snakeskin diary from her handbag. 'Miss Chanel is holding a series of garden parties. She wondered if you'd care to perform. Of course there would be a large fee.'

'Chanel . . . Leonora Chanel, the . . . ?'

The young woman's face again took on its defensive posture, dissociating her from whatever might follow. 'Miss Chanel is at Lagoon West for the summer. By the way, there's one condition I must point out – Miss Chanel will provide the sole subject matter. You do understand?'

Fifty yards away Van Eyck was dragging his damaged glider towards my car. Nolan had landed, a caricature of Cyrano abandoned in mid-air. Petit Manuel limped to and fro, gathering together the equipment. In the fading afternoon light they resembled a threadbare circus troupe.

'All right,' I agreed. 'I take your point. But what about the clouds, Miss —?'

'Lafferty. Beatrice Lafferty. Miss Chanel will provide the clouds.'

I walked around the cars with the helmet, then divided the money between Nolan, Van Eyck and Manuel. They stood in the gathering dusk, the few bills in their hands, watching the highway below.

Leonora Chanel stepped from the limousine and strolled into the desert. Her white-haired figure in its cobra-skin coat wandered among the dunes. Sand-rays lifted around her, disturbed by the random movements of this sauntering phantasm of the burnt afternoon. Ignoring their open stings around her legs, she was gazing up at the aerial bestiary dissolving in the sky, and at the white skull a mile away over Lagoon West that had smeared itself across the sky.

At the time I first saw her, watching the cloud-sculptors of Coral D, I had only a half-formed impression of Leonora Chanel. The daughter of one of the world's leading financiers, she was an heiress both in her own right and on the death of her husband, a shy Monacan aristocrat, Comte Louis Chanel. The mysterious circumstances of his death at Cap Ferrat on the Riviera, officially described as suicide, had placed Leonora in a spotlight of publicity and gossip. She had escaped by wandering endlessly across the globe, from her walled villa in Tangiers to an Alpine mansion in the snows above Pontresina, and from there to Palm Springs, Seville and Mykonos.

During these years of exile something of her character emerged from the magazine and newspaper photographs: moodily visiting a Spanish charity with the Duchess of Alba, or seated with Soraya and other members of café society on the terrace of Dali's villa at Port Lligat, her self-regarding face gazing out with its jewelled eyes at the diamond sea of the Costa Brava.

Inevitably her Garbo-like role seemed over-calculated, forever undermined by the suspicions of her own hand in her husband's death. The count had been an introspective playboy who piloted his own aircraft to archaeological sites in the Peloponnese and whose mistress, a beautiful young Lebanese, was one of the world's pre-eminent keyboard interpreters of Bach. Why this reserved and pleasant man should have committed suicide was never made plain. What promised to be a significant exhibit at the coroner's inquest, a multilated easel portrait of Leonora on which he was working, was accidentally destroyed before the hearing. Perhaps the painting revealed more of Leonora's character than she chose to see.

A week later, as I drove out to Lagoon West on the morning of the first garden party, I could well understand why Leonora Chanel had come to Vermilion Sands, to this bizarre, sand-bound resort with its lethargy, beach fatigue and shifting perspectives. Sonic statues grew wild along the beach, their voices keening as I swept past along the shore road. The fused silica on the surface of the lake formed an immense rainbow mirror that reflected the deranged colours of the sand-reefs, more vivid even than the cinnabar and cyclamen wing-panels of the cloud-gliders overhead. They soared in the sky above the lake like fitful dragonflies as Nolan, Van Eyck and Petit Manuel flew them from Coral D.

We had entered an inflamed landscape. Half a mile away the angular cornices of the summer house jutted into the vivid air as if distorted by some faulty junction of time and space. Behind it, like an exhausted volcano, a broad-topped mesa rose into the glazed air, its shoulders lifting the thermal currents high off the heated lake.

Envying Nolan and little Manuel these tremendous updraughts, more powerful than any we had known at Coral D, I drove towards the villa. Then the haze cleared along the beach and I saw the clouds.

A hundred feet above the roof of the mesa, they hung like the twisted pillows of a sleepless giant. Columns of turbulent air moved within the clouds, boiling upwards to the anvil heads like liquid in a cauldron. These were not the placid, fair-weather cumulus of Coral D, but storm-nimbus, unstable masses of overheated air that could catch an aircraft and lift it a thousand feet in a few seconds. Here and there the clouds were rimmed with dark bands, their towers crossed by valleys and ravines. They moved across the villa, concealed from the lakeside heat by the haze overhead, then dissolved in a series of violent shifts in the disordered air.

As I entered the drive behind a truck filled with *son et lumière* equipment a dozen members of the staff were straightening lines of gilt chairs on the terrace and unrolling panels of a marquee.

Beatrice Lafferty stepped across the cables. 'Major Parker – there are the clouds we promised you.'

I looked up again at the dark billows hanging like shrouds above the white villa. 'Clouds, Beatrice? Those are tigers, tigers with wings. We're manicurists of the air, not dragon-tamers.'

'Don't worry, a manicure is exactly what you're expected to carry out.' With an arch glance, she added: 'Your men do understand that there's to be only one subject?'

'Miss Chanel herself? Of course.' I took her arm as we walked towards the balcony overlooking the lake. 'You know, I think you enjoy these snide asides. Let the rich choose their materials – marble, bronze, plasma or cloud. Why not? Portraiture has always been a neglected art.'

'My God, not here.' She waited until a steward passed with a tray of tablecloths. 'Carving one's portrait in the sky out of the sun and air – some people might say that smacked of vanity, or even worse sins.'

'You're very mysterious. Such as?'

She played games with her eyes. 'I'll tell you in a month's time when my contract expires. Now, when are your men coming?'

'They're here.' I pointed to the sky over the lake. The three gliders hung in the overheated air, clumps of cloud-cotton drifting past them to dissolve in the haze. They were following a sand-yacht that approached the quay, its tyres throwing up the cerise dust. Behind the helmsman sat Leonora Chanel in a trouser suit of yellow alligator skin, her white hair hidden inside a black raffia toque.

As the helmsman moored the craft Van Eyck and Petit Manuel put on an impromptu performance, shaping the fragments of cloud-cotton a hundred feet above the lake. First Van Eyck carved an orchid, then a heart and a pair of lips, while Manuel fashioned the head of a parakeet, two identical mice and the letters 'L.C.' As they dived and plunged around her, their wings sometimes touching the lake, Leonora stood on the quay, politely waving at each of these brief confections.

When they landed beside the quay, Leonora waited for Nolan to take one of the clouds, but he was sailing up and down the lake in front of her like a weary bird. Watching this strange chatelaine of Lagoon West, I noticed that she had slipped off into some private reverie, her gaze fixed on Nolan and oblivious of the people around her. Memories, caravels without sails, crossed the shadowy deserts of her burnt-out eyes.

Later that evening Beatrice Lafferty led me into the villa through the library window. There, as Leonora greeted her guests on the terrace, wearing a topless dress of sapphires and organdy, her breasts covered only by their contour jewellery. I saw the portraits that filled the villa. I counted more than twenty, from the formal society portraits in the drawing rooms, one by the President of the Royal Academy, another by Annigoni, to the bizarre psychological studies in the bar and dining room by Dali and Francis Bacon. Everywhere we moved, in the alcoves between the marble semi-columns, in gilt miniatures on the mantelshelves, even in the ascending mural that followed the staircase, we saw the same beautiful self-regarding face. This colossal narcissism seemed to have become her last refuge, the only retreat for her fugitive self in its flight from the world.

Then, in the studio on the roof, we came across a large easel portrait that had just been varnished. The artist had produced a deliberate travesty of the sentimental and powder-blue tints of a fashionable society painter, but beneath this gloss he had visualized Leonora as a dead Medea. The stretched skin below her right cheek, the sharp forehead and slipped mouth gave her the numbed and luminous appearance of a corpse.

My eyes moved to the signature. 'Nolan! My God, were you here when he painted this?'

'It was finished before I came – two months ago. She refused to have it framed.'

'No wonder.' I went over to the window and looked down at the bedrooms hidden behind their awnings. 'Nolan was *here*. The old studio near Coral D was his.'

'But why should Leonora ask him back? They must have—'

'To paint her portrait again. I know Leonora Chanel better than you do, Beatrice. This time, though, the size of the sky.'

We left the library and walked past the cocktails and canapés to where Leonora was welcoming her guests. Nolan stood beside her, wearing a suit of white suede. Now and then he looked down at her as if playing with the possibilities this self-obsessed woman gave to his macabre humour. Leonora clutched at his elbow. With the diamonds fixed around her eyes she reminded me of some archaic priestess. Beneath the contour jewellery her breasts lay like eager snakes.

Van Eyck introduced himself with an exaggerated bow. Behind him came Petit Manuel, his twisted head ducking nervously among the tuxedos.

Leonora's mouth shut in a rictus of distaste. She glanced at the white plaster on my foot. 'Nolan, you fill your world with cripples. Your little dwarf – will he fly too?'

Petit Manuel looked at her with eyes like crushed flowers.

The performance began an hour later. The dark-rimmed clouds were lit by the sun setting behind the mesa, the air crossed by wraiths of cirrus like the gilded frames of the immense paintings to come. Van Eyck's glider rose in the spiral towards the face of the first cloud, stalling and climbing again as the turbulent updraughts threw him across the air.

As the cheekbones began to appear, as smooth and lifeless as carved foam, applause rang out from the guests seated on the terrace. Five minutes later, when Van Eyck's glider swooped down on to the lake, I could see that he had excelled himself. Lit by the searchlights, and with the overture to Tristan sounding from the loudspeakers on the slopes of the mesa, as if inflating this huge bauble, the portrait of Leonora moved overhead, a faint rain falling from it. By luck the cloud remained stable until it passed the shoreline, and then broke up in the evening air as if ripped from the sky by an irritated hand.

Petit Manuel began his ascent, sailing in on a dark-edged cloud like an urchin accosting a bad-tempered matron. He soared to and fro, as if unsure how to shape this unpredictable column of vapour, then began to carve it into the approximate contours of a woman's head. He seemed more nervous than I had ever seen him. As he finished, a second round of applause broke out, soon followed by laughter and ironic cheers.

The cloud, sculptured into a flattering likeness of Leonora, had begun to tilt, rotating in the disturbed air. The jaw lengthened, the glazed smile became that of an idiot's. Within a minute the gigantic head of Leonora Chanel hung upside down above us.

Discreetly I ordered the searchlights switched off, and the audience's attention turned to Nolan's black-winged glider as it climbed towards the next cloud. Shards of dissolving tissue fell from the darkening air, the spray concealing whatever ambiguous creation Nolan was carving. To my surprise, the portrait that emerged was wholly lifelike. There was a burst of applause, a few bars of Tannhäuser, and the searchlights lit up the elegant head. Standing among her guests, Leonora raised her glass to Nolan's glider.

Puzzled by Nolan's generosity, I looked more closely at the gleaming face, and then realized what he had done. The portrait, with cruel irony, was all too lifelike. The downward turn of Leonora's mouth, the chin held up to smooth her neck, the fall of flesh below her right cheek – all these were carried on the face of the cloud as they had been in his painting in the studio.

Around Leonora the guests were congratulating her on the performance. She was looking up at her portrait as it began to break up over the lake, seeing it for the first time. The veins held the blood in her face.

Then a firework display on the beach blotted out these ambiguities in its pink and blue explosions.

Shortly before dawn Beatrice Lafferty and I walked along the beach among the shells of burnt-out rockets and catherine wheels. On the deserted terrace a few lights shone through the darkness on to the scattered chairs. As we reached the steps a woman's voice cried out somewhere above us. There was the sound of smashed glass. A french window was kicked back, and a dark-haired man in a white suit ran between the tables.

As Nolan disappeared along the drive, Leonora Chanel walked out into the centre of the terrace. She looked at the dark clouds surging over the mesa, and with one hand tore the jewels from her eyes. They lay winking on the tiles at her feet. Then the hunched figure of Petit Manuel leapt from his hiding place in the bandstand. He scuttled past, racing on his deformed legs.

An engine started by the gates. Leonora began to walk back to the villa, staring at her broken reflections in the glass below the window. She stopped as a tall, blond-haired man with cold and eager eyes stepped from the sonic statues outside the library. Disturbed by the noise, the statues had begun to whine. As Van Eyck moved towards Leonora they took up the slow beat of his steps.

The next day's performance was the last by the cloud-sculptors of Coral D. All afternoon, before the guests arrived, a dim light lay over the lake.

Immense tiers of storm-nimbus were massing behind the mesa, and any performance at all seemed unlikely.

Van Eyck was with Leonora. As I arrived, Beatrice Lafferty was watching their sand-yacht carry them unevenly across the lake, its sails whipped by the squalls.

'There's no sign of Nolan or little Manuel,' she told me. 'The party starts in three hours.'

I took her arm. 'The party's already over. When you're finished here, Bea, come and live with me at Coral D. I'll teach you to sculpt the clouds.'

Van Eyck and Leonora came ashore half an hour later. Van Eyck stared through my face as he brushed past. Leonora clung to his arm, the day-jewels around her eyes scattering their hard light across the terrace.

By eight, when the first guests began to appear, Nolan and Petit Manuel had still not arrived. On the terrace the evening was warm and lamplit, but overhead the storm-clouds sidled past each other like uneasy giants. I walked up the slope to where the gliders were tethered. Their wings shivered in the updraughts.

Barely half a minute after he rose into the darkening air, dwarfed by an immense tower of storm-nimbus, Charles Van Eyck was spinning towards the ground, his glider toppled by the crazed air. He recovered fifty feet from the villa and climbed on the updraughts from the lake, well away from the spreading chest of the cloud. He soared in again. As Leonora and her guests watched from their seats the glider was hurled back over their heads in an explosion of vapour, then fell towards the lake with a broken wing.

I walked towards Leonora. Standing by the balcony were Nolan and Petit Manuel, watching Van Eyck climb from the cockpit of his glider three hundred yards away.

To Nolan I said: 'Why bother to come? Don't tell me you're going to fly?'

Nolan leaned against the rail, hands in the pockets of his suit. 'I'm not – that's exactly why I'm here, major.'

Leonora was wearing an evening dress of peacock feathers that lay around her legs in an immense train. The hundreds of eyes gleamed in the electric air before the storm, sheathing her body in their blue flames.

'Miss Chanel, the clouds are like madmen,' I apologized. 'There's a storm on its way.'

She looked up at me with unsettled eyes. 'Don't you people expect to take risks?' She gestured at the storm-nimbus that swirled over our heads. 'For clouds like these I need a Michelangelo of the sky . . . What about Nolan? Is he too frightened as well?'

As she shouted his name Nolan stared at her, then turned his back to us. The light over Lagoon West had changed. Half the lake was covered by a dim pall.

There was a tug on my sleeve. Petit Manuel looked up at me with his crafty child's eyes. 'Major, I can go. Let me take the glider.'

'Manuel, for God's sake. You'll kill—'

He darted between the gilt chairs. Leonora frowned as he plucked her wrist.

'Miss Chanel . . .' His loose mouth formed an encouraging smile. 'I'll sculpt for you. Right now, a big storm-cloud, eh?'

She stared down at him, half-repelled by this eager hunchback ogling her beside the hundred eyes of her peacock train. Van Eyck was limping back to the beach from his wrecked glider. I guessed that in some strange way Manuel was pitting himself against Van Eyck.

Leonora grimaced, as if swallowing some poisonous phlegm. 'Major Parker, tell him to—' She glanced at the dark cloud boiling over the mesa like the effluvium of some black-hearted volcano. 'Wait! Let's see what the little cripple can do!' She turned on Manuel with an over-bright smile. 'Go on, then. Let's see you sculpt a whirlwind!'

In her face the diagram of bones formed a geometry of murder.

Nolan ran past across the terrace, his feet crushing the peacock feathers as Leonora laughed. We tried to stop Manuel, but he raced ahead up the slope. Stung by Leonora's taunt, he skipped among the rocks, disappearing from sight in the darkening air. On the terrace a small crowd gathered to watch.

The yellow and tangerine glider rose into the sky and climbed across the face of the storm-cloud. Fifty yards from the dark billows it was buffeted by the shifting air, but Manuel soared in and began to cut away at the dark face. Drops of black rain fell across the terrace at our feet.

The first outline of a woman's head appeared, satanic eyes lit by the open vents in the cloud, a sliding mouth like a dark smear as the huge billows boiled forwards. Nolan shouted in warning from the lake as he climbed into his glider. A moment later little Manuel's craft was lifted by a powerful updraught and tossed over the roof of the cloud. Fighting the insane air, Manuel plunged the glider downwards and drove into the cloud again. Then its immense face opened, and in a sudden spasm the cloud surged forward and swallowed the glider.

There was silence on the terrace as the crushed body of the craft revolved in the centre of the cloud. It moved over our heads, dismembered pieces of the wings and fuselage churned about in the dissolving face. As it reached the lake the cloud began its violent end. Pieces of the face slewed sideways, the mouth was torn off, an eye exploded. It vanished in a last brief squall.

The pieces of Petit Manuel's glider fell from the bright air.

Beatrice Lafferty and I drove across the lake to collect Manuel's body. After the spectacle of his death within the exploding replica of their hostess's face, the guests began to leave. Within minutes the drive was full of cars. Leonora watched them go, standing with Van Eyck among the deserted tables.

Beatrice said nothing as we drove out. The pieces of the shattered glider lay over the fused sand, tags of canvas and broken struts, control lines tied into knots. Ten yards from the cockpit I found Petit Manuel's body, lying in a wet ball like a drowned monkey.

I carried him back to the sand-yacht.

'Raymond!' Beatrice pointed to the shore. Storm-clouds were massed along the entire length of the lake, and the first flashes of lightning were striking in the hills behind the mesa. In the electric air the villa had lost its glitter. Half a mile away a tornado was moving along the valley floor, its trunk swaying towards the lake.

The first gust of air struck the yacht. Beatrice shouted again: 'Raymond! Nolan's there – he's flying inside it!'

Then I saw the black-winged glider circling under the umbrella of the tornado, Nolan himself riding in the whirlwind. His wings held steady in the revolving air around the funnel. Like a pilot fish he soared in, as if steering the tornado towards Leonora's villa.

Twenty seconds later, when it struck the house, I lost sight of him. An explosion of dark air overwhelmed the villa, a churning centrifuge of shattered chairs and tiles that burst over the roof. Beatrice and I ran from the yacht, and lay together in a fault in the glass surface. As the tornado moved away, fading into the storm-filled sky, a dark squall hung over the wrecked villa, now and then flicking the debris into the air. Shreds of canvas and peacock feathers fell around us.

We waited half an hour before approaching the house. Hundreds of smashed glasses and broken chairs littered the terrace. At first I could see no signs of Leonora, although her face was everywhere, the portraits with their slashed profiles strewn on the damp tiles. An eddying smile floated towards me from the disturbed air, and wrapped itself around my leg.

Leonora's body lay among the broken tables near the bandstand, half-wrapped in a bleeding canvas. Her face was as bruised now as the storm-cloud Manuel had tried to carve.

We found Van Eyck in the wreck of the marquee. He was suspended by the neck from a tangle of electric wiring, his pale face wreathed in a noose of light bulbs. The current flowed intermittently through the wiring, lighting up the coloured globes.

I leaned against the overturned Rolls, holding Beatrice's shoulders. 'There's no sign of Nolan – no pieces of his glider.'

'Poor man. Raymond, he was driving that whirlwind here. Somehow he was controlling it.'

I walked across the damp terrace to where Leonora lay. I began to cover her with the shreds of canvas, the torn faces of herself.

I took Beatrice Lafferty to live with me in Nolan's studio in the desert near Coral D. We heard no more of Nolan and never flew the gliders again. The clouds carry too many memories. Three months ago a man who saw the derelict gliders outside the studio stopped near Coral D and walked across to us. He told us he had seen a man flying a glider in the sky high above Red Beach, carving the strato-cirrus into images of jewels and children's faces. Once there was a dwarf's head.

On reflection, that sounds rather like Nolan, so perhaps he managed to get away from the tornado. In the evenings Beatrice and I sit among the sonic statues, listening to their voices as the fair-weather clouds rise above Coral D, waiting for a man in a dark-winged glider, perhaps painted like candy now, who will come in on the wind and carve for us images of seahorses and unicorns, dwarfs and jewels and children's faces.

CHRISTINE BROOKE-ROSE

Red Rubber Gloves

From this position on my high balcony, the semi-detached beyond the garden looks more squat than it ought to in such a prosperous suburb, forming with its Siamese twin a square inverted U that faces me and boxes a wide inverted T of a back-yard, neatly divided by a hedge of roses and hydrangeas. On the left of the hedge there is a bit of lawn. On the right, only a small paved yard. The house on the left seems devoid of life, devoid, that is, of the kind of life liable to catch the eye and stop it in its casual round, mutating its idle curiosity through momentary fascination and hence, inexorably, by the mere process of reiteration, to a mild but fixed obsessiveness. As does the right-hand house.

In the angle of the square U, outside the french windows of the right-hand house, the girl sits on the edge of the red canvas bed in a pale pink bikini, carefully oiling inch after inch of her thin white body. She looks, from up here, totally naked, the pink bikini being so pale, and she sits on the edge of the red canvas bed which is set obliquely in the paved yard to face the morning sun. She has oiled the arms, the shoulders, the chest and the long midriff. Now she is doing the right leg, starting with the foot, the ankle, then the shin, as if to meet her upper oily self half way. She is oiling the right thigh. Inside the thigh. The left foot. If the heat-wave holds out she will perhaps become brown enough to contrast with the pink and so look less totally naked on the red canvas bed. The inside of the left thigh. She lies now framed in the red canvas bed, chin up, eyes closed to face the hot June sun. Round the corner from her naked body, at the square end of the inverted U, the red rubber gloves lie quiet on the kitchen window-sill.

In the morning the large rectangular windows of the house tend to reflect the sun in some at least of their thirty-two small black squares framed in cream-painted wood. And in the afternoon they are quite cast into the shade as the sun moves round to face me on my high balcony, immobilised in convalescence. I cannot therefore see much further than the beginning of the pink wash-basin in the bathroom or, in the kitchen below it, the long and gleaming double-sink unit. And the red rubber gloves, moving swiftly apart and together, vanishing and reappearing, moving apart and down. All the windows of both houses, those of the kitchen and of the bathroom above it, at each end of the square inverted U, and those of each bedroom inside the U above the french windows, are rectangular and divided into four panels, each of eight black squares, two over two over two over two, all in cream-painted frames.

The thin girl has melted away into the sun, the red canvas bed is empty.

At least, that is presumably also the lay-out of the bathroom and kitchen in the left-hand house, for the windows are mostly hidden by the apple-tree. The houses are almost identical, except for the lawn on the left of the hedge. In the back-yard of the right-hand house, a clothes-line stretches from the high wooden fence to one end of the kitchen window, and another from the same spot in the high wooden fence to the other end, forming a V with the first clothes line.

The girl, the daughter of the house, is perhaps aware that I am watching it, for the bathroom curtains have been hastily drawn. On closer scrutiny I can see that the bathroom in fact occupies only two of the framed panels in the upper window, the right-hand two, the curtains of which have been hastily drawn and are lined in white. The other two must belong to a small bedroom, the girl's bedroom perhaps. Its curtains, pulled back on either side, have a buff lining. It is midday and the cool sun of a cold July tries to pierce through the greyness to warm me in my convalescence. I call it convalescence because the doctor does and the sun is trying to shine, but I know that the paralysis will not retreat, rather will it creep up, slowly perhaps but inexorably over the years, decades even, until it reaches the vital organs.

In the kitchen window of the right-hand house, one of the panels of two squares over two over two is open to reveal a black rectangle and the beginning of the gleaming sink. Inside the sink is a red plastic bowl and on the window-sill are the red rubber gloves, now at rest.

The morning sunlight slants on all the windows, reflecting gold in some of the black squares but not in others, making each rectangular window, with its eight squares across and four squares down, look like half a chess board gone berserk to confuse the queen and all her knights. The bathroom window and the kitchen window below it form two halves of a chessboard, more or less.

In the black rectangle of the open kitchen window the sunlight gleams on the stainless steel double-sink unit, just beyond the cream-painted frame. Above the gleaming sink the red rubber gloves move swiftly, rise from the silver greyness lifting a yellow mass, plunging it into greyness, lifting it again, twisting its tail, shifting it to the right-hand sink, moving back left, vanishing into greyness, rising and moving swiftly, in and out, together and apart.

On closer scrutiny I can see that in the left-hand house the wooden frames of the thirty-two black squares, eight by four in each of the rectangular windows, are painted white. It is only the right-hand house which has cream-painted windows. They all looked the same behind the trees against the strong August sun that faces me on my high balcony. The left-hand house seems quite devoid of life. Possibly the two rectangular windows one above the other in the left-hand house, are not the windows of the bathroom and kitchen at all. It is difficult to see them through the apple-tree, and of course the goldening elm in the garden at the back of my block of flats. In the right-hand house, however, the lower room is definitely the kitchen, in the black rectangle of which the red rubber gloves move swiftly apart, shake hands, vanish into greyness, lift up a foam-white mass, vanish and reappear, move to the right, move back, plunge into greyness, rise and move swiftly right. Beyond the red rubber gloves is a pale grey shape, then blackness.

Despite so much washing activity and two clothes-lines in the back-yard I have not seen the woman yet, the mother of the girl. Surely, she must come out one day to hang out the washing on the line. I have not seen the woman yet, or the girl again, only the red rubber gloves, although the woman has been washing ceaselessly day after day since I first began to watch the house. She must have a large family, which likewise I have not seen, except for the girl sunbathing in that June heat-wave, oiling her body inch by inch, lying it seemed quite naked on the red canvas bed. But as I stare at the empty clothes-line, I know with a mild pang that I have seen shirts hanging from it, and slips, and nightdresses, many a time, without then registering the image, which only now recurs very precisely in the back of my memory. Yet I have never seen the woman herself come out to hang the washing. She must do it while I am having physiotherapy, or seeing the doctor, or eating a meal. Perhaps she waits for a moment when I am not on the balcony, to come out and hang her washing.

On the stainless steel draining board just inside the black rectangle of the open kitchen window is a red mass on a white plate. One of the red rubber gloves unfolds the mass, the other holds a carving knife, almost invisible in the redness of the glove, and cuts the meat into small square pieces on a pale blue chopping board, carefully removing the gristle. In red rubber gloves. A bit much, really. The left red rubber glove sweeps the gristle into the gleaming sink, and then moves up and down, quickly pushing, presumably, the gristle down the waste-disposal unit. One of the red rubber gloves holds the edge of the stainless steel sink, the other moves quickly all around it.

There is no doubt about it, now that the strong September sun has dimmed and gone behind a cloud, the window frames and the frames of all the small black squares inside the windows of the left-hand house are painted white. And the window frames and the frames of the small black squares in the windows of the right-hand house are painted cream.

The red rubber gloves are upstairs now, in the white washstand just beyond the cream-painted squares of the right-hand house. It is very exciting when they are upstairs. They move apart and vanish, rise and come together, shake hands, vanish and reappear. They look larger in the small wash-basin. The shape behind is white in the rosy darkness and the arms above the gloves are clearly visible. It is a rosy darkness due to the walls being probably painted pink. Inside it must be quite light. The arms are thin and white. The red rubber gloves have been removed, the wrists dip naked into the pink washbasin, one hand soaps the other arm, under the arm, the neck, the other hand soaps the first arm, under the arm, the neck.

The stainless steel is dull today, the bright reflecting squares have become black squares, removing the uneven permutations of sunlight on the two halves of the chessboard. The red rubber gloves move swiftly apart, rise from the greyness lifting a red mass, vanish and reappear. The arms above the gloves are thin and white. Despite so much washing activity I have not seen the woman yet. But then I have not been out on the balcony for quite some time, it is too cold, even with rugs. So I wheel my chair by the dining-room window and watch. Surely the woman must one day emerge to hang out all that tremendous wash. But no, the cold November drizzle is too cold and drizzly. Unless perhaps she has a spin-dryer.

The woman steps out into the paved back-yard holding in her thin white embrace the red plastic bowl full of wet clothes. She wears a black jumper and a short grey skirt, and the red rubber gloves. She is thin and has short hair. She puts down the basin and picks from it a shirt which she smooths out and hangs upon the line, upside down by the tails. And then another shirt. Then a pyjama top, with stripes. She and the girl who seemed totally naked on the red canvas bed are one and the same person.

Nobody moves at all in the house on the left. And yet the window corresponding to the bathroom and small bedroom window has one of its panels open. Through the denuded elm, books are visible on the extreme left wall.

The red rubber gloves move swiftly apart behind the cream-painted frames of the kitchen in the right-hand house. One of the squares reflects a pale December sun but otherwise all the squares are dark on the lower half of the chessboard. The red rubber gloves move swiftly apart, shake hands, vanish into a foam-grey mass, rise, vanish and reappear, move swiftly apart, vanish, rise, move apart, vanish, rise, move swiftly. In the blackness beyond the gloves the shape is emerald green.

The woman has no daughter, and no washing-machine. She is the daughter, she is the washing-machine. She is probably the spin-dryer too. Whoever she washes for so continually is never to be seen, from this position at my high dining-room window in the immobility of my convalescence. The two houses have separate roofs, high and deeply sloping in a late Edwardian style with neat little, tight little tiles of darkened red.

The red rubber gloves are also worn to chop up meat on the pale blue chopping board. A bit much, really. The meat must taste of stale detergent. The left red rubber glove sweeps the gristle into the gleaming sink, and then moves up and down pushing the gristle down the presumably waste-disposal unit. One of the red rubber gloves holds the edge of the stainless steel sink, the other moves swiftly around it.

It is three o'clock in the afternoon and the wintry sun accuses my impotence with blank undazzling orange in a dull white sky. The thin white shape appears at the bedroom window, draws the buff-lined curtains with swift brusquery. This is the first time I have seen the woman relaxing. At least, I assume she is relaxing since she has drawn the curtains. It was so jerkily done. Staring at the drawn buff curtains I know that I have seen them drawn before, without registering the image. No doubt in June already, during the heat-wave, she went up to the bedroom at three o'clock in the afternoon and drew the curtains swiftly, jerkily, in a great hurry to relax while I was dozing off. Perhaps she is not relaxing. All I saw was a quick white shape, a slip maybe, unless it was an overall, although her arms were bare. In the kitchen she sometimes wears a white overall, which makes her stand out better against the darkness of the rectangle. And of course the red rubber gloves. They lie at rest now on the kitchen window-sill just inside the small black squares, while she relaxes, thinking of black velvet or of restful landscapes as she isolates her head, and then dismisses it as she isolates her neck, and then dismisses it as she isolates her left shoulder, her left arm, flowing, flowing, out, her right arm, and then dismisses it as she isolates her left leg, and her left foot, and then dismisses it as she isolates her right leg, her right foot. That is what the physiotherapist tells me to do when I am in pain. Normal people have to do it all the way down, isolating the left leg, then the right, but I feel no pain down there at all, my legs have isolated themselves, so there's no point. It is the neck and shoulders, and the back especially, that ache. Perhaps she isolates the inside of her thigh.

The curtains are drawn open swiftly and a white shape moves away. A quick relaxation, that, merely counting to a hundred maybe, with a hundred deep breaths.

The thin white shape appears behind the cream-framed squares of the bathroom window. Briefly, for the white lined curtains are drawn with a brusque movement.

On closer scrutiny the bathroom curtains are not lined in white, but are made of plastic, the reverse side of which is white. Unless perhaps they have replaced, quite recently, the earlier bathroom curtains with the white cotton lining. It is now impossible to tell. There is a faint pink and blue pattern, ducks, possibly, or boats, brighter no doubt on the inside. Six out of thirty-two black squares reflect the pale December morning sun, Castle top left, Bishop left, White Queen on her colour, pawn one advanced two paces, pawn two advanced one pace, pawn four immobilised in dire paralysis.

The lower half of the chessboard reflects no sun. In the black rectangle of the kitchen window the red rubber gloves move swiftly apart. One of the gloves holds the edge of the stainless steel sink, the other moves swiftly around it. Three shirts are hanging on the line, upside down, and a pyjama top, male underpants, one nightie, two slips, three panties and a pale green blouse. There are no pyjama trousers.

Snow covers the two steep roofs, and all the trees and gardens. The narrow bricks of the Siamese twin houses seem unnaturally dark. The back yards look alike, no lawn now on the left, only the apple-tree, bare branched in black and white. The snow piles high on the window-sills of the left-hand house. But on the right-hand house the window sills have been swept clean and stand out dark and grey. The light is on in the kitchen, the woman clearly visible, in a blue smock over a red polo-neck. The red rubber gloves move swiftly apart, plunge into greyness and bring out a plate, a cup, another plate, another, and a saucepan, after scouring.

The snow makes map-like patterns on the dark red and steeply sloping roofs.

The red rubber gloves move swiftly apart above the gleaming sink in the dark rectangle of the open kitchen window. The April sun slants on the small black squares, whitening a few and leaving others blank, like half a chessboard gone berserk in order to confuse the queen and all her knights.

During my relapse I have thought a lot about the woman. I was unable to sit by the window but I saw her clearly in my mind's eye. Busy, always busy in her red rubber gloves. But I know. Clearly she has a lover. She receives him at three o'clock in the afternoon and swiftly draws the curtains. There is so little time.

At three o'clock in the afternoon I sit by the dining-room window now and watch the house. The lover is there, behind the curtains, caressing her face, and then her neck, her breasts, her belly and the inside of her thigh as she lies totally naked on the red counter-pane. Her belly is enormous for she is eight and a half months pregnant by him. She must have been getting bigger and bigger during my relapse, and of course before, although at that time it wouldn't have been so noticeable from this position at my dining-room window. Therefore he cannot make love to her but he caresses her. She loves me manually and I am content.

The tiny baby lies dead on the pale blue chopping board by the stainless steel sink. She cuts him up with the big carving knife and drops the small bits one by one into the waste-disposal unit which growls and grinds them into white liquid pulp.

The red rubber gloves move swiftly apart, half lost in all the blood. One hand holds the edge of the stainless steel sink, the other moves quickly around it.

The heat-wave is tremendous for late May. The woman sits on the edge of the red canvas bed in her pale pink bikini, carefully oiling her body inch by inch, the arms, the shoulders, the chest and the long midriff. Now she is doing the right leg, the shin, the thigh, the inside of the thigh. She lies on the red canvas bed, thin, white and totally naked in her invisible bikini, chin up, eyes closed to face the morning sun that pours down melting her and my left side on my high balcony. In the black rectangle of the open kitchen window the yellow rubber gloves lie on the sill, at rest.

ELIZABETH TAYLOR

In and Out the Houses

Kitty Miller, wearing a new red hair-ribbon, bounced along the Vicarage drive, skipping across ruts and jumping over puddles.

Visiting took up all of her mornings in the school holidays. From kitchen to kitchen, round the village, she made her progress, and, this morning, felt drawn towards the Vicarage. Quite sure of her welcome, she tapped on the back door.

'Why, Kitty Miller!' said the Vicar, opening it. He looked quite different from in church Kitty thought. He was wearing an open-necked shirt and an old, darned cardigan. He held a tea-towel to the door-handle, because his fingers were sticky. He and his wife were cutting up Seville oranges for marmalade and there was a delicious, tangy smell about the kitchen.

Kitty took off her coat, and hung it on the usual peg, and fetched a knife from the dresser drawer.

'You are on your rounds again,' Mr Edwards said. 'Spreading light and succour about the parish.'

Kitty glanced at him rather warily. She preferred him not to be there, disliking men about her kitchens. She reached for an orange, and watching Mrs Edwards for a moment out of the corners of her eyes, began to slice it up.

'What's new?' asked the Vicar.

'Mrs Saddler's bad,' she said accusingly. He should be at that bedside, she meant to imply, instead of making marmalade. 'They were saying at The Horse and Groom that she won't last the day.'

'So we are not your first call of the morning?'

She had, on her way here, slipped round the back of the pub and into

353

the still-room, where Miss Betty Benford, eight months pregnant, was washing the floor, puffing and blowing as she splashed grey soapy water over the flags with a gritty rag. When this job was done – to Miss Betty's mind, not Kitty's – they drank a cup of tea together and chatted about the baby, woman to woman. The village was short of babies, and Kitty visualised pushing this one out in its pram, taking it round with her on her visits.

In his office, the landlord had been typing the luncheon menus. The keys went down heavily, his finger hovered, and stabbed. He often made mistakes, and this morning had typed 'Jam Fart and Custard'. Kitty considered – and then decided against – telling the Vicar this.

'They have steak-and-kidney pie on the set menu today,' she said instead.

'My favourite!' groaned the Vicar. 'I *never* get it.'

'You had it less than a fortnight ago,' his wife reminded him.

'And what pudding? If it's treacle tart I shall cry bitterly.'

'Jam tart,' Kitty said gravely. 'And custard.'

'I quite like custard, too,' he said simply.

'Or choice of cheese and biscuits.'

'I should have cheese and biscuits,' Mrs Edwards said.

It was just the kind of conversation Kitty loved.

'Eight-and-sixpence,' she said. 'Coffee extra.'

'To be rich! To be rich!' The Vicar said. 'And what are *we* having, my dear? Kitty has caused the juices to run.'

'Cold, of course, as it's Monday.'

He shuddered theatrically, and picked up another orange. 'My day off, too!'

Kitty pressed her lips together primly, thinking it wrong for clergymen to have days off, especially with Mrs Saddler lying there, dying.

The three of them kept glancing at one another's work as they cut the oranges. Who was doing it finely enough? Only Mrs Edwards, they all knew.

'I like it fairly chunky,' the Vicar said.

When it was all done, Kitty rinsed her hands at the sink, and then put on her coat. She had given the Vicarage what time she could spare, and the morning was getting on, and all the rest of the village waiting. She was very orderly in her habits and never visited in the afternoons, for then she had her novel to write. The novel was known about in the village, and some people felt concerned, wondering if she might be another little Daisy Ashford.

With the Vicar's phrases of gratitude giving her momentum, Kitty tacked down the drive between the shabby laurels, and out into the lane.

'The Vicar's having cold,' she told Mrs De Vries, who was preparing a *tajine* of chicken in a curious earthenware pot she had brought back from Morocco.

'Poor old Vicar,' Mrs De Vries said absent-mindedly, as she cut almonds into slivers. She had a glass of something on the draining-board and often took a sip from it. 'Do run and find a drink for yourself, dear child,' she said. She was one of the people who wondered about Daisy Ashford.

'I'll have a bitter lemon, if I may,' Kitty said.

'Well, do, my dear. You know where to find it.'

As Kitty knew everything about nearly every house in the village, she did not reply; but went with assurance to the bar in the hall. She stuck a plastic straw in her drink, and returned to the kitchen sucking peacefully.

'Is there anything I can do?' she enquired.

'No, just tell me the news. What's going on?'

'Mr Mumford typed "Jam Fart and Custard" on the menu card.'

'Oh, he didn't! You've made me do the nose-trick with my gin. The *pain* of it!' Mrs De Vries snatched a handkerchief from her apron pocket and held it to her face. When she had recovered, she said, 'I simply can't wait for Tom to come home, to tell him that.'

Kitty looked modestly gratified. 'I called at the Vicarage, too, on my way.'

'And what were *they* up to?'

'They are up to making marmalade.'

'Poor darlings! They *do* have to scrimp and scratch. Church mice, indeed!'

'But isn't home-made marmalade nicer than shop?'

'Not all *that* much.'

After a pause, Kitty said, 'Mrs Saddler's on her way out.'

'Who the hell's Mrs Saddler?'

'At the almshouse. She's dying.'

'Poor old thing.'

Kitty sat down on a stool and swung her fat legs.

'Betty Benford is eight months gone,' she said, shrugging her shoulders.

'I wish you'd tell me something about people I *know*,' Mrs De Vries complained, taking another sip of gin.

'Her mother plans to look after the baby while Betty goes on going out to work. Mrs Benford, you know.'

'Not next door's daily?'

'She won't be after this month.'

'Does Mrs Glazier know?' Mrs De Vries asked, inclining her head towards next door.

'Not yet,' Kitty said, glancing at the clock.

'My God, she'll go up the wall,' Mrs De Vries said with relish. 'She's had that old Benford for years and years.'

'What do you call that you're cooking?'

'It's a *tajine* of chicken.'

'Mrs De Vries is having *tajine* of chicken,' Kitty said next door five minutes later.

'And what might that be when it's at home?'

Kitty described it as best she could, and Mrs Glazier looked huffy. 'Derek wouldn't touch it,' she said. 'He likes good, plain, English food, and no messing about.'

She was rolling out pastry for that evening's steak-and-kidney pie.

'They're having that at The Horse and Groom,' Kitty said.

'*And* we'll have sprouts. *And* braised celery,' Mrs Glazier added, not letting Mrs De Vries get away with her airs and graces.

'Shall I make a pastry rose to go on the top of the pie?' Kitty offered. 'Mrs Prout showed me how to.'

'No, I think we'll leave well alone.'

'Do you like cooking?' Kitty asked in a conversational tone.

'I don't mind it. Why?'

'I was only thinking that then it wouldn't be so hard on you when Mrs Benford leaves.'

Mrs Benford was upstairs. There was a bumping, droning noise of a vacuum cleaner above, in what Kitty knew to be Mrs Glazier's bedroom.

Mrs Glazier, with an awful fear in her heart, stared, frowning, at Kitty, who went on, 'I was just telling Mrs De Vries that after Mrs Benford's grandchild's born she's going to stay at home to mind it.'

The fact that next door had heard this stunning news first made the blow worse, and Mrs Glazier put a flour-covered hand to her forehead. She closed her eyes for a moment. 'But why can't the girl look after the little – baby herself?'

Kitty took the lid off a jar marked 'Cloves' and looked inside, sniffing. 'Her daughter earns more money at The Horse and Groom than her mother earns here,' she explained.

'I suppose you told Mrs De Vries that too.'

Kitty went to the door with dignity. 'Oh, no! I never talk from house to house. My mother says I'll have to stop my visiting, if I do. Oh, by the way,' she called back, 'You'd better keep your dog in. The De Vries's bitch is on heat.'

She went home and sat down to lamb and bubble-and-squeak.

'The Vicar's having cold, too,' she said.

'And that's *his* business,' her mother said warningly.

A few days later, Kitty called on Mrs Prout.

Mrs Prout's cottage was one of Kitty's favourite visits. Many years ago, before she was married, Mrs Prout had been a school-teacher, and she enjoyed using her old skills to deal with Kitty. Keeping her patience pliant, she taught her visitor new card games (and they were all educational), and got her on to collecting and pressing wild-flowers. She would give her pastry-trimmings to cut into shapes, and showed her how to pop corn and make fudge. She was extremely kind, though firm, and Kitty respected the rules – about taking off her Wellingtons and washing her hands and never calling on Mondays or Thursdays, because these were turning-out days when Mrs Prout was far too busy to have company.

They were very serious together. Mrs Prout enjoyed being authoritative to a child again, and Kitty had a sense of orderliness which obliged her to comply.

'They sent this from the Vicarage,' she said, coming into the kitchen with a small pot of marmalade.

'How jolly nice!' Mrs Prout said. She took the marmalade, and tilted it slightly, and it moved. Rather sloppy. But she thought no worse of the Vicar's wife for that. 'That's really *jolly* nice of them,' she said, going into the larder. 'And they shall have some of my apple jelly, in fair return. *Quid pro quo*, eh? And one good turn deserves another.'

She came out of the larder with a different little pot and held it to the light; but the clear and golden content did not move when she tipped it sideways.

'What's the news?' she asked.

'Mrs Saddler still lingers on,' Kitty said. She had called at the alms-house to enquire, but the district nurse had told her to run off and mind her own business. 'I looked in at the Wilsons' on my way here. Mrs Wilson was making a cheese and onion pie. Of course, they're vegetarians; but I have known him to sneak a little chicken into his mouth. I was helping to hand round at the De Vries's cocktail-party, and he put out his hand towards a patty. "It's chicken," I said to him in a low voice. "Nary a word," he said, and he winked at me and ate it.'

'And now you *have* said a word,' Mrs Prout said briskly.

'Why, so I have,' Kitty agreed, looking astonished.

Mrs Prout cleared the kitchen table in the same brisk way, and said, 'If you like, now, I'll show you how to make ravioli. We shall have it for our television supper.'

'Make ravioli,' cried Kitty. 'You can't *make* ravioli. Mrs Glazier buys it in a tin.'

'So Mrs Glazier may. But I find time to make my own.'

'I shall be fascinated,' Kitty said, taking off her coat.

'Then wash your hands, and don't forget to dry them properly. Isn't it about time you cut your nails?' Mrs Prout asked, in her school-mistressy voice, and Kitty, who would take anything from her, agreed. ('We all know Mrs Prout is God,' her mother sometimes said resentfully.)

'Roll up those sleeves, now. And we'll go through your tables while we work.'

Mrs Prout set out the flour bin and a dredger and a pastry-cutter and the mincer. Going back and forth to the cupboard, she thought how petty she was to be pleased at knowing that by this time tomorrow, most of the village would be aware that she made her own ravioli. But perhaps it was only human, she decided.

'Now this is what chefs call the *mise en place*,' she explained to Kitty, when she had finished arranging the table. 'Can you remember that? *Mise en place*.'

'*Mise en place*,' Kitty repeated obediently.

'Shall I help you prepare the *mise en place*?' Kitty enquired of Mrs Glazier.

'Mr Glazier wouldn't touch it. I've told you he will only eat English food.'

'But you have ravioli. That's Italian.'

'I just keep it as a stand-by,' Mrs Glazier said scornfully. She was very huffy and put out these days, especially with Mrs De Vries next door and her getting the better of her every time. Annette de Vries was French, and didn't they all know it. Mrs Glazier, as a result, had become violently insular.

'I can make ravioli,' Kitty said, letting the *mise en place* go, for she was not absolutely certain about it. 'Mrs Prout has just been teaching me. She and Mr Prout have television trays by the fire, and then they sit and crack walnuts and play cards, and then they have hot milk and whisky and go to bed. I think it is very nice and cosy, don't you?'

'Mr Glazier likes a proper sit-down meal when *he* gets back. Did you happen to see Tiger anywhere down the lane?'

'No, but I expect he's next door. I told you their bitch is on heat. You ought to shut him up.'

'It's their affair to shut *theirs* up.'

'Well, I'm just calling there, so I'll shoo him off.'

She had decided to cut short this visit. Mrs Glazier was so bad-tempered these days, and hardly put herself out at all to give a welcome, and every interesting thing Kitty told her served merely to annoy.

'And I must get on with my jugged hare,' Mrs Glazier said, making no attempt to delay the departure. 'It should be marinating in the port wine by now,' she added grandly. 'And I must make the soup and the croutons.'

'Well, then, I'll be going,' Kitty said, edging towards the door.

'And apricot mousse,' Mrs Glazier called out after her, as if she were in a frenzy.

'Shall I prepare your *mise en place*?' Kitty enquired of Mrs De Vries, trying her luck again.

'My! We *are* getting professional,' said Mrs De Vries, but her mind was really on what Kitty had just been telling her. Soup and jugged hare! She was thinking. What a dreadful meal!

She was glazing a terrine of chicken livers and wished that all the village might see her work of art, but having Kitty there was the next best thing.

'What's that?' she asked, as Kitty put the jar of apple jelly on the table.

'I have to take it to the Vicarage on my way home. It's some of Mrs Prout's apple jelly.'

Mrs De Vries gave it a keen look, and notched up one point to Mrs Prout. She notched up another when she heard about the ravioli, and wondered if she had underestimated the woman.

'I shooed that Tiger away,' Kitty said.

'The wretched cur. He is driving Topaze insane.'

Kitty mooched round the kitchen, peeking and prying. Mrs De Vries was the only one in the village to possess a *mandoline* for cutting vegetables. There was a giant pestle and mortar, a wicker bread-basket, ropes of Spanish onions, and a marble cheese-tray.

'You can pound the fish for me, if you have the energy,' said Mrs De Vries.

As this was not a house where she was made to wash her hands first, Kitty immediately set to work.

'I was just going to have pears,' Mrs De Vries said, in a half-humorous voice. 'But if the Glaziers are going in for apricot mousse I had better pull my socks up. That remark, of course, is strictly *entre nous*.'

'Then Mrs De Vries pulled her socks up, and made a big apple tart,' Kitty told her mother.

'I have warned you before, Kitty. What you see going on in people's houses, you keep to yourself. Or you stay out of them. Is that finally and completely understood?'

'Yes, Mother,' Kitty said meekly.

'My dear girl, I couldn't eat it. I couldn't eat another thing,' said Mr Glazier, confronted by the apricot mousse. 'A three-course-meal. Why, I shouldn't sleep all night if I had any more. The hare alone was ample.'

'I think Mr De Vries would do better justice to his dinner,' said Mrs Glazier bitterly. She had spent all day cooking and was exhausted. 'It's not much fun slaving away and not being appreciated. And what on earth can I do with all the left-overs?'

'Finish them up tomorrow and save yourself a lot of trouble.'

Glumly, Mrs Glazier washed the dishes, and suddenly thought of the Prouts sitting peacefully beside their fire, cracking walnuts, playing cards. She felt ill-done-by, as she stacked the remains of dinner in the fridge, but was perfectly certain that lie as she might have to to Kitty in the morning, the whole village should not know that for the second day running the Glaziers were having soup, and jugged hare, and apricot mousse.

Next day, eating a slice of apple tart, Kitty saw Mrs De Vries test the soup and then put the ladle back into the saucepan. 'What the eye doesn't see, the heart cannot grieve over,' Mrs De Vries said cheerfully. She added salt, and a turn or two of pepper. Then she took more than a sip from the glass on the draining-board, seeming to find it more to her liking than the soup.

'The Vicarage can't afford drinks,' Kitty said.

'They *do* confide in you.'

'I said to the Vicar, Mrs De Vries drinks gin while she is cooking, and he said, "Lucky old her".'

'There will be a lot of red faces about this village if you go on like this,' said Mrs De Vries, making her part of the prophecy come true at once. Kitty looked at her in surprise. Then she said – Mrs De Vries's flushed face reminding her – 'I think next door must be having the change of life. She is awfully grumpy these days. Nothing pleases her.'

'You are too knowing for your years,' Mrs De Vries said, and she suddenly wished she had not been so unhygienic about the soup. Too late now. 'How is your novel coming along?' she enquired.

'Oh, very nicely, thank you. I expect I shall finish it before I go back to school, and then it can be published for Christmas.'

'We shall all look forward to that,' said Mrs De Vries, in what Kitty considered an unusual tone of voice.

'Mrs De Vries cuts up her vegetables with a *mandoline*,' Kitty told Mrs Glazier some days later.

'I always knew she must be nuts,' said Mrs Glazier, thinking of the musical instrument.

Seeing Kitty dancing up the drive, she had quickly hidden the remains of a shepherd's pie at the back of a cupboard. She was more than ever ruffled this morning, because Mrs Benford had not arrived or sent a message. She had also been getting into a frenzy with her ravioli and, in the end, had thrown the whole lot into the dust-bin. She hated waste, especially now that her house-keeping allowance always seemed to have disappeared by Wednesday, and her husband was, in his dyspeptic way, continually accusing her of extravagance.

Kitty had been hanging about outside the almshouses for a great part of the morning, and had watched Mrs Saddler's coffin being carried across the road to the church.

'Only one wreath and two relations,' she now told Mrs Glazier. 'That's what comes of being poor. What are you having for dinner tonight? I could give you a hand.'

'Mr Glazier will probably be taking me to the Horse and Groom for a change,' Mrs Glazier lied.

'They are all at sixes and sevens there. Betty Benford started her pains in the night. A fortnight early. Though Mr Mumford thinks she may have made a mistake with her dates.'

Then Mrs Benford would never come again, Mrs Glazier thought despondently. She had given a month's notice the week before, and Mrs Glazier had received it coldly, saying – 'I think I should have been informed of this before it became common gossip in the village.' Mrs Benford had seemed quite taken aback at that.

'Well, I mustn't hang around talking,' Mrs Glazier told Kitty. 'There's a lot to do this morning, and will be from now on. When do you go back to school?'

'On Thursday.'

Mrs Glazier nodded, and Kitty felt herself dismissed. She sometimes wondered why she bothered to pay this call, when everyone else made her so welcome; but coming away from the funeral she had seen Mrs De Vries driving into town, and it was one of Mrs Prout's turning-out days. She had hardly liked to call at the Vicarage under the circumstances of the funeral, and The Horse and Groom being at sixes and sevens had made everyone there very boring and busy.

'I hope you will enjoy your dinner,' she said politely to Mrs Glazier. 'They have roast Surrey fowl and all the trimmings.'

When she had gone, Mrs Glazier took the shepherd's pie from its hiding place, and began to scrape some shabby old carrots.

'Kitty, will you stop chattering and get on with your pudding,' her mother said in an exasperated voice.

Kitty had been describing how skilfully the undertaker's men had lowered Mrs Saddler's coffin into the grave, Kitty herself peering from behind the tombstone of Maria Britannia Marlowe – her favourite dead person on account of her name.

It was painful to stop talking. A pain came in her chest, severe enough to slow her breathing, and gobbling the rice pudding made it worse. As soon as her plate was cleared she began again. 'Mrs Glazier has the change of life,' she said.

'How on earth do you know about such things?' her mother asked in a faint note.

'As *you* didn't tell me, I had to find out the hard way,' Kitty said sternly.

Her mother pursed her lips together to stop laughing, and began to stack up the dishes.

'How Mrs De Vries will miss me!' Kitty said dreamily, rising to help her mother. 'I shall be stuck there at school doing boring things, and she'll be having a nice time drinking gin.'

'Now *that* is enough. You are to go to your room immediately,' her mother said sharply, and Kitty looked at her red face reflectively, comparing it with Mrs Glazier's. 'You will have to find some friends of your own age. You are becoming a little menace to everyone with your visiting, and we have got to live in this village. Now upstairs you go, and think over what I have said.'

'Very well, Mother,' Kitty said meekly. If she did not have to help mother with the washing-up, she could get on with her novel all the sooner.

She went upstairs to her bedroom and spread her writing things out on the table and soon, having at once forgotten her mother's words, was lost in the joy of authorship.

Her book was all about little furry animals, and their small adventures, and there was not a human being in it, except the girl, Katherine, who befriended them all.

She managed a few more visits that holiday; but on Thursday she went back to school again, and then no one in the village knew what was happening any more.

KINGSLEY AMIS

Mason's Life

'May I join you?'

The medium-sized man with the undistinguished clothes and the blank, anonymous face looked up at Pettigrew, who, glass of beer in hand, stood facing him across the small corner table. Pettigrew, tall, handsome and of fully moulded features, had about him an intent, almost excited air that, in different circumstances, might have brought an unfavourable response, but the other said amiably,

'By all means. Do sit down.'

'Can I get you something?'

'No, I'm fine, thank you,' said the medium-sized man, gesturing at the almost full glass in front of him. In the background was the ordinary ambience of bar, barman, drinkers in ones and twos, nothing to catch the eye.

'We've never met, have we?'

'Not as far as I recall.'

'Good, good. My name's Pettigrew, Daniel R. Pettigrew. What's yours?'

'Mason. George Herbert Mason, if you want it in full.'

'Well, I think that's best, don't you? George . . . Herbert . . . Mason.' Pettigrew spoke as if committing the three short words to memory. 'Now let's have your telephone number.'

Again Mason might have reacted against Pettigrew's demanding manner, but he said no more than, 'You can find me in the book easily enough.'

'No, there might be several . . . We mustn't waste time. Please.'

'Oh, very well; it's public information, after all. Two-three-two, five—'

'Hold on, you're going too fast for me. Two . . . three . . . two . . .'

'Five-four-five-four.'

'What a stroke of luck. I ought to be able to remember that.'

'Why don't you write it down if it's so important to you?'

At this, Pettigrew gave a knowing grin that faded into a look of disappointment. 'Don't you know that's no use? Anyway: two-three-two, five-four-five-four. I might as well give you my number too. Seven—'

'I don't want your number, Mr Pettigrew,' said Mason, sounding a little impatient, 'and I must say I rather regret giving you mine.'

'But you must take my number.'

'Nonsense; you can't make me.'

'A phrase, then – let's agree on a phrase to exchange in the morning.'

'Would you mind telling me what all this is about?'

'Please, our time's running out.'

'You keep saying that. This is getting—'

'Any moment everything might change and I might find myself somewhere completely different, and so might you, I suppose, though I can't help feeling it's doubtful whether—'

'Mr Pettigrew, either you explain yourself at once or I have you removed.'

'All right,' said Pettigrew, whose disappointed look had deepened, 'but I'm afraid it won't do any good. You see, when we started talking I thought you must be a real person, because of the way you—'

'Spare me your infantile catch-phrases, for heaven's sake. So I'm not a real person,' cooed Mason offensively.

'I don't mean it like that, I mean it in the most literal way possible.'

'Oh, God. Are you mad or drunk or what?'

'Nothing like that. I'm asleep.'

'Asleep?' Mason's nondescript face showed total incredulity.

'Yes. As I was saying, at first I took you for another real person in the same situation as myself: sound asleep, dreaming, aware of the fact, and anxious to exchange names and telephone numbers and so forth with the object of getting in touch the next day and confirming the shared experience. That would prove something remarkable about the mind, wouldn't it? – people communicating via their dreams. It's pity one so seldom realizes one's dreaming: I've only been able to try the experiment four or five times in the last twenty years, and I've never had any success. Either

I forget the details or I find there's no such person, as in this case. But I'll go on—'

'You're sick.'

'Oh no. Of course it's conceivable there is such a person as you. Unlikely, though, or you'd have recognized the true situation at once, I feel, instead of arguing against it like this. As I say, I may be wrong.'

'It's hopeful that you say that.' Mason had calmed down, and lit a cigarette with deliberation. 'I don't know much about these things, but you can't be too far gone if you admit you could be in error. Now let me just assure you that I didn't come into existence five minutes ago inside your head. My name, as I told you, is George Herbert Mason. I'm forty-six years old, married, three children, job in the furniture business . . . Oh hell, giving you no more than an outline of my life so far would take all night, as it would in the case of anybody with an average memory. Let's finish our drinks and go along to my house, and then we can—'

'You're just a man in my dream saying that,' said Pettigrew loudly. 'Two-three-two, five-four-five-four. I'll call the number if it exists, but it won't be you at the other end. Two-three-two—'

'Why are you so agitated, Mr Pettigrew?'

'Because of what's going to happen to you at any moment.'

'What . . . Is this a threat?'

Pettigrew was breathing fast. His finely drawn face began to coarsen, the pattern of his tweed jacket to become blurred. 'The telephone!' he shouted. 'It must be later than I thought!'

'Telephone?' repeated Mason, blinking and screwing up his eyes as Pettigrew's form continued to change.

'The one at my bedside! I'm waking up!'

Mason grabbed the other by the arm, but that arm had lost the greater part of its outline, had become a vague patch of light already fading, and when Mason looked at the hand that had done the grabbing, his own hand, he saw with difficulty that it likewise no longer had fingers, or front or back, or skin, or anything at all.

ALAN SILLITOE

Mimic

I

I learned to mimic at an early age, probably at two or three when I sat in front of the fire and stared at the cat. A mimic has a long memory, fine hands, and a face he can't bear to look at in the mirror, unless he puts on somebody else's with such intensity that he cannot recognize himself there. His soul is his own, but he buries it deeply with many others because under such a mound it is finally safe. Eventually of course it is so far lost and gone that he is unable to get down to it when he wants to, but that is another matter, and finally unimportant when one knows that age and death will settle everything.

In the early days of infancy I did not know I was becoming a mimic. By all accounts I was such a handsome baby that when my mother pushed me through town in a pram men would stop to admire me and give her five shillings to buy me a new rattle. At least that was her story, though my memory is better than any story, for another line was that because she was so pretty they gave money to me as an excuse for getting off with her.

A still further version could be I was so rotten-faced and ugly they gave her money to show sympathy at her being loaded with such a terrible burden. Anyway, that's how she met her second husband, which only proves that mimics usually have pretty and wayward mothers, while they may be fair-to-ugly themselves. You can't be a mimic with a fine-featured face, but for the first few years must stare at this world and take nothing in so that your face stays flat and putty-coloured, with a button-nose, beehive-mouth, and burdock-chin that detects what sunlight hopes to make your features more heavenly to the world.

While father was at work and my mother in the scullery I'd romp on the rug for a while, then settle down and look at the cat, a black tabby with a white spot between its ears. I'd stare right into its splinter eyes till it opened its great mouth and yawned. Then, facing it on all fours, I'd open my mouth as well, full of small new teeth, stretching the side skin as far as it would go. The way the cat looked at me I knew I was successful, and because of this it seemed as if I felt alive for the first time in my life. I'll never forget this strong impression. When I mimicked, the light went on, as if somebody had sneaked up behind and slyly lifted off the dark glasses I didn't have. Finally the cat walked away, as if embarrassed.

I practised on animals for years, on the assumption, rightly I think, that if I could mimic animals so that they recognized themselves in me when I was doing it in front of them, then it would be quite easy to do it to human beings when I was ready for the changeover.

I remember at the age of nine that a young woman in our yard had a puppy, a small dark fat one that had been ill, that she wanted to get rid of. So she asked me to take it to the PDSA, gave me a shilling to put into their contribution box, and threepence to myself for the errand of taking it. The place was about a mile away, and going there I called in many sweet shops, buying chocolate at every stop. The puppy was wrapped in a towel in my arms, and after stocking up at a shop I would sit on a wall to eat the loot, and take another goz at the puppy who was going to be 'put to sleep' as the woman had said. I knew of course what that meant, and though the puppy squinted at me and licked my hand when I gave it chocolate it still looked as if it might welcome what was in store for it. I stared hard at those brown eyes, at that fat half-blind face that could never have any say in how the world was run, and between one snap of chocolate and the next I'd borrow its expression, take on that look, and show it to the puppy to let him feel he was not alone.

A mimic does what he is paid to do. By the time I got to the PDSA. I had only threepence left for the contribution box. A shilling had gone on chocolate for me and the dog, and for the dog it was the last thing it would ever eat.

On the way home a hump-backed bridge crossed a canal. I went down through a gate on to the towpath. On the opposite side was a factory wall, but on my side was a fence and an elderberry bush. The water was bottle green, and reflected both sides in it. My eyes turned from grey to brown, and I barked as the dog had barked when the woman in the white overall had taken him from me.

This isn't a story about childhood. It is about a mimic, and mimics have no childhood. In fact it would almost be fair to say that they don't even have a life of their own. There is a certain price to pay for taking on another face, another voice, even though mimicry need bring no profit. But what mimicry does give is a continuation of one's life when for some reason that life had been forfeited even before birth. Whether one had done it oneself as a spirit from another age, or whether someone in another age had got hold of your spirit before it was born and squeezed the life out of it, who can ever be able to say? One may be born innocent, but in order to make one's mark on life, one has to get rid of that innocence.

One puts one's devilries as a mimic into other people if one is guilty of what blasted one's life before birth; one takes others' devilries upon oneself if one was innocent before birth.

To borrow a face is to show no mercy to it. In order to call it your own, you leave the owner of it with nothing. Not only do you see something of an advantage in using someone else's face, but you seek to rob them of what strength they also get from wearing it. At the same time you mimic them to hide yourself. A mimic therefore can't lose, except of course that he has lost everything before birth, more than anyone else can lose unless he is a mimic too.

The first *person* I mimicked, or tried to, was my mother, and I did this by falling in love with her. This is not so easy as it sounds, especially since she had been responsible for giving me birth, but being the person with the power of life and death over me there surely wasn't any fitter person to fall in love with. But I didn't let her see it, because my way of doing it was to mimic her one day, and I expected that since she had already given me so much she wouldn't mind this at all, would be flattered by it in fact. But all she saw was that I was taking everything.

She'd just had a blinding row with my father, and he'd stormed off to see his mates in the pub. At the heart-rending smash of the door behind him she sat by the fire waiting for the kettle to boil. When it did, she burst into tears. I thought to myself that if I did the same, her misery would be halved, so I put on the same expression (the half-closed eyes and twisted mouth, hands to my face-side with two fingers over my ear) and drew tears out with almost exactly the same noise. I'd meant to let my heart flow with hers, to be with it as a sort of comfort, but what I didn't know was that I'd only irritated her, mocked her – which is what she called mimicking for many years. This barefaced imitation made it worse, though instead of increasing her tears (it could hardly do that) it stopped them altogether. This was what I had hoped for, but only in such a way as to soften her heart, not to harden her. She smacked my face: 'Don't mock me, you little bleeder. You're almost as bad as he is.' I don't need to say who 'he' was, though in spite of our similarity he never became the mimic that I did.

So I mimicked my father, seeing how my attempt at love for mother had failed. It was quite a while before I stopped tormenting my mother by only mimicking my father in front of her, and began mimicking him to his face. When I did, he laughed, and I'd never seen him in such a good mood. Life is full of surprises for a mimic. He'd loosened his belt one Sunday dinner because he was too full of beer and food. He pulled me on to his knee and kissed me, my mother looking wryly over her shoulder now and again as she washed the pots. He was so pleased at my exact imitation of him, of seeing himself so clearly in me, that he gave me a shilling.

This momentary gain went to my head and, before he could fall into a doze by the fire, I thought I would put on the best show he'd seen by mimicking my mother for him. If he could laugh at himself in me, he'd be more touched than ever to see mother in my face.

I drew myself up on the hearthrug as if I were tall and thin, curved my arms outward from my side, tilted my head, and drew in my cheeks, completely altering the shape of my mouth and putting that fire into my eyes that expected to be swamped out any second by a tidal wave.

'You've been a long time at the pub,' I said in her voice, 'don't you know your dinner's burnt? It's a wonder you couldn't smell it right from the bar.'

His eyes grew small, and the smile capsized like a boat in a gale. Before I knew where I was I was flat on my face. Then a boot got me in the ribs and I was curled up by the stairfoot floor.

Somehow, mimicking my mother in front of my father hadn't upset *her* at all, not like when I'd done it for her alone. In fact she was amused now, so when the old man lashed out at me with the old one-two of fist and boot, she cried and railed in my defence, calling him all the cruel gets under the sun.

'You leave my son alone,' she shouted, 'you drunken bully. I'll get the police in next time you kick him like that. He's never done any harm to a living soul, and you've never treated him right, either.'

Father was baffled. He'd not liked me being disrespectful, he said, as if he'd been at church instead of a pub. I hadn't any right to mock her. As for him, he could stand it because it was only a bit of a joke, but he didn't like me doing it to her, the wife and mother of the house.

By this time I'd uncurled myself from the hedgehog position (I could imitate a hedgehog very well at times) and had seated myself at the table. I wasn't crying. A mimic soon learns to stop that sort of thing, otherwise he'd never do any mimicking at all. To get kicked was one of the risks you ran. And because I wasn't in tears, they soon made up their quarrel which, after all, had only started because of me. He put more coal on the fire, and she made him some fresh tea. When that was finished they talked and laughed, and she sat on his knee. Then they went upstairs together for a Sunday sleep, and I was left downstairs alone on the hearthrug wondering where I'd gone wrong. I didn't even have the energy to mimic a strong man booting the cat out of the way because things hadn't gone too well for him at work.

Some people believe that simplicity can only come out of madness, but who wants to go through madness in order to achieve the dubious advantage of becoming simple? Only a mimic can straddle these two states and so avoid being himself. That is to say, he finds a way of not searching for himself in order to avoid discovering that he has no self, and therefore does not exist. To see finally that there is nothing behind all the faces of one's existence is to find real madness. And what simplicity is there in that?

At school, I was the sort of person of whom the other boys asked: 'Is it going to rain today?' even though I looked nothing like a sage or weatherman. But the clouds or empty sky seemed to be on my side, and I was often right when I told them one thing or the other. It wasn't so much that I could guess the weather as that I'd take a chance on saying what I thought was going to happen. This comes easy to a mimic, because every person or object that he decides to imitate has a vein of risk in it.

In my young days it took a long while for me to realize that whenever I decided to mimic someone, and actually went through the process of doing so, I was filled with a deep interest in life and did no harm to anybody. But in between times I was remote and restless in turn, and liable to delve into all kinds of mischief. If I was not inspired for weeks to mimic, and at the same time found no opportunity otherwise to work off my bilious spirit by getting into trouble, then I took ill with some current letdown of the body such as pneumonia or mumps. My father and mother would have liked to have blasted me for the bother I gave them but after I had mimicked them successfully so early on they went out of my life for ever in any important way, and I took so little notice of their rage against me that many people and other members of my family began to look on me as a saint – until my next rampage.

One Christmas at school there was a fancy-dress party before breaking up for the holidays. I went as a moth, with two great wings and white powder all over me. Some came as musketeers and spacemen, but most appeared as nothing at all, simply wearing a badge, or hat. It was an old school, but there was a stage at one end of a big classroom. I received first prize, somebody else got second, and another boy third. The other two were told to get on the stage and act out what they were supposed to be. They did their best, then I went up.

A teacher put a candle on a low table, and I became a moth, weaving around it so that everybody stopped talking and looked. Maybe the teachers told them to be quiet. It was raining in the street, and perhaps being out of it and in the warmth made it easier for me to mimic a moth, with two wings and dry powder all over me. I went round and round the candle, my eyes half closed, and the flame hardly moving. I took the moth into me, and later heard that they began to laugh. I must have known this, yet didn't know it, at the time. But I went on circling the candle, and nobody thought to stop me, to break my spell and their spell.

If life is one long quest to avoid deciding what you are, I suddenly knew that I was a moth when one whole wing was touched off by the candle.

The flame came up suddenly and without smoke, but it wasn't as swift to others as it was to me, and before more than a slight scorch was done the flame was killed stone dead by two of the teachers.

Everybody thought that my days of mimicking were done for good. So did I, because on that occasion it seemed to have got out of control, and though I thought I might like such a thing to happen at some time in my life, I wasn't ready for it yet.

Before leaving that part of my life for ever (I still can't bring myself to call it childhood) I remember a photograph of me, that showed a big self-absorbed boy of thirteen. It was taken by an uncle, and then enlarged, and my mother had it framed and put on the sideboard in the parlour where nobody went and so hardly anybody, thank God, ever looked at it. I'd been out of her care and bother for a long time, but she'd taken to liking me again. It made no difference, because once a decision is taken through a failure to mimic, nothing can alter it. Maybe I reminded her of my father who had long since gone and given place to another person, and who she still in some way liked. But I'd never mimic him for her, even so, though I could have done it so that the house would have crowed around us.

This photo seemed to have no connection with me, but everybody swore that it had, and that there couldn't be a better one. In my heart I'd come to the age where I wanted to please them, so I decided I must mimic that photo so as to become like the image on it. It wasn't long before I saw that such a thing was not feasible. If you don't know what you are, how is it possible to imitate yourself? This was the issue that burned me. I could not imitate something that had no life, not even myself if I didn't have any. And certainly judging by the photo there was no life there whatever. That was what everyone liked about it, my mother most of all, who stuck it on the sideboard in what was to her the place of honour.

Nevertheless, I looked at that photo for a long time, since other people had given it so much meaning. It was there for the world to see, above all, those who close their hearts and say: Know thyself. But I say: Get me a mirror, and according to the antics performed in it you can then (if you have that sort of desire) know everybody in the world.

But a photograph is not a mirror. You do not even see yourself as others see you. For a moment I almost went into the spirit of that photograph, but pulled myself back in time. That would have been evil. I preferred not to know what I was. There was almost triumph in that decision. If I don't know what I am, nobody can know, not even God. And if God doesn't know, then there is no God.

Rather than mimic the photograph of myself and believe in God I decided that I'd sooner be a moth.

Being such a good mimic I couldn't hold down any job for long. Sooner or later the foreman was bound to turn up when I was doing an imitation of him before all my mates. I worked harder than most though because I was so self-absorbed that nothing was too difficult or arduous for me. It was always with great regret that I was sacked.

On the other hand, all women love a mimic, except the mimic's mother, who ceases to matter by the time he becomes interested in other women. If you want to get off with a woman all you have to do is talk. Let the steamroller roll, and talk, talk, talk. Flatter her if you must, but the main thing is to talk. No woman can resist a constant stream of fulsome talk, no matter how inane and irrelevant, as long as you keep it up and make her laugh. Even if she laughs at you, it doesn't matter. By that time she's softening, you can bet.

And a mimic, even if he's so much speechless putty when left alone with himself, can mimic a funny and talkative man when the need arises. Of course, when the girl falls in love she never gets what she thinks she is getting. But then, who does? There is much wisdom in the world. Certain basic rules were formulated for me by Sam England who worked in the plywood factory where I took my first job. Never, he said, marry a girl who hates her mother, because sooner or later she will start to hate you. He also added that if you want to know what your girl-friend is going to look like in thirty years' time, look at her mother now. And if you want to know what your girl-friend expects you to look like in *ten* years' time, look at her father.

Whenever I met a girl I had to decide, by her face and talk, and the sort of home she came from, what sort of a person she'd like me to be. There weren't many girls who could ever put up with a strong silent type for the first three dates while he weighed up the situation. But after that I fell into the slot, and the talk began, the endless jokes and self-revelations that come from anyone no matter what sort he is.

If I wanted to get rid of a girl, I made an abrupt change of character.

None of them could stand this. They thought I had either gone mad, or lost my respect for them. In the soiled territory of the heart the precise configuration of the land only comes with continual and intense familiarity.

One girl I could not get rid of. I changed character no less than five times, but she wouldn't go away, so there was nothing I could do except marry her.

If there's one thing I've always found it hard to mimic it's a happy man. I've often been happy, but that was no help when I was indifferent and wanted to let someone else see that I was full of the joy of life. I knew that I had to overcome this problem and prayed that on this vital issue my talent for mimicry would not let me down.

In the very act of getting married, in order to appear happy to the girl I was to live with, I had to behave like a fool. When I should have slipped the ring on her finger I put it on mine – then on to hers. When we were declared married I attempted to kiss the best man, a fellow clerk from an office I was then working at. He fought free and pleaded with me not to be bloody silly, so then I kissed the bride, and apologized to everyone later by saying I'd been too happy to know what I was doing. They believed this, and forgave me, and I loved them so much I could have mimicked them all, one after another to the end of time.

When I changed for the sixth time it was only to mimic a man getting married. That was the one character she couldn't stand, and by the time I had come to believe in the act, and had almost grown to like it, it was the one finally by which I got rid of her. When we parted six months later I did a very tolerable job of mimicking an amicable man, who had taken one step wrong in life and wanted to go two steps back. She went home to her parents, and took the television set among all her cases in the second run of the taxi. We had always made love in the most perfect way, because I'd had enough experience to mimic that like a stallion, but it had made no difference to our final feeling for each other. She'd never been able to get through to the real me, no more than I had. And after a year of trying she imagined she never would, and I couldn't help but admire her promptitude in getting out as quickly as she did.

This is not a tale of love, or the wail of a broken marriage, or a moan about impossible human relationships. I won't dwell long on any of that.

I can go on for years telling you what all this is *not*. It'll be up to you to tell me what it is.

Ambition has never been strong in my veins. To be ambitious you have first to know what you are. Either that, or you do not have to be concerned with what you are. My talent for mimicry was an end in itself. If I could observe someone, I thought in the early days, and then become exactly the same, why should I go through years of work to accomplish it in the reality of society?

I had never any intention of working, but what society demands of you is in fact what life itself wants. So you must imitate it – instead of allowing your soul to be destroyed by believing in it. As soon as you accept something, and cease to play a role regarding it, you are done for. Your soul is in danger. You have even less chance then of ever getting to know the real nature of yourself.

The same must be with everything you are called upon to do in life, whatever action, whether it lasts a minute or a year. Mimic it, I told myself at times of danger when caught by a suspicious joy of life I was about to acquiesce to. The successful mimic is he who not only takes on a role completely so that everyone is deceived, but actually from a distance sees himself with his own eyes doing it so that he himself is never deceived. I only learned to do this later, probably after I broke up with my first wife.

One might imagine that if the main thing in life was the survival of the fittest, then one as a mimic would be wise to imitate and continue to imitate one of the fittest. But not only would that be boring, it would be inhuman, and above all foolish. We know that it is not the fittest who survive, but the wise. The wise die, but the fittest perish, and they perish early on from having settled on to one role in life. They have determined to keep it to the very end, and also to defend it to the death against those who would try to show them that the world is richer than they have made it.

It is the easiest thing in the world for me to recognize those who believe in the survival of the fittest, which means most people. It is, conversely, difficult for me to meet another person like myself, because there are so few of us.

But I once met a woman who was also a mimic. What I could never understand was why those qualities that I had, made people trust and love me, especially women. If to mimic is to betray (which it certainly is) then you would expect to be generally disliked, but strangely enough it was more often the opposite. She said exactly the same thing, except that it was especially men who loved and trusted her.

A friend of mine from the insurance office where I worked was getting married, and I met her at the reception for it. She was a thin green-eyed girl from the tobacco factory, and I listened to her during the meal mimicking the parson, for she had also been at the church. As a lesser friend of the bride's she was assigned to a more remote table, and I happened to be passing on my way back from the lavatory, where I had mimicked a disgusted man and thrown up what food I'd already eaten.

The people around her didn't know whether to be amused or offended. I was merely interested. Her face lost its pallor and grew weightier with the sombre voice she put on. She had great range of tone, and as she went through the service I took the part of bridegroom. Instead of saying 'I will,' at the correct moment, I said: 'I'm damned if I will,' and the two nearest tables joined in the applause.

The actual bride, as this went on, shook at the mouth and dropped tears on to her cheeks. The best man and the bridegroom demanded that we pack it in, but some devil was in us both, and our duet went on as if we were in the middle of a field with no audience at all. There was silence for a few minutes before the uproar. A pair of fine mimics had met, an accident of two stars clashing in interstellar space, and nothing could stop us getting to the end of the act.

The last word was with the best man. I suppose the bridegroom was saving himself for the first night. He only nodded in despair, knowing that it couldn't end in any other way. When the man hit me I pulled two chairs over and half dragged the tablecloth on to the floor. I sprang up and, mimicking an outraged partygoer whose best piece was being unjustly spat on, punched him right over the table, where his head spliced down through the four-tier cake.

The bride screamed as if her husband had been killed. I'd had enough. Grabbing the slender fingers of my fellow mimic I ran out of that doom-laden party for all I was worth, wondering how long the marriage would last after such an inauspicious beginning.

*

Our association was interesting, but disastrous from the start. We didn't live together, but shared each other's rooms. For a few months it was champagne and roses. Coming back to one of the rooms from our respective jobs we would eat a supper (imitating each other's mastication all the way through), then we would dare each other to mimic certain characters, such as an airline pilot, a policewoman, an insurance man, girl shop assistant. We played with each other, tested each other, acted God and the Devil with the deepest penetrable parts of our hearts and souls. We mimicked each other mimicking each other. We mimicked each other mimicking people we both knew. We mimicked the same person to see who could do it best. When we emptied each other we made love, and it came marvellously on such occasions. We thought we had come to the end of the road, gone over the cliff hand in hand like a couple of Gadarene swine and found we had landed in paradise.

But to think such things only means that the road is about to enter a swamp. I wanted her to marry me, but it turned out she was already married. So was I. Her husband knocked on my door one Sunday afternoon, and what could I do but ask him in? He was a van driver of thirty, but with his sweater and quiff he looked seventeen. He appeared stupid and sensitive, a not uncommon combination. 'I know you're living with him,' he said, 'but I've come to ask you to come back and live with me. That's why I've come.'

I stood up and made a quiff in my hair, threw off my jacket, and pulled the sweater down. Then I repeated his speech in exactly the same voice. It's dangerous mimicking simple people, but I couldn't resist. He must have gone through all the possible situations that could arise before he knocked at my door, but this wasn't one of them. He looked horror-struck, and leaned against the outside door. At this, Jean, who'd said nothing so far, got up and stretched her spine against the door to the kitchen with exactly the same expression.

'What's going on?' he demanded.

'What's going on?' I mimicked.

He lifted his fist as if about to fly through the room and crash against me. Jean lifted her fist and prepared to spring in exactly the same way. They would have collided and died in an apotheosis of glorious mimicry.

He turned to the door and opened it. Jean pulled at the kitchen door. We heard him running downstairs, and he never came back.

I passed him a few months later as I was walking through town. A girl was with him, and he didn't notice me in my misery. But I saw him all right because I hadn't seen anyone so obviously happy for a long time.

I followed Jean from the factory one night, and she met another man.

She'd been seeing me less and less. I'd expected it, but because we couldn't live together, could only exist like two cripples, taking turns to hold each other up, I was struck by jealousy as if a javelin had shuddered deep between my shoulder blades.

When two vampires meet, they meet for ever, until another comes to set them free. But freedom is painful, for a while. For a mimic who doesn't believe in it, it can be catastrophic.

I rang the bell of his flat one Sunday morning. As he opened the door Jean made a good imitation of the ringing noise. I saw that I was in for a bad time. Think of what situation you want from the bottom of your soul to avoid, and when you have decided what it is, consider what you'll do when it comes about.

He was grinning by the window, and Jean actually offered me a cup of tea. While she was giving it to me I could see her imitating her actions. She had learned a lot, and I wondered where. I never knew his name. To the world he was an ordinary chap in some trade or other, but to me I saw he was trying to mimic something and I didn't know what it was. I was puzzled, but sat and drank my tea.

I asked Jean how she was, but she only smiled, and didn't seem to know. I wondered if she was happy, and could only say that she was. I knew that if I asked direct questions they would combine to defeat me in mimicry, and I had no wish to bring on to myself what Jean and I had poured on to her husband. They knew this. He stayed by the window, grinning, and I withered under the stare that went with it. Nevertheless I looked up at him from time to time. His face seemed a shade paler and thinner. I would fight on my own ground, in other words get up and go – but not before I could see what he was imitating.

But the stare grew ashen and luminous, especially after I had nothing left to say. I stood up and made for the door, but Jean blocked it. Where had she met such a person?

'I'm going,' I said calmly. A mimic cannot give up the ground he stands on, without knowing that another piece of land is waiting for him. Here, I was isolated, and the ocean was wide. It wasn't an honour to be defeated at this moment, but it was essential to me as a man. In defeat one can begin to know what one is, in victory – never. 'Get out of my way.'

Behind my back I heard: 'I'm going. Get out of my way' – in my own voice exactly.

'Guess what he's mimicking?' she said.

Without turning around I saw reflected in her eyes the sky-blue bones of his skull head, and the fixed grin of the victory I'd been forced to give him.

I mimicked her: 'Guess what he's mimicking?' and didn't give her time to answer. 'A corpse,' I said, forcing her gently aside, opening the door, and walking away.

Between bouts of mimicking one person and another, my entity becomes blank. To be able to mimic someone I had to like them. That was the first rule, just as, in the reverse sense, in order to love someone you have to be able to mimic them. When I mimicked people now, they ceased to like me, if they had ever done so. But then, treachery always begins with a kiss. For these reasons I had found it impossible to imitate God, and not only because I'd never seen Him.

Later, in my isolation, I only mimicked people to myself instead of out loud or for the benefit of others. Don't force the pace. This isn't a story. Switch off if you're not with me. I'll go on as long as you can, if not longer. I've had everything: booze, pot, shock, solitary. Yet though I may be sane, and a mimic of the world, can I imitate Mr Sand or Mr Water, Mr Cloud or Mr Sky with sufficient conviction to become all of them rolled into one realistic and convincing ball?

I mimic myself trying to mimic myself when I don't know who I am or what my real self is. I sit on my own in a pub laughing inwardly because I am more king of the world than anyone else. I see faces around me both troubled and serene, and don't know which one to choose for the great grand mimic of the night. I give up trying to mimic myself, and choose a man talking earnestly to his wife. I stand in the middle of the floor. Everything is clear and steady, but no one looks at me. I talk as if the man's wife were standing two inches from my face, grinning at the jokes I'm (he's) obviously making, then looking slow-eyed and glum when she mentions the children. Somebody pushes by with an empty glass as if I don't exist. I pull him back and he knocks me down. I do exist. I live, and smile on the floor before getting up. But only he notices me, and does so no more as his glass is filled and he steps by me back to his table. It is quite a disturbance, but they don't even call the police.

Was Jean's new man mimicking himself, or was it me? I shall never know. But I would not see her again, even though she might want to take up with me. She'd been in contact with evil, and the evil had rubbed off on to her. Some of it in that short time had jumped to me and I was already trying to fight free of it.

When I was mimicking someone I was walking parallel with the frontiers of madness. When I did it marvellously well, the greater was the drop of madness below me. But I didn't know this. I was driven to mimicry by threat and fear of madness. For some months I totally lost the skill to mimic, and that's why I got a note from my doctor and presented myself at the door of the local head-hospital. They welcomed me with open arms, and I was able to begin making notes from the seven millionth bed.

I did well there, announced to all assembled that I was now going to put on a show of mimicking Doctor So-and-so, and what to me was a brilliant act for them turned out to be perfectly still flesh and a blank stare from a person who was me in the middle of the room.

I had to start again, from the beginning. In order to imitate a sneeze I was thrown on to the floor by the force of it. I turned into a dog down one side of my face, and a moth on the other.

As I came up from the pit I started to write these notes. I have written them out five times already, and on each occasion they have been snatched from me by the attendant and burned. While I write I am quiet; when I stop, I rave. That is why they are taken from me.

II

I didn't stay long: it took me two years to recover. To imitate was like learning to speak again. But my soul was filled with iron, and I went on and on. The whole world was inside of me, and on any stage I chose

I performed my masterpiece of mimicry. These were merely rehearsals for when I actually figured as the same person over and over again, a calm, precise, reasonable man who bore no relation to the real me seething like a malt-vat inside. The select audience appreciated my effort. I don't think anything was lost on them, except perhaps the truth.

No one can mimic time and make it go away, as one can sometimes make friends and enemies alike disappear when you mimic them. I had to sit with time, feed it my bones in daylight and darkness.

This great creation of mine, that I dredged up so painfully from the bottom of my soul, was someone I'd sidestepped from birth. I breathed life in him, a task as hard as if he were a stone, yet I had to perfect him and make him live, because in the looney bin I realized the trap I'd walked into.

I made a successful imitation of a sane man, and then they let me out. It felt like the greatest day of my life. I do not think my performance could have been better than it was.

An insane man can vanish like a fish in water, and hide anywhere. I am not insane, and it was never my intention to become so. But one is forced to mimic to perfection a sane man so as to become free, and what greater insanity is there than that? Yet it widens the horizons of the heart, which is no bad thing for someone who was born a mimic.

Years have passed, and in my pursuit and mimicry of sanity I have become the assistant manager of a large office. I am thirty-five years of age, and never married again. I took some winter leave and went to Switzerland. Don't ask me why – that means you, the one I'm imitating, and you, who I am not. I planned the space off work and set off for London with my pocket full of traveller's cheques and a passport. In my rucksack was a hammock, nylon groundsheet, blanket, tobacco, matches, soap, toothpaste, toothbrush, compass, a book, notebook, and pencils. That's all. I don't remember where I got such a list from but I did, and stuck to it religiously. I was determined that every action from now on should have some meaning, just as in the past every time I had ever mimicked anyone had also had some important significance. One cannot live in the world of chance. If fate will not act for you, then take it by the neck.

It was so cold I thought my head would break like an old teapot, but as I walked away from the lake and along the narrow road between banks of trees I got used to it. The walls of the mountains on either side were so steep it seemed that if anybody were foolhardy enough to climb up they would fall off and down – unless they were a fly. Perhaps I could mimic a fly, since already in the cold I had conjured a burning stove into my belly. A car passed and offered me a lift. I waved it on.

It was getting dark by five, and there wasn't much snow to be seen, a large sheet of luminous basilisk blue overhead, and behind me to the south a map-patch of dying fluorescent pink. The air was pure, you could certainly say that for it. The sun must have given the valley an hour each day, then a last wink before it vanished on its way to America.

There was snow underfoot, at certain higher places off the road, good clean snow that you could eat with honey on it. I could not see such snow and fading sun without death coming into my heart, the off-white powder humps in the dusk thrown between rock and tree-boles, flecked among the grey and scattered rooftops of a village I was coming to.

Bells were sounding from the church, a leisurely mellow music coming across the snow, so welcoming that they made me think that maybe I had had a childhood after all. I walked up the steep narrow lanes, slipping on the snow hardened into beds of ice. No one was about, though lights were in the windows of dark wooden houses.

Along one lane was a larger building of plain brick, and I went inside for something to eat. A girl stood by the counter, and said good evening in Italian. I took off my pack and overcoat, and she pointed to tables set in the room behind.

They did not ask me what I wanted but brought soup, then roast meat, bread, and cabbage. I gave in my passport, intending to stay the night. A woman walked in, tall, blonde, rawboned, and blue-eyed. She sat at another table, and fed half her meal to the cat. After my long trek from the railway station (stopping only in the town to buy a map) I was starving, and had eyes for nothing but my food. The first part of the walk was agony. I creaked like an old man, but now, in spite of my exhaustion, I felt I could walk on through the night.

I did not sleep well. In dreams I began to feel myself leaving the world. My hand was small and made of copper, tiny (like hammers that broke toffee when I was a child), and I placed it on my head that was immense and made of concrete, solid, but that suddenly started to get smaller. This was beginning to be an actual physical state, so I opened my eyes to fight it off. If I didn't I saw myself being pressed and squeezed into extinction, out of the world. It didn't seem as if I would go mad (nothing is that simple) but that I would be killed by this attrition of total insecurity. It seemed as if the earth were about to turn into concrete and roll over my body.

I got out of bed and dressed. The air in the room, which had firmly shut double windows and radiators, was stifling. When you think you're going mad it's a sign you're getting over it. The faces of everyone I'd ever mimicked or made love to fell to pieces in turn like a breaking jigsaw puzzle.

My boots bit into the snow as I closed the door behind. It wasn't yet midnight. There was a distinct ring around the full and brilliant moon. There was snow on the mountain sides, and it seemed as if just over the line of their crests a neon light was shining. I walked along the lanes of the village, in the scorching frosty cold.

To question why one is alive means that one is only half a person, but to be a whole person is to be half dead.

Sun was shining over the snow next morning as I sat by the window drinking coffee. I was near the head of the valley, and the mountain slopes opened out. Most of it was sombre forest with occasional outcrops of rock, but to the west, at a place shone on directly by the sun, I could see green space. Then nothing but rock and snow, and blue sky. My eyes were always good. I never needed glasses or binoculars, and just above the meadow before the trees began was a small hut. No smoke came from it.

I paid my bill, collected my pack, and said good-bye. At the road a cow had been hit by a car and lay dying. The car's headlamp was shattered and the animal lay in a pool of blood, moving its hoofs slightly. A group of people stood around, and the driver was showing his papers. Another man rested a notebook on the car-top to write. It was all very orderly. I pushed through and looked into the eyes of the dying animal. It did not understand. As a last gesture it bellowed, but no one was interested in it, because the end was certain. No one even heard it, I was sure. The damson eyes were full of the non-comprehension of understanding.

The mountains were reflected in one, and the village in the other – or so it seemed as I paced back and forth. Another bellow sounded, even after it was dead, and when all the people looked at me at last to make sure that the noise was coming from me and not out of the sky, I walked on alone up the road, away from the spoiled territory of the heart, and the soiled landscape of the soul.

I am wild. If I lift up my eyes to the hills a child cries. A child crying makes me sad. A baby crying puts me into a rage against it. I imagine everything. If I go into the hills and sit there, birds sing. They are made of frost, like the flowers. Insanity means freedom, nothing else. Tell me how to live and I'll be dangerous. If I find out for myself I'll die of boredom afterwards. When I look along the valley and then up it seems as if the sky is coming into land. The mountains look as tall as if they are about to walk over me. If they want to, let them. I shall not be afraid.

The wind is fresh except when it blows smoke into my face. I build a fire by the hut, boil water on it for tea. The wind is increasing, and I don't like the look of the weather.

The hut is sheltered, and when I came to it I found as if by instinct a key just under the roof. There's nothing inside, but the floor is clean, and I have my hammock as well as food. When it is dark it seems as if the wind has been moaning and prowling for days, plying its claws into every interstice of the nerves. I wanted to get out and go after it, climb the escarpment above the treeline with a knife between my teeth, and fight on the high plateau in the light of the moon, corner that diabolic wind and stab it to death, tip his carcass over the nearest cliff.

I cannot mimic either Jack Frost or a windkiller. It's too dark, pit-shadows surround me, but there's no fear because outside in the mountains the whole fresh world stretches, waiting for children like me to get up in the morning, to go out into it and be born again.

I have finished with mimicking. I always thought the time would come, but could never imagine when or where. I cannot get into anyone any more and mimic them. I am too far into myself at last, for better or worse, good or bad, till death do me part.

One man will go down into the daylight. In loneliness and darkness I am one man: a spark shot out of the blackest pitch of night and found its way to my centre.

A crowd of phantoms followed me up, and I collected them together in this black-aired hut, tamed them and tied them down, dogs, moths, mothers, and wives. Having arrived at the cliff-face of the present there's little else to say. When my store of food is finished I'll descend the mountainside and go back to the inn, where I'll think some more as I sit drinking coffee by the window, watching the snow or sunshine. I'll meet again the tall, blonde, rawboned, blue-eyed woman who fed half her meal to the cat – before setting off on my travels. Don't ask me where, or who with.

V. S. PRITCHETT

The Camberwell Beauty

August's? On the Bath Road? Twice-Five August – of course I knew August: ivory man. And the woman who lived with him – her name was Price. She's dead. He went out of business years ago. He's probably dead too. I was in the trade only three or four years but I soon knew every antique dealer in the South of England. I used to go to all the sales. Name another. Naseley of Close Place? Jades, Asiatics, never touched India; Alsop of Ramsey? Ephemera. Marbright, High Street, Boxley? Georgian silver. Fox? Are you referring to Fox of Denton or Fox of Camden – William Morris, art nouveau – or the Fox Brothers in the Portobello Road, the eldest stuttered? They had an uncle in Brighton who went mad looking for old Waterford. Hindmith? No, he was just a copier. Ah now, Pliny! He was a very different cup of tea: Caughley ware. (Coalport took it over in 1821.) I am speaking of specialities; furniture is the bread and butter of the trade. It keeps a man going while his mind is on his speciality and within that speciality there is one object he broods on from one year to the next, most of his life; the thing a man would commit murder to get his hands on if he had the nerve, but I have never heard of a dealer who had; theft perhaps. A stagnant lot. But if he does get hold of that thing he will never let it go or certainly not to a customer – dealers only really like dealing among themselves – but every other dealer in the trade knows he's got it. So they sit in their shops reading the catalogues and watching one another. Fox broods on something Alsop has. Alsop has his eye on Pliny and Pliny puts a hand to one of his big red ears when he hears the name of August. At the heart of the trade is lust but a lust that is a dream paralysed by itself. So paralysed that the only release, the only hope, as everyone knows, is disaster; a bankruptcy, a divorce, a court case, a burglary, trouble with the police, a death. Perhaps then the grip on some piece of treasure will weaken and fall into the watcher's hands and even if it goes elsewhere he will go on dreaming about it.

What was it that Pliny, Gentleman Pliny, wanted of a man like August who was not much better than a country junk dealer? When I opened up in London I thought it was a particular Staffordshire figure, but Pliny was far above that. These figures fetch very little though one or two are hard to find: The Burning of Cranmer, for example. Very few were made; it never sold and the firm dropped it. I was young and eager and one day when a collector, a scholarly man, as dry as a stick, came to my shop and told me he had a complete collection except for this piece, I said in my innocent way: 'You've come to the right man. I'm fairly certain I can get it for you – at a price.' This was a lie; but I was astonished to see the old man look at me with contempt, then light up like a fire and when he left, look back furtively at me; he had betrayed his lust.

You rarely see an antique shop standing on its own. There are usually three or four together watching one another: I asked the advice of the man next door who ran a small boatyard on the canal in his spare time and he said, 'Try Pliny down the Green: he knows everyone.' I went 'over the water', to Pliny; he was closed but I did find him at last in a sale-room. Pliny was marking his catalogue and waiting for the next lot to come up and he said to me in a scornful way, slapping a young man down, 'August's got it.' I saw him wink at the man next to him as I left.

I had bought myself a fast red car that annoyed the older dealers and I drove down the other side of Newbury on the Bath Road. August's was one of four little shops opposite the Lion Hotel on the main road at the end of the town where the country begins and there I got my first lesson. The place was closed. I went across to the bar of the hotel and August was there, a fat man of sixty in wide trousers and a drip to his nose who was paying for drinks from a bunch of dirty notes in his jacket pocket and dropping them on the floor. He was drunk and very offended when I picked a couple up and gave them to him. He'd just come back from Newbury races. I humoured him but he kept rolling about and turning his back to me half the time and so I blurted out:

'I've just been over at the shop. You've got some Staffordshire I hear.'

He stood still and looked me up and down and the beer swelled in him.

'Who may you be?' he said with all the pomposity of drink. I told him. I said right out, 'Staffordshire. Cranmer's Burning.' His face went dead and the colour of liver.

'So is London,' he said and turned away to the bar.

'I'm told you might have it. I've got a collector,' I said.

'Give this lad a glass of water,' said August to the barmaid. 'He's on fire.'

There is nothing more to say about the evening or the many other visits I made to August except that it has a moral to it and that I had to help August over to his shop where an enormous woman much taller than he in a black dress and a little girl of fourteen or so were at the door waiting for him. The girl looked frightened and ran a few yards from the door as August and his woman collided belly to belly.

'Come back,' called the woman.

The child crept back. And to me the woman said, 'We're closed,' and having got the two inside, shut the door in my face.

The moral is this: if The Burning of Cranmer was August's treasure, it was hopeless to try and get it before he had time to guess what mine was. It was clear to him I was too new to the trade to have one. And, in fact, I don't think he had the piece. Years later, I found my collector had left his collection complete to a private museum in Leicester when he died. He had obtained what he craved, a small immortality in being memorable for his relation to a minor work of art.

I know what happened at August's that night. In time his woman, Mrs Price, bellowed it to me, for her confidences could be heard down the street. August flopped on his bed and while he was sleeping off the drink she got the bundles of notes out of his pockets and counted them. She always did this after his racing days. If he had lost she woke him up and shouted at him; if he had made a profit she kept quiet and hid it under her clothes in a chest of drawers. I went down from London again and again but August was not there.

Most of the time these shops are closed. You rattle the door handle; no reply. Look through the window and each object inside stands gleaming with something like a smile of malice, especially on plates and glass; the furniture states placidly that it has been in better houses than you will ever have, the silver speaks of vanished servants. It speaks of the dead hands that have touched it; even the dust is the dust of families that have gone. In the shabby places – and August's was shabby – the dealer is like a toadstool that has grown out of the debris. There was only one attractive object in August's shop – as I say – he went in for ivories and on a table at the back was a set of white and red chessmen set out on a board partly concealed by a screen. I was tapping my feet impatiently looking through the window when I was astonished to see two of the chessmen had moved; then I saw a hand, a long thin work-reddened hand appear from behind the screen and move one of the pieces back. Life in the place! I rattled the door handle again and the child came from behind the screen. She had a head loaded with heavy black hair to her shoulders and a white heart-shaped face and wore a skimpy dress with small pink flowers on it. She was so thin that she looked as if she would blow away in fright out of the place, but instead, pausing on tiptoe, she swallowed with appetite; her sharp eyes had seen my red car outside the place. She looked back cautiously at the inner door of the shop and then ran to unlock the shop door. I went in.

'What are you up to?' I said. 'Playing chess?'

'I'm teaching my children,' she said, putting up her chin like a child of five. 'Do you want to buy something?'

At once Mrs Price was there shouting:

'Isabel. I told you not to open the door. Go back into the room.'

Mrs Price went to the chessboard and put the pieces back in their places.

'She's a child,' said Mrs Price, accusing me.

And when she said this Mrs Price blew herself out to a larger size and then her sullen face went blank and babyish as if she had travelled out of herself for a beautiful moment. Then her brows levelled and she became sullen again.

'Mr August's out,' she said.

'It is about a piece of Staffordshire,' I said. 'He mentioned it to me. When will he be in?'

'He's in and out. No good asking. He doesn't know himself.'

'I'll try again.'

'If you like.'

There was nothing to be got out of Mrs Price.

In my opinion, the antique trade is not one for a woman, unless she is on her own. Give a woman a shop and she wants to sell something; even that little girl at August's wanted to sell. It's instinct. It's an excitement. Mrs Price – August's woman – was living with a man exactly like the others in the trade: he hated customers and hated parting with anything. By middle age these women have dead blank faces, they look with resentment and indifference at what is choking their shops; their eyes go smaller and smaller as the chances of getting rid of it became rarer and rarer and they are defeated. Kept out of the deals their husbands have among themselves, they see even their natural love of intrigue frustrated. This was the case of Mrs Price who must have been handsome in a big-boned way when she was young, but who had swollen into a drudge. What allured the men did not allure her at all. It is a trade that feeds illusions. If you go after Georgian silver you catch the illusion, while you are bidding, that you are related to the rich families who owned it. You acquire imaginary ancestors. Or, like Pliny with a piece of Meissen he was said to keep hidden somewhere – you drift into German history and become a secret curator of the Victoria and Albert museum – a place he often visited. August's lust for 'the ivories' gave to his horse-racing mind a private oriental side; he dreamed of rajahs, sultans, harems and lavish gamblers which, in a man as vulgar as he was, came out, in sad reality, as a taste for country girls and the company of bookies. Illusions lead to furtiveness in every-day life and to sudden temptations; the trade is close to larceny, to situations where you don't ask where something has come from, especially for a man like August whose dreams had landed him in low company. He had started at the bottom and very early he 'received' and got twelve months for it. This frightened him. He took up with Mrs Price and though he resented it she had made a fairly honest man of him. August was to be *her* work of art.

But he did not make an honest woman of her. No one disapproved of this except herself. Her very size, growing year by year, was an assertion of virtue. Everyone took her side in her public quarrels with him. And as if to make herself more respectable, she had taken in her sister's little girl when the sister died; the mother had been in Music Hall. Mrs Price petted and prinked the little thing. When August became a failure as a work of art, Mrs Price turned to the child. Even August was charmed by her when she jumped on his knee and danced about showing him her new clothes. A little actress, as everyone said, exquisite.

It took me a long time to give up the belief that August had the Cranmer piece – and as I know now, he hadn't got it; but at last I did see I was wasting my time and settled in to the routine of the business. I sometimes saw August at country sales and at one outside Marlborough something ridiculous happened. It was a big sale and went on till late in the afternoon and he had been drinking. After lunch the auctioneer had put up a china cabinet and the bidding was strong. Some outsider was bidding against the dealers, a thing that made them close their faces with moral indignation; the instinctive hatred of customers united them. Drink always stirred August morally; he was a rather despised figure and he was, I suppose, determined to speak for all. He entered the bidding. Up went the price: 50, 5, 60, 5, 70, 5, 80, 5, 90. The outsiders were a young couple with a dog.

'Ninety, ninety,' called the auctioneer.

August could not stand it. 'Twice-Five,' he shouted.

There is not much full-throated laughter at sales; it is usually shoppish and dusty. But the crowd in this room looked round at August and shouted with a laughter that burst the gloom of trade. He was put out for a second and then saw his excitement had made him famous. The laughter went on; the wonder had for a whole minute stopped the sale. 'Twice-five!' He was slapped on the back. At sixty-four the man who had never had a nick-name had been christened. He looked around him. I saw a smile cross his face and double the pomposity that beer had put into him and he redoubled it that evening at the nearest pub. I went off to my car and Alsop of Ramsey, the ephemera man who had picked up some Victorian programmes, followed me and said out of the side of his mouth:

'More trouble tonight at August's.'

And then to change the subject and speaking for every dealer south of the Trent, he offered serious news.

'Pliny's mother's dead – Pliny of the Green.'

The voice had all the shifty meaning of the trade. I was too simple to grasp the force of this confidence. It surprised me in the following weeks to hear people repeat the news: 'Pliny's mother's dead' in so many voices, from the loving memory and deepest sympathy manner as much suited to old clothes, old furniture and human beings indiscriminately, to the flat statement that an event of business importance had occurred in my eventless trade. I was in it for the money and so, I suppose, were all the rest – how else could they live? – but I seemed to be surrounded by a dreamy freemasonry, who thought of it in a different secretive way.

On a wet morning the following spring I was passing through Salisbury on market day and stopped in the square to see if there was anything worth picking up at the stalls there. It was mostly junk but I did find a pretty Victorian teapot – no mark, I agree – with a chip in the spout for a few shillings because the fever of the trade never quite leaves one even on dull days. (I sold the pot five years later for £8 when the prices started to go mad.) I went into one of the pubs in the square, I forget its name, and I was surprised to see Marbright and Alsop there and, sitting near the window, Mrs Price. August was getting drinks at the bar.

Alsop said to me:

'Pliny's here. I passed him a minute ago.'

Marbright said: 'He was standing in Woolworth's doorway. I asked him to come and have one, but he wouldn't.'

'It's hit him hard his mother going,' Marbright said. 'What's he doing here? Queen Mary's dead.'

It was an old joke that Gentleman Pliny had never been the same since the old Queen had come to his shop some time back – everyone knew what she was for picking up things. He only opened on Sundays now and a wealthy crowd came there in their big cars – a new trend as Alsop said. August brought the drinks and stood near, for Mrs Price spread herself on the bench and never left much room for anyone else to sit down. He looked restless and glum.

'Where will Pliny be without his mother,' Mrs Price moaned into her glass and, putting it down, glowered at August. She had been drinking a good deal.

August ignored her and said, sneering:

'He kept her locked up.'

There is always a lot of talking about 'locking up' in the trade; people's minds go to their keys.

'It was kindness,' Mrs Price said, 'after the burglars got in at Sampson's, three men in a van loading it up in broad daylight. Any woman of her age would be frightened.'

'It was nothing to do with the burglary,' said August, always sensitive when crime was mentioned. 'She was getting soft in the head. He caught her giving his stuff away when she was left on her own. She was past it.'

Mrs Price was a woman who didn't like to be contradicted.

'He's a gentleman,' said Mrs Price, accusing August. 'He was good to his mother. He took her out every Sunday night of his life. She liked a glass of stout on Sundays.'

This was true, though Mrs Price had not been to London for years and had never seen this event; but all agreed. We live on myths.

'It was her kidneys,' moaned Mrs Price. One outsize woman was mourning another, seeing a fate.

'I suppose that's why he didn't get married, looking after her,' said Marbright.

'Pliny! Get married! Don't make me laugh,' said August with a defiant recklessness that seemed to surprise even himself. 'The last Saturday in every month like a clock striking he was round the pubs in Brixton with old Lal Drake.'

And now, as if frightened by what he said, he swanked his way out of the side door of the pub on his way to the Gents.

We lowered our eyes. There are myths, but there are facts. They all knew – even I had heard – that what August said was true, but it was not a thing a sensible man would say in front of Mrs Price. And – mind you – Pliny standing a few doors down the street. But Mrs Price stayed calm among the thoughts in her mind.

'That's a lie,' she said peacefully as we thought, though she was eyeing the door waiting for August to come back.

'I knew his father,' said Alsop.

We were soon laughing about the ancient Pliny, the Bermondsey boy who began with a barrow shouting 'Old Iron' in the streets, a man who never drank, never had a bank account – didn't trust banks – who belted his son while his mother 'educated him up' – she was a tall woman and the boy grew up like her, tall with a long arching nose and those big red ears that looked as though his parents had pulled him now this way now that in their fight over him. She had been a housekeeper in a big house and she had made a son who looked like an old family butler, Cockney to the bone, but almost a gentleman. Except, as Alsop said, his way of blowing his nose like a foghorn on the Thames, but sharp as his father. Marbright said you could see the father's life in the store at the back of the shop; it was piled high with what had made the father's money, every kind of old-fashioned stuff.

'Enough to furnish two or three hotels,' Alsop said. Mrs Price nodded.

'Wardrobes, tables . . .' she said.

'A museum,' said Marbright. 'Helmets, swords. Two four-posters the last time I was there.'

'Ironwork. Brass,' nodded Mrs Price mournfully.

'Must date back to the Crimean War,' said Marbright.

'And it was all left to Pliny.'

There was a general sigh.

'And he doesn't touch it. Rubbish he calls it. He turned his back on it. Only goes in for the best. Hepplewhite, marquetries, his consoles. Regency.'

There was a pause.

'And,' I said, 'his Meissen.'

They looked at me as if I were a criminal. They glanced at one another as if asking whether they should call the police. I was either a thief or I had publicly stripped them of all their clothes. I had publicly announced Pliny's lust.

Although Mrs Price had joined in the conversation, it was in the manner of someone talking in her sleep; for when this silence came, she woke up and said in a startled voice:

'Lal Drake.'

And screwing up her fists she got up and, pausing to get ready for a rush, she heaved herself fast to the door by which August had left for the Gents, down the alley a quarter of an hour before.

'The other door, missis,' someone shouted. But she was through it.

'Drink up,' we said and went out by the front door. I was the last and had a look down the side alley and there I saw a sight. August with one hand doing up his fly buttons and the other arm protecting his face. Mrs Price was hitting out at him and shouting. The language!

'You dirty sod. I knew it. The girl told me.' She was shouting. She saw me, stopped hitting and rushed at me in tears and shouted back at him.

'The filthy old man.'

August saw his chance and got out of the alley and made for the cars in the square. She let me go and shouted after him. We were all there and in Woolworth's doorway was Pliny. Rain was still falling and he looked wet and all the more alone for being wet. I walked off and, I suppose, seeing me go and herself alone and giddy in her rage she looked all round and turned her temper on me.

'The girl has got to go,' she shouted.

Then she came to her senses.

'Where is August?'

August had got to his car and was driving out of the square. She could do nothing. Then she saw Pliny. She ran from me to Pliny, from Pliny to me.

'He's going after the girl,' she screamed.

We calmed her down and it was I who drove her home. (This was when she told me, as the wipers went up and down on the windscreen, that she and August were not married.) We splashed through hissing water that was like her tears on the road. 'I'm worried for the child. I told her, "Keep your door locked." I see it's locked every night. I'm afraid I'll forget and I won't hear him if I've had a couple. She's a kid. She doesn't know anything.' I understood that the face I had always thought was empty was really filled with the one person she loved: Isabel.

August was not there when we got to their shop. Mrs Price went in and big as she was, she did not knock anything over.

'Isabel?' she called.

The girl was in the scullery and came with a wet plate that dripped on the carpet. In two years she had changed. She was wearing an old dress and an apron, but also a pair of high-heeled silver evening shoes. She had become the slut of the house and her pale skin looked dirty.

'You're dripping that thing everywhere. What have you got those shoes on for? Where did you get them?'

'Uncle Harry, for Christmas,' she said. She called August Uncle Harry. She tried to look jaunty as if she had put all her hope in life into those silly evening shoes.

'All right,' said Mrs Price weakly looking at me to keep quiet and say nothing.

Isabel took off her apron when she saw me. I don't know whether she remembered me. She was still pale, but had the shapeliness of a small young woman. Her eyes looked restlessly and uncertainly at both of us, her chin was firmer but it trembled. She was smiling too and, because I was there and the girl might see an ally in me, Mrs Price looked with half-kindness at Isabel; but when I got up to go the girl looked at me as if she would follow me out of the door. Mrs Price got up fast to bar the way. She stood on the doorstep of the shop watching me get into the car, swollen with the inability to say 'Thank you' or 'Goodbye'. If the girl was a child, Mrs Price was ten times a child and both of them standing on the doorstep were like children who don't want anyone to go away.

I drove off and for a few miles I thought about Mrs Price and the girl, but once settled into the long drive to London, the thought of Pliny supplanted them. I had been caught up by the fever of the trade. Pliny's mother was dead. What was going to happen to Pliny and all that part of the business Pliny had inherited from his father, the stuff he despised and had not troubled himself with very much in his mother's time. I ought to go 'over the water' – as we say in London – to have a look at it some time. In a few days I went there; I found the idea had occurred to many others. The shop was on one of the main bus routes in South London, a speckled early Victorian place with an ugly red brick store behind it. Pliny's father had had an eye for a cosy but useful bit of property. Its windows had square panes (1810) and to my surprise the place was open and I could see people inside. There was Pliny with his nose which looked servile rather than distinguished, wearing a long biscuit-coloured tweed jacket with leather pads at the elbows like a Cockney sportsman. There, too, was August with his wet eyes and drinker's shame, Mrs Price swelling over him in her best clothes, and the girl. They had come up from the country and August had had his boots cleaned. The girl was in her best too and was standing apart touching things in the shop, on the point of merriment, looking with wonder at Pliny's ears. He often seemed to be talking at her when he was talking to Mrs Price. I said:

'Hullo! Up from the country? What are you doing here?' Mrs Price was so large that she had to turn her whole body and place her belly in front of everyone who spoke to her.

'Seeing to his teeth,' she said, nodding at August and, from years of habit, August turned too when his wife turned, in case it was just as well not to miss one of her pronouncements, whatever else he might dodge. One side of August's jaw was swollen. Then Mrs Price slowly turned her whole body to face Pliny again. They were talking about his mother's death. Mrs Price was greedy, as one stout woman thinking of another, for a melancholy tour of the late mother's organs. The face of the girl looked prettily wise and holiday-fied because the heavy curls of her hair hung close to her face. She looked out of the window, restless and longing to get away while her elders went on talking, but she was too listless to do so. Then she would look again at Pliny's large ears with a childish pleasure in anything strange; they gave him a dog-like appearance and if the Augusts had not been there, I think she would have jumped at him mischievously to touch them, but remembered in time that she had lately grown into a young lady. When she saw him looking at her she turned her back and began writing in the dust on a little table which was standing next to a cabinet; it had a small jug on it. She was writing her name in the dust I S A B . . . And then stopped. She turned round suddenly because she saw I had been watching.

'Is that old Meissen?' she called out, pointing to the jug.

They stopped talking. It was comic to see her pretending, for my benefit, that she knew all about porcelain.

'Cor! Old Meissen!' said August, pulling his racing newspaper out of his jacket pocket with excitement, and Mrs Price fondly swung her big handbag; all laughed loudly, a laugh of lust and knowledge. They knew, or thought they knew, that Pliny had a genuine Meissen piece somewhere, probably upstairs where he lived. The girl was pleased to have made them laugh at her; she had been noticed.

Pliny said decently: 'No, dear. That's Caughley. Would you like to see it?'

He walked to the cabinet and took the jug down and put it on a table.

'Got the leopard?' said August, knowingly. Pliny showed the mark of the leopard on the base of the jug and put it down again. It was a pretty shapely jug with a spray of branches and in the branches a pair of pheasants were perching, done in transfer. The girl scared us all by picking it up in both hands, but it was charming to see her holding it up and studying it.

'Careful,' said Mrs Price.

'She's all right,' said Pliny.

Then – it alarmed us – she wriggled with laughter.

'What a funny face,' she said.

Under the lip of the jug was the small face of an old man with a long nose looking sly and wicked.

'They used to put a face under the lip,' Pliny said.

'That's right,' said August.

The girl held it out at arm's length and, looking from the jug to Pliny, she said: 'It's like you, Mr Pliny.'

'Isabel!' said Mrs Price. 'That's rude.'

'But it is,' said Isabel. 'Isn't it?' She was asking me. Pliny grinned. We were all relieved to see him take the jug from her and put it back in the cabinet.

'It belonged to my mother,' he said. 'I keep it there,' Pliny said to me, despising me because I had said nothing and because I was a stranger.

'Go into the back and have a look round if you want to. The light's on.'

I left the shop and went down the steps into the long white store-room where the white-washed walls were grey with dust. There was an alligator hanging by a nail near the steps, a couple of cavalry helmets and a dirty drum that must have been there since the Crimean War. I went down into streets of stacked up furniture. I felt I was walking into an inhuman crypt or worse still one of those charnel houses or ossuaries I had seen pictures of in one of my father's books when I was a boy. Large as the store was, it was lit by a single electric light bulb hanging from a girder in the roof and the yellow light was deathly. The notion of 'picking up' anything at Pliny's depressed me, so that I was left with a horror of the trade I had joined. Yet feelings of this kind are never simple. After half an hour I left the shop. I understood before that day was over and I was back in the room over my own place that what had made me more wretched was the wound of a sharp joy. First, the sight of the girl leaving her name unfinished in the dust had made my heart jump, then when she held the vase in her hands I had felt the thrill of a revelation; until then

I had never settled what I should go in for but now I saw it. Why not collect Caughley? That was it. Caughley; it was one of those inspirations that excite one so that every sight in the world changes; even houses, buses and streets and people are transfigured and become unreal as desire carries one away – and then, cruelly, it passes and one is left exhausted. The total impossibility of an impatient young man like myself collecting Caughley which hadn't been made since 1821 became brutally clear. Too late for Staffordshire, too late for Dresden, too late for Caughley and all the beautiful things. I was savage for lack of money. The following day I went to the Victoria and Albert and then I saw other far more beautiful things enshrined and inaccessible. I gazed with wonder. My longing for possession held me and then I was elevated to a state of worship as if they were idols, holy and never to be touched. Then I remembered the girl's hands and a violent day dream passed through my head; it lasted only a second or two but in that time I smashed the glass case, grabbed the treasure and bolted with it. It frightened me that such an idea could have occurred to me. I left the museum and I turned sourly against my occupation, against Marbright, Alsop and above all Pliny and August, and it broke my heart to think of that pretty girl living among such people and drifting into the shabbiness of the trade. I S A B – half a name, written by a living finger in dust.

One has these brief sensations when one is young. They pass and one does nothing about them. There is nothing remarkable about Caughley – except that you can't get it. I did not collect Caughley for a simple reason; I had to collect my wits. The plain truth is that I was incompetent. I had only to look at my bank account. I had bought too much. At the end of the year I looked like getting into the bankruptcy court unless I had a stroke of luck. Talk of trouble making the trade move; I was Trouble myself, dealers could smell it coming and came sniffing into my shop and at the end of the year I sold up for what I could get. It would have been better if I could have waited for a year or two when the boom began. For some reason I kept the teapot I had bought in Salisbury to remind me of wasted time. In its humble way it was pretty.

In the next six months I changed. I had to. I pocketed my pride and I got a dull job in an auctioneer's; at least it took me out of the office when I got out keys and showed people round. The firm dealt in house property and developments. The word 'develop' took hold of me. The firm was a large one and sometimes 'developed' far outside London. I was told to go and inspect some of the least important bits of property that were coming into the market. One day a row of shops in Steepleton came up for sale. I said I knew them. They were on the London Road opposite the Lion Hotel at the end of the town. My boss was always impressed by topography and the names of hotels and sent me down there. The shops were in the row where August and one or two others had had their business, six of them.

What a change! The Lion had been re-painted; the little shops seemed to have got smaller. In my time the countryside had begun at the end of the row. Now builders' scaffolding was standing in the fields beyond. I looked for August's. A cheap café had taken over his place. He had gone. The mirror man who lived next door was still there but had gone into beads and fancy art jewellery. His window was full of hanging knick-knacks and mobiles.

'It's the tourist trade now,' he said. He looked ill.

'What happened to August?'

He studied me for a moment and said, 'Closed down', and I could get no more out of him. I crossed the street to The Lion. Little by little, a sentence at a time in a long slow suspicious evening I got news of August from the barmaid as she went back and forth serving customers, speaking in a low voice, her eye on the new proprietor in case the next sentence that came out of her might be bad for custom. The sentences were spoken like sentences from a judge summing up, bit by bit. August had got two years for receiving stolen goods; the woman – 'She wasn't his wife' – had been knocked down by a car as she was coming out of the bar at night – 'not that she drank, not really drank; her weight really' – and then came the final sentence that brought back to me the alerting heat and fever of its secrets: 'There was always trouble over there. It started when the girl ran away.'

'Isabel?' I said.

'I dunno – the girl.'

I stood outside the hotel and looked to the east and then to the west. It was one of those quarters of an hour on a main road when, for some reason, there is no traffic coming either way. I looked at the now far-off fields where the February wind was scything over the grass, turning it into waves of silver as it passed over them. I thought of Isab . . . running with a case in her hand, three years ago. Which way? Where do girls run to? Sad.

I went back to London. There are girls in London too, you know. I grew a beard, reddish: it went with the red car which I had managed to keep. I could afford to take a girl down to the south coast now and then. Sometimes we came back by the Brixton road, sometimes through Camberwell and when we did this I often slowed down at Pliny's and told the girls, 'That man's sitting on a gold mine.' They never believed it or, at least, only one did. She said: 'Does he sell rings? Let us have a look.'

'They're closed,' I said. 'They're always closed.'

'I want to look,' she said, so we stopped and got out.

We looked into the dark window – it was Saturday night – and we could see nothing and as we stared we heard a loud noise coming, it seemed, from the place next door or from down the drive-in at the side of Pliny's shop, a sound like someone beating boxes or bath tubs at first until I got what it was: drums. Someone blew a bugle, a terrible squeaky sound. There was heavy traffic on the street, but the bugle seemed to split it in half.

'Boys' Brigade, practising for Sunday,' I said. We stood laughing with our hands to our ears as we stared into the dark. All I could make out was something white on a table at the back of the shop. Slowly I saw it was a set of chessmen. Chess, ivories, August – perhaps Pliny had got August's chessmen.

'What a din!' said the girl. I said no more to her for in my mind there was the long forgotten picture of Isabel's finger on the pieces, at Steepleton.

When I've got time, I thought, I will run over to Pliny's; perhaps he will know what happened to the girl.

And I did go there again, one afternoon, on my own. Still closed. I rattled the door handle. There was no answer. I went to a baker's next door, then to a butcher's, then to a pub. The same story. 'He only opens on Sundays,' or, 'He's at a sale.' Then to a tobacconist's. I said it was funny to leave a shop empty like that, full of valuable stuff. The tobacconist became suspicious.

'There's someone there all right. His wife's there.'

'No she's not,' his wife said. 'They've gone off to a sale. I saw them.'
She took the hint.

'No one in charge to serve customers,' she said.

I said I'd seen a chessboard that interested me and the tobacconist said:
'It's dying out. I used to play.'

'I didn't know he got married,' I said.

'He's got beautiful things,' said his wife. 'Come on Sunday.'

Pliny married! That made me grin. The only women in his life I had
ever heard of were his mother and the gossip about Lal Drake. Perhaps
he had made an honest woman of *her*. I went back for one last look at the
chessmen and, sure enough, as the tobacconist's wife had hinted someone
had been left in charge, for I saw a figure pass through the inner door of
the shop. The watcher was watched. Almost at once I heard the tap and
roll of a kettle drum, I put my ear to the letter box and distinctly heard
a boy's voice shouting orders. Children! All the drumming I had heard
on Saturday had come from Pliny's – a whole family drumming. Think
of Pliny married to a widow with kids; he had not had time to get his
own. I took back what I had thought of him and Lal Drake. I went off
for an hour to inspect a house that was being sold on Camberwell Green,
and stopped once more at Pliny's on the way back. On the chance of
catching him, I went to the window: standing in the middle of the shop
was Isabel.

Her shining black hair went to her shoulders. She was wearing a red
dress with a schoolgirlish white collar to it. If I had not known her by her
heart-shaped face and her full childish lips, I would have known her by
her tiptoe way of standing like an actress just about to sing a song or give
a dance when she comes forward on the stage. She looked at me daringly.
It was the way, I remembered, she had looked at everyone. She did not
know me. I went to the door and tipped the handle. It did not open. I
saw her watching the handle move. I went on rattling. She straightened
and shook her head, pushing back her hair. She did not go away. She was
amused by my efforts. I went back to the window of the shop and asked
to come in. She could not hear, of course. My mouth was opening and
shutting foolishly. That amused her even more. I pointed to something in
the window, signalling that I was interested in it. She shook her head

again. I tried pointing to other things: a cabinet, an embroidered fire-screen, a jar three feet high. At each one she shook her head. It was like a guessing game. I was smiling, even laughing, to persuade her. I put my hands to my chest and pretended to beg like a dog. She laughed at this and looked behind, as if calling to someone. If Pliny wasn't there, his wife might be, or the children. I pointed upwards and made a movement of my hands, imitating someone turning a key in a lock. I was signalling, 'Go and get the key from Mrs Pliny,' and I stepped back and looked up at a window above the shop. When I did this Isabel was frightened; she went away shouting to someone. And that was the end of it; she did not come back.

I went away thinking, Well, that is a strange thing!

What ideas people put into your head and you build fancies yourself – that woman in the bar at Steepleton telling me Isabel had run away and I imagining her running in those poor evening shoes I'd once seen, in the rain down the Bath Road, when what was more natural in a trade where they all live with their hands in one another's pockets – Pliny had married, and they had taken the girl on at the shop. It was a comfort to think of. I hadn't realised how much I had worried about what would happen to a naïve girl like Isabel when the break up came. Alone in the world! How silly. I thought, one of these Sundays I'll go up there and hear the whole story. And I did.

There was no one there except Pliny and his rich Sunday customers. I even went into the store at the back, looked everywhere. No sign of Isabel. The only female was a woman in a shabby black dress and not wearing a hat who was talking to a man who was testing the door of a wardrobe, making it squeak, while the woman looked on without interest, in the manner of a dealer's wife; obviously the new Mrs Pliny. She turned to make way for another couple who were waiting to look at it. I nearly knocked over a stack of cane chairs as I got past.

If there was no sign of Isabel, the sight of Pliny shocked me. He had been a dead man, permanently dead as wood, even clumsy in his big servile bones, though shrewd. Now he had come to life in the strangest, excited way, much older to look at, thinner and frantic as he looked about him this way and that. He seemed to be possessed by a demon. He talked loudly to people in the shop and was suspicious when he was not talking.

He was frightened, abrupt, rude. Pliny married! Marriage had wrecked him or he was making too much money; he looked like a man expecting to be robbed. He recognised me at once. I had felt him watching me from the steps going down to the store. As I came back to the steps to speak to him he spoke to me first, distinctly in a loud voice:

'I don't want any of August's men here, see?'

I went red in the face.

'What do you mean?' I said.

'You heard me,' he said. 'You know what he got.'

Wells of Hungerford was standing near, pretending not to listen. Pliny was telling the trade that I was in with August – publicly accusing me of being a fence. I controlled my temper.

'August doesn't interest me,' I said. 'I'm in property. Marsh, Help and Hitchcock. I sold his place, the whole street.'

And I walked past him looking at a few things as I left.

I was in a passion. The dirty swine – all right when his mother kept an eye on him, the poor old woman, but now – he'd gone mad. And that poor girl! I went to the tobacconist for the Sunday paper in a dream, put down my money and took it without a word and was almost out of the door when the wife called out:

'Did you find him? Did you get what you wanted?' A friendly London voice. I tapped the side of my head.

'You're telling me,' the wife said.

'Well, he has to watch everything now. Marrying a young girl like that, it stands to reason,' said the wife in a melancholy voice.

'Wears him out, at his age,' suggested the tobacconist.

'Stop the dirty talk, Alfred,' said the wife.

'You mean he married the *girl*?' I said. 'Who's the big woman without a hat – in the store?'

'What big woman is that?' asked the tobacconist's wife. 'He's married to the girl. Who else do you think – there's no one else.'

The wife's face went as blank as a tombstone in the sly London way.

'She's done well for herself,' said the tobacconist. 'Keeps her locked up like his mother, wasn't I right?'

'He worships her,' said the woman.

I went home to my flat. I was nauseated. The thought of Isabel in bed with that dressed up servant, with his wet eyes, his big raw ears and his breath smelling of onions! Innocent? No, as the woman said, 'She has done well for herself.' Happy with him too. I remembered her pretty face laughing in the shop. What else could you expect, after August and Mrs Price.

The anger I felt with Pliny grew to a rage but by the time I was in my own flat Pliny vanished from the picture in my mind. I was filled with passion for the girl. The fever of the trade had come alive in me; Pliny had got something I wanted. I could think of nothing but her, just as I remember the look August gave Pliny when the girl asked if the jug was Meissen. I could see her holding the jug at arm's length, laughing at the old man's face under the lip. And I could see that Pliny was not mad; what was making him frantic was possessing the girl.

I kept away from Pliny's. I tried to drive the vision out of my mind, but I could not forget it. I became cunning. Whenever my job allowed it – and even when it didn't – I started passing the time of day with any dealer I had known, picked up news of the sales, studied catalogues, tried to find out which ones Pliny would go to. She might be with him. I actually went to Newbury but he was not there. Bath he couldn't miss and, sure enough, he was there and she wasn't. It was ten in the morning and the sale had just started. I ran off and got into my car. I drove as fast as I could the hundred miles back to London and cursed the lunchtime traffic. I got to Pliny's shop and rang the bell. Once, then several long rings. At once the drum started beating and went on as if troops were marching. People passing in the street paused to listen too. I stood back from the window and I saw a movement at a curtain upstairs. The drumming was still going on and when I bent to listen at the letter box I could hear the sound become deafening and often very near and then there was a blast from the bugle. It was a misty day south of the river and for some reason or other I was fingering the grey window and started writing her name, I S A B . . . hopelessly, but hoping that perhaps she might come near enough to see. The drumming stopped. I waited and waited and then I saw an extraordinary sight; Isabel herself in the dull red dress, but with a lancer's helmet on her head and a side drum on its straps hanging from her shoulders and the drum sticks in her hand. She was standing upright like a boy playing soldiers, her chin up and puzzling at the sight of the letters BASI on the window. When she saw me she was confused. She immediately gave two or three taps to the drum and then bent almost double with laughter. Then she put on a straight face and played the game of pointing to one thing after another in the shop. Every time I shook my head, until at last I pointed to her. This pleased her. Then I shouted through the letter box: 'I want to come in.'

'Come in,' she said. 'It's open.'

The door had been open all the time; I had not thought of trying it. I went inside.

'I thought you were locked in.'

She did not answer but wagged her head from side to side.

'Sometimes I lock myself in,' she said. 'There are bad people about, August's men.'

She said this with great importance, but her face became ugly as she said it. She took off the helmet and put down the drum.

'So I beat the drum when Mr Pliny is away,' she said. She called him Mr Pliny.

'What good does that do?'

'It is so quiet when Mr Pliny is away. I don't do it when he's here. It frightens August's men away.'

'It's as good as telling them you are alone here,' I said. 'That's why I came. I heard the drum and the bugle.'

'Did you?' she said eagerly. 'Was it loud?'

'Very loud.'

She gave a deep sigh of delight.

'You see!' she said, nodding her head complacently.

'Who taught you to blow the bugle?' I said.

'My mother did,' she said. 'She did it on the stage. Mr Pliny – you know when Mr Pliny fetched me in his motor-car – I forgot it. He had to go back and get it. I was too frightened.'

'Isab . . .' I said.

She blushed. She remembered.

'I might be one of August's men,' I said.

'No you're not. I know who you are,' she said. 'Mr Pliny's away for the day but that doesn't matter. I am in charge. Is there something you were looking for?'

The child was gone when she put the drum aside. She became serious and practical: Mrs Pliny! I was confused by my mistake in not knowing the door was open and she busied herself about the shop. She knew what she was doing and I felt very foolish.

'Is there something special?' she said. 'Look around.' She had become a confident woman. I no longer felt there was anything strange about her. I drifted to look at the chessmen and I could not pretend to myself that they interested me, but I did ask her the price. She said she would look it up and went to a desk where Pliny kept his papers and after going through some lists of figures which were all in code she named the sum. It was enormous – something like £275 and I said, 'What!' in astonishment. She put the list back on the desk and said, firmly:

'My husband paid £260 for it last Sunday. It was carved by Dubois. There are only two more like it. It was the last thing he did in 1785.'

(I found out afterwards this was nonsense.)

She said this in Pliny's voice; it was exactly the sort of casual sentence he would have used. She looked expressionlessly and not at all surprised when I said, 'Valuable,' and moved away.

I meant, of course, that she was valuable and in fact her mystery having gone, she seemed conscious of being valuable and important herself, the queen and owner of everything in the shop, efficiently in charge of her husband's things. The cabinet in the corner, she said, in an offhand way, as I went to look at it, had been sold to an Australian. 'We are waiting for the packers.' We! Not to feel less knowing than she was, I looked around for some small thing to buy from her. There were several small things, like a cup and saucer, a little china tray, a christening mug. I picked things up and put them down listlessly and, from being indifferent, she became eager and watched me. The important, serious expression she had had vanished, she became childish suddenly and anxious: she was eager to sell something. I found a little china figure on a shelf.

'How much is this?' I said. It was Dresden; the real thing. She took it and looked at the label. I knew it was far beyond my purse and I asked her the price in the bored hopeless voice one puts on.

'I'll have to look it up,' she said.

She went to the desk again and looked very calculating and thoughtful and then said, as if naming an enormous sum:

'Two pounds.'

'It can't be,' I said.

She looked sad as I put it back on the shelf and she went back to the desk. Then she said:

'I tell you what I'll do. It's got a defect. You can have it for thirty-five shillings.'

I picked it up again. There was no defect in it. I could feel the huge wave of temptation that comes to one in the trade, the sense of the incredible chance, the lust that makes one shudder first and then breaks over one so that one is possessed, though even at that last moment, one plays at delay in a breathless pause, now one is certain of one's desire.

I said: 'I'll give you thirty bob for it.'

Young Mrs Pliny raised her head and her brown eyes became brilliant with naïve joy.

'All right,' she said.

The sight of her wrapping the figure, packing it in a box and taking the money so entranced me, that I didn't realise what she was doing or what I had done. I wasn't thinking of the figure at all. I was thinking of her. We shook hands. Hers were cold and she waved from the shop door when I left. And when I got to the end of the street and found myself holding the box I wondered why I had bought it. I didn't want it. I had felt the thrill of the thief and I was so ashamed that I once or twice thought of dropping it into a litter box. I even thought of going back and returning it to her and saying to her: 'I didn't want it. It was a joke. I wanted you. Why did you marry an awful old man like Pliny?' And those stories of Pliny going off once a month in the old days, in his mother's time, to Lal Drake that old whore in Brixton, came back to me. I didn't even unpack the figure but put it on the mantelpiece in my room, then on the top shelf of a cupboard which I rarely used. I didn't want to see it. And when in the next months – or even years – I happened to see it, I remembered her talking about the bad people, August's men.

But, though I kept away from Pliny's on Sundays, I could not resist going back to the street and eventually to the shop – just for the sight of her.

And after several misses I did see her in the shop. It was locked. When I saw her she stared at me with fear and made no signals and quickly disappeared – I suppose into the room at the back. I crossed the main road and looked at the upper part of the house. She was upstairs, standing at a window. So I went back across the street and tried to signal, but of course she could only see my mouth moving. I was obsessed by the way I had cheated her. My visits were a siege for the door was never opened now. I did see her once through the window and this time I had taken the box and offered it to her in dumb show. That did have an effect. I saw she was looking very pale, her eyes ringed and tired and whether she saw I was remorseful or not I couldn't tell, but she made a rebuking yet defiant face. Another day I went and she looked terrified. She pointed and pointed to the door but as I eagerly stepped towards it she shook her head and raised a hand to forbid me. I did not understand until, soon, I saw Pliny walking about the shop. I moved off. People in the neighbourhood must often have seen me standing there and the tobacconist I went to gave me a look that suggested he knew what was going on.

Then, on one of my vigils, I saw a doctor go to the side door down the Goods Entrance and feared she was ill – but the butcher told me it was Pliny. His wife, they said, had been nursing him. He ought to convalesce somewhere. A nice place by the sea. But he won't. It would do his wife good. The young girl has worn herself out looking after him. Shut up all day with him. And the tobacconist said what his wife had said a long time back. 'Like his poor mother. He kept *her* locked in too. Sunday evening's the only time she's out. It's all wrong.'

I got sick of myself. I didn't notice the time I was wasting for one day passed like a smear of grey into another and I wished I could drag myself away from the district, especially now Pliny was always there. At last one Saturday I fought hard against a habit so useless and I had the courage to drive past the place for once and did not park my car up the street. I drove on, taking side streets (which I knew, nevertheless, would lead me back), but I made a mistake with the one-ways and got on the main Brixton road and was heading north to freedom from myself.

It was astonishing to be free. It was seven o'clock in the evening and to celebrate I went into a big pub where they had singers on Saturday nights; it was already filling up with people. How normal, how cheerful they were, a crowd of them, drinking, shouting and talking; the human race! I got a drink and chose a quiet place in a corner and I was taking my first mouthful of the beer, saying to myself: 'Here's to yourself, my boy,' as though I had just met myself as I used to be. And then, with the glass still at my lips, I saw in a crowd at the other end of the bar Pliny, with his back half-turned. I recognised him by his jug-handle ears, his white hair and the stoop of a tall man. He was not in his dressy clothes but in a shabby suit that made him seem disguised. He was listening to a woman who had a large handbag and had bright blonde hair and a big red mouth who was telling him a joke and she banged him in the stomach with her bag and laughed. Someone near me said: 'Lal's on the job early this evening.' Lal Drake. All the old stories about Pliny and his woman came back to me and how old Castle of Westbury said that Pliny's mother had told him, when she was saying what a good son he was to her, that the one and only time he had been with a woman he had come home and told her and put his head in her laps and cried 'like a child' and promised on the Bible he'd never do such a thing again. Castle swore this was true.

I put down my glass and got out of the pub fast without finishing it. Not because I was afraid of Pliny. Oh no! I drove straight back to Pliny's shop. I rang the bell. The drum started beating a few taps and then a window upstairs opened.

'What do you want?' said Isabel in a whisper.

'I want to see you. Open the door.'

'It's locked.'

'Get the key.'

She considered me for a long time.

'I haven't got one,' she said, still in a low voice, so hard to hear that she had to say it twice.

'Where have you been?' she said.

We stared at each other's white faces in the dark. She had missed me!

'You've got a key. You must have,' I said. 'Somewhere. What about the back door?'

She leaned on the window, her arms on the sill. She was studying my clothes.

'I have something for you,' I said. This changed her. She leaned forward trying to see more of me in the dark. She was curious. Today I understand what I did not understand then; she was looking me over minutely, inch by inch – what she could see of me in the sodium light of the street lamp – not because I was strange or unusual – but because I was not. She had been shut up either alone or with Pliny without seeing another soul for so long. He was treating her like one of his collector's pieces, like the Meissen August had said he kept hidden upstairs. She closed the window. I stood there wretched and impatient. I went down the Goods Entrance ready to kick the side door down, break a window, climb in somehow. The side door had no letter box or glass panes, no handle even. I stood in front of it and suddenly it was opened. She was standing there.

'You're *not* locked in,' I said.

She was holding a key.

'I found it,' she said.

I saw she was telling a lie.

'Just now?'

'No. I know where he hides it,' she said lowering her frank eyes.

It was a heavy key with an old piece of frayed used-up string on it.

'Mr Pliny does not like me to show people things,' she said. 'He has gone to see his sister in Brixton. She is very ill. I can't show you anything.'

She recited these words as if she had learned them by heart. It was wonderful to stand so near to her in the dark.

'Can I come in?' I said.

'What do you want?' she said cautiously.

'You,' I said.

She raised her chin.

'Are you one of August's men?' she said.

'You know I'm not. I haven't seen August for years.'

'Mr Pliny says you are. He said I was never to speak to you again. August was horrible.'

'The last I heard he was in prison.'

'Yes,' she said. 'He steals.'

This seemed to please her; she forgave him that easily. Then she put her head out of the doorway as if to see if August were waiting behind me.

'He does something else, too,' she said.

I remembered the violent quarrel between August and poor Mrs Price when she was drunk in Salisbury – the quarrel about Isabel.

'You ran away,' I said.

413

She shook her head.

'I didn't run away. Mr Pliny fetched me,' she said and nodded primly, 'in his car. I told you.'

Then she said: 'Where is the present you were bringing me?'

'It isn't a present,' I said. 'It's the little figure I bought from you. You didn't charge me enough. Let me in. I want to explain.'

I couldn't bring myself to tell her that I had taken advantage of her ignorance, so I said:

'I found out afterwards that it was worth much more than I paid you. I want to give it back to you.'

She gave a small jump towards me. 'Oh please, please,' she said and took me by the hand. 'Where is it?'

'Let me come in,' I said, 'and I will tell you. I haven't got it with me. I'll bring it tomorrow, no not tomorrow, Monday.'

'Oh. Please,' she pleaded. 'Mr Pliny was so angry with me for selling it. He'd never been angry with me before. It was terrible. It was awful.'

It had never occurred to me that Pliny would even know she had sold the piece; but now, I remembered the passions of the trade and the stored up lust that seems to pass between things and men like Pliny. He wouldn't forgive. He would be savage.

'Did he do something to you? He didn't hit you, did he?'

Isabel did not answer.

'What did he do?'

I remembered how frantic Pliny had been and how violent he had sounded, when he told me to get out of his shop.

'He cried,' she said. 'He cried and he cried. He went down on his knees and he would not stop crying. I was wicked to sell it. I am the most precious thing he has. Please bring it. It will make him better.'

'Is he still angry?'

'It has made him ill,' she said.

'Let me come in,' I said.

'Will you promise?'

'I swear I'll bring it,' I said.

'For a minute,' she said, 'but not in the shop.'

I followed her down a dark passage into the store and was so close that I could smell her hair.

Pliny crying! At first I took this to be one of Isabel's fancies. Then I thought of tall, clumsy, servant-like Pliny, expert at sales with his long-nosed face pouring out water like a pump, repentant, remorseful, agonised like an animal, to a pretty girl. Why? Just because she had sold something? Isabel loved to sell things. He must have had some other reason. I remembered Castle of Westbury's story. What had he done to the girl? Only a cruel man could have gone in for such an orgy of self-love. He had the long face on which tears would be a blackmail. He would be like a horse crying because it had lost a race.

Yet those tears were memorable to Isabel and she so firmly called him 'Mr Pliny'. In bed, did she still call him 'Mr Pliny'? I have often thought since that she did; it would have given her a power – perhaps cowed him.

At night the cold white-washed store-room was silent under the light of its single bulb and the place was mostly in shadow, only the tops of stacked furniture stood out in the yellow light, some of them like buildings. The foundations of the stacks were tables or chests, desks on which chairs or small cabinets were piled. We walked down alleys between the stacks. It was like walking through a dead, silent city, abandoned by everyone who once lived there. There was the sour smell of upholstery; in one part there was a sort of plaza where two large dining tables stood with their chairs set around and a pile of dessert plates on them. Isabel was walking confidently. She stopped by a dressing-table with a mirror on it next to a group of wardrobes and turning round to face it, she said proudly:

'Mr Pliny gave it all to me. And the shop.'

'All of this?'

'When he stopped crying,' she said.

And then she turned about and we faced the wardrobes. There were six or seven, one in rosewood and an ugly yellow one and they were so arranged here that they made a sort of alcove or room. The wardrobe at the corner of the alley was very heavy and leaned so that its doors were open in a manner of such empty hopelessness, showing its empty shelves, that it made me uneasy. Someone might have just taken his clothes from it in a hurry, perhaps that very minute, and gone off. He might be watching us. It was the wardrobe with the squeaking door which I had seen the customer open while the woman whom I had thought to be Mrs Pliny stood by. Each piece of furniture seemed to watch – even the small things, like an umbrella stand or a tray left on a table. Isabel walked into the alcove and there was a greeny-grey sofa with a screwed up paper bag of toffees on it and on the floor beside it I saw, of all things, the lancer's helmet and the side drum and the bugle. The yellow light scarcely lit this corner.

'There's your drum,' I said.

'This is my house,' she said, gaily now. 'Do you like it? When Mr Pliny is away I come here in case August's men come . . .'

She looked at me doubtfully when she mentioned that name again.

'And you beat the drum to drive them away?' I said.

'Yes,' she said stoutly.

I could not make out whether she was playing the artless child or not, yet she was a woman of twenty-five at least. I was bewildered.

'You are frightened here on your own, aren't you?'

'No I am not. It's nice.'

Then she said very firmly:

'You will come here on Monday and give me the box back?'

I said: 'I will if you'll let me kiss you. I love you, Isabel.'

'Mr Pliny loves me too,' she said.

'Isab . . .' I said. That did move her.

I put my arm round her waist and she let me draw her to me. It was strange to hold her because I could feel her ribs, but her body was so limp and feeble that, loving her as I did, I was shocked and pulled her tightly against me. She turned her head weakly so that I could only kiss her cheek and see only one of her eyes and I could not make out whether she was enticing me, simply curious about my embrace or drooping in it without heart.

'You *are* one of August's men,' she said getting away from me. 'He used to try and get into my bed. After that I locked my door.'

'Isabel,' I said. 'I am in love with you. I think you love me. Why did you marry a horrible old man like Pliny?'

'Mr Pliny is not horrible,' she said. 'I love him. He never comes to my room.'

'Then he doesn't love you,' I said. 'Leaving you locked up here. And you don't love him.'

She listened in the manner of someone wanting to please, waiting for me to stop.

'He is not a real husband, a real lover,' I said.

'Yes, he is,' she said proudly. 'He takes my clothes off before I go to bed. He likes to look at me. I am the most precious thing he has.'

'That isn't love, Isabel,' I said.

'It is,' she said with warmth. 'You don't love me. You cheated me. Mr Pliny said so. And you don't want to look at me. You don't think I'm precious.'

I went to take her in my arms again and held her.

'I love you. I want you. You are beautiful. I didn't cheat you. Pliny is cheating you, not me,' I said. 'He is not with his sister. He's in bed with a woman in Brixton. I saw them in a pub. Everyone knows it.'

'No he is not. I *know* he is not. He doesn't like it. He promised his mother,' she said.

The voice in which she said this was not her playful voice; the girl vanished and a woman had taken her place and not a distressed woman, not a contemptuous or a disappointed one.

'He worships me,' she said and in the squalid store of dead junk she seemed to be illumined by the simple knowledge of her own value and looked at my love as if it were nothing at all.

I looked at the sofa and was so mad that I thought of grabbing her and pulling her down there. What made me hesitate was the crumpled bag of toffees on it. I was as nonplussed and, perhaps, as impotent as Pliny must have been. In that moment of hesitation she picked up her bugle and standing in the aisle, she blew it hard, her cheeks going out full and the noise and echoes seemed to make the shadows jump. I have never heard a bugle call that scared me so much. It killed my desire.

'I told you not to come in,' she said. 'Go away.'

And she walked into the aisle between the furniture, swinging her key to the door.

'Come back,' I said as I followed her.

I saw her face in the dressing-table mirror we had passed before, then I saw my own face, red and sweating on the upper lip and my mouth helplessly open. And then in the mirror I saw another face following mine – Pliny's. Pliny must have seen me in the pub.

In that oblong frame of mahogany with its line of yellow inlay, Pliny's head looked winged by his ears and he was coming at me, his head down, his mouth with its yellowing teeth open under the moustache and his eyes stained in the bad light. He looked like an animal. The mirror concentrated him and before I could do more than half turn he had jumped in a clumsy way at me and jammed one of my shoulders against a tall-boy.

'What are you doing here?' he shouted.

The shouts echoed over the store.

'I warned you. I'll get the police on you. You leave my wife alone. Get out. You thought you'd get her on her own and swindle her again.'

I hated to touch a white-haired man but, in pain, I shoved him back hard. We were, as I have said, close to the wardrobe and he staggered back so far that he hit the shelves and the door swung towards him so that he was half out of my sight for a second. I kicked the door hard with my left foot and it swung to and hit him in the face. He jumped out with blood on his nose. But I had had time to topple the pile of little cane chairs into the alleyway between us. Isabel saw this and ran round the block of furniture and reached him and when I saw her she was standing with the bugle raised like a weapon in her hand to defend the old man from me. He was wiping his face. She looked triumphant.

'Don't you touch Mr Pliny,' she shouted at me. 'He's ill.'

He *was* ill. He staggered. I pushed my way through the fallen chairs and I picked up one and said: 'Pliny, sit down on this.' Pliny with the bleeding face glared and she forced him to sit down. He was panting. And then a new voice joined us; the tobacconist came down the alley.

'I heard the bugle,' he said. 'Anything wrong? Oh Gawd, look at his face. What happened, Pliny? Mrs Pliny, you all right?' And then he saw me. All the native shadiness of the London streets, all the gossip of the neighbourhood came into his face.

'I said to my wife,' he said, 'something's wrong at Pliny's.'

'I came to offer Mr Pliny a piece of Dresden,' I said, 'but he was out at Brixton seeing his sister, his wife said. He came back and thought I'd broken in and hit himself on the wardrobe.'

'You oughtn't to leave Mrs Pliny alone with all this valuable stock, Mr Pliny. Saturday night too,' the tobacconist said.

Tears had started rolling down Pliny's cheeks very suddenly when I mentioned Brixton and he looked at me and the tobacconist in panic.

'I'm not interested in Dresden,' he managed to say.

Isabel dabbed his face and sent the tobacconist for a glass of water.

'No, dear, you're not,' said Isabel.

And to me she said: 'We're not interested.'

That was the end. I found myself walking in the street. How unreal people looked in the sodium light.

JEAN RHYS

Pioneers, Oh, Pioneers

As the two girls were walking up yellow-hot Market Street, Irene nudged her sister and said: 'Look at her!' They were not far from the market, they could still smell the fish.

When Rosalie turned her head the few white women she saw carried parasols. The black women were barefooted, wore gaily striped turbans and highwaisted dresses. It was still the nineteenth century, November 1899.

'There she goes,' said Irene.

And there was Mrs Menzies, riding up to her house on the Morne for a cool weekend.

'Good morning,' Rosalie said, but Mrs Menzies did not answer. She rode past, clip-clop, clip-clop, in her thick, dark riding habit brought from England ten years before, balancing a large dripping parcel wrapped in flannel on her knee.

'It's ice. She wants her drinks cold,' said Rosalie.

'Why can't she have it sent up like everybody else? The black people laugh at her. She ought to be ashamed of herself.'

'I don't see why,' Rosalie said obstinately.

'Oh, you,' Irene jeered. 'You like crazy people. You like Jimmy Longa and you like old maman Menzies. You liked Ramage, nasty beastly horrible Ramage.'

Rosalie said: 'You cried about him yesterday.'

'Yesterday doesn't count. Mother says we were all hysterical yesterday.'

By this time they were nearly home so Rosalie said nothing. But she put her tongue out as they went up the steps into the long, cool gallery.

Their father, Dr Cox, was sitting in an armchair with a three-legged table by his side.

On the table were his pipe, his tin of tobacco and his glasses. Also *The Times* weekly edition, the *Cornhill Magazine*, the *Lancet* and a West Indian newspaper, the *Dominica Herald and Leeward Islands Gazette*.

He was not to be spoken to, as they saw at once though one was only eleven and the other nine.

'Dead as a door nail,' he muttered as they went past him into the next room so comfortably full of rocking-chairs, a mahogany table, palm leaf fans, a tigerskin rug, family photographs, views of Bettws-y-Coed and a large picture of wounded soldiers in the snow, Napoleon's Retreat from Moscow.

The doctor had not noticed his daughters, for he too was thinking about Mr Ramage. He had liked the man, stuck up for him, laughed off his obvious eccentricities, denied point blank that he was certifiable. All wrong. Ramage, probably a lunatic, was now dead as a door nail. Nothing to be done.

Ramage had first arrived in the island two years before, a handsome man in tropical kit, white suit, red cummerbund, solar topee. After he grew tired of being followed about by an admiring crowd of little Negro boys he stopped wearing the red sash and the solar topee but he clung to his white suits though most of the men wore dark trousers even when the temperature was ninety in the shade.

Miss Lambton, who had been a fellow passenger from Barbados, reported that he was certainly a gentleman and also a king among men when it came to looks. But he was very unsociable. He ignored all invitations to dances, tennis parties and moonlight picnics. He never went to church and was not to be seen at the club. He seemed to like Dr Cox, however, and dined with him one evening. And Rosalie, then aged seven, fell in love.

After dinner, though the children were not supposed to talk much when guests were there, and were usually not allowed downstairs at all, she edged up to him and said: 'Sing something.' (People who came to dinner often sang afterwards, as she well knew.)

'I can't sing,' said Ramage.

'Yes you can.' Her mother's disapproving expression made her insist the more. 'You can. You can.'

He laughed and hoisted her on to his knee. With her head against his chest she listened while he rumbled gently: 'Baa baa black sheep, have you any wool? Yes, sir, yes, sir, three bags full.'

Then the gun at the fort fired for nine o'clock and the girls, smug in their stiff white dresses, had to say good night nicely and go upstairs to bed.

After a perfunctory rubber of whist with a dummy, Mrs Cox also departed. Over his whisky and soda Ramage explained that he'd come to the island with the intention of buying an estate. 'Small, and as remote as possible.'

'That won't be difficult here.'

'So I heard,' said Ramage.

'Tried any of the other islands?'

'I went to Barbados first.'

'Little England,' the doctor said. 'Well?'

'I was told that there were several places going along this new Imperial Road you've got here.'

'Won't last,' Dr Cox said. 'Nothing lasts in this island. Nothing will come of it. You'll see.'

Ramage looked puzzled.

'It's all a matter of what you want the place for,' the doctor said without explaining himself. 'Are you after a good interest on your capital or what?'

'Peace,' Ramage said. 'Peace, that's what I'm after.'

'You'll have to pay for that,' the doctor said.

'What's the price?' said Ramage, smiling. He put one leg over the other. His bare ankle was hairy and thin, his hands long and slender for such a big man.

'You'll be very much alone.'

'That will suit me,' Ramage said.

'And if you're far along the road, you'll have to cut the trees down, burn the stumps and start from scratch.'

'Isn't there a half-way house?' Ramage said.

The doctor answered rather vaguely: 'You might be able to get hold of one of the older places.'

He was thinking of young Errington, of young Kellaway, who had both bought estates along the Imperial Road and worked hard. But they had given up after a year or two, sold their land cheap and gone back to England. They could not stand the loneliness and melancholy of the forest.

A fortnight afterwards Miss Lambton told Mrs Cox that Mr Ramage had bought Spanish Castle, the last but one of the older properties. It was beautiful but not prosperous – some said bad luck, others bad management. His nearest neighbour was Mr Eliot, who owned *Malgré Tout*. Now called Twickenham.

For several months after this Ramage disappeared and one afternoon at croquet Mrs Cox asked Miss Lambton if she had any news of him.

'A strange man,' she said, 'very reserved.'

'Not so reserved as all that,' said Miss Lambton. 'He got married several weeks ago. He told me that he didn't want it talked about.'

'No!' said Mrs Cox. 'Who to?'

Then it all came out. Ramage had married a coloured girl who called herself Isla Harrison, though she had no right to the name of Harrison. Her mother was dead and she'd been brought up by her godmother, old Miss Myra, according to local custom. Miss Myra kept a sweet shop in Bay Street and Isla was very well known in the town – too well known.

'He took her to Trinidad,' said Miss Lambton mournfully, 'and when they came back they were married. They went down to Spanish Castle and I've heard nothing about them since.'

'It's not as though she was a nice coloured girl,' everybody said.

So the Ramages were lost to white society. Lost to everyone but Dr Cox. Spanish Castle estate was in a district which he visited every month, and one afternoon as he was driving past he saw Ramage standing near his letter box which was nailed to a tree visible from the road. He waved. Ramage waved back and beckoned.

While they were drinking punch on the veranda, Mrs Ramage came in. She was dressed up to the nines, smelt very strongly of cheap scent and talked loudly in an aggressive voice. No, she certainly wasn't a nice coloured girl.

The doctor tried – too hard perhaps – for the next time he called at Spanish Castle a door banged loudly inside the house and a grinning boy told him that Mr Ramage was out.

'And Mrs Ramage?'

'The mistress is not at home.'

At the end of the path the doctor looked back and saw her at a window peering at him.

He shook his head, but he never went there again, and the Ramage couple sank out of sight, out of mind.

It was Mr Eliot, the owner of Twickenham, who started the trouble. He was out with his wife, he related, looking at some young nutmeg trees near the boundary. They had a boy with them who had lighted a fire and put on water for tea. They looked up and saw Ramage coming out from under the trees. He was burnt a deep brown, his hair fell to his shoulders, his beard to his chest. He was wearing sandals and a leather belt, on one side of which hung a cutlass, on the other a large pouch. Nothing else.

'If,' said Mr Eliot, 'the man had apologized to my wife, if he'd shown the slightest consciousness of the fact that he was stark naked, I would have overlooked the whole thing. God knows one learned to be tolerant in this wretched place. But not a bit of it. He stared hard at her and came out with: "What an uncomfortable dress – and how ugly!" My wife got very red. Then she said: "Mr Ramage, the kettle is just boiling. Will you have some tea?"'

'Good for her,' said the doctor. 'What did he say to that?'

'Well, he seemed rather confused. He bowed from the waist, exactly as if he had clothes on, and explained that he never drank tea. "I have a stupid habit of talking to myself. I beg your pardon," he said, and off he went. We got home and my wife locked herself in the bedroom. When she came out she wouldn't speak to me at first, then she said that he was quite right, I didn't care what she looked like, so now she didn't either. She called me a mean man. A mean man. I won't have it,' said Mr Eliot indignantly. 'He's mad, walking about with a cutlass. He's dangerous.'

'Oh, I don't think so,' said Dr Cox. 'He'd probably left his clothes round the corner and didn't know how to explain. Perhaps we do cover ourselves up too much. The sun can be good for you. The best thing in the world. If you'd seen as I have . . .'

Mr Eliot interrupted at once. He knew that when the doctor started talking about his unorthodox methods he went on for a long time.

'I don't know about all that. But I may as well tell you that I dislike the idea of a naked man with a cutlass wandering about near my place. I dislike it very much indeed. I've got to consider my wife and my daughter. Something ought to be done.'

Eliot told his story to everyone who'd listen and the Ramages became the chief topic of conversation.

'It seems,' Mrs Cox told her husband, 'that he does wear a pair of trousers as a rule and even an old coat when it rains, but several people have watched him lying in a hammock on the veranda naked. You ought to call there and speak to him. They say,' she added, 'that the two of them fight like Kilkenny cats. He's making himself very unpopular.'

So the next time he visited the district Dr Cox stopped near Spanish Castle. As he went up the garden path he noticed how unkempt and deserted the place looked. The grass on the lawn had grown very high and the veranda hadn't been swept for days.

The doctor paused uncertainly, then tapped on the sitting-room door, which was open. 'Hallo,' called Ramage from inside the house, and he appeared, smiling. He was wearing one of his linen suits, clean and pressed, and his hair and beard were trimmed.

'You're looking very well,' the doctor said.

'Oh, yes, I feel splendid. Sit down and I'll get you a drink.'

There seemed to be no one else in the house.

'The servants have all walked out,' Ramage explained when he appeared with the punch.

'Good Lord, have they?'

'Yes, but I think I've found an old woman in the village who'll come up and cook.'

'And how is Mrs Ramage?'

At this moment there was a heavy thud on the side of the house, then another, then another.

'What was that?' asked Dr Cox.

'Somebody throwing stones. They do sometimes.'

'Why, in heaven's name?'

'I don't know. Ask them.'

Then the doctor repeated Eliot's story, but in spite of himself it came out as trivial, even jocular.

'Yes, I was very sorry about that,' Ramage answered casually. 'They

425

startled me as much as I startled them. I wasn't expecting to see anyone. It was a bit of bad luck but it won't happen again.'

'It was bad luck meeting Eliot,' the doctor said.

And that was the end of it. When he got up to go, no advice, no warning had been given.

'You're sure you're all right here?'

'Yes, of course,' said Ramage.

'It's all rubbish,' the doctor told his wife that evening. 'The man's as fit as a fiddle, nothing wrong with him at all.'

'Was Mrs Ramage there?'

'No, thank God. She was out.'

'I heard this morning,' said Mrs Cox, 'that she disappeared. Hasn't been seen for weeks.'

The doctor laughed heartily. 'Why can't they leave those two alone? What rubbish!'

'Well,' said Mrs Cox without smiling, 'it's odd, isn't it?'

'Rubbish,' the doctor said again some days later, for, spurred on by Mr Eliot, people were talking venomously and he could not stop them. Mrs Ramage was not at Spanish Castle, she was not in the town. Where was she?

Old Myra was questioned. She said that she had not seen her god-daughter and had not heard from her 'since long time'. The Inspector of Police had two anonymous letters – the first writer claimed to know 'all what happen at Spanish Castle one night': the other said that witnesses were frightened to come forward and speak against a white man.

The *Gazette* published a fiery article:

The so-called 'Imperial Road' was meant to attract young Englishmen with capital who would buy and develop properties in the interior. This costly experiment has not been a success, and one of the last of these gentlemen planters has seen himself as the king of the cannibal islands ever since he landed. We have it, on the best authority, that his very eccentric behavior has been the greatest possible annoyance to his neighbour. Now the whole thing has become much more serious . . .

It ended: 'Black people bear much; must they also bear beastly murder and nothing be done about it?'

'You don't suppose that I believe all these lies, do you?' Dr Cox told Mr Eliot, and Mr Eliot answered: 'Then I'll make it my business to find out the truth. That man is a menace, as I said from the first, and he should be dealt with.'

'Dear Ramage,' Dr Cox wrote. 'I'm sorry to tell you that stupid and harmful rumours are being spread about your wife and yourself. I need hardly say that no one with a grain of sense takes them seriously, but people here are excitable and very ready to believe mischiefmakers, so I strongly advise you to put a stop to the talk at once and to take legal action if necessary.'

But the doctor got no answer to this letter, for in the morning news reached the town of a riot at Spanish Castle the night before.

A crowd of young men and boys, and a few women, had gone up to Ramage's house to throw stones. It was a bright moonlight night. He had come on to the veranda and stood there facing them. He was dressed in white and looked very tall, they said like a zombi. He said something that nobody heard, a man had shouted 'white zombi' and thrown a stone which hit him. He went into the house and came out with a shotgun. Then stories differed wildly. He had fired and hit a woman in the front of the crowd . . . No, he'd hit a little boy at the back . . . He hadn't fired at all, but had threatened them. It was agreed that in the rush to get away people had been knocked down and hurt, one woman seriously.

It was also rumoured that men and boys from the village planned to burn down Spanish Castle house, if possible with Ramage inside. After this there was no more hesitation. The next day a procession walked up the garden path to the house – the Inspector of Police, three policemen and Dr Cox.

'He must give some explanation of all this,' said the Inspector.

The doors and windows were all open, and they found Ramage and the shotgun, but they got no explanation. He had been dead for some hours.

His funeral was an impressive sight. A good many came out of curiosity, a good many because, though his death was said to be 'an accident', they felt guilty. For behind the coffin walked Mrs Ramage, sent for post-haste by old Myra. She'd been staying with relatives in Guadeloupe. When asked why she had left so secretly – she had taken a fishing boat from the other side of the island – she answered sullenly that she didn't want any-one to know her business, and she knew how people talked. No, she'd heard no rumours about her husband, and the *Gazette* – a paper written in English – was not read in Guadeloupe.

'Eh-eh,' echoed Myra. 'Since when the girl obliged to the everybody where she go and what she do chapter and verse . . .

It was lovely weather, and on their way to the Anglican cemetery many had tears in their eyes.

But already public opinion was turning against Ramage.

'His death was really a blessing in disguise,' said one lady. 'He was evidently mad, poor man – sitting in the sun with no clothes on – much worse might have happened.'

'This is All Souls Day,' Rosalie thought, standing at her bedroom window before going to sleep. She was wishing that Mr Ramage could have been buried in the Catholic cemetery, where all day the candles burnt almost invisible in the sunlight. When night came they twinkled like fireflies. The graves were covered with flowers – some real, some red or yellow paper or little gold cut-outs. Sometimes there was a letter weighted by a stone and the black people said that next morning the letters had gone. And where? Who would steal letters on the night of the dead? But the letters had gone.

The Anglican cemetery, which was not very far away, down the hill, was deserted and silent. Protestants believed that when you were dead, you were dead.

If he had a letter . . . she thought.

'My dear darling Mr Ramage,' she wrote, then felt so sad that she began to cry.

Two hours later Mrs Cox came into the room and found her daughter in bed and asleep; on the table by her side was the unfinished letter. Mrs Cox read it, frowned, pressed her lips together, then crumpled it up and threw it out of the window.

There was a stiff breeze and she watched it bouncing purposefully down the street. As if it knew exactly where it was going.

IAN McEWAN

Pornography

O'Byrne walked through Soho market to his brother's shop in Brewer Street. A handful of customers leafing through the magazines and Harold watching them through pebble-thick lenses from his raised platform in the corner. Harold was barely five foot and wore built-up shoes. Before becoming his employee O'Byrne used to call him Little Runt. At Harold's elbow a miniature radio rasped details of race meetings for the afternoon. 'So,' said Harold with thin contempt, 'the prodigal brother . . .' His magnified eyes fluttered at every consonant. He looked past O'Byrne's shoulder. 'All the magazines are for sale, gentlemen.' The readers stirred uneasily like troubled dreamers. One replaced a magazine and walked quickly from the shop. 'Where d'you get to?' Harold said in a quieter voice. He stepped from the dais, put on his coat and glared up at O'Byrne, waiting for an answer. Little Runt. O'Byrne was ten years younger than his brother, detested him and his success but now, strangely, wanted his approbation. 'I had an appointment, didn't I,' he said quietly. 'I got the clap.' Harold was pleased. He reached up and punched O'Byrne's shoulder playfully. 'Serves you,' he said and cackled theatrically. Another customer edged out of the shop. From the doorway Harold called, 'I'll be back at five.' O'Byrne smiled as his brother left. He hooked his thumbs into his jeans and sauntered towards the tight knot of customers. 'Can I help you gentlemen, the magazines are all for sale.' They scattered before him like frightened fowl, and suddenly he was alone in the shop.

A plump woman of fifty or more stood in front of a plastic shower curtain, naked but for panties and gasmask. Her hands hung limply at her sides and in one of them a cigarette smouldered. Wife of the Month. Since gasmasks and a thick rubber sheet on the bed, wrote JN of Andover, we've never looked back. O'Byrne played with the radio for a while then switched it off. Rhythmically he turned the pages of the magazine, and stopped to read the letters. An uncircumcised male virgin, without hygiene, forty-two next May, dared not peel back his foreskin now for fear of what he might see. I get these nightmares of worms. O'Byrne laughed and crossed his legs. He replaced the magazine, returned to the radio, switched it on and off rapidly and caught the unintelligible middle of a word. He walked about the shop straightening the magazines in the racks. He stood by the door and stared at the wet street intersected by the coloured strips of the plastic walk-thro. He whistled over and over a tune whose end immediately suggested its beginning. Then he returned to Harold's raised platform and made two telephone calls, both to the hospital, the first to Lucy. But Sister Drew was busy in the ward and could not come to the phone. O'Byrne left a message that he would not be able to see her that evening after all and would phone again tomorrow. He dialled the hospital switchboard and this time asked for trainee Nurse Shepherd in the children's ward. 'Hi,' O'Byrne said when Pauline picked up the phone. 'It's me.' And he stretched and leaned against the wall. Pauline was a silent girl who once wept in a film about the effects of pesticides on butterflies, who wanted to redeem O'Byrne with her love. Now she laughed, 'I've been phoning you all morning,' she said. 'Didn't your brother tell you?'

'Listen,' said O'Byrne, 'I'll be at your place about eight,' and replaced the receiver.

Harold did not return till after six, and O'Byrne was almost asleep, his head pillowed on his forearm. There were no customers. O'Byrne's only sale was *American Bitch*. 'Those American mags,' said Harold as he emptied the till of £15 and a handful of silver, 'are *good*.' Harold's new leather jacket. O'Byrne fingered it appreciatively. 'Seventy-eight quid,' said Harold and braced himself in front of the fish-eye mirror. His glasses flashed. 'It's all right,' said O'Byrne. 'Fucking right it is,' said Harold, and began to close up shop. 'Never take much on Wednesdays,' he said wistfully as he reached up and switched on the burglar alarm. 'Wednesday's a cunt of a day.' Now O'Byrne was in front of the mirror, examining a small trail of acne that led from the corner of his mouth. 'You're not fucking kidding,' he agreed.

Harold's house lay at the foot of the Post Office Tower and O'Byrne rented a room from him. They walked along together without speaking. From time to time Harold glanced sideways into a dark shop window to catch the reflection of himself and his new leather jacket. Little Runt. O'Byrne said, 'Cold, innit?' and Harold said nothing. Minutes later, when they were passing a pub, Harold steered O'Byrne into the dank, deserted public saying, 'Since you got the clap I'll buy you a drink.' The publican heard the remark and regarded O'Byrne with interest. They drank three scotches apiece, and as O'Byrne was paying for the fourth round Harold said, 'Oh yeah, one of those two nurses you've been knocking around with phoned.' O'Byrne nodded and wiped his lips. After a pause Harold said, 'You're well in there . . .' O'Byrne nodded again. 'Yep.' Harold's jacket shone. When he reached for his drink it creaked. O'Byrne was not going to tell him anything. He banged his hands together. 'Yep,' he said once more, and stared over his brother's head at the empty bar. Harold tried again. 'She wanted to know where you'd been . . .' 'I bet she did,' O'Byrne muttered, and then smiled.

Pauline, short and untalkative, her face bloodlessly pale, intersected by a heavy black fringe, her eyes large, green and watchful, her flat small, damp and shared with a secretary who was never there. O'Byrne arrived after ten, a little drunk and in need of a bath to purge the faint purulent scent that lately had hung about his fingers. She sat on a small wooden stool to watch him luxuriate. Once she leaned forwards and touched his body where it broke the surface. O'Byrne's eyes were closed, his hands floating at his side, the only sound the diminishing hiss of the cistern. Pauline rose quietly to bring a clean white towel from her bedroom, and O'Byrne did not hear her leave or return. She sat down again and ruffled, as far as it was possible, O'Byrne's damp, matted hair. 'The food is ruined,' she said without accusation. Beads of perspiration collected in the corners of O'Byrne's eyes and rolled down the line of his nose like tears. Pauline rested her hand on O'Byrne's knee where it jutted through the grey water. Steam turned to water on the cold walls, senseless minutes passed. 'Never mind, love,' said O'Byrne, and stood up.

Pauline went out to buy beer and pizzas, and O'Byrne lay down in her tiny bedroom to wait. Ten minutes passed. He dressed after cursory examination of his clean but swelling meatus, and wandered listlessly about the sitting room. Nothing interested him in Pauline's small collection of books. There were no magazines. He entered the kitchen in search of a drink. There was nothing but an overcooked meat pie. He picked round the burnt bits and as he ate turned the pages of a picture calendar. When he finished he remembered again he was waiting for Pauline. He looked at his watch. She had been gone now almost half an hour. He stood up quickly, tipping the kitchen chair behind him to the floor. He paused in the sitting room and then walked decisively out of the flat and slammed the front door on his way. He hurried down the stairs, anxious not to meet her now he had decided to get out. But she was there. Halfway up the second flight, a little out of breath, her arms full of bottles and tinfoil parcels. 'Where d'you get to?' said O'Byrne. Pauline stopped several steps down from him, her face tilted up awkwardly over her goods, the whites of her eyes and the tinfoil vivid in the dark. 'The usual place was closed. I had to walk miles . . . sorry.' They stood. O'Byrne was not hungry. He wanted to go. He hitched his thumbs into the waist of his jeans and cocked his head towards the invisible ceiling, then he looked down at Pauline who waited. 'Well,' he said at last, 'I was thinking of going.' Pauline came up, and as she pushed past whispered, 'Silly.' O'Byrne turned and followed her, obscurely cheated.

He leaned in the doorway, she righted the chair. With a movement of his head O'Byrne indicated that he wanted none of the food Pauline was setting out on plates. She poured him a beer and knelt to gather a few black pastry droppings from the floor. They sat in the sitting room. O'Byrne drank, Pauline ate slowly, neither spoke. O'Byrne finished all the beer and placed his hand on Pauline's knee. She did not turn. He said cheerily, 'What's wrong with you?' and she said, 'Nothing.' Alive with irritation O'Byrne moved closer and placed his arm protectively across her shoulders. 'Tell you what,' he half whispered. 'Let's go to bed.' Suddenly Pauline rose and went into the bedroom. O'Byrne sat with his hands clasped behind his head. He listened to Pauline undress, and he heard the creak of the bed. He got to his feet and, still without desire, entered the bedroom.

Pauline lay on her back and O'Byrne, having undressed quickly, lay beside her. She did not acknowledge him in her usual way, she did not move. O'Byrne raised his arm to stroke her shoulder, but instead let his hand fall back heavily against the sheet. They both lay on their backs in mounting silence, until O'Byrne decided to give her one last chance and with naked grunts hauled himself on to his elbow and arranged his face over hers. Her eyes, thick with tears, stared past him. 'What's the matter?' he said in resignatory sing-song. The eyes budged a fraction and fixed on his own. 'You,' she said simply. O'Byrne returned to his side of the bed, and after a moment said threateningly. 'I see.' Then he was up, and on top of her, and then past her and on the far side of the room. 'All right then . . .' he said. He wrenched his laces into a knot, and searched for his shirt. Pauline's back was to him. But as he crossed the sitting room her rising, accelerating wail of denial made him stop and turn. All white, in a cotton nightdress, she was there in the bedroom doorway and in the air, simultaneously at every point of arc in the intervening space, like the trick photographer's diver, she was on the far side of the room and she was at his lapels, knuckles in her mouth and shaking her head. O'Byrne smiled, and put his arms around her shoulders. Forgiveness swept through him. Clinging to each other they returned to the bedroom. O'Byrne undressed and they lay down again, O'Byrne on his back, Pauline with her head pillowed on his shoulder.

O'Byrne said, 'I never know what's going on in your mind,' and deeply comforted by this thought, he fell asleep. Half an hour later he woke. Pauline, exhausted by a week of twelve-hour shifts, slept deeply on his arm. He shook her gently. 'Hey,' he said. He shook her firmly, and as the rhythm of her breathing broke and she began to stir, he said in a laconic parody of some unremembered film, 'Hey, there's something we ain't done yet . . .'

Harold was excited. When O'Byrne walked into the shop towards noon the following day Harold took hold of his arms and waved in the air a sheet of paper. He was almost shouting. 'I've worked it all out. I know what I want to do with the shop.' 'Oh yeah,' said O'Byrne dully, and put his fingers in his eyes and scratched till the intolerable itch there became a bearable pain. Harold rubbed his small pink hands together and explained rapidly. 'I'm going All American. I spoke to their rep on the phone this morning and he'll be here in half an hour. I'm getting rid of all the quid a time piss-in-her-cunt letters. I'm gonna carry the whole of the House of Florence range at £4.50 a time.'

O'Byrne walked across the shop to where Harold's jacket was spread across a chair. He tried it on. It was of course too small. 'And I'm going to call it Transatlantic Books,' Harold was saying. O'Byrne tossed the jacket on to the chair. It slid to the floor and deflated there like some reptilian air sac. Harold picked it up, and did not cease talking. 'If I carry Florence exclusive I get a special discount *and*,' he giggled, 'they pay for the fucking neon sign.'

O'Byrne sat down and interrupted his brother. 'How many of those soddin' inflatable women did you unload? There's still twenty-five of the fuckers in the cellar.' But Harold was pouring out scotch into two glasses. 'He'll be here in half an hour,' he repeated, and offered one glass to O'Byrne. 'Big deal,' said O'Byrne, and sipped. 'I want you to take the van over to Norbury and collect the order this afternoon. I want to get into this straight away.'

O'Byrne sat moodily with his drink while his brother whistled and was busy about the shop. A man came in and bought a magazine. 'See,' said O'Byrne sourly while the customer was still lingering over the tentacled condoms, 'he bought English, didn't he?' The man turned guiltily and left. Harold came and crouched by O'Byrne's chair and spoke as one who explains copulation to an infant. 'And what do I make? Forty per cent of 75p. Thirty p. Thirty fucking p. On House of Florence I'll make fifty per cent of £4·50. And that,' he rested his hand briefly on O'Byrne's knee, 'is what I call business.'

O'Byrne wriggled his empty glass in front of Harold's face, and waited patiently for his brother to fill it . . . Little Runt.

The House of Florence warehouse was a disused church in a narrow terraced street on the Brixton side of Norbury. O'Byrne entered by the main porch. A crude plasterboard office and waiting room had been set up in the west end. The font was a large ash-tray in the waiting room. An elderly woman with a blue rinse sat alone in the office typing. When O'Byrne tapped on the sliding window she ignored him, then she rose and slid aside the glass panel. She took the order form he pushed towards her, glancing at him with unconcealed distaste. She spoke primly. 'You better wait there.' O'Byrne tap-danced abstractedly about the font, and combed his hair, and whistled the tune that went in a circle. Suddenly a shrivelled man with a brown coat and clipboard was at his side. 'Transatlantic

Books?' he said. O'Byrne shrugged and followed him. They moved together slowly down long aisles of bolted steel shelves, the old man pushing a large trolley and O'Byrne walking a little in front with his hands clasped behind his back. Every few yards the warehouseman stopped, and with bad-tempered gasps lifted a thick pile of magazines from the shelves. The load on the trolley grew. The old man's breath echoed hoarsely around the church. At the end of the first aisle he sat down on the trolley, between his neat piles, and coughed and hawked for a minute or so into a paper handkerchief. Then, carefully folding the tissue and its ponderous green contents back into his pocket, he said to O'Byrne. 'Here, you're young. You push this thing.' And O'Byrne said, 'Push the fucker yourself. It's your job,' and offered the man a cigarette and lit it for him.

O'Byrne nodded at the shelves. 'You get some reading done here.' The old man exhaled irritably. 'It's all rubbish. It ought to be banned.' They moved on. At the end, as he was signing the invoice, O'Byrne said, 'Who you got lined up for tonight? Madam in the office there?' The warehouseman was pleased. His cackles rang out like bells, then tailed into another coughing fit. He leaned feebly against the wall, and when he had recovered sufficiently he raised his head and meaningfully winked his watery eye. But O'Byrne had turned and was wheeling the magazines out to the van.

Lucy was ten years older than Pauline, and a little plump. But her flat was large and comfortable. She was a sister and Pauline no more than a trainee nurse. They knew nothing of each other. At the underground station O'Byrne bought flowers for Lucy, and when she opened the door to him he presented them with a mock bow and the clicking of heels. 'A peace offering?' she said contemptuously and took the daffodils away. She had led him into the bedroom. They sat down side by side on the bed. O'Byrne ran his hand up her leg in a perfunctory kind of way. She pushed away his arm and said, 'Come on then. Where have you been the past three days?' O'Byrne could barely remember. Two nights with Pauline, one night in the pub with friends of his brother.

He stretched back luxuriously on the pink candlewick. 'You know . . . working late for Harold. Changing the shop around. That kind of thing.'

'Those dirty books,' said Lucy with a little high-pitched laugh.

435

O'Byrne stood up and kicked off his shoes. 'Don't start that,' he said, glad to be off the defensive. Lucy leaned forwards and gathered up his shoes. 'You're going to ruin the backs of these,' she said busily, 'kicking them off like that.'

They both undressed. Lucy hung her clothes neatly in the wardrobe. When O'Byrne stood almost naked before her she wrinkled her nose in disgust. 'Is that you smelling?' O'Byrne was hurt. 'I'll have a bath,' he offered curtly.

Lucy stirred the bathwater with her hand, and spoke loudly over the thunder of the taps. 'You should have brought me some clothes to wash.' She hooked her fingers into the elastic of his pants. 'Give me these now and they'll be dry by the morning.' O'Byrne laced his fingers into hers in a decoy of affection. 'No, no,' he shouted rapidly. 'They were clean on this morning, they were.' Playfully Lucy tried to get them off. They wrestled across the bathroom floor, Lucy shrieking with laughter, O'Byrne excited but determined.

Finally Lucy put on her dressing gown and went away. O'Byrne heard her in the kitchen. He sat in the bath and washed away the bright green stains. When Lucy returned his pants were drying on the radiator. 'Women's Lib, innit?' said O'Byrne from the bath. Lucy said, 'I'm getting in too,' and took off her dressing gown. O'Byrne made room for her. 'Please yourself,' he said with a smile as she settled herself in the grey water.

O'Byrne lay on his back on the clean white sheets, and Lucy eased herself on to his belly like a vast nesting bird. She would have it no other way, from the beginning she had said, 'I'm in charge.' O'Byrne had replied, 'We'll see about that.' He was horrified, sickened, that he could enjoy being overwhelmed, like one of those cripples in his brother's magazines. Lucy had spoken briskly, the kind of voice she used for difficult patients. 'If you don't like it then don't come back.' Imperceptibly O'Byrne was initiated into Lucy's wants. It was not simply that she wished to squat on him. She did not want him to move. 'If you move again,' she warned him once, 'you've had it.' From mere habit O'Byrne thrust upwards and deeper, and quick as the tongue of a snake she lashed his face several times with her open palm. On the instant she came, and afterwards lay across the bed, half sobbing, half laughing. O'Byrne, one side of his face swollen and pink, departed sulking. 'You're a bloody pervert,' he had shouted from the door.

Next day he was back, and Lucy agreed not to hit him again. Instead she abused him. 'You pathetic helpless little shit,' she would scream at the peak of her excitement. And she seemed to intuit O'Byrne's guilty thrill of pleasure, and wish to push it further. One time she had suddenly lifted herself clear of him and, with a far-away smile, urinated on his head and chest. O'Byrne had struggled to get clear, but Lucy held him down and seemed deeply satisfied by his unsought orgasm. This time O'Byrne left the flat enraged. Lucy's strong, chemical smell was with him for days, and it was during this time that he met Pauline. But within the week he was back at Lucy's to collect, so he insisted, his razor, and Lucy was persuading him to try on her underwear. O'Byrne resisted with horror and excitement. 'The trouble with you,' said Lucy, 'is that you're scared of what you like.'

Now Lucy gripped his throat in one hand. 'You dare move,' she hissed, and closed her eyes. O'Byrne lay still. Above him Lucy swayed like a giant tree. Her lips were forming a word, but there was no sound. Many minutes later she opened her eyes and stared down, frowning a little as though struggling to place him. And all the while she eased backwards and forwards. Finally she spoke, more to herself than to him. 'Worm . . .' O'Byrne moaned. Lucy's legs and thighs tightened and trembled. 'Worm . . . worm . . . you little worm. I'm going to tread on you . . . dirty little worm.' Once more her hand was closed about his throat. His eyes were sunk deep, and his word travelled a long way before it left his lips. 'Yes,' he whispered.

The following day O'Byrne attended the clinic. The doctor and his male assistant were matter-of-fact, unimpressed. The assistant filled out a form and wanted details of O'Byrne's recent sexual history. O'Byrne invented a whore at Ipswich bus station. For many days after that he kept to himself. Attending the clinic mornings and evenings, for injections, he was sapped of desire. When Pauline or Lucy phoned, Harold told them he did not know where O'Byrne was. 'Probably taken off for somewhere,' he said, winking across the shop at his brother. Both women phoned each day for three or four days, and then suddenly there were no calls from either.

O'Byrne paid no attention. The shop was taking good money now. In the evenings he drank with his brother and his brother's friends. He felt himself to be both busy and ill. Ten days passed. With the extra cash Harold was giving him, he bought a leather jacket, like Harold's, but somehow better, sharper, lined with red imitation silk. It both shone and creaked. He spent many minutes in front of the fish-eye mirror, standing sideways on, admiring the manner in which his shoulders and biceps pulled the leather to a tight sheen. He wore his jacket between the shop and the clinic and sensed the glances of women in the street. He thought of Pauline and Lucy. He passed a day considering which to phone first. He chose Pauline, and phoned her from the shop.

Trainee Nurse Shepherd was not available, O'Byrne was told after many minutes of waiting. She was sitting an examination. O'Byrne had his call transferred to the other side of the hospital. 'Hi,' he said when Lucy picked up the phone. 'It's me.' Lucy was delighted. 'When did you get back? Where have you been? When are you coming round?' He sat down. 'How about tonight?' he said. Lucy whispered in sex-kitten French, 'I can 'ardly wait . . .' O'Byrne laughed and pressed his thumb and forefinger against his forehead and heard other distant voices on the line. He heard Lucy giving instructions. Then she spoke rapidly to him. 'I've got to go. They've just brought a case in. About eight tonight then . . .' and she was gone.

O'Byrne prepared his story, but Lucy did not ask him where he had been. She was too happy. She laughed when she opened the door to him, she hugged him and laughed again. She looked different. O'Byrne could not remember her so beautiful. Her hair was shorter and a deeper brown, her nails were pale orange, she wore a short black dress with orange dots. There were candles and wine glasses on the dining table, music on the record player. She stood back, her eyes bright, almost wild, and admired his leather jacket. She ran her hands up the red lining. She pressed herself against it. 'Very smooth,' she said. 'Reduced to sixty quid,' O'Byrne said proudly, and tried to kiss her. But she laughed again and pushed him into a chair. 'You wait there and I'll get something to drink.'

O'Byrne lay back. From the record player a man sang of love in a restaurant with clean white tablecloths. Lucy brought an icy bottle of white wine. She sat on the arm of his chair and they drank and talked. Lucy told him recent stories of the ward, of nurses who fell in and out of love, patients who recovered or died. As she spoke she undid the top buttons of his shirt and pushed her hand down to his belly. And when O'Byrne turned in his chair and reached up for her she pushed him away, leaned down and kissed him on the nose. 'Now now,' she said primly. O'Byrne exerted himself. He recounted anecdotes he had heard in the pub. Lucy laughed crazily at the end of each, and as he was beginning the third she let her hand drop lightly between his legs and rest there. O'Byrne closed his eyes. The hand was gone and Lucy was nudging him. 'Go on,' she said. 'It was getting interesting.' He caught her wrist and wanted to pull her on to his lap. With a little sigh she slipped away and returned with a second bottle. 'We should have wine more often,' she said, 'if it makes you tell such funny stories.'

Encouraged, O'Byrne told his story, something about a car and what a garage mechanic said to a vicar. Once again Lucy was fishing round his fly and laughing, laughing. It was a funnier story than he thought. The floor rose and fell beneath his feet. And Lucy so beautiful, scented, warm . . . her eyes glowed. He was paralysed by her teasing. He loved her, and she laughed and robbed him of his will. Now he saw, he had come to live with her, and each night she teased him to the edge of madness. He pressed his face into her breasts. 'I love you,' he mumbled, and again Lucy was laughing, shaking, wiping the tears from her eyes. 'Do you . . . do you . . .' she kept trying to say. She emptied the bottle into his glass. 'Here's a toast . . .' 'Yeah,' said O'Byrne, 'To us.' Lucy was holding down her laughter. 'No, no,' she squealed. 'To *you*.' 'All right,' he said, and downed his wine in one. Then Lucy was standing in front of him pulling his arm. 'C'mon,' she said. 'C'mon.' O'Byrne struggled out of the chair. 'What about dinner then?' he said. 'You're the dinner,' she said, and they giggled as they tottered towards the bedroom.

As they undressed Lucy said, 'I've got a special little surprise for you so . . . no fuss.' O'Byrne sat on the edge of Lucy's large bed and shivered. 'I'm ready for anything,' he said. 'Good . . . good,' and for the first time she kissed him deeply, and pushed him gently backwards on to the bed. She climbed forward and sat astride his chest. O'Byrne closed his eyes. Months ago he would have resisted furiously. Lucy lifted his left hand to her mouth and kissed each finger. 'Hmmm . . . the first course.' O'Byrne laughed. The bed and the room undulated softly about him. Lucy was pushing his hand towards the top corner of the bed. O'Byrne heard a distant jingle, like bells. Lucy knelt by his shoulder, holding down his wrist, buckling it to a leather strap. She had always said she would tie him up one day and fuck him. She bent low over his face and they kissed again. She was licking his eyes and whispering, 'You're not going anywhere,' O'Byrne gasped for air. He could not move his face to smile. Now she was tugging at his right arm, pulling it, stretching it to the far corner of the bed. With a dread thrill of compliance O'Byrne felt his arm die. Now that was secure and Lucy was running her hands along the inside of his thigh, and on down to his feet . . . he lay stretched almost to breaking, splitting, fixed to each corner, spread out against the white sheet. Lucy knelt at the apex of his legs. She stared down at him with a faint, objective smile, and fingered herself delicately. O'Byrne lay waiting for her to settle on him like a vast white nesting bird. She was tracing with the tip of one finger the curve of his excitement, and then with thumb and forefinger making a tight ring about its base. A sigh fled between his teeth. Lucy leaned forwards. Her eyes were wild. She whispered, 'We're going to get you, me and Pauline are . . .'

Pauline. For an instant, syllables hollow of meaning. 'What?' said O'Byrne, and as he spoke the word he remembered, and understood a threat. 'Untie me,' he said quickly. But Lucy's finger curled under her crotch and her eyes half closed. Her breathing was slow and deep. 'Untie me,' he shouted, and struggled hopelessly with his straps. Lucy's breath came now in light little gasps. As he struggled, so they accelerated. She was saying something . . . moaning something. What was she saying? He could not hear. 'Lucy,' he said, 'please untie me.' Suddenly she was silent, her eyes wide open and clear. She climbed off the bed. 'Your friend Pauline will be here, soon,' she said, and began to get dressed. She was different, her movements brisk and efficient, she no longer looked at him. O'Byrne tried to sound casual. His voice was a little high. 'What's going on?' Lucy stood at the foot of the bed buttoning her dress. Her lip curled. 'You're a bastard,' she said. The doorbell rang and she smiled. 'Now that's good timing, isn't it?'

'Yes, he went down very quietly,' Lucy was saying as she showed Pauline into the bedroom. Pauline said nothing. She avoided looking at either O'Byrne or Lucy. And O'Byrne's eyes were fixed on the object she carried in her arms. It was large and silver, like an outsized electric toaster. 'It can plug in just here,' said Lucy. Pauline set it down on the bedside table. Lucy sat down at her dressing table and began to comb her hair. 'I'll get some water for it in a minute,' she said.

Pauline went and stood by the window. There was silence. Then O'Byrne said hoarsely, 'What's that thing?' Lucy turned in her seat. 'It's a steriliser,' she said breezily. 'Steriliser?' 'You know, for sterilising surgical instruments.' The next question O'Byrne did not dare ask. He felt sick and dizzy. Lucy left the room. Pauline continued to stare out the window into the dark. O'Byrne felt the need to whisper. 'Hey, Pauline, what's going on?' She turned to face him, and said nothing. O'Byrne discovered that the strap round his right wrist was slackening a little, the leather was stretching. His hand was concealed by pillows. He worked it backwards and forwards, and spoke urgently. 'Look, let's get out of here. Undo these things.'

For a moment she hesitated, then she walked round the side of the bed and stared down at him. She shook her head. 'We're going to get you.' The repetition terrified him. He thrashed from side to side. 'It's not my idea of a fucking joke,' he shouted. Pauline turned away. 'I hate you,' he heard her say. The right-hand strap gave a little more. 'I hate you. I hate you.' He pulled till he thought his arm would break. His hand was too large still for the noose around his wrist. He gave up.

Now Lucy was at the bedside pouring water into the steriliser. 'This is a sick joke,' said O'Byrne. Lucy lifted a flat, black case on to the table. She snapped it open and began to take out long-handled scissors, scalpels and other bright, tapering, silver objects. She lowered them carefully into the water. O'Byrne started to work his right hand again. Lucy removed the black case and set on the table two white kidney bowls with blue rims. In one lay two hypodermic needles, one large, one small. In the other was cotton wool. O'Byrne's voice shook. 'What is all this?' Lucy rested her cool hand on his forehead. She enunciated with precision. 'This is what they should have done for you at the clinic.' 'The clinic . . . ?' he echoed. He could see now that Pauline was leaning against the wall drinking from a bottle of scotch. 'Yes,' said Lucy, reaching down to take his pulse. 'Stop you spreading round your secret little diseases.' 'And telling lies,' said Pauline, her voice strained with indignation.

O'Byrne laughed uncontrollably. 'Telling lies . . . telling lies,' he spluttered. Lucy took the scotch from Pauline and raised it to her lips. O'Byrne recovered. His legs were shaking. 'You're both out of your minds.' Lucy tapped the steriliser and said to Pauline, 'This will take a few minutes yet. We'll scrub down in the kitchen.' O'Byrne tried to raise his head. 'Where are you going?' he called after them. 'Pauline . . . Pauline.'

But Pauline had nothing more to say. Lucy stopped in the bedroom doorway and smiled at him. 'We'll leave you a pretty little stump to remember us by,' and she closed the door.

On the bedside table the steriliser began to hiss. Shortly after it gave out the low rumble of boiling water, and inside the instruments clinked together gently. In terror he pumped his hand. The leather was flaying the skin off his wrist. The noose was riding now round the base of his thumb. Timeless minutes passed. He whimpered and pulled, and the edge of the leather cut deep into his hand. He was almost free.

The door opened, and Lucy and Pauline carried in a small, low table. Through his fear O'Byrne felt excitement once more, horrified excitement. They arranged the table close to the bed. Lucy bent low over his erection. 'Oh dear . . . oh dear,' she murmured. With tongs Pauline lifted instruments from the boiling water and laid them out in neat silver rows on the starched white tablecloth she had spread across the table. The leather noose slipped forwards fractionally. Lucy sat on the edge of the bed and took the large hypodermic from the bowl. 'This will make you a little sleepy,' she promised. She held it upright and expelled a small jet of liquid. And as she reached for the cotton wool O'Byrne's arm pulled clear. Lucy smiled. She set aside the hypodermic. She leaned forwards once more . . . warm, scented . . . she was fixing him with wild red eyes . . . her fingers played over his tip . . . she held him still between her fingers. 'Lie back, Michael, my sweet.' She nodded briskly at Pauline. 'If you'll secure that strap, Nurse Shepherd, then I think we can begin.'

ANGELA CARTER

The Courtship of Mr Lyon

Outside her kitchen window, the hedgerow glistened as if the snow possessed a light of its own; when the sky darkened towards evening, an unearthly, reflected pallor remained behind upon the winter's landscape, while still the soft flakes floated down. This lovely girl, whose skin possesses that same, inner light so you would have thought she, too, was made all of snow, pauses in her chores in the mean kitchen to look out at the country road. Nothing has passed that way all day; the road is white and unmarked as a spilled bolt of bridal satin.

Father said he would be home before nightfall.

The snow brought down all the telephone wires; he couldn't have called, even with the best of news.

The roads are bad. I hope he'll be safe.

But the old car stuck fast in a rut, wouldn't budge an inch; the engine whirred, coughed and died and he was far from home. Ruined, once; then ruined again, as he had learnt from his lawyers that very morning; at the conclusion of the lengthy, slow attempt to restore his fortunes, he had turned out his pockets to find the cash for petrol to take him home. And not even enough money left over to buy his Beauty, his girl-child, his pet, the one white rose she said she wanted; the only gift she wanted, no matter how the case went, how rich he might once again be. She had asked for so little and he had not been able to give it to her. He cursed the useless car, the last straw that broke his spirit; then, nothing for it but to fasten his old sheepskin coat around him, abandon the heap of metal and set off down the snow-filled lane to look for help.

Behind wrought iron gates, a short, snowy drive performed a reticent flourish before a miniature, perfect, Palladian house that seemed to hide itself shyly behind snow-laden skirts of an antique cypress. It was almost night; that house, with its sweet, retiring, melancholy grace, would have seemed deserted but for a light that flickered in an upstairs window, so vague it might have been the reflection of a star, if any stars could have penetrated the snow that whirled yet more thickly. Chilled through, he pressed the latch of the gate and saw, with a pang, how, on the withered ghost of a tangle of thorns, there clung, still, the faded rag of a white rose.

The gate clanged loudly shut behind him; too loudly. For an instant, that reverberating clang seemed final, emphatic, ominous as if the gate, now closed, barred all within it from the world outside the walled, wintry garden. And, from a distance, though from what distance he could not tell, he heard the most singular sound in the world: a great roaring, as of a beast of prey.

In too much need to allow himself to be intimidated, he squared up to the mahogany door. This door was equipped with a knocker in the shape of a lion's head, with a ring through the nose; as he raised his hand towards it, it came to him this lion's head was not, as he had thought at first, made of brass, but, instead, of solid gold. Before, however, he could announce his presence, the door swung silently inward on well-oiled hinges and he saw a white hall where the candles of a great chandelier cast their benign light upon so many, many flowers in great, free-standing jars of crystal that it seemed the whole of spring drew him into its warmth with a profound intake of perfumed breath. Yet there was no living person in the hall.

The door behind him closed as silently as it had opened, yet, this time, he felt no fear although he knew by the pervasive atmosphere of a suspension of reality that he had entered a place of privilege where all the laws of the world he knew need not necessarily apply, for the very rich are often very eccentric and the house was plainly that of an exceedingly wealthy man. As it was, when nobody came to help him with his coat, he took it off himself. At that, the crystals of the chandelier tinkled a little, as if emitting a pleased chuckle, and the door of a cloakroom opened of its own accord. There were, however, no clothes at all in this cloakroom, not even the statutory country-house garden mackintosh to greet his own squirearchal sheepskin, but, when he emerged again into the hall, he found a greeting waiting for him at last – there was, of all things, a liver and white King Charles spaniel crouched, with head intelligently cocked, on the Kelim runner. It gave him further, comforting proof of his unseen host's wealth and eccentricity to see the dog wore, in place of a collar, a diamond necklace.

The dog sprang to its feet in welcome and busily shepherded him (how amusing!) to a snug little leather-panelled study on the first floor, where a low table was drawn up to a roaring log fire. On the table, a silver tray; round the neck of the whisky decanter, a silver tag with the legend: *Drink me*, while the cover of the silver dish was engraved with the exhortation: *Eat me*, in a flowing hand. This dish contained sandwiches of thick-cut roast beef, still bloody. He drank the one with soda and ate the other with some excellent mustard thoughtfully provided in a stoneware pot, and, when the spaniel saw to it he had served himself, she trotted off about her own business.

All that remained to make Beauty's father entirely comfortable was to find, in a curtained recess, not only a telephone but the card of a garage that advertised a twenty-four-hour rescue service; a couple of calls later and he had confirmed, thank God, there was no serious trouble, only the car's age and the cold weather . . . could he pick it up from the village in an hour? And directions to the village, but half a mile away, were supplied, in a new tone of deference, as soon as he described the house from where he was calling.

And he was disconcerted but, in his impecunious circumstances, relieved to hear the bill would go on his hospitable if absent host's account; no question, assured the mechanic. It was the master's custom.

Time for another whisky as he tried, unsuccessfully, to call Beauty and tell her he would be late; but the lines were still down, although, miraculously, the storm had cleared as the moon rose and now a glance between the velvet curtains revealed a landscape as of ivory with an inlay of silver. Then the spaniel appeared again, with his hat in her careful mouth, prettily wagging her tail, as if to tell him it was time to be gone, that this magical hospitality was over.

As the door swung to behind him, he saw the lion's eyes were made of agate.

Great wreaths of snow now precariously curded the rose trees and, when he brushed against a stem on his way to the gate, a chill armful softly thudded to the ground to reveal, as if miraculously preserved beneath it, one last, single, perfect rose that might have been the last rose left living in all the white winter, and of so intense and yet delicate a fragrance it seemed to ring like a dulcimer on the frozen air.

How could his host, so mysterious, so kind, deny Beauty her present?

Not now distant but close at hand, close as that mahogany front door, rose a mighty, furious roaring; the garden seemed to hold its breath in apprehension. But still, because he loved his daughter, Beauty's father stole the rose.

At that, every window of the house blazed with furious light and a fugal baying, as of a pride of lions, introduced his host.

There is always a dignity about great bulk, an assertiveness, a quality of being more *there* than most of us are. The being who now confronted Beauty's father seemed to him, in his confusion, vaster than the house he owned, ponderous yet swift, and the moonlight glittered on his great, mazy head of hair, on the eyes green as agate, on the golden hairs of the great paws that grasped his shoulders so that their claws pierced the sheepskin as he shook him like an angry child shakes a doll.

This leonine apparition shook Beauty's father until his teeth rattled and then dropped him sprawling on his knees while the spaniel, darting from the open door, danced round them, yapping distractedly, like a lady at whose dinner party blows have been exchanged.

'My good fellow—' stammered Beauty's father; but the only response was a renewed roar.

'Good fellow? I am no good fellow! I am the Beast, and you must call me Beast, while I call you, Thief!'

'Forgive me for robbing your garden, Beast!'

Head of a lion; mane and mighty paws of a lion; he reared on his hind legs like an angry lion yet wore a smoking jacket of dull red brocade and was the owner of that lovely house and the low hills that cupped it.

'It was for my daughter,' said Beauty's father. 'All she wanted, in the whole world, was one white, perfect rose.'

The Beast rudely snatched the photograph her father drew from his wallet and inspected it, first brusquely, then with a strange kind of wonder, almost the dawning of surmise. The camera had captured a certain look she had, sometimes, of absolute sweetness and absolute gravity, as if her eyes might pierce appearances and see your soul. When he handed the picture back, the Beast took good care not to scratch the surface with his claws.

'Take her her rose, then, but bring her to dinner,' he growled; and what else was there to be done?

Although her father had told her of the nature of the one who waited for her, she could not control an instinctual shudder of fear when she saw him, for a lion is a lion and a man is a man and, though lions are more beautiful by far than we are, yet they belong to a different order of beauty and, besides, they have no respect for us: why should they? Yet wild things have a far more rational fear of us than is ours of them, and some kind of sadness in his agate eyes, that looked almost blind, as if sick of sight, moved her heart.

He sat, impassive as a figurehead, at the top of the table; the dining room was Queen Anne, tapestried, a gem. Apart from an aromatic soup kept hot over a spirit lamp, the food, though exquisite, was cold – a cold bird, a cold soufflé, cheese. He asked her father to serve them from a buffet and, himself, ate nothing. He grudgingly admitted what she had already guessed, that he disliked the presence of servants because, she thought, a constant human presence would remind him too bitterly of his otherness, but the spaniel sat at his feet throughout the meal, jumping up from time to time to see that everything was in order.

How strange he was. She found his bewildering difference from herself almost intolerable; its presence choked her. There seemed a heavy, sound-less pressure upon her in his house, as if it lay under water, and when she saw the great paws lying on the arm of his chair, she thought: they are the death of any tender herbivore. And such a one she felt herself to be, Miss Lamb, spotless, sacrificial.

Yet she stayed, and smiled, because her father wanted her to do so; and when the Beast told her how he would aid her father's appeal against the judgement, she smiled with both her mouth and her eyes. But when, as they sipped their brandy, the Beast, in the diffuse, rumbling purr with which he conversed, suggested, with a hint of shyness, of fear of refusal, that she should stay here, with him, in comfort, while her father returned to London to take up the legal cudgels again, she forced a smile. For she knew with a pang of dread, as soon as he spoke, that it would be so and her visit to the Beast must be, on some magically reciprocal scale, the price of her father's good fortune.

Do not think she had no will of her own; only, she was possessed by a sense of obligation to an unusual degree and, besides, she would gladly have gone to the ends of the earth for her father, whom she loved dearly.

Her bedroom contained a marvellous glass bed; she had a bathroom, with towels thick as fleece and vials of suave unguents; and a little parlour of her own, the walls of which were covered with an antique paper of birds of paradise and Chinamen, where there were precious books and pictures and the flowers grown by invisible gardeners in the Beast's hothouses. Next morning, her father kissed her and drove away with a renewed hope about him that made her glad, but, all the same, she longed for the shabby home of their poverty. The unaccustomed luxury about her she found poignant, because it gave no pleasure to its possessor and himself she did not see all day as if, curious reversal, she frightened him, although the spaniel came and sat with her, to keep her company. Today, the spaniel wore a neat choker of turquoises.

Who prepared her meals? Loneliness of the Beast; all the time she stayed there, she saw no evidence of another human presence but the trays of food that arrived on a dumb waiter inside a mahogany cupboard in her parlour. Dinner was eggs Benedict and grilled veal; she ate it as she browsed in a book she had found in the rosewood revolving bookcase, a collection of courtly and elegant French fairy tales about white cats who were transformed princesses and fairies who were birds. Then she pulled a sprig of muscat grapes from a fat bunch for her dessert and found herself yawning; she discovered she was bored. At that, the spaniel took hold of her skirt with its velvet mouth and gave it a firm but gentle tug. She allowed the dog to trot before her to the study in which her father had been entertained and there, to her well-disguised dismay, she found her host, seated beside the fire with a tray of coffee at his elbow from which she must pour.

The voice that seemed to issue from a cave full of echoes, his dark, soft rumbling growl; after her day of pastel-coloured idleness, how could she converse with the possessor of a voice that seemed an instrument created to inspire the terror that the chords of great organs bring? Fascinated, almost awed, she watched the firelight play on the gold fringes of his mane; he was irradiated, as if with a kind of halo, and she thought of the first great beast of the Apocalypse, the winged lion with his paw upon the Gospel, Saint Mark. Small talk turned to dust in her mouth; small talk had never, at the best of times, been Beauty's forte, and she had little practice at it.

But he, hesitantly, as if he himself were in awe of a young girl who looked as if she had been carved out of a single pearl, asked after her father's law case; and her dead mother; and how they, who had been so rich, had come to be so poor. He forced himself to master his shyness, which was that of a wild creature, and so she contrived to master her own – to such effect that soon she was chattering away to him as if she had known him all her life. When the little cupid in the gilt clock on the mantelpiece struck its miniature tambourine, she was astonished to discover it did so twelve times.

'So late! You will want to sleep,' he said.

At that, they both fell silent, as if these strange companions were suddenly overcome with embarrassment to find themselves together, alone, in that room in the depths of the winter's night. As she was about to rise, he flung himself at her feet and buried his head in her lap. She stayed stock-still, transfixed; she felt his hot breath on her fingers, the stiff bristles of his muzzle grazing her skin, the rough lapping of his tongue and then, with a flood of compassion, understood: all he is doing is kissing my hands.

He drew back his head and gazed at her with his green, inscrutable eyes, in which she saw her face repeated twice, as small as if it were in bud. Then, without another word, he sprang from the room and she saw, with an indescribable shock, he went on all fours.

Next day, all day, the hills on which the snow still settled echoed with the Beast's rumbling roar: has master gone a-hunting? Beauty asked the spaniel. But the spaniel growled, almost bad-temperedly, as if to say, that she would not have answered, even if she could have.

Beauty would pass the day in her suite reading or, perhaps, doing a little embroidery; a box of coloured silks and a frame had been provided for her. Or, well wrapped up, she wandered in the walled garden, among the leafless roses, with the spaniel at her heels, and did a little raking and rearranging. An idle, restful time; a holiday. The enchantment of that bright, sad, pretty place enveloped her and she found that, against all her expectations, she was happy there. She no longer felt the slightest apprehension at her nightly interviews with the Beast. All the natural laws of the world were held in suspension, here, where an army of invisibles tenderly waited on her, and she would talk with the lion, under the patient chaperonage of the brown-eyed dog, on the nature of the moon and its borrowed light, about the stars and the substances of which they were made, about the variable transformations of the weather. Yet still his strangeness made her shiver; and when he helplessly fell before her to kiss her hands, as he did every night when they parted, she would retreat nervously into her skin, flinching at his touch.

The telephone shrilled; for her. Her father. Such news!

The Beast sunk his great head on to his paws. You will come back to me? It will be lonely here, without you.

She was moved almost to tears that he should care for her so. It was in her heart to drop a kiss upon his shaggy mane but, though she stretched out her hand towards him, she could not bring herself to touch him of her own free will, he was so different from herself. But, yes, she said; I will come back. Soon, before the winter is over. Then the taxi came and took her away.

You are never at the mercy of the elements in London, where the huddled warmth of humanity melts the snow before it has time to settle; and her father was as good as rich again, since his hirsute friend's lawyers had the business so well in hand that his credit brought them nothing but the best. A resplendent hotel; the opera, theatres; a whole new wardrobe for his darling, so she could step out on his arm to parties, to receptions, to restaurants, and life was as she had never known it, for her father had ruined himself before her birth killed her mother.

Although the Beast was the source of this new-found prosperity and they talked of him often, now that they were so far away from the timeless spell of his house it seemed to possess the radiant and finite quality of dream and the Beast himself, so monstrous, so benign, some kind of spirit of good fortune who had smiled on them and let them go. She sent him flowers, white roses in return for the ones he had given her; and when she left the florist, she experienced a sudden sense of perfect freedom, as if she had just escaped from an unknown danger, had been grazed by the possibility of some change but, finally, left intact. Yet, with this exhilaration, a desolating emptiness. But her father was waiting for her at the hotel; they had planned a delicious expedition to buy her furs and she was as eager for the treat as any girl might be.

Since the flowers in the shop were the same all the year round, nothing in the window could tell her that winter had almost gone.

Returning late from supper after the theatre, she took off her earrings in front of the mirror; Beauty. She smiled at herself with satisfaction. She was learning, at the end of her adolescence, how to be a spoiled child and that pearly skin of hers was plumping out, a little, with high living and compliments. A certain inwardness was beginning to transform the lines around her mouth, those signatures of the personality, and her sweetness and her gravity could sometimes turn a mite petulant when things went not quite as she wanted them to go. You could not have said that her freshness was fading but she smiled at herself in mirrors a little too often, these days, and the face that smiled back was not quite the one she had seen contained in the Beast's agate eyes. Her face was acquiring, instead of beauty, a lacquer of the invincible prettiness that characterizes certain pampered, exquisite, expensive cats.

The soft wind of spring breathed in from the near-by park through the open windows; she did not know why it made her want to cry.

There was a sudden, urgent, scrabbling sound, as of claws, at her door.

Her trance before the mirror broke; all at once, she remembered everything perfectly. Spring was here and she had broken her promise. Now the Beast himself had come in pursuit of her! First, she was frightened of his anger; then, mysteriously joyful, she ran to open the door. But it was his liver and white spotted spaniel who hurled herself into the girl's arms in a flurry of little barks and gruff murmurings, of whimpering and relief.

Yet where was the well-brushed, jewelled dog who had sat beside her embroidery frame in the parlour with birds of paradise nodding on the walls? This one's fringed ears were matted with mud, her coat was dusty and snarled, she was thin as a dog that has walked a long way and, if she had not been a dog, she would have been in tears.

After that first, rapturous greeting, she did not wait for Beauty to order her food and water; she seized the chiffon hem of her evening dress, whimpered and tugged. Threw back her head, howled, then tugged and whimpered again.

There was a slow, late train that would take her to the station where she had left for London three months ago. Beauty scribbled a note for her father, threw a coat round her shoulders. Quickly, quickly, urged the spaniel soundlessly; and Beauty knew the Beast was dying.

In the thick dark before dawn, the station master roused a sleepy driver for her. Fast as you can.

It seemed December still possessed his garden. The ground was hard as iron, the skirts of the dark cypress moved on the chill wind with a mournful rustle and there were no green shoots on the roses as if, this year, they would not bloom. And not one light in any of the windows, only, in the topmost attic, the faintest smear of radiance on a pane, the thin ghost of a light on the verge of extinction.

The spaniel had slept a little, in her arms, for the poor thing was exhausted. But now her grieving agitation fed Beauty's urgency and, as the girl pushed open the front door, she saw, with a thrust of conscience, how the golden door knocker was thickly muffled in black crêpe.

The door did not open silently, as before, but with a doleful groaning of the hinges and, this time, on to perfect darkness. Beauty clicked her gold cigarette lighter; the tapers in the chandelier had drowned in their own wax and the prisms were wreathed with drifting arabesques of cobwebs. The flowers in the glass jars were dead, as if nobody had had the heart to replace them after she was gone. Dust, everywhere; and it was cold. There was an air of exhaustion, of despair in the house and, worse, a kind of physical disillusion, as if its glamour had been sustained by a cheap conjuring trick and now the conjurer, having failed to pull the crowds, had departed to try his luck elsewhere.

Beauty found a candle to light her way and followed the faithful spaniel up the staircase, past the study, past her suite, through a house echoing with desertion up a little back staircase dedicated to mice and spiders, stumbling, ripping the hem of her dress in her haste.

What a modest bedroom! An attic, with a sloping roof, they might have given the chambermaid if the Beast had employed staff. A night light on the mantelpiece, no curtains at the windows, no carpet on the floor and a narrow, iron bedstead on which he lay, sadly diminished, his bulk scarcely disturbing the faded patchwork quilt, his mane a greyish rat's nest and his eyes closed. On the stick-backed chair where his clothes had been thrown, the roses she had sent him were thrust into the jug from the washstand but they were all dead.

The spaniel jumped up on the bed and burrowed her way under the scanty covers, softly keening.

'Oh, Beast,' said Beauty. 'I have come home.'

His eyelids flickered. How was it she had never noticed before that his agate eyes were equipped with lids, like those of a man? Was it because she had only looked at her own face, reflected there?

'I'm dying, Beauty,' he said in a cracked whisper of his former purr. 'Since you left me, I have been sick. I could not go hunting, I found I had not the stomach to kill the gentle beasts, I could not eat. I am sick and I must die; but I shall die happy because you have come to say good-bye to me.'

She flung herself upon him, so that the iron bedstead groaned, and covered his poor paws with her kisses.

'Don't die, Beast! If you'll have me, I'll never leave you.'

When her lips touched the meat-hook claws, they drew back into their pads and she saw how he had always kept his fists clenched but now, painfully, tentatively, at last began to stretch his fingers. Her tears fell on his face like snow and, under their soft transformation, the bones showed through the pelt, the flesh through the wide, tawny brow. And then it was no longer a lion in her arms but a man, a man with an unkempt mane of hair and, how strange, a broken nose, such as the noses of retired boxers, that gave him a distant, heroic resemblance to the handsomest of all the beasts.

'Do you know,' said Mr Lyon, 'I think I might be able to manage a little breakfast today, Beauty, if you would eat something with me.'

Mr and Mrs Lyon walk in the garden; the old spaniel drowses on the grass, in a drift of fallen petals.

DORIS LESSING

Notes for a Case History

Maureen Watson was born at 93 Nelson's Way, N.1., in 1942. She did not remember the war, or rather, when people said 'The War', she thought of Austerity: couponed curtains, traded clothes, the half-pound of butter swapped for the quarter of tea. (Maureen's parents preferred tea to butter.) Further back, at the roots of her life, she *felt* a movement of fire and shadow, a leaping and a subsidence of light. She did not know whether this was a memory or a picture she had formed, perhaps from what her parents had told her of the night the bomb fell two streets from Nelson's Way and they had all stood among piles of smoking rubble for a day and night, watching firemen hose the flames. This feeling was not only of danger, but of fatality, of being helpless before great impersonal forces; and was how she most deeply felt, saw, or thought an early childhood which the social viewer would describe perhaps like this:

> Maureen Watson, conceived by chance on an unexpected granted-at-the-last-minute leave, at the height of the worst war in history, infant support of a mother only occasionally upheld (the chances of war deciding) by a husband she had met in a bomb shelter during an air raid: poor baby, born into a historical upheaval which destroyed forty million and might very well have destroyed her.

As for Maureen, her memories and the reminiscences of her parents made her dismiss the whole business as boring, and nothing to do with her.

It was at her seventh birthday party she first made this clear. She wore a mauve organdie frock with a pink sash, and her golden hair was in ringlets. One of the mothers said: 'This is the first unrationed party dress

454

my Shirley has had. It's a shame, isn't it?' And her own mother said: 'Well of course these war children don't know what they've missed.' At which Maureen said: '*I* am not a war child.' 'What are you then, love?' said her mother, fondly exchanging glances.

'I'm Maureen,' said Maureen.

'And I'm Shirley,' said Shirley, joining cause.

Shirley Banner was Maureen's best friend. The Watsons and the Banners were better than the rest of the street. The Watsons lived in an end house, at higher weekly payments. The Banners had a sweets-paper-and-tobacco shop.

Maureen and Shirley remembered (or had they been told?) that once Nelson's Way was a curved terrace of houses. Then the ground-floor level had broken into shops: a grocer's, a laundry, a hardware, a baker, a dairy. It seemed as if every second family in the street ran a shop to supply certain defined needs of the other families. What other needs were there? Apparently none; for Maureen's parents applied for permission to the Council, and the ground floor of their house became a second grocery shop, by way of broken-down walls, new shelves, a deepfreeze. Maureen remembered two small rooms, each with flowered curtains where deep shadows moved and flickered from the two small fires that burned back to back in the centre wall that divided them. These two rooms disappeared in clouds of dust from which sweet-smelling planks of wood stuck out. Strange but friendly men paid her compliments on her golden corkscrews and asked her for kisses, which they did not get. They gave her sips of sweet tea from their canteens (filled twice a day by her mother) and made her bracelets of the spiralling fringes of yellow wood. Then they disappeared. There was the new shop. Maureen's Shop. Maureen went with her mother to the sign shop to arrange for these two words to be written in yellow paint on a blue ground.

Even without the name, Maureen would have known that the shop was connected with hopes for her future; and that her future was what her mother lived for.

She was pretty. She had always known it. Even where the shadows of fire and dark were, they had played over a pretty baby. 'You were such a pretty baby, Maureen.' And at the birthday parties: 'Maureen's growing really pretty, Mrs Watson.' But all babies and little girls are pretty, she knew that well enough . . . no, it was something more. For Shirley was plump, dark – pretty. Yet their parents' – or rather, their mothers' – talk had made it clear from the start that Shirley was not in the same class as Maureen.

When Maureen was ten there was an episode of importance. The two mothers were in the room above Maureen's Shop and they were brushing their little girls' hair out. Shirley's mother said: 'Maureen could do really well for herself, Mrs Watson.' And Mrs Watson nodded, but sighed deeply. The sigh annoyed Maureen, because it contradicted the absolute certainty that she felt (it had been bred into her) about her future. Also because it had to do with the *boring* era which she remembered, or thought she did, as a tiger-striped movement of fire. *Chance*: Mrs Watson's sigh was like a prayer to the gods of Luck: it was the sigh of a small helpless thing being tossed about by big seas and gales. Maureen made a decision, there and then, that she had nothing in common with the little people who were prepared to be helpless and tossed about. For she was going to be quite different. She was already different. Not only The War but the shadows of war had long gone, except for talk in the newspapers which had nothing to do with her. The shops were full of everything. The Banners' sweets-tobacco-paper shop had just been done up; and Maureen's was short of nothing. Maureen and Shirley, two pretty little girls in smart mother-made dresses, were children of plenty, and knew it, because their parents kept saying (apparently they did not care how tedious they were): 'These kids don't lack for anything, do they? They don't know what it can be like, do they?' This, with the suggestion that they ought to be grateful for not lacking anything, always made the children sulky, and they went off to flirt their many-petticoated skirts where the neighbours could see them and pay them compliments.

Eleven years. Twelve years. Already Shirley had subsided into her role of pretty girl's plainer girl friend, although of course she was not plain at all. Fair girl, dark girl, and Maureen by mysterious birthright was the 'pretty one', and there was no doubt in either of their minds which girl the boys would try first for a date. Yet this balance was by no means as unfair as it seemed. Maureen, parrying and jesting on street corners, at bus stops, knew she was doing battle for two, because the boys she discarded Shirley got: Shirley got far more boys than she would have done without Maureen who, for her part, needed – more, *had* to have – a foil. Her role demanded one.

They both left school at fifteen, Maureen to work in the shop. She was keeping her eyes open: her mother's phrase. She wore a slim white overall, pinned her fair curls up, was neat and pretty in her movements. She smiled calmly when customers said: 'My word, Mrs Watson, your Maureen's turned out, hasn't she?'

About that time there was a second moment of consciousness. Mrs Watson was finishing a new dress for Maureen, and the fitting was taking rather long. Maureen fidgeted and her mother said: 'Well, it's your capital, isn't it? You've got to see that, love.' And she added the deep unconscious sigh. Maureen said: 'Well don't go on about it, it's not very nice, is it?' And what she meant was, not that the idea was not very nice, but that she had gone beyond needing to be reminded about it; she was feeling the irritated embarrassment of a child when it is reminded to clean its teeth after this habit has become second nature. Mrs Watson saw and understood this, and sighed again; and this time it was the maternal sigh which means: Oh dear, you are growing up fast! 'Oh *Mum*,' said Maureen, 'sometimes you just make me tired, you do really.'

Sixteen. She was managing her capital perfectly. Her assets were a slight delicate prettiness, and a dress sense that must have been a gift from God, or more probably because she had been reading the fashion magazines since practically before consciousness. Shirley had put in six months of beehive hair, pouting scarlet lips, and an air of sullen disdain; but Maureen's sense of herself was much finer. She modelled herself on film stars, but with an understanding of how far she could go – of what was allowable to Maureen. So the experience of being Bardot, Monroe, or whoever it was, refined her: she took from it an essence, which was learning to be a vehicle for other people's fantasies. So while Shirley had been a dozen stars, but really *been* them, in violent temporary transmogrifications, from which she emerged (often enough with a laugh) Shirley – plump, good-natured, and herself – Maureen remained herself through every role, but creating her appearance, like an alter ego, to meet the expression in people's eyes.

Round about sixteen, another incident: prophetic. Mrs Watson had a cousin who worked in the dress trade, and this man, unthought-of for many years, was met at a wedding. He commented on Maureen, a vision in white gauze. Mrs Watson worked secretly on this slender material for some weeks; then wrote to him: Could Maureen be a model? He had only remote connections with the world of expensive clothes and girls, but he dropped into the shop with frankly personal aims. Maureen in a white wrapper was still pretty, very; but her remote air told this shrewd man that she would certainly not go out with him. She was saving herself; he knew the air of self-esteem very well from other exemplars. Such girls do not go out with middle-aged cousins, except as a favour or to get something. However, he told Mrs Watson that Maureen was definitely model material, but that she would have to do something about her voice. (He meant her accent of course; and so Mrs Watson understood him.) He left addresses and advice, and Mrs Watson was in a state of quivering ambition. She said so to Maureen: 'This is your chance, girl. Take it.' What Maureen heard was: 'This is *my* chance.'

Maureen, nothing if not alert for her Big Chance, for which her whole life had prepared her, accepted her mother's gift of a hundred pounds (she did not thank her, no thanks were due) and actually wrote to the school where she would be taught voice training.

Then she fell into sullen withdrawal, which she understood so little that a week had gone by before she said she must be sick – or something. She was rude to her mother: very rare, this. Her father chided her for it: even rarer. But he spoke in such a way that Maureen understood for the first time that this drive, this push, this family effort to gain her a glamorous future, came from her mother, her father was not implicated. For him, she was a pretty-enough girl, spoiled by a silly woman.

Maureen slowly understood she was not sick, she was growing up. For one thing: if she changed her 'voice' so as to be good enough to mix with new people, she would no longer be part of this street, she would no longer be *Our Maureen*. What would she be then? Her mother knew: she would marry a duke and be whisked off to Hollywood. Maureen examined her mother's ideas for her and shrank with humiliation. She was above all no fool, but she had been very foolish. For one thing: when she used her eyes, with the scales of illusion off them, she saw that the million streets of London blossomed with girls as pretty as she. What, then, had fed the illusion in herself and in other people? What accounted for the special tone, the special looks that always greeted her? Why, nothing more than that she, Maureen, because of her mother's will behind her, had carried herself from childhood as something special, apart, destined for a great future.

Meanwhile (as she clearly saw) she was in 93 Nelson's Way, serving behind the counter of Maureen's Shop. (She now wondered what the neighbours had thought – before they got used to it – about her mother's fondness so terribly displayed.) She was dependent on nothing less than that a duke or a film producer would walk in to buy a quarter of tea and some sliced bread.

Maureen sulked. So her father said. So her mother complained. Maureen was – thinking? Yes. But more, a wrong had been done her, she knew it, and the sulking was more of a protective silence while she grew a scab over a wound.

She emerged demanding that the hundred pounds should be spent on sending her to secretarial school. Her parents complained that she could have learned how to be a secretary for nothing if she had stayed on at school another year. She said: 'Yes, but you didn't have the sense to make me, did you? What did you think – I was going to sell butter like you all my life?' Unfair, on the face of it; but deeply fair, in view of what they had done to her. In their different ways they knew it. (Mr Watson knew in his heart, for instance, that he should never have allowed his wife to call the shop 'Maureen's'.) Maureen went, then, to secretarial school for a year. Shirley went with her: she had been selling cosmetics in the local branch of a big chain store. To raise the hundred pounds was difficult for Shirley's parents: the shop had done badly, had been bought by a big firm; her father was an assistant in it. For that matter, it wasn't all that easy for the Watsons: the hundred pounds was the result of small savings and pinchings over years.

This was the first time Maureen had thought of the word capital in connection with money, rather than her own natural assets: it was comparatively easy for the Watsons to raise money, because they had capital: the Banners had no capital. (Mrs Watson said the Banners had had *bad luck*.) Maureen strengthened her will; and as a result the two families behaved even more as if the girls would have different futures – or, to put it another way, that while the two sums of a hundred pounds were the same, the Watsons could be expected to earn more on theirs than the Banners.

This was reflected directly in the two girls' discussions about boys. Shirley would say: 'I'm more easygoing than you.'

Maureen would reply: '*I* only let them go so far.'

Their first decisions on this almighty subject had taken place years before, when they were thirteen. Even then Shirley went further ('let them go further') than Maureen. It was put down, between them, to Shirley's warmer temperament – charitably; for both knew it was because of Maureen's higher value in the market.

At the secretarial school they met boys they had not met before. Previously boys had been from the street or the neighbourhood, known from birth, and for this reason not often gone out with – that would have been boring (serious, with possibilities of marriage). Or boys picked up after dances or at the pictures. But now there were new boys met day after day in the school. Shirley went out with one for weeks, thought of getting engaged, changed her mind, went out with another. Maureen went out with a dozen, chosen carefully. She knew what she was doing – and scolded Shirley for being so *soft*. 'You're just stupid, Shirl – I mean, you've got to get on. Why don't you do like me?'

What Maureen did was to allow herself to be courted, until she agreed at last, as a favour, to be taken out. First, lunch – a word she began to use now. She would agree to go out to lunch two or three times with one boy, while she was taken out to supper (dinner) by another. The dinner partner, having been rewarded by a closed-mouth kiss for eight, ten, twelve nights, got angry or sulky or reproachful, according to his nature. He dropped her, and the lunch partner was promoted to dinner partner.

Maureen ate free for the year of her training. It wasn't that she planned it like this; but when she heard other girls say they paid their way or liked to be independent, it seemed to Maureen wrongheaded. To pay for herself would be to let herself be undervalued: even the idea of it made her nervous and sulky.

At the end of the training Maureen got a job in a big architect's office. She was a junior typist. She stuck out for a professional office because the whole point of the training was to enable her to meet a better class of people. Of course she had already learned not to use the phrase, and when her mother did snubbed her with: 'I don't know what you mean, better *class*, but it's not much point my going into that hardware stuck upstairs in an office by myself if I can get a job where there's some life about.'

Shirley went into a draper's shop where there was one other typist (female) and five male assistants.

In Maureen's place there were six architects, out most of the time, or invisible in large offices visited only by the real secretaries; a lower stratum of young men in training, designers, draughtsmen, managers, etc., and a pool of typists.

The young men were mostly of her own class. For some months she ate and was entertained at their expense; and at each week's end there was a solemn ceremony, the high point of the week, certainly the most exciting moment in it, when she divided her wage. It was seven pounds (rising to ten in three years) and she allocated two pounds for clothes, four for the post office, and one pound for the week's odd expenses.

At the end of a year she understood two things. That she had saved something like two hundred pounds. That there was not a young man in the office who would take her out again. They regarded her, according to their natures, with resentment or with admiration for her cool management of them. But there was nothing doing *there* – so they all knew.

Maureen thought this over. If she were not taken out to meals and entertainment, she must pay for herself and save no money, or she must never go out at all. If she was going to be taken out, then she must give something in return. What she gave was an open mouth, and freedom to the waist. She calculated that because of her prettiness she could give much less than other girls.

She was using her *capital* with even more intelligence than before. A good part of her time – all not spent in the office or being taken out – went in front of her looking glass, or with the better-class fashion magazines. She studied them with formidable concentration. By now she knew she could have gone anywhere in these islands, except for her voice. Whereas, months before, she had sulked in a sort of fright at the idea of cutting herself off from her street and the neighbours, now she softened and shaped her voice, listening to the clients and the senior architects in the office. She knew her voice had changed when Shirley said: 'You're talking nice, Maureen, much nicer than me.'

There was a boy in the office who teased her about it. His name was Tony Head. He was in training to be an accountant for the firm, and was very much from her own background. After having taken her out twice to lunch, he had never asked her again. She knew why: he had told her. 'Can't afford you, Maureen,' he said. He earned not much more than she did. He was nineteen, ambitious, serious, and she liked him.

Then she was nineteen. Shirley was engaged to one of the assistants in her shop, and would be married next Christmas.

Maureen took forty pounds out of her savings and went on a tour to Italy. It was her first time out of England. She hated it: not Italy, but the fact that half the sixty people on the tour were girls, like herself, looking for a good time, and the other half elderly couples. In Rome, Pisa, Florence, Venice, the Italians mooned over Maureen, courted her with melting eyes, while she walked past them, distant as a starlet. They probably thought she was one. The courier, a sharp young man, took Maureen out to supper one night after he had finished his duties, and made it clear that her mouth, even if opened, and her breasts, were not enough. Maureen smiled at him sweetly through the rest of the trip. No one paid for her odd coffees, ices and drinks. On the last night of the trip, in a panic because the forty-pound investment had yielded so little, she went out with an Italian boy who spoke seven words of English. She thought him crude, and left him after an hour.

But she had learned a good deal for her forty pounds. Quietly, in her lunch hour, she went off to the National Gallery and to the Tate. There she looked, critical and respectful, at pictures, memorizing their subjects, or main colours, learning names. When invited out, she asked to be taken to 'foreign' films, and when she got back home wrote down the names of the director and the stars. She looked at the book page of the *Express* (she made her parents buy it instead of the *Mirror*) and sometimes bought a recommended book, if it was a best seller.

Twenty. Shirley was married and had a baby. Maureen saw little of her – both girls felt they had a new world of knowledge the other couldn't appreciate.

Maureen was earning ten pounds a week, and saved six.

There came to the office, as an apprentice architect, Stanley Hunt, from grammar school and technical college. Tallish, well-dressed, fair, with a small moustache. They took each other's measure, knowing they were the same kind. It was some weeks before he asked her out. She knew, by putting herself in his place, that he was looking for a wife with a little money or a house of her own, if he couldn't get a lady. (She smiled when she heard him using this word about one of the clients.) He tried to know clients socially, to be accepted by them as they accepted the senior architects. All this Maureen watched, her cool little face saying nothing.

One day, after he had invited a Miss Plast (Chelsea, well-off, investing money in houses) to coffee, and had been turned down, he asked Maureen to join him in a sandwich lunch. Maureen thanked him delightfully, but said she already had an engagement. She went off to the National Gallery, sat on the steps, froze off wolves and pickups, and ate a sandwich by herself.

A week later, invited to lunch by Stanley, she suggested the Trattoria Siciliana which was more expensive, as she knew quite well, than he had expected. But this meal was a success. He was impressed with her, though he knew (how could he not, when his was similar?) her background.

She was careful to be engaged for two weeks. Then she agreed to go to the pictures – 'a foreign film, if you don't mind, I think the American films are just boring.' She did not offer to pay, but remarked casually that she had nearly six hundred pounds in the post office. 'I'm thinking of buying a little business, some time. A dress shop. I've got a cousin in the trade.'

Stanley agreed that 'with your taste' it would be a sure thing.

Maureen no longer went to the Palais, or similar places (though she certainly did not conceal from Stanley that she had 'once'), but she loved to dance. Twice they went to the West End together and danced at a Club which was 'a nice place'. They danced well together. On the second occasion she offered to pay her share, for the first time in her life. He refused, as she had known he would, but she could see he liked her for offering: more, was relieved; in the office they said she was mean, and he must have heard them. On that night, taken home lingeringly, she opened her mouth for him and let his hands go down to her thighs. She felt a sharp sexuality which made her congratulate herself that she had never, like Shirley, gone 'halfway' before. Well of course, girls were going to get married to just anybody if they let themselves be all worked up every time they were taken out!

But Stanley was not at all caught. He was too cool a customer, as she was. He was still looking for something better.

He would be an architect in a couple of years; he would be in a profession; he was putting down money for a house; he was good-looking, attractive to women, and with these assets he ought to do better than marry Maureen. Maureen agreed with him.

But meanwhile he took her out. She was careful often to be engaged elsewhere. She was careful always to be worth taking somewhere expensive. When he took her home, while she did not go so far as 'nearly the whole way', she went 'everything but'; and she was glad she did not like him better, because otherwise she would have been lost. She knew quite well she did not really like him, although her mind was clouded by her response to his hands, his moustache, his clothes and his new car.

She knew, because meanwhile a relationship she understood very well, and regretted, had grown up with Tony. He, watching this duel between the well-matched pair, would grin and drop remarks at which Maureen coloured and turned coldly away. He often asked her out – but only for a 'Dutch treat' – expecting her to refuse. 'How's your savings account, Maureen? I can't save, you girls get it all spent on you.' Tony took out a good many girls: Maureen kept a count of them. She hated him; yet she liked him, and knew she did. She relied on him above all for the grinning, honest understanding of her: he did not approve of her, but perhaps (she felt in her heart) he was right? During this period she several times burst into tears when alone, without apparent reason; afterwards she felt that life had no flavour. Her future was narrowing down to Stanley; and at these times she viewed it through Tony Head's eyes.

One night the firm had a party for the senior members of the staff. Stanley was senior, Maureen and Tony were not. Maureen knew that Stanley had previously asked another girl to go, and when he asked herself, was uncertain whether she could make it until the very last moment: particularly as his inviting her, a junior, meant that he was trying out on the senior members the idea of Maureen as a wife. But she acquitted herself very well. First, she was the best-looking woman in the room by far, and the best-dressed. Everyone looked at her and commented: they were used to her as a pretty typist; but tonight she was using all her will to make them look at her, to make her face and body reflect what they admired. She made no mistakes. When the party was over Stanley and two of the younger architects suggested they drive out to London airport for breakfast, and they did. The two other girls were middle-class. Maureen kept silent for the most part, smiling serenely. She had been to Italy, she remarked, when a plane rose to go to Italy. Yes, she had liked it, though she thought the Italians were too noisy; what she had enjoyed best was the Sistine Chapel and a boat trip on the Adriatic. She hadn't cared for Venice much, it was beautiful, but the canals smelled, and there were far too many people; perhaps it would be better to go in winter? She said all this, having a right to it, and it came off. As she spoke she remembered Tony, who had once met her on her way to the National Gallery. 'Getting yourself an education, Maureen? That's right, it'll pay off well, that will.'

She knew, thinking it all over afterwards, that the evening had been important for her with Stanley. Because of this, she did not go out with him for a week, she said she was busy talking to her cousin about the possibilities of a dress shop. She sat in her room thinking about Stanley, and when thoughts of Tony came into her mind, irritatedly pushed them away. If she could succeed with Stanley, why not with someone better? The two architects from that evening had eyed her all the following week: they did not, however, ask her out. She then found that both were engaged to marry the girls they had been with. It was bad luck: she was sure that otherwise they would have asked her out. How to meet more like them? Well, that was the trouble – the drive to the airport was a bit of a fluke; it was the first time she had actually met the seniors socially.

Meanwhile Stanley showed an impatience in his courtship – and for the first time. As for her, she was getting on for twenty-one, and all the girls she had grown up with were married and had their first or even their second babies.

She went out with Stanley to a dinner in the West End at an Italian restaurant. Afterwards they were both very passionate. Maureen, afterwards, was furious with herself: some borderline had been crossed (she supposed she still could be called a virgin?) and now decisions would have to be made.

Stanley was in love with her. She was in love with Stanley. A week later he proposed to her. It was done with a violent moaning intensity that she knew was due to his conflicts over marrying her. She was not good enough. He was not good enough. They were second-best for each other. They writhed and moaned and bit in the car, and agreed to marry. Her eight hundred pounds would make it easier to buy the house in a good suburb. He would formally meet her parents next Sunday.

'So you're engaged to Stanley Hunt?' said Tony.

'Looks like it, doesn't it?'

'Caught him – good for you!'

'He's caught me, more like it!'

'Have it your way.'

She was red and angry. He was serious.

'Come and have a bite?' he said. She went.

It was a small restaurant, full of office workers eating on luncheon vouchers. She ate fried plaice ('No chips, please') and he ate steak-and-kidney pudding. He joked, watched her, watched her intently, said finally: 'Can't you do better than that?' He meant, and she knew it, better in the sense she would use herself, in her heart: he meant *nice*. Like himself. But did that mean that Tony thought *she* was nice? Unlike Stanley? She did not think she was, she was moved to tears (concealed) that he did. 'What's wrong with him then?' she demanded, casual. 'What's wrong with *you*? You need your head examined.' He said it seriously, and they exchanged a long look. The two of them sat looking goodbye at each other: the extremely pretty girl at whom everyone in the room kept glancing and remarking on, and the good-looking, dark, rather fat young accountant who was brusque and solemn with disappoinment in her. With love for her? Very likely.

She went home silent, thinking of Tony. When she thought of him she needed to cry. She also needed to hurt him.

But she told her parents she was engaged to Stanley, who would be an architect. They would have their own house, in (they thought) Hemel Hempstead. He owned a car. He was coming to tea on Sunday. Her mother forgot the dukes and the film producers before the announcement ended: her father listened judiciously, then congratulated her. He had been going to a football match on Sunday, but agreed, after persuasion, that this was a good-enough reason to stay home.

Her mother then began discussing, with deference to Maureen's superior knowledge, how to manage next Sunday to best advantage. For four days she went on about it. But she was talking to herself. Her husband listened, said nothing. And Maureen listened, critically, like her father. Mrs Watson began clamouring for a definite opinion on what sort of cake to serve on Sunday. But Maureen had no opinion. She sat, quiet, looking at her mother, a largish ageing woman, her ex-fair hair dyed yellow, her flesh guttering. She was like an excited child, and it was not attractive. *Stupid, stupid, stupid* – that's all you are, thought Maureen.

As for Maureen, if anyone had made the comparison, she was 'sulking' as she had before over being a model and having to be drilled out of her 'voice'. She said nothing but: 'It'll be all right, Mum, don't get so worked up.' Which was true, because Stanley knew what to expect: he knew why he had not been invited to meet her parents until properly hooked. He would have done the same in her place. He *was* doing the same: she was going to meet his parents the week after. What Mrs Watson, Mr Watson, wore on Sunday; whether sandwiches or cake were served; whether there were fresh or artificial flowers – none of it mattered. The Watsons were part of the bargain: what he was paying in return for publicly owning the most covetable woman anywhere they were likely to be; and for the right to sleep with her after the public display.

Meanwhile Maureen said not a word. She sat on her bed looking at nothing in particular. Once or twice she examined her face in the mirror, and even put cream on it. And she cut out a dress, but put it aside.

On Sunday Mrs Watson laid tea for four, using her own judgment since Maureen was too deeply in love (so she told everyone) to notice such trifles. At four Stanley was expected, and at 3.55 Maureen descended to the living room. She wore: a faded pink dress from three summers before; her mother's cretonne overall used for housework; and a piece of cloth tied round her hair that might very well have been a duster. At any rate, it was a faded grey. She had put on a pair of her mother's old shoes. She could not be called plain; but she looked like her own faded elder sister, dressed for a hard day's spring cleaning.

Her father, knowledgeable, said nothing: he lowered the paper, examined her, let out a short laugh, and lifted it again. Mrs Watson, understanding at last that this was a real crisis, burst into tears. Stanley arrived before Mrs Watson could stop herself crying. He nearly said to Mrs Watson: 'I didn't know Maureen had an older sister.' Maureen sat listless at one end of the table; Mr Watson sat grinning at the other, and Mrs Watson sniffed and wiped her eyes between the two.

Maureen said: 'Hello, Stanley, meet my father and mother.' He shook their hands and stared at her. She did not meet his eyes: rather, the surface of her blue gaze met the furious, incredulous, hurt pounce of his glares at her. Maureen poured tea, offered him sandwiches and cake, and made conversation about the weather, and the prices of food, and the dangers of giving even good customers credit in the shop. He sat there, a well-set-up young man, with his brushed hair, his brushed moustache, his checked brown cloth jacket, and a face flaming with anger and affront. He said nothing, but Maureen talked on, her voice trailing and cool. At five o'clock, Mrs Watson again burst into tears, her whole body shaking, and Stanley brusquely left.

Mr Watson said: 'Well, why did you lead him on, then?' and turned on the television. Mrs Watson went to lie down. Maureen, in her own room, took off the various items of her disguise, and returned them to her mother's room. 'Don't cry, Mum. What are you carrying on like that for? What's the matter?' Then she dressed extremely carefully in a new white linen suit, brown shoes, beige blouse. She did her hair and her face, and sat looking at herself. The last two hours (or week) hit her, and her stomach hurt so that she doubled up. She cried; but the tears smeared her makeup, and she stopped herself with the side of a fist against her mouth.

It now seemed to her that for the last week she had simply not been Maureen; she had been someone else. What had she done it for? Why? Then she knew it was for Tony: during all that ridiculous scene at the tea table, she had imagined Tony looking on, grinning, but understanding her.

She now wiped her face quite clear of tears, and went quietly out of the house so as not to disturb her father and mother. There was a telephone booth at the corner. She stepped calm and aloof along the street, her mouth held (as it always was) in an almost smile. Bert from the grocer's shop said: 'Hey, Maureen, that's a smasher. Who's it for?' And she gave him the smile and the toss of the head that went with the street and said: 'You, Bert, it's all for you.' She went to the telephone booth thinking of Tony. She felt as if he already knew what had happened. She would say: 'Let's go and dance, Tony.' He would say: 'Where shall I meet you?' She dialled his number, and it rang and it rang and it rang. She stood holding the receiver, waiting. About ten minutes – more. Slowly she replaced it. *He had let her down.* He had been telling her, in words and without, to be something, to stay something, and now he did not care, he had let her down.

Maureen quietened herself and telephoned Stanley.

All right then, if that's how you want it, she said to Tony.

Stanley answered, and she said amiably: 'Hello.'

Silence. She could hear him breathing, fast. She could see his affronted face.

'Well, aren't you going to say anything?' She tried to make this casual, but she could hear the fear in her voice. Oh yes, she could lose him and probably had. To hide the fear she said: 'Can't you take a joke, Stanley?' and laughed.

'A joke!'

She laughed. Not bad, it sounded all right.

'I thought you'd gone off your nut, clean off your rocker . . .' He was breathing in and out, a rasping noise. She was reminded of his hot breathing down her neck and her arms. Her own breath quickened, even while she thought: I don't like him, I really don't like him at all . . . and she said softly: 'Oh Stan, I was having a bit of a giggle, that's all.'

Silence. Now, this was the crucial moment.

'Oh Stan, can't you see – I thought it was all just boring, that's all it was.' She laughed again.

He said: 'Nice for your parents, I don't think.'

'Oh they don't mind – they laughed after you'd left, though first they were cross.' She added hastily, afraid he might think they were laughing at him: 'They're used to me, that's all it is.'

Another long silence. With all her willpower she insisted that he should soften. But he said nothing, merely breathed in and out, into the receiver.

'Stanley, it was only a joke, you aren't really angry, are you, Stanley?' The tears sounded in her voice now, and she judged it better that they should.

He said, after hesitation: 'Well, Maureen, I just didn't like it, I don't like that kind of thing, that's all.' She allowed herself to go on crying, and after a while he said, forgiving her in a voice that was condescending and irritated: 'Well, all right, all right, there's no point in crying, is there?'

He was annoyed with himself for giving in, she knew that, because she would have been. He had given her up, thrown her over, during the last couple of hours: he was pleased, really, that something from outside had forced him to give her up. Now he could be free for the something better that would turn up – someone who would not strike terror into him by an extraordinary performance like this afternoon's.

'Let's go off to the pictures, Stan . . .'

Even now, he hesitated. Then he said, quick and reluctant: 'I'll meet you at Leicester Square, outside the Odeon, at seven o'clock.' He put down the receiver.

Usually he came to pick her up in the car from the corner of the street.

She stood smiling, the tears running down her face. She knew she was crying because of the loss of Tony, who had let her down. She walked back to her house to make up again, thinking that she was in Stanley's power now: there was no balance between them, the advantage was all his.

PENELOPE FITZGERALD

The Means of Escape

St George's Church, Hobart, stands high above Battery Point and the harbour. Inside, it looks strange and must always have done so, although (at the time I'm speaking of) it didn't have the blue, pink and yellow-patterned stained glass that you see there now. That was ordered from a German firm in 1875. But St George's has always had the sarcophagus-shaped windows which the architect had thought Egyptian and therefore appropriate (St George is said to have been an Egyptian saint). They give you the curious impression, as you cross the threshold, of entering a tomb.

In 1852, before the organ was installed, the church used to face east, and music was provided by a seraphine. The seraphine was built, and indeed invented, by a Mr Ellard, formerly of Dublin, now a resident of Hobart. He intended it to suggest the angelic choir, although the singing voices at his disposal – the surveyor general, the naval chaplain, the harbourmaster and their staffs – were for the most part male. Who was able to play the seraphine? Only, at first, Mr Ellard's daughter, Mrs Logan, who seems to have got £20 a year for doing so, the same fee as the clerk and the sexton. When Mrs Logan began to feel the task was too much for her – the seraphine needs continuous pumping – she instructed Alice Godley, the Rector's daughter.

Hobart stands 'south of no north', between snowy Mount Wellington and the River Derwent, running down over steps and promontories to the harbour's bitterly cold water. You get all the winds that blow. The next stop to the south is the limit of the Antarctic drift ice. When Alice came up to practise the hymns she had to unlock the outer storm door, made of Huon pine, and the inner door, also a storm door, and drag them shut again.

The seraphine stood on its own square of Axminster carpet in the transept. Outside (at the time I'm speaking of) it was a bright afternoon, but inside St George's there was that mixture of light and inky darkness which suggests that from the darkness something may be about to move. It was difficult, for instance, to distinguish whether among the black-painted pews, at some distance away, there was or wasn't some person or object rising above the level of the seats. Alice liked to read mystery stories, when she could get hold of them, and the thought struck her now, 'The form of a man is advancing from the shadows.'

If it had been ten years ago, when she was still a school-girl, she might have shrieked out, because at that time there were said to be bolters and escaped convicts from Port Arthur on the loose everywhere. The Constabulary hadn't been put on to them. Now there were only a few names of runaways, perhaps twenty, posted up on the notice boards outside Government House.

'I did not know that anyone was in the church,' she said. 'It is kept locked. I am the organist. Perhaps I can assist you?'

A rancid stench, not likely from someone who wanted to be shown round the church, came towards her up the aisle. The shape, too, seemed wrong. But that, she saw, was because the head was hidden in some kind of sack like a butchered animal, or, since it had eyeholes, more like a man about to be hung.

'Yes,' he said, 'you can be of assistance to me.'

'I think now that I can't be,' she said, picking up her music case. 'No nearer,' she added distinctly.

He stood still, but said, 'We shall have to get to know one another better.' And then, 'I am an educated man. You may try me out if you like, in Latin and some Greek. I have come from Port Arthur. I was a poisoner.'

'I should not have thought you were old enough to be married.'

'I never said I poisoned my wife!' he cried.

'Were you innocent, then?'

'You women think that everyone in gaol is innocent. No, I'm not innocent, but I was wrongly incriminated. I never lifted a hand. They criminated me on false witness.'

'I don't know about lifting a hand,' she said. 'You mentioned that you were a poisoner.'

'My aim in saying that was to frighten you,' he said. 'But that is no longer my aim at the moment.'

It had been her intention to walk straight out of the church, managing the doors as quickly as she could, and on no account looking back at him, since she believed that with a man of bad character, as with a horse, the best thing was to show no emotion whatever. He, however, moved round through the pews in such a manner as to block her way.

He told her that the name he went by, which was not his given name, was Savage. He had escaped from the Model Penitentiary. He had a knife with him, and had thought at first to cut her throat, but had seen almost at once that the young lady was not on the cross. He had got into the church tower (which was half finished, but no assigned labour could be found to work on it at the moment) through the gaps left in the brickwork. Before he could ask for food she told him firmly that she herself could get him none. Her father was the incumbent, and the most generous of men, but at the Rectory they had to keep very careful count of everything, because charity was given out at the door every Tuesday and Thursday evening. She might be able to bring him the spent tea-leaves, which were always kept, and he could mash them again if he could find warm water.

'That's a sweet touch!' he said. 'Spent tea-leaves!'

'It is all I can do now, but I have a friend – I may perhaps be able to do more later. However, you can't stay here beyond tomorrow.'

'I don't know what day it is now.'

'It is Wednesday, the twelfth of November.'

'Then *Constancy* is still in harbour.'

'How do you know that?'

It was all they did know, for certain, in the penitentiary. There was a rule of absolute silence, but the sailing lists were passed secretly between those who could read, and memorized from them by those who could not.

'*Constancy* is a converted collier, carrying cargo and a hundred and fifty passengers, laying at Franklin Wharf. I am entrusting you with my secret intention, which is to stow on her to Portsmouth, or as far at least as Cape Town.'

He was wearing grey felon's slops. At this point he took off his hood, and stood wringing it round and round in his hands, as though he was trying to wash it.

473

Alice looked at him directly for the first time.

'I shall need a change of clothing, ma'am.'

'You may call me "Miss Alice",' she said.

At the prompting of some sound, or imaginary sound, he retreated and vanished up the dark gap, partly boarded up, of the staircase to the tower. That which had been on his head was left in a heap on the pew. Alice took it up and put it into her music case, pulling the strap tight.

She was lucky in having a friend very much to her own mind, Aggie, the daughter of the people who ran Shuckburgh's Hotel; Aggie Shuckburgh, in fact.

'He might have cut your throat, did you think of that?'

'He thought better of it,' said Alice.

'What I should like to know is this: why didn't you go straight to your father, or to Colonel Johnson at the Constabulary? I don't wish you to answer me at once, because it mightn't be the truth. But tell me this: would you have acted in the same manner, if it had been a woman hiding in the church?' Alice was silent, and Aggie said, 'Did a sudden strong warmth spring up between the two of you?'

'I think that it did.'

No help for it, then, Aggie thought. 'He'll be hard put to it, I'm afraid. There's no water in the tower, unless the last lot of builders left a pailful, and there's certainly no dunny.' But Alice thought he might slip out by night. 'That is what I should do myself, in his place.' She explained that Savage was an intelligent man, and that he intended to stow away on *Constancy*.

'My dear, you're not thinking of following him?'

'I'm not thinking at all,' said Alice.

They were in the hotel, checking the clean linen. So many tablecloths; so many aprons, kitchen; so many aprons, dining-room; so many pillow shams. They hardly ever talked without working. They knew their duties to both their families.

Shuckburgh's had its own warehouse and bond store on the harbour front. Aggie would find an opportunity to draw out, not any of the imported goods, but at least a ration of tea and bacon. Then they could see about getting it up to the church.

'As long as you didn't imagine it, Alice!'

Alice took her arm. 'Forty-five!'

They had settled on the age of forty-five to go irredeemably cranky. They might start imagining anything they liked then. The whole parish, indeed the whole neighbourhood, thought that they were cranky already, in any case, not to get settled, Aggie in particular, with all the opportunities that came her way in the hotel trade.

'He left this behind,' said Alice, opening her music case, which let fly a feral odour. She pulled out the sacking mask, with its slits, like a mourning pierrot's, for eyes.

'Do they make them wear those?'

'I've heard Father speak about them often. They wear them every time they go out of their cells. They're part of the new system, they have to prove their worth. With the masks on, none of the other prisoners can tell who a man is, and he can't tell who they are. He mustn't speak either, and that drives a man into himself, so that he's alone with the Lord, and can't help but think over his wrongdoing and repent. I never saw one of them before today, though.'

'It's got a number on it,' said Aggie, not going so far as to touch it. 'I dare say they put them to do their own laundry.'

At the Rectory there were five people sitting down already to the four o'clock dinner. Next to her father was a guest, the visiting preacher; next to him was Mrs Watson, the housekeeper. She had come to Van Diemen's Land with a seven-year sentence, and now had her ticket to leave. Assigned servants usually ate in the backhouse, but in the Rector's household all were part of the same family. Then, the Lukes. They were penniless immigrants (his papers had Mr Luke down as a scene-painter, but there was no theatre in Hobart). He had been staying, with his wife, for a considerable time.

Alice asked them all to excuse her for a moment while she went up to her room. Once there, she lit a piece of candle and burned the lice off the seams of the mask. She put it over her head. It did not disarrange her hair, the neat smooth hair of a minister's daughter, always presentable on any occasion. But the eyeholes came too low down, so that she could see nothing and stood there in stifling darkness. She asked herself, 'Wherein have I sinned?'

Her father, who never raised his voice, called from downstairs, 'My dear, we are waiting.' She took off the mask, folded it, and put it in the hamper where she kept her woollen stockings.

After grace they ate red snapper, boiled mutton and bread pudding, no vegetables. In England the Reverend Alfred Godley had kept a good kitchen garden, but so far he had not been able to get either leeks or cabbages going in the thin earth round Battery Point.

Mr Luke hoped that Miss Alice had found her time at the instrument well spent.

'I could not get much done,' she answered. 'I was interrupted.'

'Ah, it's a sad thing for a performer to be interrupted. The concentration of the mind is gone. "When the lamp is shattered . . ."'

'That is not what I felt at all,' said Alice.

'You are too modest to admit it.'

'I have been thinking, Father,' said Alice, 'that since Mr Luke cares so much for music, it would be a good thing for him to try the seraphine himself. Then if by any chance I had to go away, you would be sure of a replacement.'

'You speak as if my wife and I should be here always,' cried Mr Luke.

Nobody made any comment on this – certainly not Mrs Luke, who passed her days in a kind of incredulous stupor. How could it be that she was sitting here eating bread pudding some twelve thousand miles from Clerkenwell, where she had spent all the rest of her life? The Rector's attention had been drawn away by the visiting preacher, who had taken out a copy of the *Hobart Town Daily Courier*, and was reading aloud a paragraph which announced his arrival from Melbourne. 'Bringing your welcome with you,' the Rector exclaimed. 'I am glad the *Courier* noted it.' – 'Oh, they would not have done,' said the preacher, 'but I make it my practice to call in at the principal newspaper offices wherever I go, and make myself known with a few friendly words. In that way, if the editor has nothing of great moment to fill up his sheet, which is frequently the case, it is more than likely that he will include something about my witness.' He had come on a not very successful mission to pray that gold would never be discovered in Van Diemen's Land, as it had been on the mainland, bringing with it the occasion of new temptations.

After the dishes were cleared, Alice said she was going back for a while to Aggie's, but would, of course, be home before dark. Mr Luke, while his wife sat on with half-closed eyes, came out to the back kitchen and asked Mrs Watson, who was at the sink, whether he could make himself useful by pumping up some more water.

'No,' said Mrs Watson.

Mr Luke persevered. 'I believe you to have had considerable experience of life. Now, I find Miss Alice charming, but somewhat difficult to understand. Will you tell me something about her?'

'No.'

Mrs Watson was, at the best of times, a very silent woman, whose life had been an unfortunate one. She had lost three children before being transported, and could not now remember what they had been called. Alice, however, did not altogether believe this, as she had met other women who thought it unlucky to name their dead children. Mrs Watson had certainly been out of luck with her third, a baby, who had been left in the charge of a little girl of ten, a neighbour's daughter, who acted as nursemaid for fourpence a week. How the house came to catch fire was not known. It was a flash fire. Mrs Watson was out at work. The man she lived with was in the house, but he was very drunk, and doing – she supposed – the best he could under the circumstances, he pitched both the neighbour's girl and the baby out of the window. The coroner had said that it might just as well have been a Punch and Judy show. 'Try to think no more about it,' Alice advised her. As chance would have it, Mrs Watson had been taken up only a week later for thieving. She had tried to throw herself in the river, but the traps had pulled her out again.

On arrival in Hobart she had been sent to the Female Factory, and later, after a year's steady conduct, to the Hiring Depot where employers could select a pass-holder. That was how, several years ago, she had fetched up at the Rectory. Alice had taught her to write and read, and had given her (as employers were required to do in any case) a copy of the Bible. She handed over the book with a kiss. On the flyleaf she had copied out a verse from Hosea – 'Say to your sister, *Ruhaman*, you have obtained mercy.'

Mrs Watson had no documents which indicated her age, and her pale face was not so much seamed or lined as knocked, apparently, out of the true by a random blow which might have been time or chance. Perhaps she had always looked like that. Although she said nothing by way of thanks at the time, it was evident, as the months went by, that she had transferred the weight of unexpended affection which is one of a woman's greatest inconveniences on to Miss Alice. This was clear partly from the way she occasionally caught hold of Alice's hand and held it for a while, and from her imitation, sometimes unconsciously grotesque, of Alice's rapid walk and her way of doing things about the house.

Aggie had the tea, the bacon, the plum jam, and, on her own initiative, had added a roll of tobacco. This was the only item from the bond store and perhaps should have been left alone, but neither of the girls had ever met or heard of a man who didn't smoke or chew tobacco if he had the opportunity. They knew that on Norfolk Island and at Port Arthur the convicts sometimes killed for tobacco.

They had a note of the exact cash value of what was taken. Alice would repay the amount to Shuckburgh's Hotel from the money she earned from giving music lessons. (She had always refused to take a fee for playing the seraphine at St George's.) But what of truth's claim, what of honesty's? Well, Alice would leave, say, a hundred and twenty days for *Constancy* to reach Portsmouth. Then she would go to her father.

'What will you say to him?' Aggie asked.

'I shall tell him that I have stolen and lied, and caused my friend to steal and lie.'

'Yes, but that was all in the name of the corporeal mercies. You felt pity for this man, who had been a prisoner, and was alone in the wide world.'

'I am not sure that what I feel is pity.'

Certainly the two of them must have been seen through the shining front windows of the new terraced houses on their way up to the church. Certainly they were seen with their handcart, but this was associated with parish magazines and requests for a subscription to something or other, so that at the sight of it the watchers left their windows. At the top of the rise Aggie, who was longing to have a look at Alice's lag, said, 'I'll not come in with you.'

'But, Aggie, you've done so much, and you'll want to see his face.'

'I do want to see his face, but I'm keeping myself in check. That's what forms the character, keeping yourself in check at times.'

'Your character is formed already, Aggie.'

'Sakes, Alice, do you want me to come in with you?'

'No.'

'Mr Savage,' she called out decisively.

'I am just behind you.'

Without turning round, she counted out the packages in their stout wrapping of whitish paper. He did not take them, not even the tobacco, but said, 'I have been watching you and the other young lady from the tower.'

'This situation can't continue,' said Alice. 'There is the regular Moonah Men's prayer meeting on Friday.'

'I shall make a run for it tomorrow night,' said Savage, 'but I need women's clothing. I am not of heavy build. The flesh came off me at Port Arthur, one way and another. Can you furnish me?'

'I must not bring women's clothes to the church,' said Alice. 'St Paul forbids it.' But she had often felt that she was losing patience with St Paul.

'If he won't let you come to me, I must come to you,' said Savage.

'You mean to my father's house?'

'Tell me the way exactly, Miss Alice, and which your room is. As soon as the time's right, I will knock twice on your window.'

'You will not knock on it once!' said Alice. 'I don't sleep on the ground floor.'

'Does your room face the sea?'

'No, I don't care to look at the sea. My window looks on to the Derwent, up the river valley to the north-west.'

Now that she was looking at him he put his two thumbs and forefingers together in a sign which she had understood and indeed used herself ever since she was a child. It meant *I give you my whole heart.*

'I should have thought you might have wanted to know what I was going to do when I reached England,' he said.

'I do know. You'll be found out, taken up and committed to Pentonville as an escaped felon.'

'Only give me time, Miss Alice, and I will send for you.'

In defiance of any misfortune that might come to him, he would send

her the needful money for her fare and his address, once he had a home
for her, in England.

'Wait and trust, give me time, and I will send for you.'

In low-built, shipshape Battery Point the Rectory was unusual in being
three storeys high, but it had been smartly designed with ironwork Trafalgar
balconies, and the garden had been planted with English roses as well as
daisy bushes and silver wattle. It was the Rector's kindheartedness which
had made it take on the appearance of a human warren. Alice's small room,
as she had told Savage, looked out on to the river. Next to her, on that side
of the house, was the visiting preacher's room, always called, as in the story
of Elijah, the prophet's chamber. The Lukes faced the sea, and the Rector
had retreated to what had once been his study. Mrs Watson slept at the
back, over the wash-house, which projected from the kitchen. Above were
the box-rooms, all inhabited by a changing population of no-hopers, thrown
out of work by the depression of the 1840s. These people did not eat at the
Rectory – they went to the Colonial Families' Charitable on Knopwood
Street – but their washing and their poultry had given the grass plot the air
of a seedy encampment, ready to surrender at the first emergency.

Alice did not undress the following night, but lay down in her white
blouse and waist. One of her four shawls and one of her three skirts lay
folded over the back of the sewing chair. At first she lay there and smiled,
then almost laughed out loud at the notion of Savage, like a mummer in
a Christmas pantomime, struggling down the Battery steps and on to the
wharves under the starlight in her nankeen petticoat. Then she ceased
smiling, partly because she felt the unkindness of it, partly because of her
perplexity as to why he needed to make this very last part of his run in
skirts. Did he have in mind to set sail as a woman?

She let her thoughts run free. She knew perfectly well that Savage, after
years of enforced solitude, during which he had been afforded no prospect
of a woman's love, was unlikely to be coming to her room just for a bundle
of clothes. If he wanted to get into bed with her, what then, ought she to
raise the house? She imagined calling out (though not until he was gone),
and her door opening, and the bare shanks of the rescuers jostling in in
their nightshirts – the visiting preacher, Mr Luke, her father, the upstairs
lodgers – and she prayed for grace. She thought of the forgiven – Rahab,

the harlot of Jericho, the wife of Hosea who had been a prostitute, Mary Magdalene, Mrs Watson who had cohabited with a drunken man.

You may call me Miss Alice.

I will send for you.

You could not hear St George's clock from the Rectory. She marked the hours from the clock at Government House on the waterfront. It had been built by convict labour and intended first of all as the Customs House. It was now three o'clock. The *Constancy* sailed at first light.

Give me time and I will send for you.

If he had been seen leaving the church, and arrested, they would surely have come to tell the Rector. If he had missed the way to the Rectory and been caught wandering in the streets, then no one else was to blame but herself. I should have brought him straight home with me. He should have obtained mercy. I should have called out aloud to every one of them – look at him, this is the man who will send for me.

The first time she heard a tap at the window she lay still, thinking, 'He may look for me if he chooses.' It was nothing, there was no one there. The second and third times, at which she got up and crossed the cold floor, were also nothing.

Alice, however, did receive a letter from Savage (he still gave himself that name). It arrived about eight months later, and had been despatched from Portsmouth. By that time she was exceedingly busy, since Mrs Watson had left the Rectory, and had not been replaced.

Honoured Miss Alice,

I think it only proper to do Justice to Myself, by telling you the Circumstances which took place on the 12 of November Last Year. In the First Place, I shall not forget your Kindness. Even when I go down to the Dust, as we all shall do so, a Spark will proclaim, that Miss Alice Godley Relieved me in my Distress.

Having got to the Presbittery in accordance with your Directions, I made sure first of your Room, facing North West, and got up the House the handiest way, by scaleing the Wash-house Roof, intending to make the Circuit of the House by means of the Ballcony and its varse Quantity of creepers. But I was made to Pause at once by a

Window opening and an Ivory Form leaning out, and a Woman's Voice suggesting a natural Proceeding between us, which there is no need to particularise. When we had done our business, she said further, You may call me Mrs Watson, tho it is not my Name. – I said to her, I am come here in search of Women's Clothing. I am a convict on the bolt, and it is my intention to conceal myself on Constancy, laying at Franklyn Wharf. She replied immediately, 'I can Furnish you, and indeed I can see No Reason, why I should not Accompany you.'

This letter of Savage's in its complete form, is now, like so many memorials of convict days, in the National Library of Tasmania, in Hobart. There is no word in it to Alice Godley from Mrs Watson herself. It would seem that like many people who became literate later in life she read a great deal – the Bible in particular – but never took much to writing, and tended to mistrust it. In consequence her motives for doing what she did – which, taking into account her intense affection for Alice, must have been complex enough – were never set down, and can only be guessed at.

ALASDAIR GRAY

Five Letters from an Eastern Empire

DESCRIBING ETIQUETTE GOVERNMENT IRRIGATION
EDUCATION CLOGS KITES RUMOUR POETRY JUSTICE
MASSAGE TOWN-PLANNING SEX AND VENTRILOQUISM
IN AN OBSOLETE NATION

FIRST LETTER

Dear Mother, Dear Father, I like the new palace. It is all squares like a chessboard. The red squares are buildings, the white squares are gardens. In the middle of each building is a courtyard, in the middle of each garden is a pavilion. Soldiers, nurses, postmen, janitors and other of the servant-class live and work in the buildings. Members of the honoured-guest-class have a pavilion. My pavilion is small but beautiful, in the garden of evergreens. I don't know how many squares make up the palace but certainly more than a chessboard has. You heard the rumour that some villages and a small famous city were demolished to clear space for the foundation. The rumour was authorized by the immortal emperor yet I thought it exaggerated. I now think it too timid. We were ten days sailing upstream from the old capital, where I hope you are still happy. The days were clear and cool, no dust, no mist. Sitting on deck we could see the watchtowers of villages five or six miles away and when we stood up at nightfall we saw, in the sunset, the sparkle of the heliograph above cities, on the far side of the horizon. But after six days there was no sign of any buildings at all, just ricefields with here and there the tent of a waterworks inspector. If all this empty land feeds the new palace then several cities have been cleared from it. Maybe the inhabitants are inside the walls with me, going out a few days each year to plant and harvest, and working between times as gardeners of the servant-class.

You would have admired the company I kept aboard the barge. We were all members of the honoured-guest-class: accountants, poets and head-masters, many many headmasters. We were very jolly together and said many things we would not be able to say in the new palace under the new etiquette. I asked the headmaster of literature, 'Why are there so many headmasters and so few poets? Is it easier for you to train your own kind than ours?' He said, 'No. The emperor needs all the headmasters he can get. If a quarter of his people were headmasters he would be perfectly happy. But more than two poets would tear his kingdom apart.'

I led the loud laughter which rewarded this deeply witty remark and my poor, glum little enemy and colleague Tohu had to go away and sulk. His sullen glances amuse me all the time. Tohu has been educated to envy and fear everyone, especially me, while I have been educated to feel serenely superior to everyone, especially him. Nobody knows this better than the headmaster of literature who taught us both. This does not mean he wants me to write better than Tohu, it shows he wants me to write with high feelings and Tohu with low ones. Neither of us have written yet but I expect I will be the best. I hope the emperor soon orders me to celebrate something grand and that I provide exactly what is needed. Then you will both be able to love me as much as you would like to do.

This morning, as we breakfasted in the hold of the barge, Tohu came down into it with so white a face that we all stared. He screamed, 'The emperor has tricked us! We have gone downstream instead of up! We are coming to the great wall round the edge of the kingdom, not to a palace in the middle! We are being sent into exile among the barbarians!' We went on deck. He was wrong of course. The great wall has towers with loopholes every half mile, and it bends in places. The wall which lay along the hori-zon before us was perfectly flat and windowless and on neither side could we see an end of it. Nor could we see anything behind it but the high tapering tops of two post-office towers, one to the east, one to the west, with the white flecks of messenger pigeons whirling toward them and away from them at every point of the compass. The sight made us all very silent. I raised a finger, summoned my entourage and went downstairs to dress for disembarking. They took a long time lacing me into the ceremonial cape and clogs and afterwards they found it hard lifting me back up to the deck again. Since I was now the tallest man aboard I had to disembark first. I advanced to the prow and stood there, arms rigid by my sides, hands gripping the topknot of the doctor, who supported my left thigh, and the thick hair of Adoda, my masseuse, who warmly clasped my right. Behind me the secretary and chef each held back a corner of the cape so that everyone could see, higher than a common man's head, the dark green kneebands of the emperor's tragic poet. Without turning I knew that behind my entourage the headmasters were ranged, the first of them a whole head shorter than me, then the accountants, then, last and least, the emperor's comic poet, poor Tohu. The soles of his ceremonial clogs are only ten inches thick and he has nearly no entourage at all. His doctor, masseuse, secretary and chef are all the same little nurse.

I had often pictured myself like this, tall upon the prow, the sublime tragedian arriving at the new palace. But I had imagined a huge wide-open gate or door, with policemen holding back crowds on each side, and maybe a balcony above with the emperor on it surrounded by the college of headmasters. But though the smooth wall was twice as high as most cliffs, I could see no opening in it. Along the foot was a landing stage crowded with shipping. The river spread left and right along this in a wide moat, but the current of the stream seemed to come from under the stage. Among yelling dockers and heaped bales and barrels I saw a calm group of men with official gongs on their wrists, and the black clothes and scarlet kneebands of the janitors. They waited near an empty notch. The prow of our barge slid into this notch. Dockers bolted it there. I led the company ashore.

I recognized my janitor by the green shoes these people wear when guiding poets. He reminded us that the new etiquette was enforced within the palace walls and led us to a gate. The other passengers were led to other gates. I could now see hundreds of gates, all waist high and wide enough to roll a barrel through. My entourage helped me to my knees and I crawled in after the janitor. This was the worst part of the journey. We had to crawl a great distance, mostly uphill. Adoda and the doctor tried to help by alternately butting their heads against the soles of my clogs. The floor was carpeted with bristly stuff which pierced my kneebands and scratched the palms of my hands. After twenty minutes it was hard not to sob with pain and exhaustion, and when at last they helped me to my feet I sympathized with Tohu who swore aloud that he would never go through that wall again.

The new etiquette stops honoured guests from filling their heads with useless knowledge. We go nowhere without a janitor to lead us and look at nothing above the level of his kneebands. As I was ten feet tall I could only glimpse these slips of scarlet by leaning forward and pressing my chin into my chest. Sometimes in sunlight, sometimes in lamp-light, we crossed wooden floors, brick pavements, patterned rugs and hard-packed gravel. But I mainly noticed the pain in my neck and calves, and the continual whine of Tohu complaining to his nurse. At last I fell asleep. My legs moved onward because Adoda and the doctor lifted them. The chef and secretary stopped me bending forward in the middle by pulling backward on the cape. I was wakened by the janitor striking his gong and saying, 'Sir. This is your home.' I lifted my eyes and saw I was inside the sunlit, afternoon, evergreen garden. It was noisy with birdsongs.

We stood near the thick hedge of cypress, holly and yew trees which hide all but some tiled roofs of the surrounding buildings. Triangular pools, square lawns and the grassy paths of a zig-zag maze are symmetrically placed round the pavilion in the middle. In each corner is a small pinewood with cages of linnets, larks and nightingales in the branches. From one stout branch hangs a trapeze where a servant dressed like a cuckoo sits imitating the call of that bird, which does not sing well in captivity. Many gardeners were discreetly trimming things or mounting ladders to feed the birds. They wore black clothes without kneebands, so they were socially invisible, and this gave the garden a wonderful air of privacy. The janitor struck his gong softly and whispered, 'The leaves which grow here never fade or die.' I rewarded this delicate compliment with a slight smile then gestured to a patch of moss. They laid me flat there and I was tenderly undressed. The doctor cleaned me. Adoda caressed my aching body till it breathed all over in the sun-warmed air. Meanwhile Tohu had flopped down in his nurse's arms and was snoring horribly. I had the couple removed and placed behind a hollybush out of earshot. Then I asked for the birds to be silenced, starting with the linnets and ending with the cuckoo. As the gardeners covered the cages the silence grew louder, and when the notes of the cuckoo faded there was nothing at all to hear and I slept once more.

Adoda caressed me awake before sunset and dressed me in something comfortable. The chef prepared a snack with the stove and the food from his satchel. The janitor fidgeted impatiently. We ate and drank and the doctor put something in the tea which made me quick and happy.'

'Come!' I said, jumping up, 'Let us go straight to the pavilion!' and instead of following the path through the maze I stepped over the privet hedge bordering it which was newly planted and a few inches high.

'Sir!' called the janitor, much upset, 'Please do not offend the gardeners! It is not their fault that the hedge is still too small.'

I said, 'The gardeners are socially invisible to me.'

He said, 'But you are officially visible to them, and honoured guests do not offend the emperor's servants. That is not the etiquette!'

I said, 'It is not a rule of the etiquette, it is convention of the etiquette, and the etiquette allows poets to be unconventional in their own home. Follow me, Tohu.'

But because he is trained to write popular comedy Tohu dreads offending members of the servant class, so I walked straight to the pavilion all by myself.

It stands on a low platform with steps all round and is five sided, with a blue wooden pillar supporting the broad eaves at each corner. An obser-vatory rises from the centre of the sloping green porcelain roof and each wall has a door in the middle with a circular window above. The doors were locked but I did not mind that. The air was still warm. A gardener spread cushions on the platform edge and I lay and thought about the poem I would be ordered to write. This was against all rules of education and etiquette. A poet cannot know his theme until the emperor orders it. Until then he should think of nothing but the sublime classics of the past. But I knew I would be commanded to celebrate a great act and the greatest act of our age is the building of the new palace. How many mil-lions lost their homes to clear the ground? How many orphans were prostituted to keep the surveyors cheerful? How many captives died miserably quarrying its stone? How many small sons and daughters were trampled to death in the act of wiping sweat from the eyes of desperate, bricklaying parents who had fallen behind schedule? Yet this building which barbarians think a long act of intricately planned cruelty has given the empire this calm and solemn heart where honoured guests and servants can command peace and prosperity till the end of time. There can be no greater theme for a work of tragic art. It is rumoured that the palace encloses the place where the rivers watering the empire divide. If a province looks like rebelling, the headmaster of waterworks can divert the flow elsewhere and reduce it to drought, quickly or slowly, just as he pleases. This rumour is authorized by the emperor and I believe it absolutely.

While I was pondering, the janitor led the little party through the maze, which seemed designed to tantalize them. Sometimes they were a few yards from me, then they would disappear behind the pavilion and after a long time reappear far away in the distance. The stars came out. The cuckoo climbed down from his trapeze and was replaced by a nightwatchman dressed like an owl. A gardener went round hanging frail paper boxes of glow-worms under the eaves. When the party reached the platform by the conventional entrance all but Adoda were tired, cross and extremely envious of my unconventional character. I welcomed them with a good-humoured chuckle.

The janitor unlocked the rooms. Someone had lit lamps in them. We saw the kitchen where the chef sleeps, the stationery office where the secretary sleeps, the lavatory where the doctor sleeps, and Adoda's room, where I sleep. Tohu and his nurse also have a room. Each room has a door into the garden and another into the big central hall where I and Tohu will make poetry when the order-to-write comes. The walls here are very white and bare. There is a thick blue carpet and a couple of punt-shaped thrones lined with cushions and divided from each other by a screen. The only other furniture is the ladder to the observatory above. The janitor assembled us here, struck the gong and made this speech in the squeaky voice the emperor uses in public.

'The emperor is glad to see you safe inside his walls. The servants will now cover their ears.

'The emperor greets Bohu, his tragic poet, like a long-lost brother. Be patient, Bohu. Stay at home. Recite the classics. Use the observatory. It was built to satisfy your craving for grand scenery. Fill your eyes and mind with the slow, sublime, eternally returning architecture of the stars. Ignore trivial flashes which stupid peasants call *falling* stars. It has been proved that these are not heavenly bodies but white-hot cinders fired out of volcanoes. When you cannot stay serene without talking to someone, dictate a letter to your parents in the old capital. Say anything you like. Do not be afraid to utter unconventional thoughts, however peculiar. Your secretary will not be punished for writing these down, your parents not punished for reading them. Be serene at all times. Keep a calm empty mind and you will see me soon.

'And now, a word for Tohu. Don't grovel so much. Be less glum. You lack Bohu's courage and dignity and don't understand people well enough to love them, as he does, but you might still be my best poet. My new palace contains many markets. Visit them with your chef when she goes shopping. Mix with the crowds of low, bustling people you must one day amuse. Learn their quips and catch-phrases. Try not to notice they stink. Take a bath when you get home and you too will see me soon.'

The janitor struck his gong then asked in his own voice if we had any polite requests. I looked round the hall. I stood alone, for at the sound of the emperor's voice all but the janitor and I had lain face down on the carpet and even the janitor had sunk to his knees. Tohu and the entourage sat up now and watched me expectantly. Adoda arose with her little spoon and bottle and carefully collected from my cheeks the sacred tears of joy which spring in the eyes of everyone the emperor addresses. Tohu's nurse was licking his tears off the carpet. I envied him, for he would see more of the palace than I would, and be more ready to write a poem about it when the order came. I did not want to visit the market but I ached to see the treasuries and reservoirs and grain-silos, the pantechnicons and pantheons and gardens of justice. I wondered how to learn about these and still stay at home. The new dictionary of etiquette says *All requests for knowledge will be expressed as requests for things*. So I said, 'May the bare walls of this splendid hall be decorated with a map of the new palace? It will help my colleague's chef to lead him about.'

Tohu shouted, 'Do not speak for me, Bohu! The emperor will send janitors to lead the chef who leads me. I need nothing more and nothing less than the emperor has already decided to give.'

The janitor ignored him and told me, 'I hear and respect your request.'

According to the new dictionary of etiquette this answer means *No* or *Maybe* or *Yes, after a very long time.*

The janitor left. I felt restless. The chef's best tea, the doctor's drugs, Adoda's caresses had no effect so I climbed into the observatory and tried to quieten myself by watching the stars as the emperor had commanded. But that did not work, as he foresaw, so I summoned my secretary and dictated this letter, as he advised. Don't be afraid to read it. You know what the emperor said. And the postman who rewrites letters before fixing them to the pigeons always leaves out dangerous bits. Perhaps he will improve my prose-style, for most of these sentences are too short and jerky. This is the first piece of prose I ever composed, and as you know, I am a poet.

> *Goodbye. I will write to you again,*
> *From the evergreen garden,*
> *Your son,*
> *Bohu.*

DICTATED ON THE 27th LAST DAY OF THE OLD CALENDAR.

SECOND LETTER

Dear Mother, Dear Father, I discover that I still love you more than anything in the world. I like my entourage, but they are servants and cannot speak to me. I like the headmaster of literature, but he only speaks about poetry. I like poetry, but have written none. I like the emperor, but have never seen him. I dictated the last letter because he said talking to you would cure my loneliness. It did, for a while, but it also brought back memories of the time we lived together before I was five, wild days full of happiness and dread, horrid fights and ecstatic picnics. Each of you loved and hated a different bit of me.

*

You loved talking to me, mother, we were full of playful conversation while you embroidered shirts for the police and I toyed with the coloured silks and buttons. You were small and pretty yet told such daring stories that your sister, the courtesan, screamed and covered her ears, while we laughed till the tears came. Yet you hated me going outside and locked me for an hour in the sewing box because I wore my good clogs in the lane. These were the clogs father had carved with toads on the tips. You had given them many coats of yellow lacquer, polishing each one till a member of the honoured-guest-class thought my clogs were made of amber and denounced us to the police for extravagance. But the magistrate was just and all came right in the end.

Mother always wanted me to look pretty. You, father, didn't care how I looked and you hated talking, especially to me, but you taught me to swim before I was two and took me in the punt to the sewage ditch. I helped you sift out many dead dogs and cats to sell to the gardeners for dung. You wanted me to find a dead man, because corpse-handlers (you said) don't often die of infectious diseases. The corpse I found was not a man but a boy of my own age, and instead of selling him to the gardeners we buried him where nobody would notice. I wondered why, at the time, for we needed money for rent. One day we found the corpse of a woman with a belt and bracelet of coins. The old capital must have been a slightly mad place that year. Several corpses of the honoured-guest-class bobbed along the canals and the emperor set fire to the south-eastern slums. I had never seen you act so strangely. You dragged me to the nearest market (the smell of burning was everywhere) and rented the biggest possible kite and harness. You who hate talking carried that kite down the long avenue to the eastern gate, shouting all the time to the priest, your brother, who was helping us. You said all children should be allowed to fly before they were too heavy, not just children of the honoured-guest-class. On top of the hill I grew afraid and struggled as you tightened the straps, then uncle perched me on his shoulders under that huge sail, and you took the end of the rope, and you both ran downhill into the wind. I remember a tremendous jerk, but nothing else.

I woke on the sleeping-rug on the hearth of the firelit room. My body was sore all over but you knelt beside me caressing it, mother, and when you saw my eyes were open you sprang up, screamed and attacked father with your needles. He did not fight back. Then you loved each other in the firelight beside me. It comforted me to see that. And I liked watching the babies come, especially my favourite sister with the pale hair. But during the bad winter two years later she had to be sold to the merchants for money to buy firewood.

Perhaps you did not know you had given me exactly the education a poet needs, for when you led me to the civil service academy on my fifth birthday I carried the abacus and squared slate of an accountant under my arm and I thought I would be allowed to sleep at home. But the examiner knew his job and after answering his questions I was sent to the classics dormitory of the closed literature wing and you never saw me again. I saw you again, a week or perhaps a year later. The undergraduates were crossing the garden between the halls of the drum-master who taught us rhythms and the chess-master who taught us consequential logic. I lagged behind them then slipped into the space between the laurel bushes and the outside fence and looked through. On the far side of the freshwater canal I saw a tiny distant man and woman standing staring. Even at that distance I recognized the pink roses on the scarlet sleeves of mother's best petticoat. You could not see me, yet for a minute or perhaps a whole hour you stood staring at the tall academy fence as steadily as I stared at you. Then the monitors found me. But I knew I was not forgotten, and my face never acquired the haunted, accusing look which stamped the face of the other scholars and most of the teachers too. My face displays the pained but perfectly real smile of the eternally hopeful. That glimpse through the fence enabled me to believe in love while living without it, so the imagination lessons, which made some of my schoolmates go mad or kill themselves, did not frighten me.

The imagination lessons started on my eleventh birthday after I had memorized all the classical literature and could recite it perfectly. Before that day only my smile showed how remarkable I was. The teachers put me in a windowless room with a ceiling a few inches above my head when I sat on the floor. The furniture was a couple of big shallow earthenware pans, one empty and one full of water. I was told to stay there until I had passed the water through my body and filled the empty pan with it. I was told that when the door was shut I would be a long time in darkness and silence, but before the water was drunk I would hear voices and imagine the bodies of strange companions, some of them friendly and others not. I was told that if I welcomed everyone politely even the horrible visitors would teach me useful things. The door was shut and the darkness which drowned me was surprisingly warm and familiar. It was exactly the darkness inside my mother's sewing-box. For the first time since entering the academy I felt at home.

After a while I heard your voices talking quietly together and thought you had been allowed to visit me at last, but when I joined the conversation I found we were talking of things I must have heard discussed when I was a few months old. It was very interesting. I learned later that other students imagined the voices and company of ghouls and madmen and gulped down the water so fast that they became ill. I sipped mine as slowly as possible. The worst person I met was the corpse of the dead boy I had helped father take from the canal. I knew him by the smell. He lay a long time in the corner of the room before I thought of welcoming him and asking his name. He told me he was not an ill-treated orphan, as father had thought, but the son of a rich waterworks inspector who had seen a servant stealing food and been murdered to stop him telling people. He told me many things about life among the highest kinds of honoured-guest-class, things I could never have learned from my teachers at the academy who belonged to the lower kind. The imagination lessons became, for me, a way of escaping from the drum, chess and recitation masters and of meeting in darkness everyone I had lost with infancy. The characters of classical literature started visiting me too, from the celestial monkey who is our ancestor to Emperor Hyun who burned all the unnecessary books and built the great wall to keep out unnecessary people. They taught me things about themselves which classical literature does not mention. Emperor Hyun, for instance, was in some ways a petty, garrulous old man much troubled with arthritis. The best part of him was exactly like my father patiently dredging for good things in the sewage mud of the north-west slums. And the imperious seductive white demon in the comic creation myth turned out to be very like my aunt, the courtesan, who also transformed herself into different characters to interest strangers, yet all the time was determinedly herself. My aunt visited me more than was proper and eventually I imagined something impossible with her and my academic gown was badly stained. This was noted by the school laundry. The next day the medical inspector made small wounds at the top of my things which never quite healed and are still treated twice a month. I have never since soiled cloth in that way. My fifth limb sometimes stiffens under Adoda's caresses but nothing comes from it.

Soon after the operation the headmaster of literature visited the academy. He was a heavy man, as heavy as I am now. He said, 'You spend more days imagining than the other scholars, yet your health is good. What guests come to your dark room?'

I told him. He asked detailed questions. I took several days to describe everyone. When I stopped he was silent a while then said, 'Do you understand why you have been trained like this?'

I said I did not.

He said, 'A poet needs an adventurous, sensuous infancy to enlarge his appetites. But large appetites must be given a single direction or they will produce a mere healthy human being. So the rich infancy must be followed by a childhood of instruction which starves the senses, especially of love. The child is thus forced to struggle for love in the only place he can experience it, which is memory, and the only place he can practise it, which is imagination. This education, which I devised, destroys the minds it does not enlarge. You are my first success. Stand up.'

I did, and he stooped, with difficulty, and tied the dark green ribbons round my knees. I said, 'Am I a poet now?'

He said, 'Yes. You are now the emperor's honoured guest and tragic poet, the only modern author whose work will be added to the classics of world literature.' I asked when I could start writing. He said, 'Not for a long time. Only the emperor can supply a theme equal to your talent and he is not ready to do so. But the waiting will be made easy. The days of the coarse robe, dull teachers and dark room are over. You will live in the palace.'

I asked him if I could see my parents first. He said, 'No. Honoured guests only speak to inferior classes when asking for useful knowledge and your parents are no use to you now. They have changed. Perhaps your small pretty mother has become a brazen harlot like her sister, your strong silent father an arthritic old bore like the Emperor Hyun. After meeting them you would feel sad and wise and want to write ordinary poems about the passage of time and fallen petals drifting down the stream. Your talent must be preserved for a greater theme than that.'

I asked if I would have friends at the palace. He said, 'You will have two. My system has produced one other poet, not very good, who may perhaps be capable of some second-rate doggerel when the order-to-write comes. He will share your apartment. But your best friend knows you already. Here is his face.'

He gave me a button as broad as my thumb with a small round hairless head enamelled on it. The eyes were black slits between complicated wrinkles; the sunk mouth seemed to have no teeth but was curved in a surprisingly sweet sly smile. I knew this must be the immortal emperor.

I asked if he was blind.

'Necessarily so. This is the hundred-and-second year of his reign and all sights are useless knowledge to him now. But his hearing is remarkably acute.'

So I and Tohu moved to the palace of the old capital and a highly trained entourage distracted my enlarged mind from the work it was waiting to do. We were happy but cramped. The palace staff kept increasing until many honoured guests had to be housed in the city outside, which took away homes from the citizens. No new houses could be built because all the skill and materials in the empire were employed on the new palace upriver, so all gardens and graveyards and even several streets were covered with tents, barrels and packing-cases where thousands of families were living. I never used the streets myself because honoured guests there were often looked at very rudely, with glances of concealed dislike. The emperor arranged for the soles of our ceremonial clogs to be thickened until even the lowest of his honoured guests could pass through a crowd of common citizens without meeting them face-to-face. But after that some from the palace were jostled by criminals too far beneath them to identify, so it was ordered that honoured guests should be led everywhere by a janitor and surrounded by their entourage. This made us perfectly safe, but movement through the densely packed streets became very difficult. At last the emperor barred common citizens from the streets during the main business hours and things improved.

*

Yet these same citizens who glared and jostled and grumbled at us were terrified of us going away! Their trades and professions depended on the court; without it most of them would become unnecessary people. The emperor received anonymous letters saying that if he tried to leave, his wharves and barges would catch fire and the sewage ditches would be diverted into the palace reservoir. You may wonder how your son, a secluded poet, came to know these things. Well, the headmaster of civil peace sometimes asked me to improve the wording of rumours authorized by the emperor, while Tohu improved the unauthorized ones that were broadcast by the beggars' association. We both put out a story that citizens who worked hard and did not grumble would be employed as servants in the new palace. This was true, but not as true as people hoped. The anonymous letters stopped and instead the emperor received signed petitions from the workingmen's clubs explaining how long and well they had served him and asking to go on doing it. Each signatory was sent a written reply with the emperor's seal saying that his request had been heard and respected. In the end the court departed upriver quietly, in small groups, accompanied by the workingmen's leaders. But the mass of new palace servants come from more docile cities than the old capital. It is nice to be in a safe home with nobody to frighten us.

I am stupid to mention these things. You know the old capital better than I do. Has it recovered the bright uncrowded streets and gardens I remember when we lived there together so many years ago?

This afternoon is very sunny and hot, so I am dictating my letter on the observatory tower. There is a fresh breeze at this height. When I climbed up here two hours ago I found a map of the palace on the table beside my map of the stars. It seems my requests are heard with unusual respect. Not much of the palace is marked on the map but enough to identify the tops of some big pavilions to the north. A shining black pagoda rises from the garden of irrevocable justice where disobedient people have things removed which cannot be returned, like eardrums, eyes, limbs and heads. Half-a-mile away a similar but milkwhite pagoda marks the garden of revocable justice where good people receive gifts which can afterwards be taken back, like homes, wives, salaries and pensions. Between these pagodas but further off, is the court of summons, a vast round tower with a forest of bannerpoles on the roof. On the highest pole the emperor's scarlet flag floats above the rainbow flag of the headmasters, so he is in there today conferring with the whole college.

Shortly before lunch Tohu came in with a wood-cut scroll which he said was being pinned up and sold all over the market, perhaps all over the empire. At the top is the peculiar withered-apple-face of the immortal emperor which fascinates me more each time I see it. I feel his blind eyes could eat me up and a few days later the sweet sly mouth would spit me out in a new, perhaps improved form. Below the portrait are these words:

> *Forgive me for ruling you but someone must. I am a small weak old man but have the strength of all my good people put together. I am blind, but your ears are my ears so I hear everything. As I grow older I try to be kinder. My guests in the new palace help me. Their names and pictures are underneath.*

Then come the two tallest men in the empire. One of them is:

> *Fieldmarshal Ko who commands all imperial armies and police and defeats all imperial enemies. He has degrees in strategy from twenty-eight academies but leaves thinking to the emperor. He hates unnecessary people but says 'Most of them are outside the great wall.'*

The other is:

> *Bohu, the great poet. His mind is the largest in the land. He knows the feelings of everyone from the poor peasant in the ditch to the old emperor on the throne. Soon his great poem will be painted above the door of every townhouse, school, barracks, post-office, law-court, theatre and prison in the land. Will it be about war? Peace? Love? Justice? Agriculture? Architecture? Time? Fallen apple-blossom in the stream? Bet about this with your friends.*

I was pleased to learn there were only two tallest men in the empire. I had thought there were three of us. Tohu's face was at the end of the scroll in a row of twenty others. He looked very small and cross between a toe-surgeon and an inspector of chicken-feed. His footnote said:

Tohu hopes to write funny poems. Will he succeed?

I rolled up the scroll and returned it with a friendly nod but Tohu was uneasy and wanted conversation. He said, 'The order-to-write is bound to come soon now.'

'Yes.'

'Are you frightened?'

'No.'

'Your work may not please.'

'That is unlikely.'

'What will you do when your great poem is complete?'

'I shall ask the emperor for death.'

Tohu leaned forward and whispered eagerly, 'Why? There is a rumour that when our poem is written, the wounds at the top of our thighs will heal up and we will be able to love our masseuse as if we were common men!'

I smiled and said, 'That would be an anticlimax.'

I enjoy astonishing Tohu.

Dear parents, this is my last letter to you. I will write no more prose. But laugh aloud when you see my words painted above the doors of the public buildings. Perhaps you are poor, sick or dying. I hope not. But nothing can deprive you of the greatest happiness possible for a common man and woman. You have created an immortal,

Who lives in the evergreen garden,

Your son,

Bohu.

DICTATED ON THE 19th LAST DAY OF THE OLD
CALENDAR.

THIRD LETTER

Dear Mother, Dear Father, I am full of confused feelings. I saw the emperor two days ago. He is not what I thought. If I describe everything very carefully, especially to you, perhaps I won't go mad.

*

I wakened that morning as usual and lay peacefully in Adoda's arms. I did not know this was my last peaceful day. Our room faces north. Through the round window above the door I could see the banners above the court of summons. The scarlet and the rainbow flags still floated on the highest pole but beneath them flapped the dark green flag of poetry. There was a noise of hammering and when I looked outside some joiners were building a low wooden bridge which went straight across the maze from the platform edge. I called in the whole household. I said, 'Today we visit the emperor.'

They looked alarmed. I felt very gracious and friendly. I said, 'Only I and Tohu will be allowed to look at him but everyone will hear his voice. The clothes I and Tohu wear are chosen by the etiquette, but I want the rest of you to dress as if you are visiting a rich famous friend you love very much.' Adoda smiled but the others still looked alarmed. Tohu muttered, 'The emperor is blind.' I had forgotten that. I nodded and said, 'His headmasters are not.'

When the janitor arrived I was standing ten feet tall at the end of the bridge. Adoda on my right wore a dress of dark green silk and her thick hair was mingled with sprigs of yew. Even Tohu's nurse wore something special. The janitor bowed, turned, and paused to let me fix my eyes on his knee-bands; then he struck his gong and we moved toward the court.

The journey lasted an hour but I would not have wearied had it lasted a day. I was as incapable of tiredness as a falling stone on its way to the ground. I felt excited, strong, yet peacefully determined at the same time. The surfaces we crossed became richer and larger: pavements of marquetry and mosaic, thresholds of bronze and copper, carpets of fine tapestry and exotic fur. We crossed more than one bridge for I heard the lip-lapping of a great river or lake. The janitor eventually struck the gong for delay and I sensed the wings of a door expanding before us. We moved through a shadow into greater light. The janitor struck the end-of-journey note and his legs left my field of vision. The immortal emperor's squeaky voice said, 'Welcome, my poets. Consider yourselves at home.'

*

I raised my eyes and first of all saw the college of headmasters. They sat on felt stools at the edge of a platform which curved round us like the shore of a bay. The platform was so high that their faces were level with my own, although I was standing erect. Though I had met only a few of them I knew all twenty-three by their regalia. The headmaster of water-works wore a silver drainpipe round his leg, the headmaster of civil peace held a ceremonial bludgeon, the headmaster of history carried a stuffed parrot on his wrist. The headmaster of etiquette sat in the very centre holding the emperor, who was two feet high. The emperor's head and the hands dangling out of his sleeves were normal size, but the body in the scarlet silk robe seemed to be a short wooden staff. His skin was papier-mâché with lacquer varnish, yet in conversation he was quick and sprightly. He ran from hand to hand along the row and did not speak again until he reached the headmaster of vaudeville on the extreme left. Then he said, 'I shock you. Before we talk I must put you at ease, especially Tohu whose neck is sore craning up at me. Shall I tell a joke, Tohu?'

'Oh yes, sir, hahaha! Oh yes, sir, hahaha!' shouted Tohu, guffawing hysterically.

The emperor said, 'You don't need a joke. You are laughing happily already!'

I realized that this was the emperor's joke and gave a brief appreciative chuckle. I had known the emperor was not human, but was so surprised to see he was not alive that my conventional tears did not flow at the sound of his voice. This was perhaps lucky as Adoda was too far below me to collect them.

The emperor moved to the headmaster of history and spoke on a personal note: 'Ask me intimate questions, Bohu.'

I said, 'Sir, have you always been a puppet?'

He said, 'I am not, even now, completely a puppet. My skull and the bones of my hands are perfectly real. The rest was boiled off by doctors fifteen years ago in the operation which made me immortal.'

I said, 'Was it sore becoming immortal?'

He said, 'I did not notice. I had senile dementia at the time and for many years before that I was, in private life, vicious and insensitive. But the wisdom of an emperor has nothing to do with his character. It is the combined intelligence of everyone who obeys him.'

The sublime truth of this entered me with such force that I gasped for breath. Yes. The wisdom of a government is the combined intelligence of those who obey it. I gazed at the simpering dummy with pity and awe. Tears poured thickly down my cheeks but I did not heed them.

'Sir!' I cried, 'Order us to write for you. We love you. We are ready.'

The emperor moved to the headmaster of civil peace and shook the tiny imperial frock into dignified folds before speaking. He said, 'I order you to write a poem celebrating my irrevocable justice.'

I said, 'Will this poem commemorate a special act of justice?'

He said, 'Yes. I have just destroyed the old capital, and everyone living there, for the crime of disobedience.'

I smiled and nodded enthusiastically, thinking I had not heard properly. I said, 'Very good, sir, yes, that will do very well. But could you suggest a particular event, a historically important action, which might, in my case, form the basis of a meditative ode, or a popular ballad, in my colleague's case? The action or event should be one which demonstrates the emperor's justice. Irrevocably.'

He said, 'Certainly. The old capital was full of unnecessary people. They planned a rebellion. Field-marshal Ko besieged it, burned it flat and killed everyone who lived there. The empire is peaceful again. That is your theme. Your pavilion is now decorated with information on the subject. Return there and write.'

'Sir!' I said, 'I hear and respect your order, I hear and respect your order!'

I went on saying this, unable to stop. Tohu was screaming with laughter and shouting, 'Oh my colleague is extremely unconventional, all great poets are, I will write for him, I will write for all of us hahahaha!'

The headmasters were uneasy. The emperor ran from end to end of them and back, never resting till the headmaster of moral philosophy forced him violently onto the headmaster of etiquette. Then the emperor raised his head and squeaked, 'This is not etiquette, I adjourn the college!'

He then flopped upside down on a stool while the headmasters hurried out.

*

I could not move. Janitors swarmed confusedly round my entourage. My feet left the floor, I was jerked one way, then another, then carried quickly backward till my shoulder struck something, maybe a doorpost. And then I was falling, and I think I heard Adoda scream before I became unconscious.

I woke under a rug on my writing-throne in the hall of the pavilion. Paper screens had been placed round it painted with views of the old capital at different stages of the rebellion, siege and massacre. Behind one screen I heard Tohu dictating to his secretary. Instead of taking nine days to assimilate his material the fool was composing already.

Postal pigeons whirl like snow from the new palace, he chanted.
Trained hawks of the rebels strike them dead.
The emperor summons his troops by heliograph:
'Fieldmarshal Ko, besiege the ancient city.'
Can hawks catch the sunbeam flashed from silver mirror?
No, hahahaha. No, hahahaha. Rebels are ridiculous.

I held my head. My main thought was that you, mother, you, father, do not exist now and all my childhood is flat cinders. This thought is such pain that I got up and stumbled round the screens to make sure of it.

I first beheld a beautiful view of the old capital, shown from above like a map, but with every building clear and distinct. Pink and green buds on the trees showed this was springtime. I looked down into a local garden of justice where a fat magistrate fanned by a singing-girl sat on a doorstep. A man, woman, and child lay flat on the ground before him and nearby a policeman held a dish with two yellow dots on it. I knew these were clogs with toads on the tips, and that the family was being accused of extravagance and would be released with a small fine. I looked again and saw a little house by the effluent of a sewage canal. Two little women sat sewing on the doorstep, it was you, mother, and your sister, my aunt. Outside the fence a man in a punt, helped by a child, dragged a body from the mud. The bodies of many members of the honoured-guest-class were bobbing along the sewage canals. The emperor's cavalry were setting fire to the south-eastern slums and sabring families who tried to escape. The strangest happening of all was on a hill outside the eastern gate. A man held the rope of a kite which floated out over the city, a kite shaped like an eagle with parrot-coloured feathers. A child hung from it. This part of the picture was on a larger scale than the rest. The father's face wore a look of great pride, but the child was staring down on the city below, not with terror or delight, but with a cool, stern, assessing stare. In the margin of this screen was written *The rebellion begins.*

I only glanced at the other screens. Houses flamed, whole crowds were falling from bridges into canals to avoid the hooves and sabres of the cavalry. If I had looked closely I would have recognized your figures in the crowds again and again. The last screen showed a cindery plain scored by canals so clogged with ruin that neither clear nor foul water appeared in them. The only life was a host of crows and ravens as thick on the ground as flies on raw and rotten meat.

I heard an apologetic cough and found the headmaster of literature beside me. He held a dish with a flask and two cups on it. He said, 'Your doctor thinks wine will do you good.'

I returned to the throne and lay down. He sat beside me and said, 'The emperor has been greatly impressed by the gravity of your response to his order-to-write. He is sure your poem will be very great.' I said nothing. He filled the cups with wine and tasted one. I did not. He said, 'You once wanted to write about the building of the new palace. Was that a good theme for a poem?'

'Yes.'

'But the building of the new palace and the destruction of the old capital are the same thing. All big new things must begin by destroying the old. Otherwise they are a mere continuation.'

I said, 'Do you mean that the emperor would have destroyed the old capital even without a rebellion?'

'Yes. The old capital was linked by roads and canals to every corner of the empire. For more than nine dynasties other towns looked to it for guidance. Now they must look to us.'

I said, 'Was there a rebellion?'

'We are so sure there was one that we did not enquire about the matter. The old capital was a market for the empire. When the court came here we brought the market with us. The citizens left behind had three choices. They could starve to death, or beg in the streets of other towns, or rebel. The brave and intelligent among them must have dreamed of rebellion. They probably talked about it. Which is conspiracy.'

'Was it justice to kill them for that?'

'Yes. The justice which rules a nation must be more dreadful than the justice which rules a family. The emperor himself respects and pities his defeated rebels. Your poem might mention that.'

I said, 'You once said my parents were useless to me because time had changed them. You were wrong. As long as they lived I knew that though they might look old and different, though I might never see them again, I was still loved, still alive in ways you and your emperor can never know. And though I never saw the city after going to school I thought of it growing like an onion; each year there was a new skin of leaves and dung on the gardens, new traffic on the streets, new whitewash on old walls. While the old city and my old parents lived my childhood lived too. But the emperor's justice has destroyed my past, irrevocably. I am like a land without culture or history. I am now too shallow to write a poem.'

The headmaster said, 'It is true that the world is so packed with the present moment that the past, a far greater quantity, can only gain entrance through the narrow gate of a mind. But your mind is unusually big. I enlarged it myself, artificially. You are able to bring your father, mother and city to life and death again in a tragedy, a tragedy the whole nation will read. Remember that the world is one vast graveyard of defunct cities, all destroyed by the shifting of markets they could not control, and all compressed by literature into a handful of poems. The emperor only does what ordinary time does. He simply speeds things up. He wants your help.'

I said, 'A poet has to look at his theme steadily. A lot of people have no work because an emperor moves a market, so to avoid looking like a bad government he accuses them of rebelling and kills them. My stomach rejects that theme. The emperor is not very wise. If he had saved the lives of my parents perhaps I could have worked for him.'

The headmaster said, 'The emperor did consider saving your parents before sending in the troops, but I advised him not to. If they were still alive your poem would be an ordinary piece of political excuse-making. Anyone can see the good in disasters which leave their family and property intact. But a poet must feel the cracks in the nation splitting his individual heart. How else can he mend them?'

I said, 'I refuse to mend this cracked nation. Please tell the emperor that I am useless to him, and that I ask his permission to die.'

The headmaster put his cup down and said, after a while, 'That is an important request. The emperor will not answer it quickly.'

I said, 'If he does not answer me in three days I will act without him.'

The headmaster of literature stood up and said, 'I think I can promise an answer at the end of three days.'

He went away. I closed my eyes, covered my ears and stayed where I was. My entourage came in and wanted to wash, feed and soothe me but I let nobody within touching distance. I asked for water, sipped a little, freshened my face with the rest then commanded them to leave. They were unhappy, especially Adoda who wept silently all the time. This comforted me a little. I almost wished the etiquette would let me speak to Adoda. I was sure Tohu talked all the time to his nurse when nobody else could hear. But what good does talking do? Everything I could say would be as horrible to Adoda as it is to me. So I lay still and said nothing and tried not to hear the drone of Tohu dictating all through that night and the following morning. Toward the end, half his lines seemed to be stylized exclamations of laughter and even between them he giggled a lot. I thought perhaps he was drunk, but when he came to me in the evening he was unusually dignified. He knelt down carefully by my throne and whispered, 'I finished my poem today. I sent it to the emperor but I don't think he likes it.'

I shrugged. He whispered, 'I have just received an invitation from him. He wants my company tomorrow in the garden of irrevocable justice.'

I shrugged. He whispered, 'Bohu, you know my entourage is very small. My nurse may need help. Please let your doctor accompany us.'

I nodded. He whispered, 'You are my only friend,' and went away.

I did not see him next day till late evening. His nurse came and knelt at the steps of my throne. She looked smaller, older and uglier than usual and she handed me a scroll of the sort used for public announcements. At the top were portraits of myself and Tohu. Underneath it said:

The emperor asked his famous poets Bohu and Tohu to celebrate the destruction of the old capital. Bohu said no. He is still an honoured guest in the evergreen garden, happy and respected by all who know him. Tohu said yes and wrote a very bad poem. You may read the worst bits below. Tohu's tongue, right shoulder, arm and hand have now been replaced by wooden ones. The emperor prefers a frank confession of inability to the useless words of the flattering toad-eater.

I stood up and said drearily, 'I will visit your master.'

He lay on a rug in her room with his face to the wall. He was breathing loudly. I could see almost none of him for he still wore the ceremonial cape which was badly stained in places. My doctor knelt beside him and answered my glance by spreading the palms of his hands. The secretary, chef and two masseuses knelt near the door. I sighed and said, 'Yesterday you told me I was your only friend, Tohu. I can say now that you are mine. I am sorry our training has stopped us showing it.'

I don't think he heard me for shortly after he stopped breathing. I then told my entourage that I had asked to die and expected a positive answer from the emperor on the following day. They were all very pale but my news made them paler still. When someone more than seven feet tall dies of unnatural causes the etiquette requires his entourage to die in the same way. This is unlucky, but I did not make this etiquette, this palace, this empire which I shall leave as soon as possible, with or without the emperor's assistance. The hand of my secretary trembles as he writes these words. I pity him.

To my dead parents in the ash of the old capital, From the immortal emperor's supreme nothing, *Their son,*
Bohu.

DICTATED ON THE 10th LAST DAY OF THE OLD CALENDAR.

FOURTH LETTER

Dear Mother, Dear Father, I must always return to you, it seems. The love, the rage, the power which fills me now cannot rest until it has sent a stream of words in your direction. I have written my great poem but not the poem wanted. I will explain all this.

On the evening of the third day my entourage were sitting round me when a common janitor brought the emperor's reply in the unusual form of a letter. He gave it to the secretary, bowed and withdrew. The secretary is a good ventriloquist and read the emperor's words in the appropriate voice.

The emperor hears and respects his great poet's request for death. The emperor grants Bohu permission to do anything he likes, write anything he likes, and die however, wherever, and whenever he chooses.

I said to my doctor, 'Choose the death you want for yourself and give it to me first.'

He said, 'Sir, may I tell you what that death is?'

'Yes.'

'It will take many words to do so. I cannot be brief on this matter.'

'Speak. I will not interrupt.'

He said, 'Sir, my life has been a dreary and limited one, like your own. I speak for all your servants when I say this. We have all been, in a limited way, married to you, and our only happiness was being useful to a great poet. We understand why you cannot become one. Our own parents have died in the ancient capital, so death is the best thing for everyone, and I can make it painless. All I need is a closed room, the chef's portable stove and a handful of prepared herbs which are always with me.

'But, sir, need we go rapidly to this death? The emperor's letter suggests not, and that letter has the force of a passport. We can use it to visit any part of the palace we like. Give us permission to escort you to death by a flowery, roundabout path which touches on some commonplace experiences all men wish to enjoy. I ask this selfishly, for our own sakes, but also unselfishly, for yours. We love you, sir.'

Tears came to my eyes but I said firmly, 'I cannot be seduced. My wish for death is an extension of my wish not to move, feel, think or see. I desire *nothing* with all my heart. But you are different. For a whole week you have my permission to glut yourself on anything the emperor's letter permits.'

The doctor said, 'But, sir, that letter has no force without your company. Allow yourself to be carried with us. We shall not plunge you into riot and disorder. All will be calm and harmonious, you need not walk, or stand, or even think. We know your needs. We can read the subtlest flicker of your eyebrow. Do not even say yes to this proposal of mine. Simply close your eyes in the tolerant smile which is so typical of you.'

I was weary, and did so, and allowed them to wash, feed and prepare me for sleep as in the old days. And they did something new. The doctor wiped the wounds at the top of my thighs with something astringent and Adoda explored them, first with her tongue and then with her teeth. I felt a pain almost too fine to be noticed and looking down I saw her draw from each wound a quivering silver thread. Then the doctor bathed me again and Adoda embraced me and whispered, 'May I share your throne?'

I nodded. Everyone else went away and I slept deeply for the first time in four days.

Next morning I dreamed my aunt was beside me, as young and lovely as in days when she looked like the white demon. I woke up clasping Adoda so insistently that we both cried aloud. The doors of the central hall were all wide open; so were the doors to the garden in the rooms beyond. Light flooded in on us from all sides. During breakfast I grew calm again but it was not my habitual calm. I felt adventurous under the waist. This feeling did not yet reach my head, which smiled cynically. But I was no longer exactly the same man.

The rest of the entourage came in wearing bright clothes and garlands. They stowed my punt-shaped throne with food, wine, drugs and instruments. It is a big throne and when they climbed in themselves there was no overcrowding even though Tohu's nurse was there too. Then a horde of janitors arrived with long poles which they fixed to the sides of the throne, and I and my entourage were lifted into the air and carried out to the garden. The secretary sat in the prow playing a mouth-organ while the chef and doctor accompanied him with zither and drum. The janitors almost danced as they trampled across the maze, and this was so surprising that I laughed aloud, staring freely up at the pigeon-flecked azure sky, the porcelain gables with their coloured flags, the crowded tops of markets, temples and manufactories. Perhaps when I was small I had gazed as greedily for the mere useless fun of it, but for years I had only used my eyes professionally, to collect poetical knowledge, or shielded them, as required by the etiquette. 'Oh, Adoda!' I cried, warming my face in her hair, 'All this new knowledge is useless and I love it.'

She whispered, 'The use of living is the taste it gives. The emperor has made you the only free man in the world. You can taste anything you like.'

We entered a hall full of looms where thousands of women in coarse gowns were weaving rich tapestry. I was fascinated. The air was stifling, but not to me. Adoda and the chef plied their fans and the doctor refreshed me with a fine mist of cool water. I also had the benefit of janitors without kneebands, so our party was socially invisible; I could stare at whom I liked and they could not see me at all. I noticed a girl with pale brown hair toiling on one side. Adoda halted the janitors and whispered, 'That lovely girl is your sister who was sold to the merchants. She became a skilled weaver so they resold her here.'

I said, 'That is untrue. My sister would be over forty now and that girl, though robust, is not yet sixteen.'

'Would you like her to join us?'

I closed my eyes in the tolerant smile and a janitor negotiated with an overseer. When we moved on, the girl was beside us. She was silent and frightened at first but we gave her garlands, food and wine and she soon became merry.

We came into a narrow street with a gallery along one side on the level of my throne. Tall, elegant women in the robes of the court strolled and leaned there. A voice squeaked, 'Hullo, Bohu' and looking up I saw the emperor smiling from the arms of the most slender and disdainful. I stared at him. He said, 'Bohu hates me but I must suffer that. He is too great a man to be ordered by a poor old emperor. This lady, Bohu, is your aunt, a very wonderful courtesan. Say hullo!'

I laughed and said, 'You are a liar, sir.'

He said, 'Nonetheless you mean to take her from me. Join the famous poet, my dear, he goes down to the floating world. Goodbye, Bohu. I do not just give people death. That is only half my job.'

The emperor moved to a lady nearby, the slender one stepped among us and we all sailed on down the street.

We reached a wide river and the janitors waded in until the throne rested on the water. They withdrew the poles, laid them on the thwarts and we drifted out from shore. The doctor produced pipes and measured a careful dose into each bowl. We smoked and talked; the men played instruments, the women sang. The little weaver knew many popular songs, some sad, some funny. I suddenly wished Tohu was with us, and wept. They asked why. I told them and we all wept together. Twilight fell and a moon came out. The court lady stood up, lifted a pole and steered us expertly into a grove of willows growing in shallow water. Adoda hung lanterns in the branches. We ate, clasped each other, and slept.

I cannot count the following days. They may have been two, or three, or many. Opium plays tricks with time but I did not smoke enough to stop me loving. I loved in many ways, some tender, some harsh, some utterly absent-minded. More than once I said to Adoda, 'Shall we die now? Nothing can be sweeter than this' but she said, 'Wait a little longer. You haven't done all you want yet.'

When at last my mind grew clear about the order of time the weaver and court lady had left us and we drifted down a tunnel to a bright arch at the end. We came into a lagoon on a lane of clear water between beds of rushes and lily-leaves. It led to an island covered with spires of marble and copper shining in the sun. My secretary said, 'That is the poets' pantheon. Would you like to land, sir?'

I nodded.

We disembarked and I strolled barefoot on warm moss between the spires. Each had an open door in the base with steps down to the tomb where the body would lie. Above each door was a white tablet where the poet's great work would be painted. All the tombs and tablets were vacant, of course, for I am the first poet in the new palace and was meant to be the greatest, for the tallest spire in the centre was sheathed in gold with my name on the door. I entered. The room downstairs had space for us all with cushions for the entourage and a silver throne for me.

'To deserve to lie here I must write a poem,' I thought, and looked into my mind. The poem was there, waiting to come out. I returned upstairs, went outside and told the secretary to fetch paint and brushes from his satchel and go to the tablet. I then dictated my poem in a slow firm voice.

THE EMPEROR'S INJUSTICE

Scattered buttons and silks, a broken kite in the mud,
A child's yellow clogs cracked by the horses' hooves.
A land weeps for the head city, lopped by sabre, cracked by hooves.
The houses ash, the people meat for crows.

A week ago wind rustled dust in the empty market.
'Starve,' said the moving dust, 'Beg. Rebel. Starve. Beg. Rebel.'
We do not do such things. We are peaceful people.
We have food for six more days, let us wait.
The emperor will accommodate us, underground.

It is sad to be unnecessary.
All the bright mothers, strong fathers, raffish aunts,
Lost sisters and brothers, all the rude servants
Are honoured guests of the emperor, underground.

We sit in the tomb now. The door is closed, the only light is the red glow from the chef's charcoal stove. My entourage dreamily puff their pipes, the doctor's fingers sift the dried herbs, the secretary is ending my last letter. We are tired and happy. The emperor said I could write what I liked. Will my poem be broadcast? No. If that happened the common people would rise and destroy that evil little puppet and all the cunning, straightfaced, pompous men who use him. Nobody will read my words but a passing gardener, perhaps, who will paint them out to stop them reaching the emperor's ear. But I have at last made the poem I was made to make. I lie down to sleep in perfect satisfaction. *Goodbye, I still love you. Your son,*

Bohu.
DICTATED ON THE OLD CALENDAR'S LAST DAY.

Alasdair Gray

LAST LETTER

AN APPRECIATION OF THE POEM BY THE LATE TRA-GEDIAN BOHU ENTITLED *THE EMPEROR*'S *INJUSTICE* DELIVERED TO THE IMPERIAL COLLEGE OF HEAD-MASTERS, NEW PALACE UNIVERSITY

My Dear Colleagues, This is exactly the poem we require. Our patience in waiting for it till the last possible moment has been rewarded. The work is shorter than we expected, but that makes distribution easier. It had a starkness unusual in government poetry, but this starkness satisfies the nation's need much more than the work we hoped for. With a single tiny change the poem can be used at once. I know some of my colleagues will raise objections, but I will answer these in the course of my appreciation.

A noble spirit of pity blows through this poem like a warm wind. The destroyed people are not mocked and calumniated, we identify with them, and the third line:

A land cries for the head city, lopped by sabre, cracked by hooves, invites the whole empire to mourn. But does this wind of pity fan the flames of political protest? No. It presses the mind of the reader inexorable toward *nothing*, toward death.
This is clearly shown in the poem's treatment of rebellion:

> *We do not do such things. We are peaceful people.*
> *We have food for six more days, let us wait.*

The poem assumes that a modern population will find the prospect of destruction by their own government less alarming than action against it. The truth of this is shown in today's police report from the old capital. It describes crowds of people muttering at street corners and completely uncertain of what action to take. They have a little food left. They fear the worst, yet hope, if they stay docile, the emperor will not destroy them immediately. This state of things was described by Bohu yesterday in the belief that it had happened a fortnight ago! A poet's intuitive grasp of reality was never more clearly demonstrated.

At this point the headmaster of civil peace will remind me that the job of the poem is not to describe reality but to encourage our friends, frighten our enemies, and reconcile the middling people to the destruction of the old capital. The headmaster of moral philosophy will also remind me of our decision that people will most readily accept the destruction of the old capital if we accuse it of rebellion. That was certainly the main idea in the original order-to-write, but I would remind the college of what we had to do to the poet who obeyed that order. Tohu knew exactly what we wanted and gave it to us. His poem described the emperor as wise, witty, venerable, patient, loving and omnipotent. He described the citizens of the old capital as stupid, childish, greedy, absurd, yet inspired by a vast communal lunacy which endangered the empire. He obediently wrote a popular melodrama which could not convince a single intelligent man and would only over-excite stupid ones, who are fascinated by criminal lunatics who attack the established order.

The problem is this. If we describe the people we kill as dangerous rebels they look glamorous; if we describe them as weak and silly we seem unjust. Tohu could not solve that problem. Bohu has done with startling simplicity.

He presents the destruction as a simple, stunning, inevitable fact. The child, mother and common people in the poem exist passively, doing nothing but weep, gossip, and wait. The active agents of hoof, sabre, and (by extension) crow, belong to the emperor, who is named at the end of the middle verse:

The emperor will accommodate us, underground.

and at the end of the last:

Bright mothers, strong fathers . . . all the rude servants
Are honoured guests of the emperor, underground.

Consider the *weight* this poem gives to our immortal emperor! He is not described or analysed, he is presented as a final, competent, all-embracing force, as unarguable as the weather, as inevitable as death. This is how all governments should appear to people who are not in them.

To sum up, *THE EMPEROR'S INJUSTICE* will delight our friends, depress our enemies, and fill middling people with nameless awe. The only change required is the elimination of the first syllable in the last word of the title. I advise that the poem be sent today to every village, town and city in the land. At the same time Fieldmarshal Ko should be ordered to destroy the old capital. When the poem appears over doors of public buildings, the readers will read of an event which is occurring simultaneously. In this way the literary and military sides of the attack will reinforce each other with unusual thoroughness. Fieldmarshal Ko should take special care that the poet's parents do not escape the general massacre, as a rumour to that effect will lessen the poignancy of the official biography, which I will complete in the coming year.

I remain your affectionate colleague,
Gigadib,
Headmaster of modern and classical literature.
DICTATED ON DAY 1 OF THE NEW CALENDAR

BERNARD MacLAVERTY

Phonefun Limited

When she heard the whine of the last customer's fast spin – a bearded
student with what seemed like a year's supply of Y-fronts – Sadie Thompson changed her blue nylon launderette coat for her outdoor one and stood
jingling the keys by the door until he left. It was dark and wet and the
streets reflected the lights from the shop windows. She had to rush to get
to the Spar before it closed, and was out of breath – not that she had much
to buy – potatoes, sugar and tea-bags. In the corner shop she got her cigarettes, the evening paper and a copy of *Men Only*, which she slipped inside
the newspaper and put in her carrier bag. She slowly climbed the steep
street in the darkness because the Army had put out most of the street
lights. She turned in at Number ninety-six. The door stuck momentarily
on a large envelope lying on the mat.

She had the table set and the dinner ready for Agnes when she
came in.

'Hello, Sadie, love,' she said and kissed her on the cheek. Beside Sadie,
Agnes was huge. She wore an expensive silver-fox fur coat. Sadie did not
like the coat and had said so. It was pretty much too much for a woman
whose only job was cleaning the local primary school.

'I'm knackered,' said Agnes, kicking off her shoes and falling into the
armchair. There was a hole in the toe of her tights.

'Take off your coat, your dinner's ready,' said Sadie.

'Hang on. Let me have a fag first.'

She lit up a cigarette and put her head back in the chair. Sadie thought
she looked a putty colour. She was grossly overweight but would do nothing about it, no matter what Sadie said.

'Are you all right?'

'I'll be all right in a minute. It's that bloody hill. It's like entering the Olympics.

'If you ask me, you're carrying too much weight. When did you last weigh yourself?'

'This morning.'

'And what were you?'

'I don't know,' said Agnes laughing, 'I was afraid to look.'

With her head back like that her fat neck and chin were one. There were red arcs of lipstick on the cork-tip of her cigarette. Sadie served the mash and sausages.

'Sit over,' she said. Agnes stubbed her cigarette out and, groaning for effect, came to the table still wearing her coat.

'You'd think to hear you that you'd cleaned that school by yourself.'

'It feels like I did.' Agnes raised her fork listlessly to her mouth.

'Did the post come?'

'Yes.'

'Much?'

'It feels fat.'

'Aw God no.'

'You'll have to brighten up a bit. Don't be so glum.'

'God, that's a good one coming from you, Sadie. I don't think I've seen you smiling since Christmas.'

'I'm the brains. You're supposed to be the charm. I don't *have* to smile.' They ate in silence except for the sound of their forks making small screeches against the plate.

'I wish you'd take off your coat when you're eating. It looks that slovenly,' said Sadie. Agnes heaved herself to her feet, took off her coat and flung it on the sofa. She turned on the transistor. The news was on so she tuned it to some music.

'I need a wee doze before I brighten up. You know that, Sadie.'

'I suppose I'm not tired after a day in that bloody laundryette?'

Agnes nibbled her sausage at the front of her closed mouth, very quickly, like a rabbit. The music on the radio stopped and a foreign voice came on and babbled.

'That's a great programme you picked.'

'It's better than the Northern Ireland news.'

The foreign voice stopped and music came on again. Agnes finished what was on her plate.

'Is there anything for afters?'

'You can open some plums if you want.'

Agnes lurched out to the tiled kitchen and opened a tin of plums. She threw the circle of lid into the bucket and came back with a tin and a spoon.

'It's cold on your feet out there. There's a draught coming in under the door that would clean corn.' She ate the plums from the tin. Some juice tricked on to her chin.

'Want some?' She offered the half-finished tin to Sadie, but she refused.

'It's no wonder you're fat.'

'It oils my voice. Makes it nice for the phone.'

'I got you a *Men Only* if you run out of inspiration. It's there on the sideboard.'

'Thanks, love, but I don't think I'll need it.' Agnes drank off the last juice from the tin.

'You'll cut your lips one of these days,' said Sadie, 'don't say I didn't warn you.'

Agnes lit a cigarette and rolled one across the table to Sadie. She dropped the dead match into the tin.

'That was good,' she said. 'I'm full to the gunnels.' She slapped her large stomach with the flat of her hand in satisfaction. The foreigner began to speak gobbledegook again.

'Aw shut up,' said Sadie. 'Men are all the same no matter what they're speaking.' She twiddled the knob until she got another station with music. Almost immediately the music stopped and a man with a rich American drawl began to speak.

'Aw God, Sadie, do you remember the Yanks? He sounds just like one I had.'

'Will I ever forget them? They could spend money all right.'

'That's exactly like his voice. It's the spit of him.'

'Give us a light.' Agnes leaned over and touched Sadie's cigarette with her own. Sadie pulled hard until it was lit.

'I fancied him no end,' said Agnes. 'He was lovely. I think it was his first time but he pretended it wasn't.'

'I think you told me about him.'

'My Yankee Doodle Dandy, I called him. I still can feel the stubble of his haircut. It was like he had sandpaper up the back of his neck. Blondie. We sort of went together for a while.'

'You mean he didn't pay?'

'That kind of thing.'

'Better clear this table.' Sadie put the cigarette in her mouth, closing one eye against the trickle of blue smoke and began to remove the dirty plates. Ash toppled on to the cloth. She came back from the kitchen and gently brushed the grey roll into the palm of her other hand and dropped it into Agnes' tin. Agnes said,

'You wash and I'll dry.'

'What you mean is I'll wash and put them in the rack and then about ten o'clock you'll come out and put them in the cupboard.'

'Well, it's more hygienic that way. I saw in the paper that the tea-towel leaves germs all over them.'

'You only read what suits you.'

Sadie went out into the kitchen to wash up the dishes. She heard the programme on the radio finish and change to a service with an American preacher. It kept fading and going out of focus and was mixed up with pips of Morse Code. When she had finished she washed out the tea-towel in some Lux and hung it in the yard to dry. She could do her own washing at the launderette but she hated lugging the handful of damp clothes home. There was such a weight in wet clothes. If she did that too often she would end up with arms like a chimpanzee. When she went back into the living room Agnes was asleep in her armchair beside the radio with a silly smile on her face.

Sadie picked up the large envelope off the sideboard and opened it with her thumb and spilled out the pile of envelopes onto the table. She began to open them and separate the cheques and money. On each letter she marked down the amount of money contained and then set it to one side. Agnes began to snore wetly, her head pitched forward onto her chest. When she had all the letters opened, Sadie got up and switched off the radio. In the silence Agnes woke with a start. Sadie said,

'So you're back with us again.'

'What do you mean?'

'You were sound asleep.'

'I was not. I was only closing my eyes. Just for a minute.'

'You were snoring like a drunk.'

'Indeed I was not. I was just resting my eyes.'

The ticking of the clock annoyed Agnes so she switched the radio on again just in time to hear 'The Lord is my Shepherd' being sung in a smooth American drawl. She tuned it to Radio One. Sadie said,

'Hymns give me the creeps. That Billy Graham one. Euchh!' She shuddered. 'You weren't in Belfast for the Blitz, were you?'

'No, I was still a nice country girl from Cookstown. My Americans all came from the camp out at Larrycormack. That's where my Yankee Doodle Dandy was stationed. You stuck it out here through the Blitz?'

'You can say that again. We all slept on the Cavehill for a couple of nights. Watched the whole thing. It was terrible – fires everywhere.'

'Sadie, will you do my hair?'

Sadie took the polythene bag bulging with rollers from under the table and began combing Agnes' hair.

'It needs to be dyed again. Your roots is beginning to show.'

'I think I'll maybe grow them out this time. Have it greying at the temples.'

Sadie damped each strand of hair and rolled it up tight into Agnes's head, then fixed it with a hairpin. With each tug of the brush Agnes let her head jerk with it.

'I love somebody working with my hair. It's so relaxing.' Sadie couldn't answer because her mouth was bristling with hairpins. Agnes said,

'How much was there in the envelopes?'

'Hengy-hee oung.'

'How much?'

Sadie took the hairpins from her mouth.

'Sixty-eight pounds.'

'That's not bad at all.'

'You're right there. It's better than walking the streets on a night like this.'

'If it goes on like this I'm going to give up my job in that bloody school.'

'I think you'd be foolish. Anything could happen. It could all fall through any day.'

'How could it?'

'I don't know. It all seems too good to be true. The Post Office could catch on. Even the law. Or the tax man.'

'It's not against the law?'

'I wouldn't be too sure.'

'It's against the law the other way round but not the way we do it.'

'There. That's you finished,' said Sadie, giving the rollers a final pat in close to her head. She held the mirror up for Agnes to see but before she put it away she looked at herself. Her neck was a dead giveaway. That's where the age really showed. You could do what you liked with make-up on your face but there was no way of disguising those chicken sinews on your neck. And the back of the hands. They showed it too. She put the mirror on the mantelpiece and said,

'Are you ready, Agnes?'

'Let's have a wee gin first.'

'O.K.'

She poured two gins and filled them to the brim with tonic. Agnes sat over to the table. When she drank her gin she pinched in her mouth with the delightful bitterness.

'Too much gin,' she said.

'You say that every time.'

Agnes sipped some more out of her glass and then topped up with tonic. She began to sort through the letters. She laughed and nodded her head at some. At others she turned down the corners of her mouth.

'I suppose I better make a start.'

She lifted the telephone and set it beside her on the table. She burst out laughing.

'Have you read any of these, Sadie?'

'No.'

'Listen to this. "Dear Samantha, you really turn me on with that sexy voice of yours. Not only me but me wife as well. I get her to listen on the extension. Sometimes it's too much for the both of us." Good Gawd. I never thought there was any women listening to me.' She picked up the phone and snuggled it between her ear and the fat of her shoulder.

'Kick over that pouffe, Sadie.'

Sadie brought the pouffe to her feet. Agnes covered the hole in the toe of her tights with the sole of her other foot. She sorted through the letters and chose one.

'"Available at any time." He must be an oul' bachelor. O three one. That's Edinburgh, isn't it? Dirty oul' kilty.'

She dialled the number and while she listened to the dialling tone she smiled at Sadie. She raised her eyebrows as if she thought she was posh. A voice answered at the other end. Agnes' voice changed into a soft purr which pronounced its –ings.

'Hello is Ian there? . . . Oh, I didn't recognise your voice. This is Samantha . . . Yes, I can hold on, but not too long.' She covered the mouthpiece with her hand and, exaggerating her lips, said to Sadie, 'The egg-timer.'

Sadie went out into the kitchen and came back with it. It was a cheap plastic one with pink sand. She set it on the table with the full side on top.

'Ah, there you are again, honey,' whispered Agnes into the mouthpiece, 'are you all ready now? Good. What would you like to talk about? . . . Well, I'm lying here on my bed. It's a lovely bed with black silk sheets . . . No, it has really. Does that do something for you? Mmm, it's warm. I have the heating turned up full. It's so warm all I am wearing are my undies . . . Lemon . . . Yes, and the panties are lemon too . . . All right, if you insist . . .' Agnes put the phone down on the table and signalled to Sadie to light her a fag. She made a rustling noise with her sleeve close to the mouthpiece and picked up the phone again.

'There, I've done what you asked . . . You're not normally breathless, are you, Ian? Have you just run up the stairs? . . . No, I'm only kidding . . . I know only too well what it's like to have asthma.'

She listened for a while, taking the lit cigarette from Sadie. She rolled her eyes to heaven and smiled across the table at her. She covered the mouthpiece with her hand.

'He's doing his nut.'

Sadie topped up her gin and tonic from the gin bottle.

'Do you really want me to do that? That might cost a little more money . . . All right, just for you, love.' She laughed heartily and paused. 'Yes, I'm doing it now . . . Yes, it's fairly pleasant. A bit awkward . . . Actually I'm getting to like it. Ohhh, I love it now . . . Say what again? . . . Ohhh, I love it.'

She turned to Sadie.

'He's rung off. That didn't take long. He just came and went. Who's next?'

Sadie flicked another letter to her.

'London,' she said. 'Jerome. Only on Thursdays after eight.'

'That's today. Probably the wife's night out at the bingo.'

She dialled the number and when a voice answered she said,

'Hello Jerome, this is Samantha.'

Sadie turned over the egg-timer.

'Oh, sorry, love – say that again. Ger – o – mey. I thought it was Ger – ome. Like Ger-ome Cairns, the song writer. Would you like to talk or do you want me to . . . O.K., fire away . . . I'm twenty-four . . . Blonde . . . Lemon, mostly . . . Yes, as brief as possible. Sometimes they're so brief they cut into me.' She listened for a moment, then covering the mouthpiece said to Sadie,

'This one's disgusting. How much did he pay?'

Sadie looked at the letter.

'Ten pounds. Don't lose him. Do what he says.'

'Yes, this is still Samantha.' Her voice went babyish and her mouth pouted. 'How could a nice little girl like me do a thing like that?' . . . Well, if it pleases you.' Agnes lifted her stubby finger and wobbled it wetly against her lips. 'Can you hear that? . . . Yes, I like it . . . Yes, I have *very* long legs.' She lifted her legs off the pouffe and looked at them disapprovingly. She had too many varicose veins. She'd had them out twice.

'You *are* a bold boy, but your time is nearly up.' The last of the pink sand was caving in and trickling through. Sadie raised a warning finger then signalled with all ten. She mouthed,

'Ten pounds. Don't lose him.'

'All right, just for you . . . Then I'll have to go,' said Agnes, and she wobbled her finger against her lips again. 'Is that enough? . . . You just write us another letter. You know the box number? Good . . . I love you too, Ger – o – mey, Bye-eee.' She put the phone down.

'For God's sake give us another gin,' she said. 'What a creep!'

'It's better than walking the street,' said Sadie. 'What I like about it is that they can't get near you.'

'Catch yourself on, Sadie. If anyone got near us now they'd run a mile.'

'I used to be frightened of them. Not all the time. But there was one every so often that made your scalp crawl. Something not right about them. Those ones gave me the heemy-jeemies, I can tell you. You felt you were going to end up in an entry somewhere – strangled – with your clothes over your head.'

Agnes nodded in agreement. 'Or worse,' she said.

Sadie went on, 'When I think of the things I've had to endure. Do you remember that pig that gave me the kicking? I was in hospital for a fortnight. A broken arm and a ruptured spleen – the bastard.'

Agnes began to laugh. 'Do you remember the time I broke my ankle? Jumping out of a lavatory window. Gawd, I was sure and certain I was going to be murdered that night.'

'Was that the guy with the steel plate in his head?'

'The very one. He said he would go mad if I didn't stroke it for him.'

'What?'

'His steel plate.'

'I can still smell some of those rooms. It was no picnic, Agnes, I can tell you.'

'The only disease you can get at this game is an ear infection. Who's next?'

Sadie passed another letter to her.

'Bristol, I think.'

'This one wants *me* to breathe. God God, what will they think of next?'

'I hate their guts, every last one of them.'

'Do you fancy doing this one?' asked Agnes.

'No. You know I'm no good at it.'

'Chrissake, Sadie, you can breathe. I never get a rest. Why's it always me?'

'Because I told you. You are the creative one. I just look after the books. The business end. Would you know how to go about putting an ad in? Or wording it properly? Or getting a box number? You stick to the bit you're good at. You're really great, you know. I don't know how you think the half of them up.'

Agnes smiled. She wiggled her stubby toes on the pouffe. She said,

'Do you know what I'd like? With the money.'

'What? Remember that we're still paying off that carpet in the bedroom – and the suite. Don't forget the phone bills either.'

'A jewelled cigarette holder. Like the one Audrey Hepburn had in that picture – what was it called?'

'*The Nun's Story?*'

'No.'

'*Breakfast at Tiffany's?*'

'Yes, one like that. I could use it on the phone. It'd make me feel good.'

As Agnes dialled another number, Sadie said,

'You're mad in the skull.'

'We can afford it. Whisht now.'

When the phone was answered at the other end she said,

'Hello, Samantha here,' and began to breathe loudly into the receiver. She quickened her pace gradually until she was panting, then said,

'He's hung up. Must have been expecting me. We should get a pair of bellows for fellas like him. Save my puff.'

'I'll go up and turn the blanket on, then we'll have a cup of tea,' said Sadie. Agnes turned another letter towards herself and dialled a number.

Upstairs, Sadie looked round the bedroom with admiration. She still hadn't got used to it. The plush almost ankle-deepness of the mushroom-coloured carpet and the brown flock wallpaper, the brown duvet with the matching brown sheets. The curtains were of heavy velvet and were the most luxurious stuff she had ever touched. She switched on the blanket and while on her hands and knees she allowed her fingers to sink into the pile of the carpet. All her life she had wanted a bedroom like this. Some of the places she had lain down, she wouldn't have kept chickens in. She heard Agnes's voice coming blurred from downstairs. She owed a lot to her. Everything, in fact. From the first time they met, the night they were both arrested and ended up in the back of the same paddy-waggon, she had thought there was something awful good about her, something awful kind. She had been so good-looking in her day too, tall and stately and well-built. They had stayed together after that night – all through the hard times. As Agnes said, once you quit the streets it didn't qualify you for much afterwards. Until lately, when she had shown this amazing talent for talking on the phone. It had all started one night when a man got the wrong number and Agnes had chatted him up until he was doing his nut at the other end. They had both crouched over the phone wheezing and laughing their heads off at the puffs and pants of him. Then it was Sadie's idea to put the whole thing on a commercial basis and form the Phonefun company. She dug her fingers into the carpet and brushed her cheek against the crisp sheet.

'Agnes,' she said and went downstairs to make the tea.

She stood waiting for the kettle to boil, then transferred the tea-bag from one cup of boiling water to the other. Agnes laughed loudly at something in the living room. Sadie heard her say,

'But if I put the phone there you'll not hear me.'

She put some custard creams on a plate and brought the tea in.

'Here you are, love,' she said, setting the plate beside the egg-timer. 'He's over his time.' Agnes covered the mouth-piece and said,

'I forgot to start it.' Then back to the phone. 'I can get some rubber ones if you want me to . . . But you'll have to pay for them. Will you send the money through? . . . Goooood boy. Now I really must go . . . Yes, I'm listening.' She made a face, half laughing, half in disgust, to Sadie. 'Well done, love . . . Bye-eee, sweetheart.' She puckered her mouth and did a kiss noise into the mouthpiece, then put the phone down.

'Have your tea now, Agnes, you can do the others later.'

'There's only two more I can do tonight. The rest have special dates.'

'You can do those. Then we'll go to bed. Eh?'

'O.K.,' said Agnes. 'Ahm plumb tuckered out.'

'You're what?'

'Plumb tuckered out. It's what my Yankee Doodle Dandy used to say afterwards.'

'What started you on *him* tonight?'

'I don't know. I just remembered, that's all. He used to bring me nylons and put them on for me.'

She fiddled with the egg-timer and allowed the pink sand to run through it. She raised her legs off the pouffe and turned her feet outwards, looking at them.

'I don't like tights,' she said, 'I read somewhere they're unhygienic.'

'Do you want to hear the news before we go up? Just in case?'

'Just in case what?'

'They could be rioting all over the city and we wouldn't know a thing.'

'You're better not to know, even if they are. That tea's cold.'

'That's because you didn't drink it. You talk far too much.'

Agnes drank her tea and snapped a custard cream in half with her front teeth.

'I don't think I'll bother with these next two.'

'That's the way you lose customers. If you phone them once they'll come back for more – and for a longer time. Give them a short time. Keep them interested.' She lifted the crumbed plate and the cups and took them out to the kitchen. Agnes lit another cigarette and sat staring vacantly at the egg-timer. She said without raising her eyes,

'Make someone happy with a phone call.'

'I'm away on up,' said Sadie. 'I'll keep a place warm for you.'

Sadie was in bed when Agnes came up.

'Take your rollers out,' she said.

Agnes undressed, grunting and tugging hard at her roll-on. When she got it off she gave a long sigh and rubbed the puckered flesh that had just been released.

'That's like taking three Valium, to get out of that,' she said. She sat down on the side of the bed and began taking her rollers out, clinking hairpins into a saucer on the dressing table. Sadie spoke from the bed,

'Were you really in love with that Yank?'

'Yes, as near as possible.'

Agnes shook her hair loose and rolled back into bed. She turned out the light and Sadie notched into her back. She began to stroke Agnes' soft upper arm, then moved to her haunch.

'I've got a bit of a headache, love,' said Agnes.

Sadie turned to the wall and Agnes felt her harsh skin touch her own.

'My God, Sadie,' she said, 'you've got heels on you like pumice stones.'

SHENA MACKAY

Cardboard City

'We could always pick the dog hairs off each other's coats . . .'

The thought of grooming each other like monkeys looking for fleas sent them into giggles – anything would have.

'I used half a roll of sellotape on mine,' said Stella indignantly then, although she wasn't really offended.

'It better not have been my sellotape or I'll kill you,' Vanessa responded, without threat.

'It was His.'

'Good. *He'll* kill you then,' she said matter-of-factly.

The sisters, having flung themselves onto the train with no time to buy a comic, were wondering how to pass the long minutes until it reached central London with nothing to read. They could hardly believe that at the last moment He had not contrived to spoil their plan to go Christmas shopping. For the moment it didn't matter that their coats were unfashionable and the cuffs of their acrylic sweaters protruded lumpishly from the outgrown sleeves or that their frozen feet were beginning to smart, in the anticipation of chilblains, in their scuffed shoes in reaction to the heater under the seat. They were alone in the compartment except for a youth with a personal stereo leaking a tinny rhythm through the headphones.

With their heavy greenish-blonde hair cut straight across their foreheads and lying flat as lasagne over the hoods and shoulders of their school duffels, and their green eyes set wide apart in the flat planes of their pale faces, despite Stella's borrowed fishnet stockings which were causing her much *angst*, they looked younger than their fourteen and twelve years. It would not have occurred to either of them that anybody staring at them might have been struck by anything other than their horrible clothes. Their desire, thwarted by Him and by lack of money of their own, was to look like everybody else. The dog hairs that adhered so stubbornly to the navy-blue cloth and bristled starkly in the harsh and electric light of the winter morning were from Barney, the black and white border collie, grown fat and snappish in his old age, who bared his teeth at his new master, the usurper, and slunk into a corner at his homecoming, as the girls slunk into their bedroom.

'It's cruel to keep that animal alive,' He would say. 'What's it got to live for? Smelly old hearthrug.'

And while He discoursed on the Quality of Life, running a finger down Mummy's spine or throat, Barney's legs would splay out worse than they usually did and his claws click louder on the floor, or a malodorous cloud of stagnant pond water emanate from his coat. It was a sign of His power that Barney was thus diminished.

'We'll know when the Time has come. And the Time has not yet come,' said Mummy with more energy than she summoned to champion her elder daughters, while Barney rolled a filmy blue eye in her direction. The dog, despite his shedding coat, was beyond reproach as far as the girls were concerned; his rough back and neck had been salted with many tears, and he was their one link with their old life, before their father had disappeared and before their mother had defected to the enemy.

'What are you going to buy Him?' Vanessa asked.

'Nothing. I'm making His present.'

'What?' Vanessa was incredulous, fearing treachery afoot.

'I'm knitting Him a pair of socks. Out of stinging nettles.'

'I wish I could knit.'

After a wistful pause she started to say, 'I wonder what He would . . .'

'I'm placing a total embargo on His name today,' Stella cut her off. 'Don't speak of Him. Don't even think about Him. Right, Regan?'

'Right, Goneril. Why does He call us those names?'

'They're the Ugly Sisters in *Cinderella* of course.'

'I thought they were called Anastasia and . . . and . . .'

'Embargo,' said Stella firmly.

'It's not Cordelia who needs a fairy godmother, it's us. Wouldn't it be lovely if one day . . .'

'Grow up.'

So that was how He saw them, bewigged and garishly rouged, two pantomime dames with grotesque beauty spots and fishnet tights stretched over their bandy men's calves, capering jealously around Cordelia's high-chair. Cordelia herself, like Barney, was adored unreservedly, but after her birth, with one hand rocking the transparent hospital cot in which she lay, as a joke which they could not share, He had addressed her half-sisters as Goneril and Regan. Their mother had protested then, but now sometimes she used the names. Under His rule, comfortable familiar objects vanished and routines were abolished. Exposed to His mockery, they became ludicrous. One example was the Bunnykins china they ate from sometimes, not in a wish to prolong their babyhood but because it was there. All the pretty mismatched bits and pieces of crockery were superseded by a stark white service from Habitat and there were new forks with vicious prongs and knives which cut. Besotted with Cordelia's dimples and black curls, He lost all patience with his step-daughters, with their tendency to melancholy and easily provoked tears which their pink eyelids and noses could not conceal, and like a vivisector with an electric prod tormenting two albino mice, he discovered all their most vulnerable places.

Gypsies had travelled up in the train earlier, making their button-holes and nosegays, and had left the seats and floor strewn with a litter of twigs and petals and scraps of silver foil like confetti.

'We might see Princess Di or Fergie,' Vanessa said, scuffing the debris with her foot. 'They do their Christmas shopping in Harrods.'

'The Duchess of York to you. Oh yes, we're sure to run into them. Anyway, Princess Diana does her shopping in Covent Garden.'

'Well then!' concluded Vanessa triumphantly. She noticed the intimation of a cold sore on her sister's superior lip and was for a second glad. Harrods and Covent Garden were where they had decided, last night, after lengthy discussions, to go, their excited voices rising from guarded whispers to a normal pitch, until He had roared upstairs at them to shut up. Vanessa's desire to go to Hamleys had been overruled. She had cherished a secret craving for a tube of plastic stuff with which you blew bubbles and whose petroleum smell she found as addictive as the smell of a new Elastoplast. Now she took out her purse and checked her ticket and counted her money yet again. Even with the change she had filched fearfully from the trousers He had left sprawled across the bedroom chair, it didn't amount to much. Stella was rich, as the result of her paper round and the tips she had received in return for the cards she had put through her customers' doors wishing them a 'Merry Christmas from your Newsboy/Newsgirl', with a space for her to sign her name. She would have been even wealthier had He not demanded the money for the repair of the iron whose flex had burst into flames in her hand while she was ironing His shirt. She could not see how it had been her fault but supposed it must have been. The compartment filled up at each stop and the girls stared out of the window rather than speak in public, or look at each other and see mirrored in her sister her own unsatisfactory self.

The concourse at Victoria was scented with sweet and sickening melted chocolate from a booth that sold fresh-baked cookies, and crowded with people criss-crossing each other with loaded trolleys, running to hurl themselves at the barriers, dragging luggage and children; queuing helplessly for tickets while the minutes to departure ticked away, swirling around the bright scarves outside Tie Rack, panic-buying festive socks and glittery bow ties, slurping coffee and beer and champing croissants and pizzas and jacket potatoes and trying on ear-rings. It had changed so much from the last time they had seen it that only the late arrival of their train and the notice of cancellation and delay on the indicator board reassured them that they were at the right Victoria Station.

'I've got to go to the Ladies.'

'OK.'

Vanessa attempted to join the dismayingly long queue trailing down the stairs but Stella had other plans.

'Stell-a! Where are you going?' She dragged Vanessa into the side entrance of the Grosvenor Hotel.

'Stella, we can't! It's a HOTEL! We'll be ARRESTED . . .' she wailed as Stella's fingers pinched through her coat sleeves, propelling her up the steps and through the glass doors.

'Shut up. Look as though we're meeting somebody.'

Vanessa could scarcely breathe as they crossed the foyer, expecting at any moment a heavy hand to descend on her shoulder, a liveried body to challenge them, a peaked cap to thrust into their faces. The thick carpet accused their feet. Safely inside the Ladies, she collapsed against a basin.

'Well? Isn't this better than queuing for hours? And it's free.'

'Supposing someone comes?'

'Oh stop bleating. It's perfectly all right. Daddy brought me here once – no one takes any notice of you.'

The door opened and the girls fled into cubicles and locked the doors. After what seemed like half an hour Vanessa slid back the bolt and peeped around the door. There was Stella, bold as brass, standing at the mirror between the sleek backs of two women in stolen fur coats, applying a stub of lipstick to her mouth. She washed and dried her hands and joined Stella, meeting a changed face in the glass: Stella's eyelids were smudged with green and purple, her lashes longer and darker, her skin matt with powder.

'Where did you get it?' she whispered hoarsely as the two women moved away.

'Tracy' – the friend who had lent her the stockings, with whom Vanessa, until they were safely on the train, had feared Stella would choose to go Christmas shopping, instead of with her.

Women came and went and Vanessa's fear was forgotten as she applied the cosmetics to her own face.

'Now we look a bit more human,' said Stella as they surveyed themselves, Goneril and Regan, whom their own father had named Star and Butterfly.

Vanessa Cardui, Painted Lady, sucked hollows into her cheeks and said, 'We really need some blusher, but it can't be helped.'

'Just a sec.'

'But Stella, it's a BAR . . . we can't . . . !'

Her alarm flooded back as Stella marched towards Edward's Bar.

'We'll get DRUNK. What about our shopping?'

Ignoring the animated temperance tract clutching her sleeve, Stella scanned the drinkers.

'Looking for someone, Miss?' the barman asked pleasantly.

'He's not here yet,' said Stella. 'Come on, Vanessa.'

She checked the coffee lounge on the way out, and as they recrossed the fearful foyer it dawned on Vanessa that Stella had planned this all along; all the way up in the train she had been expecting to find Daddy in Edward's Bar. That had been the whole point of the expedition.

She was afraid that Stella would turn like an injured dog and snap at her. She swallowed hard, her heart racing, as if there were words that would make everything all right, if only she could find them.

'What?' Stella did turn on her.

'He might be in Harrods.'

'Oh yes. Doing his Christmas shopping with Fergie and Di. Buying our presents.'

Vanessa might have retorted, 'The Duchess of York to you,' but she knew better than to risk the cold salt wave of misery between them engulfing the whole day: a gypsy woman barred their way with a sprig of foliage wrapped in silver foil.

'Lucky white heather. Bring you luck.'

'Doesn't seem to have brought you much,' snarled Stella pushing past her.

'You shouldn't have been so rude. Now she'll put a curse on us,' wailed Vanessa.

'It wasn't even real heather, dumbbell.'

'Now there's no chance we'll meet Daddy.'

Stella strode blindly past the gauntlet of people rattling tins for The Blind. Vanessa dropped in a coin and hurried after her down the steps. As they went to consult the map of the Underground they almost stumbled over a man curled up asleep on the floor, a bundle of grey rags and hair and beard tied up with string. His feet, black with dirt and disease, protruded shockingly bare into the path of the Christmas shoppers. The sisters stared, their faces chalky under their makeup.

Then a burst of laughter and singing broke out. A group of men and women waving bottles and cans were holding a private crazed party, dancing in their disfigured clothes and plastic accoutrements; a woman with long grey hair swirling out in horizontal streamers from a circlet of tinsel was clasping a young man in a close embrace as they shuffled around singing 'All I want for Christmas is my two front teeth', and he threw back his head to pour the last drops from a bottle into a toothless black hole, while their companions beat out a percussion accompaniment on bottles and cans with a braying brass of hiccups. They were the only people in that desperate and shoving crowded place who looked happy.

Stella and Vanessa were unhappy as they travelled down the escalator. The old man's feet clawed at them with broken and corroded nails; the revellers, although quite oblivious to the citizens of the other world, had frightened them; the gypsy's curse hung over them.

Harrods was horrendous. They moved bemused through the silken scented air, buffeted by headscarves, furs and green shopping bags. Fur and feathers in the Food Hall left them stupefied in the splendour of death and beauty and money.

'This is crazy,' said Stella. 'We probably couldn't afford even one quail's egg.'

Mirrors flung their scruffy reflections back at them and they half-expected to be shown the door by one of the green and gold guards and after an hour of fingering and coveting and temptation they were out in the arctic wind of Knightsbridge with two packs of Christmas cards and a round gold box of chocolate Napoleons.

In Covent Garden they caught the tail end of a piece of street theatre as a green spotted pantomime cow curvetted at them with embarrassing udders, swiping the awkward smiles off their faces with its tail. A woman dressed as a clown bopped them on the head with a balloon and thrust a bashed-in hat at them. Close to, she looked fierce rather than funny. The girls paid up. It seemed that everybody in the city was engaged in a conspiracy to make them hand over their money. Two hot chocolates made another serious inroad in their finances, the size of the bill souring the floating islands of cream as they sat on white wrought-iron chairs sipping from long spoons to the accompaniment of a young man busking on a violin backed by a stereo system.

'You should've brought your cello,' said Vanessa and choked on her chocolate as she realised she could hardly have said anything more tactless. It was He who had caused Stella's impromptu resignation from the school orchestra, leaving them in the lurch. His repetition, in front of two of His friends, of an attributed reprimand by Sir Thomas Beecham to a lady cellist, had made it impossible for her to practise at home and unthinkable that she should perform on a public platform to an audience sniggering like Him, debasing her and the music.

'It's – it's not my kind of music,' she had lied miserably to Miss Philips, the music teacher.

'Well, Stella, I must say I had never thought of *you* as a disco queen,' Miss Philips had said bitterly.

Her hurt eyes strobed Stella's pale selfish face and falling-down socks as she wilted against the wall. Accusations of letting down her fellow musicians followed, and reminders of Miss Philips's struggle to obtain the cello from another school, her own budget and resources being so limited. She ignored Stella in the corridor thereafter and the pain of this was still with her, like the ominous ache in her lower abdomen. She wished she were at home curled up with a hot-water bottle.

'Bastard,' she said. 'Of all the gin joints in all the suburbs of southeast London, why did He have to walk into ours?' Mummy had brought Him home from a rehearsal of the amateur production of *Oklahoma!* for which she was doing the costumes, ostensibly for an emergency fitting of His Judd Fry outfit, the trousers and boots of which were presenting difficulties. The girls had almost clapped the palms off their hands after the mournful rendition of 'Poor Judd is Dead'. It would always be a show-stopper for them.

Stella wished she had had one of the cards from Harrods to put in the school postbox for Miss Philips, but she hadn't, and now it was too late. Vanessa bought a silver heart-shaped balloon for Cordelia, or, as Stella suspected, for herself. They wandered around the stalls and shops over the slippery cobblestones glazed with drizzle.

'How come, whichever way we go, we always end up in Central Avenue?' Vanessa wondered.

Stella gave up the pretence that she knew exactly where she was going. 'It'll be getting dark soon. We must buy *something*.'

They battled their way into the Covent Garden General Store and joined the wet and unhappy throng desperate to spend money they couldn't afford on presents for people who would not want what they received, to the relentless musical threat that Santa Claus was coming to town. 'If this is more fun than just shopping,' said Stella as they queued to pay for their doubtful purchases, quoting from the notice displayed over the festive and jokey goods, 'I think I prefer just shopping. Sainsbury's on Saturday morning is paradise compared to this.'

Stella was seduced by a gold mesh star and some baubles as fragile and iridescent as soap bubbles, to hang on the conifer in the corner of the bare front room, decked in scrawny tinsel too sparse for its sprawling branches and topped with the fairy with a scorch mark in her greying crêpe-paper skirt where it had once caught in a candle. The candles, with most of their old decorations, had been vetoed by Him and had been replaced by a set of fairy lights with more twisted emerald green flex than bulbs in evidence.

'I wish we hadn't got a tree,' Vanessa said.

'I know. Cordelia likes it, though.'

'I suppose so. That's all that matters really. I mean, Christmas is for kids, isn't it?'

Vanessa showed her the bubble bath disguised as a bottle of gin which she was buying for Him.

'Perhaps He'll drink it.'

'Early on Christmas morning, nursing a savage hangover, He rips open His presents and, desperate for a hair-of-the-dog, He puts the bottle to his lips. Bubbles come out of His nose and mouth, He falls to the floor—'

'Screaming in agony.'

'—screaming in agony, foaming at the mouth. The heroic efforts of his distraught step-daughters fail to revive him. An ambulance is called but it gets stuck in traffic. When they finally reach the hospital all the nurses are singing carols in the wards and no one can find the stomach pump. A doctor in a paper hat tells the sorrowing sisters – or are they laughing, who can tell? – that it's too late. He has fallen victim to His own greed. How much does it cost?'

'Two pounds seventy-nine.'

'Cheap at twice the price.'

After leaving the shop they collided with a superstructure formed by two supermarket trolleys lashed together and heaped with a perilous pyramid of old clothes and plastic bags and utensils and bits of hardware like taps and broken car exhausts and hubcaps, the handlebars of a bicycle fronting it like antlers and three plumes of pampas grass waving in dirty Prince of Wales feathers. The owner was dragging a large cardboard box from beneath a stall of skirts and blouses.

'What do you think he wants that box for?' Vanessa wondered.

'To sleep in, of course. He probably lives in Cardboard City.'

'Cardboard City?'

'It's where the homeless people live. They all sleep in cardboard boxes underneath the Arches.'

'What arches?'

'*The* Arches, of course. Shall we go home now?'

Vanessa nodded. They were wet and cold, and the rain had removed most of their makeup, saving them the trouble of doing it themselves before they encountered Him. The feet of Stella's stockings felt like muddy string in her leaking shoes.

They were huddled on the packed escalator, two drowned rats going up to Victoria, when Vanessa screamed shrilly.

'Daddy!'

She pointed to a man on the opposing escalator.

'It's Daddy, quick, Stella, we've got to get off.' She would have climbed over the rail if Stella hadn't held her.

'It's not him.'

'It is. It is. *Daddy!*'

Faces turned to stare. The man turned and their eyes met as they were carried upwards and he was borne inexorably down. Vanessa tried to turn to run down against the flow of the escalator but she was wedged. The man was gone for ever.

'It wasn't him, I tell you.'

Stella fought the sobbing Vanessa at the top of the stair, they were yelling at each other in the mêlée of commuters and shoppers. She succeeded in dragging her through the barrier, still crying, 'It was him. Now we'll never see him again.'

'Daddy hasn't got a beard, you know that. And he'd never wear a balaclava. Come *on*, Vanessa, we'll miss our train.'

'It was him. Let's go back, please, please.'

'Look, stupid, that guy was a down and out. A vagrant. A wino. A meths drinker. It couldn't possibly have been Daddy.'

On the home-bound train Stella carefully opened the box of chocolate Napoleons. There were so many that nobody would notice if a couple were missing. She took out two gold coins and sealed the box again. For the rest of their lives Vanessa would be convinced that she had seen her father, and Stella would never be sure. The chocolate dissolved in their mouths as they crossed the Thames.

'Where is Cardboard City?' whispered Vanessa. 'How do you get there?'

'"Follow the Yellow Brick Road . . ."'

The silver heart-shaped balloon floated on its vertical string above the heads and newspapers of the passengers.

'"Now I know I've got a heart, because it's breaking."'

'It's just a slow puncture,' Stella said. She stuck a gift label on to the balloon's puckering silver skin. It ruined the look of it, but it was kindly meant. Vanessa looked out of the window at the moon melting like a lemon drop in the freezing sky above the chimney tops of Clapham and pictured it shining on the cold frail walls and pinnacles of Cardboard City.

'I don't want Daddy to sleep in a cardboard box,' she said.

'It's a great life,' Stella said savagely. 'Didn't you see those people singing and dancing?'

BERYL BAINBRIDGE

The Longstop

Words and cricket seem to go together. Whenever I watch the game, by mistake, on television, I think it's not true that you can't get blood from a stone.

I only ever played the game once myself, in the park with some evacuees from Bootle. I was allowed to join in because I held a biscuit tin filled with shortbread that my mother had baked. They said I could have a turn if I gave them a biscuit afterwards. I didn't make any runs because I never hit the ball, and when I kept my promise and began to open the tin the evacuees knocked me over and took every piece of shortbread. They threw the tin over the wall into the gentlemen's lavatory. I had to tell my mother a six-foot-high naughty man with a Hitler moustache had chased me; she would have slapped me for playing with evacuees.

Mr Baines, who was my maternal grandfather, was a lover of cricket. Mr Jones, my father, didn't care for the game. He cared even less for my grandfather. In his humble estimation Mr Baines was a mean old bugger, a fifth columnist, and, following his self-confessed denouncing of a neighbour in Norris Green for failing to draw his curtains against the black-out, a Gauleiter into the bargain. He was also a lounge lizard, a term never satisfactorily explained, though it was true that my grandfather fell asleep between meals.

Apart from words, my father was keen on sailing ships. He subscribed to a monthly magazine on the subject. If he was to be believed, he had, when no more than a child, sailed as a cabin boy to America. In middle age, his occupation a commercial traveller, he prowled the deserted shore beyond the railway line, peering of an evening through the barbed wire entanglements at the oil tankers and the black destroyers that crawled along the bleak edge of the Irish Sea; it was a gloomy mystery to him where that fearless lad before the mast had gone.

Every week Mr Baines came for Sunday dinner. There had been a moment at the outbreak of the war when he had contemplated coming to live with us, but after three days he returned home. He said he preferred to take his chances with the Luftwaffe. His conversation during the meal was always about cricket, and mostly to do with a man called Briggs. Briggs, he said, had just missed greatness by a lack of seriousness. If only Briggs had taken batting more seriously he would have been, make no bones about it, the best all-round cricketer in England since W. G. Grace. Briggs, he informed us, took bowling and fielding in deadly earnest, but as a batsman he was a disaster; he seemed far more anxious to amuse the crowd than to improve his average.

Nobody listened to my grandfather, certainly not my father who was often heard to remark quite loudly that, had he been in control, he wouldn't give the old skinflint the time of day, let alone Sunday dinner, world without end.

However, one particular Sunday in the summer of 1944, Mr Baines, without warning, excelled himself when describing a cricketer called Ranjitsinhji.

'Just to set eyes on him,' said Mr Baines, 'was a picture in motion. The way his shirt ballooned—'

'A black chappie,' my father exclaimed, taken aback at my grandfather speaking civilly of a foreigner.

'An Indian Prince,' said Mr Baines. He was equally taken aback at being addressed in the middle of his monologue. He was used to conversing uninterrupted throughout the devouring of the black-market roast pork.

'They're two a penny,' my father said.

'More potatoes?' asked my mother, worriedly.

'Even when it wasn't windy,' continued Mr Baines, 'his shirt ballooned. Whether half a gale was blowing on the Hove ground or there wasn't enough breeze to shift the flag at Lord's, the fellow's shirt flapped like the mainsail of a six-tonner on the Solent.'

'Blithering rubbish,' said my father. He stabbed at a sprout on his plate as though it was alive.

My mother told Mr Baines that they played cricket in the park every Sunday afternoon. Not a proper team, just old men and young lads. Not what he was used to, of course. 'But,' she said, eyeing my father contemptuously, 'it will do us good to get out into the pure air.'

She didn't mean my father to come. We were never a family who went anywhere together. My father's opinion, had he voiced it, would have been that the family who stood together fell out together. Often we would attempt an outing, but between the closing of the back door and the opening of the front gate, misunderstandings occurred and plans were abruptly abandoned. She was astonished when, having washed up and taken off her pinny, she found my father in the hall putting on his trilby hat. She didn't like it, you could tell. Her mouth went all funny and the lipstick ran down at one corner. Shoulder to shoulder, more or less, we set off for the park.

I wanted to nip over the garden fence and through the blackberry bushes into Brows Lane, but my mother said my grandfather wasn't about to nip anywhere, not at his age. We trotted him down the road past the roundabout and the Council offices. The brass band was practising in the hut behind the fire station. When he heard the music, Mr Baines began to walk with his arms held stiffly at his sides, only the band kept stopping and starting and the tune came in bits, and after a little while he gave up playing at soldiers and shuffled instead. My father looked at the ground all the time; there was a grey splodge on the brim of his hat where a pigeon had done its business.

The park was quite grand, even though it had lost its ornamental gates at the entrance. My mother said they'd been removed to make into tanks. My father swore they were mouldering away in a brick field down by the Docks, along with his mother's copper kettle and a hundred thousand front railings. The park had a pavilion, a sort of hunting lodge with mullioned windows and a thatched roof. People were worried about incendiary bombs. The park keeper kept his grass roller inside and buckets of water. In front of the pavilion was a sunken bowling green, and beyond that a miniature clock-golf course. We used to ride our bikes up and down the bumps. Behind the pavilion, within a roped enclosure, was a German Messerschmitt. It had been there for two years. It hadn't crash-landed anywhere near our village; it was on loan. The park keeper was always telling the Council to tell someone to come back for it. At first we had all run round it and shuddered, but after a few weeks we hardly noticed it any more. It just perched there, propped on blocks, one wing tipped up to the sky, the cockpit half burned away, its melted hood glittering beetle-black in the sunlight.

When he saw the aeroplane, my father cried out, 'Good Lord, look at that!' He flung his arms out theatrically and demanded, 'Why wasn't I told?'

No one took any notice of him; he was always showing off. He stared up at the plane with an expression both fearful and excited, as though the monster was still flying through the air and he might yet be machine-gunned where he stood.

My mother and Mr Baines sat on wooden chairs pressed against the privet hedge. My mother was worried in case we were too near the wicket. She was for ever ducking and flinching, mistaking the white clouds that bowled across the sky for an oncoming ball. It wasn't an exciting game as far as I could tell but my grandfather sat on the edge of his chair and didn't fall asleep once. There was a man fielding who was almost as old as Mr Baines, and when the bowler was rubbing the ball up and down the front of his trousers preparing to run, the old man rested in a deck-chair on the pitch. The butcher's boy from the village shop was crouching down behind the wicket wearing a tin hat and smoking a cigarette.

'That fellow,' said Mr Baines, pointing at the elderly batsman in Home Guard uniform, 'is taking a risk. If he misses the ball he'll be out leg before or he'll get his skull stove in.'

'Heavens,' cried my mother, cringing backwards on her chair.

'Briggs used to play that sort of stroke,' said Mr Baines. 'Of course, he knew what he was doing.'

My father came and sat down beside him. He said: 'I never knew it was there. I never knew.' He still looked excited. He'd taken his hat off and there was a mark all round his forehead.

'As soon as he saw what ball it was,' Mr Baines said, 'he'd stand straight in front of the wicket and wait until it looked as if it would go straight through his body—'

'I never knew,' repeated my father. 'I never even guessed.' He was very unobservant. He'd been morosely loping to and from the railway station night and morning for twenty years and never bothered to look through the trees.

'Be quiet,' said my mother. 'We're concentrating.'

'At the last moment,' Mr Baines said, 'Briggs would hook it. Glorious stroke. Poetry in motion.'

'If I could have served,' remarked my father, 'I would have chosen the Merchant Navy.'

'Mind you,' Mr Baines said. 'It had to be a fast ball.'

'Failing that, I think I'd have fancied the Air Force,' said my father.

There wasn't anything one could reply to that piece of poppy-cock. If my father had been healthy enough to join up, he wouldn't have been any use. When Wilfred Pickles said on the wireless, 'And how old are you, luv? Ninety-seven!', my father had to blow his nose from emotion. If he happened to hear 'When the lights go on again all over the world' on Forces' Favourites, he had to go out into the scullery to take a grip on himself. According to my mother, Auntie Doris had turned him into a sissy. He was a terrible cry-baby. He cried one time when the cat went missing. My mother said that most of the time his carrying on like that was misplaced. Once he went all over Southport pressing shilling pieces into the hands of what he called 'our gallant boys in blue'. They were soldiers from the new hospital down by the Promenade. My father told them he was proud of them, that they were the walking wounded; he had a field day with his handkerchief. Afterwards it turned out there was nothing wrong with them, nothing wounded that is, it wasn't that sort of hospital. They were soldiers all right, my mother said, but they'd all caught a nasty disease from just being in the army, not from fighting or anything gallant like that, and it was certainly nothing to be proud of.

'I'm not criticising,' said Mr Baines, looking at the fielder resting in his deck-chair, 'but these fellows lack self-discipline. The true sportsman is a trained athlete. He dedicates himself to the game. Only way to succeed. Same with anything in all walks of life – cotton, fishing, banking, shipping—'

'Doesn't he ever get tired of his own voice?' said my father savagely.

I sat on the grass with my back propped against my mother's knees. I could feel her trembling from indignation. My grandfather began to clap, slapping the palms of his hands together above my head as the elderly batsman left the crease and began to trail towards the pavilion. Mr Baines was the only one applauding; there were few spectators and most of those had swivelled round the other way to look at the bowling green. The new batsman was younger and he had a gammy leg. When he heard Mr Baines clapping he glared at him, thinking he was being made fun of.

'One time,' said Mr Baines, 'Briggs got stale. The Lancashire committee suggested that he should take a week's holiday. He went to a remote village in Wiltshire—'

'Don't think I don't know what the old beggar's getting at,' said my father. 'Talking about cotton like that. Did he think I wanted to come a cropper in cotton—'

'Word got round as it will,' Mr Baines said. 'Second day there a fellow came up to Briggs and asked him how much he'd take for playing in a local match. Ten pound, said Briggs, thinking that would be prohibitive—'

The park was shimmering in sunshine. You couldn't see the boundary by the poplar trees; all the leaves were reflecting like bits of glass. The man with the gammy leg was out almost at once. I didn't know why, the bails were still standing. I couldn't follow the rules. A fat man came out in a little peaked cap. I could hear the dull clop of the ball against the bat and the click of the bowls on the green as they knocked against each other. Behind me the voices went on and on, another game in progress, more dangerous than either cricket or bowls, and the rules were always changing.

'Briggs's side lost the toss,' said Mr Baines, 'and he had to begin the bowling. His first ball was hit out of the ground for six—'

'If I'd had any appreciation all these years,' my father said, 'things might have been different. When I think how I tramp from door to door in all weathers while you and your blasted Dad put your feet up—'

'Finally he had two wickets for a hundred and fifty runs. The crowd was looking quite nasty,' Mr Baines said. 'But what finished them off was that when he went into bat he was bowled second ball.'

'All I needed was a few bob at the right moment,' said my father. 'Just a few measly quid and the old skinflint wouldn't put his hand in his pocket—'

'Don't speak about him like that,' cried my mother. 'I won't have him called names.'

'Only a stalwart policeman and the train to London saved him from a jolly good hiding,' said Mr Baines. 'He never tried village cricket again.'

'If you'd been any proper sort of woman,' groaned my father, 'you'd have been a help-mate.'

'Be quiet,' my mother cried. 'Shut your mouth.'

'You've only been a bloody hindrance,' my father shouted. He jumped up and knocked over his chair. He walked away in the direction of the aeroplane, leaving his hat on the grass.

'What's up?' I asked. Though I knew. 'Is he off home, then?'

'Ssh,' said my mother. 'He's gone for a widdle.' Her voice was all choked.

'Don't upset yourself,' said Mr Baines. 'It's not worth it.'

'He sickens me,' my mother said. 'Sickens me. Whimpering over the least thing when inside he's like a piece of rock. He's hard. He's got no pity for man nor beast.'

'Don't waste your tears,' said Mr Baines. 'You can't get blood from a stone.'

At that moment the ball flew past the wicket and, striking the ground, rolled to my grandfather's feet. He leapt up, and striding to the side of the pitch, chucked the ball at the batsman. He didn't exactly bowl it; he sort of dipped one shoulder and flung the ball like a boy skimming a stone on water. The batsman, taken by surprise at such an accurate throw, swung his bat. The scarlet ball shot over Mr Baines's shoulder and went like a bullet from a gun after my father.

When we ran up to him he was stood there in the shadow of the Messerschmitt with his hand clutched to the side of his head. The ball hadn't hit him full on, merely grazed the side of his temple. But he was bleeding like a pig.

'That's a turn-up for the book,' said Mr Baines.

DOUGLAS DUNN

Bobby's Room

Henry Pollock was the only child of only children, and his four grand-parents were dead. When he was twelve, in 1954, he and his parents left Glasgow on a motoring holiday. They stayed in a succession of hotels all over the Borders and the southwest of Scotland. At one place, they found that the hotels and guesthouses were full. It was a town Mrs Pollock particularly wanted to visit, and all the rooms were booked up for some local annual event. Mr Pollock was irate. His wife chided him for not having telephoned a reservation in advance, as, she said, she had suggested in the first place.

'We said potluck was part of the charm, did we not?' was Henry's father's riposte. Bickering in the car park lasted almost an hour.

Pollock was a tall man, powerful, proud, and successful; Henry had got used to his obstinate refusals to give in to his wife's complaints or preferences, to which, in the end, he always conformed without seeming to surrender. Harsh words when they fell out were, Henry knew, a prelude to that kind of morning on which he didn't see them until it was nearly noon. If these were mornings when he went to school, then his mother hurriedly threw his breakfast together and kissed him on the ear before running back upstairs in her kimono.

Even in the small space of the car, they managed to ignore Henry, and he knew better than to say anything.

'If you're in such a hurry to find somewhere, then why don't you drive?' his father asked Mrs Pollock.

'You know I can't. Don't be so stupid.'

'Then allow me to the judge of when we leave and when we don't. I need petrol, in any case.'

'You can't possibly need petrol. You filled up this morning in Dumfries.'

Eventually they got under way again, and after a few miles Pollock stopped the car outside a substantial stone-built villa, a house much like their own back in Glasgow; a notice board advertised that it offered accommodations.

'What do you think?' he asked.

'I think it's seen better days, that's what I think,' said Mrs Pollock, who was still simmering. Her husband went to see if there were two rooms available, and to investigate what the place was like. 'It doesn't even have a drive,' she said to Henry. 'Where will we put the car?'

'I don't see any cars,' Henry said, 'so they must have rooms.'

'When I want your opinion, I'll ask for it. *Netherbank*,' she said, sounding the name of the house as proof of its unsuitability.

Pollock returned a few minutes later. 'It's first-rate,' he said with genuine enthusiasm, leaning into the car. 'The rooms are large and spotlessly clean, very airy and spacious, and no one else is staying there.' Breezily, he listed the qualifications Mrs Pollock always insisted were necessary for a night's comfort. 'We can have the sitting room to ourselves, if we want it, and you'll find the bathroom highly acceptable. I think we should take it, Irene, it's run by a lovely old couple. You'll adore them.'

Netherbank was run by a Mrs Bawden. She was over sixty, silver-haired, round, short, respectable, and as Mrs Pollock said afterwards, very nicely spoken. She took it in her stride when Mrs Pollock asked if she could have a look at what she was offering for dinner. 'Normally, I prefer a proper restaurant. But my husband's very tired after a day's driving.'

'Some people ask me for what they call an "evening meal",' Mrs Bawden said, lifting the lid off a saucepan. 'I call it dinner. I've always called it dinner, and I won't change now. Round about here, people call lunch dinner. But I call it luncheon, and I call it luncheon at twelve-thirty. And I call tea tea. I don't know where we'll all end up if we begin to call things by the wrong names.' Mrs Pollock couldn't agree more.

They stayed for five nights. Henry knew one of the reasons his parents liked the place so much: Mrs Bawden was very obliging. Before Mrs Pollock could ask, Mrs Bawden offered to keep an eye on Henry if they

wanted to go off by themselves for a day, or go to dinner in a hotel restaurant about ten miles away which Mrs Bawden had heard was
outstanding for its seafood. 'But Mrs Bawden, you'll do yourself out of
business,' his mother said.

'No, no, I won't. You're on holiday, and it'll be my pleasure to help you
enjoy yourselves.' Mrs Pollock revelled in being the beneficiary of that
sort of consideration. Henry's parents had three days on their own without
him, and three evenings at the famous restaurant.

Henry wandered round the hills and farms, and walked the two miles to
the sea. He read, and he watched Mr Bawden at work in his garden. The old
man was hard of hearing, or said he was, and when Henry tried to talk to
him he pointed to an ear, smiled, and went back to his weeding or hoeing.

These were the last days of their holiday. His parents loved it. 'I haven't
felt so refreshed and well in years!' said Henry's mother as they drove
home. 'And Mrs Bawden – what a wonderful woman! Her cooking's
pre-war! We were lucky to find it. It's the sort of place you could drive
right past without giving it so much as a moment's notice.' After that, she
and her husband looked at each other in the way that made Henry feel
he wasn't there. A little later, Mrs Pollock started to sing. She coaxed
Henry to join in. When he didn't, she turned round and said, 'You'll grow
up to be miserable. Why won't you sing, like the rest of us?'

Two years later, there was a week in early June when Henry's father was
more thoughtful than usual. After dinner he did a lot of meditative gardening. Tired of that, he sat in the lounge with an open book on his lap.
Henry's mother brought him tea or coffee, asked him if he wanted something stronger, or something to eat, and in her busy efforts to leave him
alone made a nuisance of herself. It was obvious to Henry that his father
was making his mind up about something important. From time to time
he saw his parents talk quietly and seriously to each other. They cuddled
in the kitchen even more often than usual.

'Why don't I phone her? I kept a note of the number, you know,' he
heard his mother say one evening.

'Do you think she would?' Pollock asked her. 'It's not really what
she does.'

'Almost three months at her usual rates is probably very good business for her, especially if we add something on for her trouble. I imagine she'll be only too pleased.'

'It'd be ideal. But what do we do about the weeks of school he'll have to miss?'

'Darling, I've no intention of being left behind. It's an opportunity to travel I won't let pass by, especially since the offer specifically includes me as well. It's not as if you'll have to fork out for my fare and hotel bills. Some of us were prevented from travelling by the war, you know, not to mention marriage and motherhood.'

'If this trip's successful, there will have to be others, as a matter of course. It's a big project. It's not one bridge, it's a network. I don't look forward to going away without you, and I want you to come with me. But the best thing might be to start thinking about boarding school.'

'Were Henry younger, I'd say no, naturally. But at his age boarding school is probably a very adventurous proposition. I know it was for Alice Wylie's brother.'

Later that evening, Henry heard the telephone being used. He looked down into the hall from the top of the stairs and saw his mother leaning against the opposite wall while his father spoke into the phone. She was smoking, which she did only in company to be polite, or when she was agitated. Then she, too, went over to the phone and began to speak into it. Later, his mother called him to come down to the sitting room.

'Your mother and I have to go to Singapore,' his father said. 'We'll be gone for most of July and all of August and September. And I'm afraid it just isn't practical to take you with us.'

'You remember Mrs Bawden, and Netherbank?' His wife spoke sooner than Pollock would have liked. 'We've arranged for you to stay with her.'

'What about school?' Henry's tone of voice was meant to suggest that weeks of missed classes could be disastrous.

'Henry, you're the last person I can imagine slipping behind. A few weeks won't be a setback to you.'

His mother's way of speaking to him, her confidence in his maturity and academic excellence, made Henry want to fight back. He felt inclined to be stubborn and obstructive. 'There isn't a lot to do at Mrs Bawden's,' he said.

'We both think it's ideal.'

'We've no choice but to leave you behind.' his father said. 'We'll be happier, much happier, knowing you're somewhere we can feel easy in our minds about.'

Henry looked at his mother, hoping she would understand that he expected her to stay behind with him. She said, 'I'll talk to the headmaster on Monday. You can arrange for your teachers to give you a programme of study. You can do it on your own – I'm sure you can. And if you think you can't you're underrating yourself.' He knew enough about her to know that if at his age she had been given a 'programme of study' she'd have collapsed in tears.

Instead of making it difficult for them, he accepted it, and resigned himself. He knew why they had chosen Mrs Bawden and Netherbank. They had been happy there, and assumed that he had liked it, too. It was a place and a few days in their lives that meant something in their happiness. He wondered why they could continue to be so ignorant of his feelings. Mrs Bawden was not a complete stranger, but she was the next thing to it – the landlady of a guesthouse, a species his mother usually loathed.

'Don't feel unwanted,' his mother said. 'It would suit us better, much better, if you could come with us. But it isn't possible, so we have to make the best of it.'

When the time came, they drove him to Mrs Bawden's with suitcases, books, tennis racquet, binoculars, and field guides to the birds and wild-flowers of the British Isles. Nature study was his mother's idea. 'When I get back, I want to find you thoroughly up to the mark in country life,' she said. 'It's a wonderful opportunity for you. I've always been opposed to townies.' He tried to think of what it was she craved so determinedly that it made a trip to Singapore necessary to her.

She wept as she said goodbye. Henry felt like weeping on his own account.

'I know you won't give Mrs Bawden any trouble,' she said. It was the wrong thing to have said. Obedient to the point of filial perfection, he had never given anyone the least bit of trouble in his life.

'How long does post take from Singapore?' Mrs Pollock asked her husband.

'Airmail,' he said. 'Pretty fast.'

'Then I'll write at least once a week, and I'll expect you to do the same,' she told Henry. With that, she left for the car, dabbing at her eyes with a handkerchief.

'You haven't left me your address in Singapore,' Henry said. Pollock had to call for Mrs Bawden to bring a piece of paper for him to write it down on. He was embarrassed, talking about rush, last-minute details, oversights.

Henry had reckoned on eating alone in the dining room, like any other guest, but he ate with the Bawdens in their kitchen. 'No aunts, no uncles,' said Mr Bawden, as the old couple explored Henry's family. 'So no cousins, either. No great loss, if you ask me. A big scatter of kin makes you feel guilty at not keeping in touch, which you can't do, you know, unless you're a man of means and leisure.'

'I've second cousins,' Henry offered.

'I was closer to two of my second cousins than to any of my first,' said Mrs Bawden.

'I've never met them,' said Henry.

'Singapore's a long, long journey,' she said, pushing a bowl of cauli-flower towards him.

'Home-grown,' said Mr Bawden. 'We haven't eaten a tinned vegetable in twenty years.'

As he lay awake in bed, Henry pondered his affection for his parents, and decided it was becoming as distant and routine as his parents' love of him. They were his parents, therefore he loved them; he was their son, therefore they loved him – it was as mathematical as that. Co-operation between them was beginning to thin out, like the darkness in the triangle of dawn now at the top of the curtains. His mother prodded him to be the scholar of his class at school, and was proud of his examination victories; but she nagged him for being too studious and staying in when he should have been outside and complained of his lack of interest in sport. They expected him to be perfect, but they neglected him.

He had a different room from the one he had slept in two years before. It was at the front of the house, under the eaves; from its protruding window he could look at a small wedge of sea and the right-hand tip of an island that could be walked to at low tide over the sands. Darkness turned to a transparent grey, and objects in the room slowly became visible. Shelves in an alcove contained dozens of books of boyish interest – books on ships and the sea, the Empire, foreign countries, warlike history, wildlife, fishing, landmarks in engineering and exploration, most of them heavy and already obsolete. There was a home-made model warship on a chest of drawers. Pictures on the wall did not quite cover the cleaner paint left behind from those that had been taken down. His dressing gown, on the hook behind the door, looked like another person in the room. He imagined that the owner of the books was a long-lost son of the Bawdens, dead, probably, in the war.

'Was my room your son's?' he asked Mr Bawden, who pointed to his ear as Henry began to repeat his question.

'We thought you'd like it better than the rooms we let to the holidaymakers,' he said. 'Or *she* did. You'll find out,' he said, as if excusing himself in advance for any apparent lack of initiative on his part. 'Mrs Bawden is the boss round here. She wears the trousers.'

'Where is he?'

'I haven't the foggiest. Somewhere or other.' He jabbed his rake on the dusty ground. 'It's good soil for carrots. And there's no better earth for potatoes.'

'Is he dead?'

'Good God, no. What gave you that idea? All that's wrong with Bobby is that he's a bit wayward when it comes to writing letters. What made you think he was dead?'

Henry was embarrassed, and with no way of explaining himself. Mr Bawden shrugged and retreated into his deafness and gardening.

Mrs Bawden was obviously told of Henry's questions in the garden. At dinner she recounted Bobby's travels – his letters from Australia, where he had spent three years, the good job in Hong Kong he'd thrown up on a whim in order to go to Canada. 'We're about due a letter from him soon.'

'What's that?' her husband asked.

'I said we're about due a letter from Bobby.'

'I'll believe it when I see it,' said Mr Bawden.

When Henry offered to do Mrs Bawden's shopping, it seemed as if she had been expecting him to ask. She gave him a list, and he pedalled the two miles to the nearest shop on a bicycle that had been Bobby's.

A family of five moved in, and stayed for three nights. They were bois-terous, but their liveliness appeared toned down out of respect for someone else's house. Mrs Bawden had that effect on people. Henry kept out of their way. When he came down to say good night, Mr Bawden, alone in the kitchen with a book, directed him to the guests' sitting room. He found Mrs Bawden there with the father and mother of the visiting family.

'And this is Bobby in his uniform,' she was saying.

'My, he's a fine-looking young man.'

'And here's another one, with some friends of his from the same ship.'

'I'm off to bed now,' Henry told her.

'Good night, Henry.'

He was disconcerted by the sight of Mrs Bawden on the sofa, with a guest on either side of her, showing photographs of her son to people she had never seen before and might never see again. There was an amiable candour in her affectionate disappointment in Bobby, and it jolted Henry, who saw it as a failure of reticence, an openness that compromised her loyalty to her son. Snapshots of her son were being touted to strangers and were symptoms of an unhappiness she was too proud to notice.

'Is it all right if I take a cup of cocoa upstairs with me?' he asked Mr Bawden.

'Help yourself,' said the old man. Henry boiled the kettle and opened the cocoa tin. 'What is it, through there?' Mr Bawden asked. 'Snapshots and airmail letters?'

'What?'

'My wife, what's she doing?'

'She's talking to the guests.'

'See any photographs?'

'I think she *is* showing them photographs.'

The old man went back to his book.

Henry wondered how Mrs Bawden selected the people who were treated to her photograph albums. Perhaps everyone was, and perhaps his parents, two years before, had been shown the same photographs, with the same pride, and had listened to the same reminiscences. He felt sure that the visiting couple would have asked who Henry was, and been told that his parents had gone to Singapore, that his father was a civil engineer, and that they had stayed at Netherbank and thought it an ideal place to board their son while they were away. 'You ought to come home, Bobby,' he said to the vanished son. 'Not only does your mother miss you, but she talks about you to people she hardly knows. Worse, she's probably talking about me.'

There was a visitors' book on the hall table. Besides putting down their names and addresses, guests over the years had written their comments in a column where remarks were invited. 'We had a wonderful time.' 'Smashing food!' 'Highly recommended!' 'Excellent.' Henry leafed back to two years earlier. 'First-class!' his mother had written, in her bold, clear, self-assured handwriting. It was characteristic of her. Any time they travelled by train, his mother made it clear that they went first-class as a matter of course, and that some people did not – never would, never could.

As soon as the family of five left, Netherbank was full almost every night. His parents had found the house to their taste because they had it to themselves, and they were lucky. People often had to be told that there were no rooms left.

Henry tried to keep away from the guests as much as he could, but it was impossible not to ask Mrs Bawden each morning if there was anything she wanted him to do. 'Maybe you don't think it's man's work,' she said, 'but I could fair do with someone to strip the beds this morning and bring the linen down here for me to launder.' As the days went by he found himself aproned, pulling linen from beds, vacuuming carpets, dusting furniture, cleaning windows and mirrors, polishing the bannister.

'Next time we hear from you,' said Mr Bawden, 'you'll be running a hotel. You've taken to it. But don't tell me you like it. Believe me, I know – no one better. She's a hard woman to refuse.'

A girl from Lincolnshire, about Henry's age, passed him in the hall and said, 'You must be blind. What's that, then, if it isn't carpet fluff? There,' and she pointed. Later the same morning, egged on by a friend who was along on holiday with that family, the girl asked him, 'Is this your career? Or is it a punishment?'

'Have you been very bad?' the other girl said, giggling.

'Shoo!' Henry waved a duster at them, and they ran away delighted and laughing.

Breakfast was at seven for the Bawdens and Henry, so that they could eat before the rush of holiday families to the dining room. 'The Abercrombie children are sleeping three to a bed,' said Mrs Bawden. 'I told Mr Abercrombie it was the best I could do, and he was only too pleased to accept. The English family are just the same. There'll be eighteen for breakfast. I've never been so busy.'

'Why folk go on holidays I'll never know,' said Mr Bawden.

'Do you want me to wait on the tables?' Henry offered.

Mr Bawden gave him an uncertain look, and shook his head in a gesture of subdued bewilderment. 'Eighteen,' he said. 'She could never cook and serve at the same time – not for eighteen.'

'You ask them what they'd like,' said Mrs Bawden, patting his hand appreciatively. 'We have fruit juice. We have porridge and packet cereals. This morning we have kippers, and we have eggs, bacon, sausages, and those who want a fried breakfast are to be asked if they want black pudding with it. Some don't like it, others love it. I never need to take a note, but it might be for the best if you were to write down the orders, like a proper waiter. Eggs scrambled, fried, boiled, or poached. Tea or coffee, and toast, jam or marmalade. And if someone high and mighty asks you for kedgeree, look daft and pretend you've never even heard of it.'

'Should I get changed?'

'Put on my big white apron and you'll look the part well enough. And don't be nervous. We're not the Ritz,' she said.

Mr Bawden slipped out into the garden with his second cup of tea.

Most guests chose to come down at eight-thirty, and within the space of a few minutes the dining room was full. Henry was surprised that they could be so fussy about what to eat.

'Are the sausages fresh?' a man asked.

'I can't see Mrs Bawden serving you a bad sausage, sir.'

'What's a black pudding?'

'Black pudding,' Henry said, with a hesitant shrug.

'But what's it made of?'

'Hold on.' He asked Mrs Bawden what black puddings were made of, and Mr Bawden, rinsing his cup at the sink, raised his eyebrows.

Henry came back from the kitchen. 'Blood and lights,' he said.

'I'll have two lightly poached eggs. No, wait a minute. Did you say there were scrambled eggs? In that case, I'll have scrambled eggs.'

The two girls from Lincolnshire giggled as Henry stood in his apron with his pad and pen poised. The mother ordered them to hurry up. The father looked seriously at Henry, as if he thought he had been up to something.

By ten o'clock, Henry and Mrs Bawden were alone in the kitchen, tired out and hot and sipping tea. 'My twenty-of-everything set of breakfast china came in handy,' she said. Most of it was stacked beside the sink. 'The Lord be thanked, nobody wants lunch. Rooms next, then laundry. I don't know what I'd do without you, Henry. Next year I'll have to get a village girl to come in.'

Mr Bawden appeared with the mail.

'It's another letter from your mother!' Mrs Bawden said. She gave it to Henry. 'Go on, read it.'

His mother's cadences were in every line. They had been here, there, and seen that and other things. They had developed a taste for Chinese and Malayan food, although they'd been a bit suspicious at first.

'Is it so private that you can't read it out to me?' Mrs Bawden asked. Her husband hurried outside with a cup of tea in one hand and his watering can in the other. 'Does she say anything about the climate this time?' she said, remembering the first letter. 'Have they got over that exhausting journey? I didn't like the sound of the airport at Karachi.'

He glanced through the rest of the letter, to make sure his mother hadn't written anything embarrassing, thinking that it was only to be expected that an old woman who showed her snapshots to all and sundry would take it for granted that a letter should be shared. He read out his mother's account of the strange food, the deliciousness of which his parents had come round to accepting, and the sightseeing. '"Daddy's had to fly up to Penang for a couple of days, so I've been left on my own. Everyone's extremely kind, and I've been playing a very great deal of bridge but as yet no mah-jong, thank goodness. We've been out for dinner every night since we arrived, and I shall be quite plump when I see you next. We look forward to a quiet evening by ourselves. Our bungalow is bijou but not quite as colonial as I would have liked. I'm not very geographical, as you know, and I wasn't quite sure where Singapore was, but I know now, Henry, and I don't mind telling you that it's ABSOLUTELY TROPICAL. It was so nice of you to press a flower in your letter. It made me feel quite homesick."'

'What a nice young man you are for doing a thing like that,' said Mrs Bawden. She patted his hand. 'I knew it,' she said. 'I knew it'd be hot there.'

A girl from an Edinburgh family asked Henry if he played tennis. He said he did. She asked if there was a court. He told her where the nearest one was, two miles away in the village.

'I don't have anyone to play with,' she said. She didn't sound as if she wanted particularly to play with Henry.

Her mother appeared at the door of the sitting room. 'Are you coming with us, or are you staying behind?' The woman's voice stated these options firmly, and Henry recognized the predicaments of both girl and parents.

Mrs Bawden came to the sitting-room door.

'Have you asked him?' the woman said to her daughter.

'It's two miles away,' the girl said, meaning that the court was too far to be practical.

'We'll drop you off at the court,' said her father from inside, through a rustle of newspaper.

'You haven't had proper company for nearly a month,' Mrs Bawden said to Henry. 'Go and play tennis if you want. I can answer the door and do what needs to be done. I can manage well enough without you.'

He ran upstairs, changed, got his racquet and a box of tennis balls. When he came down, the family of three was waiting in the hall, and the front door was open. The breeze disturbed the potpourri in the bowl on the hall table.

'I'm told that your father and mother are in Singapore,' said the man when they were in the car. 'Very interesting,' he said. 'Very interesting.' Henry had the impression he had been vetted and found to be a suitable companion for the girl.

'What's your name?' he asked her as they strolled to the tennis court.

'Louise,' she said.

'I know what it's like. At least yours haven't gone to Singapore.'

'I wish they would.'

'My mother's forgotten something, and it probably hasn't dawned on her yet. I'll be fifteen in a couple of weeks and she won't be here.'

'It isn't much of a tennis court,' Louise said.

She got bored and sat down, ignoring Henry's tepid but ironic serves as they bounced close beside her. Looking at her, he thought that there might be two major ways in which only children could turn out: they became either super-obliging, obedient models of courtesy and good behaviour or, like Louise, rebelliously surly and aggrieved. He never allowed his own grievances to show, and doubted if he ever would.

'When did your father say he'd pick us up?'

'He didn't.'

'What do you think of Mrs Bawden?'

'She certainly doesn't have any secrets.'

'And Mr Bawden?'

'I didn't know there was one. I thought she was a widow.'

'No secrets?'

'I feel sorry for Bobby,' she said. 'I couldn't stand it if my parents talked about me like that.'

'She misses him,' Henry said charitably, although he was interested that Louise disapproved of Mrs Bawden's lack of reticence as much as he did.

'I think I'd like to travel,' Louise said. 'My father says that air travel will grow enormously in the next few years. I would like to be an air hostess.'

'It's Bobby's room I've got. I think I'd like him. I imagine myself talking to him. I ask him what he'd do in my circumstances.'

'And I suppose you get some sort of mysterious answer,' she said sarcastically. 'Do they have a gramophone in that house? I haven't heard a single decent record since we came away.'

'He doesn't say anything,' Henry said. 'But I see him winking at me. I don't know what it means. Do you ever try to figure out what your dreams mean?'

'Isn't there somewhere we can get lemonade or something?' she said peevishly. 'I'm parched.'

'We could buy some in the shop,' he said, 'but there isn't a café.'

'What a dump!'

'I don't think you like being in the country.'

'I don't like being with my parents. I'd rather be in the city with my friends. At least there's something to do.'

'Is your father coming back for us?'

'I doubt it. I think we're expected to walk.'

She was unsympathetic and, Henry decided, stupid. She was also unhappy. It was her unhappiness that made her interesting. Her dislikes, her petulant good looks, her tone of voice gave the impression she was festering on the edge of a bitter family insurrection. He wondered what his father had found appealing in his mother. Louise made him think that his mother might have been like her at that age, twenty years before, in the nineteen-thirties. All that would have been different was that other kinds of music, other friends were being missed.

They walked back slowly. When they reached Netherbank, Louise's father's car was parked outside with several others. Her parents were in the garden with the Bawdens. The clear light peculiar to Galloway seeped out of the hill and fields and met a great arc of early-evening light rising from the sea. Louise's parents were holding hands. Henry thought that if his parents had been there, too, he would have experienced a moment in which the significance of how people exist to each other was clear and unmistakable. People who mattered less clouded the issue. He pressed Louise's hand, but she pulled it away.

At mid-morning the following day, Louise's father said to Henry, 'Do you keep an address book? If you don't then you should. Everyone ought to. Say goodbye, you two,' he said, looking at Louise. Henry felt that Louise had given a glowing report of him to her parents, even though, in his company, she had been standoffish, pert, and sardonic. 'You should exchange addresses and keep in touch,' her father added. He was strangely open and affable.

Louise produced her address book, and Henry dictated his address to her.

'I think that's very nice,' said Mrs Bawden. 'I think it's so nice,' she said to Louise's mother, 'that young people should exchange addresses and keep in touch.'

Mr Bawden came in by the front door, surprised to find guests still in the house that late in the morning. He could hardly turn round and go out again and found himself in the company.

'They're exchanging addresses. Isn't that nice, John?' his wife said.

Mr Bawden smiled at his wife, with whose obsessive and candid garrulity he was very tenderly and very gently browned off.

'Write letters,' she urged Louise. 'Write letters and use the phone only when you have to. Letters are *much* nicer. You can keep letters, but you can't keep phone calls. Have you taken a note of Louise's address?' she asked Henry.

'My book's upstairs. I'll take it from the visitors' book.'

As Mrs Bawden went out of the front door with Louise's parents, Henry followed with Louise. 'We don't have to write,' he said.

'I'm not good at letters. If you write first, you'll have a wait for an answer.'

'I don't think I'll ever forget you,' he said, 'but I don't know if you'd understand why.' She looked at him, and laughed quietly, but she was complimented by a surprising remark that sounded serious and mature. Her wave from the departing car was curious and concerned.

Henry waved back, and then went upstairs to strip those beds that needed to be freshly made for the arrival of new guests in the late afternoon and early evening. He suspected that a time would come when his parents would regret the three months in which they had hived him off to the Bawdens. He thought about the crisis that his awakening independence would cause in their lives; still he doubted if when it arrived they would be able to trace it back to his weeks in that safe, homely, and respectable house, or to that quaint old couple who lived in daily expectation of a letter from their son Bobby, in whose room Henry slept.

GEORGINA HAMMICK

Grist

'All my love for you, Sweet*heart*,' he always said. He invariably said. 'All my love for *you*.' So when one night he didn't say it, Babe knew he didn't love her. She waited until next time – the next time his body relaxed on hers – to be sure. But it was only a formality. For by then, the space of two or three days, there were other signs. He stopped touching, fingering, you might say, with one long finger, her shoulder blades and her arms, in the way he did (as though he were drawing pictures on them). He stopped shovelling dog shit from the lawn. He didn't bring surprise whiskies to the ironing board. In their supermarket, he no longer vanished in Cereals so that he could materialize seconds later in the Pet Food aisle: 'Excuse me. You are the Most Beautiful Person in the World, and I claim my Lifetime of Happiness.' A talkative man at home, a mimic, a raconteur, he became silent. His silence grew and grew and filled the house. It was October, and the grass hidden by a weight of wet chestnut leaves, but he, usually the first to attack onerous tasks and the last to abandon them, seemed not to notice. When Babe got out the rake and barrow and started to pull the leaves into heaps, he put on his old garden coat, the garment of his she liked the best, and went for a walk by himself. (He, who'd never allowed her to take so much as a step without him!)

A horrible ten days passed, in which he pretended black was white and white black, in which he played the torturing husband in *Gaslight*, while Babe was stuck with the Ingrid Bergman role (but without Bergman's beauty: without the sure and certain hope of rescue before the credits). At the end of the ten days they had a show down. He turned everything they'd shared on its head. Then he cleared out his darkroom, packed his belongings and left.

When Babe felt able to, she drove over to Aunt's and told her about it. Not all of it, and not all at once. Babe was seeing a lot of Aunt just then. Aunt was dying, or, more accurately, living with Death. Death was giving Aunt a hard time. He followed her up and down stairs, and from sitting-room to kitchen; he had a sweetish, stomach-turning smell. He leant over her shoulder when she was playing patience or doing *The Times* crossword, he kept her awake all night. Aunt had no time for Death, and she didn't want to give him cottage room. Apart from her animals, she'd always lived alone. Depending on the strength of her pain, and on the weather, she fought or ignored him. Or she mocked him. Once, when she'd chucked Babe a cigarette and lit one for herself, she offered the packet over her shoulder. 'Go on,' she said, shaking the pack impatiently, 'take one. Feel free. It'll do you good. He's a humourless bugger,' she said to Babe.

Aunt smoked like a chimney, and the ceiling above the corner table where she did the crossword and played round after round of patience was dark brown, like the ceiling in a pub. Those who loved Aunt found this strange, it seemed out of keeping, because in all other respects Aunt was fastidious. Even with three cats and a dog, there was nothing messy about her tiny sitting room. Except for the overflowing ashtray, of course. Still, as Aunt said, you couldn't worry about getting cancer when you already had it.

Babe convinced herself that telling Aunt her troubles might, if not cheer Aunt up exactly, at least give her something else to think about (although Aunt was always interested in other people; always thinking about them). Aunt was upset by Babe's news. Upset for Babe and upset, in a way, for herself. And surprised. She hadn't seen it coming. Only the month before, Babe had brought his new book of photographs, just published, for her to see. 'That *is* nice,' Aunt had said, looking at the flyleaf on which he'd written 'Your Book, from Your Person' and underneath, his initial, enclosed by a heart. (Babe hadn't told Aunt then her worries about private, lovey-dovey inscriptions, the awful poignancy of them in secondhand bookshops: 'Binkie, Beloved Angel – All My Love for Always, Tiddles. Xmas, 1926.' 'For Clive – as fine a man as any girl could wish for – Denise.' But she had told *him*. And he'd smiled. And drawn a picture on her shoulder blades.) Aunt had sat at her table with the book of photographs, turning the pages slowly, studying each one. There were shots of Babe's grown up sons; views of her house and garden the photographer had called home. There was a whole section devoted to portraits of Babe. 'Is that really you?' Aunt had asked, peering. 'It's not the you I know. I'm not sure I want to see you in bed. Do I?' Aunt had said, of another, 'Though I must say your chins are tactfully lit.'

Aunt was upset by Babe's news. She'd grown fond of the photographer, as she always referred to him. He was interesting: he brought another world into her sitting room; he made her laugh. She was sorry she wouldn't be seeing him anymore. Having admitted that, having got it off her chest ('Look, I've got it off my chest,' she said, cough-laughing into her whisky glass) Aunt did everything she could to make Babe feel better and more positive.

'A nice fellow. Clever, certainly – though not at crosswords. Or was he?' Aunt said, 'A joke, ho ho. Generous? Oh yes. You're still hung about with his baubles, I see. Handsome, I won't deny. But a juvenile lead. Not man enough for you, Not mature enough. No. Let's have another whisky.'

They drank pints of whisky, interspersed, in Aunt's case, with painkillers and minute helpings of the creamed vegetable soup – usually carrot – those who loved Aunt took it in turns to make and bring her. Her fridge, and the box freezer above it, were full of the stuff, in little cling-filmed pots, jostling with the cod fillets Aunt fed to her cats. Every so often Aunt would leave the room, and patter, rice-paper thin, to the kitchen; and return with a fizzing glass of what looked like fruit salts which she'd set down beside her whisky on the table. Morphine every four hours; Solpadine (the fizzers) as a supplementary when the pain got unbearable; and all that whisky – why didn't it kill her?

'What did it mean, Aunt? Was none of it true? Was it a game?' Babe asked her. (Babe was still in shock; it had been so sudden.) 'Was it only a game?'

'Could be,' Aunt said. 'How do I know? Yes I do. I'm sure he meant it. I'm sure he thought he meant it, at the time. Anyway, don't you play games? You always beat me at Scrabble, I notice. I think you cheat. Don't expect me to play with you in future. Now, getting back to the crossword,' Aunt said, 'Harpo and Groucho won't do – sorry, chaps, no offence – so who were the others? Tell.'

'Chico?' Babe said. She was no good at the crossword (which Aunt regularly solved in ten minutes) but it was nice to be consulted. Aunt always consulted her. 'Then there was Karl, of course,' Babe said.

'*Karl*,' Aunt said, 'Karl. How could we forget him? Quite the funniest of the four.'

A day or so later, a postcard came to Babe's house, written all over in Aunt's famous blue felt tip: 'What say HARPO, GROUCHO, CHICO& ??? ZEPPO ??? So we don't need ~~Lenin~~ Karl (!) Come back SOON. XXX Aunt.'

Aunt's ceiling seemed to grow browner as they sat there, evening after evening, puffing away, swigging away, drunk as life peeresses. Soon snow pressed against the windows. Soon the lanes were full of it. Sometimes Babe had to stay the night, and she lay in the double bed in Aunt's spare room and listened to her cough, and heard her pad to the bathroom time and time again. The light under Aunt's door stayed on until morning.

'We laughed a lot,' Babe told Aunt. 'We were always laughing. Doubled up with it, often. Our cheekbones ached. We did have fun you know. We had a lot of fun.'

'I know you did,' Aunt said, 'I know you did. Laughter's good stuff. I approve of laughter. Tastes better than these fizzers, yuk,' Aunt said. 'A good howl can be therapeutic, too.'

Aunt didn't howl, so far as Babe knew, but she wasn't always able to laugh. Sometimes when Babe telephoned she was sharp. No, she wasn't all right, she was bloody awful. No, Babe couldn't come over. No, no, no. Not today and not tomorrow. Not any day this week.

Christmas cards began to appear on Aunt's chimneypiece. They didn't talk about them. Aunt was dreading Christmas. Not because she'd acknowledged it would be her last (she was making plans for her garden in the Spring: 'Shall I build that wall?' she kept asking, 'What do you think? Give me your views. Should I move the island bed? Should I widen the border?') but because she'd always hated festivals. Festivals were for children. Aunt had had affairs, successful and less successful, happy and not so happy; Aunt loved men and liked them, but she'd never married and she'd never had children. In the past, those who loved Aunt had begged her to spend Christmasses with them and their children (of whom she was varyingly fond) and sometimes she had, providing it didn't mean spending a night away from home. Aunt's old maroon Mini hadn't left its garage now for two weeks. She wouldn't be going anywhere of her own choosing. Her loved ones would be popping in, of course, on Christmas Eve and Christmas Day and Boxing Day; they'd all be bringing presents and booze and fags and carrot soup; Mr Timms from across the road would be coming midday to make up her fire; the doctor and the nurse would call. But there was no getting away from it: some of the time, a great deal of the time, and all of every night, Aunt was going to be – apart from the animals – alone over the Christmas holiday. With him.

Aunt still hadn't accepted her lodger. She was still taking swipes at him, still keeping him at a short arm's length. How, nobody knew. There was nothing of her. The nurse was 'dropping in' every day now, sometimes twice. The morphine was three-hourly. 'One of the advantages of teabags,' Aunt said, peering into the tea she invariably let go cold before drinking – or, increasingly, not drinking – 'is there's no risk of a tall dark stranger lurking in the cup. So there,' she said over her shoulder to him. 'Yah boo to you know who,' she said to Babe.

While Aunt was out of the room getting her fizzers, Babe peeked inside the Christmas cards on Aunt's chimneypiece. She'd thought there might be one from the photographer. He hadn't sent one to Babe, and she was trying not to think of last year, and the fun they'd had, the fun she'd thought they'd had – but Aunt, why no card for Aunt? He hadn't fallen out of love with *her*. Yet he had been fond of her, he'd said so, often. 'Aunt is a major human being,' he'd said, more than once, 'really major,' and Babe had agreed, even though, in her view, major was a word best left to military matters. No card for Aunt, no card for a really major human being, hurt. At a hurtful time, it was one of the things that hurt most. The photographer had had to write to Babe once or twice – brief, typewritten notes on practical subjects, things he'd left behind and so forth, and stamped with a second class stamp – but he'd never mentioned Aunt in these notes, he'd never asked how she was, he'd never sent her his love. Babe kept turning this over in her mind. She stayed awake pondering this. Was nothing good? Was nothing true? Was nothing real? Did nothing mean anything?

Babe couldn't talk to Aunt about this, of course, but there were other things that hurt, and she told Aunt about those.

'This exhibition is painful,' Babe said. 'All those portraits of me. More or less naked. Asleep. In bed. I'm even on the catalogue. And last week in the colour supplement there was one of *her* – his new person. Naked. In bed. We'll be beside each other, you realize, on the ICA walls. Bedfellows, so to speak. How can he do that, Aunt? Why doesn't it bother him? How can he do it so soon?'

'All grist to the photographer's mill,' Aunt said, trying to get a spoonful of carrot soup into her mouth; failing; giving up. 'Anything goes with artists. All must be sacrificed to Art – is photography Art? I'm never quite sure – nothing, no one, is safe. Anyway, they aren't portraits of you or of her, they're portraits of him. He's the subject of all his photographs, even those fuzzy landscapes. That's enough profundities for the time being. I'm not sure I like carrot soup all that much,' Aunt said, 'if I ever did. Could you pass the word round?'

'Do you think he's claimed a Lifetime of Happiness from her yet?' Babe asked Aunt over the telephone. Babe had rung Aunt to tell her Boris had come home. He'd been missing two days, unusual for him, and she'd been frantic. Aunt had been anxious about Boris too, and had rung before breakfast for news – which meant a painful descent of the stairs because she had no telephone by her bed. Those who loved Aunt were working on her to get one connected.

'I once knew a cat who was away eight months, and then just walked in,' Aunt had said before breakfast. 'What a relief,' she'd said a moment ago, when Babe had told her the glad tidings. 'Now we can all relax. Until next time.'

'Do you suppose he's sold her one?' Babe persisted. (She referred to the occasion the photographer had pretended to be a salesman, and had come to her door offering a Lifetime of Happiness on an easy instalment plan.)

'What's a lifetime?' Aunt said. She'd just 'celebrated', the one she loved best had helped her 'celebrate', her sixty-third birthday. 'What's happiness? Anyway, did *you* buy it? Did you say Ta ever so, and sign on the dotted line? I doubt it,' Aunt said. 'Not you. Too dull. Too commonplace. You'd never commit yourself to that.'

'Look, Babe,' Aunt said later, as they sat either side her fire, 'you must try and get a sense of proportion about all this. If Jim and Ted,' she said, referring to Babe's sometime husbands, 'merit a section, say, in Ted's case, and a chapter in Jim's, then the photographer is worth only a page or so in your book. I'm speaking figuratively of course. Only a page or so. Half a dozen, at the most. Remember that.' Aunt, after two stabs at it, swallowed her morphine mix, and made a face; and then chased the morphine with a swig of whisky. Just recently she'd given up all attempts at soup, no matter what variety, though she toyed with a forkful of scrambled egg, a spoonful of jelly.

'Incidentally,' Aunt said, 'how's your other book coming along? My book, I should say.' (For Babe had asked permission to dedicate the book she was writing – not writing; how could she? – to Aunt. Aunt had said yes. She was flattered, she said, not to say bowled over – though she did rather hope there wouldn't be any filth in it. No explicit bedroom scenes. Nothing a maiden aunt wouldn't be pleased to read. Babe wanted to finish the book in time for Aunt, but she knew she hadn't a hope.) 'Does the photographer appear in your book in some guise or other?' Aunt said. 'Do I? Are we both a bit of grist to your mill?'

After Aunt died, Babe said to the one Aunt loved best, the one who loved Aunt best, the one who had lost most: 'What shall we do without Aunt? What shall we do without Aunt's voice, and Aunt's laugh, and Aunt's famous blue felt tip and Aunt's postcards? How shall we manage without Aunt to tell things to?'

The one Aunt loved best and who loved Aunt best and who had lost most, the one to whom Aunt wrote not just postcards, but long letters (and had managed to do so from her hospice bed that last harrowing week) said: 'We must go on talking to Aunt. We must keep telling her things. Aunt was always interested. You can tell her about the awful men you meet, and the boring dinner parties you go to. You can tell her when Boris goes missing, and when he comes back. If you feel like cutting your throat, tell Aunt. Tell Aunt everything. Make Aunt laugh.'

Babe told Aunt. She told her funny things and sad things and boring things; and afterwards she imagined what Aunt's response would be.

For a time it worked. For a time, Babe could hear Aunt's laugh and Aunt's cough and Aunt's voice. For a time, she could see Aunt. She could see her lighting a cigarette, and padding about with a glass in her hand. She could see Aunt's hand in close-up, turning up the cards, flattening out the crossword page on the table in the corner.

Babe devised all manner of ruses to keep Aunt there, and for a time it worked, but it got harder. It got harder every day. She forgot to tell Aunt, or she couldn't face it, or she put it off. Then when she did, she couldn't always hear Aunt's reply. After two months had gone by, she couldn't see Aunt's face or Aunt's hands in the way she had; she couldn't hear Aunt's voice distinctly, she couldn't see Aunt clearly at all.

Then one day Babe went out to dinner, and when she got home, around midnight, and was having a nightcap, she told Aunt about her evening.

'Aunt,' Babe said, sitting in her easy chair, sipping her whisky, 'here's one for you. I've just been to a dinner party. Not good news, as per. No ashtrays for a start. When I asked for one, my hostess, laughing a v. false laugh, said: "You're not still a slave to that disgusting habit, surely? I thought no one in their right minds was silly enough to smoke these days," etc, etc. Then, would you believe, Bobby Gaskell – who knows the answer perfectly well – asked me why the photographer wasn't there. Had I left him at home, or something? "I got the impression he never left your side," he said. Great. Then we went in to dinner. The first course was soup. "Carrot soup!" the woman opposite me exclaimed. "My favourite! How clever of you, Annabel! Such a fiddle faddle to make, but worth it. One can never have too much carrot soup!"'

The story was supposed to make Aunt laugh, it was supposed to make Babe laugh, they were supposed to laugh together. But perhaps Babe had drunk too much claret before her nightcap; perhaps she hadn't told the story right; because though she waited in the quiet room in the quiet house, she couldn't hear anything. Babe went on sitting there, drawing on her cigarette, draining her whisky glass, listening; and eventually she thought she could hear Aunt, a long way off, saying ho ho *ho*. She thought she could hear Aunt laugh. Babe wanted to join in. She wanted to laugh with Aunt; for a moment she thought she was going to, but she didn't. She howled. She howled up the stairs and into the bathroom and while she was getting undressed and while she was taking her face off. She cried herself to sleep.

ADAM MARS-JONES

Baby Clutch

The half-dozen Walkmans that used to live on this ward, bought by a charity for the use of the patients, were walked off with in a matter of days. The next batch, if the charity decides to replace them, will have to be chained down, I expect, like books in a medieval library.

At least the television in my lover's room has a remote control; that's something. There used to be a remote for every room on the ward, but one or two have also gone walkies. Replacing them isn't a high medical priority, though perhaps it should be. Life on this ward can seem like one big game of musical chairs, as if death, being spoiled for choice, will come by preference to the person with no flowers by the bed, with no yoghurts stashed away in the communal fridge, the person whose TV has no remote control.

A television looms larger in a hospital room than it could ever do in someone's home. There are so few excuses not to watch it: visitors, coma. Once I came in and was shocked to see a nurse comforting my lover. She was bending over him with a tenderness that displaced me. My lover was sobbing and saying, 'Poor Damon.' It was a while before he could make himself understood. The nurse wasn't amused when she found out Damon was a young man on *Brookside* who'd just been killed.

She'd have been even less amused if she'd known it was the first episode of *Brookside* my lover had ever watched. He hadn't seen poor Damon alive. But I suppose it was the mother's grief having no actual content for him that let him share it so fully.

There's another television in the day-room, which even has a video recorder and a little shelf of tapes. The day-room also contains an eccentric library, *Ring of Bright Water* rubbing spines with a guide to non-nuclear defence and a fair selection of periodicals. My lover and I find ourselves

568

listing the self-descriptions we find least beguiling in the small ads of the gay press.

'Antibody-negative,' is his first contribution. He resents the assumption that good health is as intrinsic to some people as blue eyes are to others, or the condition, so common on these pages, of being 'considered attractive'.

It's my turn. 'Straight-appearing.'

'Healthy,' is second on my lover's list.

'Discreet.' What kind of boast is that, after all?

'Healthy.' My lover can't seem to get over this little preoccupation of his, so I shut myself up, without even mentioning *non-camp, looks younger, genuine* or *first-time advertiser.*

Deep down I'm pleased by the silliness of the small ads, pleased to find any evidence that there are still trivial sides to gay life. More than anything, I want there to be disco bunnies out there somewhere, still. But I expect even the disco bunnies are stoic philosophers these days, if only in their free time. What used to be the verdict on men who loved men – something about being locked in the nursery, wasn't it? There's nothing like being locked in a hospice to make the nursery look good.

We are having a respite between waves of my lover's visitors. Less than half-joking, I suggest that one of the nurses on the ward should function as a secretary, to make appointments and space the visitors out, to avoid these log-jams of well-wishers. I resent the brutal etiquette of hospital visiting, which means that a new visitor tapping hesitantly at the door instantly shuts down our intimacy. I try to be tactful, do some shopping in the area or talk to one of the other patients, but I doubt if I manage to be nice about it. Making myself scarce only encourages the other visitors to stay, to cling like leeches. I find the whole business of dealing with the visitors exhausting, and I'm not even ill.

Gently, taking care not to scare off his good fortune, my lover tells me that he is the only patient now on the ward who would benefit from a secretarial service like the one I am proposing. The other inmates have, at the most, two guests at a time. The difference may be one of character (my lover is agreed to be lovable); it may also turn out that the other patients have come back here so many times they have lost the ability to reassure their visitors, after which point the visits tend to dry up.

This is my lover's first major stay in hospital. Transfusions for anaemia don't count, even when he is there overnight. Everybody I come across refers to transfusions in the cheeriest possible terms ('just in for a top-up, are you?' is the standard phrase) though everybody also knows that transfusions can't go on for ever. That's an example of something I've been noticing recently, of how easy it is for people to rise above the fates of third parties.

I'm generally impatient with the visitors, but I make exceptions. I'm always glad to see Armchair, for instance. My lover knows so many Davids and so many Peters he gives them nicknames to tell them apart. Armchair is a Peter; other Peters are Poodle and Ragamuffin.

Armchair is, as advertised, reassuring and cosy, all the more comfortable for having one or two springs broken. Armchair is a fine piece of supportive furniture. When he phones the hospital to leave a message, he doesn't bother any more with his proper name; he just says Armchair. A nurse will come into the room and say, 'Someone called Armchair asks if it's all right to visit,' or, 'Armchair sends his love,' with a faint gathering of the eyebrows, until she's used to these messages.

Armchair is actually, in his way, my lover's deputy lover, or I suppose I mean my deputy. They met a month or two ago, while I was away, and they've slept together once or twice, but it's clear enough that Armchair would like More. It isn't a physical thing between them, exactly – my lover isn't awash with libido at the moment – but Armchair would like my lover to spend nights with him on a more permanent basis. Armchair would like to be a regular fixture at bedtime.

I wouldn't mind. It's my lover who's withdrawn a bit. But Armchair assumes I'm the problem and seems to think he's taking a huge risk by putting his hand on my lover's leg. My lover's arms are sore from the VenFlow, the little porthole the doctors keep open there, and his legs have taken over from them as the major pattable and squeezable parts. My lover's blood beneath the porthole, as we know, is full of intercepted messages of healing and distress.

Armchair looks at me with a colossal reproach. But can he really want to sit where I sit? Where I sit is sometimes behind my lover on the bed, wedging him as best I can during a retching fit, so that he is cushioned against the pain of his pleurisy. I hold on to his shoulders, which offer a reasonable guarantee of not hurting him. My medical encyclopaedia tells me that the pleura are 'richly supplied with pain fibres'. My lover has worked this out all by himself.

My lover threatens to give Armchair the yo-heave-ho. I tell him to be gentle, not to dismiss these comforting needs, and not only because Armchair too is richly supplied with pain fibres. I have my own stake in Armchair and Armchair's devotion. If Armchair stops being a fixture, I'll have to think long and hard about my own arrangements and my tender habit of spending as much time away from my lover as I possibly can. I do everything possible to look after him, short of being reliably there.

Whatever it is that ties us to each other, my lover and I, he is much too sensible to tug on it and see, once and for all, how much strain it will take. Much better to stay in doubt.

When I told my lover – he wasn't in hospital at the time – that I was thinking of spending half the week in Cambridge for a few months, he didn't say anything. It took him a while even to ask exactly how far away Cambridge is by train, and he seemed perfectly content when I said an hour and a bit – as if it counted as normal variation, in a relationship, for one party to keep himself an hour and a bit away from the other. He didn't ask if I had some grand plan, like writing a textbook, which I think I mentioned once a while back as one of my ambitions. There's something very stubborn about his refusal to call my bluff.

He knows, of course, that part-timers don't have a lot of say in their timetables (part-timers least of all), so if I've managed to fit all my teaching this term into Monday, Tuesday and Wednesday, then I've been setting it up for months.

In Cambridge I stay in the flat of an actress friend who has a short-term contract with the RSC. She's staying with friends in London herself, and all she wants is for the place to be looked after. She warned me that she might come back for the odd weekend, but she hasn't shown up yet and I've stopped expecting her, stopped cleaning madly on a Friday and filling the fridge with fine things. So all I have to do is keep the place reasonably clean, water the plants and listen from time to time to her accounts on the phone of Barbican Depression and of understudy runs that the RSC potentates never stir themselves from the Seventh Floor to see. Her flat is very near the station, which keeps my guilt to a minimum. It's not as if I was holed up in Arbury or somewhere. I'm only an hour and a bit away.

What I do here, mainly, is take driving lessons. In anyone else, learning to drive – especially after thirty – would be a move so sensible no one would notice it. With me it's different. It's a sign of a secret disorder, a malady in its own right, but only I know that.

I've always set my face against learning to drive. I've used public transport as if I'd taken a pledge to do nothing else and have always been careful not to accept lifts unless I have to. You get superstitious about favours when you can't pay them back, not in kind. If someone who has offered me a lift stays on soft drinks, I find myself refusing alcohol as if that was a helpful contribution to the evening. It's probably just irritating. I dare say people think, if he likes his drink so little he'd make a handy chauffeur, why doesn't he get his bloody licence?

I seem to have based a fair bit of my character around not being a driver. Perhaps that's why I was so disorientated when I walked through the door of the driving school that first time. It felt like learning to swim, and this the deep end. But in all fairness, the air in there would give anyone's lungs pause. All the instructors smoke away at their desks when they're on phone-duty or doing paperwork, and there's a back room that's even smokier, with a sink and a dartboard and a little fridge, not to mention a tiny microwave and a miniature snooker table.

I must say I admire the way the driving school draws a new pupil smoothly into apprenticeship. I was given a time for a two-hour consultation with an instructor, who would suggest a test date. I was certainly impressed, and mainly with myself, the competent me they were hypothesizing so suavely. It'll take more than suavity to convince me that I'm viable as a driver, but I signed up for my session of consultation just the same, rabbit paralysed by the headlights, unable to disobey the order to climb into the driving seat.

Now that I'm familiar with the place, I can't help thinking that BSM stands for British School of Macho. There's only one woman in the place, who does paperwork the whole time and smiles at me with a forlorn sweetness. The rest of the staff, I imagine, conduct their job interviews in the pub, brusquely screening out non-drinkers, non-smokers, non-eaters of meat, non-players of pool, non-tellers of jokes. I imagine them rolling back with the candidate to the driving school after closing time for some cans of Special Brew, and I imagine them huddled outside the lavatory with their fingers to their lips, when he goes to relieve himself, listening for the clinching chuckle when he sees the HIGH FIRST TIME PASS RATE sign stuck up inside the lid. I imagine them giving each other the thumbs-up sign when they hear it. And only then, after the candidate emerges from the lavatory, do I imagine them asking, 'By the way . . . can you drive?'

But somehow Keith, my instructor, slipped through their net. He does all the manly things, but he isn't a man in their sense, not at all. He's not a bachelor, but he's not by a long way a family man either, and he moved out of a perfectly nice house to live in a field.

He's a pleasantly runty fellow, brought up in a Barnardo's Home, and he still has a boyish spryness although he's in his late forties. To get from the driving school to the car, or back again at the end of the lesson, he bolts across Bridge Street, whatever the traffic's like, nipping through the smallest gaps between vehicles.

We set off in the driving school's sturdy Metro. It's white but very dirty, so someone has been able to trace the words ALSO AVAILABLE IN WHITE in dust on the coachwork. The side mirrors are both cracked, and one is even crazed. I promise myself that I'll reward the car, if and when I finally pass, and not the examiner as is customary. I'll splash out on some replacement fixtures.

Towards Keith I have absurdly mixed feelings. I trust him blindly, and have for him the sort of disproportionately solid affection that goes with the analyst's couch more often than the steering-wheel. I admire his self-control. It's not that he doesn't get irritated – when I don't lose enough speed, for instance, approaching a roundabout – but he calms down right away. It's as if he was offering me an example, in terms of temperament, of the use of the gearbox, and how to lose momentum as efficiently as possible. When I stall, he says, 'Never mind, re-start,' without any hint that he's disappointed in me. As with any indulgent parental figure, I have an urge to test his patience to the limit, to make sure that he cares underneath it all.

Once the car ran out of petrol on Queens Road, but all I could think of when I lost power was that Keith had withdrawn his faith in me, and was overruling my accelerator with the brake on the passenger side. 'Are you braking?' I cried, and he said, 'No, I'm scratching my arse as a matter of fact,' before he realized I wasn't messing him about. We weren't far from the driving school, but he's so little of a walker that he insisted on staying put. We sat there, while his eyes flickered between the windscreen and his multiple mirrors, waiting for one of the other school cars to come by and give him a lift to the petrol station. No one came, and at last, with the light dying, we had to walk after all. But I was so pleased not to have made the mistake myself that I let slip a precious opportunity for mockery – which is pretty much Keith's natural language – and I didn't tease him at all. It was nice to be the one doing the forgiving.

Alongside the exaggerated trust I feel a sharp submerged resentment towards Keith and a desire to do something atrocious, like run someone over on a crossing, while he's taking responsibility for me. In reality, he would put the brake on in a second, but I imagine myself unfastening my seat-belt after the impact and walking away, never traced for some reason though the driving school has my details, and leaving Keith to deal with the consequences.

Sometimes he sets out to provoke me, as if he wanted to bring the crisis on. He murmurs, 'Closer, son, just a little closer, and you're mine,' when a child is playing too close to the road, and remarks on the economic advantage to parents of having a child wiped out sooner rather than later, before too much money has been spent on it. But I know this is just his style of cussedness, the same style that makes him answer 'no' in the back room of the driving school to the question, 'Got a light, Keith?' even when he's busy smoking away. It seems to be his solution, as a member of the artificial tribe of driving instructors, to the problem of how to be popular, without being despised for wanting to be liked.

Keith doesn't ask why I want to learn to drive. He takes it for granted, like everybody else, that I should, though in that case he should at least be curious about why it's taken me so long to get round to it. Even if he asked, I don't think I'd tell him my own theory on the subject: that it's to do with control, and also with risk. Anything that gives me the feeling of control is obviously going to come in handy at the moment, whether or not it's a sort of control that I have historically had any use for, but I think I'm also giving myself an education in risk. Being a pedestrian, being a passenger, isn't so very safe – and rattling around on a bicycle, as I do, isn't safe at all – but behind the wheel of a car you have a different relationship with the risks that you take.

I try not to keep secrets from my lover, but I don't talk a lot about what I do in Cambridge. I'm superstitious about that. I seem to think that if I talk to him more than vaguely about Cambridge, the seal will be broken and I'll start talking about him to the people I meet in Cambridge. For the whole cock-eyed arrangement to work, I need to think of the railway line from London to Cambridge as an elaborate valve, which allows me to pass from one place to another but strips me each time of my mental luggage and preoccupations.

The ward is full of its own life, and I don't think my silence shows. The patients tend to keep their doors open, so as to make the most of whatever passes along the corridors. The staff don't tell you when someone has died, but at least if your door is open someone comes along and says, with an apologetic smile, 'Let's just close this for a moment.' I expect that other people do what I do and peek out of the window in the door, which has horizontal bars of frosting so that I can't be seen, with any luck. I try to work out, from how long it takes for the trolley to make its collection, who it is that's inside it.

I'm sure I'm not the only one making calculations, though it's not a subject that comes up a great deal in conversation at the regular Tuesday tea parties. Then the focus of attention tends to be the chocolate cake brought in every week by an ex-patient, the offering that is richest in symbolism as well as in calories, which somehow always gets finished. Even my lover puts in his few bites' worth.

There's just one man on the ward who's in a different category, a private patient who's recovering from a heart attack in a room that is costing his firm, or BUPA, £210 a day, not including the phone. He takes only short walks as yet, but sooner or later he'll come to the tea party or twig in some other way to what the problem is with everyone else in the ward. Once he asked my lover why he thought he had come down with this particularly nasty pneumonia. My lover just scratched his head, as if it had never occurred to him to wonder. But it's only a matter of time before the cardiac patient or his wife see two men holding hands. They'll be on that expensive telephone to BUPA right away, demanding to know why someone with a bad heart but otherwise good character has been sent to spend his convalescence in Sodom.

The day-room plays host to other events, as well as the tea parties. There are the art classes and the Wednesday morning discussion groups. Often there's someone over by the window on these occasions, making faces and emitting harsh sighs, but if so it's just a patient strapped into the emetic aqualung of pentamidine, grimacing with controlled disgust as he inhales through a mask filled with bitter gas. Sometimes it's even a discharged patient, coming back for a few lungfuls of fly-killer to keep the bugs at bay.

Through the open doors, at various times of the week, come the visitors who aren't quite friends. There's a manicurist, for one, who asks her clients, when she's finished, if they'd like a dab of nail polish. She quietens any protest by saying brightly, 'Some does and some doesn't, so I always ask.' The first time she offered her services to my lover, she'd broken her wrist and had her arm in a sling. She couldn't work, obviously, so what she was really offering was manicure counselling, rather than manicure as such. My lover said, to comfort her, 'I bite my nails anyway,' and she said, to comfort him, 'Well, you do it very well.'

An aromatherapist comes round from time to time to rub essential oils into people. She doesn't rub very hard, and my lover longs for a real massage, but it isn't easy telling her to be merciless. His pentamidine drip has brought his blood pressure right down, and it's easy to see how she might get the idea he should be handled with care – seeing he needs to be helped if he wants to go as far as the lavatory, which is three steps away. The aromatherapist takes away the pillows and blankets, and gets my lover to lie face down, with his feet where his head usually goes.

I get a shock every time I visit my lover after she has laid her too-gentle hands on him. It's as if there was some new symptom that could spin him bodily round, from end to end and top to bottom, casting him down passive and aromatic, his eyes half-closed, on the crumpled sheets.

In the evenings, there are volunteers manning the hot-drinks trolley. They're noticeably more generous with the tea and the coffee than the domestics who push the trolley during the day, who can make visitors feel about as welcome as bedsores. With the evening trolley-pushers, I don't have to pretend that it's my lover who wants the drink if it's me who does really, and we don't scruple to ask for two if we're in the mood. The evening staff don't look right through me if I sit up on the bed next to my lover in my usual slightly infantile posture, facing the other way down the bed and hugging his big feet. This is the arrangement we've evolved now that so much of him is sore that a hug calls for as much careful docking as a refuelling in deep space. For him to see my face has become proportionally more important, as our bodies have had their expressiveness so much restricted.

My lover's soreness is dying down; I can tell because the fidgeting has gone out of his feet. I ask, in an interviewer's tenderly wheedling voice, 'What strikes you most about the whole terrible situation?'

Obligingly he answers, 'It brings out the best in people. And the worst.'

'What, you mean the best *and* the worst?'

'Both. The two.'

He's getting drowsy from the drugs he's on, as the chemical invasions of his body get the better of the surgical ones.

There's a hesitant knock on the door, and when I say to come in, this evening's volunteer stands in the doorway and asks what we want in the way of tea and coffee. I see him flinch when he spots the bag of blood on its wheeled stand, and the tube going into my lover's arm. But I notice too a quickening of interest in my lover, in the few seconds before our volunteer leaves the room to get the drinks from the trolley. Even before my lover murmurs, 'Isn't he gorgeous?' I have realized that the volunteer is very much my lover's type. He bears a passing resemblance to Joy Adamson's husband in the film of *Born Free*, a furry-faced scoutmaster on safari.

But now the volunteer returns with the teas and keeps his eyes turned down from the blood-drip. My lover has noticed his aversion and asks kindly, 'Does the blood bother you?'

'A bit.'

'Just a bit?'

'A lot.' Finally he admits that he sometimes feels faint. My lover looks affectionately at the sump of blood suspended above his arm and drawls, from the drastic languor of his medication, 'Just think of it as a big plastic kidney.' The volunteer resists the cue to look at the blood-bag, with the result that he continues to look deeply into my lover's eyes.

My lover pats the side of the bed. 'Do you have a moment to sit down?' I move over so that my lover can move his legs out of the volunteer's way, but my lover leaves his legs where they are, so the volunteer must make contact or else perch on the very edge of the bed.

The volunteer sits quiet for a moment, then clears his throat. 'Do you mind if I ask you a question?' he asks.

'Feel free,' my lover says. 'You're the guest.'

'Well, you're having a transfusion, and what I can never work out is, what happens to the blood you have extra, when you get someone else's on top of your own?'

'Yes, I used to wonder about that,' admits my lover. 'What happens is, they put another tube in your big toe, and drain the old blood out of there.' He gives the sheet a tug to loosen it from the bottom of the bed. 'Do you want a look?'

For the moment, the volunteer wants to go on looking at my lover's face.

'Don't you think you should?' my lover goes on. 'Shouldn't you try to overcome this silly fear of yours, if you're going to do the sort of work you're doing? Wouldn't that be the responsible thing?'

Mesmerized, the volunteer looks down at my lover's foot under the sheet. My lover pulls the sheet away from his foot. The big toe is pink and normal-looking. My lover looks startled and says, 'Oh, *Christ*, it must have come out, *now* we're in trouble, can you see it anywhere?' The volunteer casts his eyes desperately this way and that.

For some time I have been sending my lover signals of mild reproach about the wind-up job that is giving him so much pleasure; finally he gives in to them. He drapes the sheet over his feet again and says, 'Actually, since you ask, I pee away the surplus.' He smiles at the volunteer, who smiles back, at first incredulously and then with wonder at my lover's healthy sense of mischief.

My lover asks him please to tuck in the sheet around his feet, since it seems to have come adrift.

When the volunteer has gone at last, my lover says again, 'Isn't he gorgeous?' He looks thoughtful. 'But he can't be gay. That's never a gay beard. It's too overgrown.'

'I'm afraid you're right.'

'And you saw those corduroys.'

'Cords are a bad sign. Still . . .'

My lover sighs. 'At least he's not mutton dressed as lamb. He's mutton all right. But he has definite mutton appeal.' It sounds like an advert for stock cubes. 'He just can't be gay, that's all.'

My lover has a fantasy about living in the country with a vet who drives a half-timbered Morris Traveller, and this stranger comes close enough to set it off. A half-timbered Morris Traveller is apparently a car which even animals recognize as the appropriate vehicle for a person who will take care of them, so that they quieten down, even if their injuries are severe – or so my lover says – when they hear its engine note, some time before the car comes into view.

There is something I recognize as authentic in this fantasy of my lover's. It has about it the whiff of self-oppression, which we are as quick to recognize in each other as other couples, I imagine, are at spotting egg-stains on ties or lipstick on collars. The imaginary vet is classified by fantasy as virile and caring, in a way no man could be who loved other men, while my lover enters the picture as a damaged animal, a creature who can't hope to be treated as an equal but who accepts subordinate status, the price of tenderness.

All the same, the volunteer pays a number of return visits. He goes on holiday to Malta for a week and phones the hospital twice, so that the cordless phone – a treat that testifies to the volunteer's special status – is delivered to my lover's room, its aerial extended and gleaming. My lover has exercised once again his knack for being loved. The volunteer out of *Born Free*, meanwhile, is awarded a mark of privilege, a nickname: the Vet. Now my conversations with my lover have an extra layer of mysteriousness to nurses who hear me asking him if he's seen the Vet today. The Vet turns out to be older than he looks, in his mid-forties, so that he could almost be my lover's father. There's certainly something fatherly about the Vet when he sits on the bed and plays absent-mindedly with the hairs on my lover's leg. Sitting there, he might indeed be a father, trying to put off explaining the facts of life to an adolescent son, or a public-school housemaster explaining the meaning of confirmation.

One day I give my lover a bath; feeling clean, after all, is the nearest that people on this ward can come to feeling well. My lover is dizzy and unsteady on his feet, so I use a wheelchair to carry him back along the corridor to his room. I return the wheelchair to the bathroom right away, like a good boy, and the Vet must have arrived just while I was down the corridor, because when I come back I see that the door is closed. I look through the window and see the Vet perched on the bed, conducting his usual earnest conversation with my lover's leg. So I kill time doing a tour of the ward.

I offer to buy the patient in the room next to my lover's some of the ice-lollies he sucks when his mouth flares up, but he's well supplied at the moment, and his thrush doesn't even seem too bad. In fact he's unusually perky altogether. It was his birthday last week, and his ex-lover continued the custom they'd had by bringing him one practical present (a toasted-sandwich-maker) and one pampering present: a big bottle of essence of violets from Jermyn Street. I'm mean enough, by the way, to think that ex-lovers can afford to be generous when they visit; I look on them the way lifers in a prison must look on youngsters who are in for a short sharp shock.

The sandwich-maker was taken home, and the essence bottle was wrapped in a flannel and put by the basin, where a cleaner smashed it two days later. She burst into tears, and he told her not to worry about it, but in fact he wants to be reimbursed, and if the hospital doesn't have the relevant insurance he wants it taken out of the cleaner's wages. So now he's unpopular with the staff, but he's sticking to his guns. If dirty looks were radiotherapy he'd have lost a lot of hair by now, but the sense of defending a principle has given his health a definite boost.

When I return to my lover's room and peep through the window, the conversation shows no sign of stopping, so I leave them to it and go back to his neighbour's room, where the basin still smells like a florist's. There was something I glimpsed on the window sill a minute ago that puzzled me, and I summon up the nerve to ask about it.

It's a soft toy in the shape of a fat scheming cat, but a cat that seems to have two tiny hoops of wire fixed high on its stomach.

'That's my hospital Garfield,' explains the neighbour with a little embarrassment. 'I only use it in hospital.'

'No, I don't mean that,' I say, 'I mean, what are those?' I point at the little hoops.

He blushes outright and shyly opens his pyjama jacket. 'What you really mean is, what are these?'

His nipples have little inserted hoops of their own, and the hospital Garfield is indeed, as I thought incredulously at first glance, a soft toy with an erotic piercing.

My lover's neighbour nods at his customized toy. 'The nurses have this great sense of humour,' he says. 'They did that while I was out.'

I am slow to take in the information he is giving me. It is a few moments before I realize that by 'out' he means not just *socially unavailable* but *profoundly unconscious*.

I keep away from my lover as long as I plausibly can. Purely from a medical point of view, flirtation is likely to have a beneficial effect on his low blood pressure. A little teasing romance may actually make him stronger at the knees.

From my own point of view I feel not jealousy, but a definite tremor of worry. My lover's instinct for help is profound and I trust it. If he thinks I'm capable, then I am. But if he enlists the Vet, I lose confidence. It's not that I don't want to share the load. I'd love to. But if my lover is hedging his bets, then I suddenly fear that he has good reason. Perhaps he now realizes I will crack up or get ill myself. My equilibrium falters, and the glands of selfish worry, that I have been suppressing for the duration, flare up at once and all together.

On subsequent visits, the Vet consolidates his burly charisma in my lover's eyes by turning out to own the right cars. He doesn't drive a Morris Traveller as such – that would be a little bit spooky. But he does buy glamorous or gloriously dowdy cars cheap in auctions, and garages them with friends or in fields when they need a little more work than he can do, handy though he is. He drives an Alfa that costs him more in insurance every year than he paid in the first place. One of these days he knows that the police will pull him over and ask him ever so nicely not to wear it in public again. Waiting in various locations for a little more cash or an elusive spare part are a Bentley, an Aston Martin and a Wolseley.

My lover has a passion for fast and/or classic cars. Before I knew him he owned an MG – he put an old phone in it, in fact, the kind you crank, and used to mime conversations at traffic-lights in summer, with the top down. This was before the days of car phones, let alone the days of commercially made imitation car phones – which I think makes it all right.

I don't follow my lover's car conversations with the Vet. I don't begin to understand what makes one car boxy but lovable, and another one nippy but a little Japanese about the hips.

There must be something about cars that makes people use a different register, almost a different language. Keith, my instructor, uses a whole mysterious vocabulary of phrases, so that I had to learn to understand his language, if not actually to speak Instructor, before I could really begin learning to drive. He mutters, 'Baby clutch . . . *baby* clutch,' when he wants me to be subtle with my left foot, and, 'Double gas . . . TREBLE gas,' when he wants me to be brash with my right. When I'm fumbling between gears he prompts me ('then three . . . then two'), and when I've finally got it right and married speed to ratio, he says with mild put-on surprise, 'It works!' or else he gives a sort of jeer of approval ('Yeeeeah!'). If I don't need prompting for a minute or so, he'll murmur, 'Looking good' or, 'I'm almost impressed.' More often he gets me to slow down, with a warning 'Cool it,' or to speed up – for which he mutters, 'It's not happening' and makes gestures with his hands, sweeping them forwards.

I used to interpret the phrase and the gesture the wrong way, as if what Keith wanted was for the road to be taken away from in front of him, but I suppose that was just my old reluctance surfacing again in the lightest of disguises. I've got it worked out now and give the accelerator a squeeze. If I've been slow to understand him and to deliver the speed he requires, Keith gets more direct. The phrases for this are 'Let's piss off out of here' or 'Give it a bit of poke.'

If I take my time before changing up, he goes 'mmmm', with a sharp intonation that says what-are-you-waiting-for? If I'm not properly positioned in my lane, he makes a flick of the hand to guide me in the right direction. Often, when I've misjudged a manoeuvre or underestimated a hazard, he says, with a quiet satisfaction, '*Not* a good gear.' To remind me of the mirror he sometimes taps it with his forefinger or mutters – there seems no obvious reason for his choice of language – '*Spiegel*'.

I start to relax in the lesson at the point where Keith lights up his first cigarette. I'm sure he's got enough of a craving that he'd light up sooner or later, whatever sort of idiot I was being, but I become more competent knowing he's felt able to focus his attention on the cigarette packet and the matches for a few seconds. Unless of course it's my terrible driving that makes the comfort of a cigarette so hugely attractive.

Keith opens the window a crack and leans forward to adjust the heating. I take every move he makes as a looming comment on my driving, so I'm absurdly relieved when he's only making adjustments to the car's interior climate. Then Keith talks. It's as if he's trying to simulate the distractions of traffic, when we're on a clear road. There's nothing I find harder than giving talking a low priority; left to my instincts, I'd rather be attentive in the conversation than safe on the road. It's not that I get flustered when he's really trying to put me off my stride – like the time he asked, 'When you going to get married, then?' after he had warned me he was about to request an emergency stop, and before he actually smacked the dashboard to give me my cue. That question doesn't faze me, though I gather it's pretty much guaranteed to make the young men botch their manoeuvre. But I'm interested in Keith and what he has to say, and when he stops talking because there's tricky work ahead I can't wait to get the hazards behind me, whatever they are, and go back to what he's saying.

Sometimes Keith talks about nothing, anything, the daily papers, and how he's going to give up the *Sun* when they stop running their Bingo game – unless of course they announce another. He wrote a letter to the *Sun*'s Grouse of the Week column just recently, which they didn't print, complaining about a doctor in the news who'd overturned the car giving his daughter a driving lesson in the grounds of his house. It was taking a living away from driving instructors, that was Keith's Grouse, and served the doctor right, and what would *he* think if people started doing operations on each other in their kitchens?

Sometimes he talks about his history, about Barnardo's and the army and home-ownership.

'I had a lovely house in an acre, lovely car, two-car garage, garden with a rockery and floodlights – spent a grand on landscaping – fruit trees, currant bushes, but it wasn't what I wanted, none of it. I think I worked that out before I finished laying the rockery, but I still installed those bloody floodlights.'

He moved out from the house he shared with Sue and took up with

Olga. Olga is the battered mobile home where he lives, parked in a muddy field a few miles out of town. She's a hulk, but he seems well set up there, in his way. We went out there once, on a lesson; I needed practice, apparently, manoeuvring in muddy conditions, and Keith certainly needed a Calor Gas container picked up and taken for refilling. We had a cup of tea in Olga while we were at it, though his eyes narrowed with distrust at the idea that anyone could drink it without sugar. He takes four spoonfuls and gives the tea-bag a good drubbing with the spoon, as if the point of the procedure was not to infuse a drink but actually to wash the tea-bag free of stains.

Laundry is one of the few services that he's not found a way of doing for himself. He does any telephoning he needs at the driving school, and even brings his electric razor in to work for recharging with BSM current. He leaves the right change for milk and newspapers in Olga's mighty glove compartment and has them delivered right into her cab. But laundry is one thing that's beyond him and so he pops over to Sue's every week or so (and takes a bath while he's at it). He has a 'leg-over' while he's there, but to hear him talk about it, that leg-over isn't the linchpin of the arrangement. I imagine Sue in front of her mirror on one of the evenings Keith is expected – he doesn't always turn up, but he knows how to keep just enough on the right side of her that she doesn't come to find him, her horn sounding furiously all the way from the main road as her car crawls into the treacherous field where Olga sits. I imagine her powdering her face and wondering whether she should try some new perfume. She doesn't know it's Ariel that arouses Keith's senses, not Chanel.

I need a pee after my cup of tea. Keith shows me the lavatory, which is chemical and tucked away in a low cupboard. Keith can stand up in most parts of Olga, but there's nowhere that the roof's high enough to give my head clearance. To use the lavatory, I have to kneel and face forward. Keith gives me a little privacy by going to the cab, where he hasn't bothered to put up cork tiling. He presses a hand to the roof and says, 'Some mornings the condensation's unbelievable in here. It's like Niagara bastard Falls.'

Only when I'm finished with my rather awkward pee does he mention that personally, *personally*, speaking for himself, he finds it more convenient to piss in a bottle and then pour it away, though of course everybody's different, aren't they? There's a coffee jar, scrupulously clean and free of labels, tucked away at the side of the lavatory, which I suspect is his chosen bottle. I wish I'd spotted it earlier, though I doubt if I'd have had the nerve to use it.

Before we leave, Keith shows me his photo album. It's like anybody's photo album – anybody who wasn't thought worthy of a photograph before he joined the army, who built a raft in Malaya based on what people built in films when they were marooned, who had four children by two wives before there was ever a Sue, who kept sheep and chickens for a while in Devon – except that nothing's in order. It's the sort of album where each thick page has a thick sheet of Cellophane to hold the pictures down, no need of photo corners, and Keith seems to like keeping even the past provisional. Perhaps on non-bath evenings he amuses himself by rearranging the photographs, shuffling the blurred sheep and the precise soldiers, the blurred children. In every picture that shows Keith, he is pointing out of the frame, insisting that the real subject is out there somewhere, refusing to be the focus of the composition.

On the way back to town, he gets me to do some emergency stops. If it's at all possible, he synchronizes them with young women walking alone. He smacks the dashboard just before we pass. The woman usually glares at us as we stop dead right next to her and then she relaxes into a pitying half-smile when she sees it's only a learner driver. No real threat. Then her face goes half-way back to its original expression, when she sees that Keith is staring at her with a defiant hunger. At times like this, I am able to look at Keith outside the terms of our sealed-in little relationship, outside its flux of resentment and dependence, and he seems, I must admit, like a pretty ordinary little shit.

Even when I have passed my test and put Keith behind me, I can't imagine that I'll do a lot of driving. Public transport is enough to get me to the hospital, though I sometimes use my bicycle on a Sunday, partly for the exercise and partly to dramatize my errand, if I'm bringing something for my lover. On the bicycle I can feel like a courier whose package will make a difference to the person waiting for it.

My lover keeps the television on all the time, just turning up the sound when there's something he actually wants to watch. At the moment, a weatherman is standing in front of two maps of the country. I expect they represent the weather tonight and tomorrow. But the weatherman, if he wanted, could also show us the weather of our two healths. His vocabulary of symbols is meagre but it will stretch. My map will be full of smiling suns and light refreshing breezes, a fantasy of summer; my lover's map a nightmare winter, chock-a-block with gales and freezing showers. My lover looks without interest at the screen as it changes. Some of his calm is really exhaustion, but some of his calm is really calm. It helps that he's still in touch socially with the few people he exposed to risk. With a bravery that to me seems insane, they've all taken the test, and they all tested negative.

He keeps a list of his sexual partners, does my lover, though it's not so detailed he could use it to track people down if he'd lost touch. I only found out about it recently. It's at the back of his diary, but then I only found out about the diary recently. Suddenly there was this battered book on the bed, and my lover was saying, oh yes, he always used to keep a diary, he'd just got out of the habit. He'd just now come across it and was taking a look.

Even my lover had to admit, after a little reading, that his diary-keeping had never been regular; he wrote in his diary only when a relationship was on the rocks. It took tears to get the words flowing and then he would write what were in effect letters to his lovers, full of sombre accusations and depressive spite. He even read me a detailed account of my own selfishness. This was his version of a crisis of which I have no version, since I survived it by not noticing.

I asked if I could look at the diary, and he passed it across. At the back of the book there was a list of numbers and names, starting with '1. John in Toyota Corolla.' Number two was Mark, and number three was Mark and Ben. The list went into the low forties before it met a scrawl, twice underlined: *'Enough of this rubbish.'* The list-making impulse had started to falter even before then. Two numbers in the thirties were entered as 'What was the name?' and 'Macho Letdown'.

My lover gave me a beady look as I read his diary and asked, 'Are you the sort of person who reads people's diaries?'

I didn't know there was any other sort of person, but I avoided the question by holding the book up and waving it. 'The evidence against me is strong.'

'I mean, when the owner's not around?'

'Only if I can find it.' I've only made a couple of searches since then – as much to see if he was bothered enough to hide it as because I'm curious – and I haven't found it, so I suppose the answer to the question is, Yes, he was bothered enough.

The limitations on my lover's future make his past the more precious, and I find that I'm a bit bothered, after all, that I don't know where his diary is.

I bring my lover hot thick soups, in a big old-fashioned vacuum flask with a wide neck. Conventional soups bear the same relationship to my soup as the sun bears to those collapsed stars whose every speck outweighs it. An oxtail is a wispy thing compared to what I make of it with the strong rendering of my pressure cooker. My soups are concentrated expressions of the will to nourish.

But tonight my lover is not to be nourished. 'You know I hate innards,' he says, pushing the plate of soup away almost as soon as I've poured it.

I'm ashamed that I don't know my lover's preferences as well as I should, but I'm also offended and I protest. 'Oxtail isn't innards!'

'It's as good as.'

'Oxtail couldn't be further from innards. Be reasonable. If cows kept their tails on the inside how could they deal with flies?'

Even as I say this, I realize that talk of flies is among the poorer triggers of appetite. The ward is full of tiny insects, as it happens, sustained out of season by the warmth and the abundance of fruit.

Even unmolested, the fruit would look incongruous beside the stack of moulded cardboard vomit-bowls on my lover's bedside table. They look, with their broad rims turned down at one side, like jaunty little hats, as if they were there for use in a big dance production number. We've tried to bring them into our private world by referring to them as 'Berkeleys' or 'Astaires', but the name that has stuck, *vomit-hats*, leaves them uncomfortably real. These homely objects resist the final push into euphemism.

Our little tussle over the soup reminds me of how poorly matched we are in habits and appetites. We don't even have the same taste in bread. I like wholemeal, but his stomach can deal most easily with inflated plastic white, and naturally I give way to him. All the same, I'd have thought somebody could make a killing out of couples like us, by producing a hybrid loaf that combined the two, all the goodness and bran sucked out of each alternate slice and shunted into the next one.

In this way among others, we don't present a united front. Our team-work seems ragged, while the illness we're fighting is ruthlessly co-ordinated. But then it's only recently, since he came into hospital in fact, that I have thought of him, truly, as my lover.

Before then I compared him in my mind – often very flatteringly, it's true – with other men past or possible. But now I compare him only with the world as it will be when he is subtracted from it, not with rival beds but with his bed, empty. That is what locks the phrase in place: my lover.

My lover and I never used pet names or endearments before his first visit to hospital, but how stupid it sounds when I say so. It's like saying *I never had much use for pot plants and cushions before I came to live in this condemned cell.* Except that the unstoppable progress of medical science has taken our condemned cell and turned it into a whole suite of con-demned cells.

Our endearment system is based round the core-word *pie*, derived from the phrase *sweetie-pie* but given its independence in a whole series of verbal caresses. The turning-point in its history was my buying an Easter egg with the message piped on it, 'WITH LOVE TO MY SWEETIE PIE'. This was at a time when a raised patch on the roof of my lover's mouth had been diagnosed as a cancer, a separate sentence on his mouth that his tongue must read and remember every time it makes contact, and I wanted to go to meet him armed with more than a hug. It comforted me to watch the woman at Thorntons in Cambridge – where a free message in icing was a seasonal offer – at work on the egg with her expert nozzle of fon-dant and her smile of romantic voyeurism. The smile would have hardened on her lips like painted sugar if she knew she was decorating a sweet to take the bitterness out of a malignancy.

Pie was the word that stuck, the last part of the inscribed egg that my lover would have eaten, I'm sure, if he hadn't kept the whole thing intact, as a totem of chocolate. *Pie* stuck to a number of phrases, private ones at first and then sentences of ordinary conversation, by slip of tongue to start with and afterwards defiantly, mixing embarrassment and the refusal to be embarrassed. *Pie* functions as pet name (*dear one*), as interrogative (*are you awake?*), as exclamation (*how could you say such a thing!*).

So near have I approached to that which I vowed I would never use, the edged endearment of the grown-up, the *darling* of protest if not yet the *darling* of bitter reproach.

Pie is allied by assonance with *my* (*my Pie*), by alliteration with expressive adjectives: *poor Pie, precious Pie, pretty Pie.*

Occasionally it appears in phrases of estrangement, though its use acts as a guarantee that estrangement is reversible: *crusty Pie, poison Pie, piranha Pie.*

Written down and rationalized as an irrational number – π – it loses a little of its sugar. Transposed into fake Italian *mio Pio* – it acquires a register almost operatic. As a double diminutive – as *pielet* or *pilot* – it brings into play a fresh set of overtones.

Perhaps endearment, verbal sweetness so concentrated nothing else can survive, will prevent infection, the way honey does. Honey yanks the moisture out of bacteria with the violence of its osmosis. Honey has been found uncorrupt in the tombs of the Pharaohs, though it had been left there to be used, after all, to sweeten the darkness of the dead.

Who could have thought when the treasures were laid out in the vault that the bees' modest embalming would last so well, that their glandular syrup of flowers would turn out so nearly eternal?

My lover raises the remote control panel and turns the television off. Late at night, the nurses stop being so demanding, and even Armchair and the Vet can be relied on to stay away. My lover and I don't have to be so guarded in our behaviour.

This is the time we draft our imaginary letters to newspapers and public figures, our radical complaints and proposals. My lover wants to live long enough to be the only survivor of an air crash, so that he can say at the press conference, where he will have an arm in plaster – perhaps only a finger – 'You see? God doesn't hate me after all. Whatever *you* think.' In the meantime he will settle for composing imaginary letters to the papers, setting the record straight day by day.

Sometimes one or the other of us will shed some tears, but we haven't properly settled the agenda of our crying. We're both New Men, I suppose that's what it comes down to, so we have a lot of respect for tears and what they represent. Crying is a piece of expressive behaviour that needs no apology and isn't, absolutely isn't, a demand for attention. We pride ourselves on being able to ask for affection straight out, without needing to break down to do it. There's something a little crass about a hug as a response to tears. A hug can be an act of denial, even, and neither of us is going to make that mistake. We claim the right to cry uncomforted, letting the discharge do its work uninterrupted.

But in practice, I get so distressed by his tears, and he by mine, that we regress just as fast as we possibly can, and smother the expressiveness that we have so much respect for under a ton of hugs.

Endlessly we reformulate our feelings for each other. This is the same superstition that makes people put up bumper stickers – *Keep Your Distance, Baby on Board, I* ♥ *my* π – to make the roads safe and life go on for ever.

Fate is a dual-control Metro, that much I know, but I'm not clear about who's in which seat. It may be me, or it may be my lover, that squeezes the brake when we approach a bend too fast, or who pops the clutch in to prevent a stall. 'Baby clutch,' I can hear a familiar voice saying in my ear, '*baby*-baby clutch,' as we move off up the hill to where we must go.

GEORGE MACKAY BROWN

Three Old Men

The old man came out of his house and it was a dark night. A few snow-flakes drifted on to his head.

'Well,' he said, 'I don't know why I want to leave the fire on a cold night like this. I want to get to the village but why I don't remember.'

He guessed his way along the track going down from the hill, and once he stumbled and almost fell into the wet ditch.

'Well, thank you, staff, for keeping me on my feet,' said the old man to his stick. 'A fine thing, if they found us in the morning, you and me in a drift in the ditch, as stiff and cold as one another.'

The old man laughed, and he went slowly down the cart road from the hill to the village. He felt happy, though now the snow was in his beard, and he struck out with his staff and startled a star from a way-side stone.

At the crossroads, half-way to the village, a shadow lingered. The shadow declared itself to be a man, because there was the small flame of a match being applied to a pipe. The face shone fitfully once or twice and was part of the night again.

'What's an old man like you doing out in a night like this?' said the voice at the crossroads, and the seeker in the darkness recognised Ben, the retired skipper, from the far end of the island. They had sat in the same classroom at the village school, but they hadn't seen each other for thirty years, the time Ben was at sea, and now only occasionally at the island regatta or the agricultural show.

'The truth is,' said the old man from the hill, 'I don't rightly remember. I know I have some errand to the village, and maybe it'll come back to me before I get to the bridge.'

'Well,' said Ben, 'we might as well walk on together. I expect it's drink you're after, to keep out the cold. We can hold each other up on the way home.'

The two old men laughed. The skipper had a smell of hot rum on his breath. Could he be wanting more grog in the inn?

'I just thought,' said Ben, 'I would like to stretch my legs under the stars. Only there's not a star to be seen. It's as black as the ace of spades.'

The two old men went arm-in-arm along the track. Sometimes one or the other of them would give a bark of laughter or a cry of annoyance as his foot struck against a stone in the middle of the road.

The snow was falling thicker than ever. The old sailor passed his tobacco pouch to the old shepherd, but Sam had left his pipe at home. The match spurted, and the flame showed the hollowed cheeks of Ben as he drew in the smoke, before a falling snowflake fell on the burning match – a drifting moth – and quenched it.

It was the darkest night of winter, and such a snow cloud was drifting across the island that they couldn't see the lights of the village.

But they knew the general direction.

Once they both left the road and sallied against a barbed wire fence, and one of the travellers got a deep scrape on his hand, and a fencing post knocked the burning pipe out of the other's mouth.

Then they said one or two uncomplimentary things about the farmer who had been so inconsiderate as to put up his fence in that particular place. Ben found his pipe in the snow drift. Sam shook beads of blood from his hand.

They went on, grumbling and laughing.

'I hear trouble,' said the old shepherd.

'I hear nothing,' said the old skipper, 'but then I'm hard of hearing since that last trip I made to China.'

What came to them through the darkness was music – a fragment of a reel played on a fiddle – a scratching and a scraping that could only be made by Willie the miller.

'Well,' said Willie as the skipper and the shepherd came up to him where he stood at the buttress of the bridge over the burn, 'I thought I would be playing tonight to an owl and an otter maybe. But here come two old men. Imagine that.'

On the three old men walked together. And the snow fell thicker about them.

The miller put his trembling fiddle inside his coat.

The shepherd drew his scarf across his mouth.

There was a lighthouse miles away across the Pentland Firth, in Scotland. It pulsed regularly. The sky was clear to the south.

Sometimes one or other of them would say something, but the snow muffled the words. They struggled on, arm in arm, lifting heavy feet out of the drifted ruts.

Ben said, in the ringing voice he had once used on the quarter deck, 'I think we're in for a real blizzard. I feel it in my bones.'

It was as if his words put out the lighthouse. They could see its flashings no more. The night was thickening.

They stopped at the crown of the brae to get their breath.

'I'd have been right enough,' said the miller, 'playing this fiddle to the cat at home.'

In the slow wavering downward flake-drift their faces were three blurs.

'I'll tell you something,' said Ben. 'When I was in India a long while ago, I bought a piece of ivory from a merchant in Bombay. Well, I have a lot of interesting objects from all over the world at home. But this piece of ivory I always liked best. It has a bunch of grapes carved on it. Tonight I thought to myself, "Ben, what's the use of a houseful of treasures to an old man like you? You might be dead before the first daffodils in April." So I put the carving in my pocket and came out like an old fool into this blizzard.'

The three men stood there in the heart of the snowstorm.

'Well now,' said Sam the shepherd, 'that's a very strange thing you've said, Ben. I'll tell you why. I had three golden sovereigns put away in a stone jar on the mantelpiece. It had been there for twenty years. It was to pay for my funeral, that money. It struck me this afternoon at sunset – "They'll have to bury you anyway, Sam," I said to myself. "You're too old now for a pauper's grave. Why don't you take the money," I said to myself, "and give it to the living?" . . . '

The three old men laughed, a muffled threefold merriment on the crown of the island.

The snow fell thicker still.

593

Willie the miller said, 'I tell you what – I've been working on a new fiddle tune since harvest. I think it's the best music I ever made. I call it *Milling the Barley*. I thought, "I'm going to play this reel somewhere where it'll be truly appreciated" . . . But where could that be?'

'We'd better be getting on then,' said Ben.

So they linked arms and put their heads into the slow black drift. Here and there the snow was up to their knees.

'Watch where you're going,' said Willie, as if the other two were responsible for their wayward progress.

Then they were all in a deep drift, topsy-turvy, a sprawl and a welter and struggle of old men!

They got to their feet, pulling at each other, shaking the snow off their coats, wheezing and grumbling.

'I tell you what,' said Ben, 'we've lost the road altogether. We'd best go carefully. We might be over the crag and into the sea before we know.'

They could hear, indeed, the surge and break of waves against the cliff, but whether near or far-off was hard to say, on such a night.

'We're lost, that's what it is,' said Sam.

Just then the snow cloud was riven, and in a deep purple chasm of sky a star shone out, and before the cloud closed in again they saw the farmhouse Skeld with a lamp in the window.

'We're on a true bearing,' said Ben the skipper. 'But what that star was I don't know.'

The snow was falling thicker than ever as they came to the first houses of the village.

Now they could hear the hullabaloo from the inn bar, shouts and mauled bits of song and the clash and clank of pewter, and the innkeeper calling, 'Less noise! I want no rows or fighting tonight. The policeman's on his way.'

The three were aware of a lantern near the end of the kirk, and when it was near enough the lantern light splashed the face of Tommy Angel, the boy who sometimes kept the inn fires going and washed the glasses and swept the floor.

'I was sent to meet you,' said Tommy, 'and take you to the place.'

They could have found their own way to the inn, with all that clamour and noise coming from the lighted door.

'Lead on, Tommy,' said Sam the shepherd.

The boy led them round the inn to the byre behind, where the inn-keeper stabled his beasts in winter.

The old men could just see, through the veils of snow, the glim of a candle inside.

A. S. BYATT

Racine and the Tablecloth

When was it clear that Martha Crichton-Walker was the antagonist? Emily found this word for her much later, when she was a grown woman. How can a child, undersized and fearful, have enough of a self to recognize an antagonist? She might imagine the malice of a cruel stepmother or a jealous sister, but not the clash of principle, the essential denial of an antagonist. She was too young to have thought-out beliefs. It was Miss Crichton-Walker's task, after all, to form and guide the unformed personality of Emily Bray. Emily Bray's ideas might have been thought to have been imparted by Martha Crichton-Walker, and this was in part the case, which made the recognition of antagonism peculiarly difficult, certainly for Emily, possibly for both of them.

The first time Emily saw Miss Crichton-Walker in action was the first evening of her time at the school. The class was gathered together, in firelight and lamplight, round Miss Crichton-Walker's hearth, in her private sitting-room. Emily was the only new girl: she had arrived in mid-year, in exceptional circumstances (a family illness). The class were thirteen years old. There were twenty-eight of them, twenty-nine with Emily, a fact whose significance had not yet struck Emily. The fireside evening was Miss Crichton-Walker's way of noticing the death of a girl who had been in the class last term and had been struck by peritonitis after an operation on a burst appendix. This girl had been called Jan but had been known to the other girls as Hodgie. Did you hear about Hodgie, they all said to each other, rushing in with the news, mixing a kind of fear with a kind of glee, an undinted assurance of their own perpetuity. This was unfortunate for Emily; she felt like a substitute for Hodgie, although she was not. Miss Crichton-Walker gave them all pale cocoa and sugar-topped buns, and told them to sit on the floor round her. She spoke gently about their friend Hodgie whom they must all remember as she had been, full of life, sharing everything, a happy girl. She knew they were shocked; if at any later time they were to wish to bring any anxieties or regrets to her, she would be glad to share them. Regrets was an odd word, Emily perhaps noticed, though at that stage she was already willing enough to share Martha Crichton-Walker's tacit assumption that the girls would be bound to have regrets. Thirteen-year-old girls are unkind and in groups they are cruel. There would have been regrets, however full of life and happy the lost Hodgie had been.

Miss Crichton-Walker told the girls a story. It made a peaceful scene, with the young faces turned up to the central storyteller, or down to the carpet. Emily Bray studied Miss Crichton-Walker's appearance, which was firmly benign and breastless. Rolled silver curls, almost like a barrister's wig, were aligned round a sweet face, very soft-skinned but nowhere slack, set mild. The eyes were wide and very blue, and the mouth had no droop, but was firm and even, straight-set. Lines led finely to it but did not carve any cavity or depression: they lay lightly, like a hairnet. Miss Crichton-Walker wore, on this occasion and almost always, a very fine woollen dress, nun's veiling with a pleated chest, long fitted sleeves, and a plain white Peter Pan collar. At her neck was a simple oval silver brooch. There was something essentially girlish – not skittish, or sullen, or liquid, but unmarked, about this face and body, which were also those of a neat, elderly woman.

The story was allegorical. It was about a caddis-grub which scuttled about on the floor of a pond, making itself a makeshift tube-house of bits of gravel, twigs and weed to cover its vulnerable and ugly little grub body. Its movements were awkward and painful, its world dank and dimly lit. One day it was seized with an urge to climb which it could not ignore. Painfully it drew its squashy length out of its abandoned house and made its way, bursting and anguished, up a tall bulrush. In the bright outer air it hardened, cased in, and then most painfully burst and split, issuing forth with fine iridescent wings and darting movements, a creature of light and air. Miss Crichton-Walker enjoyed this tale of contrasts. Emily Bray could not make out – she was never much to make out, it was her failing – what the other girls thought or felt. Always afterwards she imagined the dead Hodgie as grub-like and squashy. During the telling she imagined the others as little girls, although she herself was the smallest in size, puny and stick-like. They all sat in their dressing-gowns and pyjamas, washed and shapeless. Later in the dormitory they would chatter agitatedly, full of opinions and feelings, pointing fingers, jutting chins. Here they were secret and docile. Miss Crichton-Walker told them they had had a peaceful evening together and that had been good. Emily Bray saw that there were two outsiders in the room. There was herself, set aside from the emotion that was swimming around, and there was Miss Crichton-Walker who wanted them all to be sharing something.

Every Wednesday and every Sunday the school walked into the centre of the cathedral city to go to church. On Wednesday they had their own service, shared with their brother school, Holy Communion and Morning Prayer. On Sunday they made part – a large part – of the general congregation. There were rules about walking through the city; they did not go in a crocodile, but were strictly forbidden to walk more than two abreast through the narrow streets. Three laughing girls, horseplaying perhaps, had once swept over an old lady outside Boot's, had fractured frail bones and been cautioned by the Police. A result of this reasonable ruling was that it was important for each girl to have a partner, someone to walk with, a best friend. Girls of that age choose best friends naturally, or so Emily had observed, who had not had a best friend since her days in the junior school, before her unfortunate habits became pronounced. The church-walking added forms and rituals to the selection and rejection of best friends. Everyone knew if a couple split up, or a new couple was formed. Emily discovered quickly enough that there was a floating population of rejects, rag, tag, bobtail, who formed feebler ties, *ad hoc* partnerships, with half an eye on the chance of a rift between a more acceptable pairing. She assumed she would belong with these. She had no illusions about her chance of popularity in the class. The best she could hope for was decent anonymity. She also knew that decent anonymity was unlikely. When the exam results came, she would be found out. In the interim, she realized quickly enough the significance of the size of the class, twenty-nine girls. There would always be a final reject, one running round when all the musical chairs were occupied. That one would be Emily Bray.

*

You might suppose that grown-up, intelligent schoolmistresses would be capable of seeing the significance of twenty-nine, or that it might be possible for Emily to point it out, or recall it to them, if they did not. You also almost certainly know enough about conventional institutional rigours to be unsurprised that it was quite impossible for Emily to say anything coherent when, as happened regularly, she was caught up in the street and reprimanded for tagging along in a threesome. (Walking anywhere alone was an unthinkable and serious offence.) She dreaded Wednesdays and Sundays, working herself up on Tuesdays and Saturdays to beg, with mortified mock-casual misery, to be allowed to come along. After she began to get exam results, the situation, as she had foreseen, worsened. With appalling regularity, with unnatural ease and insulting catholicity, Emily Bray came first in almost everything except maths and domestic science. She came first in the theoretical paper of the domestic science, but her handiwork let her down. She was a simply intellectual creature. She was physically undeveloped, no good at sport, no one to chatter to about sex, or *schwärmerei*, delicious shoes or pony club confrontations. She had an image of herself in their minds as a kind of abacus in its limited frame, clicking mnemonics, solving problems, recording transactions. She waited to be disliked and they duly disliked her. There were clever girls, Flora Marsh for example, who were not so disliked: Flora was peaceably beautiful, big and slender and athletic and wholesome, genuinely modest, wanting to be mother of six and live in the country. Flora had a horse and a church partner, Catherine, she had known since she was five. Flora's handwriting was even and generous, flowing on in blue running curves and rhythmic spaces. Emily Bray wrote hunched over the page, jabbing at it with a weak-nibbed fountain pen. There was never a misspelled word, but the whole was blotted and a little smeared and grimy, the lines uneven, the characters without settled forms. In Emily's second year Miss Crichton-Walker addressed their class on its work and said in front of all of them that it was her habit always to read the best set of exam papers. In this case that was, as they all knew, Emily Bray's but she was afraid that she had had to return these unfinished since she was distressed by the aggressive handwriting. The papers were a disgrace in other ways too, nastily presented, and dirty. If Emily would be kind enough to make a fair copy she would be delighted to read them. She delivered this

judgment, as was her habit, with a slight smile, not deprecating, not miti-
gating, but pleased and admiring. Admiring the accuracy of her own
expressions, or pleased with the placing of the barb? It did not occur to
young Emily to ask herself that question, though she noted and remembered the smile accurately enough to answer it, when she was ready, when
her account was made up. But the child did not know what judgment the
woman would make, or indeed that the woman would judge. The child
believed she was shrugging off the judgment of herself. Of course the
paper was dirty: schools thought dirt mattered; she believed it did not.
She opposed herself like a shut sea-anemone, a wall of muscle, a tight
sphincter. It is also true, changing the metaphor, that the judgment
dropped in heavily and fast, like a stone into a pond, to rest unshifted on
the bottom.

She noted the word, aggressive, as on that earlier occasion she had
noted 'regrets'. She remembered writing those speedy, spattered pages – an
essay on Hamlet's delays, a character-analysis of Emma Woodhouse. She
had written for pleasure. She had written for an imaginary ideal Reader,
perfectly aware of her own strengths and failings, her approximations to
proper judgments, her flashes of understanding. If she had thought for
ten minutes she would have known that no such Reader existed, there
was only Miss Harvey and beyond Miss Harvey Miss Crichton-Walker.
But she never yielded those ten minutes. If the real Reader did not exist
it was necessary to invent Him, and Emily did so. The pronoun is an
accurate rendering of Emily's vaguest intimation of his nature. In a female
institution where justice, or judgment, was Miss Crichton-Walker, benign
impartiality seemed to be male. Emily did not associate the Reader with
the gods worshipped in the cathedral on Sundays. God the Judge and
God the Friend and God the rushing wind of the Spirit were familiars
of Miss Crichton-Walker invoked with an effort of ecstasy in evening
prayers in the school, put together with music and branched stone and
beautiful words and a sighing sentiment in the choir stalls. Emily could
not reasonably see why the propensity to believe this myth should have
any primary guarantee of touching at truth, any more than the propensity
to believe Apollo, or Odin, or Gautama Buddha, or Mithras. She was not
aware that she believed in the Reader, though as she got older she became
more precise and firm about his attributes. He was dry and clear, he was

all-knowing but not messily infinite. He kept his proportion and his place. He had no face and no imaginary arms to enfold or heart to beat: his nature was not love, but understanding. Invoked, as the black ink spattered in the smell of chalk dust and dirty fingers, he brought with him a foreign air, sunbaked on sand, sterile, heady, tolerably hot. It is not too much to say that in those seemingly endless years in that place Emily was enabled to continue because she was able to go on believing in the Reader.

She did not make a fair copy of her papers for Miss Crichton-Walker. She believed that it was not really expected of her, that the point to be made had been made. Here she may have been doing Miss Crichton-Walker an injustice, though this is doubtful. Miss Crichton-Walker was expert in morals, not in *Hamlet* or *Emma*.

When she was fifteen Emily devised a way of dealing with the church walk. The city was mediaeval still in many parts, and, more particularly, was surrounded with long stretches of city wall, with honey-pale stone battlements, inside which two people could walk side by side, looking out over the cathedral close and the twisting lanes, away down to the surrounding plain. She discovered that if she ducked back behind the church, under an arched gateway, she could, if she went briskly, walk back along the ramparts almost all the way, out-flanking the mainstream of female pairs, descending only for the last few hundred yards, where it was possible to dodge through back streets to where the school stood, in its pleasant gardens, inside its own lesser barbed wall. No one who has not been an inmate can know exactly how powerful is the hunger for solitude which grows in the constant company, day and night, feeding, washing, learning, sleeping, almost even, with partition walls on tubular metal stems, excreting. It is said women make bad prisoners because they are not by nature communal creatures. Emily thought about these things in the snatched breathing spaces she had made on the high walls, but thought of the need for solitude as hers only, over against the crushing others, though they must all also, she later recognized, have had their inner lives, their reticences, their inexpressive needs. She thought things out on that wall, French grammar and Euclid, the existence of males, somewhere else, the purpose of her life. She grew bold and regular – there was a particular tree, a self-planted willow, whose catkins she returned to each week, tight dark reddish buds, bursting silvery grey, a week damp and glossy grey fur and then the full pussy willow, softly bristling, powdered with bright yellow in the blue. One day when she was standing looking at these vegetable lights Miss Crichton-Walker and another figure appeared to materialize in front of her, side by stiff side. They must have come up one of the flights of steps from the grass bank inside the wall, now bright with daffodils and crocus; Emily remembered them appearing head-first, as though rising from the ground, rather than walking towards her. Miss Crichton-Walker had a grey woollen coat with a curly lambskin collar in a darker pewter; on her head was a matching hat, a cylinder of curly fur. There were two rows of buttons on her chest; she wore grey kid gloves and sensible shoes, laced and rigorous. She stood there for a moment on the wall and saw Emily Bray by her willow tree. There was no question in Emily's mind that they had stared at each other, silently. Then Miss Crichton-Walker pointed over the parapet, indicating some cloud formation to her companion, of whose identity Emily formed no impression at all, and they passed on, in complete silence. She even wondered wildly, as she hurried away back towards the school, if she had not seen them at all.

She had, of course. Miss Crichton-Walker waited until evening prayers to announce, in front of the school, that she wanted to see Emily Bray, tomorrow after lunch, thus leaving Emily all night and half a day to wonder what would be said or done. It was a school without formal punishments. No one wrote lines, or sat through detentions, or penitently scrubbed washroom floors. And yet everyone, not only Emily Bray, was afraid of committing a fault before Miss Crichton-Walker. She could make you feel a real worm, the girls said, the lowest of the low, for having illegal runny honey instead of permitted hard honey, for running across the tennis lawns in heavy shoes, for smiling at boys. What she could do to those who cheated or stole or bullied was less clear and less urgent. On the whole they didn't. They were on the whole nice girls. They accepted Miss Crichton-Walker's judgment of them, and this was their heavy punishment.

Emily stood in front of Miss Crichton-Walker in her study. Between their faces was a silver rose bowl, full of spring flowers. Miss Crichton-Walker was small and straight in a large upright arm chair. She asked Emily what she had been doing on the wall, and Emily said that she had no one to walk home from church with, so came that way. She thought of adding, most girls of my age, in reasonable day schools, can walk alone in a city in the middle of the morning, quite naturally, anybody might. Miss Crichton-Walker said that Emily was arrogant and unsociable, had made little or no effort to fit in with the community ever since she came, appeared to think that the world was made for her convenience. She set herself against everything, Miss Crichton-Walker said, she was positively depraved. Here was another word to add to those others, regrets, aggressive, depraved. Emily said afterwards to Flora Marsh, who asked what had happened, that Miss Crichton-Walker had told her that she was depraved. Surely not, said Flora, and, yes she did, said Emily, she did, that is what she *thinks*. You may have your own views about whether Miss Crichton-Walker could in sober fact have uttered the word depraved, in her soft, silvery voice, to an awkward girl who had tried to walk alone in mid-morning, to look at a pussy-willow, to think. It may be that Emily invented the word herself, saying it for bravado to Flora Marsh after the event, though I would then argue, in defence of Emily, that the word must have been in the air during that dialogue for her to pick up, the feeling was there, Miss Crichton-Walker sensed her solitude as something corrupt, contaminating, depraved. What was to be done? For the next four weeks, Miss Crichton-Walker said, she would walk back from church with Emily herself. It was clear that she found this prospect as disagreeable as Emily possibly could. She was punishing both of them.

What could they say to each other, the awkward pair, one shuffling downcast, one with a regular inhibited stride? Emily did not regard it as her place to initiate any conversation: she believed any approach would have been unacceptable, and may well have been right. You will think that Miss Crichton-Walker might have taken the opportunity to draw Emily out, to find out why she was unhappy, or what she thought of her education. She did say some things that might have been thought to be part of such a conversation, though she said them reluctantly, in a repressed, husky voice, as though they were hard to bring out. She was content for much the larger part of their four weeks' perambulation to say nothing at all, pacing it out like prison exercise, a regular rhythmic pavement-tapping with which Emily was compelled to try to keep time. Occasionally spontaneous remarks broke from her, not in the strained, clutching voice of her confidential manner, but with a sharp, clear ring. These were remarks about Emily's personal appearance for which she felt – it is not too strong a word, though this time it is mine, or Emily's; Martha Crichton-Walker is innocent of uttering it – she felt disgust. 'For the second week running you have a grey line round your neck, Emily, like the scum you deposit round the rim of the bath.' 'You have a poor skin, Emily. Ask Sister to give those blackheads some attention: you must have an abnormal concentration of grease in your nasal area, or else you are unusually skimpy in your attention to your personal hygiene. Have you tried medicated soap?' 'Your hair is lank, Emily. I do not like to think of the probable state of your hatband.' 'May I see your hands? I have never understood how people can bring themselves to bite their nails. How unpleasant and profitless to chew away one's own flesh in this manner. I see you are imbrued with ink as some people are dyed with nicotine: it is just as disagreeable. Perhaps the state of your hands goes some way to explain your very poor presentation of your work: you seem to *wallow* in ink to a quite unusual extent. Please purchase a pumice stone and a lemon and scour it away before we go out next week. Please borrow a knife from the kitchen and prise away the boot-polished mud from your shoe-heels – that is a lazy way of going on that does not deceive the eye, and increases the impression of slovenliness.'

None of these remarks was wholly unjust, though the number of them, the ingenuity with which they were elaborated and dilated on, were perhaps excessive? Emily imagined the little nose sniffing at the armpits of her discarded vests, at the stains on her pants. She sweated with anxiety inside her serge overcoat, waiting outside Miss Crichton-Walker's study, and imagined Miss Crichton-Walker could smell her fear rising out of the wool, running down her lisle stockings. Miss Crichton-Walker seemed to be without natural exudations. A whiff of lavender, a hint of mothball.

She talked to Emily about her family. Emily's family do not come into this story, though you may perhaps be wondering about them, you might need at least to know whether the authority they represented would be likely to reinforce that of Miss Crichton-Walker, or to present some counter-balance, some other form of moral priority. Emily Bray was a scholarship girl, from a large Potteries family of five children. Emily's father was a foreman in charge of a kiln which fired a curious mixture of teacups thick with lilies of the valley, dinner plates edged severely with gold dagger-shapes, and virulently green pottery dogs with gaping mouths to hold toothbrushes or rubber bands. Emily's mother had, until her marriage, been an elementary school teacher, trained at Homerton in Cambridge, where she had developed the aspiration to send her sons and daughters to that university. Emily was the eldest of the five children; the next one, Martin, was a mongol. Emily's mother considered Martin a condign punishment of her aspirations to betterment. She loved him extravagantly and best. The three younger ones were left to their own resources, much of the time. Emily felt for them, and their cramped, busy, noisy little life, some of the distaste Miss Crichton-Walker felt for her, perhaps for all the girls. There are two things to note in this brief summing-up – a hereditary propensity to feel guilty, handed down to Emily from her briefly ambitious mother, and the existence of Martin.

Miss Crichton-Walker knew about Martin, of course. He had been part of the argument for Emily's scholarship, awarded on grounds of social need, in line with the principles of the school, rather than academic merit. Miss Crichton-Walker, in so far as she wanted to talk to Emily at all, wanted to talk about Martin. Tell me about your brothers and sisters, dear, she said, and Emily listed them, Martin, thirteen, Lorna, ten, Gareth, eight, Amanda, five. Did she miss them, said Miss Crichton-Walker, and Emily said no, not really, she saw them in the holidays, they were very noisy, if she was working. But you must love them, said Miss Crichton-Walker, in her choking voice, you must feel you are, hmm, not properly part of their lives? Emily did indeed feel excluded from the bustle of the kitchen, and more confusedly, more anxiously, from her mother's love, by Martin. But she sensed, rightly, that Miss Crichton-Walker wished her to feel cut off by the privilege of being at the school, guilty of not offering the help she might have done. She described teaching Amanda to read, in two weeks flat, and Miss Crichton-Walker said she noticed Emily did not mention Martin. Was that because she was embarrassed, or because she felt badly about him? She must never be embarrassed by Martin's misfortune, said Miss Crichton-Walker, who was embarrassed by Emily's inkstains and shoe-mud most sincerely, she must acknowledge her own. I do love him, said Emily, who did, who had nursed and sung to him, when he was smaller, who suffered from his crashing forays into her half-bedroom, from scribbled-on exercises, bath-drowned books. She remembered his heavy amiable twinkle. We all love him, she said. You must try to do so, said Miss Crichton-Walker.

Miss Crichton-Walker had her lighter moments. Some of these were part of the school's traditional pattern, in which she had her traditional place, such as the telling of the school ghost story at Hallowe'en, a firelit occasion for everyone, in the stark dining-room, by the light of two hundred candles inside the grinning orange skins of two hundred swedes. The girls sat for hours hollowing out these heads, at first nibbling the sweet vegetable, then revolted by it. For days afterwards the school smelled like a byre: during the story-telling the roasting smell of singed turnip overlay the persisting smell of the raw scrapings. For an hour before the storytelling they had their annual time of licence, running screaming through the dark garden, in sheets and knitted spiderwebs, jointed paper skeletons and floating batwings. The ghost story concerned an improbable encounter between a Roman centurion and a phantom cow in a venerable clump of trees in the centre of which stood an old and magnificent swing. Anyone meeting the white cow would vanish, the story ran, as in some other time the centurion had vanished, though imperfectly, leaving traces of his presence among the trees, the glimpsed sheen on a helmet, the flutter of his leather skirting. There was always a lot of suppressed giggling during Miss Crichton-Walker's rendering of this tale, which, to tell the truth, lacked narrative tension and a conclusive climax. The giggling was because of the proliferate embroidered legends which were in everyone's mind of Miss Crichton-Walker's secret, nocturnal, naked swinging in that clump of trees. She had once very determinedly, in Emily's presence, told a group of the girls that she enjoyed sitting naked in her room, on the hearth by the fire in the evening. It is very pleasant to feel the air on your skin, said Miss Crichton-Walker, holding her hands judicially before her chest, fingertips touching. It is natural and pleasant. Emily did not know what authority there was for the legend that she swung naked at night in the garden. She had perhaps once told such a group of girls that she would *like* to do so, that it would be good and pleasant to swoop unencumbered through the dark air, to touch the lowest branches of the thick trees with naked toes, to feel the cool rush along her body. There were in any case now several stories of her having been solidly seen doing just that, urging herself to and fro, milky-white in the dark. This image, with its moon face and rigid imperturbable curls was much more vivid in Emily's mind at Hallowe'en than any ghostly cow or centurion. The swing, in its wooden authority and weight, reminded Emily of a gibbet. The storytelling, more vaguely, reminded her of the first evening and the allegorizing of Hodgie's death.

Their first stirrings of appetite and anxiety, directed at the only vaguely differentiated mass of the brother school's congregation, aroused considerable efforts of repressive energy in Miss Crichton-Walker. It was said that under a previous, more liberal headmistress, the boys had been encouraged to walk the girls back from church. No one would even have dared to propose this to her. That there were girls who flouted this prohibition Emily knew, though only by remote hearsay. She could not tell one boy from another and was in love with Benedick, with Pierre, with Max Ravenscar, with Mr Knightley. There was an annual school dance, to which the boys were brought in silent, damp-palmed, hunched clumps in two or three buses. Miss Crichton-Walker could not prevent this dance: it was an ancient tradition: the boys' headmaster and the governors liked it to exist as a sign of educational liberality. But she spoke against it. For weeks before the arrival of the boys she spent her little Saturday evening homilies on warning the girls. It was not clear, from what she said, exactly what she was warning against. She was famous in the Lower Sixth for having managed explicitly to say that if any boy pressed too close, held any girl too tightly, that girl must say composedly 'Shall we sit this one out?' Girls rolled on their dormitory beds gasping out this *mot* in bursts of wild laughter and tones of accomplished parody. (The school was full of accomplished parodists of Miss Crichton-Walker.) They polished their coloured court shoes, scarlet and peacock, and fingered the stiff taffeta folds of their huge skirts, which they wore with demure and provocative silk shirts, and tightly-pulled wide belts. In later years Emily remembered as the centre of Miss Crichton-Walker's attack on sexual promptings, on the possibilities of arousal, a curiously elaborate disquisition on the unpleasantness and unnatural function of the female razor. She could not bring herself to mention the armpits. She spoke at length, with an access of clarity and precision, about the evil effects on the skin of frequent shaving of the legs, which left 'as I know very well, an unsightly dark stubble, which then has to be treated more and more frequently, once you have shaved away the first natural soft down. Any gardener will tell you that grass grows coarser after it has once been cut. I ask all the girls who have razors in the school to send them home, please, and all girls to ask their parents not to send such things through the post.' It was also during the weeks preceding the dance that she spoke against deodorants, saying that they were unnecessary for young girls and that the effects of pro-longed chemical treatment of delicate skin were not yet known. A little talcum powder would be quite sufficient if they feared becoming heated.

I am not going to describe the dance, which was sad for almost all of them, must have been, as they stood in their resolutely unmingled ranks on either side of the grey school hall. Nothing of interest really happened to Emily on that occasion, as she must, in her secret mind, have known it would not. It faded rapidly enough in her memory, whereas Miss Crichton-Walker's peculiar anxiety about it, even down to her curious analogy between razors and lawn-mowers, remained stamped there, clear and pungent, an odd and significant trace of the days of her education. In due course this memory accrued to itself Emily's later reflections on the punning names of depilatories, all of which aroused in her mind a trace-image of Miss Crichton-Walker's swinging, white, hairless body in the moonlight. Veet. Immac. Nair. Emily at the time of the static dance was beginning to sample the pleasures of being a linguist. Nair sounded like a Miltonic coinage for Satanic scaliness. Veet was a thick English version of French rapidity and discreet efficiency. Immac, in the connexion of Miss Crichton-Walker, was particularly satisfying, carrying with it the Latin, maculata, stained or spotted, immaculata, unstained, unspotted, and the Immaculate Conception, which, Emily was taught at this time, referred to the stainless or spotless begetting of the Virgin herself, not to the subsequent self-contained, unpunctured, manless begetting of the Son. The girls in the dormitories were roused by Miss Crichton-Walker to swap anecdotes about Veet, which according to them had 'the – most – terrible – *smell*' and produced a stinking slop of hairy grease. No one sent her razor home. It was generally agreed that Miss Crichton-Walker had too little bodily hair to know what it was to worry about it.

Meanwhile, and at the same time, there was Racine. You may be amused that Miss Crichton-Walker should simultaneously ban ladies' razors and promote the study of *Phèdre*. It is amusing. It is amusing that the same girls should already have been exposed to the betrayed and betraying cries of Ophelia's madness. 'Then up he rose, and doffed his clothes, and dupped the chamber door. Let in the maid that out a maid, never departed more.' It is the word 'dupped' that is so upsetting in that little song, perhaps because it recalls another Shakespearean word that rhymes with it, Iago's black ram tupping the white ewe, Desdemona. Get thee to a nunnery, said Hamlet, and there was Emily, in a nunnery, never out of one, in a rustle of terrible words and delicate and gross suggestions, the stuff of her studies. But that is not what I wanted to say about Racine. Shakespeare came upon Emily gradually, she could accommodate him, he had always been there. Racine was sudden and new. That is not it, either, not what I wanted to say.

Think of it. Twenty girls or so – were there so many? – in the A level French class, and in front of each a similar, if not identical small, slim greenish book, more or less used, more or less stained. When they riffled through the pages, the text did not look attractive. It proceeded in strict, soldierly columns of rhymed couplets, a form disliked by both the poetry-lovers and the indifferent amongst them. Nothing seemed to be happening, it all seemed to be the same. The speeches were very long. There appeared to be no interchange, no battle of dialogue, no action. *Phèdre*. The French teacher told them that the play was based on the *Hippolytus* of Euripides, and that Racine had altered the plot by adding a character, a young girl, Aricie, whom Hippolytus should fall in love with. She neglected to describe the original play, which they did not know. They wrote down, Hippolytus, Euripides, Aricie. She told them that the play kept the unities of classical drama, and told them what these unities were, and they wrote them down. The Unity of Time = One Day. The Unity of Space = One Place. The Unity of Action = One Plot. She neglected to say what kind of effect these constrictions might have on an imagined world: she offered a half-hearted rationale she clearly despised a little herself, as though the Greeks and the French were children who made unnecessary rules for themselves, did not see wider horizons. The girls were embarrassed by having to read this passionate sing-song verse aloud in French.

Emily shared their initial reluctance, their near-apathy. She was later to believe that only she became a secret addict of Racine's convoluted world, tortuously lucid, savage and controlled. As I said, the imagination of the other girls' thoughts was not Emily's strength. In Racine's world, all the inmates were gripped wholly by incompatible passions which swelled uncontrollably to fill their whole universe, brimming over and drowning its horizons. They were all creatures of excess, their secret blood burned and boiled and an unimaginably hot bright sun glared down in judgment. They were all horribly and beautifully interwoven, tearing each other apart in a perfectly choreographed dance, every move inevitable, lovely, destroying. In this world men and women had high and terrible fates which were themselves and yet greater than themselves. Phèdre's love for Hippolyte was wholly unnatural, dragging her world askew, wholly inevitable, a force like a flood, or a conflagration, or an eruption. This art described a world of monstrous disorder and excess and at the same time ordered it with iron control and constrictions, the closed world of the classical stage and the prescribed dialogue, the flexible, shining, inescapable steel mesh of that regular, regulated singing verse. It was a world in which the artist was in unusual collusion with the Reader, his art like a mapping trellis between the voyeur and the terrible writhing of the characters. It was an austere and adult art, Emily thought, who knew little about adults, only that they were unlike Miss Crichton-Walker, and had anxieties other than those of her tired and over-stretched mother. The Reader was adult. The Reader saw with the pitiless clarity of Racine – and also with Racine's impersonal sympathy – just how far human beings could go, what they were capable of.

After the April foolery, Miss Crichton-Walker said she would not have believed the girls were capable of it. No one, no one Emily knew at least, knew how the folly had started. It was 'passed on', in giggled injunctions, returning again embroidered to earlier tellers. It must have originated with some pair, or pairs, of boys and girls who had managed to make contact at the static dance, who had perhaps sat a few waltzes out together, as Miss Crichton-Walker had bidden. The instruction they all received was that on Sunday April 1st the boys were to sit on the girls' side of the church and vice versa. Not to mingle, that is. To change places *en bloc*, from the bride's side to the bridegroom's. No rationale was given for this jape, which was immediately perceived by all the girls and boys involved as exquisitely funny, a kind of epitome of disorder and misrule. The bolder spirits took care to arrive early, and arrange themselves decorously in their contrary pews. The others followed like meek sheep. To show that they were not mocking God, the whole congregation then worshipped with almost unnatural fervour and devotion, chanting the responses, not wriggling or shifting in their seats. The Vicar raised his eyebrows, smiled benignly, and conducted the service with no reference to the change.

Miss Crichton-Walker was shocked, or hurt, to the quick. It was as though, Emily thought very much later, some kind of ritual travesty had happened, the Dionysiac preparing of Pentheus, in his women's skirts, for the maenads to feast on. Though this analogy is misleading: Miss Crichton-Walker's anguish was a kind of puritanical modesty. What outraged her was that, as she saw it, she, and the institution of which she was the head, had been irrevocably shamed in front of the enemy. In the icy little speech she made to the school at the next breakfast she did not mention any insult to the church, Emily was almost sure. Nor did she dart barbs of precise, disgusted speech at the assembled girls: she was too upset for that. Uncharacteristically she wavered, beginning 'Something has happened . . . something has taken place . . . you will all know what I am speaking of . . . ' gathering strength only when she came to her proposed expiation of the sin. 'Because of what you have done,' she said, 'I shall stand here, without food, during all today's meals. I shall eat nothing. You can watch me while you eat, and think about what you have done.'

Did they? Emily's uncertainty about the thoughts of the others held for this extraordinary act of vicarious penance, too. Did they laugh about it? Were they shocked and anxious? Through all three meals of the day they ate in silence, forks clattering vigorously on plates, iron spoons scraping metal trays, amongst the smell of browned shepherd's pie and institutional custard, whilst that little figure stood, doll-like, absurd and compelling, her fine lips pursed, her judicial curls regular round her motionless cheeks. Emily herself, as always, she came to understand, reacted with a fatal doubleness. She *thought* Miss Crichton-Walker was behaving in an undignified and disproportionate manner. She *felt*, gloomily and heavily, that she had indeed greatly damaged Miss Crichton-Walker, had done her a great and now inexpiable wrong, for which Miss Crichton-Walker was busily heaping coals of fire on her uncomprehending but guilty head. Miss Crichton-Walker was atoning for Emily's sin, which Emily had not, until then, known to be a sin. Emily was trapped.

When the A-level exams came, Emily developed a personality, not perhaps, you will think, a very agreeable one. She was approaching a time when her skills would be publicly measured and valued, or so she thought, as she became increasingly aware that they were positively deplored, not only by the other girls, but by Miss Crichton-Walker. The school was academically sound but made it a matter of principle not to put much emphasis on these matters, to encourage leadership, community spirit, charity, usefulness and other worthy undertakings. Girls went to university but were not excessively, not even much praised for this. Nevertheless, Emily knew it was there. At the end of the tunnel – which she visualized, since one must never allow a metaphor to lie dead and inert, as some kind of curving, tough, skinny tube in which she was confined and struggling, seeing the outside world dimly and distorted – at the end of the tunnel there was, there must be, light and a rational world full of aspiring Readers. She prepared for the A level with a desperate chastity of effort, as a nun might prepare for her vows. She learned to write neatly, overnight it seemed, so that no one recognized these new, confident, precisely black unblotted lines. She developed a pugnacious tilt to her chin. Someone in her form took her by the ears and banged her head repeatedly on the classroom wall, crying out 'you don't even have to try, you smug little bitch . . . ' but this was not true. She struggled secretly for perfection. She read four more of Racine's plays, feverishly sure that she would, when the time came, write something inadequate, ill-informed about his range, his beliefs, his wisdom. As I write, I can feel you judging her adversely, thinking, what a to-do, or even, smug little bitch. If I had set out to write a story about someone trying for perfection as a high diver, perhaps, or as a long distance runner, or even as a pianist, I should not so have lost your sympathy at this point. I could have been sure of exciting you with heavy muscles going up the concrete steps for the twentieth or thirtieth time, with the smooth sheet of aquamarine always waiting, the rush of white air, white air in water, the drum in the eardrums, the conversion of flesh and bone to a perfect parabola. You would have understood this in terms of some great effort of your own, at some time, as I now take pleasure in understanding the work of televised snooker players, thinking a series of curves and lines and then making these real, watching the balls dart and clatter and fall into beautiful shapes, as I also take pleasure in the skill of the cameramen, who can show my ignorant eye, picking out this detail and that, where the beautiful lines lie, where there are impossibilities in the way, where the danger is, and where success.

Maybe I am wrong in supposing that there is something inherently distasteful in the struggles of the solitary clever child. Or maybe the reason is not that cleverness – academic cleverness – is distasteful, but that writing about it is déjà-vu, wearisome. That's what they all become, solitary clever children, complaining writers, misunderstood. Not Emily. She did not become a writer, about her misunderstood cleverness or anything else.

Maybe you are not unsympathetic at all, and I have now made you so. You can do without a paranoid narrator. Back to Miss Crichton-Walker, always in wait.

On the evening before the first exam, Miss Crichton-Walker addressed to the whole school one of her little homilies. It was summer, and she wore a silvery grey dress, with her small silver brooch. In front of her was a plain silver bowl of flowers – pink roses, blue irises, something white and lacy and delicate surrounding them. The exams, she told the school, were due to begin tomorrow, and she hoped the junior girls would remember to keep quiet and not to shout under the hall windows whilst others were writing. There were girls in the school, she said, who appeared to attach a great deal of importance to exam results. Who seemed to think that there was some kind of exceptional merit in doing well. She hoped she had never allowed the school to suppose that her own values were wrapped up in this kind of achievement. Everything they did mattered, mattered very much, everything was of extreme importance in its own way. She herself, she said, had written books, and she had embroidered tablecloths. She would not say that there was not as much lasting value, as much pleasure for others, in a well-made tablecloth as in a well-written book.

While she talked, her eyes appeared to meet Emily's, steely and intimate. Any good speaker can do this, can appear to single out one or another of the listeners, can give the illusion that all are personally addressed. Miss Crichton-Walker was not a good speaker, normally: her voice was always choked with emotion, which she was not so much sharing as desperately offering to the stony, the uncaring of her imagination. She expected to be misunderstood, even in gaudier moments to be reviled, though persisting. Emily understood this without knowing how she knew it, or even that she knew it. But on this one occasion she knew with equal certainty that Miss Crichton-Walker's words were for her, that they were delivered with a sweet animus, an absolute antagonism into which Miss Crichton-Walker's whole cramped self was momentarily directed. At first she stared back angrily, her little chin grimly up, and thought that Miss Crichton-Walker was exceedingly vulgar, that what mattered was not exam results, God save the mark, but *Racine.* And then, in a spirit of almost academic justice, she tried to think of the virtue of tablecloths, and thought of her own Auntie Florence, in fact a great-aunt. And, after a moment or two, twisted her head, broke the locked gaze, looked down at the parquet.

In the Potteries, she had many great-aunts. Auntie Annie, Auntie Ada, Auntie Miriam, Auntie Gertrude, Auntie Florence. Auntie Florence was the eldest and had been the most beautiful. She had always looked after her mother, in pinched circumstances, and had married late, having no children of her own, though always, Emily's mother said, much in demand to look after other people's. Her mother had died when Florrie was fifty-four, demented and senile. Her husband had had a stroke, that year, and had lain helplessly in bed for the next ten, fed and tended by Auntie Florrie. She had had, in her youth, long golden hair, so long she could sit on it. She had always wanted to travel abroad, Auntie Florrie, whose education had ceased formally at fourteen, who read Dickens and Trollope, Dumas and Harriet Beecher Stowe. When Uncle Ted died at last, Aunt Florrie had a little money and thought she might travel. But then Auntie Miriam sickened, went off her feet, trembled uncontrollably and Florrie was called in by her children, busy with their own children. She was the one who was available, like, Emily's mother said. She had always been as strong as a horse, toiling up and down them stairs, fetching and carrying for Gran, for Uncle Ted, and then for poor Miriam. She always looked so wholesome and ready for anything. But she was seventy-two when Miriam died and arthritis got her. She couldn't go very far. She went on with the embroidery she'd always done, beautiful work of all kinds, bouquets and arabesques and trellises of

flowers in jewelled colours on white linen, or in white silk on white pil-
lowcases, or in rainbow colours and patterns from every century, Renaissance,
Classical, Victorian, Art Nouveau, on satin cushion covers. If you went to
see her you took her a present of white satin to work on. She liked heavy
bridal satin best. She liked the creamy whites and could never take to the
new glaring whites in the nylon satins. When she was eighty-five the local
paper had an article in it about her marvellous work, and a photograph of
Auntie Florrie in her little sitting-room, sitting upright amongst all the
white rectangles of her needlework, draped on all the furniture. Aunt Florrie still wore a woven crown of her own thinning hair. She had a good
neighbour, Emily's mother said, who came in and did for her. She couldn't
do much work, now, though. The arthritis had got her hands.

After Miss Crichton-Walker's little talk, Emily began to cry. For the first
half-hour of the crying she herself thought that it was just a nervous reaction, a kind of irritation, because she was so strung-up for the next day's
examination, and that it would soon stop. She cried at first rather noisily
in a subterranean locker-room, swaying to and fro and gasping a little,
squatting on a bench above a metal cage containing a knot of canvas
hockey boots and greying gym shoes. When bed-time came, she thought
she ought to stop crying now, she had had her time of release and respite.
She must key herself up again. She crept sniffing out into the upper corridors, where Flora Marsh met her and remarked kindly that she looked
to be in a bad way. At this Emily gave a great howl, like a wounded creature, and alarmed Flora by staggering from side to side of the corridor as
though her sense of balance were gone. Flora could get no sense out of
her: Emily was dumb: Flora said perhaps she should go to the nursery,
which was what they called the sick bay, should see Sister. After all, they
had A-level Latin the next day, she needed her strength. Emily allowed
herself to be led through the already-darkened school corridors, moaning
a little, thinking, inside her damp and sobbing head in a lucid tic-tac, that
she was like an ox, no, like a heifer it would have to be, like Keats's white
heifer in the Grecian urn . . . lowing at the skies . . . Dusty round white
lamps hung cheerlessly from metal chains.

Sister was a small, wiry, sensible widow in a white coat and flat rubber-soled
shoes. She made Emily a cup of Ovaltine, and put her into an uncomfortable

but friendly cane armchair, where Emily went on crying. It became clear to all three of them that there was no prospect of Emily ceasing to cry. The salt tears flooded and filmed her eyes, brimmed over and ran in wet sheets down her face, flowing down her neck in cold streamlets, soaking her collar. The tic-tac in Emily's mind thought of the death of Seneca, the life simply running away, warm and wet, the giving up. Sister sent Flora Marsh to fetch Emily's things, and Emily, moving her arms like a poor swimmer in thick water, put on her nightdress and climbed into a high hospital bed in the nursery, a hard, cast-iron headed bed, with white cotton blankets. The tears, now silent, darkened and gathered in the pillow. Emily put her knees up to her chin and turned her back on Sister, who pulled back some wet hair, out of her nightdress collar. What has upset her, Sister asked Flora Marsh. Flora didn't know, unless it was something the Headmistress had said. Emily heard them at a huge distance, minute in a waste of waters. Would she be fit to take her exams, Flora asked, and Sister replied, with a night's sleep.

Emily was double. The feeling part had given up, defeated, abandoned to the bliss of dissolution. The thinking part chattered away toughly, tapping out pentameters and alexandrines with and against the soothing flow of the tears. The next morning the feeling part, still watery, accepted tea and toast shakily from Sister; the thinking part looked out craftily from the cavern behind the glistening eyes and stood up, and dressed, and went wet-faced to the Latin exam. There Emily sat, and translated, and scanned, and constructed sentences and paragraphs busily, for a couple of hours. After, a kind of wild hiccup broke in her throat and the tears started again, as though a tap had been turned on, as though something, everything, must be washed away. Emily crept back to the nursery and lay on the iron bed, cold-cheeked and clammy, buffeted by a gale of tags from Horace, storm-cries from *Lear*, domestic inanities from Mrs Bennett, subjunctives and conditionals, sorting and sifting and arranging them, tic-tac, whilst the tears welled. In this way she wrote two German papers, and the English. She was always ready to write but could never remember what she had written, dissolved in tears, run away. She was like a runner at the end of a marathon, moving on will, not on blood and muscle, who might, if you put out a hand to touch him, fall and not rise again.

*

She received a visit. There was an empty day between the English and the final French, and Emily lay curled in the iron bed, weeping. Sister had drawn the blinds half-way down the windows, to close out the glare of the summer sun, and the cries of tennis players on the grass courts out in the light. In the room the air was thick and green like clouded glass, with pillars of shadow standing in it, shapes underwater. Miss Crichton-Walker advanced precisely towards the bedside, bringing her own shadow, and the creak of rubber footsteps. Her hair in the half-light glistened green on silver: her dress was mud-coloured, or seemed so, with a little, thickly-crocheted collar. She pulled out a tubular chair and sat down, facing Emily, her hands folded composed in her lap, her knees tightly together, her lips pursed. Crying had not thickened Emily's breathing but vacated its spaces: Miss Crichton-Walker smelled very thinly of moth-balls, which, in the context, Emily interpreted as the sharp mustiness of ether or chloroform, a little dizzy. She lay still. Miss Crichton-Walker said, 'I am sorry to hear that you are unwell, Emily, if that is the correct term. I am sorry that I was not informed earlier, or I should have come to see you earlier. I should like you to tell me, if you can, why you are so distressed?'

'I don't know,' said Emily, untruthfully.

'You set high store by these examinations, I know,' said the mild voice, accusing. 'Perhaps you overreached yourself in some way, overextended yourself, were overambitious. It is a pity, I always think, to force young girls to undergo these arbitrary stresses of judgment when it should surely be possible more accurately to judge the whole tenor of their life and work. Naturally I shall write to the Board of Examiners if you feel – if I feel – you may not quite have done yourself justice. That would be a great disappointment but not a disaster, not by any means a disaster. There is much to be learned in life from temporary setbacks of this kind.'

'I have sat all my papers,' said Emily's drugged, defensive voice. Miss Crichton-Walker went on.

'I always think that one real failure is necessary to the formation of any really resolved character. You cannot expect to see it that way just now, but I think you will find it so later, if you allow yourself to experience it fully.'

Emily knew she must fight, and did not know how. Half of her wanted to respond with a storm of loud crying, to drown this gentle concerned voice with rude noise. Half of her knew, without those words, that that way was disaster, was capitulation, was the acceptance of this last, premature judgment. She said, 'If I don't talk, if I just go on, I think I may be all right, I think.'

'You do not seem to be all right, Emily.'

Emily began to feel faint and dizzy as though the mothballs were indeed anaesthetic. She concentrated on the area below the judging face: the little knots and gaps in the crochet work, which lay sluggish and inexact, as crochet, even the best, always will, asymmetrical daisies bordered with little twisted cords. Little twisted cords of the soft thick cotton were tied at Miss Crichton-Walker's neck, in a constricting little bow that gathered and flounced the work and then hung down in two limp strands, each nearly knotted at its end. Where was Racine, where was the saving thread of reasoned discourse, where the Reader's dry air? The blinds bellied and swayed slightly. A tapestry of lines of verse like musical notation ran through Emily's imagination as though on an endless rolling scroll, the orderly repetitious screen of the alexandrine somehow visually mapped by the patterning of Aunt Florrie's exquisite drawn-thread work, little cornsheaves of threads interspersed by cut openings, tied by minute stitches, a lattice, a trellis.

> *C'était pendant l'horreur d'une profonde nuit.*
> *Ma mère Jézabel devant moi s'est montrée*
> *Comme au jour de sa mort pompeusement parée . . .*

Another bedside vision, highly inappropriate. The thinking Emily smiled in secret, hand under cheek.

'I think I just want to keep quiet, to concentrate . . . '

Miss Crichton-Walker gathered herself, inclining her silver-green coils slightly towards the recumbent girl.

'I am told that something I said may have upset you. If that is so, I am naturally very sorry. I do not need to tell you that what I said was well-meant, and, I hope, considered, said in the interest of the majority of the girls, I believe, and not intended to give offence to any. You are all equally my concern, with your varying interests and gifts. It may be that I felt the need of others more at that particular time than your need: perhaps I believed that you were better provided with self-esteem than most. I can assure you that there was no personal application intended. And that I said nothing I do not wholly believe.'

'No. Of course not.'

'I should like to know whether you did take exception to what I said.'

'I don't want to—'

'I don't want to leave you without clearing up this uncomfortable matter. I would hate – I would be very distressed – to think I had caused even unintentional pain to any girl in my charge. Please tell me if you thought I spoke amiss.'

'Oh no. No, I didn't. No.'

How reluctant a judge, poor Emily, how ill-equipped, how hopeless, to the extent of downright lying, of betraying the principles of exactness. The denial felt like a recantation without there having been an affirmation to recant.

'So now we understand each other. I am very glad. I have brought you some flowers from my little garden: Sister is putting them in water. They should brighten your darkness a little. I hope you will soon feel able to return to the community. I shall keep myself informed of your well-being, naturally.'

The French papers were written paragraph by slow paragraph. Emily's pen made dry, black, running little marks on the white paper: Emily's argument threaded itself, a fine line embellished by bright beads of quotations. She did not make it up; she knew it, and recognized it, and laid it out in its ordered pattern. Between paragraphs Emily saw, in the dark corners of the school hall, under dusty shields of honour, little hallucinatory scenes or tableaux, enacting in doorways and window embrasures a charade of the aimlessness of endeavour. She wrote a careful analysis of the clarity of the exposition of Phèdre's devious and confused passion and looked up to see creatures gesticulating on the fringed edge of her consciousness like the blown ghosts trying to pass over the Styx. She saw Miss Crichton-Walker, silvery-muddy, as she had been in the underwater blind-light of the nursery, gravely indicating that failure had its purpose for her. She saw Aunt Florrie, grey and faded and resigned amongst the light thrown off the white linen cloths and immaculate bridal satins of her work, another judge, upright in her chair. She saw Martin, of whom she thought infrequently, on an occasion when he had gleefully tossed and rumpled all the papers spread on her little table, mild, solid, uncomprehending flesh among falling sheets of white. She saw even the long racks of ghost-glazed, unbaked pots, their pattern hidden beneath the blurred film of watery clay, waiting to go into the furnace of her father's kiln and be cooked into pleasantly clean and shining transparency. Why go on, a soft voice said in her inner ear, what is all this fuss about? What do you know, it asked justly enough, of incestuous maternal passion or the anger of the gods? These are not our concerns: we must make tablecloths and endure. Emily knew about guilt, Miss Crichton-Walker had seen to that, but she did not know about desire, bridled or unbridled, the hooked claws of flame in the blood. She wrote a neat and eloquent paragraph about Phèdre's always-present guilt, arching from the first scene to the end, which led her to feel terror at facing Minos her father, judge of the Underworld, which led her ultimately to feel that the clarity of her vision dirtied the light air, the purity of daylight. From time to time, writing this, Emily touched nervously the puffed sacs under her swollen eyes: she was struggling through liquid, she could not help irrelevantly seeing Phèdre's soiled clarity of gaze in terms of her own over-wept, sore vision, for which the light was too much.

In another place, the Reader walked in dry, golden air, in his separate desert, waiting to weigh her knowledge and her ignorance, to judge her order and her fallings-off. When Emily had finished her writing she made her bow to him, in her mind, and acknowledged that he was a mythical being, that it was not possible to live in his light.

Who won, you will ask, Emily or Miss Crichton-Walker, since the Reader is mythical and detached, and can neither win nor lose? Emily might be thought to have won, since she had held to her purpose success-fully: what she had written was not gibberish but exactly what was required by the scrupulous, checked and counter-checked examiners, so that her marks, when they came, were the highest the school had ever seen. Miss Crichton-Walker might be thought to have won, since Emily was diag-nosed as having broken down, was sent home under strict injunctions not to open a book, and was provided by her mother with a piece of petit-point to do through the long summer, a Victorian pattern of blown roses and blue columbine, stretched across a gripping wooden hoop, in which she made dutiful cross after cross blunt-needled, tiny and woollen, pink, buff, crimson, sky-blue, royal blue, Prussian blue, creating on the underside a matted and uncouth weft of lumpy ends and trailing threads, since finishing off neatly was her weakest point. Emily might be thought to have won in the longer run, since she went to university indeed, from where she married young and hastily, having specialized safely in French language. If Emily herself thought that she had somehow lost, she thought this, as is the nature of things, in a fluctuating and intermittent way, feeling also a steady warmth towards her mild husband, a tax inspector, and her two clever daughters, and beyond that a certain limited satisfaction in the translation work she did part-time for various international legal bodies.

One day, however, she was called to see the deputy head of her eldest daughter's school, a shining steel and glass series of cubes and prisms, very different from her own dark, creeper-covered place of education. The deputy head was birdlike, insubstantial and thin in faded denim; his thin grey hair was wispy on his collar; his face was full of mild concern as he explained his anxieties about Emily's daughter. You must try to understand, he told Emily, that just because you are middle-class and university-educated, you need not expect your daughter to share your priorities. I have told Sarah myself that if she wants to be a gardener we shall do everything we can to help her, that her life is her own, that everything all the girls do here is of great importance to us, it all matters equally, all we want is for them to find themselves. Emily said in a small, dull voice that what Sarah wanted was to be able to do advanced French and advanced maths and that she could not really believe that the school had found this impossible to timetable and arrange. The deputy head's expression became extensively gentler and at the same time judicially set. You must allow, he told Emily, that parents are not always the best judge of their child's aptitudes. You may very well – with the best of intentions, naturally – be confusing Sarah's best interests with your own unfulfilled ambitions. Sarah may not be an academic child. Emily dared not ask him, as she should have done, as furious Sarah, frustrated and rebellious, was expecting her to do, if he *knew* Sarah, on what he was founding this judgment. Sarah's French, she said, is very good indeed; it is my subject, I know. She has a natural gift. He smiled his thin disbelief, his professional dismissal, and said that was her view, but not necessarily the school's. We are here to educate the whole human being, he told Emily, to educate her for life, for forming personal relations, running a home, finding her place in society, understanding her responsibilities. We are very much aware of Sarah's needs and problems – one of which, if I may speak frankly, is your expectations. Perhaps you should try to trust us? In any case, it is absolutely impossible to arrange the timetable so that Sarah may do both maths and French.

That old mild voice sounded through this new one: Emily walked away through the glassy-chill corridors thinking that if it had not been for that earlier authority she would have defied this one, wanting to stone the huge, silent panes of glass and let the dry light through, despising her own childishness.

At home, Sarah drew a neat double line under a geometric proof, laid out for the absent scanning of an unfalteringly accurate mind, to whose presence she required access. What Sarah made of herself, what Sarah saw, is Sarah's story. You can believe, I hope, you can afford to believe, that she made her way into its light.

MARTIN AMIS

Career Move

When Alistair finished his new screenplay, *Offensive from Quasar 13*, he submitted it to the *LM*, and waited. Over the past year, he had had more than a dozen screenplays rejected by the *Little Magazine*. On the other hand, his most recent submission, a batch of five, had been returned not with the standard rejection slip but with a handwritten note from the screenplay editor, Hugh Sixsmith. The note said:

> I was really rather taken with two or three of these, and seriously tempted by *Hotwire*, which I thought close to being fully achieved. Do please go on sending me your stuff.

Hugh Sixsmith was himself a screenplay writer of considerable, though uncertain, reputation. His note of encouragement *was* encouraging. It made Alistair brave.

Boldly he prepared *Offensive from Quasar 13* for submission. He justified the pages of the typescript with fondly lingering fingertips. Alistair did not address the envelope to the Screenplay Editor. No. He addressed it to Mr Hugh Sixsmith. Nor, for once, did he enclose his curriculum vitae, which he now contemplated with some discomfort. It told, in a pitiless staccato, of the screenplays he had published in various laptop broadsheets and comically obscure pamphlets; it even told of screenplays published in his university magazine. The truly disgraceful bit came at the end, where it said 'Rights Offered: First British Serial *only*.'

Alistair spent a long time on the covering note to Sixsmith – almost as long as he had spent on *Offensive from Quasar 13*. The note got shorter and shorter the more he worked on it. At last he was satisfied. There in the dawn he grasped the envelope and ran his tongue across its darkly luminous cuff.

That Friday, on his way to work, and suddenly feeling completely hopeless, Alistair surrendered his parcel to the sub-post office in Calchalk Street, off the Euston Road. Deliberately – very deliberately – he had enclosed no stamped-addressed envelope. The accompanying letter, in its entirety, read as follows: 'Any use? If not – w.p.b.'

'W.p.b.' stood, of course, for 'waste-paper basket' – a receptacle that loomed forbiddingly large in the life of a practising screenplay writer. With a hand on his brow, Alistair sidled his way out of there – past the birthday cards, the tensed pensioners, the envelopes, and the balls of string.

When Luke finished the new poem – entitled, simply, 'Sonnet' – he xeroxed the printout and faxed it to his agent. Ninety minutes later he returned from the gym downstairs and prepared his special fruit juice while the answering machine told him, among many other things, to get back to Mike. Reaching for an extra lime, Luke touched the preselect for Talent International.

'Ah. Luke,' said Mike. 'It's moving. We've already had a response.'

'Yeah, how come? It's four in the morning where he is.'

'No, it's eight in the evening where he is. He's in Australia. Developing a poem with Peter Barry.'

Luke didn't want to hear about Peter Barry. He bent, and tugged off his tank top. Walls and windows maintained a respectful distance – the room was a broad seam of sun haze and river light. Luke sipped his juice: its extreme astringency caused him to lift both elbows and give a single, embittered nod. He said, 'What did he think?'

'Joe? He did backflips. It's "Tell Luke I'm blown away by the new poem. I just know that 'Sonnet' is really going to happen."'

Luke took this coolly. He wasn't at all old but he had been in poetry long enough to take these things coolly. He turned. Suki, who had been shopping, was now letting herself into the apartment, not without difficulty. She was indeed cruelly encumbered. Luke said, 'You haven't talked numbers yet. I mean like a ballpark figure.'

Mike said, 'We understand each other. Joe knows about Monad's interest. And Tim at TCT.'

'Good,' said Luke. Suki was wandering slenderly towards him, shedding various purchases as she approached – creels and caskets, shining satchels.

'They'll want you to go out there at least twice,' said Mike. 'Initially to discuss . . . They can't get over it that you don't live there.'

Luke could tell that Suki had spent much more than she intended. He could tell by the quality of patience in her sigh as she began to lick the sweat from his shoulderblades. He said, 'Come on, Mike. They know I hate all that L.A. crap.'

On his way to work that Monday Alistair sat slumped in his bus seat, limp with ambition and neglect. One fantasy was proving especially obdurate: as he entered his office, the telephone on his desk would actually be *bouncing* on its console – Hugh Sixsmith, from the *Little Magazine*, his voice urgent but grave, with the news that he was going to rush Alistair's screenplay into the very next issue. (To be frank, Alistair had had the same fantasy the previous Friday, at which time, presumably, *Offensive from Quasar 13* was still being booted round the floor of the sub-post office.) His girlfriend, Hazel, had come down from Leeds for the weekend. They were so small, he and Hazel, that they could share his single bed quite comfortably – could sprawl and stretch without constraint. On the Saturday evening, they attended a screenplay reading at a bookshop on Camden High Street. Alistair hoped to impress Hazel with his growing ease in this milieu (and managed to exchange wary leers with a few shambling, half-familiar figures – fellow screenplay writers, seekers, knowers). But these days Hazel seemed sufficiently impressed by him anyway, whatever he did. Alistair lay there the next morning (her turn to make tea), wondering about this business of being impressed. Hazel had impressed him mightily, seven years ago, in bed: by not getting out of it when he got into it. The office telephone rang many times that Monday, but none of the callers had anything to say about *Offensive from Quasar 13*. Alistair sold advertising space for an agricultural newsletter, so his callers wanted to talk about creosote admixes and offal reprocessors.

He heard nothing for four months. This would normally have been a fairly good sign. It meant, or it might mean, that your screenplay was receiving serious, even agonized, consideration. It was better than having your screenplay flopping back on the mat by return post. On the other hand, Hugh Sixsmith might have responded to the spirit and the letter of Alistair's accompanying note and dropped *Offensive from Quasar 13* into his waste-paper basket within minutes of its arrival: four months ago. Rereading his fading carbon of the screenplay, Alistair now cursed his own (highly calibrated) insouciance. He shouldn't have said, 'Any use? If not – w.p.b.' He should have said, 'Any use? If not – s.a.e.'! Every morning he went down the three flights of stairs – the mail was there to be shuffled and dealt. And every fourth Friday, or thereabouts, he still wrenched open his *LM*, in case Sixsmith had run the screenplay without letting him know. As a surprise.

'Dear Mr Sixsmith,' thought Alistair as he rode the train to Leeds. 'I am thinking of placing the screenplay I sent you elsewhere. I trust that . . . I thought it only fair to . . .' Alistair retracted his feet to accommodate another passenger. 'My dear Mr Sixsmith: In response to an inquiry from . . . In response to a most generous inquiry, I am putting together a selection of my screenplays for . . .' Alistair tipped his head back and stared at the smeared window. 'For Mudlark Books. It seems that the Ostler Press is also interested. This involves me in some paperwork, which, however tedious . . . For the record . . . Matters would be considerably eased . . . Of course if you . . .'

Luke sat on a Bauhaus love seat in Club World at Heathrow, drinking Evian and availing himself of the complimentary fax machine – clearing up the initial paperwork on the poem with Mike.

Everyone in Club World looked hushed and grateful to be there, but not Luke, who looked exhaustively displeased. He was flying first class to LAX, where he would be met by a uniformed chauffeur who would convey him by limousine or courtesy car to the Pinnacle Trumont on the Avenue of the Stars. First class was no big thing. In poetry, first class was something you didn't need to think about. It wasn't discussed. It was statutory. First class was just business as usual.

Luke was tense: under pressure. A lot – maybe too much – was riding on 'Sonnet'. If 'Sonnet' didn't happen, he would soon be able to afford neither his apartment nor his girlfriend. He would recover from Suki before very long. But he would never recover from not being able to afford her, or his apartment. If you wanted the truth, his deal on 'Sonnet' was not that great. Luke was furious with Mike except about the new merchandizing clause (potential accessories on the poem – like toys or T-shirts) and the improved cut he got on tertiaries and sequels. Then there was Joe.

Joe calls, and he's like, 'We really think "Sonnet"'s going to work, Luke. Jeff thinks so too. Jeff's just come in. Jeff? It's Luke. Do you want to say something to him? Luke. Luke, Jeff's coming over. He wants to say something about "Sonnet".'

'Luke?' said Jeff. 'Jeff. Luke? You're a very talented writer. It's great to be working on "Sonnet" with you. Here's Joe.'

'That was Jeff,' said Joe. 'He's crazy about "Sonnet".'

'So what are we going to be talking about?' said Luke. 'Roughly.'

'On "Sonnet"? Well, the only thing we have a problem on "Sonnet" with, Luke, so far as I can see, anyway, and I know Jeff agrees with me on this – right, Jeff? – and so does Jim, incidentally, Luke,' said Joe, 'is the form.'

Luke hesitated. Then he said, 'You mean the form "Sonnet"'s written in.'

'Yes, that's right, Luke. The sonnet form.'

Luke waited for the last last call and was then guided, with much unreturned civility, into the plane's nose.

'Dear Mr Sixsmith,' wrote Alistair,

> *Going through my files the other day, I vaguely remembered sending you a little effort called Offensive from Quasar 13 – just over seven months ago, it must have been. Am I right in assuming that you have no use for it? I might bother you with another one (or two!) that I have completed since then. I hope you are well. Thank you so much for your encouragement in the past.*
>
> *Need I say how much I admire your own work? The austerity, the depth. When, may I ask, can we expect another 'slim vol.'?*

He sadly posted this letter on a wet Sunday afternoon in Leeds. He hoped that the postmark might testify to his mobility and grit.

Yet, really, he felt much steadier now. There had been a recent period of about five weeks during which, Alistair came to realize, he had gone clinically insane. That letter to Sixsmith was but one of the many dozens he had penned. He had also taken to haunting the Holborn offices of the *Little Magazine*: for hours he sat crouched in the coffee bars and sandwich nooks opposite, with the unsettled intention of springing out at

Sixsmith – if he ever saw him, which he never did. Alistair began to wonder whether Sixsmith actually existed. Was he, perhaps, an actor, a ghost, a shrewd fiction? Alistair telephoned the *LM* from selected phone booths. Various people answered, and no one knew where anyone was, and only three or four times was Alistair successfully connected to the apparently permanent coughing fit that crackled away at the other end of Sixsmith's extension. Then he hung up. He couldn't sleep, or he thought he couldn't, for Hazel said that all night long he whimpered and gnashed.

Alistair waited for nearly two months. Then he sent in three more screenplays. One was about a Machine hitman who emerges from early retirement when his wife is slain by a serial murderer. Another dealt with the infiltration by the three Gorgons of an escort agency in present-day New York. The third was a heavy-metal musical set on the Isle of Skye. He enclosed a stamped-addressed envelope the size of a small knapsack.

Winter was unusually mild.

'May I get you something to drink before your meal? A cappuccino? A mineral water? A glass of sauvignon blanc?'

'Double decaf espresso,' said Luke. 'Thanks.'

'You're more than welcome.'

'Hey,' said Luke when everyone had ordered. 'I'm not just welcome any more. I'm more than welcome.'

The others smiled patiently. Such remarks were the downside of the classy fact that Luke, despite his appearance and his accent, was English. There they all sat on the terrace at Bubo's: Joe, Jeff, Jim.

Luke said, 'How did "Eclogue by a Five-Barred Gate" do?'

Joe said, 'Domestically?' He looked at Jim, at Jeff. 'Like – *fifteen?*'

Luke said, 'And worldwide?'

'It isn't *going* worldwide.'

'How about "Black Rook in Rainy Weather"?' asked Luke.

Joe shook his head. 'It didn't even do what "Sheep in Fog" did.'

'It's all remakes,' said Jim. 'Period shit.'

'How about "Bog Oak"?'

'"Bog Oak"? Ooh, maybe twenty-five?'

Luke said sourly, 'I hear nice things about "The Old Botanical Gardens".'

They talked about other Christmas flops and bombs, delaying for as long as they could any mention of TCTs ''Tis he whose yester-evening's high disdain', which had cost practically nothing to make and had already done a hundred and twenty million in its first three weeks.

'What happened?' Luke eventually asked. 'Jesus, what was the publicity budget?'

'On "'Tis"?' said Joe. 'Nothing. Two, three.'

They all shook their heads. Jim was philosophical. 'That's poetry,' he said.

'There aren't any other sonnets being made, are there?' said Luke.

Jeff said, 'Binary is in post-production with a sonnet. "Composed at — Castle". *More* period shit.'

Their soups and salads arrived. Luke thought that it was probably a mistake, at this stage, to go on about sonnets. After a while he said, 'How did "For Sophonisba Anguisciola" do?'

Joe said, '"For Sophonisba Anguisciola"? Don't talk to me about "For Sophonisba Anguisciola".'

It was late at night and Alistair was in his room working on a screenplay about a high-IQ homeless black man who is transformed into a white female junk-bond dealer by a South Moluccan terrorist witchdoctor. Suddenly he shoved this aside with a groan, snatched up a clean sheet of paper, and wrote:

Dear Mr Sixsmith,

It is now well over a year since I sent you Offensive from Quasar 13. *Not content with that dereliction, you have allowed five months to pass without responding to three more recent submissions. A prompt reply I would have deemed common decency, you being a fellow-screenplay writer, though I must say I have never cared for your work, finding it, at once, both florid and superficial. (I read Matthew Sura's piece last month and I thought he got you bang to rights.) Please return the more recent screenplays, namely* Decimator, Medusa Takes Manhattan *and* Valley of the Stratocasters, *immediately.*

He signed it and sealed it. He stalked out and posted it. On his return he haughtily threw off his drenched clothes. The single bed felt enormous, like an orgiast's four-poster. He curled up tight and slept better than he had done all year.

So it was a quietly defiant Alistair who the next morning came plodding down the stairs and glanced at the splayed mail on the shelf as he headed for the door. He recognized the envelope as a lover would. He bent low as he opened it.

> *Do please forgive this very tardy reply. Profound apologies. But allow me to move straight on to a verdict on your work. I won't bore you with all my personal and professional distractions.*

Bore me? thought Alistair, as his hand sought his heart.

> *I think I can at once give the assurance that your screenplays are unusually promising. No: that promise has already been honoured. They have both feeling and burnish.*
>
> *I will content myself, for now, by taking* Offensive from Quasar 13. *(Allow me to muse a little longer on* Decimator.*) I have one or two very minor emendations to suggest. Why not telephone me here to arrange a chat?*
>
> *Thank you for your generous remarks about my own work. Increasingly I find that this kind of exchange – this candour, this reciprocity – is one of the things that keep me trundling along. Your words helped sustain my defences in the aftermath of Matthew Sura's vicious and slovenly attack, from which, I fear, I am still rather reeling. Take excellent care.*

'Go with the lyric,' said Jim.

'Or how about a ballad?' said Jeff.

Jack was swayable. 'Ballads are big,' he allowed.

It seemed to Luke, towards the end of the second day, that he was winning the sonnet battle. The clue lay in the flavour of Joe's taciturnity: torpid but unmorose.

'Let's face it,' said Jeff. 'Sonnets are essentially hieratic. They're strictly period. They answer to a formalized consciousness. Today, we're talking consciousnesses that are in *search* of form.'

'Plus,' said Jack, 'the lyric has always been the natural medium for the untrammelled expression of feeling.'

'Yeah,' said Jeff. 'With the sonnet you're stuck in this thesis-antithesis-synthesis routine.'

Joan said, 'I mean what are we doing here? Reflecting the world or illuminating it?'

It was time for Joe to speak. 'Please,' he said. 'Are we forgetting that "'Tis" was a sonnet, before the rewrites? Were we on coke when we said, in the summer, that we were going to go for the *sonnet*?'

The answer to Joe's last question, incidentally; was yes; but Luke looked carefully round the room. The Chinese lunch they'd had the secretary phone out for lay on the coffee table like a child's experiments with putty and paint and designer ooze. It was four o'clock and Luke wanted to get away soon. To swim and lie in the sun. To make himself especially lean and bronzed for his meeting with the young actress Henna Mickiewicz. He faked a yawn.

'Luke's lagged,' said Joe. 'Tomorrow we'll talk some more, but I'm pretty sure I'm recommitted to the sonnet.'

'Sorry,' said Alistair. 'Me yet again. Sorry.'

'Oh yes,' said the woman's voice. 'He *was* here a minute ago . . . No, he's there. He's there. Just a second.'

Alistair jerked the receiver away from his ear and stared at it. He started listening again. It seemed as if the phone itself were in paroxysm, all squawk and splat like a cabby's radio. Then the fit passed, or paused, and a voice said tightly but proudly, 'Hugh Sixsmith?'

It took Alistair a little while to explain who he was. Sixsmith sounded surprised but, on the whole, rather intrigued to hear from him. They moved on smoothly enough to arrange a meeting (after work, the following Monday), before Alistair contrived to put in: 'Mr Sixsmith, there's just one thing. This is very embarrassing, but last night I got into a bit of a state about not hearing from you for so long and I'm afraid I sent you a completely mad letter which I . . .' Alistair waited. 'Oh, you know how it is. For these screenplays, you know, you reach into yourself, and then time goes by and . . .'

'My dear boy, don't say another word. I'll ignore it. I'll throw it away. After a line or two I shall simply avert my unpained eye,' said Sixsmith, and started coughing again.

Hazel did not come down to London for the weekend. Alistair did not go up to Leeds for the weekend. He spent the time thinking about that place

in Earls Court Square where screenplay writers read from their screenplays
and drank biting Spanish red wine and got stared at by tousled girls who
wore thick overcoats and no make-up and blinked incessantly or not at all.

Luke parked his Chevrolet Celebrity on the fifth floor of the studio car
park and rode down in the elevator with two minor executives in tracksuits
who were discussing the latest records broken by "'Tis he whose
yester-evening's high disdain'. He put on his dark glasses as he crossed the
other car park, the one reserved for major executives. Each bay had a name
on it. It reassured Luke to see Joe's name there, partly obscured by his
Range Rover. Poets, of course, seldom had that kind of clout. Or any clout
at all. He was glad that Henna Mickiewicz didn't seem to realize this.

Joe's office: Jim, Jack, Joan, but no Jeff. Two new guys were there. Luke
was introduced to the two new guys. Ron said he spoke for Don when
he told Luke that he was a great admirer of his material. Huddled over
the coffee percolator with Joe, Luke asked after Jeff, and Joe said, 'Jeff's
off the poem,' and Luke just nodded.

They settled in their low armchairs.

Luke said, 'What's "A Welshman to Any Tourist" doing?'

Don said, 'It's doing good but not great.'

Ron said, 'It won't do what "The Gap in the Hedge" did.'

Jim said, 'What did "Hedge" do?'

They talked about what 'Hedge' did. Then Joe said, 'Okay. We're going
with the sonnet. Now. Don has a problem with the octet's first quatrain,
Ron has a problem with the second quatrain, Jack and Jim have a problem
with the first quatrain of the sestet, and I think we *all* have a problem
with the final couplet.'

Alistair presented himself at the offices of the *LM* in an unblinking trance
of punctuality. He had been in the area for hours, and had spent about
fifteen quid on teas and coffees. There wasn't much welcome to overstay
in the various snack bars where he lingered (and where he moreover imagined himself unfavourably recollected from his previous *LM* vigils),
holding with both hands the creaky foam container, and watching the
light pour past the office windows.

As Big Ben struck two, Alistair mounted the stairs. He took a breath

so deep that he almost fell over backwards – and then knocked. An elderly office boy wordlessly showed him into a narrow, rubbish-heaped office
that contained, with difficulty, seven people. At first Alistair took them
for other screenplay writers and wedged himself behind the door, at the
back of the queue. But they didn't look like screenplay writers. Not much
was said over the next four hours, and the identities of Sixsmith's sup-
plicants emerged only partially and piecemeal. One or two, like his
solicitor and his second wife's psychiatrist, took their leave after no more
than ninety minutes. Others, like the VAT man and the probation officer,
stayed almost as long as Alistair. But by six forty-five he was alone.

He approached the impossible haystack of Sixsmith's desk. Very hurriedly he started searching through the unopened mail. It was in Alistair's
mind that he might locate and intercept his own letter. But all the envelopes, of which there were a great many, proved to be brown, windowed,
and registered. Turning to leave, he saw a Jiffy bag of formidable bulk
addressed to himself in Sixsmith's tremulous hand. There seemed no reason not to take it. The old office boy, Alistair soon saw, was curled up in
a sleeping-bag under a worktable in the outer room.

On the street he unseamed his package in a ferment of grey fluff. It
contained two of his screenplays, *Valley of the Stratocasters* and, confusingly,
Decimator. There was also a note:

> *I have been called away, as they say. Personal ups and downs. I shall ring
> you this week and we'll have – what? Lunch?*

Enclosed, too, was Alistair's aggrieved letter – unopened. He moved on.
The traffic, human and mechanical, lurched past his quickened face. He
felt his eyes widen to an obvious and solving truth: Hugh Sixsmith was
a screenplay writer. He understood.

After an inconclusive day spent discussing the caesura of 'Sonnet''s opening line, Luke and his colleagues went for cocktails at Strabismus. They
were given the big round table near the piano.

Jane said, 'TCT is doing a sequel to '"Tis".'
Joan said, 'Actually it's a prequel.'
'Title?' said Joe.

'Undecided. At TCT they're calling it "'Twas".'

'My son,' said Joe thoughtfully, after the waiter had delivered their drinks, 'called me an asshole this morning. For the first time.'

'That's incredible,' said Bo. '*My* son called me an asshole this morning. For the first time.'

'So?' said Mo.

Joe said, 'He's six years old, for Christ's sake.'

Phil said, 'My son called me an asshole when he was five.'

'My son hasn't called me an asshole yet,' said Jim. 'And he's nine.'

Luke sipped his Bloody Mary. Its hue and texture made him wonder whether he could risk blowing his nose without making yet another visit to the bathroom. He hadn't called Suki for three days. Things were getting compellingly out of hand with Henna Mickiewicz. He hadn't actually promised her a part in the poem, not on paper. Henna was great, except you kept thinking she was going to suddenly sue you anyway.

Mo was saying that each child progresses at its own rate, and that later lulls regularly offset the apparent advances of the early years.

Jim said, 'Still, it's a cause of concern.'

Mo said, 'My son's three. And he calls me an asshole all the time.'

Everybody looked suitably impressed.

The trees were in leaf, and the rumps of the tourist buses were thick and fat in the traffic, and all the farmers wanted fertilizer admixes rather than storehouse insulation when Sixsmith finally made his call. In the interim, Alistair had convinced himself of the following: before returning his aggrieved letter, Sixsmith had *steamed it open and then resealed it.* During this period, also, Alistair had grimly got engaged to Hazel. But the call came.

He was pretty sure he had come to the right restaurant. Except that it wasn't a restaurant, not quite. The place took no bookings, and knew of no Mr Sixsmith, and was serving many midday breakfasts to swearing persons whose eyes bulged over mugs of flesh-coloured tea. On the other hand, there was alcohol. All kinds of people were drinking it. Fine, thought Alistair. Fine. What better place, really, for a couple of screenplay writers to . . .

'Alistair?'

Confidently Sixsmith bent his long body into the booth. As he settled, he looked well pleased with the manoeuvre. He contemplated Alistair with peculiar neutrality, but there was then something boyish, something consciously remiss, in the face he turned to the waiter. As Sixsmith ordered a gin and tonic, and as he amusingly expatiated on his weakness for prawn cocktails, Alistair found himself wryly but powerfully drawn to this man, to this rumpled screenplay writer with his dreamy gaze, the curious elisions of his somewhat slurred voice, and the great dents and bone shadows of his face, all the faulty fontanelles of vocational care. He knew how old Sixsmith was. But maybe time moved strangely for screen-play writers, whose flames burnt so bright . . .

'And as for my fellow artisan in the scrivener's trade: Alistair. What will *you* have?'

At once Sixsmith showed himself to be a person of some candour. Or it might have been that he saw in the younger screenplay writer someone before whom all false reticence could be cast aside. Sixsmith's estranged second wife, it emerged, herself the daughter of two alcoholics, was an alcoholic. Her current lover (ah, how these lovers came and went!) was an alcoholic. To complicate matters, Sixsmith explained as he rattled his glass at the waiter, his daughter, the product of his first marriage, was an alco-holic. How did Sixsmith keep going? Despite his years, he had, thank God, found love, in the arms of a woman young enough (and, by the sound of it, alcoholic enough) to be his daughter. Their prawn cocktails arrived, together with a carafe of hearty red wine. Sixsmith lit a cigarette and held up his palm towards Alistair for the duration of a coughing fit that turned every head in the room. Then, for a moment, understandably disorientated, he stared at Alistair as if uncertain of his intentions, or even his identity. But their bond quickly re-established itself. Soon they were talking away like hardened equals – of Trumbo, of Chayevsky, of Towne, of Eszterhas.

Around two thirty, when, after several attempts, the waiter succeeded in removing Sixsmith's untouched prawn cocktail, and now prepared to serve them their braised chops with a third carafe, the two men were arguing loudly about early Puzo.

Joe yawned and shrugged and said languidly, 'You know something? I was never that crazy about the Petrarchan rhyme scheme anyway.'

Jan said, '"Composed at — Castle" is ABBA ABBA.'

Jen said, 'So was "'Tis". Right up until the final polish.'

Jon said, 'Here's some news. They say "Composed at — Castle" is in turnaround.'

'You're not serious,' said Bo. 'It's released this month. I heard they were getting great preview reaction.'

Joe looked doubtful. '"'Tis" has made the suits kind of antsy about sonnets. They figure lightning can't strike twice.'

'ABBA ABBA,' said Bo with distaste.

'Or,' said Joe. 'Or . . . or we go unrhymed.'

'*Un*rhymed?' said Phil.

'We go blank,' said Joe.

There was a silence. Bill looked at Gil, who looked at Will.

'What do you think, Luke?' said Jim. 'You're the poet.'

Luke had never felt very protective about 'Sonnet'. Even its original version he had regarded as little more than a bargaining chip. Nowadays he rewrote 'Sonnet' every night at the Pinnacle Trumont before Henna arrived and they started torturing room service. 'Blank,' said Luke. 'Blank. I don't know, Joe. I could go ABAB ABAB or even ABAB CDCD. Christ, I'd go AABB if I didn't think it'd tank the final couplet. But blank. I never thought I'd go *blank.*'

'Well, it needs something,' said Joe.

'Maybe it's the pentameter,' said Luke. 'Maybe it's the iamb. Hey, here's one from left field. How about syllabics?'

At five forty-five Hugh Sixsmith ordered a gin and tonic and said, 'We've talked. We've broken bread. Wine. Truth. Screenplay-writing. I want to talk about your work, Alistair. Yes, I do. I want to talk about *Offensive from Quasar 13.*'

Alistair blushed.

'It's not often that . . . But one always knows. That sense of pregnant arrest. Of felt life in its full . . . Thank you, Alistair. Thank you. I have to say that it rather reminded me of my own early work.'

Alistair nodded.

Having talked for quite some time about his own maturation as a screenplay writer, Sixsmith said, 'Now. Just tell me to shut up any time you like. And I'm going to print it anyway. But I want to make one *tiny* suggestion about *Offensive from Quasar 13.*'

Alistair waved a hand in the air.

'Now,' said Sixsmith. He broke off and ordered a prawn cocktail. The waiter looked at him defeatedly. 'Now,' said Sixsmith. 'When Brad escapes from the Nebulan experiment lab and sets off with Cord and Tara to immobilize the directed-energy scythe on the Xerxian attack ship – where's Chelsi?'

Alistair frowned.

'Where's Chelsi? She's still in the lab with the Nebulans. On the point of being injected with a Phobian viper venom, moreover. What of the happy ending? What of Brad's heroic centrality? What of his avowed love for Chelsi? Or am I just being a bore?'

The secretary, Victoria, stuck her head into the room and said, 'He's coming down.'

Luke listened to the sound of twenty-three pairs of legs uncrossing and recrossing. Meanwhile he readied himself for a sixteen-tooth smile. He glanced at Joe, who said, 'He's fine. He's just coming down to say hi.'

And down he came: Jake Endo, exquisitely Westernized and gorgeously tricked out and perhaps thirty-five. Of the luxury items that pargeted his slender form, none was as breathtaking as his hair, with its layers of pampered light.

Jake Endo shook Luke's hand and said, 'It's a great pleasure to meet you. I haven't read the basic material on the poem, but I'm familiar with the background.'

Luke surmised that Jake Endo had had his voice fixed. He could do the bits of the words that Japanese people were supposed to find difficult.

'I understand it's a love poem,' he continued. 'Addressed to your girlfriend. Is she here with you in L.A.?'

'No. She's in London.' Luke found he was staring at Jake Endo's sandals, wondering how much they could possibly have cost.

A silence began its crescendo. This silence had long been intolerable when Jim broke it, saying to Jake Endo, 'Oh, how did "Lines Left Upon a Seat in a Yew-Tree, Which Stands Near the Lake of Easthwaite, on a Desolate Part of the Shore, Commanding a Beautiful Prospect" do?'

'"Lines"?' said Jake Endo. 'Rather well.'

'I was thinking about "Composed at — Castle",' said Jim weakly.

The silence began again. As it neared its climax Joe was suddenly reminded of all this energy he was supposed to have. He got to his feet saying, 'Jake? I guess we're nearing our tiredness peak. You've caught us at kind of a low point. We can't agree on the first line. First line? We can't see our way to the end of the first *foot*.'

Jake Endo was undismayed. 'There always are these low points. I'm sure you'll get there, with so much talent in the room. Upstairs we're very confident. We think it's going to be a big summer poem.'

'No, we're very confident too,' said Joe. 'There's a lot of belief here. A lot of belief. We're behind "Sonnet" all the way.'

'Sonnet?' said Jake Endo.

'Yeah, sonnet. "Sonnet".'

'"Sonnet"?' said Jake Endo.

'It's a sonnet. It's called "Sonnet".'

In waves the West fell away from Jake Endo's face. After a few seconds he looked like a dark-age warlord in mid-campaign, taking a glazed breather before moving on to the women and the children.

'Nobody told me,' he said as he went towards the telephone, 'about any *sonnet*.'

The place was closing. Its tea trade and its after-office trade had come and gone. Outside, the streets glimmered morbidly. Members of the staff were donning macs and overcoats. An important light went out. A fridge door slammed.

'Hardly the most resounding felicity, is it?' said Sixsmith.

Absent or unavailable for over an hour, the gift of speech had been restored to Alistair – speech, that prince of all the faculties. 'Or what if . . .' he said. 'What if Chelsi just leaves the experiment lab earlier?'

'Not hugely dramatic,' said Sixsmith. He ordered a carafe of wine and enquired as to the whereabouts of his braised chop.

'Or what if she just gets wounded? During the escape. In the leg.'

'So long as one could avoid the wretched cliché: girl impeded, hero dangerously tarrying. Also, she's supernumerary to the raid on the Xerxian attack ship. We really want her out of the way for that.'

Alistair said, 'Then let's kill her.'

'Very well. Slight pall over the happy ending. No, no.'

A waiter stood over them, sadly staring at the bill in its saucer.

'All right,' said Sixsmith. 'Chelsi gets wounded. Quite badly. In the arm. *Now* what does Brad do with her?'

'Drops her off at the hospital.'

'Mm. Rather hollow modulation.'

The waiter was joined by another waiter, equally stoic; their faces were grained by evening shadow. Now Sixsmith was gently frisking himself with a deepening frown.

'What if,' said Alistair, 'what if there's somebody passing who can *take* her to the hospital?'

'Possibly,' said Sixsmith, who was half standing, with one hand awkwardly dipped into his inside pocket.

'Or what if,' said Alistair, 'or what if Brad just gives her *directions* to the hospital?'

Back in London the next day, Luke met with Mike to straighten this shit out. Actually it looked okay. Mike called Mal at Monad, who had a thing about Tim at TCT. As a potential finesse on Mal, Mike also called Bob at Binary with a view to repossessing the option on 'Sonnet', plus development money at rolling compound, and redeveloping it somewhere else entirely – say, at Red Giant, where Rodge was known to be very interested. 'They'll want you to go out there,' said Mike. 'To kick it around.'

'I can't believe Joe,' said Luke. 'I can't believe I knocked myself out for that flake.'

'Happens. Joe forgot about Jake Endo and sonnets. Endo's first big poem was a sonnet. Before your time. "Bright star, would I were steadfast as thou art". It opened for like one day. It practically bankrupted Japan.'

'I feel used, Mike. My sense of trust. I've got to get wised up around here.'

'A lot will depend on how "Composed at — Castle" does and what the feeling is on the "'Tis" prequel.'

'I'm going to go away with Suki for a while. Do you know anywhere where there aren't any shops? Jesus, I need a holiday. Mike, this is all bullshit. You know what I *really* want to do, don't you?'

'Of course I do.'

Luke looked at Mike until he said, 'You want to direct.'

*

When Alistair had convalesced from the lunch, he revised *Offensive from Quasar 13* in rough accordance with Sixsmith's suggestions. He solved the Chelsi problem by having her noisily eaten by a Stygian panther in the lab menagerie. The charge of gratuitousness was, in Alistair's view, safely anticipated by Brad's valediction to her remains, in which sanguinary revenge on the Nebulans was both prefigured and legitimized. He also took out the bit where Brad declared his love for Chelsi, and put in a bit where Brad declared his love for Tara.

He sent in the new pages, which three months later Sixsmith acknowledged and applauded in a hand quite incompatible with that of his earlier communications. Nor did he reimburse Alistair for the lunch. His wallet, he had explained, had been emptied that morning – by which alcoholic, Sixsmith never established. Alistair kept the bill as a memento. This startling document showed that during the course of the meal Sixsmith had smoked, or at any rate bought, nearly a carton of cigarettes.

Three months later he was sent a proof of *Offensive from Quasar 13*. Three months after that, the screenplay appeared in the *Little Magazine*. Three months after that, Alistair received a cheque for £12.50, which bounced.

Curiously, although the proof had incorporated Alistair's corrections, the published version reverted to the typescript, in which Brad escaped from the Nebulan lab seemingly without concern for a Chelsi last glimpsed on an operating table with a syringe full of Phobian viper venom being eased into her neck. Later that month, Alistair went along to a reading at the Screenplay Society in Earls Court. There he got talking to a gaunt girl in an ash-stained black smock who claimed to have read his screenplay and who, over glasses of red wine and, later, in the terrible pub, told him he was a weakling and a hypocrite with no notion of the ways of men and women. Alistair had not been a published screenplay writer long enough to respond to, or even recognize, this graphic proposition (though he did keep the telephone number she threw at his feet). It is anyway doubtful whether he would have dared to take things further. He was marrying Hazel the following weekend.

In the new year he sent Sixsmith a series – one might almost say a sequence – of screenplays on group-jeopardy themes. His follow-up letter in the summer was answered by a brief note stating that Sixsmith was no longer employed by the *LM*. Alistair telephoned. He then discussed the matter with Hazel and decided to take the next day off work.

It was a September morning. The hospice in Cricklewood was of recent design and construction; from the road it resembled a clutch of igloos against the sheenless tundra of the sky. When he asked for Hugh Sixsmith at the desk, two men in suits climbed quickly from their chairs. One was a writ-server. One was a cost-adjuster. Alistair waved away their complex requests.

The warm room contained clogged, regretful murmurs, and defiance in the form of bottles and paper cups and cigarette smoke, and the many peeping eyes of female grief. A young woman faced him proudly. Alistair started explaining who he was, a young screenplay writer come to . . . On the bed in the corner the spavined figure of Sixsmith was gawkily arranged. Alistair moved towards it. At first he was sure the eyes were gone, like holes cut out of pumpkin or blood orange. But then the faint brows began to lift, and Alistair thought he saw the light of recognition.

As the tears began, he felt the shiver of approval, of consensus, on his back. He took the old screenplay writer's hand and said, 'Goodbye. And thank you. Thank you. Thank you.'

Opening in four hundred and thirty-seven theatres, the Binary sonnet 'Composed at—Castle' did seventeen million in its first weekend. At this time Luke was living in a two-bedroom apartment on Yokum Drive. Suki was with him. He hoped it wouldn't take her too long to find out about Henna Mickiewicz. When the smoke cleared he would switch to the more mature Anita, who produced.

He had taken his sonnet to Rodge at Red Giant and turned it into an ode. When that didn't work out he went to Mal at Monad, where they'd gone for the villanelle. The villanelle had become a triolet, briefly, with Tim at TCT, before Bob at Binary had him rethink it as a rondeau. When the rondeau didn't take, Luke lyricized it and got Mike to send it to Joe. Everyone, including Jake Endo, thought that now was surely the time to turn it back into a sonnet.

Luke had dinner at Rales with Joe and Mike.

'I always thought of "Sonnet" as an art poem,' said Joe. 'But sonnets are so hot now I've started thinking more commercially.'

Mike said, 'TCT is doing a sequel *and* a prequel to "'Tis" and bringing them out at the same time.'

'A sequel?' said Joe.

'Yeah. They're calling it "'Twill".'

Mike was a little fucked up. So was Joe. Luke was a little fucked up too. They'd done some lines at the office. Then drinks here at the bar. They'd meant to get a little fucked up. It was okay. It was good, once in a while, to get a little fucked up. The thing was not to get fucked up too often. The thing was not to get fucked up to excess.

'I mean it, Luke,' said Joe. He glittered potently. 'I think "Sonnet" could be as big as "—".'

'You think?' said Luke.

'I mean it. I think "Sonnet" could be another "—".'

'"—"?'

'"—".'

Luke thought for a moment, taking this in. '"—" . . .' he repeated wonderingly.

CANDIA McWILLIAM

The Only Only

The first ferry for a week was fast to the quay, the thick rope springs hold-ing it to, looped fore and aft over iron cleats the height of children. The weather had been so hard and high that there was seaweed all over the island, brought in by the wind, and the east wall of each house was drifted up to the roof. The children dug in to these drifts and made blue caves to sit in, smoothing till the cave's inner ice melted and set to a clear lucent veneer.

Seven children lived on the island and attended the school together. Sandy was the only only among them; the rest had brothers or sisters. She was a girl of eight born to the teacher Euphemia and her husband Davie, who set and lifted lobsterpots for his main living, though the ferry com-pany kept him on a retainer to attend the arrival and departure of the ferry, three times a week when the sea would let it through. Davie'd to hook up and untie the boat, watch for the embarkation of livestock and the safe operation of the davits on the quay. He had an eye to the secure delivery of post and to the setting in place of the gangplank so that it would hold in a swell.

He liked his job. It involved him with everyone who lived on the island and he was careful to respect this. If he knew that the father of a child off just now inside its mother on the ferry to be born on the mainland was not the man with his arm around the woman as the ship parted from the land, he did not say. Davie was not an islander born, although Euphe-mia was; she could remember her grandmother skinning fulmars to salt them for the winter and she herself could feel if the egg of a gull might be taken for food or if it was fertilised and packed with affronted life. Davie had boiled up a clutch of eggs once and they had sat down to them with a salad and pink potatoes from outdoors; the tapping and the faint window of membrane had seemed right enough, but when he'd got through to the boiled halfmade chick with its eggtooth sticking out like a sail needle's hook, he'd got sick. He still looked away when a seal heaved up the rocks to die after a gashing; the thickness of the blubber inside gave him a lurch, like seeing the legs above an old woman's stocking tops. In death a seal keeps its enthusiastic expression; the human face falls to neutral peace, but the seal appears to trust even death.

Because there had been no boat for some time, everyone was on the pier today. It was a social occasion although it was so cold. Something seemed to have slowed the sea, its salt particles surrendering to the grip ice has on water. On the Atlantic coast of the island, rockpools were freezing over, the crabs moving in under sea lettuce to escape seizure by the ice. Among the blue-brown mussels that clustered around the stanchions of the pier hung icicles at low tide. The sea was unusually quiet, hushed by the cold from lapping or thrashing the shingle or the harbour walls. Only the hardiest boats were still down in the water, fishing boats and a clam skiff that had been neglected and had taken in water that was now a hard slope of grey ice halfway up to the gunwales.

On the slip where the smaller boats came alongside there was a tangle of nets and a pile of polythene fishboxes. Yellow, orange, mauve and electric blue, the nets were neatly trimmed with a white buzz of rime. The impression of a deserted, frozen harlequinade was emphasised by a pair of red heavy-duty gloves lying on the weed next to a single yellow seaboot.

Sandy stood with Euphemia in a group of women. People asked the teacher about their children; in such a community there was no chance of going unnoticed. Talk was the pastime, talk and work the currency. Euphemia was pleased to be among women, with her daughter. When, as now, she was irked at her man she did not tell, or it would have been round the place before tea.

She wanted him to give up the boat and come into teaching at the school with her. She could not see the future in working on the pier. It took up a good day three times a week, when the following up had been done, the cargo counted, the letters sorted and settled in the red Land Rover to be taken round the only road by the post; and by the time drink had been taken, with the purser maybe, or with whoever came off the boat or was in the bar off a fishing boat.

He was a good man, but where did these boat days go? Whereas, should he come in with her at the teaching, they would see their work as it grew day by day. And he could still do the lobsters, if there were any left in the sea. With the French and the Russians and the warm-water breeders at it, the sea was full of mostly red herrings, forget the silver darlings.

Sandy now, she would see more of her father if he came in with the teaching, and then Euphemia maybe, when it was all settled, would get down to having another baby.

The purple line at the horizon lay over the slow grey sea. The air smelt of weed, cigarettes and diesel; the post office van was idling and the men gathered around it in their oilskins, smoking for the warmth. The children of the island were standing against the rail at the end of the pier, their feet kicking against the robust wire barrier with a bright harsh chiming. Six of them red-headed, in shades of red from orangeade to a bracken mixed with rough briar brown, and one of them with the crow-black hair that does not shine and goes with blue eyes. The children were waiting to wave, even those who were waving no one off; it was the boat, which was the presiding event of their lives, that they wished to acknowledge.

Against the folding evening clouds, and frosted by their departing rims of hard light, the shining ruby-juice red of Sandy's straight hair and the drained white of her face seemed to Euphemia to be stamped like a royal seal set to important words. It was not easy to think of Sandy with a brother or a sister. But Euphemia did not approve of only children; especially not here, where circumstances were already isolated in the world's eyes. It was not possible to imagine loving Sandy any less or loving any child more than Sandy was loved; it was hard to imagine the love that Davie and she bore for their child stretching to accommodate more, but Euphemia was convinced that this would occur naturally, without pain, like passing through a door into a new room with open windows.

The ferry was loaded. The gangplank was lifted on its ropes and let down to the pier for rolling and storage in the metal waiting room at the end where the children hung and bobbed and cuffed one another's bright heads. A long plaintive blast warned that the boat must soon go and the children hollered back to it through cupped hands. Lights were coming on in the boat; soon the dark would land over them all, steaming across the water from the purple edge of the sea.

Davie was checking that goods had been properly exchanged, the gang-mower sent to the mainland for fixing by June time, the cowcake fetched up out of the hold, the canned goods and frozen gear stowed ready for the shop, the box of specially requested medicaments boxed up for the doctor, the beer rolled into the pub's Bedford van; detail was what mattered in this job, and he took a pride in it.

In the restful numbed cold silence, people began to prepare themselves to make farewell and to depart for their homes. The moment the children loved was coming, when they could wave to the boat as it pulled out and away from the island, seagulls over the wake like bridesmaids. They stood and waited at the pier end, looking out to sea.

There was a creak, a sodden tugging groaning. The seagulls gathered. The eighty people on the pier experienced the shared illusion that it was they and not the boat who moved. The rudder of the ship was churning deep under the water which, astern, showed silvery green below its surface and white above. The air was still enough for a hundred separate lifted voices to reach the ears intended as the twenty souls on the boat looked down to the crowd on the pier. The children waited.

The stern spring of the boat cracked free of the cleat from which Davie had forgotten to lift it. After the first tearing report of the bust rope came the whipping weight of sixty yards of corded hemp and steel, swinging out through its hard blind arc at the height of a good-sized child.

'Lie down, get down, for God's sake,' yelled a man. The women fell to the ground. Unless they were mothers, when they ran for their little ones to the end of the pier as the thick murderous rope lashed out, rigid and determined as a scythe to cut down all that stood in its way.

Sandy lay under her mother's heart, hearing it in the coat that covered them both. The concrete of the pier seemed to tremble with the hard commotion of the rope's passing over them.

Snapped out of her dreams, Euphemia held her only child.

The boat continued to move away, its briefly lethal rope trailing behind it, a lone seaman at the winch above, coiling it in to usefulness. The black ferrous patina on the big cleat had burned off under the seething tension of the rope; its stem was polished by force through to a pale refined metal blue. The children from the end of the pier comforted their mothers, who stared out to the disappearing ship seeing, abob in the water, the heads of children cut off at the neck, their frozen sweetness of face under the streaming curtailed hair; red, red, red, red, red, red or black, and to grow no more.

JANICE GALLOWAY

last thing

we were
coming

coming back from the pictures with half a packet of sweeties still coming round the corner at the Meadowside with Mary saying she was feart to go up the road herself Mary is feart for everything but so I said I'll take you because I'm bigger than her the film thing we'd saw at the pictures that Halloween thing wasny really scary I don't think but Mary saying she hated all the screaming the big knife was horrible one time her brother pushed one under the toilet door she said and told her to slit her wrists but he's not right Billy he works a place they make baskets or something he's not right in the head so I said I'll take you up the road offering her a sweetie it got stuck to the back of her teeth and she was laughing kidding on her mouth was glued shut and she couldn't talk only make these moaning noises because her mouth was all stuck together when this shape a big kind of shadow thing started it came out of the close at the corner of the main street right where the street-light is at the corner a big shape coming out and turning into a man he was only a wee bit bigger than Mary so maybe he was a boy really and he said

I've lost my mate

just like that he said and away back in again away in the close he had come out I just looked but I couldn't see him but he was definitely there you could hear him saying it again in there I've lost my mate only a wee thin voice with no body now but you couldn't see maybe he was round the back garden or something and I thought he must be lost too the man maybe not from here with him speaking funny the way he did not know-ing you didn't wander about in people's gardens this terrible idea of being lost and maybe not knowing where you were and not being able to find the person who had come with you like losing the only thing you understood and I went in Mary was kind of hanging back she didn't like people she's an awful feart kind of person Mary she gets rows from her mother for talking to folk she gets rows for just being there but I went in away after the sound of the voice that had lost its friend and was maybe lonely I went in after the voice and I couldn't see him at first it was too dark too

dark off the main road and I didn't like it was too

dark I couldn't hear anything any

more and I was nearly shouting for Mary to come too it was frightening expecting to go in and help somebody and suddenly they weren't there to be helped and it was like a dark tunnel between nothing and where she was out there so I was about to shout her when something

some thing wrapped it

self around my neck I didn't know just felt the tilt backwards and couldn't work out why I was unsteady on my feet till the thing went tight in my neck like a piece of pipe or something it was blocked a stuck thing poking into where I needed to breathe and my legs going soft like they wouldn't be able to hold me up I just went like a dolly because I got a surprise not knowing what it was till I was being dragged backwards back

wards away from the road the streetlight out there the yellowness kind of slipping further away because somebody some body was dragging me by the neck a man he said YOU'RE COMING WITH ME but his voice wasn't right like he was choking or crying maybe something was wrong it was definitely the man saying YOU'RE COMING WITH ME and he shoved one of his hands up under my jersey I could feel the big shape of his hand sort of pulling my jersey under my jacket and going up onto my belly and it made me stop and breathe wrong it was so unexpected his hand there then he pushed me round the edge out the close altogether against the wall so then I could feel the wall being crumbly thon way plaster goes after years with the wee bits of moss growing through it crumbling through to the grey stuff underneath you think it would have felt scratchy but it wasn't it was just this stuff disintegrating under where he was pushing me back against the wall so it was hard to keep breathing right with his hand pushing under my chin so all I could see was the sky a funny colour with the orange off the streetlight making

wee grains in it like off milk but right then right that minute something
kind of turned in my head something kind of clicked and I wanted to
look him right in the eye

it was what I really wanted to do I wanted to
just see his face just
look him in the eye he was pushing my face so hard my nose was running he was hurting my wrists but I kind of pushed my head straight till
I could see because I wanted to see his face I wanted to stare at him he
was cutting off where I was trying to breathe and know I just wanted him
to know to see me and know what he was doing the noise of Mary greeting from the street out there I could hear her in the place by the close
mouth Mary a terrible coward and not even sure where I lived and even
if she found it I was scared she got a row so would I for being out I could
get a row easy for there being marks on my neck maybe hit I wondered
if it looked like lovebites or hit for not being back on time the face of the
man rising a single eye in enough light to glisten seeing me watching him
and thinking it will make a difference if he can see me so I looked at him

right into his eyes I looked right at him
keeping
my sights

clear

and

last thing

still

ALI SMITH

miracle survivors

When the thaw set in they found one man still alive who'd been buried
in the snow for over a week. His skin was blue and his pulse so submerged
that the man from the rescue services almost missed the beat altogether
and took him for dead. His clothes were stuck to his skin under his arms
and at his chest and neck and crotch.

In town that year the snow had reached over two foot high and out of
town had lain thicker than most living people could remember. The main
news on television, between the sports results and the *Generation Game*,
ran a report about the white Christmas there was going to be in the
Highlands, and the radio said not to travel, and if you had to, to carry a
spade in the boot of your car.

Several people had suffocated in their cars trying to keep warm with
the ignition left on, snow piling round them on the gone roads, snow
creeping up the windscreens and blotting the windows out. One couple,
found sitting in the front seats with their arms frozen round each other,
looked like they'd just fallen asleep. The bodies of other people surfaced
near their abandoned cars as the slow work of the thaw went on. But the
old man, still breathing, just, they found by chance at the side of the
Culloden road while they were searching for somebody else. Nobody on
the list of people missing matched his description. Well that's no surprise
now, is it? he said to the nurse afterwards. It's not as if I told anyone I
was planning to be missing now, did I?

Macpherson, Thomas, she wrote on the form. She wrote Not Known
in the spaces marked date of birth and next of kin. She wrote the word
Traveller in both the space marked occupation and the space marked
address. I've been all over, the man told her hoarsely as she wrote. I've

been to Iceland, I was there once and you know there wasn't any dark at
all. It was all daylight. I'm not making that up. I had a bath in a hot spring.
What's your name? Well, Margaret, it was fine and warm under the snow,
Maggie, is it Meg you get called, it had the makings of a fine bed, if you'd
only been there yourself to keep me warm. Don't get me wrong now, I'm
not meaning anything by it, just a thought, and a polite thought, and a
very nice one too.

The nurse told the reporters what his first words had been when he
came round: No Wonder. *No Wonder Says Miracle Survivor. He wanted to
say something so I put my head to his ear to hear and he whispered the words
'no wonder' to me, said Nurse Margaret Gallagher (22).* Afterwards, when
he was well enough to be photographed, the old man explained that it
wasn't wonder he'd said, it was vinegar: No Vinegar. He'd been in the
ditch and dug himself down in the snow to make room, and where he
was digging, he said, he'd found a half-eaten bag of chips someone must
have thrown out of a car window on to the verge.

Can you describe to us how it felt under the snow? the reporters asked.

Oh, it was fine and dandy, the man said. I had a good rest.

The papers sent their photographers back to take his picture again, this
time still wrapped in the tinfoil hospital blanket and holding a fish supper.
My father's father, he told the photographers, knew a lad that went down
on the *Titanic*. My father's father went through two fortunes. My father's
father would have had enough to go on the *Titanic* himself if he'd wanted,
the man said.

By the end of the week the nurses were squabbling over who'd get to
put the lotion on, who'd get to shave him, who'd get to do his feet. One
day one of them showed him a photograph of her boyfriend. Oh he's a
handsome young stag, the old man said, you'll have a herd of big-eyed
bairns out of him and you'll be together for a long time, look at him, he'll
live to be a hundred years and be loyal to you for more than seventy.

The next day all the nurses, even the men, and some from the other
wards, were in and out of his room showing him their photographs.

The younger nurses took to sitting on the edge of his bed whenever
they had a break; the Sister gave three of them a dressing-down about it
one morning, going in there on the thinnest pretext just dodging their
work and making more work for others. The nurses looked at the ground

so as not to look at each other; she'd be angrier if any of them was to laugh now. But the Sister leaned forward and spoke in a quite different voice. Has he told any of you what it was like, what it was really like being under there all that time? Does he remember anything about it? She looked from one kirby-gripped white-hatted head to the next; they were sitting up, looking up now, they all spoke at once. Has he said at all how they actually came to find him in amongst all that snow? the Sister asked, low, insistent.

It was the tree he broke the branch off, Shona said. He says the snow was so high, Sister, that he could just reach up and break the branch off, and all the snow from the other branches shook down on to him and nearly knocked him over, nearly buried him there and then, he says, but he stuck the stick as far as he could through the snow into the ground and tied a bit of his coat on to it.

Oh, the Sister said. Sort of like a flag, do you mean?

The others told the Sister their versions of the story. Just ask him, Sister, just ask him yourself, he'll tell you, Shona said. Shona was especially fond of Tom. Shona means great beauty, he'd told her. To everything there is a season, Shona, and you'll have three babies, three girls, and they'll each go through their lives like nobody else in the world and make you happy, so they will, mark my words. And at the new year, be sure and not lend anybody anything or pay anybody anything you owe them. You'll end up lending and paying all year. Whatever else you do lend no one your matches, and don't be taking rubbish out of the house. The things you do on New Year's Day make your luck for the rest of the year, now, so make sure your first-foot is tall and dark and very handsome. I'll be your first-foot this year, shall I, eh, Shona?

Shona pulled one of the decorations down off the wall and wrote her address on the back of a piece of paper chain.

Later that week Sandra (noble beauty) and Fiona (fine boned and prosperous) were tucking him in, one on each side, when he said, I'll be needing my clothes back now.

They looked at each other across the bed. You're not fit to go yet, Tom, Fiona said. Your clothes are burnt, Tom, Sandra said. We'd to send them for burning. And we'd to cut them off you anyway, you couldn't have put them on again even if they hadn't been burnt.

What about my boots? the man asked.

Against the wishes of the doctors, in the clothes of the fathers and brothers of nurses and with folded pound notes in so many of his pockets, the man left the hospital on the last day of the year.

Twenty minutes to midnight, twenty years later, and Dawn is about to break in to a newsagent's on the deserted station concourse. Not break in exactly, since they have a key though they're not sure what it's for. This girl Tina who Dawn's been hanging about with for the past while for safety in numbers lifted it off one of the men who run the shop when she was doing him a favour earlier. Tina swears she's seventeen though Dawn suspects she's nearer fifteen. Anyway Tina's favours have been keeping them warm all week. Tonight it's freezing cold again, too cold for snow.

It's weird to see the station so empty. There's nobody down there, not a soul, just them and the great scuffed space of the floor shining from the lights left on in the shops, their windows all cheap with tinsel. The front of the newsagent's has a metal shutter down. Tina rattles the padlock then looks around as the sound echoes across the concourse. Round the back in the dark they try the delivery door and the key turns. The door has a panel that's been blocked off by a big plank of wood; someone's tried breaking in here before.

Tina makes straight for the Mars Bars. Behind the counter Dawn finds a convector heater and switches it on with her foot. She puts her face in the blast of air as it warms, and her hand by a telephone under the counter. She picks the receiver up. She listens to the dialling tone.

Can't be new year yet, she says. There's no crossed lines.

In the light from the display window she fills her pockets with packs of cigarettes, and she tries the till, just to see, but it won't open. She chooses a box of matches with care, and sits on a stack of newspapers while she lights a cigarette. She looks at Tina, sitting on the floor in her dirty pink jacket with the *Broons* annual open in her hands and all the racks of magazines behind her.

Princess Tina, Dawn says, and blows smoke out and up.

Tina looks at her blankly. Throw me them, she says. The matches and all.

You're too young, Dawn says. It's bad for you.

Tina has a list of swears the like of which Dawn has never heard before, not even in any of the places she's been over the last few months. Tina sounds like she's from Glasgow though Dawn's not very good at accents; she could be from anywhere down here. I'll bet she's Glaswegian, though, Dawn thinks. I mean, she really knows stuff, even if she is younger than me.

The swears stream through the air at Dawn until the cigarettes land at Tina's feet. And the matches, Tina says.

Dawn reaches behind the counter for a new box and throws them over. Tina bends the *Broons* annual open on her knee to keep her place, lights a cigarette.

Did you ever read that one when you were wee, Dawn says, where they have these posh people coming round for tea and the mother is all up to high doh about the state of their house and the posh people seeing it? The one where they all have to stand in a funny way, like the tall one has to stand with his hand covering the damp patch on the ceiling and one of the girls has to lean against the wall with her elbow to cover something else, and someone else has to stand on the patch that's in the carpet? That's a really funny one.

Tina doesn't look up. On the front cover of the book there's pink-purple pretend tartan; the Broons are gathered for a family portrait. In yellow, the words say Scotland's Happy Family. It's not even the real Broons any more, Dawn thinks, Daphne's supposed to be uglier than that. She feels dull suddenly, like something angry in a dark tweed coat is thudding itself at her from behind a wall of misty glass or ice. On the back cover, the Bairn is asleep on Paw's lap in a big chair.

They always have one about new year on the very last page, Dawn says.

Tina flicks to the back and reads the page hard. Aye, she says eventually, so there is.

Dawn stubs out the cigarette on the papers she's sitting on. The date she stubs the cigarette out near is December 31st. All over the front are the things that have happened over the last year. People who've been shot or killed. OJ. That house where they buried those girls. Princess Di. Dawn puts another cigarette to her mouth, looks around the shop. There's so much stuff in here. Cold drinks and books and all those magazines, sweets and chocolate and postcard racks and batteries and things for cameras, and things for tourists, tartan things, fluffy white dogs wearing tam o'shanters, dolls dressed up as pipers. She wipes the ash and picks the black burnt bits off the top newspaper, smooths down the burnt place with her hand.

Tina is coughing hard. After she finishes she says, is it new year now?

I think so, Dawn says. She looks at the inside of the silver metal shutter over the front of the shop. I wonder who'll first-foot us, she says. Tina laughs, and coughs. She always coughs like that when she gets in somewhere warm.

What were you doing this time last year? Dawn asks.

Jesus Christ, *I* don't know, Tina says, and looks at Dawn as if she's said something really stupid. She lies back on the splay of shiny covered magazines; she looks like women do when they lie back in luxurious baths on adverts on tv.

No, Dawn says. It's important. What you do on New Year's Day makes your luck for the whole year.

Tina sits up. I know what we could do, she says.

What? says Dawn.

We could phone our horoscopes, Tina says.

For the next while they listen to long messages on the ends of the numbers they find in the women's magazines. Tina is Sagittarius, Dawn is Leo. They are both going to have a year filled with changes in their careers and on the domestic front. Tina phones a thing she calls the itching line and they hold the phone between them to hear an oriental-sounding man telling her she will meet her master in the street, and that two mountains sit between her and the future.

Aye, Tina says, that'll be right.

Then Tina closes her eyes and punches in a number at random. It rings at the other end, and someone answers. Happy new year, Tina shouts down the phone. Happy new year from Tina and Dawn.

She does this three or four times. It's Tina, she says to one person. Dawn can hear it's a man's voice. *Tina*, Tina says. From that party. I'm really hurt you don't remember me.

At another number there's someone playing the pipes at the tinny other end of the phone; happy new year, they both scream, happy new year, a lot of people at the other end shout. Tina gets them to tell her the address. That sounded like a good laugh, she says to Dawn.

Yeah, Dawn says. She gives the receiver to Tina, pushes it to Tina's ear as she presses a combination of numbers for her. Then she steps back, goes over to the magazine racks and watches from there.

Hi, Tina says to the voice that answers. Happy new year. It's Tina. Don't you know me? It's Tina and her friend—

She looks over at Dawn, sees Dawn's face.

It's Tina and her friend Denise, she says. No, never mind, you won't, it's been a long time. We're just calling to wish you a very happy new year. All the best for ninety-six. And many more of them and all. Cheers now. Bye.

Tina puts the phone down.

Who answered it? Dawn asks.

A woman, Tina says. She didn't know who we were or anything. I told her happy new year from both of us.

Then Tina and Dawn spend half an hour spelling out, in tubes of peppermints and packets of chewing gum across the floor of the shop, the words HAPPY NEW YEAR FROM THE SEXY SUPER MODELS WE WERE HERE BUT YOU WERE NOT YOUR LOSS. They stand back to look at what they've written. They tidy the magazines back on to the shelves and keep the ones they want to take with them. With chocolate and more cigarettes in their pockets, with their magazines and with one of the disposable cameras from the peg above the lottery machine, they lock the door behind them and head for the party with the pipes that they heard down the other end of the phone.

Morning is coming up now, grey and clear. As they go along the road they take photos of each other and of the people who drunkenly pass them. One man has his photo taken with his arm round Dawn, calls her darling and gives her a fiver when she asks. When the roll of pictures jams to an end in the camera Tina tosses it over a hedge into someone's garden. Well, she says, that's what they're for, you're supposed to throw them away.

They link arms, laughing. All the way down the road, looking for an address that Tina's not sure she remembers right, they laugh about how the man who runs the newsagent's in the station will be getting the biggest phone bill he's ever had, and what he'll think when he gets into his shop and finds their message, and how he'll remember it every new year, maybe be telling his customers and his family and friends all about it for years and years to come.

TESSA HADLEY

Buckets of Blood

The coach journey from Cambridge to Bristol took six hours. Hilary Culvert was wearing a new purple skirt, a drawstring crêpe blouse and navy school cardigan, and over them her school mac, because it was the only coat she had. The year was 1972. In the toilets at Oxford bus station where they were allowed to get out she had sprayed on some perfume and unplaited her hair. She worried that she smelled of home. She didn't know quite what home smelled like, as she still lived there and was used to it; but when her sister Sheila had come back from university for Christmas she had complained about it.

—You'd think with all these children, Sheila had said,—that at least the place would smell of something freshly nasty. Feet or sweat or babies or something. But it smells like old people. Mothballs and Germolene: who still uses mothballs apart from here?

Hilary had been putting Germolene on her spots; this was the family orthodoxy. She put the little tube aside in horror. Sheila had looked so different, even after only one term away. She had always been braver about putting on a public show than Hilary was: now she wore gypsy clothes, scrumpled silky skirts and patchwork tops with flashing pieces of mirror sewn in. Her red-brown hair was fluffed out in a mass. She had insisted on washing her hair almost every day, even though this wasn't easy in the vicarage: the old Ascot gas heater only dribbled out hot water, and there were all the younger children taking turns each night for baths. Their father had remonstrated with Sheila.

—There's no one here to admire you in your glory, he said.—You'll only frighten the local boys. Save your efforts until you return to the fleshpots.

—I'm not doing it for anyone to admire, said Sheila.—I'm doing it for myself.

He was a tall narrow man, features oversized for the fine bones of his face, eyes elusive behind thick-lensed glasses; he smiled as if he was squinting into a brash light. His children hadn't been brought up to flaunt doing things for themselves, although the truth was that in a family of nine a certain surreptitious selfishness was essential for survival.

Now Hilary in her half-term week was going to visit Sheila in the fleshpots, or at Bristol University, where she was reading Classics. A lady with permed blue-white hair in the seat next to her was knitting baby clothes in lemon-yellow nylon wool which squeaked on her needles; Hilary had to keep her head turned to stare out of the window because she suffered terribly from travel sickness. She wouldn't ever dream of reading on a coach, and even the flickering of the knitting needles could bring it on. The lady had tried to open up a conversation about her grandchildren and probably thought Hilary was rude and unfriendly. And that was true too, that was what the Culverts were like: crucified by their shyness and at the same time contemptuous of the world of ordinary people they couldn't talk to. Outside the window there was nothing to justify her fixed attention. The sky seemed never to have lifted higher all day than a few feet above the ground; rolls of mist hung above the sodden grass like dirty wool. The signs of spring coming seemed suspended in a spasm of unforgiving frozen cold. It should have been a relief to leave the flatlands of East Anglia behind and cross into the hills and valleys of the west, but everywhere today seemed equally colourless. Hilary didn't care. Her anticipation burned up brightly enough by itself. Little flames of it licked up inside her. This was the first time she had been away from home alone. Sheila was ahead of her in their joint project: to get as far away from home as possible, and not to become anything like their mother.

At about the same time that Sheila and Hilary had confided to each other that they didn't any longer believe in God, they had also given up believing that the pattern of domestic life they had been brought up inside was the only one, or was even remotely desirable. Somewhere else people lived differently; didn't have to poke their feet into clammy hand-me-down wellingtons and sandals marked by size inside with felt-tip pen; didn't have to do their homework in bed with hot-water bottles because the storage heaters in the draughty vicarage gave out such paltry warmth. Other people didn't have to have locked money boxes for keeping safe anything precious, or have to sleep with the keys on string around their necks; sometimes anyway they came home from school to find those locks picked or smashed. (The children didn't tell on one another; that was their morality. But they hurt one another pretty badly, physically, in pursuit of justice. It was an honour code rather than anything resembling Christian empathy or charity.) Other people's mothers didn't stoop their heads down in the broken way that theirs did, hadn't given up on completed sentences or consecutive dialogue, didn't address elliptical ironical asides to their soup spoons as they ate.

Their mother sometimes looked less like a vicar's wife than a wild woman. She was as tall as their father but if the two of them were ever accidentally seen standing side by side it looked as if she had been in some terrible momentous fight for her life and he hadn't. Her grey-black hair stood out in a stiff ruff around her head; Sheila said she must cut it with the kitchen scissors in the dark. She had some kind of palsy so that her left eye drooped; there were bruise-coloured wrinkled shadows under her eyes and beside her hooked nose. Her huge deflated stomach and bosom were slapped like insults on to a girl's bony frame. She was fearless in the mornings about stalking round the house in her ancient baggy underwear, big pants and maternity bra, chasing the little ones to get them dressed: her older children fled the sight of her. They must have all counted, without confessing it to one another: she was forty-nine, Patricia was four. At least there couldn't be any more pregnancies, so humiliating to their suffering adolescence.

As girls, Sheila and Hilary had to be especially careful to make their escape from home. Their older brother Andrew had got away, to do social policy at York and join the Young Socialists, which he told them was a Trotskyite entrist group. He was never coming back, they were sure of it. He hadn't come back this Christmas. But their sister Sylvia had married an RE teacher at the local secondary modern school who was active in their father's church and in the local youth clubs. Sylvia already had two babies, and Sheila and Hilary had heard her muttering things to herself. They remembered that she used to be a jolly sprightly girl even if they hadn't liked her much: competitive at beach rounders when they went on day trips to the coast, sentimentally devoted to the doomed stray dogs she tried to smuggle into their bedroom. Now, when they visited her rented flat in Haverhill, her twin-tub washing machine was always pulled out from the wall, filling the kitchen with urine-pungent steam. Sylvia would be standing uncommunicatively, heaving masses of boiling nappies with wooden tongs out of the washer into the spin tub, while the babies bawled in the battered wooden playpen that had been handed on from the vicarage.

In the coach, aware of her reflection in the window from time to time when the scenery was dun enough behind to make a mirror out of it, Hilary sat up very straight. She and Sheila had practised with one another, remembering never to lapse into the crumpled unawareness that smote their mother if ever for a moment she left off being busy. She was almost always busy. She had driven Hilary in to catch her coach that morning only because she had to go in to Cambridge anyway, to buy replacement school shorts and other uniform from Eaden Lilley for the boys. The boys had larked around in the back seats of the ropy old Bedford van that was their family transport, kicking at each other's shins and dropping to wriggle on their bellies about the floor, so that their mother – who drove badly anyway, with grindings of the gears and sudden brakings – spent the whole journey deploring fruitlessly, and peering to try and locate them in the rear-view mirror. She had taken to wearing dark glasses when she went anywhere outside her home, to cover up the signs of her palsy. She stopped the van on Parker's Piece and had to get out to open the door on Hilary's side because the handle was broken. Hilary had a vivid idea of how her mother must appear to strangers: the sticking-up hair and dark glasses and the worn once-good coat she never had time to button up; her jerky burrowing movements, searching for money or lists in bags or under the van seats; her cut-glass enunciations, without eye contact, of bits of sentences that never became any whole message. When Hilary walked away with her suitcase to take her place in the little huddled crowd of waiting travellers she wouldn't look to see if any of them had been watching.

Bristol bus station was a roaring cavern: everything was greasy and filthy with oil, including the maimed pigeons. Green double-decker city buses reversed out of the bays and rumbled off, important with illumination, into the evening. A whole day's light had come and gone on the journey. Hilary looked excitedly for Sheila while she shuffled down the aisle on the coach. She wasn't worried that she couldn't see her right away. 'Whatever you do don't go off anywhere,' Sheila had instructed her. 'Stay there till I come.'

Someone waited slouching against the metal railing while she queued for her suitcase, then stepped forward to confront her when she had it: a young man, short and soft-bodied, with lank light brown hair and a half-grown beard, wearing a pinstriped suit jacket over jeans. He also had bare feet, and black eye make-up.

—Are you Hilary?

He spoke with a strong northern accent.

Hilary felt the disapproving attention of the blue-rinsed knitting lady, focused on his make-up and his feet. She disdained the disapproval, even though in the same instant she judged against the man with Culvert passionate finality. 'What an unappealing little dwarf of a chap,' she thought, in her mother's voice. Of course her thought didn't show. To him she would look only like the sum of what she was outwardly: pale with bad skin, fatally provincial, frightened, with girls' school gushing manners.

—Yes.

—Sheila couldn't be here. She's unwell. You have to come with me.

He swung away without smiling or otherwise acknowledging her; he had only ever looked perfunctorily in her face, as if he was checking basics. She had to follow after him, out through the bus station back entrance into a twilit cobbled street and then up right beside a high grim wall that curved round to join a busier road. The tall buildings of a hospital with their lighted windows rose sobering and impassive against the evening sky, where the murky day in its expiring was suddenly brilliantly deep clear blue, studded already with one or two points of stars. The man walked ahead and Hilary followed, hurrying, struggling with her suitcase, three or four steps behind. The suitcase was an old leather one embossed with her grandfather's intials; he had taken it to ecumenical conferences in the thirties. Because the clasps were liable to spring open she had fastened an elastic Brownie belt around it.

Unwell! Unwell was the word they had to use to the games mistress at school when they weren't having showers because they had a period.

Hilary saved the joke up to amuse Sheila. Then she was flooded with doubt; why had she followed this rude man so obediently? She should have at least questioned him, asked him where Sheila was and what was wrong with her. Sheila had told her to wait, whatever happened, at the bus station. She opened her mouth to protest to him, to demand that he explain to her, and take a turn carrying the case. Then stubbornly she closed it again. She knew what a squeak would come out of it if she tried to attract his attention while she was struggling along like this. And if she put the case down and stopped she was afraid he'd go on without noticing she was no longer behind him, and then she would be truly lost in an unknown city, with nowhere to spend the night, and certainly not enough money to pay for anywhere. She could perhaps have hired a taxi to take her to Sheila's hall of residence, although she wasn't sure what that would cost either. She had never been in a taxi in her life, and would never have the courage to try and signal to one. And what if Sheila wasn't at the hall of residence?

Pridefully she marched on, though her breath was hurting in her chest and her hand without its glove – they were somewhere in her shoulder bag but she couldn't stop to find them – was freezing into a claw on the case handle. Her arm felt as if it was being dragged from her shoulder. It wasn't clothes that made her case heavy, but some books Sheila had asked her to bring. Every forty paces – she began to count – she swapped her case and shoulder bag from hand to hand, and that gave a few moments of relief. She fixed her eyes on the back of the rumpled pinstriped jacket. Once or twice, on the zebra crossings, he looked back to check for her. Luckily his bare feet seemed to slow him down somewhat, probably because he had to keep an eye out for what he might be walking in. There were quite a few people on the streets, even though the shops were closed; sometimes he held back to let a crowd go by, perhaps because he was afraid of someone stepping on his toes. Perversely Hilary started slowing down too whenever this happened. She was damned now if she wanted to catch up with him. Even if he stopped to wait for her, now, she thought that she would stop too and wait, as if the distance between them had become a fixed relationship, an invisible rigid frame of air connecting them and holding them apart in the same grip.

She thought she recognised the streets that they were walking through.

When their father had driven Sheila over with her things at the start of the autumn term, Hilary had come with them; she had wanted to be able to picture where Sheila was, when she wasn't at home. This shopping area was on a hill behind the city centre: it had seemed lively and fashionable, with tiny boutiques, cafés, a department store whose long glass windows were stuck with brown and yellow paper leaves. She had seen Sheila taking it all in from her front seat in the van, satisfied with her choice, impatient to be left alone to explore. At home they could only ever get lifts in to Cambridge every so often, and anyway their shopping there was dogged by waiting parents, ready with ironic comments on whatever the girls chose to buy with their money. Dimly in the dusk now, Hilary could see the Victorian Gothic university tower where it ought to be, over to her right. Manor Hall residence where Sheila had a room should be somewhere off to the left, up past a little triangle of green grass. The pinstriped jacket struck off left, and Hilary was relieved. They must arrive soon, and she would be able to put her case down, and be rid of her dreadful companion.

The road he took didn't lead up past any triangle of grass but downhill; it was wide, busy with fast through traffic but not with people. They left the shops behind and it seemed all at once to be completely night; the pavement ran alongside a daunting high wall to their left. The steep hills and old high walls of this city were suddenly sinister and not quaint, as if they hid dark prisons and corruptions in their folds. Hilary followed the pinstriped jacket in a grim, fixed despair. In spite of the cold she was sweating, and her chest was racked. She thought that catastrophe had overtaken her. She had made an appalling mistake when she meekly followed this man out of the bus station, like a trusting child, like an idiot. The only form of dignity left to her was not to falter, or make a worse fool of herself screaming and running, not to break the form of the rigid relationship in which they moved. She thought he might be taking her somewhere to kill her with a knife. She wouldn't say a word to save her life; she might swing at him with her grandfather's suitcase. Or she imagined drugs, which she didn't know anything about: perhaps drug addicts recruited new associates by bundling strangers into their den and injecting them with heroin. She didn't ever imagine rape or anything of that sort, because she thought that as a preliminary to that outrage there would have to be some trace of interest in her, some minimal sign of a response to her, however disgusted.

The pinstriped jacket crossed the road, darting between cars. Following, Hilary hardly cared if she was hit. He struck off up a narrow precipitous hill with tall toppling houses facing on to the pavement on either side. Because of the effort of climbing she had her head down and almost walked into him when he stopped outside a front door. He pushed the door and it swung open. The house inside was dark.

—In here, he said, and led the way.

Hilary followed.

In the hall he switched on a light: a bare bulb hung from the ceiling. The place was desolate: ancient wallpaper washed to colourlessness hung down in sheets from the walls. Even in her extremity, though, she could tell that this had been an elegant house once. City lights twinkled through a tall arched window. The stairs wound round and round a deep stairwell, up into blackness; the handrail was smooth polished wood. Everything smelled of a mineral decay. They climbed up two flights, their footsteps echoing because there was no stair carpet. He pushed another door.

—She's in there.

Hilary didn't know what she expected to find.

Sheila was sitting with a concentrated face, rocking backwards and forwards on a double bed which was just a mattress on bare floorboards. She was wearing a long black T-shirt, her hair was scraped carelessly back and tied with a scarf. The room was lit by another bare bulb, not a ceiling pendant this time but a lamp-base without a shade, which cast leering shadows upwards. It was warm: an electric radiator painted mustard yellow was plugged in the same socket as the lamp. Hilary felt herself overheating at once, her face turning hot red, after her exertions in the cold outside.

—Thank God you've come, Hills, Sheila said.

She sounded practical rather than emotional. That at least was reassuring.

Pinstripe stepped into the room behind Hilary. He put on a shifty uncomfortable smile, not quite looking straight at Sheila, focusing on the dark tangle of sheets and blankets that she seemed to have kicked to the bottom of the bed.

—D'you want anything? Tea?

Sheila shook her head.—I'm only throwing it up.

—D'you want anything?

Hilary couldn't believe he was actually talking to her.—No, I'm fine, thanks, she said.

—I'll be downstairs, he said.—If you need anything.

They heard the sound of his footsteps retreating. Hilary put down her case: her hand for quite a few minutes wouldn't ease from its frozen curled position.—Shuggs: what's going on?

Sheila groaned: not in answer to the question, but a sound ripped from inside her, a low and embarrassing rumble as if she didn't care what anybody heard. She rocked fiercely.

—I'm miscarrying a pregnancy, she said when the spasm seemed to have passed.—It's a fine mess. Blood everywhere. Buckets of blood. You'll have to help get rid of everything.

—I can't believe this, Hilary said. She felt she was still somewhere inside the Bluebeard story she had been imagining on her way from the bus station. For a few pure moments she blazed with anger against Sheila. It wasn't fair, for Sheila to have spoiled her visit with this, her so looked-forward-to chance to get away. Sheila's mission had been clear and certain: to cut herself free of all the muffling dependencies of home and childhood. If she could succumb to anything so predictable as this melodrama – just what their parents would have warned against if only they hadn't been too agonised to find the words – what hope was there?

—What are you doing here? she demanded.—What is this place?

—It's a squat, said Sheila calmly.—Neil's squat. I told them at Manor Hall that I was going away for a few days. They're not to ever know anything about this, obviously.

—You'd be kicked out.

—Uh-oh, said Sheila, attentive to something inside her. Then she lunged from the bed to sit on something like a chamber pot in the crazy shadows on the far side of the room. Hilary tried not to hear anything. – Oh, oh, Sheila groaned, hugging her white legs, pressing her forehead to her knees.

—They wouldn't kick me out, she said after a while.—It's not that.

—And who's Neil?

—That's him, you idiot. You've just walked in with him.

Hilary hadn't moved from where she stood when she first came in, or even made any move to unbutton her mac. She felt as if there was an unpassable waste of experience between her and her sister now, which couldn't be crossed. Sheila had joined the ranks of women submerged and knowing amid their biology. She realised with a new shock that Sheila must have had sexual intercourse, too, in order to be pregnant.

—I don't want Mum to know, that's why, Sheila said.—I'll simply kill you if you ever tell anyone at home.

—I wouldn't, said Hilary coldly.

—I just can't bear the idea of her thinking that this is the same thing, you know? The same stuff that's happened to her. Because it isn't.

Hilary was silent. After a long while Sheila stood up stiffly from the chamber pot. She stuffed what looked like an old towel between her legs, and moving slowly, bent over as if she was very old, she lay down on the bed again, on her side this time, with her eyes closed.

—You could take it down to the lavatory for me. It's a flight and a half down, door on the right.

Hilary didn't stir.

—Please, Hills. You could cover it with a newspaper or something.

—Did you do this deliberately? Hilary said.—Is this an abortion?

—No. It just happened. I might have done it deliberately, but I didn't need to. I'd only just realised that I was pregnant. I've only missed two periods, I think. I never keep track.

—Who is the father of it?

Sheila's eyes snapped open incredulously.—Who do you think? she said.—I wouldn't have just sent any old person to get you.

Hilary helped. Several times she carried the chamber pot down one and a half flights of stairs, holding the banister rail, watching her feet carefully in the gloom (there was only the one bulb in the hallway, which Neil had switched on when they first came in). She covered whatever was inside the pot with a piece of newspaper, then tipped it into the lavatory without looking and flushed the chain. Thankfully it had a good strong flush. She stood listening to voices downstairs, a long way off as if they came from underground, from a basement room perhaps: Neil's voice and others, male and female, subdued but nonetheless breaking out into laughter

sometimes. Opening off the landing above the lavatory Hilary found a
filthy bathroom, with a torn plastic curtain at the window, overgrown
with black mould. An ancient rusted red-painted reel wound with canvas
rope was secured to the wall beside the window, with instructions on how
to lower it as an escape harness in case of fire. She ran the bath taps for
a while, but although the pipes gave out buckings and bellowing noises
and hiccuped gouts of tea-coloured cold water into the grit and dirt in
the bottom of the bath, she couldn't get either tap to run hot.

—There's no hot water, Sheila said.—This is a squat: what did you
think? Everyone goes into the halls to bathe. We're lucky to have electricity: one of the guys knew how to reconnect it. You could ask Neil for the
electric kettle. What do you want hot water for anyway?

—I thought you might like a wash. I thought I could put some things
in to soak.

—Don't worry about it. I'll wash in the morning. We can take all this
stuff to the launderette later.

Although they had always lived so close together in the forced intimacy
of the vicarage, where there was only one lavatory and fractious queues
for the bathroom in the mornings, the sisters had been prudish in keeping
their bodily functions hidden from one another. This was partly in scalded
reaction to their mother, who poked curiously in the babies' potties to
find swallowed things, and delivered sanitary towels to the girls' room
with abandoned openness, as if she didn't know that the boys saw. They
had even always, since they stopped being little girls, undressed quickly
with their backs turned, or underneath their nightdresses. It was a surprise
how small the step seemed, once Hilary had taken it, over into this new
bodily intimacy of shared secret trouble and mess. Sheila's pains, she
began to understand, had a rhythm to them: first a strong pang, then a
pause, then a sensation as if things were coming away inside her. After
that she might get ten or fifteen minutes' respite. When the pain was at
its worst, Hilary rubbed her back, or Sheila gripped her hand and squeezed
it, hard and painfully, crushing the bones together.

—Damn, damn, damn, she swore in a sing-song moan while she rocked
backwards and forwards; tears squeezed out of her shut eyes and ran down
her cheeks.

—Are you sorry? Hilary said, humbled.

—How could I possibly be sorry? Sheila snapped.—You think I want a *baby*?

She said the pains had begun at three in the afternoon. She told Hilary at some point that if they were still going on in the morning they would have to call an ambulance and get her into hospital: she explained in a practical voice that women could haemorrhage and die if these things went wrong. By ten o'clock, though, the worst seemed to be over. There hadn't been any bad pains for over an hour, the bleeding was almost like a normal period. When Neil came upstairs Sheila wanted a cup of tea and a hot-water bottle.

—You'll have to take Hilary out, she told him,—and buy her something to eat.

Hilary had eaten some sandwiches on the coach at lunchtime. She hadn't had anything since then; she didn't feel hungry but she felt light-headed and her hands were shaking.

—I'm fine, she said hastily.—I don't want anything.

—Don't be so silly. Buy her some fish and chips or something.

Hilary was too tired not to be obedient. She put on her mac and followed Neil downstairs, as if their fatal passage round the city had to recommence. At least this time she wouldn't be carrying her case. She waited on the street outside; he said he had to fetch the others.

—By the way, he added, not looking at her,—I shouldn't mention anything. They just think Sheila's got a tummy bug. They'd be upset.

—OK, Hilary mumbled. Furiously she thought to herself that she wouldn't have spoken to his friends about her sister if he had tortured her. 'You silly little man,' she imagined herself saying. 'How dare you think I care about upsetting them?' She tipped back her head and looked up the precipitous fronts of the houses to the far-off sky, studded with cold stars.

She noticed that Neil had put on shoes to come out this time: a pair of gym shoes, gaping without laces. His friend Julian had jug ears and long dyed blond hair; Gus was shy and lumpish, like a boy swelled to man-size without his face or body actually changing to look grown-up. Becky was a pretty girl in a duffel coat, who giggled and swivelled her gaze too eagerly from face to face: she couldn't get enough of her treat, being the only girl and having the attention of three men. She knew instinctively that Hilary didn't count. Even her patronising was

670

perfunctory: she reminisced about her own A levels as if she was reaching back into a long-ago past.

—You've chosen all the easy ones, you clever thing! My school forced me to do double maths, it was ghastly.

—Are you sure you're not hungry? Neil said to Hilary as they hurried past a busy chip shop with a queue.—Only if we don't stop we're in time for the pub. You could have some crisps there.

Hilary gazed into the bright steamy window, assaulted by the smell of the chips, weak with longing.—Quite sure, she said. She had never been into a pub in her life. There was a place in Haverhill where some of the girls went from school, but she and Sheila had always despised the silly self-importance of teenage transgression. It was impossible to imagine ever wanting to enter the ugly square red-brick pub in the village, where the farm labourers drank, and the men from the estate who worked in the meat-packing factory. Neil's pub was a tiny cosy den, fumy light glinting off the rows of glasses and bottles. The stale breath of it made Hilary's head swim; they squeezed into red plush seats around a table. Neil didn't ask her what she wanted, but brought her a small mug of brown beer and a packet of crisps and one of peanuts. She didn't like the taste of the beer but because the food was so salty she drank it in thirsty mouthfuls, and then was seized by a sensation as if she floated up to hang some little way above her present situation, graciously indifferent, so that her first experience of drunkenness was a blessed one.

When the pub closed they came back to the house and sat around a table in the basement kitchen by candlelight: the kitchen walls were painted crudely with huge mushrooms and blades of grass and giant insects, making Hilary feel as if she was a miniature human at the deep bottom of a forest. She drank the weak tea they put in front of her. The others talked about work and exams. Becky was doing biological sciences, Gus was doing history, Julian and Neil seemed to be doing English. Hilary couldn't believe that they sounded just like girls at school, scurrying in the rat-run of learning and testing, trying to outdo one another in protestations of how little work they'd done. Not once did any of them actually speak seriously about their subjects. Hilary felt so deeply disappointed in university life that on the spot she made up her mind to dedicate herself to something different and nobler, although she wasn't clear what. Neil and Julian were concentrating upon sticking a brown lump of something on a pin and roasting it with a match. From her indifferent distance she supposed this must be drugs, but she wasn't frightened of that now.

—Don't tell your daddy the vicar what you've seen, said Neil.

She was confused – did the others know what had happened after all? – until she realised that he meant the brown lump.

—Are you two really from a vicarage? asked Becky.—It's like something out of a book.

—We can't offer the respectability that Hilary's used to, Neil said.— She'll have to slum it here for a few days.

Hilary could see that Neil was the centre of all the others' attention. At least he had not joined in when the others were fluttering and fussing about their work; he had smiled to himself, licking the edges of little pieces of white paper and sticking them together as if none of it bothered him. He had an air as if he saw through the sham of it all, as if he came from a place where the university didn't count for much: she could see how this had power over the others. He didn't say much but when he spoke it was with a deliberate debunking roughness that made the others abject, ashamed even of the feel in their mouths of their own nice eager voices.

Becky told Neil flirtatiously that he would have to be on his best behaviour, while Hilary was staying.—No swearing, she said.—'Cause I can see she's a nice girl.

—Fuck, he said.—I hadn't thought of that. Fuck that.

Hilary thought of the farm boys at home, who called sexual words when she and Sheila had to walk past them in their school uniform. She had always thought, however much it tortured her, that they had an obscure right to do it because of their work. In the winter mornings from the school bus you could see the frozen mists rising up out of the flat colourless fields, and figures bent double with sacks across their shoulders, picking Brussels sprouts, or sugar beeting. But Neil was here, wasn't he, at university? He'd crossed over to their side, the lucky side. Whatever she thought of her life, she knew it was on the lucky side, so long as she wasn't picking Brussels sprouts or meat-packing.

No one had said anything since she arrived about where Hilary was to sleep. Sheila was supposed to have booked a guest room for her at Manor Hall, but of course she couldn't go there now. When she couldn't hold herself upright at the kitchen table any longer she climbed upstairs to ask what she should do, but Sheila was asleep, breathing evenly and deeply. Her forehead was cool. Hilary kept all her clothes on and wrapped herself in an old quilt that Sheila had kicked off; she curled up to sleep on the floor beside the bed. At some point in the night she woke, frozen rigid and harrowed by a bitter draught blowing up through the bare floorboards; she climbed into the bed beside Sheila who snorted and heaved over. Under the duvet and all the blankets it smelled of sweat and blood, but it was warm. When she woke again it was morning and the sun was shining.

—Look at the patterns, Sheila said.

She was propped up calmly on one elbow on the pillow, and seemed returned into her usual careful self-possession. Hilary noticed for the first time that the room was painted yellow; the sun struck through the tall uncurtained windows and projected swimming squares of light on to the walls, dancing with the movements of the twiggy tops of trees which must be growing in a garden outside.

—Are you all right? she asked.

Sheila ignored the question as if there had never been anything wrong.

—How did you get on with everybody last night?

—We went to a pub.

—Oh, which one? She interrogated Hilary until she was satisfied that it must have been the Beaufort.—We often go there, she said enthusiastically.—It's got a great atmosphere, it's really local.

—When I told them we lived in a vicarage, Hilary said,—one of them asked if we were Catholics.

—That's so funny. I bet I know who that was. What did you think of Neil?

Hilary was cautious.—Is he from the north?

—Birmingham, you idiot. Couldn't you tell? Such a pure Brummie accent.

—He wasn't awfully friendly.

Sheila smiled secretively.—He doesn't do that sort of small talk. His dad works as a toolsetter at Lucas's, the engineering company. No one in his family has been to university before. His parents don't have money, compared to most of the students here. He gets pretty impatient with people, you know, who just take their privilege for granted.

Hilary felt like a child beside her sister. What had happened yesterday marked Sheila as initiated into the adult world, apart from her, as clearly as if she was signed with blood on her forehead. She supposed it must be the unknown of sexual intercourse which could transform things in this way that children couldn't see: Neil's self-importance into power, for instance. At the same time as she was in awe of her sister's difference, Hilary also felt a stubborn virgin pride. She didn't want ever to be undone out of her scepticism, or seduced into grown-up credulous susceptibility.

—But doesn't he think that we're poor, too? she asked fiercely.—Have you told him? Does he have any idea?

—It's different, said Sheila with finality.—It's just different.

When Hilary drove in the summer with her father in the Bedford van, to pick up Sheila and all her things at the end of her first year, she was waiting for them of course at Manor Hall, as if there had never been any other place, any squat whose kitchen was painted with giant mush-rooms. Hilary understood that she was not ever to mention what had happened there, not even when she and Sheila were alone. Because they never wore the memory out by speaking of it, the place persisted vividly in her imagination.

She had stayed on in that house for almost a week: she had arrived on Monday and her return ticket was for Saturday. Sheila rested for the first couple of days, sleeping a lot, and Hilary went out on her own, exploring, going round the shops. On Sheila's instructions she took several carrier bags of bloody sheets and towels to the launderette, where she sat reading Virginia Woolf while the washing boiled. There seemed to be a lot of hours to pass, because she didn't want to spend too much time in Sheila's room; she shrank from the possibility of getting in the way between Sheila and Neil. A couple of times she went to the cinema in the afternoon by herself. They all went out to pubs every evening and she got used to drinking beer, although she didn't get to like it. While the others joked and drank and smoked she sat in a silence that must have looked gawky and immature, so that she was sure Sheila despaired of her, although Sheila must also surely have known that she found the conversation impossible to join because it was so tepid and disappointing, gossip mostly about people she'd never met. Sheila, who had been aloof and not popular at school, seemed to be working hard to make these people like her. She made herself brighter and funnier and smaller than her real self, Hilary thought. She surrounded Neil in particular with such efforts of admiration, prompting him and encouraging him and attributing ideas to him, while he smiled in lazy amusement, rolling up his eternal cigarettes. At least they weren't all over each other, they didn't cling together in public. Hilary even feared for Neil, thinking that he shouldn't trust her sister, he should wonder what dark undertow might follow after such a glittering bright flood.

By the end of the week Sheila was well enough to go to lectures again, and on the Saturday she came to the bus station to see Hilary off. She insisted on carrying Hilary's suitcase, which swung in her hand as light as if there was nothing in it, now that their father's old dictionaries of classical mythology had been unloaded.

—I didn't feel anything, you know, Sheila said as they walked, as if she was picking up on some discussion they had only broken off a few moments before, although in fact they hadn't talked once, since it was over, about what had happened to her.—I mean, apart from physically. Just like a tummy upset. That's all it was: a nuisance.

—All right, if you say so.

For the first time Sheila talked about her studies. She had to write an essay on the *Oresteia* which she said was all about the sex war, female avenging Furies and male reason.

—*The gods are disgusted at you*, she said gleefully.—Apollo to the Furies. *Apoptustoi theosis. Never let your filth touch anything in my sacred shrine.*

When Hilary was in her seat in the coach, Sheila stayed hanging around outside the window although Hilary signed to her to go, there was no need to wait. They laughed at one another through the glass, helpless to communicate: for the first time they were in tune together as they used to be. Sheila mouthed something and Hilary mimed elaborately: frowned, shook her head, shrugged her shoulders. She couldn't understand. Sheila put her face close to the glass and cupped her hands round her mouth, shouting. She was wearing a woollen knitted hat with knitted flowers, pulled down over her ears.

—Give my love to everybody!

Hilary saw that all of a sudden her sister didn't want her to go. She was seized then by an impulse to struggle off the coach, to stay and fight, as if Sheila had after all been abducted by a Bluebeard: she felt focused as a crusader in her opposition to Neil. She even half turned round in her seat, as if to get out. But there was a man in the seat beside her, she would have had to ask him to move, he was settled behind his newspaper. The moment and the possibility passed. The coach reversed, the sisters waved frantically, and then Sheila was gone and Hilary subsided into her solitude, keeping her face averted from the man who had seen too much of her excitement, and whose newspaper anyway would make her sick if she accidentally read any of the headlines.

Above the city buildings the sky was blue and pale with light, drawn across by thin skeins of transparent cloud. Beyond the outskirts of the city everything was bursting with the spring growth which was further on over here than in the east. The tips of the hedgerows and the trees, if they hadn't yet come into leaf, gave off a red haze where the twigs swelled and shone. It seemed extraordinary to Hilary that her life must at some point soon change as completely and abruptly as Sheila's had, so that everything familiar would be left behind. She sat with bubbles of excitement rising in her chest. The scruffy undistinguished countryside outside the coach window seemed to her beautiful. It desolated her to think that when she was dead she wouldn't be able to see it: cows, green hummocky fields, suburban cottages of weathered brick, a country factory with smashed windows, an excited spatter of birds thrown up from a tree. Then she started to see these things as if she was dead already, and they were persisting after her, and she had been allowed back, and must take in everything hungrily while she had the chance, every least tiny detail.

ADAM MAREK

The 40-Litre Monkey

I once met a man with a forty-litre monkey. He measured all his animals by volume. His Dalmatian was small, only eighteen litres, but his cat, a Prussian Blue, was huge – five litres, when most cats are three. He owned a pet shop just off Portobello Road. I needed a new pet for my girlfriend because our last two had just killed each other.

'The ideal pet,' the owner told me, 'is twelve litres. That makes them easy enough to pick up, but substantial enough for romping without risk of injury. What did you have?'

'A gecko,' I replied. 'I guess he was about half a pint.'

'You use imperial?' The man smirked and gestured towards a large vivarium in the corner. 'Iguana,' he said. 'Six litres, and still growing.'

'Oh right,' I said. 'I also had a cat. She must have been four litres, maybe more.'

'Are you sure?' he asked. 'Was she a long hair, because they look big, but when you dunk them they're small, like skinny rats.'

'She was a short hair,' I said.

'How old?'

'Four.'

'That volume would have dropped anyway, unless you mixed tripe with her food. Did you do that?'

'No,' I said. 'She ate tuna fish.'

'No pet ever got voluminous eating tuna,' he smiled, almost sympathetic.

'What's the biggest thing you've got?' I asked.

'That would have to be my forty-litre monkey,' he smiled.

'May I see it?'

'You doubt my veracity?'

'Not at all. Is it a secret monkey?'

'No, he's not a secret monkey. I've shown him in South America, Russia, and most of Western Europe.'

'What sort of monkey is it?'

'He is a baboon,' he said, raising his eyebrows.

'A baboon? What do they usually scale in at?'

'Twenty-three litres.'

'How did yours get so big?'

'I won't tell you. Have you any idea how many thirty-litre monkeys I got through before I hit on the right combination?'

I shrugged my shoulders. The man rubbed his brow between his thumb and forefinger, as if wondering why he was even talking to me, the owner of a dead half-pint gecko. I was getting claustrophobic and started to leave, when he grabbed my arm and said, 'Would you like to see my monkey?'

I nodded that I would. He locked the front door and led me up a narrow staircase. Names were written on every step, and alongside, a volume: Edgar 29 litres; Wallace 32 litres; Merian 34 litres. Also on every step were paper bags of feed, books and files, stacked up against the wall, so that I had to put each foot directly in front of the other to walk up, and I kept catching my ankle with the edge of my heel.

'So how did your pets die, anyway?' the man asked.

'The cat managed to slide the door of the gecko's tank open. She tried to eat him whole, and he stuck in her throat.'

'Hmph,' the man laughed.

The man took me to a door, which was covered in stickers of various animal organisations I'd never heard of: Big Possums of Australasia, American Tiny Titans. The door had a keypad, which he shielded with one hand as he punched the code with the other. A pungent stench of meat and straw and bleach poured out of the room, and I heard a soft sucking noise, like air drawn into a broken vacuum, but I may have imagined this.

Being in the room felt like being suffocated in an armpit. Something was shuffling about in a cage in the corner, grunting softly. The perimeter of the room was like the staircase, with books, files and bags of dried foodstuffs piled up the walls. The floor was covered in black linoleum, and the section in front of the door was rough with thousands of scratches. Opposite the door was an archway, which led into a bright bathroom. He had a huge glass tank in there with units of measurement running up the sides and extra marks and comments written in marker pen.

'He's over there,' the man said. 'Stay here, and I'll let him out.'

'Does he bite?' I asked.

'Not any more.'

The man took a key from his back pocket, which was attached to a chain and belt loop. The lock undid with a satisfying click. He opened the cage door a little and crouched in front. He whispered something to the baboon, but I couldn't hear what he said. He nodded his head, as if receiving a response from the monkey, then moved back, staying in his crouched position.

The bad air in the room was making me feel sick.

'Why is it so dark in here?' I asked.

'Light makes him too active. He burns off all that volume when the light's on,' he replied.

The man stayed crouched down, and began to bob his backside up and down, as if he were rubbing an itch up against a tree. He patted the floor with his hands, staring all the while into the cage.

A shape shuffled out. I'd never seen a regular-size baboon, so had no point of reference for his size, but he was big, big and greasy.

'Why is his fur all slicked down like that?' I asked.

'Vaseline,' the man replied. 'Baboon hair is slightly absorbent. If he soaks up water that makes less volume.'

'So you grease him up to make him waterproof?'

'Yes.'

'Is that legal?'

The man looked at me like I was an idiot.

The baboon came further out of the cage. The man put something in his own mouth. The baboon shifted back nervously at first, but then skipped in and took the food from his lips. He looked at me while he ate. His face seemed to be saying, 'I know I look ridiculous, but if you say anything, I'll pull your arm off.'

'What's his name?' I asked.

'Don't speak so loudly,' he whisper-spat. 'He's called Cooper.'

'So what's next,' I asked. 'A fifty-litre monkey?'

'You can't get a baboon that size. Not without steroids.'

'Do they make monkey steroids?'

'Are you mocking me?' The man stood up. The baboon raised his arms and hooted. The man squatted down again and bowed his head, looking back at me and suggesting I do the same.

I squatted down. The smell became worse. It hung near the floor like a fog.

'Do many people do this, grow big monkeys, I mean?'

'Not many. In this country anyway.'

'How many would you say there are around the world?'

'It's hard to say,' the man said. 'Not everyone competes, but there are about sixty regulars I guess.'

'And is this a record monkey?'

'By half a litre.'

'So have you got like an arch rival? An enemy monkey grower?' I couldn't help smiling when I said this. The man seemed to be having a crisis. He didn't know whether to be angry, or to be excited. I think this must have been the first time anyone had wanted to see his monkey.

'There's a guy from Thailand. He claimed he had a forty-three litre monkey, but he'd put putty in its armpits and stuffed golfballs up its bum.'

'You're kidding.'

'It's quite common. They're a lot stricter about it now though.'

The baboon settled close to the man and allowed him to stroke its greasy head.

'Who's they?' I asked. 'Is there some kind of governing body?'

'Yes, the BMG.'

'What's that stand for, the Big Monkey Group?' I laughed.

'Yes. They're a part of the Big Animal Group. People compete with almost every animal you could think of. I specialise in baboons, but I dabble in cats and guinea pigs too. They're cheaper to transport long distance, and they take less time to grow.'

I was glad that it was dark because my eyes were watering.

'Do you want me to measure him?' the man asked.

'What, now? In the tank?'

The man nodded.

'No, don't worry. You're okay. I wouldn't want to get Cooper all wet for nothing.'

'It's no trouble.'

'No really. It's fine,' I said.

'But how do you know I'm not lying to you?'

'I trust you.'

'Would you know a forty-litre monkey when you saw one?'

'No, but at a guess, I'm sure that he's about . . .'

'Not about. Exactly. He's exactly forty litres. I'll show you.'

The man scooped Cooper up in his arms. The baboon wrapped his long arms around the man's neck. His blue shirt became smeared with Vaseline.

'It's really okay. I believe you,' I said.

The man ignored me and went into the bathroom. He pointed to the water level, which was exactly on the zero position, and then lowered the monkey in. I expected him to freak out, but instead, he went limp, as if dead.

'How come he's like that?' I asked.

'If he moved around, he might splash water out of the tank. Instant disqualification. Getting them to be still can be even harder than getting them large,' he said.

Cooper grasped the man's index fingers and remained still as the water covered his throat, his mouth, and then his whole head. When the water level cut a line across the baboon's forearms, the man let him go. Cooper pulled his arms down below the surface. The water made a soft plopping sound. The man ducked down to look at the monkey through the tank. He clapped his hands twice, and Cooper stuck his arms out to either side, pressing against the glass and holding himself below the water.

His hair stayed flat against his body. Air bubbles clung to the corners of his eyes and to his nostrils. His black-ringed eyes darted around while his head stayed still, as if the monkey was just a suit, and there was something alive inside it, something that didn't like water.

'There, you see?' the man said.

I looked at the water level. 'It says thirty-nine,' I said.

'Don't be stupid,' he snapped, but then he looked at the meniscus and gasped. It was a sound of pain, of betrayal. His intake of breath and the way he stared at the baboon were loaded with hurt.

The baboon stayed beneath the surface of the water. The man looked him up and down and around the tank, looking for a reason for the reading. He walked around the tank, looking for spilt water.

'Is he waiting for some kind of signal to come up?' I asked. Cooper's eyes were frantic.

The man ignored me, still trying to see a reason why the reading would be low. He scrambled around the tank, his hands wrestling each other.

'Should I clap or something?' I asked.

The man looked at me, and then at the monkey, and clapped twice. The baboon let go of the sides of the tank and rose up. His head broke the surface and he wheezed for breath, panic over his face, as if he knew he was guilty of something awful.

The man grabbed his wrists and dragged him out. He was being much less delicate with Cooper than before he went in the tank.

'What did you do?' he snapped. 'What did you do?' The baboon shook some of the water off of his oiled skin. 'Did you make yourself sick?'

'Bastard monkey,' he spat.

'Surely it's not his fault,' I said.

'Oh, you think?' The man smiled, and then turned nasty. 'What the hell do you know about monkeys, huh?'

I shrugged my shoulders, and the man turned his attention back to the monkey. He dropped Cooper to the ground, and the baboon bounded across the room. The man muttered to himself as he grabbed a paper sack from the floor. He poured something that looked like muesli into a bowl, and then squeezed a bright yellow liquid over it. He dumped the bowl on the floor while he used both hands to unscrew a large tub, out of which he scooped two spoonfuls of a gelatinous substance. He mixed this into the bowl, all the while muttering to himself. He took the bowl to a cabinet, which was full of droppers and bottles like a medicine cabinet. He put drops of this in and a sprinkling of that, and popped a capsule of something else in, then stirred it all up and slid it across the floor to the baboon.

The baboon looked at the bowl, and then at the man. He turned away and slunk into the cage.

'Oh, you're not hungry,' he said. 'Maybe you're happy being a thirty-nine-litre monkey? Is that what you're telling me? Why are you doing this?'

The man looked like he was caught between crying and bleeding from his ears.

'I should probably go,' I said. 'Thanks for showing me your monkey.'

'Is that some kind of joke,' the man turned to me. 'Thanks for showing me your thirty-nine-litre monkey? Is that what you're trying to say?' His fists were bunched.

'I'm not trying to say anything. I think you've got a lovely monkey, whatever volume he is.'

I don't know what I'd said to him, but he went crazy. His face flushed bright red and the tendons in his neck went taut. He actually reached his arms out towards me and stretched his fingers, as if he were going to strangle me. I backed away towards the door, preparing myself to sprint.

But then a cloud seemed to pass behind his eyes. He began tapping the side of his left palm and whispering to himself. And this had an immediate calming effect. He took a deep breath.

'I apologise for displaying inappropriate emotion,' he said.

'That's . . . okay,' I said.

The man locked up Cooper's cage, shoulders hunched, and his posture repentant. He spoke to Cooper in a soft voice. I could not hear the words, or see the baboon's face, but the shuffling sounds in the cage calmed, giving me the impression that they were making their peace. 'Let us sort out a new pet for your girlfriend,' the man said as he stood up and ushered me to the door, huffing air through his nose.

The air in the shop, which had been thick when I first entered, was fresh compared to the poisonous fug of Cooper's room. 'Look around,' he said. 'I'll give you a very good deal.'

I paced around the shop, sidestepping to get through the tight spaces between display shelves, and looked at the eyes of cockatoos and kittens and rabbits and snakes. Nothing made an impression on me. My mind was blank. I couldn't shake the image from my head of Cooper beneath the water, his hands pressed against the glass sides of the tank.

'I don't know,' I said. 'You're the expert. What do you think my girl-friend would like?'

At this, the muscular plates of his face slid around an expression of pure delight. 'Yes. Yes!' He said, jabbing a triumphant finger into the air. 'I have it.' And he went through a beaded curtain into a back room, coming back moments later with a small cage covered in a thick, dark cloth.

The man lifted up the corner of the cloth and urged me to peer inside. I could see nothing in there at first, but as I pressed my nose against the metal bars, my eyes adjusted and I could see, sat on a smooth branch, a small possum-like creature. Its long tail was wrapped around the branch, and as I inhaled, it turned its enormous eyes to me.

'Wow,' I said. 'What is it?'

'She is a Madagascan nightingale lemur. Very rare. At dusk, she sings a song that would send lions to sleep.'

'That's perfect,' I said. 'Thank you.'

We were discussing the price, when the man put one palm up in the air, and the index finger of his other hand to his lips. 'Wait,' he said. 'Do you hear that? She is about to start singing.'

JON McGREGOR

The Remains
Friskney

Are believed to still be intact. Are understood to be within an area of approximately seventeen square miles. Are believed to have been concealed. Are either partially or completely buried. Are likely to be without clothes or jewellery or other possessions. May not be suitable for visual identification. Will be treated as a critical evidential scene. Have been the subject of much intrusive and unhelpful press speculation. Continue to be a key focus of questioning. Will be located using a combination of aerial surveillance and ground-penetrating radar. May be beautifully preserved, tanned and creased and oiled, by the action of the rich peated ground. May be laid in a resting position with legs together and hands folded and head turned gently to one side. Are of course still a concern to everyone in the department. May be intact. Have continued to be a topic of periodic speculation from time to time over the years. May be crammed into a box or bag or case. May need to be identified by recourse to dental records. May be wholly or partially lost due to action by animal or animals. May be wrapped in a silken winding sheet and buried with jewellery and other possessions pressed neatly into the folded hands. Must be in a location known to person or persons as yet unidentified. Could well be recoverable given the relinquishing of certain key details known to person or persons unknown. May have been visited from time to time by the perpetrator or individuals known to the perpetrator. Are either partial or complete. May ultimately need to be recovered using a team from the forensic archaeology department. Are not currently a priority in this challenging period of strained resources. Have yet to be found. Continue to be the subject of an open case file. Have yet to be found. Have yet to be found. Have yet to be found. Have been destroyed by water.

Have yet to be found. Have yet to be found. Have yet to be found. Have yet to be found. Have yet to be found. Have yet to be found. Have yet to be found. Have yet to be found. Have been destroyed by earth. Have yet to be found. Have yet to be found. Will not give you what you need. Have yet to be found. Have yet to be found. Have yet to be found. Have yet to be found. Have no further purpose to serve. Have yet to be found. Have yet to be found. Have yet to be found. Have yet to be found. Have been destroyed by fire. Have yet to be found. Have yet to be found. Have yet to be found. Have yet to be found. Have yet to be found. Have yet to be found. Have yet to be found. Have yet to be found. Have yet to be found. Have yet to be found. Have yet to be found. Have yet to be found. Have yet to be found. Have yet to be found. Have yet to be found. Have yet to be found. Will not bring her back. Have yet to be found. Have yet to be found. Have yet to be found. Have yet to be found. Have yet to be found. Have yet to be found. Have yet to be found. Have yet to be found. Have yet to be found. Have yet to be found. Have yet to be found. Have yet to be found. Have yet to be found. Have yet to be found. Have yet to be found. Have yet to be found. Have yet to be found. Have yet to be found. Have gone. Have yet to be found. Have yet to be found. Have yet to be found. Have yet to be found. Have yet to be found. Have yet to be found. Have yet to be found. Have yet to be found. Have yet to be found. Are gone. Have yet to be found. Have yet to be found. Have yet to be found. Have yet to be found. Have yet to be found. Have yet to be found. Is gone. Have yet to be found. Have yet to be found. Have yet to be found. Have yet to be found. Have yet to be found. Have yet to be found. Have yet to be found. Have yet to be found. Are gone. Have yet to be found. Have yet to be found. Have yet to be found. Have yet to be found. Have yet to be found. Is gone. Have yet to be found. Have yet to be found. Have yet to be found. Have yet to be found. Have yet to be found. Have yet to be found. Have yet to be found. Have yet to be found. Have yet to be found. Have yet to be found. Have yet to be found. Have yet to be.

ZADIE SMITH

The Embassy of Cambodia

0—1

Who would expect the Embassy of Cambodia? Nobody. Nobody could have expected it, or be expecting it. It's a surprise, to us all. The Embassy of Cambodia!

Next door to the embassy is a health centre. On the other side, a row of private residences, most of them belonging to wealthy Arabs (or so we, the people of Willesden, contend). They tend to have Corinthian pillars on either side of their front doors, and – it's widely believed – swimming pools out the back. The embassy, by contrast, is not very grand. It is only a four- or five-bedroom north London suburban villa, built at some point in the 1930s, surrounded by a red-brick wall, about eight feet high. And back and forth, cresting this wall horizontally, flies a shuttlecock. They are playing badminton in the Embassy of Cambodia. Pock, smash. Pock, smash.

The only real sign that the embassy is an embassy at all is the little brass plaque on the door (which reads: 'THE EMBASSY OF CAM-BODIA') and the national flag of Cambodia (we assume that's what it is – what else could it be?) flying from the red-tiled roof. Some say, 'Oh, but it has a high wall around it, and this is what signifies that it is not a private residence, like the other houses on the street, but rather an embassy.' The people who say so are foolish. Many of the private houses have high walls, quite as high as the Embassy of Cambodia – but they are not embassies.

0——2

On 6 August, Fatou walked past the embassy for the first time, on her way to a swimming pool. It is a large pool, although not quite Olympic size. To swim a mile you must complete eighty-two lengths, which, in its very tedium, often feels as much a mental exercise as a physical one. The water is kept unusually warm, to please the majority of people who patronize the health centre, the kind who come not so much to swim as to lounge poolside or rest their bodies in the sauna. Fatou has swum here five or six times now, and she is often the youngest person in the pool by several decades. Generally, the clientele are white, or else South Asian or from the Middle East, but now and then Fatou finds herself in the water with fellow Africans. When she spots these big men, paddling frantically like babies, struggling simply to stay afloat, she prides herself on her own abilities, having taught herself to swim, several years earlier, at the Carib Beach Resort, in Accra. Not in the hotel pool – no employees were allowed in the pool. No, she learned by struggling through the rough grey sea, on the other side of the resort walls. Rising and sinking, rising and sinking, on the dirty foam. No tourist ever stepped on to the beach (it was covered with trash), much less into the cold and treacherous sea. Nor did any of the other chambermaids. Only some reckless teenage boys, late at night, and Fatou, early in the morning. There is almost no way to compare swimming at Carib Beach and swimming in the health centre, warm as it is, tranquil as a bath. And, as Fatou passes the Embassy of Cambodia, on her way to the pool, over the high wall she sees a shuttlecock, passed back and forth between two unseen players. The shuttlecock floats in a wide arc softly rightwards, and is smashed back, and this happens again and again, the first player always somehow able to retrieve the smash and transform it, once more, into a gentle, floating arc. High above, the sun tries to force its way through a cloud ceiling, grey and filled with water. Pock, smash. Pock, smash.

0——3

When the Embassy of Cambodia first appeared in our midst, a few years ago, some of us said, 'Well, if we were poets perhaps we could have written some sort of an ode about this surprising appearance of the embassy.' (For embassies are usually to be found in the centre of the city. This was the first one we had seen in the suburbs.) But we are not really a poetic people. We are from Willesden. Our minds tend towards the prosaic. I doubt there is a man or woman among us, for example, who – upon passing the Embassy of Cambodia for the first time – did not immediately think: 'genocide'.

0—4

Pock, smash. Pock, smash. This summer we watched the Olympics, becoming well attuned to grunting, and to the many other human sounds associated with effort and the triumph of the will. But the players in the garden of the Embassy of Cambodia are silent. (We can't say for sure that it is a garden – we have a limited view over the wall. It may well be a paved area, reserved for badminton.) The only sign that a game of badminton is under way at all is the motion of the shuttlecock itself, alternately being lobbed and smashed, lobbed and smashed, and always at the hour that Fatou passes on her way to the health centre to swim (just after ten in the morning on Mondays). It should be explained that it is Fatou's employers – and not Fatou – who are the true members of this health club; they have no idea she uses their guest passes in this way. (Mr and Mrs Derawal and their three children – aged seventeen, fifteen and ten – live on the same street as the embassy, but the road is almost a mile long, with the embassy at one end and the Derawals at the other.) Fatou's deception is possible only because on Mondays Mr Derawal drives to Eltham to visit his mini-market there, and Mrs Derawal works the counter in the family's second mini-mart, in Kensal Rise. In the slim drawer of a faux-Louis XVI console, in the entrance hall of the Derawals' primary residence, one can find a stockpile of guest passes. Nobody besides Fatou seems to remember that they are there.

Since 6 August (the first occasion on which she noticed the badminton), Fatou has made a point of pausing by the bus stop opposite the embassy for five or ten minutes before she goes in to swim, idle minutes she can hardly afford (Mrs Derawal returns to the house at lunchtime) and yet seems unable to forgo. Such is the strangely compelling aura of the embassy. Usually, Fatou gains nothing from this waiting and observing, but on a few occasions she has seen people arrive at the embassy and watched as they are buzzed through the gate. Young white people carrying rucksacks. Often they are scruffy, and wearing sandals, despite the cool weather. None of the visitors so far have been visibly Cambodian. These young people are likely looking for visas. They are buzzed in and then pass through the gate, although Fatou would really have to stand on top of the bus stop to get a view of whoever it is that lets them in. What she can say with certainty is that these occasional arrivals have absolutely no effect on the badminton, which continues in its steady pattern, first gentle, then fast, first soft and high, then hard and low.

0—5

On 20 August, long after the Olympians had returned to their respective countries, Fatou noticed that a basketball hoop had appeared in the far corner of the garden, its net of synthetic white rope rising high enough to be seen over the wall. But no basketball was ever played – at least not when Fatou was passing. The following week it had been moved closer to Fatou's side of the wall. (It must be a mobile hoop, on casters.) Fatou waited a week, two weeks, but still no basketball game replaced the badminton, which carried on as before.

0—6

When I say that we were surprised by the appearance of the Embassy of Cambodia, I don't mean to suggest that the embassy is in any way unique in its peculiarity. In fact, this long, wide street is notable for a number of curious buildings, in the context of which the Embassy of Cambodia does not seem especially strange. There is a mansion called GARYLAND, with something else in Arabic engraved below GARYLAND, and both the English and the Arabic text are inlaid in pink-and-green marble pillars that bookend a gigantic fence, far higher than the embassy's, better suited to a fortress. Dramatic golden gates open automatically to let vehicles in and out. At any one time, GARYLAND has five to seven cars parked in its driveway.

There is a house with a huge pink elephant on the doorstep, apparently made of mosaic tiles.

There is a Catholic nunnery with a single red Ford Focus parked in front. There is a Sikh institute. There is a faux-Tudor house with a pool that Mickey Rooney rented for a season, while he was performing in the West End fifteen summers ago. That house sits opposite a dingy retirement home, where one sometimes sees distressed souls, barely covered by their dressing gowns, standing on their tiny balconies, staring into the tops of the chestnut trees.

So we are hardly strangers to curious buildings, here in Willesden and Brondesbury. And yet still we find the Embassy of Cambodia a little surprising. It is not the right sort of surprise, somehow.

0—7

In a discarded *Metro* found on the floor of the Derawal kitchen, Fatou read with interest a story about a Sudanese 'slave' living in a rich man's house in London. It was not the first time that Fatou had wondered if she herself was a slave, but this story, brief as it was, confirmed in her own mind that she was not. After all, it was her father, and not a kidnapper, who had taken her from Ivory Coast to Ghana, and when they reached Accra they had both found employment in the same hotel. Two years later, when she was eighteen, it was her father again who had organized her difficult passage to Libya and then on to Italy – a not insignificant financial sacrifice on his part. Also, Fatou could read English – and speak a little Italian – and this girl in the paper could not read or speak anything except the language of her tribe. And nobody beat Fatou, although Mrs Derawal had twice slapped her in the face, and the two older children spoke to her with no respect at all and thanked her for nothing. (Sometimes she heard her name used as a term of abuse between them. 'You're as black as Fatou.' Or 'You're as stupid as Fatou.') On the other hand, just like the girl in the newspaper, she had not seen her passport with her own eyes since she arrived at the Derawals', and she had been told from the start that her wages were to be retained by the Derawals to pay for the food and water and heat she would require during her stay, as well as to cover the rent for the room she slept in. In the final analysis, however,

Fatou was not confined to the house. She had an Oyster Card, given to her by the Derawals, and was trusted to do the food shopping and other outside tasks, for which she was given cash and told to return with change and receipts for everything. If she did not go out in the evenings that was only because she had no money with which to go out, and anyway knew very few people in London. Whereas the girl in the paper was not allowed to leave her employers' premises, not ever – she was a prisoner.

On Sunday mornings, for example, Fatou regularly left the house, to meet her church friend Andrew Okonkwo at the 98 bus stop and go with him to worship at the Sacred Heart of Jesus, just off the Kilburn High Road. Afterwards Andrew always took her to a Tunisian café, where they had coffee and cake, which Andrew, who worked as a night guard in the City, always paid for. And on Mondays Fatou swam. In very warm water, and thankful for the semi-darkness in which the health club, for some reason, kept its clientele, as if the place were a nightclub, or a midnight Mass. The darkness helped disguise the fact that her swimming costume was in fact a sturdy black bra and a pair of plain black cotton knickers. No, on balance she did not think she was a slave.

o—8

The woman exiting the Embassy of Cambodia did not look especially like a New Person or an Old Person – neither clearly of the city nor the country – and of course it is a long time since this division meant anything in Cambodia. Nor did these terms mean anything to Fatou, who was curious only to catch her first sighting of a possible Cambodian anywhere near the Embassy of Cambodia. She was particularly interested in the woman's clothes, which were precise and utilitarian – a grey shirt tucked tightly into a pair of tan slacks, a blue mackintosh, a droopy rain hat – just as if she were a man, or no different from a man. Her straight black hair was cut short. She had in her hands many bags from Sainsbury's, and this Fatou found a little mysterious: where was she taking all that shopping? It also surprised her that the woman from the Embassy of Cambodia should shop in the same Willesden branch of Sainsbury's where Fatou shopped for the Derawals. She had an idea that Oriental people had their own, secret establishment and shopped there. (She believed the Jews did, too.) She both admired and slightly resented this self-reliance, but had no doubt that it was the secret to holding great power, as a people. For example, when the Chinese had come to Fatou's village to take over the mine, an abiding local mystery had been: what did they eat and where did they eat it? They certainly did not buy food in the market, or from the Lebanese traders along the main road. They made their own arrangements. (Whether back home or here, the key to surviving as a people, in Fatou's opinion, was to make your own arrangements.)

But, looking again at the bags the Cambodian woman carried, Fatou wondered whether they weren't in fact very old bags – hadn't their design changed? The more she looked at them the more convinced she became that they contained not food but clothes or something else again, the outline of each bag being a little too rounded and smooth. Maybe she was simply taking out the rubbish. Fatou stood at the bus stop and watched until the Cambodian woman reached the corner, crossed and turned left towards the high road. Meanwhile, back at the embassy the badminton continued to be played, though with a little more effort now because of a wayward wind. At one point it seemed to Fatou that the next lob would blow southwards, sending the shuttlecock over the wall to land lightly in her own hands. Instead the other player, with his vicious reliability (Fatou had long ago decided that both players were men), caught the shuttlecock as it began to drift and sent it back to his opponent – another deathly, downward smash.

0—9

No doubt there are those who will be critical of the narrow, essentially local scope of Fatou's interest in the Cambodian woman from the Embassy of Cambodia, but we, the people of Willesden, have some sympathy with her attitude. The fact is if we followed the history of every little country in this world – in its dramatic as well as its quiet times – we would have no space left in which to live our own lives or to apply ourselves to our necessary tasks, never mind indulge in occasional pleasures, like swimming. Surely there is something to be said for drawing a circle around our attention and remaining within that circle. But how large should this circle be?

It was the Sunday after Fatou saw the Cambodian that she decided to put a version of this question to Andrew, as they sat in the Tunisian café eating two large fingers of dough stuffed with cream and custard and topped with a strip of chocolate icing. Specifically, she began a conversation with Andrew about the Holocaust, as Andrew was the only person she had found in London with whom she could have these deep conversations, partly because he was patient and sympathetic to her, but also because he was an educated person, presently studying for a part-time business degree at the College of North West London. With his student card he had been given free, twenty-four-hour access to the Internet.

'But more people died in Rwanda,' Fatou argued. 'And nobody speaks about that! Nobody!'

'Yes, I think that's true,' Andrew conceded, and put the first of four sugars in his coffee. 'I have to check. But, yes, millions and millions. They hide the true numbers, but you can see them online. There's always a lot of hiding; it's the same all over. It's like this bureaucratic Nigerian government – they are the greatest at numerology, hiding figures, changing them to suit their purposes. I have a name for it: I call it "demonology". Not "numerology" – "demonology".'

'Yes, but what I am saying is like this,' Fatou pressed, wary of the conversation's drifting back, as it usually did, to the financial corruption of the Nigerian government. 'Are we born to suffer? Sometimes I think we were born to suffer more than all the rest.'

Andrew pushed his professorial glasses up his nose. 'But, Fatou, you're forgetting the most important thing. Who cried most for Jesus? His mother. Who cries most for you? Your father. It's very logical, when you break it down. The Jews cry for the Jews. The Russians cry for the Russians. We cry for Africa, because we are Africans, and, even then, I'm sorry, Fatou' – Andrew's chubby face creased up in a smile – 'if Nigeria plays Ivory Coast and we beat you into the ground, I'm laughing, man! I can't lie. I'm celebrating. Stomp! Stomp!'

He did a little dance with his upper body, and Fatou tried, not for the first time, to imagine what he might be like as a husband, but could see only herself as the wife, and Andrew as a teenage son of hers, bright and helpful, to be sure, but a son all the same – though in reality he was three years older than she. Surely it was wrong to find his baby fat and struggling moustache so off-putting. Here was a good man! She knew that he cared for her, was clean and had given his life to Christ. Still, some part of her rebelled against him, some unholy part.

'Hush your mouth,' she said, trying to sound more playful than disgusted, and was relieved when he stopped jiggling and laid both his hands on the table, his face suddenly quite solemn.

'Believe me, that's a natural law, Fatou, pure and simple. Only God cries for us all, because we are *all* his children. It's very, very logical. You just have to think about it for a moment.'

Fatou sighed, and spooned some coffee foam into her mouth. 'But I still think we have more pain. I've seen it myself. Chinese people have never been slaves. They are always protected from the worst.'

Andrew took off his glasses and rubbed them on the end of his shirt. Fatou could tell that he was preparing to lay knowledge upon her.

'Fatou, think about it for a moment, please: what about Hiroshima?'

It was a name Fatou had heard before, but sometimes Andrew's superior knowledge made her nervous. She would find herself struggling to remember even the things she had believed she already knew.

'The big wave . . .' she began, uncertainly – it was the wrong answer. He laughed mightily and shook his head at her.

'No, man! Big bomb. Biggest bomb in the world, made by the USA, of course. They killed five million people in *one second*. Can you imagine that? You think just because your eyes are like this' – he tugged the skin at both temples – 'you're always protected? Think again. This bomb, even if it didn't blow you up, a week later it melted the skin off your bones.'

Fatou realized she had heard this story before, or some version of it. But she felt the same vague impatience with it as she did with all accounts of suffering in the distant past. For what could be done about the suffering of the distant past?

'OK,' she said. 'Maybe all people have their hard times, in the past of history, but I still say—'

'Here is a counterpoint,' Andrew said, reaching out and gripping her shoulder. 'Let me ask you, Fatou, seriously, think about this. I'm sorry to interrupt you, but I have thought a lot about this and I want to pass it on to you, because I know you care about things seriously, not like these people—' He waved a hand at the assortment of cake eaters at other tables. 'You're not like the other girls I know, just thinking about the club and their hair. You're a person who thinks. I told you before, anything you want to know about, ask me – I'll look it up, I'll do the research. I have access. Then I'll bring it to you.'

'You're a very good friend to me, Andrew, I know that.'

'Listen, we are friends to each other. In this world you need friends. But, Fatou, listen to my question. It's a counterpoint to what you have been saying. Tell me, why would God choose us especially for suffering when we, above all others, praise his name? Africa is the fastest-growing Christian continent! Just think about it for a minute! It doesn't even make sense!'

'But it's not him,' Fatou said quietly, looking over Andrew's shoulder to the rain beating on the window. 'It's the Devil.'

o——II

Andrew and Fatou sat in the Tunisian coffee shop, waiting for it to stop raining, but it did not stop raining and at three p.m. Fatou said she would just have to get wet. She shared Andrew's umbrella as far as the Overground, letting him pull her into his clammy, high-smelling body as they walked. At Brondesbury station Andrew had to get the train, and so they said goodbye. Several times he tried to press his umbrella on her, but Fatou knew the walk from Acton Central to Andrew's bedsit was long and she refused to let him suffer on her account.

'Big woman. Won't let anybody protect you.'

'Rain doesn't scare me.'

Fatou took from her pocket a swimming cap she had found on the floor of the health club changing room. She wound her plaits into a bun and pulled the cap over her head.

'That's a very original idea,' Andrew said, laughing. 'You should market that! Make your first million!'

'Peace be with you,' Fatou said, and kissed him chastely on the cheek.

Andrew did the same, lingering a little longer with his kiss than was necessary.

0——12

By the time Fatou reached the Derawals' only her hair was dry, but before going to get changed she rushed to the kitchen to take the lamb out of the freezer, though it was pointless – there were not enough hours before dinner – and then upstairs to collect the dirty clothes from the matching wicker baskets in four different bedrooms. There was no one in the master bedroom, or in Faizul's or Julie's. Downstairs a television was blaring. Entering Asma's room, hearing nothing, assuming it empty, Fatou headed straight for the laundry basket in the corner. As she opened the lid she felt a hand hit her hard on the back; she turned around.

There was the youngest, Asma, in front of her, her mouth open like a trout fish. Before Fatou could understand, Asma punched the huge pile of clothes out of her hands. Fatou stooped to retrieve them. While she was kneeling on the floor, another strike came, a kick to her arm. She left the clothes where they were and got up, frightened by her own anger. But when she looked at Asma now she saw the girl gesturing frantically at her own throat, then putting her hands together in prayer and then back to her throat once more. Her eyes were bulging. She veered suddenly to the right; she threw herself over the back of a chair. When she turned back to Fatou her face was grey and Fatou understood finally and ran to her, grabbed her round her waist and pulled upwards as she had been taught in the hotel. A marble – with an iridescent ribbon of blue at its centre, like a wave – flew from the child's mouth and landed wetly in the carpet's plush.

Asma wept and drew in frantic gulps of air. Fatou gave her a hug, and worried when the clothes would get done. Together they went down to the den, where the rest of the family was watching *Britain's Got Talent* on a flat-screen TV attached to the wall. Everybody stood at the sight of Asma's wild weeping. Mr Derawal paused the Sky box. Fatou explained about the marble.

'How many times I tell you not to put things in your mouth?' Mr Derawal asked, and Mrs Derawal said something in their language – Fatou heard the name of their God – and pulled Asma on to the sofa and stroked her daughter's silky black hair.

'I couldn't breathe, man! I couldn't call nobody,' Asma cried. 'I was gonna die!'

697

'What you putting marbles in your mouth for anyway, you idiot?' Faizul said, and unpaused the Sky box. 'What kind of chief puts a marble in her mouth? Idiot. Bet you was bricking it.'

'Oi, she saved your life,' said Julie, the eldest child, whom Fatou generally liked the least. 'Fatou saved your life. That's deep.'

'I woulda just done this,' Faizul said, and performed an especially dramatic Heimlich to his own skinny body. 'And if that didn't work I woulda just start pounding myself karate style, bam bam bam bam bam—'

'Faizul!' Mr Derawal shouted, and then turned stiffly to Fatou, and spoke not to her, exactly, but to a point somewhere between her elbow and the sunburst mirror behind her head. 'Thank you, Fatou. It's lucky you were there.'

Fatou nodded and went to leave, but at the doorway to the den Mrs Derawal asked her if the lamb had defrosted and Fatou had to confess that she had only just taken it out. Mrs Derawal said something sharply in her language. Fatou waited for something further, but Mr Derawal only smiled awkwardly at her, and nodded as a sign that she could go now. Fatou went upstairs to collect the clothes.

o—13

'To keep you is no benefit. To destroy you is no loss' was one of the mottoes of the Khmer Rouge. It referred to the New People, those city dwellers who could not be made to give up city life and work on a farm. By returning everybody back to the land, the regime hoped to create a society of Old People – that is to say, of agrarian peasants. When a New Person was relocated from the city to the country, it was vital not to show weakness in the fields. Vulnerability was punishable by death.

In Willesden, we are almost all New People, though some of us, like Fatou, were, until quite recently, Old People, working the land in our various countries of origin. Of the Old and New People of Willesden I speak; I have been chosen to speak for them, though they did not choose me and must wonder what gives me the right. I could say, 'Because I was born at the crossroads of Willesden, Kilburn and Queen's Park!' But the reply would be swift and damning: 'Oh, don't be foolish, many people were born right there; it doesn't mean anything at all. We are not one people and no one can speak for us. It's all a lot of nonsense. We see you standing on the balcony, overlooking the Embassy of Cambodia, in your dressing gown, staring into the chestnut trees, looking gormless. The real reason you speak in this way is because you can't think of anything better to do.'

0—14

On Monday, Fatou went swimming. She paused to watch the badminton. She thought that the arm that delivered the smashes must make a movement similar to the one she made in the pool, with her clumsy yet effective front crawl. She entered the health centre and gave a guest pass to the girl behind the desk. In the dimly lit changing room, she put on her sturdy black underwear. As she swam, she thought of Carib Beach. Her father serving snapper to the guests on the deck, his bow tie always a little askew, the ugly tourists, the whole scene there. Of course, it was not surprising in the least to see old white men from Germany with beautiful local girls on their laps, but she would never forget the two old white women from England – red women, really, thanks to the sun – each of them as big as two women put together, with Kweku and Osai lying by their sides, the boys hooking their scrawny black bird-arms round the women's massive red shoulders, and dancing with them in the hotel 'ballroom', answering to the names Michael and David, and disappearing into the women's cabins at night. She had known the boys' real girlfriends; they were chambermaids like Fatou. Sometimes they cleaned the rooms where Kweku and Osai spent the night with the English women. And the girls themselves had 'boyfriends' among the guests. It was not a holy place, that hotel. And the pool was shaped like a kidney bean: nobody could really swim in it, or showed any sign of wanting to. Mostly, they stood in it and drank cocktails. Sometimes they even had their burgers delivered to the pool. Fatou hated to watch her father crouching to hand a burger to a man waist-high in water.

The only good thing that happened in Carib Beach was this: once a month, on a Sunday, the congregation of a local church poured out of a coach at the front gates, lined up fully dressed in the courtyard and then walked into the pool for a mass baptism. The tourists were never warned, and Fatou never understood why the congregants were allowed to do it. But she loved to watch their white shirts bloat and spread across the surface of the water, and to hear the weeping and singing. At the time – though she was not then a member of that church, or of any church except the one in her heart – she had felt that this baptism was for her, too, and that it kept her safe, and that this was somehow the reason she did not become one of the 'girls' at the Carib Beach Resort. In almost two years – between her father's efforts and the grace of an unseen and unacknowledged God – she did her work, and swam Sunday mornings at the crack of dawn, and got along all right. But the Devil was waiting.

She had only a month left in Accra when she entered a bedroom to clean it one morning and heard the door shut softly behind her before she could put a hand to it. He came, this time, in Russian form. Afterwards, he cried and begged her not to tell anyone: his wife had gone to see the Cape Coast Castle and they were leaving the following morning. Fatou listened to his blubbering and realized that he thought the hotel would punish him for his action, or that the police would be called. That was when she knew that the Devil was stupid as well as evil. She spat in his face and left. Thinking about the Devil now made her swimming fast and angry, and for a while she easily lapped the young white man in the lane next to hers, the faster lane.

o—15

'Don't give the Devil your anger, it is his food,' Andrew said to her, when they first met, a year ago. He handed her a leaflet as she sat eating a sandwich on a bench in Kilburn Park. 'Don't make it so easy for him.' Without being invited, he took the seat next to hers and began going through the text of his leaflet. It was printed to look like a newspaper, and he started with the headline: 'WHY IS THERE PAIN?' She liked him. They began a theological conversation. It continued in the Tunisian café, and every Sunday for several months. A lot of the things he said she had heard before from other people, and they did not succeed in changing her attitude. In the end, it was one thing that he said to her that really made the difference. It was after she'd told him this story:

'One day, at the hotel, I heard a commotion on the beach. It was early morning. I went out and I saw nine children washed up dead on the beach. Ten or eleven years old, boys and girls. They had gone into the water, but they didn't know how to swim. Some people were crying, maybe two people. Everyone else just shook their heads and carried on walking to where they were going. After a long time, the police came. The bodies were taken away. People said, "Well, they are with God now." Everybody carried on like before. I went back to work. The next year I was in Rome. I saw a boy who was about fifteen years old knocked down on his bike. He was dead. People were screaming and crying in the street. Everybody crying. They were not his family. They were only strangers. The next day, it was in the paper.'

And Andrew replied, 'A tap runs fast the first time you switch it on.'

0—16

Twenty more laps. Fatou tried to think of the last time she had cried. It was in Rome, but it wasn't for the boy on the bike. She was cleaning toilets in a Catholic girls' school. She did not know Jesus then, so it made no difference what kind of school it was – she only knew she was cleaning toilets. At midday, she had a fifteen-minute break. She would go to the little walled garden across the road to smoke a cigarette. One day, she was sitting on a bench near a fountain and spotted something odd in the bushes. A tin of green paint. A gold spray can. A Statue of Liberty costume. An identity card with the name Rajib Devanga. One shoe. An empty wallet. A plastic tub with a slit cut in the top meant for coins and euro notes – empty. A little stain of what looked like blood on this tub. Until that point, she had been envious of the Bengali boys on Via Nazionale. She felt that she, too, could paint herself green and stand still for an hour. But when she tried to find out more the Bengalis would not talk to her. It was a closed shop, for brown men only. Her place was in the toilet stalls. She thought those men had it easy. Then she saw that little sad pile of belongings in the bush and cried; for herself or for Rajib, she wasn't sure.

Now she turned on to her back in the water for the final two laps, relaxed her arms and kicked her feet out like a frog. Water made her think of more water. 'When you're baptized in our church, all sin is wiped, you start again': Andrew's promise. She had never told Andrew of the sin precisely, but she knew that he knew she was not a virgin. The day she finally became a Catholic, 6 February 2011, Andrew had taken her, hair still wet, to the Tunisian café and asked her how it felt.

She was joyful! She said, 'I feel like a new person!'

But happiness like that is hard to hold on to. Back at work the next day, picking Julie's dirty underwear up off the floor inches from the wicker basket, she had to keep reminding herself of her new relationship with Jesus and how it changed everything. Didn't it change everything? The following Sunday she expressed some of her doubt, cautiously, to Andrew.

'But did you think you'd never feel sad again? Never angry or tired or just pissed off – sorry about my language. Come on, Fatou! Wise up, man!'

Was it wrong to hope to be happy?

o—17

Lost to these watery thoughts, Fatou got home a little later than usual and was through the door only minutes before Mrs Derawal.

'How is Asma?' Fatou asked. She had heard the girl cry out in the night.

'My goodness, it was just a little marble,' Mrs Derawal said, and Fatou realized that it was not in her imagination: since Sunday night, neither of the adult Derawals had been able to look her in the eye. 'What a fuss everybody is making. I have a list for you – it's on the table.'

o—18

Fatou watched Andrew pick his way through the tables in the Tunisian café, holding a tray with a pair of mochas on it and some croissants. He hit the elbow of one man with his backside and then trailed the belt of his long, silly leather coat through the lunch of another, apologizing as he went. You could not say he was an elegant man. But he was generous, he was thoughtful. She stood up to push a teetering croissant back on to its plate. They sat down at the same time, and smiled at each other.

'A while ago you asked me about Cambodia,' Andrew said. 'Well, it's a very interesting case.' He tapped the frame of his glasses. 'If you even wore a pair of these? They would kill you. Glasses meant you thought too much. They had very primitive ideas. They were enemies of logic and progress. They wanted everybody to go back to the country and live like simple people.'

'But sometimes it's true that things are simpler in the country.'

'In some ways. I don't really know. I've never lived in the country.'

I don't really know. It was good to hear him say that! It was a good sign. She smiled cheekily at him. 'People are less sinful in the country,' she said, but he did not seem to see she was flirting with him, and began upon another lecture.

'That's true. But you can't force people to live in the country. That's what I call a Big Man Policy. I invented this phrase for my dissertation. We know all about Big Man Policies in Nigeria. They come from the top and they crush you. There's always somebody who wants to be the Big Man, and take everything for themselves, and tell everybody how to think and what to do. When, actually, it's he who is weak. But if the Big Men see that *you* see that *they* are weak they have no choice but to destroy you. That is the real tragedy.'

Fatou sighed. 'I never met a man who didn't want to tell everybody how to think and what to do,' she said.

Andrew laughed. 'Fatou, you include me? Are you a feminist now, too?'

Fatou brought her mug up to her lips and looked penetratingly at Andrew. There were good and bad kinds of weakness in men, and she had come to the conclusion that the key was to know which kind you were dealing with.

'Andrew,' she said, putting her hand on his, 'would you like to come swimming with me?'

0—19

Because Fatou believed that the Derawals' neighbours had been instructed to spy on her, she would not let Andrew come to the house to pick her up on Monday, instead leaving as she always did, just before ten, carrying misleading Sainsbury's bags and walking towards the health centre. She spotted him from a long way off – the road was so straight and he had arrived early. He stood shivering in the drizzle. She felt sorry, but also a little prideful: it was the prospect of seeing her body that had raised this big man from his bed. Still, it was a sacrifice, she knew, for her friend to come out to meet her on a weekday morning. He worked all night long and kept the daytime for sleeping. She watched him waving at her from their agreed meeting spot, just on the corner, in front of the Embassy of Cambodia. After a while, he stopped waving – because she was still so far away – and then, a little later, he began waving again. She waved back, and when she finally reached him they surprised each other by holding hands. 'I'm an excellent badminton player,' Andrew said, as they passed the Embassy of Cambodia. 'I would make you weep for mercy! Next time, instead of swimming we should play badminton somewhere.' Next time, we should go to Paris. Next time, we should go to the moon. He was a dreamer. But there are worse things, Fatou thought, than being a dreamer.

0——20

'So you're a guest and this is your guest?' the girl behind the desk asked.

'I am a guest and this is another guest,' Fatou replied.

'Yeah . . . that's not really how it works?'

'Please,' Fatou said. 'We've come from a long way.'

'I appreciate that,' the girl said. 'But I really shouldn't let you in, to be honest.'

'Please,' Fatou said again. She could think of no other argument.

The girl took out a pen and made a mark on Fatou's guest pass.

'This one time. Don't tell no one I did this, please. One time only! I'll need to cross off two separate visits.'

For one time only, then, Andrew and Fatou approached the changing rooms together and parted at the doors that led to the men's and the women's. In her changing room, Fatou got ready with lightning speed. Yet somehow he was already there on a lounger when she came out, eyes trained on the women's changing-room door, waiting for her to emerge.

'Man, this is the life!' he said, putting his arms behind his head.

'Are you getting in?' Fatou asked, and tried to place her hands, casually, in front of her groin.

'Not yet, man, I'm just taking it all in, taking it all in. You go in. I'll come in a moment.'

Fatou climbed down the steps and began to swim. Not elegant, not especially fast, but consistent and determined. Every now and then she would angle her head to try to see if Andrew was still on his chair, smiling to himself. After twenty laps, she swam to where he lay and put her elbows on the tiles.

'You're not coming in? It's so warm. Like a bath.'

'Sure, sure,' he said. 'I'll try it.'

As he sat up his stomach folded in on itself and Fatou wondered whether he had spent all that time on the lounger to avoid her seeing its precise bulk and wobble. He came towards the stairs; Fatou held out a hand to him, but he pushed it away. He made his way down and stood in the shallow end, splashing water over his shoulders like a prince fanning himself, and then crouching down into it.

'It is warm! Very nice. This is the life, man! You go, swim – I'll follow you.'

Fatou kicked off, creating so much splash she heard someone in the adjacent lane complain. At the wall, she turned and looked for Andrew. His method, such as it was, involved dipping deep under the water and hanging there like a hippo, then batting his arms till he crested for air, and then diving down again and hanging. It was a lot of energy to expend on a short distance, and by the time he reached the wall he was panting like a maniac. His eyes – he had no goggles – were painfully red.

'It's OK,' Fatou said, trying to take his hand again. 'If you let me, I'll show you how.' But he shrugged her off and rubbed at his eyes.

'There's too much bloody chlorine in this pool.'

'You want to leave?'

Andrew turned back to look at Fatou. His eyes were streaming. He looked, to Fatou, like a little boy trying to disguise the fact he had been crying. But then he held her hand, under the water.

'No. I'm just going to take it easy right here.'

'OK,' Fatou said.

'You swim. You're good. You swim.'

'OK,' Fatou said, and set off, and she found that each lap was more distracted and rhythmless than the last. She was not used to being watched while she swam. Ten laps later, she suddenly stood up halfway down the lane and walked the rest of the distance to the wall.

'You want to go in the Jacuzzi?' she asked him, pointing to it.

In the hot tub sat a woman dressed in a soaking tracksuit, her head covered with a headscarf. A man next to the woman, perhaps her husband, stared at Fatou and said something to the woman. He was so hairy he was almost as covered as she was. Together they rose up out of the water and left. He was wearing the tiniest of Speedos, the kind Fatou had feared Andrew might wear, and was grateful he had not. Andrew's shorts were perfectly nice, knee-length, red and solid, and looked good against his skin.

'No,' Andrew said. 'It's great just to be here with you, watching the world go by.'

O—21

That same evening, Fatou was fired. Not for the guest passes – the Derawals never found out how many miles Fatou had travelled on their membership. In fact, it was hard for Fatou to understand exactly why she was being fired, as Mrs Derawal herself did not seem able to explain it very precisely.

'What you don't understand is that we have no need for a nanny,' she said, standing in the doorway of Fatou's room – there was not really enough space in there for two people to stand without one of them being practically on the bed. 'The children are grown. We need a housekeeper, one who cleans properly. These days, you care more about the children than the cleaning,' Mrs Derawal added, though Fatou had never cared for the children, not even slightly. 'And that is of no use to us.'

Fatou said nothing. She was thinking that she did not have a proper suitcase and would have to take her things from Mrs Derawal's house in plastic bags.

'And so you will want to find somewhere else to live as soon as possible,' Mrs Derawal said. 'My husband's cousin is coming to stay in this room on Friday – this Friday.'

Fatou thought about that for a moment. Then she said, 'Can I please use the phone for one call?'

Mrs Derawal inspected a piece of wood that had flaked from the doorframe. But she nodded.

'And I would like to have my passport, please.'

'Excuse me?'

'My passport, please.'

At last Mrs Derawal looked at Fatou, right into her eyes, but her face was twisted, as if Fatou had just reached over and slapped her. Anyone could see the Devil had climbed inside poor Mrs Derawal. He was lighting her up with a pure fury.

'For goodness' sake, girl, I don't have your passport! What would I want with your passport? It's probably in a drawer in the kitchen somewhere. Is that my job now, too, to look for your things?'

Fatou was left alone. She packed her things into the decoy shopping bags she usually took to the swimming pool. While she was doing this, someone pushed her passport under her door. An hour later she carried her bags downstairs and went directly to the phone in the hall. Faizul walked by and lifted his hand for a high-five. Fatou ignored him and dialled Andrew's number. From her friend's voice she knew that she had woken him, but he was not even the slightest bit angry. He listened to all she had to say and seemed to understand, too, without her having to say so, that at this moment she could not speak freely. After she had said her part, he asked a few quick technical questions and then explained clearly and carefully what was to happen.

'It will all be OK. They need cleaners in my offices – I will ask for you. In the meantime, you come here. We'll sleep in shifts. You can trust me. I respect you, Fatou.'

But she did not have her Oyster Card; it was in the kitchen, on the fridge under a magnet of Florida, and she would rather die than go in there. Fine: he could meet her at six p.m. at Brondesbury Overground station. Fatou looked at the grandfather clock in front of her: she had four hours to kill.

'Six o'clock,' she repeated. She put the phone down, took the rest of the guest passes from the drawer of the faux-Louis XVI console and left the house.

'Weighed down a bit today,' the girl at the desk of the health club said, nodding at Fatou's collection of plastic bags. Fatou held out a guest pass for a stamp and did not smile. 'See you next time,' this same girl said, an hour and a half later, as Fatou strode past, still weighed down and still unwilling to be grateful for past favours. Gratitude was just another kind of servitude. Better to make your own arrangements.

Walking out into the cold grey, Fatou felt a sense of brightness, of being washed clean, that neither the weather nor her new circumstances could dim. Still, her limbs were weary and her hair was wet; she would probably catch a cold, waiting out here. It was only four thirty. She put her bags on the pavement and sat down next to them, just by the bus stop opposite the Embassy of Cambodia. Buses came and went, slowing down for her and then jerking forward when they realized that she had no interest in getting up and on. Many of us walked past her that afternoon, or spotted her as we rode the bus, or through the windscreens of our cars, or from our balconies. Naturally, we wondered what this girl was doing, sitting on the damp pavement in the middle of the day. We worried for her. We tend to assume the worst, here in Willesden. We watched her watching the shuttlecock. Pock, smash. Pock, smash. As if one player could imagine only a violent conclusion and the other only a hopeful return.

Author Biographies

P. G. WODEHOUSE (1881–1975) was one of the most prolific, popular and original English novelists of the twentieth century. The child of old English gentry, he spent most of his childhood in boarding schools. He was unable to go to Oxford because of a fall in the value of the Indian rupee. A brief and unsuccessful period working for the Hong Kong and Shanghai Bank was followed by writing columns, stories for boys, and novels. A trip to New York left a lasting mark and encouraged him to develop his writing in the direction of musical comedies. In 1914, Wodehouse married a daunting woman named Ethel, and from the end of the Great War onwards, amassed colossal popularity and an immense fortune. They lived in France until captured by invading German forces, who interned him in concentration camps before releasing him and persuading him to make comic radio talks from Berlin. There were calls for him to be hanged as a traitor from wartime Britain, to which he never returned. He was given an honorary doctorate by Oxford University and, in 1975, shortly before his death, a knighthood.

'MALACHI' (MARJORIE) WHITAKER (1895–1976) was the daughter of a Bradford bookbinder. She wrote energetically from an early age, though most of her early work is lost; an early novel fell overboard from a channel steamer. She married Leonard Whitaker, a businessman, and adopted two children, saying later that 'the only physical result of our union was that I was left with the itch'. She began to write under her pen name in 1926, and subsequently published four collections of short stories and an extraordinary autobiography, *And So Did I*, in 1939. After this, she announced her retirement from writing and published nothing else new for her remaining thirty-seven years.

JACK COMMON (1903–68) was the son of a Newcastle engine driver. From intermittent casual employment, he acquired a reputation as a powerful debater in socialist causes. He was encouraged by John Middleton Murry at *The Adelphi*, of which he ultimately became the editor. Primarily an essayist and polemicist, he retained a strong interest in working-class voices. After the war, he worked as a screenplay writer, but never made a living. He had to work at a mushroom nursery in the 1950s, despite publishing two impressive and much-praised autobiographies. By the end of his life, his views of class conflict were so out of fashion as to make him unpublishable.

ELIZABETH BOWEN (1899–1973) was born of an old Anglo-Irish family, in Ireland, but grew up in Hythe. In 1923, she married Alan Cameron, an educational administrator. Their marriage was unconsummated. She started to publish fiction in 1923. In 1933, she embarked on an affair with the Oxford don Humphry House. That and subsequent affairs, with Sean O'Faolain and May Sarton, fed into her novels and fiction of emotional trauma and rejection. In 1952, she and Alan moved to her ancestral home, Bowen's Court, where he died. Afterwards, Bowen had a stretch of success as a literary hostess before having to sell the house to a local farmer, who demolished it.

EVELYN WAUGH (1903–66) was the son of a Hampstead publisher. His elder brother, Alec, was also a novelist. A legendarily disgraceful undergraduate career led to a period teaching boys in an awful boarding school, interspersed with Bright Young Things debauchery in London. His first novels, brilliant farces, were written during a brief marriage to a woman also called Evelyn. Subsequent novels darkened and showed the influence of a profound Roman Catholic faith. With his second wife, Laura, he had six children. He was a celebrated wit and practical joker who was generally found grossly offensive in person. In later years, he lived as an English country gentleman in a form so exaggerated many people concluded it was meant as a joke; he required tailors to make suits from cloth previously reserved for flat caps. He had an appalling war, having to be removed from frontline service in case one of his men took the opportunity to shoot him in the back. Drug-fuelled delirium provided him with the theme of a great late novella, *The Ordeal of Gilbert Pinfold*. He died at home in the lavatory on Easter Sunday, shortly after having received Communion in the old rite. The reforms of the Second Vatican Council had partly estranged him from his chosen church.

JAMES HANLEY (1901–85) was born in Dublin but moved with his family to Liverpool at the age of seven. At twelve he left school and joined the merchant navy, enlisting in the army and working as a docker and on the railway or on the racecourse from the late 1920s. His novels began to be published in 1930. His second novel, *Boy*, was the subject of prosecution for obscenity and defended by E. M. Forster. He was prolific, and his work was so bleak that it never found popularity among readers, although he was regarded with considerable respect by his peers.

T. H. WHITE (1906–64) was born in Bombay, and had a traumatic childhood. His alcoholic father and the furious beatings laid on at his public school made their mark on his adult personality. He became a schoolmaster at the newly founded Stowe School before retreating to 'a feral state' in a rural cottage. His adult novels were succeeded by the first in a Malory-influenced tetralogy, *The Sword in the Stone*. He moved to Ireland during the war, and, to avoid taxation, to Alderney afterwards. Financial success because of the Broadway musical *Camelot* and the animated Disney film *The Sword in the Stone* brought White misery, and he died alone on board ship in Piraeus. His friends concede that he was a sexual sadist, but furiously deny that he could have been homosexual.

LESLIE HALWARD (1905–76) was of working-class origins, born in Birmingham. He left school at fifteen, and worked as a toolmaker, labourer and plasterer before starting to write stories for magazines and for the BBC, as well as radio plays. His autobiography, *Let Me Tell You* (1938), tells of a passion for music. It was written shortly after Halward married his wife Gwen, after a long engagement, and describes how they moved into a house called O Providence, after a novel by his best man, John Hampson, a fellow member of the Birmingham Group of writers.

JULIAN MACLAREN-ROSS (1912–64), immortalized as 'X Trapnel' in his friend Anthony Powell's sequence *A Dance to the Music of Time*, has come to be synonymous with the bohemian culture of Soho and Fitzrovia in the 1940s and 1950s. He was the son of a gentleman 'of independent means' and lived in France as a child. Having run through any inherited money, he worked as a vacuum-cleaner salesman. His stories and plays were accepted by the BBC and Cyril Connolly's *Horizon*. Military service ended with imprisonment for absence without leave, and subsequent apotheosis as a Soho dandy in white suit and silver-topped cane. His *Memoirs of the Forties*, assembled after his early death by Alan Ross, offers an unparalleled view of the time and place.

ALUN LEWIS (1915–44) was the son of a Glamorgan schoolmaster. After university in Aberystwyth and Manchester, he became a schoolmaster himself before joining the army in 1940. He married in 1941 before being posted to India. There, he fell in love with a Freda Aykroyd. In March 1944, shortly before the start of his first patrol against the Japanese, he shot himself.

'HENRY GREEN' (HENRY YORKE) (1905–73) was a patrician novelist who created one of the most extraordinary and original prose styles in the English language. After school and Oxford, where he was reputed to have seen two different films every day for two years, he worked on the factory floor of the family engineering works, Pontifex and Sons, in Birmingham. He wrote his novels unobtrusively, during his lunch hour. His first novel, *Blindness* (1926), was written while still at school. The eight novels and volume of autobiography that followed establish him as an experimental modernist. He took up a post as a fireman during the London Blitz, and claimed once to have entered a burning house to discover a young woman ignoring the conflagration around in favour of sexual congress with an Alsatian. After *Doting* (1952), he wrote no more novels, instead concentrating on heavy drinking in and around his Belgravia house, where he was often mistaken for a derelict.

SYLVIA TOWNSEND WARNER (1893–1978) was the daughter of a Harrow schoolmaster, and became a musicologist of high accomplishment. Friendship with David Garnett and T. F. Powys led to the publication of her first poems and a novel, *Lolly Willowes*. In 1930, she met and fell in love with the poet Valentine Ackland. The two women lived together in Dorset for the rest of their lives, where Valentine was often mistaken for a man by the slower inhabitants of the county. They were devoted to advanced causes, and travelled together to Barcelona during the Spanish Civil War to work for the Red Cross. Sylvia had a long association with the *New Yorker*, which published many of her short stories. The startling differences between the style, subject and effect of her eight novels has sometimes confused readers, during her life and subsequently.

W. SOMERSET MAUGHAM (1875–1965) had a stammer in youth, and learned French (perfectly) and German (imperfectly, in Heidelberg, where he was first seduced by a man). He qualified as a doctor, but immediately published a modestly successful novel, and gave up medical practice. His first major success was a play, *Lady Frederick*. From then until 1933, he concentrated on the theatre, developing a parallel career as a successful novelist, often on imperial themes, from *Of Human Bondage* (1915) onwards. He amused his contemporaries greatly by marrying a woman, Syrie Wellcome (née Barnardo) in 1917. They divorced in 1929, after which Maugham settled down in the South of France with a succession of heavily drinking queens of doubtful temperament. Sometimes guests, observing handsome naked boys swimming in the pool at the Villa Mauresque, were surprised to be handed a note on a silver salver by the butler, reading in Maugham's hand, 'You may look, but you may not touch'. His latter days were darkened by an inadvertently hilarious memoir, in which he pretended to be heterosexual, and by the constant presence of his sponging nephew Robin Maugham, memorably described by Patrick White as resembling 'a wizened cow's twat'.

ROALD DAHL (1916–90) was born in Glamorgan, the son of prosperous Norwegians. He was damaged by his father's early death and by a brutal regime at his public school. An adventurous early life travelling to Newfoundland and Tanganyika culminated in a wartime career in the Royal Air Force in Africa. Dahl's romantic accounts of RAF life, often inaccurate in detail, led to an unusual friendship with F. D. Roosevelt. His bizarre and often cruel stories were widely read. In 1953, Dahl married Patricia Neal, the film actress. Their family life had tragic aspects, including a son whose skull was smashed at four months (Dahl invented a life-saving medical pump) and a daughter who died at seven. In 1967, he turned to writing books for children, starting with *James and the Giant Peach* and *Charlie and the Chocolate Factory*, much disapproved of by the establishment of children's literature. He also wrote the script for the best of all James Bond movies, *You Only Live Twice*. Stories of his deliberate offensiveness, experienced at first hand, abound.

L. A. G. STRONG (1896–1958) was the son of a professional Devon family. He suffered from poor health, which interrupted his education. A career as a schoolmaster continued until the success of his first published novel. Thereafter, he was a successful and popular novelist and writer of short fiction of unusual subtlety. He also wrote biographies, literary criticism and a work on the speaking of English. The near-total decline of his reputation after his death is something of a puzzle, given his writing's consistent quality and penetration.

T. F. POWYS (1875–1953) was one of eleven children, including two other celebrated novelists, John Cowper Powys and Llewellyn Powys. His father and both grandfathers were clergymen. He became a farmer and biblical commentator. He wrote much fiction before achieving publication. He was very prolific, and much of his fiction, often taking the form of fables set in an allegorical and luminous version of Dorset, has never been published.

GRAHAM GREENE (1904–91) was the son of a headmaster. He attempted suicide while still a schoolboy, and was sent for psychiatric treatment by his parents. He was converted to Catholicism by his first wife, and wrote his first novel, a historical romance, while a sub-editor at *The Times*. In 1932, he wrote a novel designed to be popular, *Stamboul Train*, by establishing a firm routine of 500 words a day. It worked. Thereafter, until the 1950s, Greene divided his books, rather misleadingly, into 'novels' and 'entertainments'. During the Second World War, he was involved in intelligence and counter-espionage, where he worked with Kim Philby. An energetic traveller in every part of the world, he gave MI6 unofficial help for many years. Post-war statements of sympathy for the Soviet Union did not fool knowledgeable observers. His last years were spent in tax exile in France and Switzerland.

G. F. GREEN (1911–77) was the child of a well-to-do family, but his observations of working-class life were so acute and sympathetic as to lead Alan Sillitoe to describe him as a 'proletarian' writer. In the Second World War, he was posted to Ceylon, but this ended in disaster when he was caught *in flagrante* with a Sinhalese rickshaw-puller. His talent was damaged by heavy drinking, but he stopped altogether in 1957. He was an austere and slow-working writer. His later years were spent restoring a handsome Georgian house in Somerset.

ANGUS WILSON (1913–91) was born in Bexhill-on-Sea, and had a borderline respectable childhood, moving from hotel to hotel. He was left-wing, and theatrical in temperament. He worked at the British Library until called up to work at the code-breaking unit at Bletchley Park during the war. After a nervous breakdown, he was advised to write as therapy. His collections of short stories touched a fashionable nerve after the war, and during the 1950s his novels were also successful. He undertook a busy public life on committees and attending international conferences, although the quality of his novels declined. In 1970 he established an early, although not the first, MA in Creative Writing in Britain. He was knighted in 1980.

RHYS DAVIES (1901–78) was the son of a grocer in a mining district of Wales. He left school at fourteen, and began working in his parents' shop. After five years, he moved to Cardiff and subsequently, in 1924, to London. He published his first collection in 1927. His life was peripatetic and on the borders of success, much admired by many of his contemporaries but dogged by bad luck and the looming prospect of failure. He often wrote from a woman's point of view, and despite setting the vast majority of his fiction in Wales, never lived there after the age of twenty-three. His best friend was the novelist Anna Kavan, whose legacy supported his last years.

FRANCIS KING (1923–2011) was born in Switzerland, the son of an Indian official, and spent his childhood with a succession of relations in England. He was a prodigy of a novelist, and his first book was published while he was still an undergraduate. A career with the British Council was combined with a busy novelistic practice, and gave him useful insights into foreign cultures, especially that of Japan. His novels are often brilliant, but sometimes curiously foul-tempered in final effect. One of the best, *A Domestic Animal*, ran into trouble when a male Labour MP of King's acquaintance, Tom Skeffington-Lodge, recognized himself thinly disguised as a ridiculous Dame Winifred Harcourt. He sued for libel, and King lost his house to legal costs. Ten years later, King portrayed Skeffington-Lodge in even more venomous, and recognizable, terms as another ridiculous woman in a novel, bringing another legal action for libel. When asked what on earth he was thinking of, he merely said 'Oh, I thought he wouldn't have the stomach to go through all that again.'

WILLIAM SANSOM (1912–76) was the son of a naval architect in Dulwich. He was christened Norman Trevor, but understandably changed his name once he was able. He worked in raffish professions, including as a night-club pianist and advertising copywriter. His writing career took off after the Second World War, and for a long period he published at least one book a year. He wrote in the former billiards room of his substantial house in Maida Vale. He married the actress daughter of an accountant, subsequently working as a literary scout. The marriage was tempestuous, driven by heavy drinking on both parts. His wife sent him a note during his last illness in hospital claiming that if he ever came out, he would find that she had destroyed all his papers. She hadn't, in fact.

SAMUEL SELVON (1923–94) was the son of a cocoa merchant in Trinidad. He worked for the Trinidad *Sunday Guardian* and the *Evening News* until 1950, when he moved to London. He lived in Britain during the period of his best writing, producing a matchless account of the lives of the Windrush generation, until he moved to Canada in 1978. There, for a time, he had to work as a janitor at the University of Calgary, which subsequently appointed him Writer in Residence.

MURIEL SPARK (1918–2006) was the daughter of a fitter in Edinburgh, a 'gentile Jewess' as she described herself – her father but not her mother was Jewish. In 1937 she departed for Southern Rhodesia to marry a man called Spark she had met at a dance. In Africa, he turned out to be violent and frightening, even to the generally dauntless Mrs Spark. In 1944 she took a troop ship to Liverpool. She occupied various posts in the London literary world. In 1954 she experienced paranoid hallucinations due to reliance on slimming pills. Her first novel, *The Comforters*, addresses the experience. In the early 1960s, her publishers, hypnotized by Spark, offered to buy her a house. A Roman Catholic convert, she was extraordinarily chic in both appearance and intellectual capacity. The excellence of her novels continued without diminishment to the end, the later ones being written in Italian exile with the domestic support of a companion, Penelope Jardine.

ROBERT AICKMAN (1914–81) was the son of a Hampstead architect. His grandfather met his father in a public toilet, and encouraged him to marry his daughter despite thirty years difference in age. Aickman was isolated and depressive throughout his early life, and married a girl he met in an opera queue out of sympathy. After they divorced in 1957, she became a nun. Aickman, in 1946, set up the Inland Waterways Association to preserve and restore British canals. After 1951 he published a series of macabre stories and novels. He is described as a man 'at odds with the modern world' and one who, autocratic in his public life, 'did not suffer fools gladly'. This may or may not be a euphemism.

V. S. NAIPAUL (1932–) was born in Trinidad, the son of a journalist. He won a scholarship to Oxford, where he was lonely and insecure. Relying on his wife, Pat, he pursued a career in writing and as an occasional presenter on the BBC. His first books, beautifully conceived and written, were published by André Deutsch. They quickly won prizes, and by the time of *A House for Mr Biswas* (1961) the greatness of its author was accepted. Afterwards, Naipaul began to travel, including his first trip to his ancestral India. The sequence of non-fiction that followed was unsparing and sometimes, as in the case of *Among the Believers* (1981), startlingly prophetic. His novels pursue the large topic of the consequences of imperialism lucidly and without undue sentiment. Although his public persona has given rise to much controversy in recent years, he is often and justly regarded as one of the greatest novelists in English since the Second World War.

J. G. BALLARD (1930–2009) was born in Shanghai, the son of the manager of a calico print works. He and his family were interned in a prison camp when the Japanese army occupied Shanghai. Afterwards, Ballard moved with his mother to England, where he went through boarding school and Cambridge in a very independent spirit. Like many writers, he trained as a doctor. From 1951 onwards he wrote visionary science fiction. In 1955 he married and in 1959 he moved to Shepperton. In 1964 his wife died suddenly while they were on holiday in Spain, leaving Ballard to bring up three children alone. He drank whisky from 9 a.m. onwards, once the children were at school. The later works bring experimental modernism into the previously safe world of British science fiction. His last years were spent in a cloud of admiration, by which time the chaotic semi-detached house in Shepperton had become a legendary destination for the ambitious writers of Sunday newspaper profiles.

CHRISTINE BROOKE-ROSE (1923–2012) was born in Geneva and brought up in Brussels. She was educated at Somerville College,

Oxford and University College London. She worked from 1968 to 1988 at the University of Paris, Vincennes, and was married three times. She was regarded in Britain as a proponent of an English-language version of the French *nouveau roman*.

ELIZABETH TAYLOR (1912–73) was the daughter of an insurance inspector. On leaving school, she worked as a governess, marrying John Taylor, a chocolate manufacturer, in 1936. After a passionate affair with a fellow communist, she began to publish novels in 1945. Her subsequent life was spent maintaining important literary connections from a slight distance – Ivy Compton-Burnett, Elizabeth Bowen, Kingsley Amis and especially Robert Liddell were friends – and in living a respectable upper-middle class life in Penn in Buckinghamshire. Although she was successful in her lifetime, and one of the English writers that the *New Yorker* strongly supported, she was often subject to casual dismissal. Her reputation has grown considerably since her death.

KINGSLEY AMIS (1922–95) was the son of a clerk at Colman's, the mustard manufacturer. He was educated at the City of London School and at St John's, Oxford, where he formed a lifelong friendship with Philip Larkin. From 1942 he served in the army. He married Hilary Bardwell in 1948 and returned to academic study. Although his B.Litt thesis was failed, he managed to get a job at the University of Swansea. Soon afterwards, Amis published *Lucky Jim*, an immediate and enormous success. Amis's subsequent career has fascinated a series of generations for its leap from left-wing causes to staunch Tory, and for its energetic engagement with genre in a confrontational and frequently masterly manner. He left his first wife for the novelist Elizabeth Jane Howard. He was a noted philanderer and spectacular drunk, as well as the most gifted mimic of his generation. When his second marriage broke up acrimoniously, he moved in with his first wife and her third husband Lord Kilmarnock, who acted as housekeepers and carers. He took considerable pleasure in asking a peer of the realm to make him a cup of tea, or to mix up some Fybogel constipation cure.

ALAN SILLITOE (1928–2010) was born the son of a labourer. His childhood was scarred by abuse, and by poverty when his father lost his job. He left school at fourteen, but was furthered by self-education in the public libraries; he was always regarded by his peers as being exceptionally well read. He had to leave the RAF when he contracted tuberculosis. He moved with his companion Ruth Fainlight to the South of France and then Majorca. Robert Graves suggested to Sillitoe that he should write about his own world; the result, *Saturday Night and Sunday Morning,* was a huge success. In later years, his varied and immensely inventive work sometimes baffled reviewers who believed that working-class writers should not venture beyond their obvious subject matter. He was highly regarded behind the Iron Curtain, but misunderstood as much there as at home: he took the opportunity in 1969 to attack human rights abuses in the USSR during a speech to the Soviet Writers' Union.

V. S. PRITCHETT (1900–97) is the greatest of all British writers of short stories. Born the son of a feckless migratory man with fantasies about business success, Pritchett spent a childhood moving from lodging to lodging. At fifteen he left school for a job in a tannery in Bermondsey. At nineteen, he moved to Paris with the wish to become a painter, acquiring French. He returned to London and took up a job as foreign correspondent for the *Christian Science Monitor.* His first collection of short stories, *The Spanish Virgin,* was published in 1930. His novels were not successful, but his short stories and his book-reviewing quickly put him in the first rank of English writers. His life from the 1940s onwards was one of recollection and contemplation, and from his writing and from visiting professorships in America he was able to buy a substantial house in Regent's Park. He rescued and preserved his beloved wife Dorothy from a serious patch of alcoholism. Two volumes of memoirs are masterpieces.

'JEAN RHYS' (ELLA WILLIAMS) (1890–1979) was born in Dominica, the daughter of a Welsh doctor. In 1907 she was sent to England for her education, choosing to enter the Academy of Dramatic Art. When asked to leave because of her ineradicable Caribbean accent, she became a chorus girl. A series of affairs followed, and a dangerously late abortion. She married and moved to Paris, and started to publish novels. Her first novel, *Quartet,* was an account of her affair with the novelist, Ford Madox Ford. Her husband, also a novelist published his own account of the affair. She returned to England and lived with, then married, her literary agent while developing a heavy drinking habit. She and her husband lost all their money, and any contact with the literary world. After the war her husband died. Rhys lived in Beckenham with his cousin, often being prosecuted for bohemian behaviour. In 1949 and again in 1956 adverts were placed in the press asking for any news of the whereabouts of this forgotten author. In 1966, with the strong support of new friends, *Wide Sargasso Sea* was published and hailed as a masterpiece.

IAN McEWAN (1948–) was the son of a Scots major in the army. He was educated at the University of Sussex and was one of the first pupils of the University of East Anglia's Creative Writing Programme. His work has gone from gleefully macabre short stories to high-minded statements of principles. He is a Labour supporter and an enthusiastic secularist. In his novel *Saturday,* about a day in the life of a Labour-supporting brain surgeon resident in the same impressive Fitzrovia house that McEwan lives in, a murderous rapist is dissuaded from his beastly intentions by a character reading *Dover Beach* out loud.

ANGELA CARTER (1940–92) was the daughter of a journalist, born in Eastbourne. She spent much of her childhood in Yorkshire at her grandmother's house, which contained three copies of *Foxe's Book of Martyrs,* the young Carter's favourite reading. She started and soon after finished work as a reporter on a local paper in Croydon: factual reportage was not her strong point. She married very young, and took a degree in English literature, specializing in mediaeval romances. She used the money from the Somerset Maugham Award for her third novel to leave her husband and go to Japan. She was a highly original essayist and novelist, and her experiences were unusually wide for the increasing professionalized occupation of novelist – she worked as a bar hostess in Ginza in Tokyo. From the 1970s onwards, she relied upon the support of university fellowships in Sheffield, Brown in the USA and Adelaide in Australia. She married a potter and lived in South London until her early death. Shortly afterwards, it was reported that more PhD theses were being written on her work in the UK than on the entire eighteenth century.

DORIS LESSING (1919–2013) was born in Iran, the daughter of a soldier and clerk at the Imperial Bank of Persia. Most of her early life was spent in Southern Rhodesia (now Zimbabwe). Lessing married twice, and left her second husband to travel to London with her younger son in 1949. In London, she was an active communist and political campaigner against apartheid and nuclear arms. Her first novel was published in 1950. Over the next sixty years, she maintained an argumentative, inspiring presence in London, publishing novels of every sort, picking intellectual fights, making an example of herself and giving every sign of enjoying an energetic disagreement. 'How pleasant to be a Dame! I would adore it,' she wrote to a government official, turning down a DBE. She died shortly after the death of her younger son, Peter, for whom she had cared for many years.

PENELOPE FITZGERALD (1916-2000) was born in the Bishop's Palace at Lincoln, the daughter of a famously intellectual English family. Her father was editor of *Punch*, one uncle was one of the cryptographers who broke the code of the Enigma machine, and another was the most famous English Catholic divine of the twentieth century. She married a catastrophic wastrel in 1942, who was expelled from the Bar for petty theft and perhaps went to prison. During this time, Fitzgerald abandoned a series of rented houses, lived in a houseboat on the Thames (which sank) and was reduced to a hostel for the homeless with her three children, while teaching at a crammer. Towards the end of her husband's life she took to writing first biographies, and then after his death, a brilliant series of novels. Most people found her gaze a complex experience: kindly, unforgettably penetrating, disconcerting, and decidedly daunting.

ALASDAIR GRAY (1934–) was born in Glasgow, the son of a factory worker. He studied at the Glasgow School of Art from 1952 to 1957, and subsequently taught there. He established a career as an artist, and his first writings were plays, broadcast on radio and television in 1968. For many years, he worked slowly on his novel *Lanark*, finally published in 1981 and the object of great admiration, not only among Scottish nationalists. His books are objects of unusual beauty; his motto, 'Work as if you live in the early days of a better nation', migrated from the pages of his books to the wall of the Scottish Parliament.

BERNARD MacLAVERTY (1942–) was born in Belfast and grew up in an extended Roman Catholic family. His father was a sign painter who often worked for cinemas. At school he was a member of a skiffle band. After school, he worked as a technician in the anatomy laboratory at Queen's University, where he joined a writers' group that included Philip Hobsbaum, Michael Longley and Derek Mahon. He took a degree as a mature student and first published a book in 1977.

SHENA MACKAY (1944–) was born in Edinburgh but grew up in Hampstead and Shoreham in Kent. A novelistic prodigy, she published her first fiction, two brilliant novellas, the year after leaving school. She worked as an office junior and subsequently in an antique shop owned by the art critic David Sylvester's parents. A Soho period followed with connections in the Colony Rooms, and the friendship of Francis Bacon. Her first creative period came to an end in 1971, before she resumed publishing in 1983. Her subjects are the pleasures of ordinary life, touched with metropolitan and bohemian glamour. She lives in Southampton.

BERYL BAINBRIDGE (1932–2010) was the daughter of a commercial agent and a mother who, after her father's bankruptcy, made it clear that she had married beneath her. She was expelled from school at fourteen for illustrating a dirty limerick. On leaving school, she worked as an ASM and subsequently an actor in the theatre. Her final role was as Ken Barlow's girlfriend in *Coronation Street*. Bainbridge married a Roman Catholic artist, and subsequently had an affair with a man called Sharp, who when his daughter was born said he was going to get a book out of the car, and never came back. In 1967 she began to publish fiction. Her publisher was Colin Haycraft, who despised novelists. He made an exception for Bainbridge, who he had a long affair with. After Haycraft's death, she started to receive proper payment for her novels for the first time. Her house contained a stuffed water buffalo in the hallway and a life-sized papier-mâché figure of Neville Chamberlain in her bedroom.

DOUGLAS DUNN (1942–) was born in Clydeside, the son of a tyre company executive. He worked as a librarian, initially in Glasgow but subsequently in America, where he started reviewing poetry and was mysteriously called up for the Vietnam War, which he ignored and was labelled a deserter. Returning to the UK, he started a degree at the University of Hull, meeting Tom Paulin and the librarian Philip Larkin. His wife died, tragically young, in 1981, giving rise to the poetry collection *Elegies* (1985), a classic.

GEORGINA HAMMICK (1939–) is the daughter of a military attaché, whose identical twin, Amanda Vesey, is an artist and illustrator. A formative experience was travelling across the Atlantic in December 1948, away from rationing to the sight of a glittering New York in the snow. She lives in Peckham with a greedy Romanian street dog and a flock of goldfinches which choose not to migrate in winter. Her first collection, *People for Lunch*, a masterpiece, was greatly admired by both Bernard Levin and Adam Mars-Jones.

ADAM MARS-JONES (1954–) was born in London. His father was a High Court Judge. Mars-Jones told his father that he was homosexual on the last day of 1977, to which his father insisted that Mars-Jones had masturbated when he had glimpsed Jacqueline Bissett in a Truffaut film. Shortly afterwards, Mars-Jones went to America, returning after having written a volume of short stories about a serial killer, his father, an upper-class eccentric and the Queen. He was included in lists of best British novelists in 1983 and 1993, despite not having published a novel. Subsequently he published one short one and two very long ones, named after abstruse items of punctuation.

GEORGE MACKAY BROWN (1921–96) was born the son of a tailor and postman in Orkney. He started to write after an attack of tuberculosis, in the form of verse and articles for the *Orkney Herald*. For twenty years, serious attacks of ill health delayed Brown's educational development and writing. In 1961 he became a Roman Catholic. He spent time in Edinburgh, where he made important literary connections, but left Orkney only unwillingly.

A. S. BYATT (1936–) was born in Sheffield, one of four remarkable children: her siblings are the novelist Margaret Drabble, the art historian Helen Langdon and the QC Richard Drabble. The family moved to York. Byatt's education was Quaker. After Cambridge and Oxford, Byatt lectured at London University, and was first published by Cecil Day-Lewis. Between a sequence of exceptional novels, Byatt edited the predecessor to this anthology, the *Oxford Book of the English Short Story*.

MARTIN AMIS (1949–) is the son of the novelist Kingsley Amis. A peripatetic childhood, including periods in America, led to the prospect of academic failure. On returning to school after taking a part in the movie of Richard Hughes' *A High Wind in Jamaica*, Amis was expelled for truancy. A spell in crammers got him into Oxford, and subsequently a career in literary journalism. Among his less celebrated publications are a book about the early video game Space Invaders and the screenplay to *Saturn 3*. His second novel, *Dead Babies*, was retitled *Dark Secrets* in paperback in order not to offend any dead babies, or anyone who knew any. Manufactured controversies about his teeth, his divorces, his advances, his views on Islam increasingly affected the public reception of his novels, whatever their quality.

CANDIA McWILLIAM (1955–) was born in Edinburgh, the daughter of a classically educated modernist who worked for the Scottish

National Trust. Her mother died in tragic circumstances. She was adopted by a family on Colonsay, and took a job working for *Vogue*. She had a celebrated prose style, was a famous beauty of exceptional intelligence and married first an English earl, then a brilliant Oxford don. Three dazzling novels and a volume of short stories over nine years were followed by a long silence. The reasons for that, including a savage drink problem, were set out in a scarifying memoir, *What To Look For In Winter*. In 2006, following a year judging the Booker Prize, a rare medical condition caused McWilliam to go blind, but she was cured after some years by radical surgery.

JANICE GALLOWAY (1955–) was born in Saltcoats in Scotland. Her father was a bus driver and her mother a cleaner. She read Music and English at Glasgow University before working as a schoolteacher. Her mother enabled her to have an abortion so that she could continue her education. She was Writer in Residence at four prisons and has been Research Fellow at the British Library. Her father was killed in a fireworks accident.

ALI SMITH (1962–) was born in Inverness. She studied at the University of Aberdeen and then at Cambridge for a PhD, unfinished. She worked as a university lecturer and currently lives in Cambridge.

TESSA HADLEY (1956–) was born in Bristol. She was educated at Cambridge and became a teacher, first in a school then in extramural evening classes. She wrote while bringing up her children. Her first novel, *Accidents in the Home*, was published in 2002. Her short stories have been regularly published by the *New Yorker*.

ADAM MAREK (1974–) is the son of a merchant sailor and was born because of confusion between time zones and the required timing of the contraceptive pill. His conception was announced by a Ouija board. He worked at a pillow factory and a film production company. He began writing with the W. H. Smith Young Writers' Competition, in which he was highly commended at the age of eleven.

JON McGREGOR (1976–) was born in Bermuda. He studied Media Technology and Production at Bradford University. He moved to Nottingham and lived on a narrowboat. His novels and volumes of short stories have been awarded many prizes. From October 2013, he announced his intention to refuse to use all technological communication other than the telephone.

ZADIE SMITH (1975–) was born in London. She changed her name from Sadie in 1989. She was educated at Hampstead Comprehensive School and King's, Cambridge, where she occasionally performed as a singer and actor. Her first novel was taken on by a publisher very soon after her leaving university. From 2002 onwards she started spending time in America, and lived for a year in Rome. Interest in her daily existence was often in excess of that experienced by most writers of fiction. Her media profile often started to include facts invented by bored and possibly delusional journalists, such as the possession of a non-existent whirlpool bath driving a non-existent neighbour to a non-existent psychosis.

Acknowledgements

'Bind Your Hair', Robert Aickman.

First published in Robert Aickman, *Dark Entries: Curious and Macabre Ghost Stories* (London: Collins, 1964). Reprinted by permission of HarperCollins Publishers Ltd. Copyright © Robert Aickman, 1964.

'Mason's Life', Kingsley Amis.

First published in *The Sunday Times Magazine* (24 December 1972) and then in Harry Harrison and Brian W. Aldiss (eds.), *Best SF: 1973* (New York: G. P. Putnam's Sons, 1974). Reprinted by permission of the Wylie Agency (UK) Ltd. Copyright © Kingsley Amis, 1972.

'Career Move', Martin Amis.

First published in *The New Yorker* (29 June 1992) and then in Martin Amis, *Heavy Water and Other Stories* (London: Jonathan Cape, 1998). Reprinted by permission of the Wylie Agency (UK) Ltd. Copyright © Martin Amis, 1998.

'The Longstop', Beryl Bainbridge.

First published in Michael Meyer (ed.), *Summer Days: Writers on Cricket* (London: Eyre Methuen, 1981). Reprinted by permission of Johnson & Alcock Ltd. Copyright © The Estate of Beryl Bainbridge, 1981.

'The Cloud-Sculptors of Coral D', J. G. Ballard.

First published in *The Magazine of Fantasy and Science Fiction* (December 1967) and then in Judith Merril (ed.), *SF12* (New York: Delacorte Press, 1968). Reprinted by permission of the Wylie Agency (UK) Ltd. Copyright © J. G. Ballard, 1967.

'The Dancing-Mistress', Elizabeth Bowen.

First published in Elizabeth Bowen, *Joining Charles and Other Stories* (London: Constable and Co., 1929). Reprinted by permission of Curtis Brown Group Ltd, London, on behalf of The Beneficiaries of the Estate of Elizabeth Bowen. Copyright © Elizabeth Bowen, 1929.

'Red Rubber Gloves', Christine Brooke-Rose.

First published in John Burke (ed.), *Tales of Unease* (London: Pan Books, 1966). Reprinted by permission of The Christine Brooke-Rose Estate. Copyright © Christine Brooke-Rose, 1966.

Acknowledgements

'Racine and the Tablecloth', A. S. Byatt.

First published in A. S. Byatt, *Sugar and Other Stories* (London: Chatto & Windus, 1987). Reprinted by permission of The Random House Group Limited. Copyright © A. S. Byatt, 1987.

'The Courtship of Mr Lyon', Angela Carter.

First published in British *Vogue* (1979) and then, revised, in Angela Carter, *The Bloody Chamber and Other Stories* (London: Victor Gollancz, 1979). Reprinted by permission of The Estate of Angela Carter, c/o Rogers, Coleridge & White, 20 Powis Mews, London W11 1JN. Copyright © Angela Carter, 1979.

'Nineteen', Jack Common.

First published in *The Adelphi* (September 1931). Reprinted by permission of Sally Magill. Copyright © Jack Common, 1931.

'Someone Like You', Roald Dahl.

First published in *Town & Country* (November 1945) and then in Roald Dahl, *Over to You* (London: Hamish Hamilton, 1946). Reprinted by permission of David Higham Associates. Copyright © Roald Dahl, 1945.

'A Human Condition', Rhys Davies.

First published in *The New Yorker* (24 September 1949) and in Rhys Davies, *Boy with a Trumpet* (London: William Heinemann, 1949). Reprinted by permission of Dr Meic Stephens, Secretary, The Rhys Davies Trust. Copyright © Rhys Davies, 1949.

'Bobby's Room', Douglas Dunn.

First published in *The New Yorker* (16 January 1984) and then in Douglas Dunn, *Secret Villages* (London: Faber & Faber, 1985). Reprinted by permission of Faber & Faber Ltd. Copyright © Douglas Dunn, 1985.

'The Means of Escape', Penelope Fitzgerald.

First published in Marsha Rowe (ed.), *Infidelity* (London: Chatto & Windus, 1993). Reprinted by permission of The Estate of Penelope Fitzgerald, c/o Rogers, Coleridge & White, 20 Powis Mews, London W11 1JN. Copyright © Penelope Fitzgerald, 1993.

'last thing', Janice Galloway.

First published in Janice Galloway, *Where You Find It* (London: Jonathan Cape, 1996). Reprinted by permission of Blake Friedmann. Copyright © Janice Galloway, 1996.

'Five Letters from an Eastern Empire', Alasdair Gray.

First published in *Words Magazine* (1979) and then in Alasdair Gray, *Unlikely Stories, Mostly* (Edinburgh: Canongate Books, 1983). Reprinted by permission of Canongate Books Ltd. Copyright © Alasdair Gray, 1979.

Acknowledgements

'A Wedding', G. F. Green.

First published in *The Spectator* (6 August 1937) and then in Edward J. O'Brien (ed.), *The Best British Stories of 1938, and the Yearbook of the British, Irish and Colonial Short Story* (Boston and New York: Houghton Mifflin Co., 1938). Reprinted by permission of the G. F. Green Estate. Copyright © G. F. Green, 1937.

'The Lull', Henry Green.

First published in *New Writing and Daylight* (Summer 1943) and then in John Lehmann (ed.), *Pleasures of New Writing: An Anthology of Poems, Stories and Other Prose Pieces from the Pages of New Writing* (London: John Lehmann, 1952). Reprinted by permission of The Random House Group Limited. Copyright © Henry Green, 1943.

'The Hint of an Explanation', Graham Greene.

First published in *Commonweal* and *The Month* (both in February 1949) and then in Graham Greene, *Twenty-One Stories* (London: William Heinemann, 1954). Reprinted by permission of David Higham Associates. Copyright © Graham Greene, 1949.

'Buckets of Blood', Tessa Hadley.

First published in *Granta 89: The Factory* (Spring 2005) and then in Tessa Hadley, *Sunstroke and Other Stories* (London: Jonathan Cape, 2007). Reprinted by permission of The Random House Group Limited. Copyright © Tessa Hadley, 2007.

'Old Sweat', Leslie Halward.

First published in *The Left Review* (August 1937) and then in Edward J. O'Brien (ed.), *The Best British Stories of 1938, and the Yearbook of the British, Irish and Colonial Short Story* (Boston and New York: Houghton Mifflin Co., 1938). Reprinted by permission of A. R. Halward. Copyright © Leslie Halward, 1937.

'Grist', Georgina Hammick.

First published in Georgina Hammick, *People for Lunch* (London: Methuen, 1987). Reprinted by permission of the author and The Sayle Literary Agency. Copyright © Georgina Hammick, 1987.

'The German Prisoner', James Hanley.

First published in a limited edition, James Hanley, *The German Prisoner*, with an introduction by Richard Aldington (London: Privately printed, [1930]). Reprinted by permission of David Higham Associates. Copyright © James Hanley, 1930.

'The Mouse', Francis King.

First published in The Listener (1951) and then in Francis King, *So Hurt and Humiliated and Other Stories* (London: Longmans, 1959). Reprinted by permission of A. M. Heath & Co. Ltd. Copyright © Francis King, 1951.

Acknowledgements

'Notes for a Case History', Doris Lessing.
   First published in Doris Lessing, *A Man and Two Women* (London: MacGibbon & Kee, 1963). Reprinted by permission of HarperCollins Publishers Ltd. Copyright © Doris Lessing, 1963.
'Private Jones', Alun Lewis.
   First published in Alun Lewis, *The Last Inspection and Other Stories* (London: Allen & Unwin, 1942). Reprinted by permission of HarperCollins Publishers Ltd. Copyright © Alun Lewis, 1942.
'Pornography', Ian McEwan.
   First published in *The New Review* (February 1976) and then in Ian McEwan, *In Between the Sheets* (London: Jonathan Cape, 1978). Reprinted by permission of the author, c/o Rogers, Coleridge & White, 20 Powis Mews, London W11 1JN. Copyright © Ian McEwan, 1978.
'The Remains', Jon McGregor.
   First published in Jon McGregor, *This Isn't the Sort of Thing That Happens to Someone Like You* (London: Bloomsbury Publishing, 2012). Reprinted by permission of Bloomsbury Publishing plc. Copyright © Jon McGregor, 2012.
'Cardboard City', Shena Mackay.
   First published in Shena Mackay, *Dreams of Dead Women's Handbags* (London: Heinemann, 1987). Reprinted by permission of Little, Brown and Rogers, Coleridge & White, 20 Powis Mews, London W11 1JN. Copyright © Shena Mackay, 1987.
'Three Old Men', George Mackay Brown.
   First published in *The Tablet* (21 December 1991) and then in George Mackay Brown, *Winter Tales* (London: John Murray, 1995). Copyright © George Mackay Brown, 1991.
'Death of a Comrade', Julian Maclaren-Ross.
   First published in *Tribune* (28 August 1942) and then in *Julian Maclaren-Ross: Selected Stories* (Stockport: Dewi Lewis Publishing, 2004). Reprinted by permission of The Estate of Julian Maclaren-Ross. Copyright © Julian Maclaren-Ross, 1942.
'Phonefun Limited', Bernard MacLaverty.
   First appeared: Glasgow Theatre Club, Tron Theatre, 1981; BBC Radio, Northern Ireland, 1982; and then in Bernard MacLaverty, *A Time to Dance and Other Stories* (London: Jonathan Cape Ltd, 1982). Reprinted by permission of the author, c/o Rogers, Coleridge & White, 20 Powis Mews, London W11 1JN. Copyright © Bernard MacLaverty, 2013.

Acknowledgements

'The Only Only', Candia McWilliam.
> First published in Andrew Motion and Candice Rodd (eds.), *New Writing 3* (London: Minerva, in association with the British Council, 1994). Copyright © Candia McWilliam, 1994.

'The 40-Litre Monkey', Adam Marek.
> First published in the Bridport Prize Anthology 2003, and then in Adam Marek, *Instruction Manual for Swallowing* (Manchester: Comma Press, 2007). Reprinted by permission of Comma Press. Copyright © Adam Marek, 2007.

'Baby Clutch', Adam Mars-Jones.
> First published in *Granta 27: Death* (Summer 1989) and then in Giles Gordon and David Hughes (eds.), *Best Short Stories 1990* (London, Heinemann, 1990). Reprinted by permission of United Agents. Copyright © Adam Mars-Jones, 1992.

'Winter Cruise', W. Somerset Maugham.
> First published (as 'The Captain and Miss Reid') in *Cosmopolitan* (June 1943) and then in W. Somerset Maugham, *Creatures of Circumstance* (London: William Heinemann, 1947). Reprinted by permission of United Agents LLP on behalf of The Royal Literary Fund. Copyright © W. Somerset Maugham, 1943.

'The Perfect Tenants', V. S. Naipaul.
> First published in V. S. Naipaul, *A Flag on the Island* (London: André Deutsch, 1967). Reprinted by permission of the Wylie Agency (UK) Ltd. Copyright © V. S. Naipaul 1967, renewed 1995.

'The Key of the Field', T. F. Powys.
> First published in a limited edition, T. F. Powys, *The Key of the Field* (Furnival Books, 1), with a foreword by Sylvia Townsend Warner (London: William Jackson (Books) Ltd, 1930) and then in *The Furnival Book of Short Stories* (London: Joiner & Steele, 1932). Reprinted by permission of Pollinger Limited on behalf of The Estate of T. F. Powys. Copyright © T. F. Powys, 1930.

'The Camberwell Beauty', V. S. Pritchett.
> First published in V. S. Pritchett, *The Camberwell Beauty [and Other Stories]* (London: Chatto & Windus, 1974). Reprinted by permission of Peters Fraser & Dunlop (www.petersfraserdunlop.com) on behalf of The Estate of V. S. Pritchett. Copyright © V. S. Pritchett, 1974.

'Pioneers, Oh, Pioneers', Jean Rhys.
> First published (as 'Dear, Darling Mr Ramage') in *The Times* (28 June 1969) and then in Jean Rhys, *Sleep It Off Lady* (London: André Deutsch, 1976). Copyright © Jean Rhys Ltd, 1969.1

'A Contest of Ladies', William Sansom.
> First published (as 'A Contest of Ladies: A Summer Idyll') in *The Cornhill*

Magazine (Summer 1952) and then in William Sansom, *A Contest of Ladies* (London: The Hogarth Press, 1956). Reprinted by permission of Greene and Heaton. Copyright © William Sansom, 1952.

'Knock on Wood', Samuel Selvon.

First published in *Evergreen Review*, 3, 9 (1959). Reprinted by permission of The Estate of Samuel Selvon. Copyright © Samuel Selvon, 1959.

'Mimic', Alan Sillitoe.

First published in *Encounter* (January 1969) and then in A. D. Maclean (ed.), *Winter's Tales 15* (London: Macmillan, 1969). Reprinted by permission of The Estate of Alan Sillitoe, c/o Rogers, Coleridge & White, 20 Powis Mews, London W11 1JN. Copyright © Alan Sillitoe, 1973.

'miracle survivors', Ali Smith.

First published in Ali Smith, *Other Stories and other stories* (London: Granta Books, 1999). Reprinted by permission of the Wylie Agency (UK) Ltd. Copyright © Ali Smith, 1999.

'The Embassy of Cambodia', Zadie Smith.

First published in Great Britain by Hamish Hamilton (London, 2013) and in the USA in *The New Yorker* (11 February 2013). Reprinted by permission of the author, c/o Rogers, Coleridge & White, 20 Powis Mews, London W11 1JN. Copyright © Zadie Smith, 2013.

'Bang-Bang You're Dead', Muriel Spark.

First published in Muriel Spark, *Voices at Play: Stories and Ear-Pieces* (London: Macmillan and Co., 1961). Reprinted by permission of David Higham Associates. Copyright © Muriel Spark, 1961.

'The Rook', L. A. G. Strong.

First published in *The Fortnightly Review* (November 1931) and in L. A. G. Strong, *The English Captain and Other Stories* (New York: Alfred A. Knopf, 1931). Reprinted by permission of Peters Fraser & Dunlop (www.petersfraserdunlop.com) on behalf of The Estate of L. A. G. Strong. Copyright © L. A. G. Strong, 1931.

'In and Out the Houses', Elizabeth Taylor.

First published in *The Saturday Evening Post* (14 December 1968) and then in Elizabeth Taylor, *The Devastating Boys and Other Stories* (London: Chatto & Windus, 1972). Reprinted by permission of Johnson & Alcock Ltd. Copyright © The Estate of Elizabeth Taylor, 1968.

'The Trumpet Shall Sound', Sylvia Townsend Warner.

First published in Sylvia Townsend Warner, A *Garland of Straw: Twenty-Eight Stories* (New York: Viking Press, 1943). Reprinted by permission of

Acknowledgements

The Estate of Sylvia Townsend Warner. Copyright © Sylvia Townsend Warner, 1943.

'Cruise', Evelyn Waugh.

First published in *Harper's Bazaar* (London) (February 1933) and then in *Work Suspended and Other Stories Written before the Second World War* (London: Chapman & Hall, 1948). Reprinted by permission of the Wylie Agency (UK) Ltd. Copyright © The Estate of Laura Waugh, 2011.

'Courage', Malachi Whitaker.

First published in Malachi Whitaker, *Honeymoon and Other Stories* (London: Jonathan Cape, 1934). Reprinted by permission of Michael Whitaker. Copyright © Malachi Whitaker, 1934.

'The Point of Thirty Miles', T. H. White.

First published in T. H. White, *The Maharajah and Other Stories* (London: Macdonald, 1981). Reprinted by permission of David Higham Associates. Copyright © T. H. White, 1981.

'The Wrong Set', Angus Wilson.

First published in Angus Wilson, *The Wrong Set and Other Stories* (London: Secker & Warburg, 1949). Reprinted by permission of Curtis Brown Group Ltd, London, on behalf of The Beneficiaries of the Estate of Angus Wilson. Copyright © Angus Wilson, 1949.

'Unpleasantness at Bludleigh Court', P. G. Wodehouse.

First published in *The Strand Magazine* (February 1929) and then in *Mr Mulliner Speaking* (London: Herbert Jenkins, 1929). Reprinted by permission of The Random House Group Limited. Copyright © P. G. Wodehouse, 1929.

Every effort has been made to trace the copyright-holders of the copyright material in this book and credit the sources of the stories. Penguin regrets any oversight and upon written notification will rectify any omission in future reprints or editions. The editor and publisher gratefully acknowledge the above for permission to reprint stories.